About the Editor

BILL TONELLI has worked as reporter and editor for several magazines including *Esquire, Rolling Stone,* and *Us Weekly.* He is the author of *The Amazing Story of the Tonelli Family in America,* and lives and works in New York.

ALSO BY BILL TONELLI

The Amazing Story of the Tonelli Family in America:
Twelve Thousand Miles in a Buick in Search of Identity, Ethnicity,
Geography, Kinship and Home

THE ITALIAN
AMERICAN READER

EDITED BY

BILL TONELLI

Foreword by Nick Tosches

Perennial Currents
An Imprint of HarperCollinsPublishers

To my children

A hardcover edition of this book was published in 2003 by William Morrow, an imprint of HarperCollins Publishers.

First Perennial Currents edition published 2005.

Designed by Richard Oriolo

The Library of Congress has catalogued the hardcover edition as follows:
The Italian American Reader : a collection of outstanding fiction, memoirs, journalism, essays, and poetry / edited by Bill Tonelli ; foreword by Nick Tosches.—
1st ed.
p.   cm.
ISBN 0-06-000666-8
1. American literature—Italian American authors. 2. Italian Americans—Literary collections. I. Tonelli, Bill.
PS508.173 P67 2003
810.8'0851—dc21   2002029358
ISBN 0-06-000667-6 (pbk)

05   06   07   08   09   ❖/RRD   10   9   8   7   6   5   4   3   2   1

CONTENTS

SEX, LOVE, AND GOOD LOOKS

FOOD

POP

DEATH

WORK

GOD

EACH OTHER

EVERYBODY ELSE

FOREWORD

by Nick Tosches

THE FIRST LUMINATION OF ITALIAN AMERICAN LITERATURE was but a lone, faint glow of candlelight in the dark chambers of history. Though veiled by mystery and the passing of centuries, the tale of this light is a tale that I love to rekindle; for it is the tale of a writer who lived and wrote as one, in the beautiful spirit of the wandering and windswept soul of all Italian-blooded writing: a spirit in which writing, the breath of life, the quietus of death, and the immanence, breezes, and storms of the never-ending are naturally, inexorably bound.

He was a Jew, born as Emanuele Conegliano, in 1749, in the now vanished town of Ceneda, north of Venice. At the age of fourteen, when his widowed father took another wife, who was Catholic, his family, as required by law, converted to the Cross. Young Emanuele took the name of the officiating bishop. As Lorenzo Da Ponte, he entered a seminary, became a scholar of Hebrew, classical Greek, and Latin. Ordained at twenty-four, he was assigned to a church in Venice, where he befriended and caroused with Casanova. The priest arranged brothel entertainments, deflowered the fairest of his flock, and twice planted his offspring in the womb of a married woman. But it was his verse that brought down upon him the wrath of the authorities, who declared certain of his rhymes to be dangerously seditious. After fleeing to Vienna, he was tried and condemned in absentia. In Vienna, he met Mozart, and it was as the librettist for the composer's operas *La Nozze di Figaro, Don Giovanni,* and *Così Fan Tutte* that Lorenzo Da Ponte and his verse found immortality. Following Mozart's death, in 1791, Da

Ponte moved to Trieste, where, though still a Roman Catholic priest, he is believed to have proposed marriage to a British lady. It is not known whether they were wed, but they did present themselves as husband and wife, and as Anglicans. On Casanova's advice, the couple moved to London, where for a dozen years Da Ponte wrote, translated, doctored plays and libretti, and operated a rare-book shop. Fleeing arrest for debt, he escaped, in 1804, to the United States, where he opened a grocery store in Philadelphia.

In time, after further misadventures, Lorenzo Da Ponte ended up affiliated with Columbia College, the successor to King's College, in downtown Manhattan, in the block bounded by Church Street, College Place, Barclay Street, and Murray Street. (Later, in 1897, after taking over the lands of the Bloomingdale Asylum for the Insane, far uptown, in Morningside Heights, the college would become Columbia University.) There, he lectured on Dante and held the school's first, nonpaying professorship of Italian literature. He published several volumes: his *Storia della lingua e letteratura italiana in New York* (1827); *The Memoirs of Lorenzo Da Ponte* (1829), which offered a foretaste of the full *Memoirs*, published posthumously; and *A History of the Florentine Republic* (1833).

His Italian Opera House, which opened at the northwest corner of Church and Leonard Streets in the autumn of 1833, was a great failure and was abandoned after eight months and a loss of nearly thirty thousand dollars. The elderly Da Ponte died broke in New York in the summer of 1838. His funeral was held at the old St. Patrick's Cathedral, on Mulberry Street, near the heart of what would come to be Little Italy; and he was buried, probably in the tomb of a friend, in the old Catholic cemetery on East Eleventh Street. By the end of the 1800s, the deteriorating old graveyard fell victim to the new century. The caskets and bones that lay under its ground were dug up, hauled off, and dumped in Calvary Cemetery in godforsaken Queens. The remains of Lorenzo Da Ponte, whose grave had been unmarked, were as lost as the memory of him.

The first, faint, and errant glow of candlelight was extinguished, and it was a long time until the light of Italian American literature was renewed.

Quite unlike Da Ponte, the waves of Italian immigrants that came to the United States in the latter years of the nineteenth century and the early years of the twentieth were for the most part unlettered laborers fleeing poverty and hard times in the agricultural southern provinces.

I have a copy of the birth certificate of my grandmother Laurina Cicchetti, who was born in Abruzzi in 1896. On this document, there are clues about her parents, whom I never knew. Her mother is described as a *contadina*—a peasant; her father, a *mugnaio*—a miller. But the descriptive that pronounces itself most strongly is *analfabeta*—illiterate. It was in the new land that she married my grandfather Filippo Tosches, who came to New York in 1899 from the hill town of Casalvecchio di Puglia, which is to this day one of the rare places where one can commonly encounter the ancient Albanian-Italian surname of Tosches.

It was one of my grandparents' generation, an unskilled laborer who learned to put the language of his new homeland to writing, who can be said to be the father of modern Italian American literature.

The word *Bohemian* has fallen to a trite, hackneyed ruin; but this figurative sense of the word originally denoting natives of Bohemia and gypsies long ago well filled a gaping hole in our vocabulary. As defined by the *Westminster Review* in 1862: "The term 'Bohemian' has come to be very commonly accepted in our day as the description of a certain kind of literary gipsey, no matter in what language he speaks, or what city he inhabits." Included in this definition was a hint of the social and cultural outlaw or outcast: "A Bohemian is simply an artist or littérateur who, consciously or unconsciously, secedes from conventionality in life and in art."

Bertolotti's was a trattoria-saloon-café run by Angelo Bertolotti and his wife at 85 West Third Street, in Greenwich Village. It was the joint that marked the beginning and became the heart of the Village's transformation, simultaneously, into an Italian and a Bohemian neighborhood, bringing together and serving as the shared haven and hangout of both communities of social outsiders.

Emanuele Carnevale (1897–1942) supported himself as a dishwasher in the Greenwich Village of that golden age. Radical Italian American political and social theorists such as Carlo Tresca (1879–1943) and Arturo Giovannitti (1884–1959) had published poetry, most notably Giovannitti's *Arrows in the Gale* of 1914; but these men were rare, academic exceptions. It is with Carnevale that the true Italian American lifeblood begins to flow. His sole book, *Tales of a Hurried Man* (1925), made an impact on modern American poetry. Praised in his day by William Carlos Williams and others, he since has been all but forgotten. But I can often feel a current, if only spiritual, running from Carnevale to Gregory Nunzio Corso (1930–2001), a greater, wilder, and more lyrical poet, born to teenage Italian-immigrant parents in the Greenwich Village of Carnevale's and Bertolotti's day.

Meanwhile, out west, John Fante (1909–1983), also a son of Italian immigrants, in early stories such as "The Odyssey of a Wop" and collections such as *Dago Red* (1940), forged a rotgut-poetic prose that resounded in the fiction of his admirer Charles Bukowski. In the 1950s and 1960s the names grew numerous: from John Ciardi (1916–1986) to Mario Puzo (1920–1999), from Corso to Gilbert Sorrentino, to mention only those who present themselves at this moment to my wandering mind. And to this wandering mind comes, too, the memory of laughter shared with Puzo over how he had fabricated "godfather" as a Mafia term, and how even the FBI had come to accept this fairy-tale terminology as *una vera parola della malavita*. And yet it is the private joke of *The Godfather,* and not his beautiful earlier novel, *The Fortunate Pilgrim,* for which the fable-hungry masses remember Mario. To somewhat bend the meaning of those words to which Lorenzo Da Ponte gave life: *così fan tutte.*

The one thing that the best Italian American writers have in common is that they are, above all, writers pure and uncostumed of their ethnicity, no matter how conscious of, inescapable from, or proud of that ethnicity they may be. We live in an age in which too much writing, almost all of it mediocre or worse, seems to address or express a sense of this ethnic "experience" or that. As with all real writers, real Italian American writers have sought always to express what lies beyond the accidents of blood and geography that not so much define us as divide us.

Early on, in the dark river of my youth, I wanted to become a writer. It seemed a most unlikely thing. In my neighborhood, there were few books, many bookies. I was discouraged from reading, on the grounds that it would "put ideas in your head."

There was, of course, a certain wisdom in that.

But I am happy that I was hardheaded. And I am very happy now, these many years later, to be a part of this book.

—New York City, December 2001

INTRODUCTION

M USIC?
You want to start with music?

Music's easy! I can draw a more or less straight line from Caruso to Sinatra, from Italian in America to Italian American, and once we get to Ol' Blue Eyes we're headlining the big room of 20th-century popular culture, so let's hear it too for Dino, Perry Como, Tony Bennett et Al (Martino). From there it's a quick left to Bobby Darin, and then you're next door to Dion with or without the Belmonts, followed by the rest of Italo-rock (who *else* put the wop in doo-wop?), including the South Philly holy trinity of Fabian, Frankie Avalon, Bobby Rydell, and James Darren (I know it's a crowded trinity but hey, we were poor). From there you make that big falsetto leap up—*ohh-WAH-ahh!*—to those sons of Vivaldi, the Four Seasons, who were, in some dark corners of the culture map, whether you like it or not, considered to be genuine rivals to that other quartet of the era, the Naples to their Florence, you could say. In the midsixties came the great flowering renaissance of the artform (Florence won), and with that the recognizably, blatantly Italianate sonic influence vanishes, seemingly left in the dust—except that the presence of Italian American creative figures in popular music has remained huge. It's just that ever since and unto now, it's pretty much impossible to isolate or identify: You've got a long list of names (including your Trey Anastasio of Phish, your Rivers Cuomo of Weezer, your Frank Zappa, Madonna, Jon Bon Jovi, Ani De Franco, Gwen Stefani, Joey Fatone, Mike Viola, on and on) with nothing apparent in common aside from that ultimate vowel.

Which is as it should be: Over the course of decades a style matures into an aesthetic, which then builds and broadens and deepens and develops and expands and absorbs until *pow!* it explodes into a thousand manifestations in which the original impulse is at once everywhere and nowhere to be found. The pattern was thereby established, and it mirrored the path of American ethnic assimilation itself—hang together awhile for protection and sustenance, then, once the weather breaks and the natives warm up, light out for the open road and do your own thing.

Anyway, like I said, music's easy. You want to discuss the contribution of Americans of the Italian persuasion to global mass culture, pop/rock edition, and I can bend your ear for hours.

Movies? Here, too, I can sling vowels all day and never break a sweat. I can't exactly account for the long drought that comes right after Capra, Frank and ends with Coppola, Francis Ford, but once you get to the '70s, stand back, because from Scorsese to DePalma to Cimino to Tarantino, from DeNiro to Pacino to Buscemi to Heather Matarazzo (*Heather Matarazzo!* In one beautiful, unforgettable name, the story of our great mutt nation is told), there's an awful lot of Italian energy that's gone into American mythology-making. As in music, there's an Italo canon (six essential films—the three Godfathers and the Mean Streets/Raging Bull/Good Fellas trilogy) which, once established, provides the fertile bed in which a thousand flowers (*Heather!*) bloom and now, thanks to David Chase and "The Sopranos," has even brought us back to where we started, still explaining America to itself better than anyone else.

In fact, take just Sinatra and the Mario Puzo/Coppola collaboration and you've got two indisputable all-time high points of twentieth-century American culture. So what more do you want from us? What's left to prove? Theater? Dancing? I don't know dance, but then neither do you. Art? Over my head, and anyway I have to get around to my point here sooner or later.

Writing? Okay, this is the problem. This is the thing. Because in this particular branch of the expressive arts, while there have been Italians scuffling alongside everybody else, and even some superstars who hit the long ball, it has never quite come together as it did in music and movies. It has failed to attain that moment of *coalescence*.

Why is this so? The question of insufficient Italian contribution to American letters has been raised before, most memorably a few years back, on the front page of the *New York Times Book Review,* by Gay Talese, one of the big-ticket literary figures we've got. The generation of immigrants' children did, in fact, produce a number of noteworthy scribblers—the novelist John

Fante, the poet John Ciardi, Puzo, Talese (he was too modest to say, so I will), a handful more—but after that, Talese wondered aloud: *What happened?* As I say, there have been plenty of writers who happen to be of Italian blood, among them the uncontested god of the post-modern novel, but taken all together, as a tribe, they were not numerous enough, or voluminous enough, or courageous or contagious enough, to create a body of work that hung together like a widely acknowledged *literature*. Or so Talese observed.

In response to his essay, an intramural protest rose up from some of what *litterateurs* (or is it *literati?*) as existed, saying no way, Gay, we Italian American writers *are too* here, working long and hard and well, but the keepers of the castle have ignored and marginalized and relegated us to the sidelines of American cultural life, boo hoo hoo. In other words: *It's not our fault!* Of course, the truth is that pretty much *all* writers are ignored and marginalized and so on—it's like the default position of the late-twentieth/early twenty-first centuries, and if they do get any attention it's practically a miracle, a freak occurrence. Books have been getting their asses kicked by moving images and recorded sound for nearly a century now, and it's never going to get any better.

Besides, none of these conditions stopped American Jews from creating a literature of *their* own, one that dominated the postwar reading life of the country as a whole. (On the other hand, if the Jews had been able to produce a Sinatra, would they have bothered with a Bellow or a Roth?)

Even before Talese broke the silence, this particular vacuum had been noticed. In 1974, Rose Basile Green published her critical survey of the subject, *The Italian American Novel: A Document of the Interaction of Two Cultures.* In that book's foreword, Mario Pei, a novelist and educator, made some interesting observations of his own regarding the lack of an Italian American literature. He pointed out that the Western Hemisphere had been widely explored by Italians (Columbus, Vespucci, Cabot, Verrazzano) operating under the flags of other nations. After which, the languages and cultures of certain European countries took root throughout the New World and elsewhere—English in the U.S., Canada, New Zealand, and Australia; French in Canada, Haiti, parts of Africa and southeast Asia; Spanish throughout North, Central and South America. Portuguese is the native tongue of Brazil, which accounts for half the land mass of South America, and what the hell has Portugal done lately?

Whereas Italian, Pei couldn't help but notice, the language *and* the culture, achieved no such influence away from home. Italy managed one imperialistic conquest, over poor Ethiopia, and even that was through in a flash.

And while, for example, a worthy Spanish-language literature sprang forth in Latin America, there is no such branch of writing in Italian thriving anywhere outside of Italy, despite the fact that it disgorged roughly one-quarter of its population around the turn of the twentieth century, most of it highly concentrated in pockets of North and South Americas.

Even historically, the greatest storytellers of Italian blood have not tilled the fields of the long-form written narrative. Granted, the novel was not the rage back in the day of Ovid or Dante, but two relatively contemporary colossi never wrote a single word—and still the old tales as told by Verdi and Puccini persist. Puzo spun a terrific and popular yarn, but chances are it would be forgotten by now were it not for the involvement of Coppola, who turned *The Godfather* into something transcendent, just as Italy postwar was served most brilliantly not by its authors but by its moviemakers. In the century or so of the existence of the Nobel Prize for literature, Italians have won it six times: Thrice by poets (Giuseppe Carducci, Salvatore Quasimodo and Eugenio Montale), twice by playwrights (Luigi Pirandello and Dario Fo), and just once by a novelist—Grazia Deledda, in 1926. Italy today still does not possess a voracious book culture—of all Italians old enough to read, only 42 percent make it all the way through one book a year. In the southern part of the country, the ancestral home of most Italian Americans, the number is even smaller—just 32 percent read a book a year.

Migration to America improved that habit, and began doing so almost as soon as the educated children of the uneducated immigrants were old enough to express themselves in writing. This would have been in the late 1930s, a bit of bad timing that was just one more reason for the lack of a secure Italian place at the table of American letters. The first appearance of three of Italian America's most gifted sons, authors whose work remains in print today, happens in the late '30s to early '40s: Pietro DiDonato's proletarian masterpiece, *Christ in Concrete,* comes out in 1939, as does John Fante's breakthrough second novel, *Ask the Dust.* In 1943 Jerre Mangione publishes his landmark novel-memoir, *Mount Allegro.* So we have the first flowering of Italian American literature taking place simultaneously with World War II, a time, you may recall, when Italy took the side of Hitler against the U.S. and the forces of freedom and decency.

This, you can guess, didn't do much to promote the good name of Italian culture hereabouts.

Scholars have yet to fully explore how deeply World War II drove Italian American culture into hiding. Nor have they explained the near-miraculous turnaround as America began its warm (and continuing) embrace of Italy and its offspring a quarter-century after the war ended. Americans of German and, to a lesser extent, Japanese extraction still occasionally bear the stigma of those days, whereas it's hard to find anyone who blames Italians for the evil of the era.

At the time, however, more than 600,000 Italians living in America were deemed "enemy aliens," and thousands were interned as potential threats to national security, locked away in camps far from the coasts, where they presumably might have made mischief. They went after Joe DiMaggio's father! Banished him from the coastal waters of northern California where he had once made his living as a fisherman, where he earned the sustenance to grow a Joltin' Joe. Overall it was a nervous time to be Italian in this country. The men and women of my parents' generation, who came of age around World War II, tended to be fervently American, if only to convince everybody else whose side they were on. This probably made ostentatious tribalism, even in reading habits, seem like a bad idea.

After the war, America was ready for some new voices, setting the stage for all the ethnic, racial and other outsiders who began telling their tales in the '50s, '60s and '70s. By then, however, the seminal Italian American moment had come and gone.

Which is not to say that outside forces are completely or even largely to blame for the lack of a widely recognized literature. In his essay, Talese wondered if there might be some aspects of the Italian American nature—of our character, our culture, our soul—that could account for the lack of a strong tradition of written expression. Here he spoke mostly from personal experience, but it rang true when he pointed out that in order to be a writer you need to be, to some extent, an antisocial creature, because you spend so much of your time either alone reading or alone writing. You also need to be comfortable revealing (even under the guise of fiction) matters of home and heart that might normally be thought of as private. And these two traits, Talese ventured, are maybe the weakest suits in the Italian American hand.

Vile, pernicious stereotypes! And like most stereotypes, containing some brave truth. Traditionally, southern Italians *do* esteem the group, the gang, the neighborhood, the team, the family, thereby separating the world into two factions: us and them. A sane attitude, by the way, and one without which the beleaguered southern part of Italy might not have outlasted centuries of occupation by hostile foreigners. This insularity, this conformity, these weren't just whims—they were (and maybe still are) excellent survival mechanisms. In Italy, small villages (like Nereto, in the province of Teramo, my grandfather's birthplace) are called by the name of *Comune*—as in commune. In America, my grandmother's highest praise for girls I brought home, usually reserved for the ones who had the ambition and nerve to engage her in conversation, was to comment, "She was *very* sociable." To the textbook Italian American, as more than one writer in this volume has pointed out, together is wholesome and alone is ill.

The justly celebrated southern Italian taciturnity, especially in the face of nosy outsiders, is likewise imported and ingrained. By now, thanks to an overdose of bad gangster movies, the word *omerta* has entered into the lingo as the mafia's oath of secrecy when it comes to criminal doings. But this discretion is a central pillar of southern Italian peasant culture itself, true for gangsters and grandmas alike. It's all part of the same wisely self-protective villager's mindset. At its heart it states simply this: *If you want to know the worst about me you'll have to figure it out yourself, because I'm not telling.* Given this fundamental trait, is it any wonder that so far we've produced no Italian American *Portnoy*? If Philip Roth had been one of ours, his grandmother would have chopped him up and buried the pieces under her tomato plants.

And that's assuming she'd read the book, of course, because along with everything else, the southern Italian hotbeds of immigration tended to be places where literacy and education were low. Nonexistent, even. What Nick Tosches wrote in his foreword, others have echoed: There was a suspicion that you have to be careful with books, because they can put thoughts in an impressionable young head. To that viewpoint, reading amounts to an act of deviance and defiance. Whereas music and movies, both in the creating and the consuming, seem better suited to inherently social Italian American natures. Frankly, having spent an awful lot of my waking existence either reading or writing, a life of working on movie sets or in doowop quartets looks like more fun.

At any rate, if people don't read, they won't write. And writers alone can't create a literature—they need readers. This is what really seemed to rankle, with justification, all those aggrieved and frustrated Italian American authors—not only were they being ignored by the culture at large, but even their cousins weren't paying all that much attention.

If any of this had been different, you might already know the name George Panetta. He's been dead for thirty years, but back in his time he was really something—the son of Calabrese immigrants whose day job was as a successful creative figure at Young & Rubicam, the giant advertising agency, during a period (the '50s and '60s) when Madison Avenue was a vibrant force in the life of America. But he was also a playwright, winner of an Obie Award in the 1957–58 season for best off-Broadway comedy, a work called *Comic Strip*. He was a book-writer, too—he wrote a funny and earthy short novel about a family of Calabrese immigrants called *We Ride a White Don-*

key, and a collection of stories based on his job titled *Viva Madison Avenue!* (It was a Broadway play, too.) He even wrote a few kids' books in there—he was prolific for the sensible reason that he needed the money, allegedly to support a racetrack habit—but my point here is that he was a gifted writer who worked hard and well and successfully in a very public arena.

On top of all that he was a memorable character, according to Harriett Wasserman, who knew him when she worked for Panetta's literary agent, Henry Volkening. Panetta was short and stocky and funny and sweet, she remembers. "Once, I took him to lunch, and he reached for the check. So I grabbed it away and said, 'Oh, no, I'm your agent—*I'll* pay for lunch.' And he said, 'A dame is picking up my tab? This has never happened to me before!'"

Don't feel too guilty if you run to your shelves and find no George Panetta there—none of his books has been in print for decades. He's dead and forgotten (or nearly so). If no lasting readership materialized for him, and no champion of his work later came forward to keep the flame burning, what hope did any of his literary paisans have?

That's not to say that we Italian Americans should read and revere him or anybody else just because of some coincidence of ethnicity. That's the danger down at the other extreme—that you become known and loved too much for your ancestry and too little for anything else. John Ciardi famously called the WASP lion of letters Robert Lowell a son of a bitch after Lowell praised Ciardi as an Italian American poet. Ciardi, who was an influential cultural figure and public artist (a poet with a network TV show, if you can imagine), felt damned by Lowell's qualified praise, and who can blame him for being a little touchy? Today, of course, people are shocked to think of Don DeLillo as having any ethnicity at all, and while Talese has written journalism and memoirs about Italian American life, he began doing so only after first securing his high reputation in the bloodless meritocracies of the *New York Times* and *Esquire* circa four decades ago—where, if anything, being of southern Italian lineage was strike one and two.

Sinatra achieved perfect balance in these matters: In his personal life, he seemed to be 100 percent prewar guinea from Jersey. Professionally, however, he was an American artist, end of story. He wore subtle English suits, sang with impeccable diction, and never performed or recorded songs in Italian, a temptation to play the goomba card that others failed to resist. He didn't want you to like him because of where his grandfathers were born. Did Joe DiMaggio set the record hitting streak by an Italian American ballplayer? Does Antonin Scalia sit on the Italian American Supreme Court?

That skinny little hyphen—history's trailer hitch—is what held us together, sure, but maybe it's also what held us back.

And yet.

And yet?

AND YET HERE WE ARE with a big, fat book of outstanding work by American writers who happen to be of Italian ancestry. At this point I probably owe you a few words about what I chose and why I chose it, but allow me to back all the way up to why I undertook this in the first place.

My initial motive in assembling this volume was not to deem anybody worthier than anybody else, or to make the case for particular writers or books. (Because if that *were* my goal, you can bet your ass I'd have included something from *The Amazing Story of the Tonelli Family in America*, published in hardcover by Addison-Wesley in 1994, ISBN 0-201-62455-9, now out of print, dormant though not dead, meaning that if enough people buy this anthology maybe I can still get a paperback deal and give my poor book the shot at immortality it truly deserves.)

No, it begins because I was a kid in a time and place when finding a journalist or novelist with an Italian-sounding name was kind of an unusual event and therefore (to me) a big deal. I have the vivid memory of teenage Thursdays scanning the *South Philadelphia Review,* a weekly paper, searching for the column by Tom Cardella (who's still writing there, a true Italo-litero hero). When I first noticed him, something went *click* inside my brain. The fact that he could be funny and sly and honest and even ironic about who he was and how he lived only heightened my joy. A little later, reading *Philadelphia Magazine,* I discovered the gifted journalists Gaeton Fonzi and Jim Riggio, and the clicking grew louder. It made me feel as though maybe I had a shot at working somewhere in the word trades.

Do young readers still operate that way? I hope not—nobody ever truly was excluded from writing (not a real exclusive field to begin with) because of who their grandparents were.

But you know how it is when you're a kid—you're looking outside, hoping to find some plausible version of yourself already functioning in the world of adults. These writers became, in a way, like alter egos, or, more precisely, like alternate fathers. My father worked all his life as a welder in the High Voltage department of the General Electric plant at 70th and Elmwood in Southwest Philly. There he made switchgear equipment, gargantuan machinery that went into electrical generating plants. I visited on GE's open-house days, and it was an awesome sight—everything was huge and dark and deadly, capable of zapping you into a small pile of cinders with a couple million volts. It thrilled me to see the armor my father wore, heavy, scarred cladding topped by a steel helmet with a thick glass window—arrayed thusly, blazing torch in gloved hand, he became god-like to my eyes: Vulcan Tonelli, the blue-collar deity of fire and molten metal. But I knew there was no way I could manage thirty years on that job. I'd hit the wrong button and cremate myself inside of thirty minutes.

So if I couldn't find me there, where *was* I? That's where those other fathers, the ones who worked with a notebook and a typewriter, came in handy. Maybe I was there? Later, when I first started working as a reporter, my father casually told me what, in his youth, he had dreamed of becoming: a writer.

As I say, all these events happened a long time ago, but still, to this day—reflexively, helplessly—I scour the horizon for writers with names ending in vowels, and despite my better judgment, I'm always happy when I find a good one. If a collection like this needs a stated reason to exist, let this primal and earnest one bear the weight: I wanted to share a reader's happiness. I'm standing too close to say whether any of this amounts to an Italian American literature—that will be for you and your cousin Louie to determine, and anyway what difference would it make?—but I did find a big world of terrific writing that struck me as having a thing or two in common.

One aspect of Italian American culture that Gay Talese didn't discuss explicitly (though he hinted at it) is its energetic skepticism where nonconformity is concerned. I mean *any* kind of human eccentricity, but especially the variety found in most writers—the one characterized by the watchful, detached footing that is the big gun of the authorial arsenal. As a result, Italian Americans don't follow the literary path lightly. Certainly, nothing encourages you down that particular lonesome road, and so, in my experience, there tend to be no dilettantes or lightweights among Italian American oddballs. The ones who do emerge (and survive) tend to be fierce and stubborn and battle-hardened and purposeful—even the funny ones. (Even the poets are tough!) They don't write as though they expect a great deal of sentimental indulgence from the reader. And, sharing a trait with their brethren in music and movies, they keep in mind that if you're going to take the stage you had better be entertaining, along with whatever else it is you're trying to be. It makes for some vigorous, efficient storytelling.

Another thing I noticed was that the best writing by Italian Americans tended not to exist in books intent on telling anyone what it was like to *be*

Italian American. You can find terrific novels by Irish or black authors that manage to articulate, with great, lasting power, an entire ethnicity's experience in America. To the best of my knowledge, no such dispatch has been written by an Italian American. Maybe we still refuse to trade on our secrets—if old habits die hard, old Italian habits die hardest. We have always taken a special pleasure in understatement, indirection and subtle deceptions, I think. It's probably in our blood, or close enough. This may be damning to the possibility of a literature, but for my purposes that discovery was liberating. It allowed me to forsake the most obvious qualification for inclusion herein, when I decided that subject didn't matter: If an Italian American wrote it, it was eligible, regardless of what it was about, even if it had absolutely nothing to do with "being" Italian. If ancestry counts for anything meaningful, I figured, then it must count no matter what a writer writes. There are several authors included here who cautioned me that they feel no connection whatsoever to their roots and have never seen themselves as Italian at all. Fine by me, I said—that's just one more way of being Italian. One writer, a really famous one, at first rejected the invitation to be in this anthology. The reason: This particular writer has always despised the idea of hyphenated citizenship and (in Ciardi-like fashion) feels actively insulted by the Italian American label. Perfect, I replied—this book *needs* that kind of bad attitude.

Sometimes I even decided against using something that felt like a natural choice—I could easily have taken John Fante's justifiably famous story, "Odyssey of a Wop," but instead I chose something even better, from his novel *Ask the Dust*. As a literary influence on other authors (primarily Charles Bukowski, who was himself fairly influential), the novel earns its position high among anything ever written by an Italian American. If you love this excerpt, I hope you'll go out and find the stories. I also resisted the temptation to instruct—for a while I intended to represent Jerre Mangione with an excerpt of *La Storia*, the Italian American history that he and novelist Ben Morreale wrote together. I was going to use the chapter about a little-remembered moment in 1891 when eleven innocent Sicilian immigrants were lynched by a racist mob in New Orleans. But, as important as that chapter may be, it's not really Mangione at his best, and so instead I went with a memoir of his Sicilian-American youth (hoping, again, that some readers will find *La Storia* as a result).

Italians have been depicted strangely over the course of the century or so we've been Americans in any serious number. Our time of genuine suffering at the hands of this bruising country passed more or less unchronicled, by ourselves or anyone else. And even now, in an era that supposedly values cultural diversity and authenticity, the portrait of Italian Americans is monotonous and observed from a safe distance. It's understandable—the mobster, the urban brute, the little old lady shoving a plate of rigatoni under your nose, these are vivid characters. And I don't care what the anti-defamation mafia would have you think, nobody loves those characters better than Italian Americans do. But enough already! It gets to be like a minstrel show after a while. We should be free to be mobsters and brutes and pushy old broads, but also free to go wherever else our natural inclinations lead us. There are many more Italian American CPAs than hit men (not that I want to watch a cable TV series about accountants).

Of course, the question then arises: If we're not those memorable figures from central casting, who are we? The immigrants of olden days asked no such question: they were constantly being reminded that they were Italians. Their children lived the compelling drama of all new Americans. But we are . . . *who*? If we wish, we can claim the label of Italian American, but that's an imprecise and unstable mixture: We're a whole other thing. That's partly what I was looking for as I gathered this anthology—writing that addressed the questions of who and what we are and how we live as they have confronted us over the past seven decades, without the cheap comfort of nostalgia for a time and way of life that probably never existed. We're going to have to navigate the future using the past, but who are we *today*? This book contains nearly 70 answers to that question.

The oldest work in this collection is from 1939, but overall it skews toward the contemporary. There are nine or ten dead writers, which feels about right to me, enough tribute to the ancestral words but not too much. When it comes to the old books, we have the test of time working for us—if something holds up after sixty years it must possess some true virtue. The *Bibliography of the Italian American Book*, a 2000 publication of the Italian American Writers Association, was my only reference work as I prepared this collection, and it would have been a harder, lonelier job without it. According to this document, there have been at least 1,500 book-length works of writing (not counting cookbooks) by Italian American authors, nearly all created during the last 60 years of the twentieth century, by roughly 500 or so authors. This anthology strains its capacity with 68 contributors, meaning I've been forced to leave out roughly 90 percent of all Italian American writers, and probably two-thirds of the good ones.

Beyond that, of course, there are the perversities and blind spots of my own taste. I resolved from the start that I wouldn't include anything if I didn't really love it, regardless of its literary or historical importance or its reputation among other readers. But even with that standard I ended up leaving out a lot of very good work, some of which I enjoyed as much as the stuff I've included. The only writing that I felt, going in, was absolutely essential is also the oldest—Pietro DiDonato's *Christ in Concrete*, which came out as a book in '39 but was first glimpsed (the opening chapter) in *Esquire* two years earlier. That this classic is even still in print (in paperback) is a minor miracle and testament to its power. I read this first in my twenties, was blown away, put it aside, re-read it in the course of assembling this collection, and was blown away again. I love everything in this book, but my absolute favorite piece is another one that's been around awhile, "Suit," a story by the aforementioned George Panetta. I mention this mainly as a reader service—it's way in the back of the book, but I don't want you to miss it.

The organizing principle of this collection suggested itself—once I arranged all the pieces on a very large table, they began to group themselves as you see them here: under headings of home, Mom and Pop, love, sex and good looks, God, work, death, food, each other, and everybody else. Better than chronological or alphabetical, I thought, and satisfyingly elemental as themes go. When you try to go beyond these realms of life, you find there's not much left.

Aside from whatever literary goals I had in editing this collection, I think I also wanted to repay my long-overdue reader's debt. I wanted to give something back to the writers, like a chance to get their noses out of their belly buttons, to have a few belts and relax a little—we could bring back some of the dead ones, let them dust themselves off and wet their whistles and have a few laughs. I figured the writers would talk to us readers, but they would, across the pages, talk to each other, too, maybe get a little rowdy and make some noise, like it's a party—I wanted to interrupt the dirty joke Mario Puzo was telling to Don DeLillo, Victoria Gotti, Camille Paglia and John Fante and tell them all to stand still a minute so I could take their picture. I'm just the guy who rented the hall and hired the caterer and—okay, mercifully, the party's begun and the band is playing, so I'll shut up. Listen: *Ohh-WAH-ahh . . .*

—Bill Tonelli
July 31, 2002

Bronzini didn't own a car, didn't drive a car, didn't want one, didn't need one, wouldn't take one if somebody gave it to him. Stop walking, he thought, and you die.

HOME

Don DeLillo

Underworld

BRONZINI THOUGHT THAT WALKING WAS an art. He was out nearly every day after school, letting the route produce a medley of sounds and forms and movements, letting the voices fall and the aromas deploy in ways that varied, but not too much, from day to day. He stopped to talk to cardplayers in a social club and watched a woman buy a flounder in the market. He peeled a tangerine and wondered how a flatfish lying glassy on flaked ice, a thing scraped with a net from the dim sea, could seem so eloquent a fellow creature. Its deadness was a force in those bulging eyes. Such intense emptiness. He thought of the old device of double take, how it comically embodies the lapsed moment where a life used to be.

He watched an aproned boy wrap the fish in a major headline.

Even in this compact neighborhood there were streets to revisit and men doing interesting jobs, day labor, painters in drip coveralls or men with sledgehammers he might pass the time with, Sicilians busting up a sidewalk, faces grained with stone dust. The less a job pays, Bronzini thought, the harder the work, the more impressive the spectacle. Or a waiter having a smoke during a lull, one of those fast-aging men who are tired all the time. The waiters had tired lives, three jobs, backaches and bad feet. They were more tired than the men in red neckerchiefs who swung the heavy hammers. They smoked and coughed and told him how tired they were and looked for a place on the sidewalk where they might situate the phlegm they were always spitting up.

He ate the last wedge of tangerine and left the market holding the spiral rind in his hand. He walked slowly north glancing in shop windows. There were silver points of hair in his brush mustache, still so few they were countable, and he wore rimless spectacles with wire temples because at thirty-eight, or so said his wife, he wanted to convince himself he was older, settled in his contentments, all the roilsome things finally buttoned and done.

He heard voices and looked down a side street filled with children playing. A traffic stanchion carried a sign marking the area a play street and blocking the way to cars and delivery trucks. With cars, more cars, with the status hunger, the hot horsepower, the silver smash of chrome, Bronzini saw that the pressure to free the streets of children would make even these designated areas extinct.

He imagined a fragment of chalked pavement cut clean and lifted out and elaborately packed—shipped to some museum in California where it would share the hushed sunlight with marble carvings from antiquity. *Street drawing; hopscotch; chalk on paved asphalt; Bronx, 1951.* But they don't call it hopscotch, do they? It's patsy or potsy here. It's buck-buck, not johnny-on-the-pony. It's hango seek—you count to a hundred by fives and set out into alleyways, shinnying up laundry poles and over back fences, sticking your head into coal bins to find the hiding players.

Bronzini stood and watched.

Girls playing jacks and jumping double dutch. Boys at boxball, marbles and ringolievio. Five boys each with a foot in a segmented circle that had names of countries marked in the wedges. China, Russia, Africa, France and Mexico. The kid who is *it* stands at the center of the circle with a ball in his hand and slowly chants the warning words: *I de-clare a-war u-pon.*

Bronzini didn't own a car, didn't drive a car, didn't want one, didn't need one, wouldn't take one if somebody gave it to him. Stop walking, he thought, and you die.

George the Waiter stood smoking near the service entrance of the restaurant where he worked. He was a face on a pole, a man not yet out of his thirties who carried something stale and unspontaneous, an inward tension that kept him apart. Over the spare body a white shirt with black vest and black trousers and above the uniform his jut features looking a little bloodsucked.

Bronzini walked over and took up a position next to George and they stood without speaking for a long moment in the odd solidarity two strangers might share watching a house burn down.

Three boys and a girl played down-the-river against the side of a building, each kid occupying a box formed by separations in the sidewalk. One of them slap-bounced a ball diagonally off the pavement so that it hit up against the wall and veered off into another player's box.

He was George the Waiter in a second sense, that his life seemed suspended in some dire expectation. What is George waiting for? Bronzini couldn't help seeing a challenge here. He liked to educe comment from the untalkative man, draw him forth, make him understand that his wish to be friendless was not readily respected here.

Then the second player bounced the ball into someone else's box, hitting it hard or lightly, slicing at the lower half of the ball to give it English, and so on up and down the river.

"The thing about these games," Bronzini said. "They mean so much while you're playing. All your inventive skills. All your energies. But when you get a little older and stop playing, the games escape the mind completely."

In fact he'd played only sporadically as a child, being bedridden at times, that awful word, and treated for asthma, for recurring colds and sore throats and whooping cough.

"How we used to scavenge. We turned junk into games. Gouging cork out of bottle caps. I don't even remember what we used it for. Cork, rubber bands, tin cans, half a skate, old linoleum that we cut up and used in carpet guns. Carpet guns were dangerous."

He checked his watch as he spoke.

"You talk about the cork," George said.

"What was the cork for?"

"We used the cork to make cages for flies. Two flat pieces of cork. Then we got straight pins from the dressmaker which were all over the floor of the shop."

"My god you're right," Bronzini said.

"We stuck the pins between the cork discs. One disc is the floor, one is the ceiling. The pins are the bars."

"Then we waited for a fly to land somewhere."

"A horsefly on a wall. You cup your hand and move it slowly along the wall and come up behind the fly."

"Then we put the fly in the cage."

"We put the fly in the cage. Then we put in extra pins," George said, "sealing the fly."

"Then what? I don't remember."

"We watched it buzz."

"We watched it buzz. Very educational."

"It buzzed until it died. If it took too long to die, somebody lit a match. Then we put the match in the cage."

"My god what terror," Bronzini said.

But he was delighted. He was getting George to talk. How children adapt to available surfaces, using curbstones, stoops and manhole covers. How they take the pockmarked world and turn a delicate inversion, making something brainy and rule-bound and smooth, and then spend the rest of their lives trying to repeat the process.

Directly across the street George the Barber was sweeping the floor of his shop. Voices from Italian radio drifting faintly out the open door. Bronzini watched a man walk in, a custodian from the high school, and George put away the broom and took a fresh linen sheet out of a drawer and had it unfolded and sail-billowing, timed just right, as the man settled into the chair.

"Maybe you heard, Albert. The hunchback died, that used to carve things out of soap."

"We're going back a few years."

"He carved naked women out of soap. Like anatomical. The hunchback that used to sit outside the grocery."

"Attilio. You'd give him a bar of soap, he'd carve something."

"What's-his-name died, the softball player, the pitcher that threw windmill. He had shrapnel from the war. He had shrapnel actually in his heart from the war. That only now killed him."

"Jackie somebody. You and he."

"We used to work together at the beach. But I barely knew him."

George used to sell ice cream at the beach. Bronzini saw him many times deep-stepping through the sand with a heavy metal cooler slung over his shoulder and a pith helmet rocking on his head. And white shirt and white ducks and the day somebody got a cramp while George sold Popsicles in section 10.

"Remember the drowned man?" Bronzini said.

They were playing salugi in the street. Two boys snatched a schoolbook belonging to one of the girls, a Catholic school girl in a blue pinafore and white blouse. They tossed the book back and forth and she ran from one boy to the other and they threw the book over her head and behind her back. The book had a thick brown kraft cover that Bronzini was sure the girl had made herself, folding and tucking the grainy paper, printing her name in blue ink on the front—name and grade and subject. *Salugi*, they cried, that strange word, maybe some corruption of the Italian *saluto*, maybe a mock salutation— hello, we've got your hat, now try and get it back. Another boy joined the game and the girl ran from one to the other, scatterhanded, after the flying book.

Or Hindi or Persian or some Northumbrian nonce word sifting down the centuries. There was so much to know that he would die not knowing.

"What about the kid?" George said. "I'm hearing things that I don't know if it's good or what."

"He's coming along. I'm pleased one day, exasperated the next."

"I have respect for people that can play that game. When I think to myself this kid is how old."

"I try not to lose sight of that very thing, George."

"I hear he beats experienced players. This could be good or bad. Not that I'm the expert here. But I'm thinking maybe he should be in the street with those other kids."

"The street is not ready for Matty."

"You should impress into him there's other things."

"He does other things besides playing chess. He cries and screams."

George didn't smile. He was standing off, faded into old brooding, and he sucked the last bland fumes from his cigarette. One drag too many. Then he dropped the butt and stepped on it with the tap toe of his way-weary shoe, the border of uniformed George, rutted and cut across the instep.

"Time I showed my face inside. Be good, Albert."

"We'll talk again," Bronzini said.

He walked across the street so he could wave to George the Barber. How children adapt, using brick walls and lampposts and fire hydrants. He watched a girl tying one end of her jump rope to a window grille and getting her little brother to turn the other end. Then she stood in the middle and jumped. No history, no future. He watched a boy playing handball against himself, hitting Chinese killers. The hi-bounce rubber ball, the pink spaldeen, rapping back from the brick facade. And the fullness of a moment in the play street. Unable to imagine you will ever advance past the pencil line on the kitchen wall your mother has drawn to mark your height.

The barber waving back. Bronzini went to the corner past a man unloading jerry cans of Bulgarian sheep cheese from the trunk of a beat-up car. He walked north again, the savor of sweet peel in his hand. He realized he was still holding the fruit rind. It made him think of Morocco. He'd never been there or much of anywhere and wondered why the frailest breath of tangerine might bring to mind a reddish sandscape flashing to infinity.

Buck buck how many horns are up?

The clear cry reached him as he tossed the skin toward some cartons stacked at a cellar entrance. They are jumping on the backs of their playpals. It is usually the fattest boy who serves as cushion, standing against a wall or pole while the boys on one team stoop head to end and their rivals run and jump one by one and come yowing down. With the stooped boys swaying under the weight, the leader of the mounted team holds fingers aloft and calls out the question. How many horns are up? Bronzini tried to recall whether the padded boy, the slapped and prodded roly-poly, the one who dribbles egg cream down his chin—is he officially called the pillow or the pillar? Bronx boys don't know from pillars, he decided. Make him the mothery casing stuffed with down.

Twenty past four. The appointment was ten minutes hence and he knew that even if he arrived after the specified time he would not be late because Father Paulus was certain to be later. Bronzini envied the blithe arrivals of life's late people. How do they manage the courage to be late, enact the rude dare repeatedly in our waiting faces? A goat and four rabbits were hung upside down in a window, trussed at the hind legs, less affectingly dead than the flounder in the market—dumb scuzzy fur with nothing to impart. Envy and admiration both. He took it that these people refuse to be mastered by the pettier claims of time and conscience.

The butcher appeared at the door of his shop, flushed and hoarse, loud, foul, happy in his unwashed apron, a man who lived urgently, something inside him pushing outward, surging against his chest wall.

"Albert, I don't see you no more."

"You're seeing me now. You see me all the time. I bought a roast last week."

"Don't tell me last week. What's last week?"

The butcher called to people walking by. He called across the street to insult a man or engage a particular woman with knowing references. The rasping spitty sandblast voice. Other women twisted their mouths, amused and disgusted.

"What are you feeding that genius of yours?"

"He's not mine," Bronzini said.

"Be thankful. That was my kid I drive him out to the country and leave him on a hillside. But I wait for the dead of winter."

"We let him chew on a crayon once a week."

"Feed the little jerk some capozella. It makes him ballsy."

The butcher gestured at the whole lamb hanging in the window. Bronzini imagined the broiled head hot from the oven and sitting on a plate in front of Matty. Two cooked heads regarding each other. And Albert is telling the boy he has to eat the brain and eyes and principal ganglia. Or no more chess.

"It puts some lead in his pencil."

The butcher stood at the corner of the window looking well-placed among the dangled animals, his arms crossed and feet spread. Bronzini saw an aptness and balance here. The butcher's burly grace, watch him trim a chop, see how he belongs to the cutting block, to the wallow of trembling muscle and mess—his aptitude and ease, the sense that he was born to the task restored a certain meaning to these eviscerated beasts.

Bronzini thought the butcher's own heart and lungs ought to hang outside his body, stationed like a saint's, to demonstrate his intimate link to the suffering world.

"Be good, Albert."

"I'll be in tomorrow."

"Give my best to the woman," the butcher said.

Bronzini checked his watch again, then stopped at a candy store to buy a newspaper. He was trying to be late but knew he could not manage it. Some force compelled him to walk into the pastry shop not only on time but about two and a half minutes early, which translated to a wait of roughly twenty minutes for the priest. He took a table in the dim interior and unfolded the *Times* across the scarred enamel.

A girl brought coffee and a glass of water.

The front page astonished him, a pair of three-column headlines dominating. To his left the Giants capture the pennant, beating the Dodgers on a dramatic home run in the ninth inning. And to the right, symmetrically mated, same typeface, same-size type, same number of lines, the USSR explodes an atomic bomb—*kaboom*—details kept secret.

He didn't understand why the *Times* would take a ball game off the sports page and juxtapose it with news of such ominous consequence. He began to read the account of the Soviet test. He could not keep the image from entering his mind, the cloud that was not a cloud, the mushroom that was not a mushroom—the sense of reaching feebly for a language that might correspond to the visible mass in the air. Suddenly there the priest was, coming in a flurry, Andrew Paulus S.J., built low and cozy, his head poked forward and that glisten of spittle in his smile.

He had books and folders slipping down his hip but managed to extend a cluster of scrubbed fingers, which Albert gripped in both hands, pressing and shaking, half rising from his chair. It took a moment of clumsy ceremony with overlapping salutations and unheeded questions and a dropped book and a race to retrieve it before the two men were settled at the table and all the objects put away. The priest heaved, as they say, a sigh. He wore a roman collar fitted to a biblike cloth called a rabat and over this a dark jacket with pocket square and he could have been George the Waiter's tailored master in black and white.

"How late am I?"

"You're not late at all."

"I'm doing a seminar on knowledge. Wonderful fun but I lose track."

"No, you're early," Bronzini said.

"How we know what we know."

You had to look hard at Andrew Paulus to find a trace of aging. Unfurrowed and oddly aglow, with a faint baked glaze keeping his skin pink and fresh. Hair pale brown and fringed unevenly across the forehead in boyish bangs. Bronzini wondered if this is what happens to men who forswear a woman's tangling touch and love. They stay a child, preserved in clean and chilly light. But there were parish priests everywhere about, leaky-eyed and halting, their old monotones falling whispery from the pulpit. He decided this man was not youthful so much as ageless. He must be thirty years senior to Albert and not an eyelid ever trembles or a bristly whit of gray shows at the jawline.

"Did you see the paper, Father?"

"Please, we know each other too well. You're required to call me Andy now. Yes, I stole a long look at someone's *Daily News*. They're calling it the Shot Heard Round the World."

"How did we detect evidence of the blast, I wonder. We must have aircraft flying near their borders with instruments that measure radiation. Or well-placed agents perhaps."

"No no no no. We're speaking about the home run. Bobby Thomson's heroic shot. The tabloids have dubbed it for posterity."

Bronzini had to pause to take this in.

"The Shot Heard Round the World? Is the rest of the world all that interested? This is baseball. I was barely aware. I myself barely knew that something was going on. Heard round the world? I almost missed it completely."

"We may take it that the term applies to the suddenness of the struck blow and the corresponding speed at which news is transmitted these days. Our servicemen in Greenland and Japan surely heard the home-run call as it was made on Armed Forces Radio. You're right, of course. They're not talking about this in the coffeehouses of Budapest. Although in fact poor Ralph Branca happens to be half Hungarian. Sons of immigrants. Branca and Thomson both. Bobby himself born in Scotland, I believe. You see why our wins and losses tend to have impact well beyond our borders."

"You follow baseball then."

"Only in distant memory. But I did devour today's reports. It's all over the radio. Something propelled this event full force into the public imagination. All day a steady sort of ripple in the air."

"I don't follow the game at all," Bronzini said.

He fell into remorseful thought. The girl appeared again, sullen in a limp blouse and shuffling loafers. Only four tables, theirs the only one occupied. The plain decor, the time-locked thickness in the air, the trace of family smell, even the daughter discontented—all argued a theme, a nonpicturesqueness that Albert thought the priest might note and approve.

"But baseball isn't the game we're here to discuss," Paulus said.

In other shops the priest had made an appreciative show of selecting a pastry from the display case, with moans and exclamations, but was subdued today, gesturing toward the almond biscotti and asking the girl to bring some coffee. Then he squared in his chair and set his elbows firmly on the table, a little visual joke, and framed his head with cupped hands—the player taut above his board.

"I've been taking him to chess clubs," Bronzini said, "as we discussed last time. He needs this to develop properly. Stronger opponents in an organized setting. But he hasn't done as well as I'd expected. He's been stung a number of times."

"And when he's not playing?"

"We spend time studying, practicing."

"How much time?"

"Three days a week usually. A couple of hours each visit."

"This is completely ridiculous. Go on."

"I don't want to force-feed the boy."

"Go on," Paulus said.

"I'm just a neighbor after all. I can push only so hard. There's no deep tradition here. He just appeared one day. Shazam. A boy from another planet, you know?"

"He wasn't born knowing the moves, was he?"

"His father taught him the game. A bookmaker. Evidently kept all the figures in his head. The bets, the odds, the teams, the horses. He could memorize a scratch sheet. This is the story people told. He could look at a racing form with the day's entries, the morning line, the jockeys and so on. And he could memorize the data of numerous races in a matter of minutes."

"And he disappeared."

"Disappeared. About five years ago."

"And the boy is eleven, which means daddy barely got him started."

"Adequate or not, on and off, I have been the mentor ever since."

The priest made a gesture of appeasement, a raised hand that precluded any need for further explanation. The girl brought strong black coffee and a glass of water and some biscuits on a plate.

"The mother is Irish Catholic. And there's another son. One of my former students. One semester only. Bright, I think, but lazy and unmotivated. He's sixteen and can quit school any time he likes. And I'm speaking on behalf of the mother now. She wondered if you'd be willing to spend an hour with him. Tell him about Fordham. What college might offer such a boy. What the Jesuits offer. Our two schools, Andy, directly across the road from each other and completely remote. My students, some of them don't know, they remain completely unaware of the fact that there's a university lurking in the trees."

"Some of my students have the same problem."

Bronzini remembered to laugh.

"But what a waste if a youngster like this were to end up in a stockroom or garage."

"You've made your plea. Consider your duty effectively discharged, Albert."

"Dip your biscotto. Don't be bashful. Dip, dip, dip. These biscuits are direct descendants of honey and almond cakes that were baked in leaves and eaten at Roman fertility rites."

"I think the task of reproducing the species will have to devolve upon others. Not that I would mind the incidental contact."

Bronzini leaning in.

"In all seriousness. Have you ever regretted?"

"What, not marrying?"

Bronzini nodding, eyes intent behind the lenses.

"I don't want to marry." And now it was the priest's turn to lean forward, shouldering down, sliding his chin near the tabletop. "I just want to screw," he whispered electrically.

Bronzini shocked and charmed.

"The verb to screw is so amazingly, subversively apt. But conjugating the word is not sufficient pastime. I would like to screw a movie star, Albert. The greatest, blondest, biggest-titted goddess Hollywood is able to produce. I want to screw her in the worst way possible and I mean that in every sense."

The small toothy head hovered above the table in defiant self-delight. Bronzini felt rewarded. On a couple of past occasions he'd taken the priest into shops and watched him taste the autumnal pink Parma ham, sliced transparently thin, and he'd offered commentaries on pig's blood pastry and sheets of salt cod. The visitor showed pleasure in the European texture of the street, things done the old slow faithful way, things carried over, suffused with rules of usage. This is the only art I've mastered, Father—walking these streets and letting the senses collect what is routinely here. And he walked the priest into the acid stink of the chicken market and pushed him toward the old scale hung from the ceiling with a lashed bird in the weighing pan, explaining how the poultryman gets twenty cents extra to kill and dress the bird—say something in Latin, Father—and he felt the priest's own shudder when the deadpan Neapolitan snapped the chicken's neck—a wiry man with feathers in his shirt.

"If I were not so dull a husband we might sit here and tell stories into the night."

"Yours real, mine phantasmal."

The priest's confession was funny and sad and assured Albert that he was a privileged companion if not yet a trusted friend. He enjoyed being a guide to the complex deposits around them, the little histories hidden in a gesture or word, but he was beginning to fear that Andy's response would never exceed the level of appreciative interest.

"And when you were young."

"Was I ever in love? Smitten at seven or eight, piercingly. The purest stuff, Albert. Before the heavy hormones. There was a girl named something or other."

"I know a walk we ought to take. There's a play street very near. I think you'd enjoy a moment among the children. It's a dying practice, kids playing in city streets. We'll finish here and go. Another half cup."

He signaled the girl.

"Do you know the famous old painting, Albert? Children playing games. Scores of children filling a market square. A painting that's about four hundred years old and what a shock it is to recognize many games we played ourselves. Games still played today."

"I'm pessimistic, you think."

"Children find a way. They sidestep time, as it were, and the ravages of progress. I think they operate in another time scheme altogether. Imagine standing in a wooded area and throwing stones at the top of a horse chestnut tree to dislodge the sturdiest nuts. Said to be in the higher elevation. Throwing stones all day if necessary and taking the best chestnut home and soaking it in salt water."

"We used vinegar."

"Vinegar then."

"We Italians," Albert said.

"Soak it to make it hard and battle-worthy. And poke a hole through the nut with a skewer and slip a tough bootlace through the hole, a lace long enough to wind around the hand two or three times. It's completely vivid in my mind. Tie a knot, of course, to keep the chestnut secured to the lace. A rawhide lace if possible."

"Then the game begins."

"Yes, you dangle your chestnut and I bash it by launching my own with a sort of dervishy twirl. But it's finding the thing, soaking the thing, taking the time. Time as we know it now had not yet come into being."

"I tramped through the zoo every year at this time to gather fallen chestnuts," Bronzini said.

"Buckeyes."

"Buckeyes."

"Time," the priest said.

Across the room the girl filled the cups from a machine. Father Paulus waited for her to slide his cup across the table so he could let the aromatic smoke drift near his face.

Then he said, "Time, Albert. Both of you must be willing, actually, to pay a much higher price. Hours and days. Whole days at chess. Days and weeks."

Bronzini had his opening, finally.

"And if I'm not willing? Are you? Or not able. If I'm not able to do it. Not equal to the job. Are you, Andy?"

The priest looked at the knot in Albert's tie.

"I thought you wanted advice."

"I do."

"Please. Do you think I'd even consider tutoring the boy? Albert, please. I have a life, such as it is."

"You're far more advanced than I, Father. You're a tournament player. You understand the psychology of the game."

Paulus sat upright in his chair, formally withdrawing, it seemed, to a more objective level of discourse.

"Theories about the psychology of the game, frankly, leave me cold. The game is location, situation and memory. And a need to win. The psychology is in the player, not the game. He must enjoy the company of danger. He must have a killer instinct. He must be prideful, arrogant, aggressive, contemptuous and dominating. Willful in the extreme. All the sins, Albert, of the noncarnal type."

Chastened and deflated. But Albert felt he had it coming. The man's remarks were directed at his own genial drift, of course, not the boy's. His complacent and easy pace.

"He shows master strength, potentially."

"Look, I'm willing to attend a match or two. Give you some guidance if I can. But I don't want to be his teacher. No no no no."

Now the grandmother appeared with an opened bottle of anisette crusted at the rim. When Bronzini asked how she was feeling she let her head rock back and forth. The liqueur was a gesture reserved for select customers and took earning over time. She poured an ashy dram into each demitasse and the priest colored slightly as he seemed to do in the close company of people who were markedly different. Their unknown lives disconcerted him, making his smile go stiff and bringing to his cheeks a formal flush of deference.

She left without a word. They watched her glide moon-slow into the dimmed inner room.

"I don't know what to tell you about the older brother," Paulus said.

"Never mind. I asked only because the mother asked. It will all straighten itself out."

"We have an idea, some of us, that's taking shape. A new sort of collegium. Closer contact, minimal structure. We may teach Latin as a spoken language. We may teach mathematics as an art form like poetry or music. We will teach subjects that people don't realize they need to know. All of this will happen somewhere in the hinterland. We'll want a special kind of boy. Special circumstances," Paulus said. "Something he is. Something he's done. But something."

When they stood to leave and the priest was gathering his books, Bronzini took his cup, the priest's, and drained it of sediment, tipping his head quickly—espresso dregs steeped in anisette.

They shook hands and made vague plans to stay in touch and Father Paulus started on the short walk back to the Fordham campus and Albert realized he'd forgotten his own suggestion about visiting the play street nearby. Too bad. They might have ended on a mellower note.

But when he walked past the street it was nearly emptied out. A few boys still playing ringolievio, haphazard and half speed, the clumsy fatboy trapped in the den, always caught, always *it*, the slightly epicene butterfat bulk, the boy who's always reaching down to lift a droopy sock and getting swift-kicked by the witlings and sadists.

Is that what being *it* means? Neutered, sexless, impersonalized?

Dark now. Another day of games all ended, or nearly all—he could hear the boys' following voices as he made his way down the avenue. And when it ends completely we find ourselves abandoned to our sodden teens. What a wound to overcome, this passage out of childhood, but a beautiful injury too, he thought, pure and unrepeatable. Only the scab remains, barely seen, the exuded substance.

Ringolievio Coca-Cola one two three.

A faint whiff of knishes and hot dogs from the luncheonette under the bowling alley. Then Albert crossed the street to Mussolini Park, as the kids called it, where a few old men still sat on benches with their folded copies of

Il Progresso, the fresh-air inspectors, retired, indifferent or otherwise idle, and they smoked and talked and blew their noses in the street, leaning over the curbstone with thumb and index finger clamped to old shnozzola, discharging the stringy stuff.

Albert wanted to linger a while but didn't see anyone he knew and so he joined the small army of returning workers coming around the bend from Third Avenue, from the buses and elevated train.

Time, finally, to go home.

Theresa Maggio

Ciolino

∽◦∾

I WAS ON A MISSION: to find the smallest mountain towns in Sicily. Tiny jewels, remote and isolated, tourists seldom see them. But they are the island's hidden treasure, and the secret spring of Sicilian endurance.

One town led to another. I'd stare at my map, now flannel soft at the edges, and look for a small dot with an appealing name, get on a bus and go. That's how I came to Polizzi Generosa, four thousand people in a town teetering on a peak in the Madonie Mountains, a quiet world of mist and moss on old stones.

I liked Polizzi so much I rented an apartment there for two weeks. One day I explained to Signora Riccobene, the grocer, about my search. "If you're looking for a small town," she said, "you must go to Locati." Her daughters, twin pharmacists, owned a drugstore there. I checked my map; Locati didn't rate a dot, my kind of town. If I wanted to go, all I had to do was meet Antonietta and Rosaria at six the next morning, and they would drive me there.

For several days I made their pharmacy my base camp and there I met the black-shawled women and men bent over canes who came in to fill prescriptions. One thousand people lived in Locati and soon only the old would be left; the young leave for school and desk jobs in the city. No one wants to be a farmer anymore.

Rosaria and Antonietta were kind to their aged customers and always listened to their sorrows. Seventy-year-old Signora Maria, a regular, had lived most of her life alone in a thatched stone hut in a village much smaller than

Locati. A stroke had forced her to move to town three years before, but she still longed for her abandoned home in the wheat fields of Ciolino.

One afternoon the sisters planned a surprise. They closed up shop, picked up Signora Maria and drove us to her old home. The summer landscape slid by under a matte blue sky—tawny fields of wheat, furrows of freshly turned earth, the rustling gray-green crowns of olive trees. Signora Maria hadn't seen her home since she'd locked its door and left it. Slight, with blue eyes and gray hair, she stared out at the land and told us her life.

She had never married. A peasant farmer's only child, she had lived with her parents on a dirt road in the middle of wide wheat fields. Her family was too poor to own a car, so when they needed supplies, her father took Maria on the donkey and walked to Locati, the closest town with stores. They had to cross a river with no bridge, so they waded across it. "It was all mud," she said. "When it rained, you couldn't walk."

Her father died when she was seven, leaving only the house and the donkey. Maria was heartbroken when her mother sold the beast and they waded one last time through the river to Locati, where there might be work. For the next two years, Maria's mother had heart trouble. Then she died, and Maria was alone. She walked back to Ciolino and raised herself in the thatched stone hut.

"I worked in the wheat harvest. They used to sing," she said as we wound past orchards of almonds and pears. Maria gleaned the fields, the miller ground her grain and she baked round loaves in the communal domed brick oven at the end of her street. To give Maria a trade, a kindly woman had taught her how to give injections painlessly. People paid her with pasta, bread and sacks of grain. "We all respected one another," she said.

There were seventy families in her village then. At Carnevale they would dance until dawn. But Maria spent most of her time alone, cooking, baking, sewing, cleaning and washing for one. "You were a little girl," I said. "Didn't you ever have time for fun?" She had; in her spare time she memorized long folk poems. Once learned, a poem was hers forever, the one thing that couldn't be taken from her.

She was quiet a moment, then the words bubbled up from sixty years before and Signora Maria began a folk epic in rhymed, rhythmic quartets. It told of heroes and villains and women in love, a story about courage and poverty, true friends and betrayal. She recited for ten minutes, as if in a trance, using stage whispers and shouts that once would have lured her neighbors to gather and listen.

The sign at the turn for Ciolino said: "Beyond this point the streets have no names." And, as far as we could see, no trees, no houses, only the sinewy ripple of wheat stalks, plush as puma fur, in fields vast and golden. Now only twenty families remained.

Signora Maria's old neighbors, who knew we were coming, met us at the door of the square stone house they had built and roofed with red tiles. They had abandoned their traditional straw hut years before for the conveniences of modern living. Signora Maria stepped out of the car and looked worriedly at her old house next door. It seemed to have sprouted from the ground and now was going back to it. The straw roof, once stiff as a broom, was bowed and rotting. When it buckled, the world it once sheltered, her girlhood, would be gone forever. Our hostess put her arm around Maria and led us into her own house to a trestle table laden with crusty bread, homemade cheese, plates of sliced mortadella and bowls of black olives. Her husband, a farmer, opened a door off the dining room, flung his arm wide and showed us his treasure: a storeroom stacked to the ceiling with plump burlap sacks of hard Sicilian durum.

Signora Maria ate little but waited politely until the table was cleared. Then she fished a skeleton key from her purse, walked to her cottage, pushed open the door and stepped in.

The only light came through the cracks in the thatching. It was a single large room whose beamed ceiling came to a point high above its center. The beams rose from limestone block walls built to chest level. The stone floor was stuccoed smooth. The rest of the house was of straw.

The twins, the neighbors, their son and I traipsed about in this relic of another time. I lay on the floor and took pictures of the roof beams, then walked around taking notes. No one thought to leave Maria alone with her memories.

The house was as she had left it. Her bed was on the wall opposite the door, a quilt still folded at its foot. A broom leaned against the wall. Wooden vegetable crates had been her dresser drawers, a bedside table her only furniture. A curtain on a clothesline divided the room. Her eyes followed a sunbeam up to the roof.

"When it rained, it never leaked," she said.

She led us to the outdoor kitchen she had built with her own hands—two stone walls with a tiled roof and an iron pot hung over a fire pit. Signora Maria had lived here without electricity or plumbing. There was the galvanized bucket she had used to haul water from the well; the tall terra-cotta amphora she had filled with oil, its pointed bottom snugged in a sand bed, as on Phoenician trading ships; the white enameled bowl where she had bathed; the shard of mirror where she combed her hair; the fingernail brush on a nail. Niches carved in the wall were her dish drainers. A caned wooden chair was set in a corner, covered with cobwebs.

Signora Maria was on her knees, under the bed, searching for something.

With the broomstick she pulled out a brown leather book bag. She stood up, wiped the dust from it with her sleeve and hugged it. She would not say what she thought was in it, and she would not open it before us.

A few days later I called the twins from a phone booth in Sperlinga, where some people still live in cave homes in a cliff. Rosaria answered the phone.

"What was in the book bag?" I asked.

"They were the poems," she said.

W. S. DI PIERO

Oregon Avenue on a Good Day

Some nights I dream the taste
of pitch and bus fumes and leaf meal
from my old exacting street.
This time home, I'm walking to find

I don't know what. Something always
offers itself while I'm not watching.
I'm hoping for a certain completion,
of housefronts or myself. I don't want

the standard gold of ginkgo leaves,
or weeping cherries, O how beautiful,
but fused presence, a casual fall
of light that strikes and spreads

on enameled aluminum siding, brick,
spangled stonework, fake fieldstone
and clapboard, leftover Santa lights,
casements trimmed in yellow fiberglass,

our common dream of the *all*
and the *only this*, that's exactly
what I can't find. The best of it
is a racy, homely metric unplanned

line to line, building up a scene:
husband and wife inside, plus kids, suppertime,
pine paneling where scratchy exterior light
rises sweetly above a TV voice.

MICHAEL MARTONE

Ten Little Italies of Indiana

ᗒᗕ

1. THE KNIGHTS OF COLUMBUS HALL: COLUMBUS

SETTLED BY BAKUNIN ANARCHISTS FLEEING BOSTON in the wake of the Sacco and Vanzetti trial, the Italian community of Columbus stealthily blended in with the Hoosier natives of this town by dyeing their hair blond and changing all family names, en masse, to "Streeter," only to emerge seventy years later from behind the many folds of secrecy (garlic, for example, was cultivated in various basements by means of full-spectrum lighting and early experiments in hydroponic gardening) to take its place in the rich ethnic tapestry that is contemporary Columbus. The construction of the Knights of Columbus Hall marked the Streeters' proud return to ethnic identity. Taking full advantage of the noblesse oblige of local business giant, Cummins Engine, which provides architectural fees for any civic building built within the town, the newly organized Knights commissioned Michael Graves to render their vision in a postmodern meeting hall located near the Philip Johnson Mason Lodge and the Frank Gehry Third African Methodist Episcopal Church. Immediately recognizable by the hermaphrodite xebec rigging of the faux nautical "sails," really campanili, embroidered with red Spanish crosses, the hall quotes, architecturally, the nautical superstructure of the club's namesake's smallest vessel, the *Nina*. The cavernous Bingo Hall hosted the Bingo World Series in 1987 and again five years later in 1992. A mild hybrid of garlic, out of tradition, is still cultivated in the basement.

2. CAMOUFLAGE FASHION CENTER: MILAN

Settled by Carabiniere of the Italian alpine troops of the Second World War after their release from POW camps at Fort Benjamin Harrison, Milan (pronounced MY lan) supports a thriving apparel industry specializing in the production of camouflage garments. It was in the workshops and lofts of Milan that such famous sartorial patterns of deception as "Northern European Snow," a white rip-stopped gabardine splotched with dabs of gray and black and "Arab Chunk Cookie Dough," made famous during the Gulf War, were developed for the military. The domestic outdoorsman market also benefits from Milanese designers' keen eye. A stunning innovation was the recent development of the bright safety orange hooded synthetic twill sweatshirt which still incorporates the patented outline of disrupting dazzle splashes in cinnabar-tinted umber and incarnadine-influenced sienna. With runway seasons both in fall and spring, the houses of Milan display their creations for buyers who flock to this small Indiana town to catch the first glimpse of these new interpretations of light and natural habitat. There to the beat of martial music one might witness the introduction of such fabrics as "Gray Grid," a distorting plaid that defeats the images generated by star scopes and night vision goggles or "Baby-flage," a line of waffle weave pajamas, sleepers, nightgowns, Onesies, and long johns decorated with a woodland array of primary colors which allows an infant to fade into its toy-rich background.

3. THE PURDUE UNIVERSITY ITALIAN SANDWICH RESEARCH KITCHEN AND SUB SHOP EXPERIMENT STATION: AMO

Settled by shoemakers from Brindisi, Amo is now the home of Purdue University's Italian Sandwich Research Kitchen and Sub Shop Field Experiment Station. Here, new recipes for flavored cheeses and spiced meats originating in the experimental food laboratories of the West Lafayette campus are tested in a variety of combinations and with a myriad of condiments and toppings upon an eager volunteer lunch population. Of interest is the extensive collection, displayed and mouth-wateringly preserved in the main building's lobby, of regional species of the genre, collected during class trips by the local 4-H. Under glass and neatly labeled are examples of the *Italian* of the Southern Midwest, the *Italian Sandwich* and the *Small Italian* of Southern Maine as well as the *Sub*, the *Submarine*, the *Hoagie* of Delaware

Valley, the *Trunk*, the *Grinder* of New England, the *Bomber* of upstate New York with its distinctive layer of coleslaw, the *Atomic Rod*, the *Wedge*, the *Herk*, the *Blimpie*, the *Cuban Sandwich* of Miami, the greater and lesser *Po' Boy* and *Poor Boy* of the Delta, the *Zep*, the *Stromboli*, the *Mario*, and rare *Meatless*, the *Urp* and the *Grilled Urp*, the *Weasel* and the *Hot Wombat*, the *Podburger* of Omaha, the *Montegolfer*, the *Whole Toledo*, the *Torpedo*, the *Hero*, the *Anchovy Anaconda*, and last but not least the local *Last*, named for the foot-long blocks of wood lasts, used by cobblers to mold leather for shoes.

4. THE GROTTO OF OUR LADY OF KRYLON: CHURUBUSCO

Settled by immigrants from Queens, New York, Churubusco is the site of the first appearance, west of the Alleghenies, of graffiti (a freehand red tag, "RR123," affixed to a dust bin behind Kinze's Hardware Store downtown) on Pentecost Sunday, 1979. Churubusco was also the site, that same year, of the subsequent visitation in one of Oscar Yoder's soybean fields, of the Virgin Mary, arrayed in a pastel disco-inspired raiment, instructing Oscar's son, Oder, that believers should protect and nurture all writing on walls. It fell to Father Johnny Raucci, pastor of St. Pat's, to begin construction of a shrine, still being built, commemorating the miracle and perpetuating the Mother of God's imperatives. The Grotto employs in its facades a mosaic design made up of a variety of empty aerosol lacquer cans imbedded in stucco walls covered already with layers of spray-painted inscriptions reaching a depth of two inches on some exterior surfaces of the basilica. It is here that Cardinal Primo Casaburo stopped briefly on his second tour of North America to try his hand with a yellow "Kilroy was here" in the narthex. Among the Grotto's many relics is a color Xerox reproduction of the Shroud of Turin, a synthetic stone cast of Lord Byron's scratched signature taken from the Temple of Poseidon at Sunian, Greece, which itself shows multiple defacement, and the scorched metacarpal and distal phalanx of the index finger of Saint Stencil of Trans Alpine Gaul, patron saint of vandals and sackers.

5. THE LEANING TOWER OF PAOLI: PAOLI

Settled by refugees from the Kingdom of the Two Sicilies after an abortive attempt to integrate with the second utopian experiment at New Harmony,

Indiana, Paoli, named for the Corsican patriot, Pasquale de Paoli, who led the struggle for independence from Genoa, is notable also for the famous leaning tower. The fifty-foot tower, actually an abandoned wood stave barrel tank once used by the L&N railroad to water steam engines when Paoli served as a division point and coaling station on the Louisville to Chicago sub-mainline, took on its characteristic three-degree cant when wooden joists of one of its four support pylons were pilfered, after the tank was no longer used, in an abortive parquet bread board scheme of the mid 1950s. The citizens of Paoli, refusing to demolish the local landmark, instead buttressed the weakened legs with hydraulic jacks which overcorrected the initial tilt and left the structure at its current angle. The Italianate tromp l'oeil column was added during the Johnson administration to commemorate the visit of the First Lady, Lady Bird Johnson, during her promotion of a national beautification project. The tower, used today mainly as a test platform upon which high school physics students from around the state re-create the gravitational experiments of Galileo Galilei, is known as one of the Seven Wonders of Indiana.

6. OLD WORLD LAWN ORNAMENTS: LOOGOOTEE

Settled by the descendants of Carrara masons lured to this country during the heyday of the booming limestone construction materials business, the artisans of Loogootee, for years, dressed and finished stones quarried for such famous buildings as New York's Rockefeller Center and the Empire State Building. With the decline of the stone industry after the Second World War, the Loogootee shops turned their talents to the fabrication of life-sized, painted and unpainted lawn statuettes and figurines sculpted in slag limestone gleaned from the abandoned quarries. Loogootee pieces, their subjects caught in the readily identifiable naturalistic style of the local studios and posed in the characteristic gestures of wide-eyed frenetic action or deep doe-eyed contemplation, are found on the finest lawns of North America including the Reagan ranch in California, the American Gothic House in Eldon, Iowa, and throughout Colonial Williamsburg and Henry Ford's Greenfield Village. In New York City, one may view the Henry Moore–inspired cherubic bunny series in the permanent collection of the Museum of Modern Art as well as the famous assemblage of Jockeys on the front porch of "21." Not to be missed, the annual blessing of the lawn ornaments at the Church of St. Francis, which takes place during the patron saint's feast day in early October and corresponds with the height of the region's fall foliage splendor.

7. THE ONLY ACTIVE VOLCANO IN THE STATE: MOUNT ETNA

Settled by Sicilians accustomed to living in the shadow of an active volcano, Mount Etna nestled at the foot of the 429-foot hill shelters several dozen families still engaged in the traditional peasant occupations of their forbears. There, on the fertile slopes of Mount Etna, the entire national crop of anise is cultivated annually each fall. Also in production are gourmet table grapes and raisins hybridized for use in chocolate-covered confections. The region's groves produce the specialty salad olive, a variety, due to the tendency of its fruit to break apart or split upon ripening, ideal as an ingredient in a green lettuce salad. Mount Etna, currently erupting particulate ash and steam, has attracted a colony of landscape painters who come to the area to employ what has been called "Hoosier Light" in oils and watercolors to accent their renderings of the summit's brooding romantic nature.

8. THE RUINS OF ROME: ROME CITY

Settled by the families of extras appearing in the films of the Italian neo-realist cinema who emigrated when the worldwide interest in such movies waned in the face of the French new wave and Japanese samurai productions, Rome City today still retains some of the feel of the old country homeland recently devastated by Allied bombing and peopled by malnourished and homeless displaced persons. As if caught in time, the crumbling facades are just that—facades—lovingly re-created by the industry's settings for the *Combat* television series of the 1960s. Each summer, the city holds its annual Bicycle Thief Days, which features midnight showings of the movie viewed by an audience, enthusiastically dressed as various members of the film's cast, who talk back to the screen, reciting verbatim and in chorus, huge chunks of dialogue while weeping profusely.

9. THE CANALS OF CHAIN O'LAKES: CHAIN O'LAKES STATE PARK, WAWAKA, ALTONA, SYRACUSE, LARGO, AND ENVIRONS

Settled by Venetians who had been recruited to complete, secretly, the Wabash and Erie Canal after the canal's and the state's bankruptcy and collapse last century in the face of emerging railroad competition. To this day the Venetians operate a clandestine transportation network of waterborne cargo that extends throughout Indiana and on into all the cities and states of the Ohio River watershed and Great Lakes basin. The public waterways are awash with these "Liquid Gypsies" employing slow-moving pontoon catamarans, bass boats, cabin cruisers, inboard family runabouts, canoes, Sunfish, and inflatable dinghies to move their enormous contraband. It is said that theirs is a floating metropolis. Business is conducted by means of buoyant two-story diving ramps on the choppy waters of Lake Wauwausee. Biology and English classes of the public high schools are taught on lashings of drifting inner tubes meandering along the Mississinewa. The solemn ritual of Extreme Unction is performed by wet-suited priests on natant, paddle-powered funeral parlors wafting placidly along the Eel. These Venetians, as were their Old World ancestors, are famous for their handmade glass. At night along the rivers and canals, the viaducts and mill ponds, one may observe the deep red fires of their furnaces reflected in the water. There, the sudden glowing expansion, the twinkling of fireflies as the molten glass is blown into globes used as floats to suspend gossamer drift nets, dredging the channels for river perch, carp, pike, blue gill, and catfish.

10. THE LITTLEST LITTLE ITALY: FORT WAYNE

Settled by Antonio Martone who, at seventeen years of age, fled the influenza outbreak of Naples in 1919 and the real possibility that he would spend the rest of his life as a streetcar motorman, who got off the train at Fort Wayne thinking he had reached his original destination of Chicago and stayed, living the rest of his life at 322 Brandriff Street, right behind the Nickel Plate roundhouse, where, at the same location ten years later, he opened an Italian grocery offering imported cheeses, meats, olive oils, pine and hazel nuts, and wines as well as produce grown in his own backyard, such as plum tomatoes, basil, chard, pole beans, spinach, sweet peppers, and okra along with the noodles he would roll out in his basement assisted by his wife, Madeline, who was brought from the old country, their marriage brokered by relations in Chicago, and who was Antonio's only customer for years at the store, running a tab she never paid and he never expected she should pay, and where they would sit in the kitchen drinking mineral water, grappa, and coffee and ate, occasionally, Madeline's famous chocolate cake and where, also, they raised three children, a boy, Junior, and two girls, Mary and Carmella, who learned a little of the language and married Americans and moved away from where their parents would never move after moving so far away from their own birthplaces and who would never move again from Brandriff Street, listening to the trains whistling to each other in the yard while they themselves worked in their garden where they also listened to the lilt of the neighborhood kids playing, riding their bikes up and down the cinder alley, making fun of the singsong Italian accents made by the old couple by picking up the accent from the Martones working in their gardens, shouting to each other, making fun of the foreigners and their language, naturally, but also finding, in what was left of it, a curious beauty that tasted strange and sweet on their young tongues.

DON DE GRAZIA

American Skin

W HEN THINGS GOT TOO CRAZY with the cops I suggested to
Timmy Penn that we go to college, but he just laughed and said skin-
heads were working-class for life. Aside from my dad, who was in prison at
the time, I looked up to Tim more than anyone. Aside from my dad.

When I was a kid my dad made a stack of cash, sold all his all-night din-
ers, and moved our family from Taylor Street in Little Italy out to an old
farmhouse surrounded by thick woods, hidden meadows, and an overgrown
orchard. In a hilly clearing beside the house sat a red barn, and a long,
white-roofed stable where we kept the animals—Shetland ponies, some
sheep, a gander, a goat, and an army of dogs. My mom was pregnant with my
sister. My parents spent their time raising me and Stacy, and my dad wrote
poetry. Haiku poetry. I'm serious. As I grew up he became very well-
respected in the Haiku world.

The locals were American Gothic, with strip malls and attitude. They
thought we were hippies. My dad grew a beard and my mom let her plat-
inum Jackie O hairdo grow out to natural brown, and wore it in two braided
ropes, like an Indian. It might sound funny, but my dad didn't consider him-
self a hippie at all. The sixties had their own effect on every man, I guess.

Have you ever seen a lilac bush in bloom? My dad liked to call our place
"Lilac Farm." Back behind our house there were so many lilac bushes that,
from inside, they filled up every windowpane in spring. Purple and flowery
with that candy scent floating all around. It only lasted a very short time
though, before all the little flowers turned brown and stank like shit. Lilac
Farm was a good name for that place.

The house sat beneath a grove of giant oaks, and on fall nights we would drift asleep to acorns lightly raining on the roof. Summer mornings I'd cross through the wildflowers and rolling hills of our south meadow to a spring-fed pond, wade through the cattails near the shore to a tiny island, and dive through the sun-warmed surface to the chill underneath, down to the smooth clay bottom, to the silent icy gush of the spring.

We went on long walks exploring our woods—crossing little streams on rocks that stuck out of the water—and picked apples off the trees. We milked the goat, and drank wine at every dinner. My dad would make a fire and play guitar at night. He'd play "The Wabash Cannonball." It was some kind of place to live.

But one day things went badly for us out there in the woods. I was at the high school when it happened. That November it stayed dark as dusk all day. It's a very strange thing to walk out of natural darkness into electric light in the middle of the morning.

I skipped first period study hall as usual to hang out in the library, so when I heard my name over the intercom just before second period, I assumed I'd finally been caught. No big deal. In-school suspension. I'd get to spend a couple days just reading instead of going to class.

I decided to grab some books before going to the office. I turned the corner and saw a gym teacher and a uniformed cop with a dog going through my locker. I stopped and backtracked in shock, but I can't say it was a total surprise. I'd seen the packages of marijuana in my dad's desk, and Jack Wappler came up from the city with the stuff about this time every month. Those men sifting through my locker gave shape to a vague uneasiness I'd always had within me.

The hundred steps or so down that empty hallway felt like a walk across a lunar landscape. The bell rang and kids poured out of every room. I reached a door and slipped outside.

I ran home and I remember it being so terribly cold that my face burned and the wind whistled. But aside from that there was no sound or pain or weight or anything for the whole four miles.

I thought only of the bricks of pot I'd seen in my dad's desk, and knew I was just scaring myself—this was something minor or a mistake and my dad would know what to do—but when I was nearly home, about to collapse, I saw a cop car parked at the end of our driveway. The woods were so thick, and our house was set so far back that you couldn't see it from the road. So I ducked under an old barbed-wire fence and into the woods, and trudged through the snow and between the branches of the apple trees that hung heavy with white. After about four hundred yards I could see our house. There were a bunch of cops and men in suits (IRS, I was later told) strolling in and out, some of them carrying my dad's business files and stuff. I wasn't thinking clearly, but I knew not to come out of the woods. I pictured them rummaging through my locker and remembered my dad scoffing as his beatnik buddy Mickey Silver told stories of police planting drugs on war protesters—sending them off to prison where they were gang-raped for years.

They stayed the whole day, and so did I, staring out from the woods. All I had on was jeans and a sweater and gym shoes and no gloves. To this day my fingers and toes hurt badly when it gets cold out.

By nightfall they were gone. I crept back to the end of the driveway. The squad car had left. Lying in a blue-plastic sleeve, half-buried in snow by tire tracks, was our afternoon paper. I've always wondered if the delivery man felt any kind of irony as he tossed it, or if he even knew at all.

With numb fingers I slid off the plastic and read by the moonlight. It made the bottom of the front page.

For years no one listened, but following a significant drug bust this morning in unincorporated Harding County, a group of concerned community members say persistence finally paid off.

Alex and Teresa Verdi, of 90405 Dairy Lake Rd., were arrested, along with Jack Wappler of Chicago, and charged with intent to distribute nearly 2 kilos of marijuana, with an estimated street value of $75,000.

Later, even after I met Tim Penn and learned the business end of drugs, I always wondered how they came up with a dollar amount like that from three pounds of weed. The nearest I can figure now is "street value" meant what three pounds was worth if you rolled it all into toothpick joints and sold them in prison.

If convicted the three face a possible maximum sentence of 12 years. Wappler's black 1985 New Yorker and the Verdis' 1980 Ford Van were seized. The vehicles, authorities stress, along with the Verdis' property—three buildings set on 40 acres zoned for farming—can and will be sold at public auction upon conviction under current statutes.

"We want to send a clear message that the trafficking of narcotics will not be tolerated in this community," says Harding County Sheriff's

Investigator Lt. Dennis Richter, who headed the investigation in con-
junction with the Illinois State Troopers and Cook County Sheriff's
Police. Community members—including a mail deliverer and a former
employee of the Verdis'—say officials only paid heed to their suspi-
cions after they took matters into their own hands, reportedly keeping
the Verdis' residence under surveillance as part of an unofficial
neighborhood-watch initiative.

The Verdis' 17-year-old-son, a junior at Harding High School, is
being sought for questioning regarding the possibility that marijuana
was funneled into the school, which has reported a marked increase in
drug abuse. If charged, Richter says, the son will be tried as an adult.
The Verdis' daughter, 11, was brought to Cook County and placed in
state care until relatives are reached.

"*What* relatives?" I mouthed, lips thick with cold. I tore the article out
and dropped the rest of the paper in the snow. Them seeking *me* seemed
ridiculous. I didn't do anything. But I was seventeen. Was I custody of the
state too?

When I got back to the house I saw right off that they shot Lovie, the queen
of all our dogs—a massive bitch mastiff, fiercely protective of our family. She
wouldn't let them in, so they shot her. They could have used a knockout dart or
something, but why bother, right? Half her head was caved in and her brains
had spilt out into the snow. I went right down to the stable and came back with
a wheelbarrow, a shovel, and a pickax. I turned the barrow on its side and rolled
Lovie's big body in. Then I righted it, and shoveled the bloody snow and brains
up on top of her. I remember that I started to cry as I was burying her in the
woods by a frozen stream, but I only started. The clay I was digging in was rock
solid, and I thought my fingers would break off every time I swung that pickax
down from over my head with both hands as hard as I could.

After it was done I walked back to the house and broke through the yel-
low tape the police put across the door. It was dark inside, but I could see by
the moon that the furniture had been turned over and there were papers
scattered everywhere. The electricity was out—a branch somewhere in the
woods had fallen on the lines again—and a faucet had been left running in
the kitchen, so there was no hot water left. There was cooking gas, though,
so I found some matches and lit the old stove's pilot light. I boiled big kettles
of water and poured them into the bathtub until it was full. Then I stripped
off my wet shoes and socks and wet clothes and climbed on in.

I was scared. In the water I decided it didn't matter that I'd never sold any
drugs, or that my father was only part of a little communal buy. My dad

laughed at Mickey, but I believed what he'd said about cops. There was a feeling falling and rising inside of me, tightening and relaxing—like everything out there was over, but nothing was settled. I stayed in the tub, seething in the dark, till long after the water'd turned ice-cold. Then I dressed and left.

But before I left I thought of something. For all their searching, they didn't find my dad's small shotgun. He kept it with a box of shells in the tackroom, wrapped up in a horse blanket underneath my sister's little red saddle for the pony that had once been mine.

I loaded the gun and paced around out front of the house for a while, blindheaded, shouting things I can't remember, then headed down to the stable and unlocked all the pens. I let the ponies out and the dogs could pretty much go as they pleased but the Irish wolfhound who was goofy we had to chain up so I unlatched his collar. Still holding the shotgun in one hand, I grabbed the handle of a five-pronged digging-fork and went out to the shed where we kept the feed and ripped big holes in all the bags and left the door wide open. Then I went to the barn and climbed the ladder to the loft and tossed all the bales of hay out onto the snow. I kicked the loose hay strewn on the loft floor into a pile, and felt for the matches in my jeans.

When the fire was burning good up there I went down to let the sheep out, but they wouldn't leave. I don't know where I expected them to go—it was freezing cold out—but the sight of them huddled there in the corner of the pen baaing set me off and I chased them outside with the fork.

With an armful of hay I started another small fire in the stable around an old dried-out wooden beam which caught pretty quick. I went back to the house to the tackroom and lit one there too. As the same blue-black smoke poured from the windows of all three buildings I grabbed the shotgun and started off through our north woods toward the highway. I heard something behind me and saw the wolfhound following and smiling with reflective eyes and without thinking I roared at the dog and fired the shotgun up in the air. It released a bright blue fountain of flame and sparks in the black woods and I saw nothing but spots for a full minute. I heard the wolfhound yelp and bolt back toward the house and when I could see right again, I heaved the gun into the dark and crashed my way through the bushes and branches and, covered with snow and burrs, I ran across the neighboring cornfield to the corner of 73 and 41, where the truckers slept.

An old fellow was pissing up against the side of his eighteen-wheeler. His name was Virgil Sickles, as I recall, and he said he could take me as far as Chicago.

LISA LENZO

Within the Lighted City

$\backsim\!\sim\!\sim$

MY PARENTS' APARTMENT DOOR, hung with a wreath of copper bells, stands open to the outer hallway. We walk in, and Marly drops her boots on the tiled floor of the inner hall and runs down the corridor to the computer room. As I set down the rest of our stuff (our ancient suitcase, my running shoes, my books, and a bag of presents), I hear my brothers talking from the other direction, and I'm so eager to see them that I straighten up and walk toward them without stopping to take off my coat. They look up at me, the four of them sprawled on the white leather couches and chair. "Nice coat, Annie," Dan says with surprise.

Arthur sits in his chair and mumbles something, and my other three brothers laugh.

"What?" I ask the group of them. "What did you say?" I ask Arthur, walking over to the chair across which his lanky body is draped.

"Never mind," Arthur says, his face slightly peeved, a look designed, I'm sure, to milk more humor from his remark.

"C'mon, *tell* me," I say, pushing Arthur's knee with my hand. "What did you say about my coat? What's wrong with it?" I really want to know what Arthur thinks; he's a year older than me, and, even though I'm thirty-one, I still tend to look up to him. Maybe the coat is too old-fashioned, too long, or maybe the flared cut is a little extreme. Or maybe it's too gaudy. It's fake cherry red, the color of a maraschino.

"Nothing's wrong with it," Arthur says.

"Then what did you say about it?"

Dan, who is twenty-nine, leans toward me from the couch. "He said, 'Yeah, well, I still want to see the receipt.'" Mike and Zachary laugh again, it seems in homage to the original delivery.

I turn back to Arthur. "What do you mean—are you saying that I stole it?"

"No, no," Dan says. "He meant that you got it at the Salvation Army or somewhere."

I go over the exchange in my head: *Nice coat, Annie; Yeah, well, I still want to see the receipt.* "They give receipts at the Salvation Army," I say.

This brings a loud laugh from Zachary, my youngest brother. At six feet three and two hundred pounds, Zach is also the largest of my brothers, but I used to take care of him when I could lift him up by his armpits, and when he sees me looking at him sternly he explains, "You're completely familiar with how the Salvation Army operates."

Finally it's becoming clear to me what this whole thing is about: my brothers are teasing me for being so cheap. I don't think they've stopped to consider that, while I've been cheap all my life, since my divorce and return to school habitual scrimping has become a necessity.

"Tell the truth, Ann," Dan says. "Did you buy it new?"

"No, but I didn't buy it at the Salvation Army. I bought it at this second-hand store that has a lot nicer stuff."

"What did I tell you?" Arthur says, and he sets his lips in a stiff line and folds his arms across his chest.

"Well, what's wrong with that?" I ask. "Like you're Mr. *GQ*." I push Arthur's foot this time, and he resettles it to the floor. He is wearing his usual art student clothes: paint- and glaze-spattered gym shoes and T-shirt and jeans.

"We were just having fun with you, Nini," Mike, my oldest brother, says. "It's a pretty coat, and it looks really nice on you."

"Well, thanks," I say. I throw a glare sidelong at Arthur.

"I never said it wasn't nice," Arthur says.

"Maybe I'll go hang it up now, unless someone has something to add."

"Nope," Dan says, "I think that was it. But wait a minute, let me check—"

I walk back to the hallway and unbutton my coat. I bought it a week ago, to wear for Toby. He hasn't seen me in it yet. We live on opposite sides of the state, and though we've been corresponding for two and a half years, I've only seen him once in that time: we met for lunch north of Detroit near the high school where Toby teaches, ten weeks after the summer conference at which Toby and I first met. At that second meeting, after we ate lunch, Toby and I walked through a chilly park and talked of becoming lovers. He said he couldn't imagine abandoning his wife and his daughter, and though I left my husband partly as a result of meeting Toby, I only wanted to have an affair, I told Toby, if it could lead to marriage. We didn't kiss during that walk, and we kept our hands at our sides. Mine were cold, and I wanted to shove them into the pockets of my down coat, but I kept them out, hoping that Toby would take one in his.

I drove home to my new apartment feeling angry and determined: angry at Toby for inviting me all the way across the state just to reject me, and determined to find love elsewhere. And I did find it, or at least something close to it for a while, first, for a few months, with a fellow student at Western Michigan, and then, for a year and a half, with a married man from Grand Haven who replaced Toby, the man I loved and hoped to marry, until the affair ended. Still, Toby and I continued to write each other, every couple of months during my affair with Lowell, and more frequently after it ended. Our letters were full of warmth and solicitude and occasional flares of anger, our sexual feelings cloaked in friendship or pushed down under the surface.

I thought I had given up on ever becoming Toby's lover. Then, just before I came home for Christmas, Toby wrote me a letter that was different from all the others; he wrote inviting me to lunch while I was in Detroit, and, though he is still married, from the tone of this letter and other things written in it, it seemed that he was inviting me to more than just lunch. I wrote him back that I felt funny about leaving Marly with my family, since they would want to know where I was going and with whom. I could lie to them, of course, but my family is nosy, and I'm not good at hiding the truth, and while I don't care if my brothers know that I'm thinking about starting an affair, I am worried about making my mom feel bad. My dad had an affair years ago through which I watched my mom suffer. It took her years to completely recover. That didn't stop me from having an affair with Lowell, and it might not stop me this time, either, but I don't want to use my parents' apartment as the launching pad for my transgression.

As I hung up my coat in the hall closet, my mom appears at my side. "There you are," she says, giving me a hug and a kiss. "I knew you were here, because Marly came running back." She smiles. "At least I figured Marly didn't get here by herself."

"Good figuring, Mom," I say. Marly is eight, and we've just driven in from Saugatuck, three and a half hours away. "Where's Dad?" I ask.

"At the airport, picking up Grandma."

"He went all by himself?"

"Yeah—Grandma's getting kind of old for a lot of excitement. Ralphy thought it would be more restful if he got her alone." My grandma is eighty-seven. My dad is fifty-eight, a little old to be called Ralphy, but my mom changes everyone's name so that it ends in a long *e* sound. Her children, from the top down, are Mikey, Artie, Annie, Danny, and Zachary. Mike's fiancée, Sarah, is Sary, and Zachary's wife, Sasha, is Sashy. Dan's daughters, Ruth and Greta, are Ruthie and Grettie, and Nicole, my dad's daughter from his affair, is Nicki. Nicole lives with her mother, but she visits "Dad and Rosie," as she calls them, two evenings a week and for parts of the holidays.

"Where's everybody else?" I ask.

"Oh, let me see," my mom says. "I was just showing Sary a computer program for calculus, Sashy's in the bathroom, I think, Marly and Nicki are playing with the dress-up clothes, and I'm not sure where all of your brothers are."

"I know where *they* are. What about Greta and Ruth? Are they going to come after all, or not?"

"No, I guess they're going to stay with their mom, and we'll see them at New Year's."

"She had them last Christmas," I say. "It's Dan's turn."

"I know," my mom says. "But, well, it's up to Danny to stand up for himself."

I rub my mom's back with my palm, simply glad to see her. She's so non-interfering. And she has a genius IQ, yet she says things like "Danny stand up for himself," when Dan hasn't stood in ten years. He's used a wheelchair to get around since he was nineteen, when his legs were severed at a summer factory job.

"Are you hungry?" my mom asks. "We're going to eat as soon as Ralphy and Grandma get here, but do you want a little something to snack on for now?"

"No," I say, "I'll wait."

"Well, I'm going to go see how Sary's doing with that program. I was just getting her started."

My mom returns to the rear of the apartment, and I step from the small, bright square of hallway into the living room, which is suddenly dark. Someone has turned off the overhead lights as well as the lights of the tree, and one of the white leather couches has been pushed aside to reveal the view out the two walls of windows. My brothers are sitting on the remaining couch and the chair, both of which have been shifted to the center of the room, and the shapes of their bodies are outlined by the white leather glowing around their still forms.

Outside, the night is brightened by the lights of downtown Detroit. We are six stories up, and, looking straight out, all I can see is blackness lit by lights shining from every direction, lower than my parents' windows, and higher, and at the same level. Seeing the darkness lit up without any apparent relation to gravity makes it seem as if the apartment is floating; it feels as if we are hanging suspended in the darkness, above and below and within the lighted city. The soft grayness inside the apartment makes it feel as if I am floating, too, as if I'm not attached to anything.

My spell flits off like a dream when I squeeze between Zachary and Dan. Zachary pats my left thigh, and Dan takes my right hand. We are all lined up facing the river: Zachary, then me, then Dan, then Mike, then Arthur on the chair to our right. Arthur is talking about the Canadian Club sign on Canada's shore, a mile away, which blinks on and off at the far left edge of the windows. It is made of orange neon and blinks with a pulsing rhythm.

"I wonder how many alcoholics have apartments facing that sign," Arthur says. "I wonder how many of them were alcoholics *before* they began reading that sign a thousand times a night. I wonder if I start drinking again, if I can sue Canadian Club."

"Are you worried about starting to drink again?" Dan asks.

"Hell no," Arthur says. "I wouldn't anyway, but what with this other drug I have to take, there's no way."

Arthur is taking fourteen hundred milligrams of Tegretol a day in an attempt to control his epilepsy, which began to surface as faint leg spasms ten years ago and has grown in the two years since he's quit using alcohol and other drugs into seizures that grip and shake his whole body. After a seizure strikes, it takes Arthur a week or longer to recover his energy, and sometimes he stutters for months, and while he hasn't suffered any permanent brain damage, his neurologist says that he likely will if the seizures continue to occur. They keep switching Arthur's medications and upping the dosages. He hasn't had a seizure now for almost three months, but over the summer he lasted three months and one week, and then two seizures struck ten days apart.

"Look at how black the river is," I say. It's a thick, black line dividing Windsor from Detroit.

"There a boat," Mike says. "All the way to the right."

"Oh, cool," Arthur says. "A barge." The barge has been outlined in lights, as if for Christmas.

"Mmmm, this looks cozy," Sasha says, appearing from around the side of the couch and settling into Zachary's lap. "Oh, hi, Annie!" She leans down and gives me a kiss. "When did you get in?"

"Just a little while ago."

Zach pats Sasha's butt, then points his huge index finger at the barge. "How often do those pass by?" he asks Arthur. Arthur lives with our parents. Zach and Sasha live in San Diego and only fly back to Detroit once or twice a year.

"Not too often, I don't know," Arthur says. "But then, how often do I sit here looking out? I'm at school or my studio most of the day, and when I'm home I'm usually doing something. Probably all kinds of things happen out there when I'm not looking."

"I know what you mean," Dan says. "Six or seven spaceships were out there when I got here today. They were circling the RenCen. One landed on top. Then the other six started shooting it out. Three of them went up in flames and fell into the river. Then the rest of them zoomed off." He looks around at the rest of us. "You didn't see it? Nobody else saw it?" Arthur reaches over from his chair and noogies Dan's part-bald, part-bristly head.

"What are you guys talking about, anyway?" Marly asks. She has slipped around the edge of the couch and is standing in front of Sasha and Zach.

"Hi, Marly!" Sasha says. "Hi, sweetie!" She leans forward and gives Marly a kiss. Marly is wearing a round straw hat tied on with a scarf, with three or four more silky scarves draped around her neck. The rest of her, except for her thin arms and her face, is lost in yards of dark cloth.

"We're talking about flying saucers," Mike says. "Have you ever seen one?"

"*I* haven't," Marly says, "but some people in Saugatuck have. They fly over Lake Michigan at night and blink their lights."

"C'mere, my little-favorite-anorexic *niece*," Dan says, grabbing Marly's wrist.

Marly screeches with delight, and Dan draws her onto his lap.

"Did I ever tell you about this anorexic I met while I was at Cornell?" Arthur asks.

"You make it sound like you went to the university," Dan says. "Why don't you just say, 'When I was locked up for doing drugs'?"

"Actually, I was a walk-in," Arthur says. "The anorexics weren't walk-ins, though. They were all young girls, and their parents had signed them in, at $300 a day."

"You're joking," Mike says.

"It was so expensive because they had to be watched round the clock to make sure they didn't make themselves vomit."

"Oh, gross," Marly says.

"I'm with you," Sasha says. "Marly, come sit on our laps."

Dan tightens his arms around Marly. "No, she's mine, I had her first. Well, all right—go on." He passes Marly, smiling, her legs dragging and the blue cloth trailing, over me to Sasha.

"Speaking of anorexics," Sasha says, "look who could absolutely *not* be mistaken for an anorexic anymore. Darlin', you look gorgeous," she says to Nicole, who is standing in front of us now.

"Thank you," Nicole says. My little sister is thirteen and just beginning to put on a little weight all over, including on her breasts and her hips. She is draped sari-style in shimmering, light cloth, and her head is wrapped in a white turban-style twist.

"Hey, baby, you can come sit on my lap," Arthur says.

"No thanks," Nicole says, patting a yawn. "I think I'll sit on the couch."

"Ha! She knows better already," Zach says.

"Arthur the *ladies'* man," Dan says, holding out his hand for Arthur to slap.

"Look who's talking," Arthur says, ignoring Dan's hand. "Or, as Mom would say, 'Look at the pot calling the kettle black.'"

"Hey, don't be putting me in your league, buddy," Dan says. "You're way up there with Wilt the Stilt and Magic Johnson."

"Not anymore," Arthur says. "I've cut way back. And the way you've been adding on, pretty soon you're going to pass me."

"What are you talking about?" Dan says. "I've never even had a one-night stand. I might not be perfect, but I'm not like you—at least I always start out with good intentions."

"Yeah, and I'm sure all the three-month stands you've had since your divorce were thrilled about your good intentions when you blew them off."

"Can you guys change the subject?" I ask, worried about the questions that Marly will ask me later.

"I don't think Arthur's epilepsy is from too much drugs," Dan says. "I think it's from too much sex."

"Thanks for the insight," Arthur says. "I'll pass it on to my neurologist."

"Maybe he can do a study," Dan says. "You can be the sex maniac, and I can be the control."

"C'mon, Dan," I say. "If Greta and Ruth were here, would you be talking like this?"

"Probably," Dan says. Then he looks at me and says, "Okay, sorry."

"*Any*how," Arthur says, "as I was starting to say, I got to know a couple of anorexics at Cornell because when they reach a certain weight they're allowed to play volleyball with the addicts. And this one anorexic told me that she used to come home from school every day, take one Cheerio out of the box, and cut it into eight pieces with an Exacto knife. Then she'd eat each tiny little piece, one at a time, by placing it on the center of her tongue and closing her mouth. She wouldn't chew or swallow. It took fifteen minutes for each eighth of a Cheerio to dissolve, so it took her two hours to eat one Cheerio."

"You're making this up," Zach says.

"This is what she told me," Arthur says. "And she said that when her mom came home, her mom would beg her to eat, and she'd say, 'Mom, I've been eating ever since I got home from school.'"

We all laugh; then Sasha says, "That's sad."

"It's crazy," Marly says. "I eat a whole bowlful of Cheerios at one time."

"Then how come you're so scrawny?" Dan asks.

"Don't call her scrawny," I say. "She's naturally thin. She's perfect."

"Yeah, be quiet, Dan," Arthur says, "or we'll get out those old family slides where you've got those little toothpick arms and legs."

"Well, at least my legs were fatter than they are *now*," Dan says, looking down at the space where his lower legs used to be, his hugely muscled upper body angled over what he calls his "nubs": ten inches of thigh whose rounded, healed ends poke out of his cutoff sweats. "Yeah, Marly, don't go on any diets," Dan says. "That's the mistake I made. I was trying to lose just a little off my belly, but, well, I guess may aim was off, plus I got slightly carried away." He looks into Marly's face and attempts a guileless smile.

"What do you think I am, three years old?" Marly says. Over our laughter she asks, "Uncle Dan, can I play in your chair?"

"Don't you think you're a little old for *playing*?" Dan says. "Yeah, you can. But be careful—it's not mine. I'm just test-driving it before I deliver it to a customer."

"Can I use it, too?" Nicole asks.

"Yeah, sure. No popping wheelies, though. You want to goof around, wait till tomorrow, and I'll get you a chair out of my van."

But before the girls get up from our laps, the front door opens loudly. Our dad has always opened doors more loudly than anyone else. "Grandma's here," Mike says.

We listen to the harmonious voices of our grandma and our mom greeting each other. Then our dad's voice booms out: "How come all the lights are off in here?"

Our dad appears before us, a silhouette against our view, the lights from the city outlining the wisps of hair that spring up from his mostly bald head. Though the whole front of him is in darkness, you can still vaguely see his large nose and his chin and the overall intensity of his face. "What did you do with the other couch?" he demands.

"We sold it," Dan says.

"Jesus Christ, how many of you are sitting on one damn couch?"

"Just about the whole damn family," Arthur says.

Dan pats his lap. "There's room for you, Old Man."

Our dad sighs, his body loosening just slightly. Then his normal intensity returns. "*Annie*," he says, with happy surprise. "And *Marly*. It's so dark in here, I didn't see you." He leans down and kisses us. "Well, good, everybody's here then." He turns toward the hall. "Rosie! When are we going to eat?"

"*I'm* cooking dinner, Old Man," Arthur says.

"Then what are you doing just sitting around?"

"Enjoying the view, not to mention waiting for you. It's all done, I just need to take it out of the oven."

"Well, take it out of the goddamned oven, I'm starving."

"*Relax*, Old Guy," Arthur says. "You just got here."

"Do they make Ritalin for adults?" Dan asks.

"Quaaludes," Arthur says. "Reds. Alcohol. Heroin."

"I'm going to go say hi to Grandma," Mike says. He stands.

Marly puts her lips to my ear and whispers, "Do I have to kiss her?"

"You don't have to, but it would be nice. Why don't you want to?"

Marly whispers again. "She's so *old*."

"Hey, no secrets around here," Dan says.

"Well then we'll take our secrets elsewhere."

"Before everybody takes off," our dad says, "a couple of you move the couches back to where they belong." He flicks on the lights, and everyone stands except for Dan, who hops onto the floor and lifts an arm of the couch.

ALL TWELVE OF US ARE sitting around the rosewood table, which has been extended to its full length so that it fills up the alcove off the living room. We're pretty much wedged into our seats, eating lasagna and passing bread, everyone talking at once. My grandma is sitting across from me and a couple of settings down, and my attention wanders from the table chatter as I watch her. I can see why Marly is afraid to kiss her—as Marly pointed out to me when we retreated to the computer room, my grandma does resemble a dead person. The wrinkled flesh of her face has shrunk close to the bone, as if the skeleton she will become is already emerging, and her normally tan complexion has a faded, yellowish cast, except for her cheekbones, which are colored the same brilliant red as her lips. If she held still and closed her eyes, you could mistake her for a corpse made up by an overzealous mortician.

But my grandma doesn't close her eyes, which are large and one hundred percent lucid, and she doesn't hold still as she eats, and though she moves slowly, her movements are fluid. She is a tiny woman, at four feet eleven inches, four inches shorter than me. We're the two shortest adults in the family, except for Dan, of course, though he was six feet before his accident, and now the immense breadth of his muscled shoulders and chest makes him seem anything but small. Besides being short, I am like my grandma in other ways: thin, dark, and, as Toby has called me, Italianate, with large, shadowed eyes, full lips, and a big nose.

I am also like my grandma in that we both tend to worry, which she is doing, I notice, as she eats bites of the lasagna. It's an exotic creation, with a blanket of sautéed carrots and another of sautéed eggplant laid down between the usual layers, and I think at first that our grandma is perturbed that Arthur has altered one of her specialties. Her large eyes seem larger and darker than usual, her brow is more furrowed, and even as she eats her lips are puckered in a sort of pout. She isn't speaking, but you have to speak quickly and loudly in our family if you want to be heard.

It's our habit to save the salad for last, and the whole table is quiet for a moment when we dig into our greens. During this moment of quiet, my grandma speaks. All I catch is, "So little respect."

"What? What did you say, Ma?" my dad asks.

"The way they talk to you—your sons," my grandma says. "My grandsons. The names they call you."

My dad squints and leans forward as he struggles to grasp what his mother is getting at; more than once he's said that he became a psychiatrist so that he could figure his mother out. "Oh, you mean calling me 'Old Man'? Are you worrying about that again, Ma? It's nothing, Ma. They're just fooling around."

Grandma doesn't answer right away. We are all watching her big, troubled eyes and her worried mouth. "You never spoke that way to your father," she says. The rest of us remain silent. My brothers and I have been calling our dad "Old Man" since we were teenagers. This is the first time that I, anyway, have heard our grandma object.

My mom breaks the silence cheerfully. "Times are different now, Mom. Kids joke more with their parents, and it isn't considered disrespectful."

"We don't mean anything by it, Grandma," Arthur says.

Our grandma shrugs. "He never in all his life spoke like that to his father."

"That's because my father was a full-blooded Sicilian," my dad says. "These punks think they can take advantage of me because I'm only half Sicilian, but they're *wrong*." His arm flashes to his left and wraps around Zachary's head, then he pulls Zachary's huge head down to his armpit and begins clamping it rhythmically, mashing his tight curls, squeezing his cheekbones. Zachary submits; beneath our dad's forearms, he is grimacing or grinning.

My grandma looks at her son sorrowfully. "You never fought with your father, either."

"That's because I knew better than to pick a fight with a Sicilian."

"Oh, Ralph, how you talk. Your father was the gentlest man in all of Queens."

My mom speaks up again, trying to explain. "They're not being disrespectful, Mom. When they call him 'Old Man,' they mean it affectionately."

My grandma shrugs, unhappily. Michael, who is sitting next to her, drapes his arm across the back of her chair. "It's okay, Grandma, really it is. Remember when we used to have long hair, and we told you it was just the style? It's the same thing. This is just the style."

"Then why is Arthur's hair *still* long?" Grandma asks.

"Yeah, Arthur, what's *wrong* with you?" Dan says.

Arthur tips back his head. His straight, dark-blond hair is gathered into a long tail. "Hey, Dan," he says, "what's wrong with *you*?" Dan is almost as bald as our dad.

"Don't get disrespectful with me, pal," Dan says. "This is the style."

I WAKE IN THE NIGHT at the clicking of my grandma's rosary.

"Grandma, what's the matter?" I ask.

"Oh, I'm so sorry I woke you," she says.

I'm sharing a bed with my grandma because she's too old to sleep on a couch or on the floor and too small to need a double bed all for herself. It's Arthur's bed. Arthur has given the bed up for our grandma, and I guess I could feel lucky to be allotted the other half, but getting paired with our grandma reminds me that I have no true other half to sleep with and that I haven't had for some time.

"I'm so sorry I woke you," my grandma says again.

"That's okay, Grandma, I'm a light sleeper," I answer, thinking that if I'm going to be awakened in the middle of the night by someone lying next to me, I want it to be a man—a man waking me up on purpose, wanting to do something more interesting than work a rosary.

"Are you worried about something, Grandma?" I ask.

"No," my grandma says, sounding mournful.

"Then why are you praying in the middle of the night?"

My grandma sighs. "To bore myself to sleep. God forgive me."

I turn away from her so she can't see my smile.

"I'm so sorry I woke you," she says again.

"That's okay, Grandma."

"I'll put it away now." I hear her rosary clacking and sliding onto the night table. She falls back to sleep before I do.

I lie awake thinking about Toby, wishing I'd said yes. Yes to lunch and to whatever else. He will be in Canada visiting relatives by tomorrow, so it's too late for me to change my mind. Of course, I think, breathing quietly on my side, I always change my mind when it's too late. There was a man who fell in love with me when Marly was a baby, and even though I had started to fall in love with him and my marriage was dying, I ran away from him, figuratively and almost literally—I hurried away down the street while Al followed me and spoke to me from the other side. This is crazy, I thought as I quickened my stride; I was on my way to Penney's to buy my husband and myself some socks, and I had a one-year-old baby at home waiting for me.

A year after Al followed me, calling to me, he became engaged to someone else; by the time I was free, he'd been remarried for several years.

At least I didn't tell Toby no, never—I said maybe we could meet for lunch after the holidays. Maybe I'd drive to the Detroit area without stopping to see my parents, or maybe he could meet me halfway across the state. He said he would like that very much and would see what we could arrange.

I WAKE AGAIN AT THE sound of my grandma's snoring. My grandma is so tiny that the shape of her almost disappears beneath the covers, yet she snores as loudly as a full-size person. I think of what my mom has told me about getting my dad to stop: first she tries nudging him with her elbow, next she pokes him with her finger, and if he still keeps it up, she barks out his name. "What?" he'll say. "Stop snoring," she'll order, and he'll fall back to sleep and be quiet for a while.

I lie on my back listening to my grandmother. Then I turn toward her face. Arthur has stuck a nightlight into the outlet over the bed, because when he wakes in the dark he sometimes forgets where he is, he thinks he is in one of the apartments or houses of his drug-addict years and that he is still an addict; with the light on, seeing our parents' old dresser draped with his clothes and his own artwork, his junk-shop Jesus art, and his nieces' drawings on the walls, he remembers where he is and doesn't panic.

Using drugs all those years has made him like a Vietnam veteran, I think: too much damage has occurred for the past to contain; it keeps leaking into the present. But maybe everybody's past is like that, it just leaks in more subtly. I wonder how much of my grandma's past still leaks or floats into her present. She seems too small to contain all the years she has lived. And in the light from Arthur's nightlight, which my grandma has switched on in case she has to get up to use the bathroom, she seems too fragile for me to touch, let alone elbow or poke.

Besides, if she wakes up she'll be mortified at having woken me again. She always makes such a big deal out of everything; when one of us catches a cold, even, she treats it like a calamity. She still talks about the loss of Dan's legs as if it happened last month, and when someone refers to mine or Dan's or Arthur's divorces, her face takes on the suffering look of Mary at the death of Jesus. She never gets over anything, not even halfway. Sometimes it seems that she doesn't even make an attempt. I love my grandma, but despite our resemblances, I'm very different from her. And as I stare at her lined and sunken cheeks (her teeth, a full set, are in a jar on the night table) I realize that, even though she held me when I was a baby and has hugged and kissed me every year of my life since, I don't know her well enough to touch her while she is sleeping.

I turn onto my back and, as my grandma snores, I pass the time by looking at Arthur's collection of junk-shop religious art. In deference to our grandma, Arthur has taken down the religious art that he has made himself, such as *The Last Breakfast*, in which Jesus and his disciples are consuming bananas, Diet Coke, and Cap'n Crunch. But he has left up his less inflammatory ceramic wall sculptures; Greta's, Ruth's, and Marly's drawings; and a collection of religious kitsch that looks as if it has been lifted from the walls of our grandma's apartment.

Of four pieces, there are two crucifixes hanging high up in the shadows. (I'm thankful that, in the limited light of the nightlight, I can't see their dripping blood.) On the wall across the room is a print of Jesus walking on water with his unpierced hands at his sides and his smooth, broad feet just barely dimpling the water's surface. And closer to me, on the wall to my left, is a print of Jesus in which his heart has been pierced by thorns and risen to the surface of his chest. Jesus's heart is lying right on top of his skin or else the skin has disappeared; either way, his heart is exposed to the air. Thin yellow lines painted around it signify that it glows with an ethereal light, or that despite its being pierced and exposed it continues to beat. My grandma has told me that the heart is glowing and bleeding and exposed like that because Jesus loves us so much, but it makes me think of when I was a child visiting my grandmother and I slept in a room with a crucifix over the bed: my parents were raising us kids as atheists and I didn't know who Jesus was, and I was afraid that whoever had done that to that man would come in the night and get me.

Perhaps because of this memory, staring at the exposed heart makes me feel a little squeamish. I close my eyes to block it out. This magnifies the sound of my grandma's snoring, which reminds me of a death rattle except that it keeps starting up again. I know that I'll never fall back to sleep with that sound, so, gathering up my pillow and timing my exit with one of my grandma's snores, I slip from the bed and go out into the living room.

Halfway across the living room, I stop and stare out. The lights of the city and the darkness they shine in seem alive. The bright yellow lights shimmer and so does the liquid black air; it's as if I can see their molecules moving. If I open a window, it seems that I might hear sound—music, maybe, or humming.

Inside the living room the air is gray and sleepy, motionless and utterly quiet. The white couches glow faintly around the still forms of Arthur and Dan. Zach and Sasha are sleeping side by side on the floor. The rest of my family are paired off in other rooms: my parents in their own bed at the back of the apartment, Marly and Nicole on the floor of the computer room, and Mike and Sarah at the Renaissance Center, which towers like a black-and-gold fortress outside the windows, half a mile across the sky. Standing by myself in the middle of the living room, the only one up and awake, it seems that the pairs in the other rooms have floated off to other worlds, and even the ones within my sight seem as far beyond my reach as if they have fallen under a spell.

I scavenge the blanket that Dan has thrown off (his broad, compact body keeps itself warm) and lie down on the strip of carpet behind the couch next to the largest wall of windows; I lie on my back on the thick, padded carpet and look up and out at the black-and-yellow night and wonder where Toby is, and if he is awake. Probably he is sleeping. I want him awake and lying down with me, even though my strip of carpet is so narrow that my hand rests on its knotted fringe.

I haven't seen Toby in more than two years, yet I still remember the brush of his lips on my neck and the softness of his mouth as we kissed. I remember how soothing his arms felt around me, even though—stupidly, I think now—we remained standing. I want to lie down with him and feel the whole weight and length of him pressed hard against my body. I would remove my flannel nightgown. We wouldn't need one inch of extra space. And if we wanted more room and privacy, we could walk across the sky to the Renaissance Center and slip through a window onto a big, empty bed. I want to make love with Toby on a wide, blank bed without thinking about anyone else, and then I want to fall asleep with him, I want to feel his arms holding me and his skin against my skin as we drift off to the same place.

WHEN I WAKE AGAIN, IT'S still night, but the darkness outside the windows seems quieter, and faded, and though it is quiet, too, inside the apartment, and from the stillness I can tell that my whole family is still asleep, they don't seem so far away from me anymore. I feel that if I call to any one of them they will wake right up and answer me. Maybe the only difference between now and before is that now the night is almost over, it's actually morning already. Soon we'll get up, one and two at a time, and sit around and eat breakfast and read the paper.

I'm drifting back to sleep again when it occurs to me that if my grandma wakes and finds me gone she'll want to know why I left her. I'll have to tell her the truth, or else make something up. I can say that the bed was too soft or the nightlight too bright, but chances are she won't believe me. She'll feel bad for having driven me off, and I'll feed bad for making her feel bad, and, on top of all this bad feeling, I'll have to listen to her apologize for the rest of the day.

I peel back my blanket and am about to get up from the floor when Dan calls to me from the other side of the couch: "Annie? Is that you?"

"Yeah."

I hear him scrambling and feel the couch moving a little; then a hand closes around my foot and feels its shape. "I thought you were Greta or Ruth at first," Dan says. "They're the ones who usually sneak up on me and steal my blankets."

"I didn't steal it," I say. "It was lying at the end of the couch."

"Yeah, sure."

"You can have it back."

"No, go ahead and keep it," Dan says. "I'm not cold."

"I don't need it anymore," I say. "I'm going back to the bed."

"Will you two be quiet?" Arthur calls from the other couch. "Annie, what are you doing out here anyway?"

"Grandma was snoring."

Arthur laughs.

"Yeah, you think it's funny, you try sleeping with her," I say.

"I'm trying to cut back on the number of women I sleep with," Arthur says.

"Well, I'd rather be sleeping with a man. Just one." *A certain one*, I think but don't add. I told Arthur and Dan a long time ago about meeting Toby, and they know that falling in love with him was the last thing I did before

Ray asked me to leave our marriage and our house. I think of telling my brothers now about Toby's latest letter and asking them for advice. But I know that I'm not going to figure out what to do just yet, no matter what advice anyone gives me. I'm afraid of making the same mistake that I made by running away from Al, whom I can see now, from a distance of seven years, would have been a good husband for me. And I'm just as afraid of making the opposite mistake, as I did by getting involved with my lover from Grand Haven, who was not unhappily married, as I naively assumed, but only wanted a supplement to his marriage.

I set Dan's blanket on the arm of his couch, pick up my pillow, and start across the room.

"Ann," Dan calls, trying to catch me before I reach the hall.

I stop and turn back toward him.

"Want to go running tomorrow?" he asks. He means that I'll run and he'll wheel.

"I'm out of shape," I say. "I'd never keep up."

"You could borrow Mom's bike," Dan says. We've done this before; Dan gets a good workout, while I ride at a fairly leisurely pace.

"I don't know," I say. "I might be too tired."

"The cold air will wake you up," Dan says.

"I might be too beat. I haven't gotten much sleep tonight."

"All the more reason to get your butt out there," Dan says. "Fresh air and exercise are good for insomnia."

"Well, I'll see how I feel in the morning."

"You can hold on to the back of my chair and just coast," Dan says. "Or I'll wheel alongside you and turn the pedals with my hands. Or you can just junk the bike, and Zach will carry you on his back."

I laugh, imagining riding Zach horsey-back through the streets. "Okay," I say.

"The weather's supposed to stay mild," Dan says. "Above freezing, anyway. We'll go in the morning, when Mike and Sarah get back from the Ren-Cen. They wanted to come, too."

"It's not going to be above freezing in the morning," Arthur says.

"Do you want to go, Arthur?" Dan asks.

"Nah," Arthur says.

"You could run," I say, thinking that if Arthur started to seize, we'd be there to cushion his fall and to help him home after it was over.

"I haven't run in years," Arthur says.

"You could borrow Dad's bike," I say.

"And his helmet," Dan says. "We could run around you, in formation."

"Maybe," Arthur says.

"We can run by those old warehouses between Jefferson and the river," Dan says. "There's hardly any traffic. We'll have the streets to ourselves."

"It sounds like it would be fun," Arthur says. "I'll think about it. I'll sleep on it."

I hug my pillow under my arm and walk back to Arthur's room and stop in the hallway and look in. The yellow light from the nightlight is bathing the walls with a soft glow and casting a bright circle on the bed. My grandma is lying on her side, facing the door. Her wrinkled face is still and her large eyes are closed.

I step around to the bed's far side, keeping my gaze lowered so I won't see the exposed heart, and lift the covers and slip in, and as the blankets settle over me with their soothing, protective weight, I try not to think about Toby for now.

But as soon as I close my eyes, he appears in my vision; I see him as he looked more than two years ago, during the last half hour of the conference. He is sitting across from me at the small table in his room, wearing khaki pants and a maroon corduroy shirt. He isn't looking at me. His hands are shaking. In another second our conversation will falter, and he'll stand up and walk to me and ask me to stand, too, and I'll soar with the possibility, opening as suddenly as our mouths, of us being together in the future.

I try not to feel that hope now. It's been over two years since I've even seen Toby's face, and though in his last letter he said he'd like to arrange to meet me again, in his first letter he warned me: *Don't make any plans that have me in them, Annie, because you'll only hurt yourself to imagine them.* Something has changed for him since then, but I don't know what has changed or how much, and whatever it is that is different now, I'm afraid that his first words are still true—that my plans with him in them will not become real.

I turn onto my side on my half of the bed and try to turn my thoughts away from him again; I think of how, in a couple of hours, I'll get up and get dressed and ride my mother's bike down by the old warehouses, with Dan, and maybe Arthur, and Mike, Sarah, and Zach. And as I curl up on my side, looking forward to the coming morning, imagining the gray, rippling surface of the river and the grimy walls and dark windows of the old warehouses, sleep drifts toward me once more, loosening my body and my breath. I open my eyes and close them again, taking in with me the soft glow of the room and my grandmother breathing quietly beside me.

ANTHONY GIARDINA

The Cut of His Jib

〜〜〜

W HEN I WAS FIFTEEN YEARS OLD, I mowed lawns for the sum-
mer. My biggest job (eleven dollars) was the house on the corner of
our street. The man was a lawyer; his name was Matt Romano. He might
have been thirty-seven then, a lean, tall, handsome man whose good looks—
and this was nothing unusual, a characteristic of certain men of the time—
bore a faint whiff of the criminal.

No one else on the street was quite like him, though. The men were
older, for one thing. My father was older. They were Italian men who had
started poor, worked hard, and "risen," so that they'd been able to move from
their cramped neighborhoods to this woodsy, "exclusive" hill. Here, they
bought half-acre lots and built their big, modern houses, most of them act-
ing as their own contractors. A common style had been agreed to for all the
houses: two-story, split-level. The Delosas lived across the street, and the
Zagamis. On our side there were us and the Noceras. It was all very serious,
living there. You felt, distinctly, your father's pride in having ascended.

The house at the end of the street was vacant for the first few months
after we moved in. Deluria, the contractor, had built it on spec, and rumor
had it he was asking too much. We, the families, big with our new sense of
ourselves as landed gentry, sat around our tables after dinner and discussed
such things. The side yard of the vacant house sloped downward, following
the curve of the hill. The ledge that had had to be blasted in order to build
some of these houses obtruded in spots, with vegetation sprouting from it.
The house had, perhaps, more grandeur than the other houses because of

this, and because of the number of trees in the back. Amidst them, Deluria had planted a fountain, an angelic woman pouring water from a jug. Couples came on Sundays to look at the house, but none of them seemed quite up to the task of living in it. The Sunday Matt Romano came, the air had a heightened quality; that is the way I remember it, though I know some parts of my memory are the result of additions, things gathered to the central, bare fact because they seem, now, appropriate. We had moved into our house in midfall and this was the beginning of spring. Lawns had only just been seeded, so the way I remember it—all the families gathered on green lawns, standing like alerted shepherds to view the coming of the Romanos—cannot be exact. More likely it was me standing alone in my driveway, while a family stepped out of a gold car, a Mercury Cougar, I think. First, a man who looked like he'd just emerged from the cover of a novel, in a blue double-breasted blazer and cream-colored slacks. Then a wife, with honey blond hair and sunglasses, followed by two daughters, dark-haired, like him. They carried about them an air of difference; something made you look at them as if, were you only to stare hard enough, you'd find something out. She was with them that day, I remember that much with absolute assurance. She emerged from the car last, a smaller, darker woman, much younger than his wife but too old to be his daughter. She wore sunglasses as well, but she removed hers. She took them off and glanced across the seeded lawn at us, for only a second's lapse. My father must have come out and joined me by then, because I remember it was the two of us staring at her.

HE WAS, FROM THE BEGINNING, a kind of odd duck. I never heard those words used, but I imagine hearing them used in an overheard conversation, my father and mother talking, my father and one of the men. This is what should have happened. They ought to have stepped back and understood him, dismissed him with one of the functional phrases they had invented for such men. Instead, they did what was natural for them: they accepted him. He became, almost immediately, a part of the crowd. They socialized on Saturday nights, nearly every week, in one or another of the neighbors' basements (but these were not basements, understand; they were "lower levels," carpeted, with big pool tables and pine paneling). My father's idea of a good time was to gather all the men into his office as soon as they arrived and ask them to take off their clothes and get into women's dresses and wigs. Then the men, dressed as women, would come out and dance for their wives, the "girls," who would sit together on couches and giggle uproariously. From our rooms upstairs, my sisters and I would hear them and sometimes creep to the banister and watch these hairy, half-exposed men in scanty costumes, from the bottom of which their boxer shorts showed. In dresses and wigs, they looked more like men than they would have in their regular party clothes. That was the nature of the game; I understood, early on, that it was all about sexual display.

My father loved to tell the story of the first time Matt Romano came to one of these parties. He grabbed him by the arm, took him into his office, and said, "Take off your pants." "You should have seen his face!" My father laughed. He is a simple man, my father; when he laughs, his face goes red. He believes deeply, I think, that every man is at heart the same man, with the same desires, save for those few who are so perverse that they must be set aside from the rest. "And then," my father went on, "in the next minute, he did it!" It was Matt Romano's initiation as ordinary man. He removed his blue double-breasted blazer and the cream-colored slacks and put on a dress and a wig. I did not watch this particular party, but I saw other scenes enough like it so that I can imagine how Matt Romano would have arranged his face into a pose of easy mirth, so much like the others that anyone would have been fooled. Then he would have gone out and bared his legs, and the men would have laughed, very hard, and put their hands on his shoulders, and laughed again.

Very soon, his name began to change. I had thought, on first hearing it, that it had a certain elegance that put him at a distance from the others. And they spoke it, too, that way at first, with a kind of perplexed respect. Who was this man, this newcomer, this lawyer who had moved in among them? His practice was in Boston. Much was made of that, his city life, his professional life, his physical removal from the cement trucks and Laundromats and muddy construction sites of my father and his cronies. It is easy enough to imagine him as he might have existed in those days, in his office with its view of the harbor. In my image, he is speaking on the phone, leaning forward, scratching the side of his nose, a familiar habit of his. Several stories below, the water runs slate gray, smoky in the afternoon light. Yet I can't hold the image without seeing him turn away from the things on his desk, the crisp papers, the letter opener. He looks down and away, riveted by something. There in the harbor, my father and Steve Delosa are out on my father's Chris-Craft, fishing for flounder off of Rainsford Island. They are wearing fishing jackets, funny hats; in their hands are cans of beer. He is staring at them intently; there is something he is trying to figure out, a desire he is probing. Already, they have put a spin on his name, something that does not displease him. In their flat Boston pitch they stress the *an* in Rom*a*no. All its languor, its otherworldliness, is being ironed out. They are making him, in all the ways they know how to, just like them.

There is only the fact of Sundays to stand in the way of this ongoing absorption: on Sundays she comes, the slender, dark-haired girl in sunglasses. She wears dresses that cling to her small body, and she moves with the cautious precision of someone crippled in youth. Very soon, it seems, everyone knows her name. "Did Dolores visit the Romanos today?" my mother might ask my father on a Sunday evening, as if she hadn't herself looked and seen. And the name will not be reduced, not the way they have reduced his name. The word *Dolores* cannot be bitten down on; it comes out, in spite of their best attempts, sounding ambiguous, dreamlike, a word from another place, one they have steadfastly determined not to visit.

Dolores was Matt Romano's secretary. That explanation arrived a month or so after the Romanos moved in. I don't know when the neighbors began to wonder about their Sunday arrangement, but I know the explanation, the business relationship, was spoken of with relief. After that, all forms of apocrypha sprang up. She was an orphaned girl for whom the Romanos had agreed to stand as substitute family. Her relations lived far away, in "California." The weekends were hard for her. She had nowhere else to go.

A snapshot: it is early summer, before Matt Romano has asked me to start mowing his lawn. I am in my backyard. I do not know what I am doing. Perhaps when you are fifteen, you only watch; it is your principal task, whatever other functions your body might be performing. It is your obsession to figure out the world. Matt Romano and Dolores are alone in the backyard, and from two houses away I can see them. They are walking among the trees in the Romanos' backyard, the miniature forest of tall maples. Her dress is blue and belted; she is wearing a straw hat. He is walking slightly ahead of her and gesturing. His long arm goes out, as if to make a point; he turns to her. For a moment he considers her the way I was later to see him consider many things, as if from a far remove, something passing briefly over his face that to an outsider might resemble contempt. Then something else. The afternoon, for two or three seconds only, is heavy with an essence that I know, even at fifteen, he believes to be at the heart of life. If I had now to put a name on that thing I was made aware of, I would fumble, I would choose a useless word like *confusion*. Like *ambivalence*. But at that instant, as I stand in the presence of it, I seem to understand that there is no need to name it. It is simply there, on Matt Romano's face as I view it from a distance, a seeing into life that troubles him deeply, yet that he is brave enough to hold on to for these few seconds. Then he moves past it—his body does, anyway; they sit on the edge of the fountain and resume their conversation. He goes on gesturing with his arms. Dolores sits upright, listening attentively but at the same tie with an air of distraction, as though the important thing was said a while ago, and she is struggling to absorb it while only pretending to hear the words he is saying now. Through all of this, I have remained unseen.

IN JULY, AT SOMEONE'S COOKOUT, he spoke to me for the first time.

"I hear you're a pretty good lawn mower," he said.

I don't remember answering. It was a bit of a surprise to come face-to-face with the fact that we inhabited the same universe, that he existed in dimensions identical to mine, was capable of taking me in, even of making a request. But some arrangement must have been made that afternoon, because I began mowing their lawn on Wednesdays. He had offered eleven dollars. The figure was irresistible; his largesse, everything that was impressive about him, was in it. His lawn took half a day. He was at work while I did it. I was fastidious, careful with things like edges and rocks, and I lost myself, always, in the rhythm of the humming machine. Every once in a while I would gaze up at the house, trying to get a closer look. A cedar deck rose on stilts at the far end. Through the window, I could see the cathedral ceiling, the hanging chandelier that would have lit their living room. His daughters were not girls who often played outside, but occasionally the younger one—she must have been five or six at the time—would come out and talk to me. I wanted to say nothing that would offend her, nothing she could report to her father that might cause me to lose this job, so we had a series of careful conversations in which most of our time was spent merely staring at one another. When the mowing was done, I trimmed the borders with clippers and went over the whole lawn carefully to check for any spots I'd missed. After the first time, I made the mistake of going up to the back door and standing before Stella Romano, too embarrassed to ask for money but assuming she would know what I was there for.

At first, she looked at me, then past me, as if I'd come to tell her about some problem with the lawn. And it was as though this worried her: the lawn wasn't her domain.

"I'm finished," I said.

She looked at me again, still not comprehending. Then she finally seemed to get it and laughed in her light, dismissive way. It was mid-afternoon, but she wore a dress, and jewelry. Beyond that, the little girls watched TV in the den.

"You'll have to come back tonight," she said.

I came back after I saw his car in the driveway, and that was the ritual I followed all summer. I left an hour for their dinner, which was later than ours, so that by the time I crossed the two yards I had to leave the very comfortable scene of our house at dusk, the television on in our family room and the yellow evening light coming in, while my sisters painted their nails and my mother did the dishes. My father, his gaze fixed absently on the screen, had set this time aside for what remained of his dream life. I looked forward to the moment when I had some excuse to leave them, to cross the two lawns in the deepening light. Something in that family room at that hour gave me cause for fear. I never probed it, or never far; something was stopped there, something had achieved perfection. I felt oddly freed by the feeling of unsettledness I had as I climbed the steps to the back landing of the Romanos'.

There, the scene was always repeated, always the same—Matt Romano would answer the door and look at me as if he had never seen me before and had no idea what I was there for. Seconds would pass; he would focus, then seem displeased by the fact that had finally risen into his consciousness. I was the boy who mowed their lawn, the neighbor's son come looking for money. He seemed, in his half-unbuttoned white shirt and black dress pants, to have emerged recently from a scene of violence. There was about him an agitation that made me think at any second a wild gesture might spring forth, though he would only reach into his pocket and count out eleven dollars, and as he spoke, in the transparent effort he made to be kind, I came to know that he was only drunk. Behind him, there might have been some noise, a woman's whimpering, though I am quite sure I am reading this in. The single instance Stella Romano appeared behind him, it was the cagey, frightened look of a keeper that she wore; she drew him back when he began to speak to me. His words were slurred; I doubt I even heard him. She must have been afraid, though, of what he might say. She drew him back with one hand, and as I turned to her I lost the haunted look in his eyes, the look that drunks get when they want, terribly, to be understood. There seemed to be in it some message meant directly for me. But it, too, was lost. One or the other of them shut the door.

IT DOESN'T SEEM AT ALL strange to me how little my life that summer had to do with the outside world, the world of my peers, how fully and simply I inhabited that neighborhood. I don't think my evening bike rides ever took me beyond the street, or the sand pits that announced foundations that would soon be built on the newly cleared lots opening into the forest. I circled the houses and studied hard, noticed small architectural flaws—the Zagamis had left too much foundation showing, so had my father—and grew attuned to an unnameable melancholy that settled over me as I stared at new brick and stone at dusk. Sometimes I wandered through the skeletons of houses that were still just wood, naming the rooms. If I saw a man walking past—Steve Delosa with his dog, Al Zagami whistling—I would stare hard at that, too, waiting for the image to reveal its deeper truth. The intuition that guided my days was that something was about to be shown to me, some fact about life I had to be alert for, a thing that might free me from what, even then, I could see was not a usual infatuation.

In September, they decided to throw themselves a ball. It did not seem extraordinary, though a far cry from the parties where the men dressed as women. The women were to purchase gowns; the men, tuxedos. I don't think the ball was the Romanos' idea exactly, but I believe it was because of the Romanos that a change occurred. Within a year, the raucous Saturday night cross-dressing became a thing of the past.

There was a school dance that Saturday night, but I didn't go. Instead, I sat in my house and waited for my parents to appear, dressed for the occasion. The Noceras joined my parents for a preball drink, but there was tension as soon as they came in. Elena Nocera seemed uncomfortable, as if waiting to be sprung from the tight white gown she wore, to put her feet up and make one of the ribald comments that were her trademark. Charlie Nocera, too, looked fidgety in his tuxedo. But my father moved about the rooms, appearing purposefully stiff, as though guided by the stately measures of a piece of music none of the rest of us could hear. "Have a brandy, Charlie?" he asked, and went to pour it. Charlie Nocera put his hands in his pockets. Elena made a joke. My mother, in her yellow gown, sat as if in a trance.

When they had all gone into the Romanos', I stood at the foot of their lawn to see what I could of the party. A bay window, twelve feet across, cast its light onto the lawn. A single birch rose up in front, stark and long-trunked. Through its leaves, I watched the pastel women pass, the men in black suits. Matt himself came for a moment and stood at the window. I don't believe he saw me. One hand was in the pocket of his tuxedo pants, the other held a long-stemmed drink. On his face was that by now familiar, wistful suggestion that what was most dear to him, most essential, existed elsewhere. I was sure he was going to step away, come outside, drive off. Around his body was that slight, subliminal blurring, as in a film, where you know an action is forthcoming, and I understood it was the action I'd been waiting for. I might have been coaxing him, hoping for the gesture, the tug of the rope with which all the scenery might be lifted and the mechanics of this world revealed to me so that I might see it, at last, for the blunt thing it was. But all he did was turn away. He went back to the party. The movement of the room seemed to slow down and gather around him, as if he had gotten lost on an outing, stopped somewhere to get a closer look at some amazing, briefly glimpsed thing, and now the others had formed a party to carry him away from it.

I AM SORRY TO SAY that after that night, or soon after, I began to change. A new school year had begun, different from the one before; circumstances converged in a way that made me grow more interested in myself, less so in the world around me. I lost the perfect outward attunement of a fifteen-year-old boy, and never again recovered it. Or let me say, instead, that I found it, or had it thrust on me, on only two other occasions, so that what might have been a rich, dark, satisfying story becomes instead jagged, a thing of snapshots.

The first occurred at another cookout, during another summer, and it was the only time I saw Matt Romano flare up, openly declare his independence from the others, though when I say "flare up," that's too much; it was subtler than that. The Noceras had built a pool; there were gatherings on Sundays, celebrations, really, of Charlie Nocera's deepening success in the construction business. No one else had a pool. Charlie Nocera's grin grew foxier, wider in those days. You see this gathering of energy in certain men, the moment when they peak. The children are still young, the pool is new, all the calls are for them. He began to take some of the limelight away from Matt Romano. Perhaps Matt sensed this and was annoyed; perhaps that's the explanation for his behavior that day. I don't know. We all leaped into the pool, one nearly on top of the other, but after a time I sat in a lounge chair, wrapped in a towel, taking time off from my growing fascination with myself to pay attention to the men.

They were talking: Matt Romano, my father, Charlie Nocera, Steve Delosa. The women were elsewhere and the chatter was aggressive, punctuated by laughter, then softening, drifting, falling back into the rhythms of the summer afternoon. Matt Romano began a story. It always surprised me to hear him talk. Whenever he opened his mouth and spoke, I was made certain that I had invented him, invented, at least, the dreaming, wraithlike figure who hovered over the neighborhood but was never quite one with it.

When he spoke, he was a coarse man whose eyes revealed the desperation of someone wanting merely to be liked. I turned away. I remember, though, when he'd finished, registering on some level that his story had failed to make the desired impression. The men seemed disturbed by it. Matt had told a story about a rascal, a business cheat he half-admired. The story ended, the men made a kind of silent grumble, then Matt said, in afterthought, "I liked the cut of his jib."

I turned back then, I had to, because some sixth sense told me I was about to witness a scene. Charlie Nocera was sitting, his hands folded, leaning slightly forward, with his thumbs flicking at one another. He was grinning, but the grin had passed its point of animation and some darker assessment was taking place in his eyes. Hatred would be too strong a word for it, but it was not impossible to imagine, from that look, that in other circumstances he might be about to get up and hit Matt Romano. My father leaned back in his chair with one finger pressing against the side of his lips—his thoughtful, impatient pose. Steve Delosa glanced off at the neighboring trees, waiting for something to pass.

All of this took place in a matter of seconds, and within it, I saw Matt Romano watch them all, quietly defiant. "The cut of his jib." It was not language any of them would ever have used; he had brought it from somewhere else and held it before them like a sign of his dual citizenship, his ability to escape their little world, if it came to that. They all knew this: they were antagonists at heart. All their silent acceptance of Dolores, of his transgression of the rules, felt about to erupt. Instead, the unexpected, habitual thing happened. It was as though a bird, emerging from its egg, went backward, covered itself over, so that the egg, though newly whole, revealed its network of cracks. Someone said something, to offset the tension. Matt Romano's face turned grim. Whatever he was seeking took its form in the space between him and the men. He considered it, then lowered his eyes. He leaned back in his chair and crossed his legs. From a distance, it might have appeared as though an ease had returned to the scene. A breeze made the tops of the trees move. Elena Nocera, grinning widely, came out with iced tea.

FINALLY, WE ARE ALL ON the water, in my father's boat. It is a twenty-seven-foot cabin cruiser, docked in Gloucester. The family sleeps on it Saturday nights in summer; on Sundays the neighbors come. Before noon, they emerge at the top of the ramp, holding coolers, picnic baskets. But now I am no longer interested in them. It is two summers later, 1967; they have gone from being gods to becoming jokes. Not their fault, entirely, or mine. Even beyond my seventeen-year-old consciousness, a passage was going on. They were all suburban Democrats in Ban-Lon pants, and they were being moved, ungently, from the center of the visible universe to some laughable periphery.

Still, they acted as though they hardly knew this. On Sundays they cooked steaks and drank beer and appeared to me on the other side of the smoke from the grill, men whose clothes no longer fit so well, women out-living their usefulness. My invisibility, once so precious to me, seemed another count against them. I could not understand how they remained so fascinated by themselves and each other. I felt they should turn to me, and stare, perhaps ask a question about the life I was about to go off and seize.

In one of the home movies of his later years, my father did something private, for himself. I came upon it once by accident, looking for something else. On a day when they must have been alone together on the boat, he filmed my mother. She is not doing anything dramatic or particularly interesting. For long stretches, she eats, she puts on sunglasses, she sits staring upward at the sun. She faces him and speaks. There is no sound to the film, so there is only her mouth moving, and the sight of her body, in a one-piece bathing suit. The light is overbright, the water an impossible blue. He holds the camera a long time on her, as though not willing to turn away.

But that was later, all my understanding came later. That day in 1967 I was entirely blind to it. Dolores was still there among them. She might have been thirty then. If there had been delicacy and ripeness to her at the beginning, it was starting to go. Her belly fell into tight ridges that clung to her ribs when she sat. Though she didn't speak often, her voice, when she did, no longer sounded hopeful and tentative and waiting to hear the great defining thing. She was like someone's niece who ought to have been at another party, one with young lawyers and daiquiris, but no one had the grace to tell her so. It had to come through an action.

It was a big party that day: us, the Noceras, the Delosas, Matt Romano, Stella, and Dolores. Six children altogether. It was my job to steer, which I didn't mind doing. I kept a transistor radio at the helm: Top 40 blocked them out. They sat in deck chairs; the women put on kerchiefs to keep their hair from blowing in their faces.

We made a wide circle of the harbor, then edged under the narrow bridge into the Annisquam River toward Wingaersheek Beach. For the most part, that day would have been a day like any other. We always anchored the boat along the mile-long tongue of white sand that stretches from the mouth of Wingaersheek. The dinghy we carried on our stern would have brought the women in to shore. Then, laughter as they tried to go from dinghy to sand without getting wet, and my father, on the outboard motor, would have made a joke, and shaken the boat, to make them nervous.

The men usually chose to swim in, to make big awkward dives and thrash through the water, then emerge, sleek-headed and dripping, before a dry, fully clothed woman. Then the women would have stripped down to their bathing suits, blankets would have been laid out, cigarettes lit.

The only awkwardness—too familiar now for anyone to pay much attention—would have been Matt Romano's emergence from the sea. Dolores stood waiting. She watched him swim in, always, as if at any moment he might be lost forever. Stella would not be so overt: she'd busy herself with the children, the two dark-haired girls. Age had made them lithe, more physical, and Stella was awkward as she ran after them. Little attention as I paid (I stayed on the boat, with one of my sisters; we read paperbacks), I can see the choice as it might have appeared to him that day. Stella, who had put on weight, who rarely in those days allowed herself to be seen in a bathing suit. A yellow or pale green dress flapping against her white legs, the jewelry she was never without—necklace, rings—making a sparkle in the sun. Her hair would fly backward in the wind, her profile standing out, unadorned. Then Dolores, at a distance, arms crossed, a bit impatient. Still, nothing attached to her, no children; she was merely what she was, a woman who had waited a long time for him to make up his mind. One of the men might have come up to her and made a joke—"Look, he's not as quick as he used to be!"—and then she would have laughed edgily and looked at Matt Romano splashing through the sea until some presentiment of the hugeness of her risk made her shiver. Seeing this, his mind would be made up for him, at least for the moment, and he'd go to her, to reassure.

Out of the corner of her eye, Stella would catch sight of this and pretend not to notice. As practiced at acceptance as the neighbors had become by then, there had to be a moment—very brief, a hairline fracture—when the facade began to crack. Steve Delosa would put out a cigarette, with disgust, in the sand. Everyone would know what he meant, awareness traveling like a shared tremor among them. Matt Romano would register it.

But after a while things would slacken, the rhythms of the afternoon would take hold. Cigarettes would be smoked, conversational topics broached. What might have compelled them in the summer of 1967? The advent of the hippies in San Francisco? Lyndon Johnson's escalation of the

Vietnam War? A sale at Penney's? The words would have floated on the air, the way they do on a beach, important for a moment, then gone. Elena Nocera would have lain back and made a joke about her legs. One of the men would have adjusted his bathing suit to free his balls. They'd've watched the younger couples as they strolled this length of sand, or made note of the other vessels, or turned in the opposite direction from shore, where the dune grass glistened in the white heat.

It would have been that kind of afternoon. Insignificant. The sun would have gradually lowered in the sky, and it would have been lost, a day gone. Half a mile distant, blankets would have been gathered off the crowded beach, the small exodus to cars begun, thoughts returning to Monday, to the question and the problem of work. For them merely a reflex, that, and then a deeper sinking into the day, the stretching out of legs. What anxiety did "work" have for any of them? Headaches, yes. Problems with suppliers, arguments, but all this would come and go, it was tomorrow's business. They were lucky, and they knew it. They had survived to this point in their lives, rich enough, without encountering any of the stickier problems—all but the Romanos, that is. Tonight the men would make love to their wives the way older men do in summer, when the rising of the skin seems to have less to do with a particular woman than with the quality of the day, and you try to get to it in the last light, when the vestiges of some old existence, one you perhaps never actually lived, are to be found in the edges and crannies of the act itself. On the beach the men would have thought of all that, and the group stayed later than anyone else.

By the time they finally gathered their things, the water would have darkened, fishing boats coming in with their entourage of gulls, and their bodies would have gone heavy, resistant to the transition back to boat, to car. My father pulled the dinghy, loaded with women, through the shallows until the water reached midway up his thighs, then he heaved himself onboard. Another joke, more laughter, his head with its gray nest of hair and then his body, as he half-stood to jerk the motor into life, flinging toward me the brief, unwelcome awareness that he was still vital, still fucked my mother, a terrible thing to know but something he was resplendent with as he pointed the dinghy toward the boat, where I waited with my sister and our novels. The women's faces on the dinghy, the sun behind them, were red, their hair lightened by the salt, and their bodies had the soft-shoulderedness of women who had recently been pleasured. It was as if my father were riding his harem across this weedy patch of sea, a harem of contented, middle-aged women.

Only one thing was interesting that day: Dolores, among them, on the dinghy, and I don't think I'd even remember how she looked if it wasn't the last time I was to see her. Straight-backed with resistance, she sat in sunglasses, her proud little body thinner than anyone else's. She would not give herself over to the happy ease of that boat; if once she'd felt close enough to them to joke, to share secrets, those days were over. She had grown careful to mark out her boundaries and to move within them with precision, so that while the thighs of Mary Delosa and my mother might have been touching, their sweatshirted shoulders blurred and indistinguishable, you saw all the space around Dolores.

They came to the boat and unloaded, my father made playful little grabs for their calves, and immediately they busied themselves, putting away blankets, getting out robes to welcome their children, who were still onshore with the men. None of them watched what was going on there, not at the beginning.

My father had returned to shore and was in the process of getting each of the children loaded into the boat, outfitting them first with life preservers. There was just room, with children on their laps, for the three men as well, though it made the boat ride low. After lifting his daughters in, Matt Romano put up his hand in a gesture of refusal. My father made an answering gesture, beckoning him in. These were repeated, until Matt Romano stepped away from the boat. My father looked at him a moment, unmoving, with just the focus of the others on the boat to tell me he was saying something. Matt Romano lowered his hands into the water, and my father started up the motor. Someone, one of the women, said, "He's going to swim," and then another—not Stella, not Dolores—said, unworried, factual, "It's too far."

The tide had come in enough so that the distance was, in fact, significant. I didn't doubt, though, that he would make it. He was no more than forty then and had a strong body. He moved out to where the water was waistdeep and watched the progress of the dinghy until my father had reached us and we all had begun helping the children onboard. Only when everyone was recovered did he begin his swim, and I was prescient enough even then to understand that, for some reason, he wanted us to watch him.

My father was still standing on the dinghy, but after Matt Romano had swum twenty or thirty feet he decided there was no reason not to lift it and hook it to the back of the boat. As he did so, a look passed over his face, an annoyed look. Charlie Nocera had come and stood beside me to watch his neighbor swim. I could feel the tension of his body even a foot away, and it wasn't an ordinary tension. Something was happening. It could have been the most commonplace of things—a man swimming a long distance—or it could have turned into something else. Charlie and my father didn't know yet. That there was something remarkable about Matt Romano—his occasional, yet highly dramatic, insistence that life could be lived differently than they lived it—was the grit of sand under their suits, the thing they would remove if they could. Yet it was elusive, it might not be at all what they thought it was, so they were denied the clean action that would stop him in his tracks. They could only wait and see.

So he swam, and we watched him, the black knot of his hair dipping, then rising, his Indian's beak of a nose coming up, his wide back glistening in the sun, until someone started to notice what was happening.

It was barely detectable at first. He was veering off course, but just slightly, and it could have been no more than a trick of light that he appeared to be making no progress toward us. We were so taken in by his impressive swimming that it didn't seem quite possible that another force—an invisible one—might be rendering all that beautiful effort in vain. "The current's taking him," one of the men said, finally. He began to slow down after a while and then you could see it more clearly, how it was pulling him, the late-afternoon tug of the tide, so strong on that part of the river. He must have been fifty feet upriver of us when he lifted his head.

She was beside me then, nestled between me and Charlie Nocera but not aware of either of us. She had come to the railing to look, and still there was that space around her, as if she believed this display was for her alone.

It had that quality to it, his moment of failure, because I believed the same thing, that it was for me. His head was lifted now and he was looking at us as though not yet willing to ask for help. Instead, he seemed deliberately to choose this moment, to hold it still and out of time, as a kind of invitation to all of us to see him for what he was; to be accepted for all that he could not quite do.

We all took it in; there was a silence on the boat. I was disappointed, above all other things. I had needed, very badly, to see him as someone capable of breaking free of this world, if he only chose, but now, as I watched him, watched his face, which made no effort to excuse his moment of shame, I saw that he had been caught by it, was, in fact, the same as them, in love with something closer to death than to life. Finally, he let the current carry him up the river until it deposited him on the shore.

As we watched this, I felt the movement of Dolores's body in front of me. She'd gone very close to the railing. Now her shoulders lowered, and the bumps of the vertebrae along her back receded. It was enough to let me know something. My father let the dinghy into the water again; his expression was more satisfied now. The rest of us watched to make sure Matt Romano made it to shore, and then my father, floating, asked, "Anybody want to come for a ride?"

As it turned out, both of the other men wanted to come with him. Matt had been carried far upriver, so as they steered toward him they made a diagonal into the sun. I remember their rounded, coarse backs on the boat. I remember, too, how it occurred to me that, for them, this was not entirely unexpected, this turn of events, that all along they had known what would happen to him, and had treated him more or less like a child who would, in time, understand. Only I had been fooled into believing there was, for him, some possibility of escape.

IT TOOK TWENTY YEARS BEFORE the life he gave himself over to that day finally killed him. Heart trouble had apparently started much earlier, but more than for most men, the passage from age fifty to sixty had a wasting effect. My wife and I went to visit him and Stella when we were newly married; they had dogs then. We were big with our romance, and all I remember my wife and me doing was talking about ourselves, giving details of our domestic arrangements, our studio apartment in New York, places we had traveled and were going to travel. He listened, and at one point I thought I saw the old contemptuous look come over his face. It was just after Christmas, and he lifted one of the opened boxes in their living room. I leaned forward, relieved, thinking he was going to show me one of his gifts, when suddenly, and with majestic fierceness, he used it to sidearm one of the dogs.

That's all much later; I'm getting ahead. But there wasn't a lot left to that day really. Memory closes down on it, as if it wants to see the end there. He's onshore, waiting for them, his hands on his hips. He doesn't look embarrassed. He's standing straight, merely waiting. Maybe he's calmer now. Something has been settled on, after a long effort. They come in close, the three men, and move over for him, and he steps in and settles among them on the boat, and the four of them ride toward us, black, faceless figures with the sun behind them, and when I look again, she is not there anymore. Without my quite knowing it, Dolores has slipped from her position before me, so that as the dinghy comes very near, I feel a shiver of apprehension that there is no longer anything standing between me and him.

JOHN GIORNO

Age of Innocence

∾⸞⸏∿

O N D E C E M B E R 2 5 , 1 9 6 4 , I W E N T home for Christmas dinner with
my mother and father in Roslyn Heights, on the north shore of Long
Island. I was twenty-eight years old, and it was a little depressing that I was
still doing it. I was in bondage, required to do the right thing, slavery to fam-
ily values. I drove from my apartment at 255 East Seventy-fourth Street,
New York, in my 1954 MG TD, pale yellow, dirty and banged up, and really
cool. I had a hangover, and grit my teeth for the Italian-American Christmas
dinner.

I arrived about eleven-thirty on a cold, dry, sunny morning. Number 16
Old Brick Road, Norgate in East Hills, a ranch house built in 1949 using
Frank Lloyd Wright's ideas, surrounded by 250-year-old oak trees and beau-
tiful gardens, in an affluent suburb, was an upper-middle-class dream
house. It was decorated for Christmas: the tree laden with ornaments,
wreaths, holly from the garden, pine garland over the mantel of the marble
fireplace, and a wood fire burning. My mother was in the kitchen cooking
the elaborate Italian dinner and my father was setting the dining room table.
We greeted each other happily and cheerfully, "Merry Christmas!" I really
liked them and we got along really well. We exchanged presents, and gos-
siped. A typical American family.

The energy of the Christmas preparations was infectious and wonderful.
I joined in, as usual, doing what I wanted first. I put mistletoe over the fire-
place above the eighteenth-century portrait of Don Nicolo Maria Panevino,
one of my ancestors. Then I took over from my father and finished setting

the dining room table for ten guests, thirteen altogether. I brought out more silver.

A great feast! Offering vast amounts of food and drink was the joy of generosity. Everything was nonverbal. The Christmas celebrations were primordial, were about more than the birth of Christ, more than the new year, and the guests coming to dinner were gods and goddesses.

My parents were Catholic, but didn't go to church. My father had gone to Christmas Eve mass, but my mother was too busy. As a child, I had an Irish Catholic nanny who made me say Our Fathers and Hail Marys every day. When I was eight years old, I said to my parents, "I don't want to do it anymore!" They said, "Don't do it, if you don't want." That concluded me being Catholic.

The portrait was my secret magic spot. My great-great-great-grandfather, Don Nicola Maria Panevino, on my father's mother's side of the family, was born in 1771 in Aliano. He was a famous judge and His Excellency the governor of Basilicata, a region of southern Italy. He must have been very politically skillful to deal with the new king of Naples, Ferdinand II, on the one side, and the feudal landowners he represented on the other. Through him, the ancient Panevino family got more landholdings and were one of the ruling families of Basilicata for about a hundred years.

Being a famous judge, he must have been wise; being the governor of Basilicata, he must have been ruthless.

Their moment of glory had finished about a hundred years before 1964 and was forgotten. Nobody remembered anything. Their descendants in New York were working class, with no special qualities, and some disabling gentility. The painting had been brought to New York by my grandmother's brother Vincenzo Panevino in the 1880s, bequeathed to his son Emil, then to my father, and to me. It hung for fifty years over the fireplace at 16 Old Brick Road, until 2001, when I brought the painting to my home at 222 Bowery, and sold the house.

My mother, Nancy Giorno, was a fashion designer and had a very successful career with Arnold Scaasi, Bill Blass, Hattie Carnegie, Elizabeth Arden, and other famous ones. Her genius lay in her ability to work with great fashion designers, transforming their ideas into cloth, understanding what was wanted before they knew they wanted it, and made it happen. She knew how to make an idea brilliantly real, with the help of sample hands and other people. My mother, born in 1910, was an early career woman. She was very well paid. She was the driving force in the family, and brought money and vitality.

My father, Amedeo Giorno, born in 1901, owned a reweaving business, employing highly skilled Italian women repairing torn and damaged fine cloth and textiles. It was what remained of the successful custom tailor business started by my grandfather John Giorno in the 1880s. My father barely supported the family.

My grandfather Giovanni Giorno (not yet John Giorno, until 1895), married my grandmother in 1888. The story was they met during the blizzard of 1888. They both lived in an apartment building at 143 Mott Street, on the corner of Spring Street, in Little Italy, two blocks from 222 Bowery, where I have lived for forty years. The blizzard was on March 12, 1888, and ended on March 13. The snow was four feet deep drifting to twelve. New York was paralyzed. My grandmother Maria Panevino was frightened, and called to a young man in the street, who she knew lived in the building, and asked him to take a letter to her cousin. She threw it down to him, and that was how they met. They were married four months later on July 12, 1888. My grandfather was nineteen years old and my grandmother twenty-seven, a spinster in those years. She came from the noble family, and for her brother Vincenzo Panevino to allow the marriage, my grandfather must have already been successful, as a young tailor; or maybe, just to get her married; or maybe they fucked while the blizzard stopped New York, and she was pregnant, and she hooked him.

Number 222 Bowery was built in 1884 by the YMCA, and called The Young Men's Institute. It was the first of the modern-day YMCAs. Previously, the Ys were soup kitchens and shelters for the homeless. Cleveland Dodge and the Pyne brothers, young gentlemen just graduated from Princeton, had the idea and got together with forty-four-year-old Cornelius Vanderbilt II and created The Young Men's Institute, to help men seventeen years or older from immigrant families get a better start in life with gymnastics, classes in music and poetry, language, carriage building, etc. An organization intended to promote the physical, intellectual, and spiritual health of young workingmen in the densely crowded Bowery. The building was Romanesque-Revival, built by Cornelius Vanderbilt's railroad architect Bradford Gilbert. The rich guys built a palazzo for the beggars. The Bowery and surroundings were a sea of squalor and deplorable conditions, filth and disease, abuse, the suffering of all the immigrants. The Young Men's Institute was a safe haven and joy to countless young men until it closed in 1932.

It became an artists' loft building beginning with Fernand Léger in the early 1940s, and Rothko in the 1950s, Michael Goldberg and Lynda Benglis, and other artists. William Burroughs and I liked to think that the gay sublife, sex and homosexual love, that must have happened there—it was a Y, like in the gay rock song "YMCA"—were carried on splendidly during our years. The building became a co-op. I own three lofts, the second-and third-floor lofts, and the Bunker of Burroughs, or locker room on rear mezzanine floor, where I live and work.

I believe that my grandfather John Giorno, who lived two and a half blocks away at Mott and Spring Streets, visited 222 Bowery many times, frequented my lofts, came often, participating in the activities from 1885 to 1888. It was designed for ambitious, upwardly mobile boys like my grandfather. He had emigrated from Taranto in southern Italy when he was twelve, in 1881. He was trying to better himself. Maybe he was a member of the Y, and maybe it was good for him and changed his life. He married my grandmother in 1888, and maybe he stopped going to The Young Men's Institute. Or maybe he took her there to the events to which ladies were invited. She would have liked going to a brand-new, palazzo-style building that was two and a half blocks from where she lived.

From his noble mother Maria Panevino Giorno, my father, Amedeo—Middy, as everyone called him, her youngest son—received the qualities of gentleness, modesty, a love of reading and music, and generosity. Most important, Middy spent his whole life helping others. An unending stream of people from Italy—who had problems, and didn't know what to do about something, and could barely speak English, and were suffering—and my father did something, guided them, fixed it, free, no charge, from kindness and compassion, and didn't talk about it.

As a child, my father took me to the gala opera benefits organized by Michael Sisca and La Follia di New York, an opera society and magazine. The great singers of the day—Renata Tebaldi and Mario Del Monaco, Jussi Björling, Maria Callas, and countless others, and Enrico Caruso in the old days—sang at Carnegie Hall, Town Hall, Hunter College, union auditoriums in bad times, and Alice Tully Hall. La Follia was started in 1893 by Mike's parents, Alessandro and Marziale Sisca, who were friends of my grandparents. The gala concerts were spectacular. In the 1940s, the greatest singers ran over between acts from the Metropolitan Opera on West Thirty-ninth Street, and later, from Lincoln Center, and were happy to offer themselves. I saw them running breathless in the door. Each year, Mike and La Follia outdid the year before.

I sat in the audience and listened to the magnificent voices and music, which were like a drug that took me to a god-world for a brief moment, and left me back with nothing. It was very different from the suffering of every day in a horrible school in New York. In the 1940s and 1950s, I was lost in emptiness, imprisoned in ignorance, without a clue; and the music and voices were a glimpse of the possibility of liberation, as were alcohol, pop music, and poetry.

Backstage at the concerts, the great singers were infinitely deferential and respectful of Michael Sisca, and loved him. La Follia meant something to them. Mr. Sisca was very kind and I liked him. He remembered my grandparents and treated me as a young prince. I went almost every year, a ten-year-old, twelve, a twenty-year-old at Columbia College. I was devoted to them in a Proustian context.

One year, we went into a dressing room full of cigarette smoke and sweet, pathetic, old Italian men. My father introduced me. An old man called Il Maestro, with long, white, stale yellow hair and a shabby black suit, said, "We expect great things from you!"

I got a sinking feeling. Oh, no! But they'll all be dead, and never know, so let them have it. "Thank you," I said graciously. I was fourteen, and impeccably dressed.

On December 25, 1964, everyone arrived about one-thirty or two in a flurry of mink coats, blue overcoats, and fedoras. In the 1950s and 1960s, the men drank dry gin martinis, and from the 1970s on, they drank Scotch. The women always drank Manhattans. I drank vodka and soda, lots of red wine, and cognac. Large quantities of alcohol were consumed. They were conservative people, and liked drinking, and had a good time.

Old friends, my parents had known them from before I was born. The ten or twelve people usually were the same ones for Christmas, Easter, and Thanksgiving, and they always came to our house. Judge Paul P. Rao and his lifelong girlfriend, and after forty years, his wife, Catherine. He was chief judge of the U.S. Customs Court and had been the first Italian in a cabinet post, appointed by President Truman as deputy attorney general. Catherine, or Doll, was very beautiful and very glamorous. She put enormous amounts of hot red pepper on her pasta and she drank a lot. She and I got drunk together and laughed endlessly. She was a joy. She was over the top, so she was transcendent.

There was Judge John Cannella, of the U.S. First District Court and his wife, Ida. He had been an all-American football player at Fordham University, and was one of the famous heroes called the Four Pillars of Granite, and he played for the New York Giants; then he went to law school and became a brilliant and compassionate judge. I had a special close, personal bond with him for more than fifty years.

There were Evelyn and Geraldine De Julian, two lesbian sisters. One was a guidance counselor in a New York City public school, smart and compassionate, and the other worked for a bank. Mae Windecker, who had divorced the heir to Diamond Alkalai, a midwestern chemical fortune, and her daughter, Judy, and son, John, who was two years younger than me, and her husband, Reggie Petassi.

Over the years, other friends came. They all were my family for more than fifty years; I grew up with them. They were my aunts and uncles. My blood relatives, I saw mostly at funerals, and I refused to go to weddings. My parents' friends were well intentioned and funny and I loved them.

Having drinks, I was sitting with Judge Rao, who loved me as a son. Ever since I was a teenager, whenever I wanted a favor, I asked him. He was very powerful in New York Democrat politics and got anything done instantly. It was wonderful being on the receiving side of privilege.

"If I may give some words of advice," said Judge Rao, who had adopted the dignified bearing of Roosevelt and Harriman and the New York patricians, but without marbles in his mouth. "Never slam the door."

It was brilliant. "Ahhh! Like don't burn your bridges." We laughed and laughed. "It's an oxymoron!" I often thought of Judge Rao's words, in the years that came, when my anger ended something. When you slammed a door, you were not welcome back.

"Paul, darling," said my mother, drinking a Manhattan. "Come to dinner!"

The Italian-American Christmas dinner ritual was overabundance. Many courses and side dishes, lasagna, lamb and ham, etc. There was a table of Christmas sweets: cakes and candies, chocolate flourless cake (my favorite), fruitcakes, etc., candy canes and red ribbon, and Christmas candles. A grand offering to the gods, with roots going back five thousand years to prehistory, the celebrations that happened on the days after the Winter solstice. These friends of my parents were deities in a samsara god world, and celebrated the seasons in their worldly spiritual way.

"I saw a photo of Johnny sleeping in a magazine," said Evelyn. We were seated at the dining room table. I was the star of Andy Warhol's first movie, *Sleep.* It had been released in September 1964, and the publicity was just hitting in December. "The *Ladies' Home Journal!* It was the funniest thing!"

"And I'm in *Harper's Bazaar* next month," I said. Everyone laughed. I refused to think about what they thought of Andy's movie of me sleeping for eight hours. The fact that I was famous was enough. I was gay. My parents and their friends were all worldly smart and knew gay people. Even though I looked straight, more or less, they must have known. We never talked about that. And it was okay with me.

My own personal sufferings: a poet, gay, incarcerated in this world, and lonely all the time. No matter how much love anyone gave me, it was not quite enough or what I wanted, love from my mother and father and friends, fans of the poet, and the prodigious amount of fabulous promiscuous sex. I was missing something, missing an understanding of the empty nature of awareness and phenomena.

I also knew that I lived a somewhat fortunate life, with a little money and privilege; so I refrained from making negative judgments. As I was benefiting, I was a little tolerant, and respectful in their world. I didn't feel compromised. In my poems and in my world, I did as I damned pleased in your face, hell yes.

I had to endlessly endure the Christmas, Easter, and Thanksgiving dinners. Even though I loved my family, their mindless drivel didn't interest me and got on my nerves. And their bourgeois attachment to worldly nonsense, sometimes gross and crude. The fact that I was required to do what was expected of me was depressing. I kept drinking wine until it ended.

The Christmas, Thanksgiving, and Easter dinners at 16 Old Brick Road went on for almost fifty years. I saw them all grow old and die, one by one. My father died in 1986 at age eighty-five, and over the next fifteen years everyone else did, until there was nobody left, only me and my eighty-nine-year-old mother alone, eating whatever burned food she managed to cook in the filthy house. I visited her, and if everything was okay, there was no problem. I was in complete denial of her increasing old-age dementia. In 1999, after several small strokes, I had to put her in a nursing home. That was expensive, and she was well taken care of as she became more feeble.

During the next three years, I moved my archive from the attic to a storage facility and sorted through the enormous number of things before I sold the house. This was almost the best time. They were all dead and gone, with their grasping ignorance that had rattled in my head. I had seen it through to the end and was happy it was over. I did not miss them. What a relief! I did Tibetan Nyingma Buddhist meditation practice sitting on the couch in the living room. The house was empty and peaceful, and totally wonderful. I wrote this. Everything came to a slow close.

She was filled with a savage, exultant joy, a knowledge

that only her death could loosen this child from her.

MOM

⌇⌇⌇

MARIO PUZO

The Fortunate Pilgrim

IN THE HEAVY SUMMER DARKNESS SIGHING with the breath of
sleeping children, Lucia Santa pondered over her life. Marrying a second
husband, she had brought sorrow to her first child. She knew Octavia held
her guilty of not showing proper grief. But you could not explain to a young
virginal daughter that her father, the husband whose bed you shared, whom
you were prepared to live with the rest of your life, was a man you did not
really like.

He had been the master, but a chief without foresight, criminal in his
lack of ambition for his family, content to live the rest of his life in the slum
tenements a few short blocks from the docks where he worked. Oh, he had
made her shed many tears. The money for food he had always given, but the
rest of his pay, savings-to-be, he spent on wine and gambling with his
friends. Never a penny for herself. He had committed such an act of gen-
erosity in bringing Lucia Santa to the new country and his bed, beggar that
she was without linen, that he had no need to be generous again. One deed
served a lifetime.

Lucia Santa remembered all this with a vague resentment, knowing it was
not all truth. His daughter had loved him. He had been a handsome man.
His beautiful white teeth chewed sunflower seeds and the little Octavia
would accept them from his mouth as she never did from her mother. He
had loved his daughter.

The truth was simple. He had been a kind, hardworking, ignorant, plea-
sure-loving man. Her feeling had been the feeling of millions of women
toward improvident husbands. That men should control the money in the

house, have the power to make decisions that decided the fate of infants—what folly! Men were not competent. More—they were not serious. And she had already begun the struggle to usurp his power, as all women do, when one terrible day he was killed.

But she had wept. Oh, how she had wept. A grief compounded with terror. Not grief for departed lips, eyes, hands, but a wail for her shield against this foreign world, a cry for the bringer of her children's bread, the protector of the infant in her womb. These widows tear their hair and gash their cheeks, scream insane laments, do violence, and wear mourning for the world to see. These are the real mourners, for true grief is thick with terror. They are *bereaved*. Lovers will love again.

His death was comically grotesque. While a ship was being unloaded, the gangplank had given way high above the water, plunging five men and untold tons of bananas down into the river mud. Human limbs and banana stalks buried together. Never rising once.

She dared herself to think it: he had given them more dead than alive. In the darkness, now, years later, in mockery of her younger self, she smiled grimly. At what her younger self would think of such thoughts. But the court had awarded each of the children a thousand dollars—even Vincent not yet born but only too visible to the world. The money in trust, because here in America there was wisdom; not even parents were given charge of their children's monies. She herself had received three thousand dollars that no one on the Avenue knew about except Zia Louche and Octavia. So it was not all in vain.

Not to be spoken of, not to be thought of even now, were those months with the child in her belly. A child whose father had died before he was born, like the child of a demon. Even now she was struck with a terrible superstitious fear; even now, thirteen years later, tears sprang beneath her eyelids. She wept for herself as she was then, and for the unborn child, but not for the death of her husband. Her daughter Octavia could never know or understand.

And then the most shameful: only a year after her husband's death, only six months after the birth of that dead husband's son, she—a grown woman—had for the first time in her life become passionate about a man, the man who was to become her second husband. In love. Not the spiritual love of young girls or priests; not the emotion for heroes in romances that could be told to a young girl. No; love was the word for the hot flesh, the burning loins, feverish eyes and cheeks. Love was the feel of turgid, spongy flesh. Ah, what madness, what foolishness for the mother of children. Thank Jesus Christ in heaven she was beyond that now.

And for what? Frank Corbo was thirty-five, never married; slender, wiry, and with blue eyes; considered odd for being unwedded at that age, odd also in his reticence, his silent nature and lonely pride—that pride so ludicrous in those who are helpless before society and fate. The neighbors, searching for a widow's mate and feeder of four hungry mouths, thought him capable of any foolishness and a fine candidate. He worked steadily on the early morning shifts of the railroad gangs, and his afternoons were free for courting. There would be no scandal.

So the neighbors, out of kindness and self-preservation, brought them together, with conscience clear that both would make a good bargain.

The courtship was surprisingly young and innocent. Frank Corbo knew only the quick, cold whore's flesh; he would come to a marriage bed fresh with love, with a boy's eagerness. He pursued the mother of the three children as he would a young girl, making himself even more ridiculous in the eyes of the world. In the late afternoons he visited her as she sat before the tenement, guarding her playing and sleeping children. Sometimes he would take supper with them and leave before the children were put to bed. Finally one day he asked Lucia Santa to marry him.

She gave him an arch look, treating him like a young boy. She said, "Aren't you ashamed to ask me, with a baby still in the carriage from my first husband?" And for the first time she saw that dark look of hate. He stammered out that he loved her children as he loved her. That even if she did not marry him he would give her money for the children. In fact, he made good money on the railroad and always brought the children ices and toys. He had sometimes even given her money to buy the children clothing. At first she had tried to refuse, but he had become angry and said, "What is it, you don't wish to be friends with me? You think I'm like other men? I don't care for money—" and started to tear up the dirty green bills. For some reason this had brought tears to her eyes. She had taken the money from him, and he had never presumed on his gifts. It was she who became impatient.

ONE SUNDAY IN SPRING, INVITED, Frank Corbo came to the midday meal, the feast of the week for Italian families. He brought with him a gallon of biting homemade Italian wine and a box of cream pastries, *gnole* and *soffiati*. He wore a shirt, a tie, a many-buttoned suit. He sat at table with children about him: shy, awkward, more timid than they.

The spaghetti was coated with Lucia Santa's finest tomato sauce, the meatballs were beautifully round and peppered with garlic and fresh parsley. There was the dark green lettuce with olive oil and red wine vinegar, and then walnuts to eat with the wine. Everything had a bite to it of herbs and

garlic and strong black pepper. They all stuffed themselves. Finally the chil-
dren went down to the street to play. Lucia Santa should have kept them
with her in the house to avoid scandal, but she did not.

And so in the golden afternoon with sunlight streaming through the long
railroad flat, with the poor infant Vincenzo's eyes shielded from sin by a con-
veniently placed pillow, they sealed their fate on the living room couch, the
mother only slightly distracted by her children's voices rising sweetly from
the street below.

Ah, delight, delight, the taste of love. After so long an abstinence the ani-
mal odor was an aphrodisiac, a bell to ring in the coming joy; even now, so
many years later, the memory was fresh. And in that act of love she had been
the master.

The man so harsh, so strong against the world, had wept on her breast, and
in the fast-fading sunlight she understood that in all his thirty-five years of life
he had never received a caress with real tenderness. It was too much for him.
He had changed afterward. He had come too late to love, and he despised his
weakness. But for that one afternoon she forgave him many things, not every-
thing; and cared for him as she had never cared for her first husband.

There was very little trouble until his first child was born. His natural love
for Gino became cancerous, murdering his love for wife and stepchildren,
and he became evil.

But in the first year of marriage, in the trust of love, he told her of his
childhood in Italy as the son of a poor tenant farmer. He had often been
hungry, often cold, but what he could never forget was that his parents made
him wear cast-off shoes which were too small. His feet became horribly
deformed, as if every bone had been broken and then bound together in one
grotesque lump. He showed her his feet as if to say, "I keep nothing from
you; you needn't marry a man with such feet." She had laughed. But she did
not laugh when she learned that he always bought twenty-dollar shoes,
beautiful brown-grained leather. The act of a true madman.

His parents were a rarity in Italy, drunken peasants. They relied on him to
work the farm and give them their bread. When he fell in love with a young
girl of the village, the marriage was forbidden. He ran away and lived in the
woods for a week. When they found him, he was little more than an animal.
He was in shock and was committed to a mental institution. After a few
months he was released, but he refused to return to his home. He immi-
grated to America, where in the densest city in the world he lived a life of
the most extreme loneliness.

He took care of himself; he never became ill again. In his life of solitude and hard work he found safety. As long as he did not become emotionally entangled with other human beings, he was safe, as something immobile is to some degree safe from the dangers of motion. But this love which brought him back to life brought him back to danger, and perhaps it was this knowledge, animal-like, felt rather than known, that had made him so weak that Sunday afternoon.

Now, after twelve years of life together, the husband was as secretive with her as he had always been with other people.

OCTAVIA STRETCHED OUT ON HER narrow bed. She wore her rayon slip as a nightdress. The room was too small for any additional furniture except a tiny table and a chair, but it had a door she could close.

She was too hot and too young to sleep. She dreamed. She dreamed of her real father.

Oh, how she had loved him, and how angry she had been that he let himself be killed, left her alone with no one to love. At the end of each day she had met him in front of the tenement and kissed his dirty bearded face, its black stubble so hard it bruised her lips. She carried his empty lunch pail up the stairs and sometimes cajoled from him the wicked steel clawed baling hook of the longshoreman.

And then in the house she set his plate for dinner, jealously placing the fork with the straight tines, the sharpest knife, his small wineglass polished and flashing like a diamond. Fussing until the exasperated Lucia Santa smacked her away from the table so that food could be served. And Larry, sitting in his high chair, could never interfere.

Even now, so many years later, waiting for sleep, the thought like a cry, "Why weren't you more careful?" Reproaching him for his sinful death, echoing her mother, who sometimes said, "He didn't take care of his family. He didn't take care of his money. He didn't take care of his life. He was careless in everything."

Her father's death had brought the thin blue-eyed stranger with his slanting, uneven face. The second husband, the stepfather. Even as a child she had never liked him, accepted his gifts distrustfully, stood with Larry in hand, holding him, hiding behind the mother's back, until he patiently found her. Once he had made a gesture of affection and she shrank away from his hand like an animal. Larry was the favorite until his own children came. He never liked Vincent for some reason, the lousy bastard—hateful, hateful.

But even now she could not blame her mother for marrying, could not hate her mother for bringing so much sorrow. She knew why her mother married this evil man. She knew.

IT WAS ONE OF THE most terrible times of Lucia Santa's life, and much of the distress that followed her husband's death was the fault of friends, relatives, and neighbors.

They had, every one, kept after Lucia Santa to let the newborn infant, Vincent, be taken care of by a rich cousin, Filomena, in New Jersey. Just for a little while, until the mother regained her strength. "What a boon to that childless couple. And she can be trusted, Filomena, your own first cousin from Italy. The child would be safe. And the rich Filomena's husband would then certainly consent to be godfather and assure the child's future." And how they had spoken in tones of most sorrowful pity, so tenderly, "And you, Lucia Santa, everyone worries about you. How meager you are. Not yet recovered from the birth. Still grieving over your beloved husband and torn to rags by lawyers over the settlement. You need a rest from care. Treat yourself well for your children's sake. What if you should die?" Oh, no threat was too much for them. "Your children would perish or go into a home. They could not be sent to the grandparents in Italy. Guard your life, your children's only shield." And they went on and on. And the child would be back in a few months, no, a month, perhaps a few weeks. Who could tell? And Filomena would come Sundays, her husband drove a *Forda*. They would bring her to their beautiful home in Jersey to visit the baby Vincenzo. She would be an honored guest. Her other children would have a day in the country, in the fresh air. *La la la la.*

Now. How could she deny them or herself or her children? Even Zia Louche nodded her warty head in agreement.

Only little Octavia began to weep, saying over and over again with childish despair, "They won't give him back." Everyone laughed at her fear. Her mother smiled and patted Octavia's short black curls, ashamed now of her own reluctance.

"Only until I am well," she told the little girl. "Then Vincenzo will come home."

Later the mother was not able to understand how she had come to let the child go. True, the shock of her husband's death and a midwife's harshness at Vincenzo's birth had left her weak. But this never excused her in her own mind. It was an act that gave her so much shame, made her despise herself so much that whenever she had a difficult decision to make, she recalled that one act, to make sure she would not be cowardly again.

And so little Vincent had gone away. The strange Aunt Filomena had come one noon when Octavia was in school, and when Octavia came home the crib was empty.

She had wept and screamed, and Lucia Santa had given *one* the left hand, *two* the right hand, fine, heavy slaps across the face, making her little daughter's ears ring, saying, "Now, there is something to make you cry." Her mother was glad to get rid of the baby. Octavia hated her. She was evil, like a stepmother.

But then came that terrible beautiful day that had made her love and trust her mother. Part of it she saw herself as a little girl, but the story had been told innumerable times, so that now it seemed to Octavia as if she had seen everything. For naturally it was told; it became a legend of the family, mentioned in an evening of gossip, spread out at the Christmas table over walnuts and wine.

The trouble started after only a week. Filomena did not come that first Sunday, there was no automobile to take Lucia Santa to visit her infant son. Only a telephone message to the candy store. Filomena would come the following week, and to show her good heart and regret there would be a money order for five dollars in the mail, a small peace offering.

Lucia Santa brooded that dark Sunday. She went to take counsel with her neighbors on the floors below. They reassured her, urged her not to think foolish things. But as the day wore on she became more and more somber.

Early Monday morning she said to Octavia, "Run. Go to Thirty-first Street and get Zia Louche." Octavia wailed, "I'll be late for school." Her mother replied, "Today you are not going to your beautiful school"—saying it with such menace that the girl flew from the house.

Zia Louche came, a shawl around her head, a blue wool-knitted jacket reaching to her knees. Lucia Santa served the ceremonial coffee, then said, "Zia Louche, I am going to see the little one. Care for the girl and Lorenzo. Do me this favor." She paused. "Filomena did not come yesterday. Do you think I should go?"

In later years Lucia Santa always insisted that if Zia Louche had reassured her she would not have gone that day, and that for the honest answer she would always remain in the old woman's debt. For Zia Louche, nodding her old crone's head like a repentant witch, said, "I gave you bad advice, Signora. People are saying things I don't like." Lucia Santa begged her to speak out, but Zia Louche would not, because it was all gossip, nothing to be repeated to an anxious mother. One thing could be noted, though: the promise to send five dollars. The poor did well not to trust such charity. Best to go, set everyone's mind at rest.

In the gay light of winter, the mother walked to the Weehawken Ferry at Forty-second Street, and for the first time since coming from Italy, she rode water again. In Jersey, finding a streetcar, she showed a slip of paper with the address on it, and then walked many blocks until a friendly woman took her by the hand and guided her to the dwelling of Filomena.

Ah, what a pretty house it was for the devil to live in. It had a pointed roof, like nothing she had ever seen in Italy, as if it were a plaything, not to be used for people full grown. It was white and clean, with blue shutters and a closed-in porch. Lucia Santa was suddenly timid. People so well off would never practice treachery on a poor woman like herself. The breaking of the Sunday promise could be explained in many ways. Still, she knocked on the side of the porch. She went through the screen door and knocked on the door of the house. She knocked again and again.

The stillness was frightening; as if the house were deserted. Lucia Santa went weak with fear. Then, inside the house, her baby began to wail, and she was ashamed of her terrible, ridiculous suspicion. Patience. The baby's wailing turned to shrieks of terror. Her mind went blank. She pushed against the door and went into the hallway and up the stairs, tracing those shrieks to a bedroom.

How pretty the room was; the prettiest room Vincenzo would ever have. It was all in blue, with blue curtains, a blue crib, a white stuffed toy horse standing on a little blue bureau. And in that beautiful room her son lay in his own piss. No one to change him, no one to quiet his shrieks of terror.

Lucia Santa took him in her arms. When she felt the lump of flesh warm and soaked in its own urine, when she saw the wrinkled rose face and the jet-black infant hair, she was filled with a savage, exultant joy, a knowledge that only her death could loosen this child from her. She stared around the pretty room with the dumb anger of an animal, noting all its assurances of permanency. Then she opened a bureau drawer and found some clothing to dress the baby. As she did so, Filomena came bursting into the room.

Then, then what a drama was played. Lucia Santa accused the other of heartlessness. To leave an infant alone! Filomena protested. She had only gone to help her husband open the grocery store. She had been gone fifteen minutes—no, ten. What a terrible, unlucky chance. But had not Lucia Santa herself sometimes left her infant alone? Poor people could not be as careful as they wished (how Lucia Santa sneered when Filomena included herself among the poor); their babies must be left to cry.

The mother was blind to reason, blind with an agonizing, hopeless rage, and could not say what she felt. When her child was left crying at home, it was flesh and blood of its own that came to the rescue. But what could a baby think if left alone and only a strange face appeared? But Lucia Santa said simply, "No, it's easy to see that since this is not your own blood you don't care to put yourself out. Go help in the store. I will bring my baby home."

Filomena lost her temper. Shrew that she was, she shouted, "What of our bargain, then? How would I appear to my friends, that I can't be trusted with your child? And what of all this I have bought, money thrown into air?" Then, slyly, "And we both know, more was meant than said."

"What? What?" Lucia Santa demanded. Then it all came out.

There had been a cruel plot to do a kindness. The neighbors had all assured Filomena that, given time, the helpless widow, forced to work for her children's bread, would gradually relinquish all claims to her infant son and let Filomena adopt the baby. They were deviously cautious, but made it understood that Lucia Santa even hoped for such good fortune. Nothing could be said outright, of course. There were delicate feelings to consider. Lucia Santa cut all this short with wild laughter.

Filomena played another tune. Look at the new clothes, this pretty room. He would be the only child. He would have everything, a happy childhood, the university, become a lawyer, a doctor, even a professor. Things that Lucia Santa could never hope to give. What was she? She had no money. She would eat dirt with her bread her whole life long.

Lucia Santa listened, stunned, horrified. When Filomena said, "Come, you understood why I would send you money every week," the mother drew back her head like a snake and spat with full force into the older woman's face. Then, child in her arms, she fled from the house. Filomena ran after her, screaming curses.

That was the end of the story as it was told—with laughter, now. But Octavia always remembered more clearly the part never told: her mother's arriving home with the baby Vincent in her arms.

She entered the house feverish with cold, her coat wrapped around the sleeping infant, her sallow skin black with the blood of anger, rage, despair. She was trembling. Zia Louche said, "Come. Coffee waits. Sit down. Octavia, the cups."

Baby Vincent began to cry. Lucia Santa tried to soothe him, but his shrieks grew greater and greater. The mother, furious with guilt, made a dramatic gesture, as if to hurl the infant away; then she said to Zia Louche, "Here, take him." The old crone began to coo to the baby in a cracked voice.

The mother sat at the round kitchen table. She rested her head on her hand, hiding her face. When Octavia came with the cups she said, still shielding her face, "See. A little girl knows the truth and we laugh." She caressed her daughter, her fingers full of hatred, hurting the tender flesh. "Listen to the children in the future. We old people are animals. Animals."

"Ah," Zia Louche crooned, "coffee. Hot coffee. Calm yourself." The baby continued to wail.

The mother sat still. Octavia saw that a terrible rage at the world, at fate, made her unable to speak. Lucia Santa, her sallow skin darkening, held back her tears by pressing her fingers in her eyes.

Zia Louche, too frightened to speak to the mother, scolded the infant. "Come, weep," she said. "Ah, how good it feels. How easy it is, eh? You have the right. Ah, how fine. Louder. Louder." But then the child became still, laughing at that toothless, wrinkled face mirrored from the other side of time.

The old crone shouted in mock anger, "Finished so soon? Come. Weep." She shook the baby gently, but Vincent laughed, his toothless gums a mockery of hers.

Then the old woman said slowly, in a sad, singsong voice, "*Miserabile, miserabile*. Your father died before you were born."

At these words the mother's control broke. She pressed her nails tightly into the flesh of her face, and the great streaming tears mingled with the blood of the two long gashes she made in her cheeks. The old crone chirped, "Come, Lucia, some coffee now." There was no answer. After a long time the mother lifted her dark face. She raised her black-clad arm to the stained ceiling and said in a deadly earnest voice filled with venom and hate, "I curse God."

Caught in that moment of satanic pride, Octavia loved her mother. But even now, so many years later, she remembered with shame the scene that followed. Lucia Santa had lost all dignity. She cursed. Zia Louche said, "Shh—shh—think of the little girl who listens." But the mother rushed out of the apartment and down the four flights of stairs, screaming obscenities at the kind neighbors, who immediately locked the doors she pounded on.

She screamed in Italian, "Fiends. Whores. Murderers of children." She ran up and down the stairs, and out of her mouth came a filth she had never known she knew, that the invisible listeners would eat the tripe of their parents, that they committed the foulest acts of animals. She raved. Zia Louche gave baby Vincent into Octavia's arms and went down the stairs. She grabbed Lucia Santa by her long black hair and dragged her back to her home. And though the younger woman was much stronger, she let herself descend into howls of pain, collapsing helplessly by the table.

Soon enough she took coffee; soon enough she calmed and composed herself. There was too much work to do. She caressed Octavia, murmuring, "But how did you know, a child to understand such evil?"

Yet when Octavia had told her not to marry again, saying, "Remember I was right about Filomena stealing Vinnie," her mother only laughed. Then she stopped laughing and said, "Don't fear. I'm your mother. No one can harm my children. Not while I live."

Her mother held the scales of power and justice; the family could never be corrupted. Safe, invulnerable, Octavia fell asleep, the last image flickering: her mother, baby Vincent in her arms returning from Filomena's, raging, triumphant, yet showing guilty shame for ever having let him go.

JOHN CIARDI

The Shaft

At first light in the shadow, over the roach
like topaz on the sill, over the roofs,
the Old North Church spire took its time to heaven
where God took His to answer.
                 I took my drink
at clammy soapstone round a drain of stinks
and slid back into bed, my toes still curled
from the cold lick of linoleum. Ma was first,
shaking the dead stove up. Then Pa,
a rumble hocking phlegm. When the cups clattered
I could get up and climb him and beg *biscotti*
while Ma sipped cups of steam and scolded love.

The shaft went down four darks from light to light,
through smells that scurried, from the sky-lit top
where I built cities of kindling, to cobbly streets
that curved away as men go, round their corners,
to what they do after they kiss their sons.
Where *did* he go? He kissed me and went down,
a step at a time, his derby like a bob.
And then pulled under. And the day begun.

Later, when days were something that had names,
I went there with her, out of my sky-lit first
on the top landing, to the falling streets.

The stores were cellars and they smelled of cheese,
salami, and olive brine. Dark rows of crates,
stacked back to damp brick where the scurries were,

made tunnels in whose sides the one-eyed beans
were binned so deep I could lose all my arm
into their sliding buttons. In a while
I got my cookie and knew I had behaved.
Then up the shaft again, through its four darks
to the top landing where we lived in light.
A latched-on fence playpenned a world I made
of slant and falling towns. Until his derby
rose from the shaft and all the kitchen steamed.

God's cellar was one more dark. A tallow deep
where nickels clinked at racks of burning flowers.
Black shawls kneeled there whispering to the dead,
and left the prayer still burning when they rose.
He had such gold saints by Him in His dark:
why was God so dusty? Was He making
the dead from dust again because she prayed
and made me pray? Would all the dead be made
back to the shawls draped on those altar rails,
and come home singing up their shafts of dark?

I kissed the stone he changed to in his flowers.
But when he stayed away she would not waste
the prayers she lit but got him back in me.
His letters came. From God and Metropolitan.
A piecemeal every week. And he had bought us
half a house in Medford—out of the shaft
and into green that had a river through it.

And still he would not come back, the garden summer
nothing to him, the fruit with nothing to say.
My aunt and uncle bought the other half.

God had a house there, too, but would not speak
His first Italian to her. She came home
and spoke the rest to Pa, hissing all night
how much she was afraid. Or a dream rattled
and speared her to a scream, and the girls woke crying,
and ran to fetch her water, while I lay

guilty of happiness, half deep in books,
learning to guess how much hysteria
could be a style of acting, and how much
have its own twisted face, and how much more
could be the actress acting what she was,
panting and faint but gripping the glass of water
they always ran to fetch and watch her drink
till she sank back exhausted by medication
and let herself be fussed to sleep again,
satisfied as long as she was feared for.

So all was well. And if a glass of water
and the girls' fears were medicine enough,
why the girls would wake, the pipes would not run dry.

I lost her, and I lost them, shutting out
more night-rattling and more day-squalls
than I had sky for, there behind my books.
I made a cave of them and crept inside
and let the weather blow away unheard.

They had to run those weathers of the dark
forked day and night by lightnings of her nerves.
Not they, nor I, guessed half those howling years
the lightnings were her staff and they her sheep
to frighten close, all madness being fear.

And still they grew away because they grew.
And she came stalking after like a witch
when they strolled after supper. They found her out,
flitting from tree to tree with the black cat
of sniffed suspicion sliding at her feet,
a shadow in a shadow, and they led her
foot-blistering hikes through nowhere and back home,
slowing to let the shadow flit away
around the corner, slide into the house,
be dumped in a back closet, and not be there
to mar her innocence when she looked up
from sorting sorted socks at the kitchen table,

or sweeping the swept floor, and breathing hard,
but half believing their straight-faced innocence
as they clacked by to shut a bedroom door
on gales of whispering with giggly showers.

I read my book and guessed and didn't care.
An oaf in a madhouse. Keeping my escape
but staying on for meals. She learned at last
suspicion makes sore feet. But she wasn't finished.
Not while she still could faint and not come to
till everyone was crying in a circle
of guilt and glasses of water and grand opera.
I didn't know she was crazy. That we all were.

Nor that I dropped my book and lost my place.
I knew she had fainted and we were to blame.

Then, one night when the girls had invitations
her black cat hissed at, she stood in the doorway
ranting to turn them back, and when they argued,
she turned her eyes up, started breathing hard
and settled to the floor across the sill.
She had her act so polished by that time
she could sink like a dropped sheet, all one motion
and down without a thud. It was well done—

It took me in and sent me running for water—
but by whatever tells truth to the badgered,
it was too well done. When I came running back,
the girls had clucked her gently to one side,
pillowed her head, smoothed on a comforter,
and bent to kiss her cheek, cooing, "Poor Ma.
A nap will do her good." And off they clattered,
squeezing their giggles tight. Then even I—
the oaf of the litter—got it. I found the glass
still in my hand, started to put it down,
then drank it off. And, having watched that much,
sat down to watch the rest.
                    Were her eyes closed?

The girls' heels clicked across the porch and off it.
The last click jerked her upright in a rage,
but to one side, in case the girls looked back.
She hadn't seen me and I guessed she meant
to be found lying there when the girls came home.
God, what a weapon! I could *hear* her glower,
her lips grimacing vows to kill a saint.
"Have a good nap?" I said.

                       She snapped around,
head and body together in one shriek.
My skin crawled on a rasp of shame too late.
Then she was on me like her blackest cat,
its claws turned into fists. She beat so hard
it hurt me not to hurt. She'd hurt herself
unless I stopped her. Well, I'm an actor, too,
from a family of actors, I told myself,
and tried to clown it away. "Hey, Ma, lay off.
You'll hurt your wrist again. Come on, let's dance!"
The thing was to catch her mood and turn it around.
I picked her up—she weighed about ten pounds—
waltzed her across the room, her fists still going,
then settled her soft as dandelion fuzz on cushions.
"Just like your father, pig!" she tried to scold,
but her glower was out.

                   "So what? So it didn't work.
So now you can stop fainting. So what's lost?—
your stage career? It was a lousy act."

I'd kept my head just far enough above books
to guess my best chance was to play her husband.
"Just like your father," she scowled, but her grimace
quivered halfway to a smile. I thought I'd won.
But it slipped past a smile, turned into a giggle,
and out through a mad laughter to a scream
that had no actress in it but the fear
I was no husband to, and could not be.

—And gasped at last, since comedy is all,
to hiccups that went on until she lay

where comedy is nothing, strewn like lint
blown down into the bottom of a well
I could remember like the smell of tallow
inside a dark where racks of burning flowers
swallowed black shawls to altar rails of bone
down every turn and landing of the shaft.

If God still spoke her language there, I hope
she heard enough to promise her the light
I didn't know how to light her when I tried.

She did ease into age with half a smile
mending inside her. But her eighties raveled.
Her wits went back to muttering, and she sat
hugging a raggedy doll that would not light back
husband or son. And never saw us again
although we came and stood there in the shaft
bringing her pastries that oozed down her chin,
candies we had to wash out of her fist,
and jokes she did not hear the nurses laugh at.
She hugged her final dark to a rag God
who spoke in broken weathers to no wits.
And then we turned my father's grave and laid her
to take her time to Heaven in her last faint.

And there's a life, God knows, no soul would choose.
And if I send love after it, what's that
but one more scurry sounding down the shaft?

FRANK LENTRICCHIA

Johnny Critelli

Ⲥⲟⲥⲛ

I SIT HERE IN THIS SPARE ROOM, in Clearwater, Florida, and I have questions on my mind. Who told my son to put our real names in a book? What am I supposed to do? Sue my own son? First he wrote nine books nobody could understand in the family, not even my nephew Tommy, who went to college. You want to know what I did with those nine books? I lined them up on top of the television. I took the pictures of his children off. I took the picture off of the first one he married whose father was a Jew. I took the second wife off who was a Lebanese. I took off my fiftieth wedding anniversary. The first two wives call me for the holidays, but my husband won't talk to them. After I talk to them he won't talk to me. Then I won't talk to him. This goes on for a couple of days. And now when we're practically in our eighties and my husband has diabetes on top of everything else he suddenly has to write a real book that normal people might read. You know what he should do with this *Edge of Night?* Do I have to spell it out? Sideways! And if it doesn't fit up there, I'll borrow my husband's ball peen hammer. What's wrong with an Italian girl that he never likes one? And now this new one he's with now, she claims she's Catholic. I think she's supposed to be Irish. I'm going to take a picture of this tall Irish girl. I'm going to tell her I can't put it on top of the television because there's no more room. I'll tell her even though he's my son I'm warning you, wise up fast before he puts you in a book too. He'll murder you just like everybody else. I don't talk the way he makes me talk. Does anybody? There's no room for anybody on top of the television except himself and one nice little knickknack. Maybe he'll die first, God forbid, because if he doesn't he's going to throw our dead bodies in the city dump, then put all his television books inside the coffins instead of us. He'll ship the coffins up to Utica. He'll make them write on the stone, Buried here are my wonderful parents, my wonderful children, my wonderful wives, and if you don't believe it just dig up the coffins and look inside and you'll see my whole family who I love so much, including the wonderful Irish girlfriend, may they all be nice to one another. After he kills me in his book he expects me to love him for what he did. I'll tell you one thing. I saw his penis when he was a kid plenty of times. Naturally, I'm his mother. I was never that impressed. He'll never be the man his father was. If his father were younger he'd sweep this Irish one right off of her feet, in no time she'd go for him. I went for my husband, didn't I? Oh, my husband will defend Frank, because that's what men do, but they have no love for one another. How can they? Have you ever heard of Johnny Critelli? I heard of him once. He died a long time ago. But I never heard of his mother. He made her up. He told me on my birthday that I was based on Critelli's mother. I said to him, Who the hell is Critelli's mother? What do you mean based? He said back, She doesn't exist, Ma, that's why I based you on her. Can you understand that? Is he saying I don't exist? He claims in this *Edge of Night* that he's black! He claims that he's an Italian Negro. I thank God for one thing, that I don't have to be the Irish girlfriend. I exist. I don't tell people I'm black. The Lentricchia men and their friends play cards together, they go fishing together, they watch ball games together, day and night on television. Now they even watch that goddamn golf together. How quiet they are when they watch! They have to watch constantly because they're afraid of each other. They're pathetic and I think my son finally realizes it. I got my own television now in here so to hell with them, they don't faze me. I never met the mother of the Irish one, I don't even know her name and what is she doing already who barely knows my son? She's sending my son shirts. She'll send the shirts. Then one of these days after he gets four or five shirts in the mail from UPS he'll send her one of his books for the top of the television and she'll put it up there. Because what choice does she have? Did I, the real mother, have a choice? In your eighties, which I'm almost in, you want to look at nice memories on top of your television. You want to look at a little happiness. This skinny little book he just wrote, you don't want to see that thing. [She pauses.] I hope he loves me. The Irish girlfriend, she's going to have to tell him she likes this book. [She pauses.] I better wash this bathrobe more, if you wear a bathrobe as much as I do you better wash it once a week. At least I still go to the toilet by myself. Will somebody do a person like me a favor and tell me who is my son? I think at this age I have a right to know. You lose a name here and there, you lose your mind. His book reminds me that even the good things I remember hurt me now, and this is what I see when I watch television alone in this spare room.

NOT THAT LONG AFTER WE got married, this was in 1936, there was a woman in the summertime while he sat on the grass eating his lunch with his friends where he worked. She sat on the grass ten feet in front of him, without underwear on. She let her dress go over her knees. She raised her knees opening up looking into the sun in front of my husband who was eating with the sun on his back, looking into her. She wanted my husband and now she was doing this just in case he didn't know, because now he would know, now he'll get hard eating his lunch that I made, looking into her so wide open. I'll tell you what happened. He never got hard. She told someone, who told my husband's friend, who told my husband that he must have ice water in his veins. I have to say something. We don't look like we used to, we almost have no shapes anymore. In my opinion we look like ugly blobs. Maybe I should let them cremate me, but I don't want to burn even when I'm dead. Naturally he got hard. I admit it. We may not look it now but we had plenty. The things he did were wonderful. Ice water my ass! My husband's friend said she said that my husband stared at her vagina like he was a statue, except she didn't say vagina. When I heard she stated that he stared, then I knew everything. I know what staring means. You should have seen my husband's father, who my son is looking like more every day. Naturally he started to get hard, a healthy man in his twenties. He saw it and she was a beautiful woman. But when she opened up wide in the grass, he was thinking about something else, that's why he was staring, because I saw him staring a million times and I used to ask about it. Are you bored with me, honey? Do you want me to kiss your neck? He was in his mind playing tennis, for God sakes! In his mind tennis on his lunch hour, that's what staring used to mean in those days, and it still does. She was ignorant of tennis, that was her big problem. When we were young he worked from eight to six loading things too heavy for him on boxcars all day long without complaining. He was like a rail. He came home exhausted, but not too exhausted. At five-forty-five sharp the next morning every morning my husband's friend who was his boss picked him up so they could play. They had to play. My husband didn't learn to drive until he was in his late thirties. When did he have the time? Eight until six on the boxcars. Weekends helping out all day at Rachel's store. From six in the morning until almost eight he and his boss played tennis, plus late Sunday afternoons they had to do it too. They always had to do it. They even did it in the winter when there wasn't too much snow. I made his lunch the night before: six sandwiches, I'm telling you the truth, a piece of fruit, a thermos of coffee and two cookies, but who can put on weight or learn to drive doing what he did? A pound of macaroni just for him, he practically ate us into the poorhouse in the Depression. Oh he got hard, in the sunlight she glistened all over because she wanted my husband to put it in, he saw himself coming on a strange woman before it actually got in, his semen jumping out all over her belly and bush, then he finished jamming it hard all the way in as far as he could, jamming it. He wanted to split that wide-open bitch wide open! He saw this when he was playing tennis on the grass in his mind eating my lunch. But she was ignorant, that was her only problem. Before he came in his pants, the tennis came first. My husband thought he was that famous tennis player he bombasted me about during supper, who turned out to be a homosexual. I said to him when it all came out, Did you read the front page yet? He got arrested! He's a big queer! My husband said to me, What's that got to do with it? Are you jealous of Big Bill? Are you thinking something you're afraid to say? Now I'll tell *you* something! My boss and I are pretty evenly matched, but I beat him almost every time and he never takes it out on me on the job. That's what tennis is, he said. What do you know? I don't care if he sucks his own cock off, because what's that got to do with tennis? Then he threw a box of macaroni against the wall as hard as he could. Macaroni flying all over the kitchen! I was scared because my husband never uses bad words. When he looked between her legs the tennis in his mind definitely started to lose, then it started to win, then it won. And it was the best tennis he ever played, looking into that bag. Ice water? My husband was tempted, but he kept eating my sandwich and he kept playing, and then that's all he was doing, playing like the tall handsome queer. That beautiful bag wanted him, but she didn't understand Big Bill. He loved Big Bill. I think it helped that he was eating my sandwich, he likes what I make him eat. With me and Big Bill my husband has everything he needs. As far as my son goes, he can write this down, but he didn't tell this story. I didn't tell it either, as far as that goes, my husband told it. I just made the sandwiches. Tell me something. What does my son do? Because why should he get the credit?

I REMEMBER THE LIGHT ON top of the ambulance in the dark going around and around. This was in August of 1949. Then the people on our block must have all come rushing out of their houses the way they always did whenever an ambulance or a police car stopped on our block. They were standing in the driveway staring down at me. Eva the big mouth next door was the head one as usual, in her housecoat, which she was usually bare under that summer. I felt drowsy and the funny thing was, this is what I remember better than anything, I had no cares for my family. Isn't that something? They were wheeling me down the driveway in one of those stretchers with wheels on and I was on a cloud. I didn't know where my daughter was. My mother-in-law must have been taking care of her in the kitchen giving her cookies, and I have to admit that it didn't matter one way or the other where she was. My husband who was walking beside me wasn't looking at me, he was looking at the driveway in his T-shirt. I didn't want to say, Frank, look at me, I'm your wife. He had finally filled out nice, his muscles in his chest and arms were very beautiful. I don't have any idea to this day what he was going through because we never had a conversation concerning this, but I'm positive he wasn't playing tennis in his mind for a change, but who knows for sure. I heard my son's voice say somewhere in the dark what's wrong with my mother. My son was nine then, playing outside in the dark. He must have seen the light on top of the ambulance. I heard Eva say to him there was too much blood. That's all she said. There was too much blood. My husband kept looking at the driveway and walking and saying nothing. The crowd didn't talk and I couldn't see my son, who must have been in the crowd staring. I heard these things going down the driveway but I didn't belong to these things for a change. I was just going to sleep in August with all those blankets on me and that's all it was. They must have thought I was cold. I wasn't cold or hot. I wasn't anything for a change. Back then people were different with their kids. We didn't tell them I was pregnant. It was too embarrassing back then to talk like that. Besides, because of the risk we didn't want to disappoint them. I was told to stay in bed because Dr. Panzone said I might not keep it because of the spotting a little too much. That night I started to get terrible cramps and the spotting became a river. After I soaked the mattress they called an ambulance. I was just full of blood down there. Two children without trouble, now this. You know when I stopped wanting to have another one? The true answer is never. Through my fifties and sixties and even these days once in a blue moon I wish I had another one. They always say you should be grateful for what you have, but I keep thinking about the one who died inside me. I guess I became my baby's coffin, didn't I? My son was old enough to have been told about what happened, but he wasn't told until his late twenties. We didn't have the words to talk to a nine-year-old like that. My husband could have taken him with us in the ambulance, so what if I died right there? But then we would have been forced to say something to him in the ambulance. He would have seen them put that thing on my face. I don't think he needed to see that. Why didn't Eva at least lie? You don't tell a nine-year-old there's too much blood when in the dark his mother is going down a driveway into an ambulance out of the blue. I'm mad now, but I wasn't mad then. You should see my husband's face when I say I wouldn't mind having another one. I could use a cat or dog. This morning on *Donahue* I heard a woman professor say something that was very intelligent. She said what happened to me should be called a natural abortion. When she applied that word to me, I felt like slapping her face. I never had a picture of it in an album. I can't even have one in my mind. I've tried hard to make up a face in my mind. My son is so damn stubborn, I can't tell you, or I would ask him to do me a big favor. I would like to ask my son if he has to write about us and make half of it up why can't you make me one in your mind, Frank, make me one in your mind and then put it in words in a book where I can read it every day. Make a picture of a face close up. Make it six months old, who cares whether a girl or boy, and let it be healthy, and say I nursed it until it was ten. *[She pauses.]* I went to the toilet, and it fell out of me in pieces. *[She pauses.]* Write me a baby, Frank. Is that so hard to do if you're a writer?

FELIX STEFANILE

The Catch

YOUR COLLEGE LEARN YOU BE SMART, talk fancy. You go with the girls, talk fancy. You tell your mother, Ma, why you got the bun on your head, old fashion. Your college learn you don't respect your mother. Some college. Now you say this girl you live together, marriage never mind, old fashion. Your mother cry, and with the beads pray pray and pray. What you think, she ask me. You know what I think, boy? I think if you was pig we raise by and by we sell you for money now, not your mother cry.

STEVEN VARNI

Going Under

∽∾∾

MY MOTHER LAY IN A HOSPITAL on the opposite edge of town from where we lived. The same place she'd stayed a couple of times before, with vague never-explained ailments, when I'd been too young to visit hospitals. Now I was with my father and he drove on the road that ran alongside the big canal, filled with dirty water and crossed every now and then by concrete footbridges—where the watergates were. It was a brutally hot Sunday in mid-September and there were small clusters of Okies on almost every bridge we passed, wearing ragged cutoffs (and T-shirts, if they were girls), clowning around and jostling for their turns to slide with the rushing water down the gates' short falls. At St. Stephen's School we were lectured on canal safety every spring and fall, and my father always said that swimming in the canals was as filthy as washing your face in a mud puddle, so I knew it was something only Okies did. Kids from public schools and shabby families who weren't taught of the dangers: of the big branches, old rotting shrubs, and discarded ropes that would tangle your feet so you couldn't swim. Kids who were never warned of—or were too stupid to heed—the whirlpools that would swirl around you until you didn't have the strength left to resist them. Watery tornadoes, I'd always imagined, that would catch hold of you and spin you down to the canal's slimy floor.

The kids' faces were disfigured in shouts, but I could hear nothing. My father had the windows up against the heat. From the air conditioner came streams smelling sickly-metallic and dusty, carrying the scent of whatever had settled unseen inside the vents and the hoses that coiled beneath the dashboard. The sun had faded the top of the gray dashboard to a whitish color, with dirty-looking swipes where I'd once used a rag soaked with Windex to try to clean the layer of dust that always coated it. The armrest on the driver's side door was blackened from my father's forearm. There was a map of Arizona, a penlight, and a cracked collapsible travel cup in the glove box. A St. Stephen's Church bulletin, rigid, forgotten, curled beneath the passenger seat. These last things I knew from the few times my father left his car at home, when I crawled around inside it knowing he would be gone for the entire afternoon and I'd have time to pretend the long silver Buick was a submarine, so that anytime I left its confines I had to hold my breath or drown. (The whole Central Valley had once been a sea, a certain teacher always used to remind us: "Our crops flourish in its *ancient sedimentary bed*.") But on this afternoon the Buick seemed more like a submarine than ever before. It was cold inside the car, beneath a dingy cloudless sky, and the only sound was the air conditioner, whose air was strangely unnatural enough to seem unnecessary, as though it provided the only environment— man-made—in which I could survive, separate from everything outside, from the wet Okies whom I couldn't even hear as I sat without a word and no thought of a word or even a look at my brooding father.

We crossed an overpass spanning the 99 Highway, passed a Kmart and a Putt-Putt Golf course, then the road and canal were bordered on either side by tall plank fences and cinder-block walls, above which I could see the rooflines and chimneys of houses. We passed the neighborhood, where Richie Smith lived, of skinny short trees that provided no shade and whose useless presence made the sun and heat seem all the more intense. One summer I'd gone to Richie's house for his birthday party. A "Swimming Party," the invitation said. It was held in the backyard, with traffic sounds rushing over the fence, beside a large mudhole that Richie and his older brother, Rusty, had dug. I'd forgotten my swim trunks, so I sat and watched Richie and Darrel Shreef and Harry Burnet and others splash and slip around, and was watched in turn by Richie's father, who sat in a lawn chair beneath the lone tree, a can of Shasta cola resting between his thighs. I'd rejected a pair of Rusty's shorts—much too big—that he'd offered to let me borrow. So he sat and glared at me. "What's the matter," he'd said finally, after I'd refused for the third time, "pool's not good enough for you? Shorts not good enough for you?" He had the same small nose as Richie and the same accent, the same kind of face that always looked a little bruised, the same crew cut.

I looked nothing like my father. In all the photos I'd ever seen of him his hair was short and grew straight back from the broad almost flat horizon of his hairline. It was black and gray, like the engines of the trucks and forklifts at his warehouse. My hair was reddish brown and had to be cut often because it grew in erratic curls over the tops of my ears. It had been even curlier when I was a baby, and blond, and my mother had saved clippings from that time, in a blank envelope in the top drawer of her dresser. When my mother left for the hospital with my father it was nighttime and I slept on the couch beneath an afghan, sick with the flu. I woke to my parents' voices, to my mother, carrying a small tan box of an overnight case, and my father waiting at the door, his hand on the knob. Then my mother quickly left the room, walking toward the opposite end of the house, and my father followed. When she entered again I was more awake. She came into the room alone, but I knew my father would follow and I waited for him. She noticed me watching her and from the middle of the room said, "I'm going now. I'm going to the hospital, I won't be long, everything will be fine. Everything will be fine." She looked toward the kitchen door as she said this—not at me—anticipating my father's entrance. She took short, hesitant, nervous steps, forward and back, side to side, moving constantly, but going nowhere. Her eyes darted between the kitchen doorway and her hands, joined together on the handle of the overnight case—both looking for my father and looking to avoid him when he entered, which he soon did. Then he was at the door again, Mary, red-eyed, stood in the doorway to the kitchen, and my mother said, "This is all for the best. Everything will be fine, it's okay, you'll see. Everything will be better, don't worry about me, I'll be home soon, see you soon." And she stepped toward me for just a moment, bent at the waist, still keeping her distance, and gave a quick tug at a curl by my ear. Then both of my parents were gone.

Toward the center of town the rooftops receded from the road and the trees became tall, dark green, dense with leaves. In this neighborhood my mother's mother lived, on a short narrow street shaded by great branches that arched over it from either side and met above its middle to form a cover, like the plaster vault of St. Stephen's Church. It was where I always spent New Year's Eve and my parents' anniversary—nights when my parents stayed out late. But I spent nonholidays there, too. I liked my grandmother's house: small and white, with plain unassuming pillars on its low porch, a trim little unfenced yard in the front, and a rose garden and larger plot of lawn bordered by a tall brick wall and a white garage in the back. One heavy arm of her neighbor's cherry tree stretched over the corner formed by the garage and brick wall, and in the corner opposite, in a niche near the house, stood a tall statue of the Virgin Mary with one bare foot on the throat of a sea serpent, writhing, with fins and long curling tail. This was painted in life-like colors. Inside the house she had an unused pink ashtray with the words CATALINA ISLAND curving above a picture of a sailboat, and a copper statue of the Empire State Building. A crucifix hung above the door of the bedroom where I slept, and on the wall was an old beige photograph of my dead grandfather in a tie and jacket, with a smooth smiling face. When we walked to the shopping centers strung by their large parking lots along Ralston's main boulevard, MacAffee, she insisted I walk between her and the street, where a gentleman was supposed to walk—"so if someone throws garbage out of a passing car it will soil the man, not the lady." Every time we went shopping she bought me something. Sometimes we took the bus, as if we were in a big city.

But this time my mother went into the hospital I didn't stay at my grand-mother's house as I had before. During those times my grandmother had helped me make cards for my mother, letting me use her ancient typewriter, heavy as lead, on which she wrote to her friends and relatives back East and in Italy. When I was still learning to read she used to spell each word for me, patiently letting me hunt among the round keys—so much like a patch of clover—for the right letters. This time my father wanted me with him, and he and Mary and I sat together silently at late dinners, after he got home from work. On nights when he went straight from work to the hospital, Mary and I would eat TV dinners, then she'd talk on the phone (sometimes to Paul, at college) or have her best friend over, and they'd have long pained discussions in the rarely used living room, sitting cross-legged at the feet of furniture which existed, for the most part, only for display, while I watched television in the den. Sometimes Mary would ask about my new teacher, or if there were any new students this year, or any changes at school. Then, inevitably, she'd abruptly say, *This is all for the best. It'll be okay*—and I'd be unable to stand her anymore. I'd wish she'd just leave me alone, go into the kitchen, make a phone call.

At MacAffee Boulevard, beneath which the canal disappeared, my father had to stop for a red light, and I began to think about swimmers who must have tried to swim underwater from one side of the four-lane road to the other. One day at school, Sean Koons had said he'd done it. He always made claims like this and I rarely believed any of them. But there must have been some swimmers who really had done it—or at least tried. Maybe someone on a dare. Or in a game of Truth or Dare, which I hated because its whole point was to frighten and humiliate. Someone could probably do it, even though the water was so dirty that he wouldn't be able to open his eyes and would just have to try to swim, blindly, as straight as possible from the start. Whenever my grandmother and I crossed the canal on our walks down MacAffee, I tried to estimate how long it would take to make this swim. Today, though, as my father's car idled at the intersection, I imagined a swimmer who ran out of air beneath the middle of the road and kicked up toward the water's surface only to find no surface and no air and no light. Someone who came up fast, breathless and scared, and slammed into the bottom of the road, where he'd stay for the rest of time, floating against the concrete that vibrated with the cars passing above. I wondered how many bodies were trapped in this way, and imagined how creepy it would be if someone on a dare got tangled up with these rotting corpses. But possibly there was just a slender layer of air between the bottom of MacAffee and the water's surface, maybe an inch or two, so that a swimmer who ran out of air could, if he rose slowly enough, carefully raise his face close to the road's underside and breathe. And maybe just tread water like that, his head lifted, only his nose and mouth above the surface, and try to remember—in the midst of all those failed and decaying swimmers—the way out.

Across MacAffee the trees of the older neighborhoods remained big and green for a while, then gradually began to thin and shrink, then—just before orchards that stretched out of town—we reached the hospital, four stories high beside the canal. As we drove through the parking lot I saw my mother's three aunts coming out of the hospital doors. My father cursed. My great-aunts all lived in moldy-smelling houses, and held birthday parties for their grandchildren in the center of Almeda Park, at the wooden picnic benches and tables, where everyone could see them carrying on. Their husbands (two were still living) worked for the post office, and were always home from work by four o'clock. These men—both non-Italians—did foolish things and laughed at themselves. The bald, squat one, Fred, spent all his free time playing with model trains in a room filled with plaster-of-paris mountains and miniature redwoods, tiny towns and scaled-down warehouses and little men. "None of that family works too hard," my father would say to my mother after weddings. And whenever my mother visited them, she'd always embarrass me with how loudly she laughed and talked.

My great-aunts didn't seem to see us, though, and left together in one car. I followed my silent father from the harsh light and heat of the parking lot into the cool hospital, then past the gift shop whose toy-filled windows made me think it might be fun to be sick if people would bring you things. Even though the toys and games in the window looked shoddy, down-sized, I could sense the extra pleasure that would come from a gift-shop toy brought to you in a hospital when you had good reason to stay in bed beneath fresh sheets and watch television, good reason to do nothing at all except receive gifts.

I tried to imagine how my mother would look, lying in bed in a hospital gown with tubes in her arms or maybe her nose, like her father beneath his clear little tent before he died. She didn't look sick before she left, didn't suddenly collapse, soaked with sweat, as he had. I was sicker than she was, in bed with the flu—she was active, busy. On the day before I became sick, she took down from the wall behind my father's recliner all the school and baby and wedding photos, Paul's high school graduation portrait, pulled all the nails out, hammered in new ones, then rehung the photos. The next day while I lay in bed, home from school, I heard her take them all down again, heard the hammering, then saw, later, that she'd altered their placement again. Then, finally, the day before she left she did it all once more: pulled out the nails, hammered in new ones, moved our family photos. I was lying on the couch and she worked without paying any attention to me. By this time, after all the rearranging, it had become a challenge for her to conceal the holes in the plaster. I couldn't help but watch her—it was like she was doing a puzzle.

At the fourth floor the elevator opened to two couches near a large tinted window, two coffee tables covered with magazines, and, to the left, a broad hallway ending abruptly in a wall with a door in its center. The door was closed, and had a small square window, crisscrossed by wire. Cut out of the left side of the hallway, before the door, was a nurses' station.

My father walked with me to a couch, told me to sit down.

"I'll bring your mother out," he said, awkwardly standing over me. He took a step back—a better angle to talk. "She wanted to see you. I'll go get her. Just a minute." He gave a quick half-smile—a grimace, actually—dropped his head, turned, and walked to the nurse behind her counter. They spoke briefly, then he stepped in front of the door, his back to me, his head upright, painfully still, until the nurse, distracted for a few moments by a ringing phone, buzzed the door unlocked and he quickly pulled it open and disappeared behind it.

When I was four years old my mother took me to visit my grandfather in the special care section of a nursing home and I saw a man, tottering down the hall, who wore an oxygen mask over his nose and mouth and cradled a slender scubalike tank in his arms. I imagined, for a minute, my mother coming out in a mask like that. But I knew it wouldn't happen. I wondered if she had a roommate. If she had a television. Or if she had her own room, like her father, where everything was quiet and there was no TV, where he'd sat almost straight up beneath the clear tent, eyes frozen on nothing. When our St. Stephen's pastor, Father Alvarez, went into the hospital for an operation the whole school said prayers for him each morning before class. Twice in one week we took time out of math to make cards for him. It was almost like a holiday—but serious. I'd written a card for my mother, but realized now that I'd left it at home. No one at school knew my mother was in the hospital.

I turned on the couch, looked out the window at the brimming canal. Two kids on bikes rode along the edge of it. When the canals were empty, in the winter, I'd go with a bunch of other kids to ride our bikes up and down the canal near our school. The trick was to set off from the top at an angle, then slant down one side and up the other. If you went straight down you'd be thrown over your handlebars when your front wheel hit the place where the canal's sloping side met its floor. One day Richie Smith came to school with half of his face bruised and said he "ate it" at the canal. But I never saw anyone actually go over the handlebars. Frankie Banelli, a runty, big-headed asthmatic kid, once had his pedals in the wrong position so that halfway down the side a pedal hit concrete and made his whole bike jump. He didn't come close to falling—still, he never went down the side again. But Sean Koons was the best canal rider. He'd lift his feet from the pedals as he set off, and angle down and up with both of them resting on his handlebars. He'd do it standing: his feet on the bike seat, legs straight, and head and shoulders so far forward (he still had to use his hands to steer) that it looked like the slightest bump would pitch him into the concrete. He was at least a year younger than anyone else at the canal, and he dipped Copenhagen. Before and after school his lower lip bulged with it, revealing some of the soft shiny redness of the inside of his mouth and the black of the finely ground peppery-smelling tobacco. He dipped when he rode. He was fearless.

But, though no one else seemed to remember, Sean Koons had been very different when he first appeared at school, with his mother. On that day he'd been pale and skinny and small, holding on to his mother's hand, timidly. And his mother had worn a muddy-colored coat, all askew, and her short dark hair lay flat against one side of her head, as though she'd just risen from a nap. She was older than any other mother I'd seen at school, confused-looking, and she moved with the hesitancy of a foreigner, slowly approaching the door of the school, risking only a few steps down the hall, before coming outside again, and looking all around for assistance, for signs. I expected her to have an accent. She walked up to a group of us on the edge of the playground, still moving feebly, still pulling Sean along, and asked us where the front office was. And when I heard her voice, unaccented, but sounding as lost and exhausted as she looked, and saw close-up the alien and shabby kind of helplessness in which she was clothed, older as she was and strange, with Sean at the end of her arm, and having to ask a smart-ass like Harry Burnet for directions, my breath was forced from me by a sudden shame, so I could never remember if Harry gave her the right directions or lied to her or anything that he said. I remembered only the laughter and jokes that followed her away.

The waiting room was noiseless, except for the nurse thumbing through papers, or answering the softly ringing phone. I slumped on the couch, stared dumbly at the glossy magazines on the table before me, let the photos on their covers blur into a jumble of formless colors, the words—as though I didn't know how to read—scatter into letters, meaningless shapes.

Perhaps I wouldn't see my mother today after all. I hoped I would not.

But the door near the nurses' station buzzed, then came the noise of someone fumbling with the knob. Through the wires on the window I saw the top of my mother's head, then a glimpse of my father's face and shoulder as he reached around from behind her to help. The door opened and my mother stood still in its frame. She wore her heavy red bathrobe from home, wrapped tightly around her same old off-white nightgown. Her face was very pale, except for deep pink at the edges of her eyelids. My father, from behind, touched the small of her back and she vaguely smiled at me, then started toward me slowly and unsteadily—walking, with great effort, as if she waded to me through water, waist-high.

Jay Parini

II. Ida Parini (1890–1976)

A drowning was the one thing she remembered
from the other side,
how the roiling sea gave up a girl
one morning on the beach
in old Liguria, where she was born.

The body was like alabaster, cool;
the hair was dandled by the lurid waters,
to and fro. She'd known the girl
"not very well."

       If pressed, she'd say
Liguria was full of shaggy rats; her father
shot them with a long-nosed pistol.
It was not so hard to leave all this.

The crossing she remembered wave by wave.
The maggoty old meat, the swampy water,
how her cousin died of fever
on the mid-Atlantic,
though she suffered "less than one might think."

Her parents left her lonely at the docks
with someone twice her age or more.
He had golden cuff-links, ivory teeth.
They married in Manhattan
as her parents sailed to Argentina,
where an earthquake swallowed their last days.
"It was not as if I really knew them."

She was left alone in Pennsylvania
with her five small sons.
She did not complain, though once or twice
I found her sitting by the swollen river
near her house, her long hair down.
When I would ask her what was wrong
she would say she'd lost so many people
she had scarcely known.
It was "not as bad as I imagined,
but you sometimes wonder what was meant."

JAY PARINI

Grandmother in Heaven

In a plume-field, white above the blue,
she's pulling up a hoard of rootcrops
planted in a former life and left to ripen:
soft gold carrots, beets, bright gourds.
There's coffee in the wind, tobacco smoke
and garlic, olive oil and lemon.
Fires burn coolly through the day,
the water boils at zero heat.
It's always almost time for Sunday dinner,
with the boys all home: dark Nello,
who became his cancer and refused to breathe;
her little Gino, who went down the mines
and whom they had to dig all week to find;
that willow, Tony, who became so thin
he blew away; then Julius and Leo,
who survived the others by their wits alone
but found no reason, after all was said,
for hanging on. They'll take their places
in the sun today at her high table,
as the antique beams light up the plates,
the faces that have lately come to shine.

Maria Laurino

Clothes

AT THE CORNER OF MADISON AVENUE and Sixty-eighth Street
stand a pair of buildings that once told the story of contemporary fash-
ion through the vision of two Italians, one born in the genteel "civic" north,
the other from the rugged "uncivic" south of Italy. In a simpler time perhaps,
before the designer Giorgio Armani moved into his colossal flagship store a
few blocks away, before Gianni Versace opened his own fashion palace on
Fifth Avenue and ultimately became a household name because of his bru-
tal murder, these two competed for customers, staking out like feuding
neighbors their starkly different stylistic territory. The pull and tug of these
men, archrivals, master weavers of myth, reminds me of my youth and the
role that clothes played in our household. Not that we knew anything about
haute couture when I was growing up. But we did know something about
good taste and bad taste.

Above the red brick entrance to the old Armani boutique is a large airy
window in the shape of an arch; it resembles a church window, simple and
Protestant, a fitting image for the northern Italian often thought of as the
high priest of Milanese fashion. To wear the name Giorgio Armani is to bear
an imprimatur of luxury and distinction. To enter an Armani shop is to step
into the land of taste, a subdued world where shades of beige quietly rule,
and in their elegance and beauty conquer.

Next door, the charcoal gray Versace boutique is embellished with sixteen
faux Corinthian columns, each crowned with a silver cornice. The Versace
window display, always a kaleidoscope of colors, one spring season featured

mannequins draped in bright orange, accessorized with matching-color patent leather bags and shiny spike-heeled shoes; these were fiery warriors next to Armani's neutral goddesses. Showy gewgaws adorned the clothes inside; Versace's gold Medusa-head emblem fastens belts, buttons sweaters, and clamps purses shut.

Gianni Versace made an extraordinary career for himself by breaking the rules of fashion, openly defying what Roland Barthes called the "taboo of an aesthetic order," tweaking the tasteful upturned nose of Armani clothes. Or as *Vogue* editor in chief Anna Wintour once put it: "Versace was always sort of the 'mistress' to Armani's wife."

Armani was said to have grumbled about the direction of Italian fashion led by Versace, a trend that some of their colleagues playfully labeled "the good taste of bad taste." But it would be impossible to understand the source of the Armani-Versace rivalry without recognizing that the style of both designers was derived in part from the contradictory outlook of a country deeply divided by class.

MY GUARDIANS OF FASHION, MY mother and my aunt, would never have made a Versace-like mistake. They would not have worn a bright orange dress with matching patent leather sandals or overdecorated sweaters, sure signs of lower-class Italian-American taste. I would become their model, and they would dress me to look delicate, refined, a picture of good taste.

For many years, my mother and my aunt divided up the duty of dressing me. My aunt took the first decade, my mother watched over the next two. My aunt, a widow in her forties, lived alone in a small apartment and spent most of her paycheck from a clerical job at Western Electric on clothes for herself. She also delighted in dressing her brother's child, and my earliest clothes memories are a swirl of pastels: baby pink, blue, and yellow, the colors of my Easter suits, light wools that hung tentatively on my tiny body, as if the sheep were surprised by the tender age of their new home. Dresses, jackets, skirts, and blouses. Soft cottons, cool wools, cuddly bouclés.

My closet filled with clothes allowed me to dress up and to make believe, replacing toys as the child's suspension bridge into the land of wonder, providing me with a passageway to an imaginary, grown-up world. I was much more preoccupied with the interchangeable satin ribbons that accessorized my new straw hat than dolling up a Barbie, and I deliberated with great care over what color to wear each week. I would carry my head high as I walked into church on Sundays, with a touch of forest green or burgundy wrapped above the brim to accent a navy coat.

Early on I learned about the age barrier to dressing for success. In kindergarten, I carried home a handwritten note from my teacher informing my mother that I was inappropriately dressed; my clothes were too good for a five-year-old who spent half of her day crawling and napping on a floor mat. Because girls were not allowed to wear pants, I needed play dresses, but a less fancy outfit (a housedress?) could never fit my aunt's image of what I should look like at school. The dresses were so pretty that we ignored the teacher's comment and I learned to kneel on the floor like a Japanese princess at tea.

Each fashion season, my aunt would buy me dresses and colorful tights to match and bring them to our house, except on special occasions, like the week before Easter, when she would take me shopping and out to lunch at her favorite department store, Haynes in Newark, New Jersey. I would sit in the plain Haynes lounge with its faded wallpaper and wait for a gray-haired waitress to deliver my tuna fish melt, all of which seemed resplendent to me. Afterward, we would shop.

"I like this one," I'd say with an eight-year-old's authority, and point to a two-piece electric yellow knit. My aunt let me try it on, along with several others, but she had already chosen my Easter dress. The outfit I picked out looked "cheesy," she said. I assumed she meant it bore a color resemblance to Cheddar cheese, and tried to convince myself that her choice was better than mine.

My mother trusted my aunt to buy me clothes, but I could never tell how much she liked her sister-in-law's taste, although she always accepted the gifts with thanks and praise. The two women looked very different, my mother with her salt-and-pepper short-cropped hair and old cotton housedresses, and my aunt, who wore her dyed red hair in a flip and always came to visit us in a new outfit. My mother's hands were red and chafed from the soapy water she used to clean the dishes and floor each day; my aunt's fingernails were painted in creamy ivory, and she stared at them often, although I never knew whether she was admiring their luster or mourning the absence of the wedding band she once wore. While my mother envied my aunt's freedom to pamper herself, I think she always believed that her own taste was finer, with her eye for simple, elegant cuts. Yet she was raising three children and my father's wallet was emptier. My mother did understand the essential role that clothes could play in fashioning a look and a life of refinement and beauty. She may have had a limited wardrobe, but she had much greater expectations for her daughter.

I can recall best one outfit of my mother's: a khaki-colored suit worn with either a plain black or white scoop-necked cotton shirt. She believed in buying "one nice thing," a finely made suit that could be used many times, rather than several cheaper items. Minimalism guided her choices because she feared excess, afraid as she was of looking Italian-American, or *gavone* (pronounced "gah-vone"). *Gavone*, which we used as both adjective and noun, was southern Italian dialect derived from the Italian word *cafone*, or ignorant person. The word meant to us—if one can ever interpret precisely the variable nuances of dialect—low-class. (I didn't realize until years later that *cafone* was the label northern Italians used to mock poor southerners.) *Gavone* outfits combined a sexiness and tackiness that left me awestruck in their excessive splendor.

I had an early encounter with this look as a child at a cocktail party my parents gave prior to a church event. One relative entered our house wearing a tight orange cardigan with a plunging V-neck, a gold cross that dangled between her breasts, clinging black pants, and high-heeled sandals. "That's quite a sweater," my mother laughed nervously, and she did seem to like the cardigan despite its audaciousness. I stood close to this relative for most of the evening, impressed by her full figure, admiring the way her body looked, but disturbed that she had worn this outfit to a gathering attended by a priest. She had Gianni Versace in her bones before the designer ever sold his first pair of skintight pants.

Italian-American clothes were colorful and baroque, often worn by women with jet-black hair piled high on the head: tops in turquoise, chartreuse, shocking pink, purple, and coral (an especially popular color at weddings) and clashing pants; dresses dripping with brocades; gold shoes. Like any adolescent who follows fashion trends as if they were the Holy Grail, for years I amused myself flipping through magazines trying to determine that fine line between *gavone* and chic. Beautiful models wore raging reds, shocking pinks, and deep purples, yet those same colors could create that over-the-top Italian-American look. How would I know if I was *gavone* or chic?

Today it amuses me when a design that fits my childhood image of Italian-American taste is labeled haute couture. Yet many of the top designers are Italian, some came from the poorest regions of southern Italy, and how else is fashion created but from memory, the palette of colors, textures, and objects appropriated from one's youth?

CLOTHES CONJURED FOR ME THE dual demons of pride and embarrassment, of joy and fear. Like any girl, I loved dressing up, but at five, after being told about the note from my teacher, I had a vague feeling that my clothes were inappropriate, that there was too much effort spent in trying to make me look right, putting me in dresses when play clothes would do. And

I never was allowed to forget the value of good clothes, which made it hard to act like a child.

My aunt once bought me a pair of royal blue tights that matched a cotton dress, and I put the gift aside, awaiting the perfect spring day to wear them. When I finally deemed my legs ready for this swathe of blue, I tripped that day during recess and tore a hole at the knee, which protruded beneath the fabric like a gibbous moon. I wept the rest of the afternoon, anticipating a reprise of my mother's angry, oft-repeated lecture: "You don't deserve good clothes." (Who deserves good clothes? People who can afford to tear them? Children who don't fall down when they play?)

Soon I began to dislike the way clothes looked on me because my once skinny body had grown plump. My normally quiet father grew talkative about the issue of my weight. He was fearful that his daughter would suffer the sad fate of his secretary, who had been engaged to a doctor but had, after ballooning in size, ended up marrying a mozzarella maker. While I was eating vanilla ice cream drenched in Hershey's syrup and topped with Reddi Wip, he muttered that I was becoming "as fat as a house," perhaps envisioning my future of kneading and tossing dough for a demanding husband in a full apron stained with milky curds.

By the time I reached the age of ten or eleven, my aunt had grown tired of buying clothes for me, showing up with less and less until she stopped altogether. A chubby girl wasn't as fun to dress, and buying clothes had become a costlier proposition. My aunt explained that an adolescent was too difficult to shop for, and she would wait until I became "a perfect size ten." I believed her, having no sense of the little deceits adults commit when they trap themselves in a box and, upon grasping its dimensions and limitations, desperately wish to escape.

"When you're a perfect ten [the size that she wore], I'll know how to shop for you," my aunt repeated. Her explanation had the cadence of a lullaby, pacifying my anxieties about my body and promising a better future. So I naively dreamed of turning into a lady, becoming the "perfect ten," pleasing my elders, and awakening a few years later to walk down the runway of my aunt's taste and charge card.

Because clothes played such a large part in my mother's anxieties about becoming an American, I'm sure that her mixed feelings about leaving my early dressing to my aunt were compounded by her own fear of having to shop for me. "Your sister spoiled her. She got used to good things," my mother would say to my father, who knew that there was no acceptable answer.

"And now we have to buy her nice clothes," she'd conclude to the air. My mother understood that the choice of what to wear could allow you to be something you are not, that fabric and style could transcend class labels, providing the essential threads for a Pygmalion tale. My aunt had the perfect arrangement, according to my mother's fantasy of the single woman's life: she spent very little money on housing, living in a small apartment in an urban area of New Jersey; her success was measured by the clothes she wore in the world.

My mother's sensitivity to the transformative power of clothes was part and parcel of her second-generation instinct to assimilate, and like most children of immigrants, she juggled the difficulties of leaving the Old World to adapt to the New. While she loved her parents, they spoke with a heavy accent and looked like Italian immigrants. Her responsibility to act like a dutiful daughter and her desire to adopt the image of an American suburban housewife and mother could be mutually exclusive, and she lacked the confidence—or the ability to create the *bella figura*—needed to pull off the latter. In trying to abandon the stereotype of the Italian—the greaseball, the *gavone*—mixed messages abounded in our household. My mother wanted to maintain tradition, keep the spirit of our humble origins, but at the same time reject a look that we labeled lower-class.

If ancestry could be masked in the weave of a classic style, then her daughter, educated and well dressed, could achieve dreams beyond my mother's reach. But clothes choices need validation, and my mother, isolated and alone in our house, was ill at ease shopping in a department store. "I don't trust my taste," she said, explaining that she envied women who always knew what they wanted. She would dither and nervously wander among the racks, and ultimately feel helpless until she found a saleswoman to affirm the choices in her hand.

My mother had one story about clothes that she repeated like a Scheherazade tale, hoping its message could redeem a lost part of herself. The time was several years before her marriage, those strange days of contained independence for a young woman engaged to an army officer stationed in Europe; the place, a cozy sweater shop far from the horrors her fiancé was facing. There the manager put my mother in charge of selecting the finest sweaters delivered to his shop. He would seek her opinion and showcase the cottons and wools that she had picked; always, she said, he would compliment her choices. The store gave my mother a place to nurture an identity that thrived on the notion of possessing good taste.

The story sadly reminded me of her brief working life, stopped short by marriage and children. As a teenager I wanted to say, "What do you care what that stupid man thought anyway? Why does his judgment, not yours, mean that you have good taste?" But I knew better than to respond. The image of those pretty sweaters comforted my mother like a blanket of luxurious wool during years of servitude to a husband of immeasurable silences and children who grew old too soon.

Children never want to see their parents' youthful possibilities, and perhaps that was the reason why I refused to imagine this scene in the sweater shop. I understood and accepted her fashion advice as a mother's advice, a gauge that set limits to the child's limitless wants. But as a daughter, I didn't think about her youthful investment, how she looked in clothes before she was married, the persona she adapted by wearing what she chose, and, most unimaginably, how men saw what covered her body. In her married life, my mother abandoned clothes that she may have chosen in that sweater shop, clothes that could heighten her dark-haired allure. I, too, agreed with her choices. Her judgment would mute my love of the bright and bold.

GIANNI VERSACE WAS THE FASHION world's great success story. Born the son of a dressmaker from Reggio di Calabria, by the time of his death he had reportedly built an $800 million empire. He was inspired by, and dressed, many muses, including a vampy Madonna, a curvaceous Elizabeth Hurley, and a royally sensual Princess Di. Versace left southern Italy by the age of twenty to design costumes for the theater, and early on in his career he pronounced his clear differences with the reigning king of Italian fashion, Giorgio Armani.

In a *New Yorker* profile published shortly after Versace's death, the writer Andrea Lee offered accounts of Versace's past that were as varied as his color palette. Versace described to Lee what it was like to grow up in the "romantic atmosphere of a rich bourgeois family: Father was a businessman who loved opera and literature; Mother was the glamorous, free-spirited proprietress of an important dressmaking atelier."

In a *New York Times* article he remarked, "When you are born in a place and there is beauty all around, a Roman bath, a Greek remain, you cannot help but be influenced by the classical past." Versace's descriptions of Reggio di Calabria served to polish the shabby image of the Italian boot, reclaiming its stature as the land of Greek antiquity where Pythagoras dreamed and poets honored Scylla and Charybdis, not the dreary villages plagued by *la miseria*, the abounding poverty that defines so much of the south.

The Versace Italian myth became emblazoned in stone, a fitting tribute to a man who chose the Medusa head as his fashion logo: the King of Fashion wanted his family business to be run like the Medicis, he once said. He was about "class, not mass," a newspaper columnist wrote. Richard Martin, curator of the Costume Institute at the Metropolitan Museum of Art, described Versace: "To say that he lives like a prince is not to say merely that he lives affluently, but that he is a modernized version of the Renaissance tradition of the learned, artistically discriminating cultural leader." The death of this prince for the 1990s was eclipsed only by that of a real princess the following month.

Later in the *New Yorker* profile, Lee offered a revised version of the Versace family history. A sportswear designer who had known Versace for decades commented, "There was no rich background, no grand, high-fashion atelier. They were a simple family: the father sold appliances, and the mother made dresses in her little shop. It was a *merceria-abbigliamento* [a small clothing shop that also sells buttons and accessories] and its name, if I recall, was Vogue. The rest is fantasy."

While the blue-eyed Giorgio Armani, born in Piacenza, an hour away from Milan, grew up surrounded by upper-class Italian style, the nearest capitals for the young Versace would have been Naples, hundreds of miles north, and Palermo, farther south, both considered by northerners to be embarrassments of corruption and decay, and, until designers like Gianni Versace and Dolce & Gabbana came on the scene, the last places to look for inspiration to dress the elegant fashion consumer.

Versace was surrounded by the tastes of southern Italy. It is the taste of poor and working-class people; it is Barthes's "profusion of elements," the composition of bad taste. Bright Mediterranean colors, the earthy sensuality of peasants, the excessive pageantry of the religious south, and a baroque style that rejected simplicity as a metaphor for the Teutonic, northern way of life were images a young Versace would have internalized.

"What is Versace all about?" a *New York Times* fashion writer asked. "Quite simply, a lot. Of everything. Full-blast prints. All-out beadwork. Poufs and big, floating skirts (the underwiring is sometimes so wide it looks as if a curtain fell over a bicycle)."

The *gavone* Italian-American look had to have originated in the tastes of southern Italy, carried from one generation to the next. As Gianni Versace rose to the highest echelons of the fashion world, he blotted out his rustic past but achieved success by using attributes of peasant style in his designs.

Fashion writers often described Versace as subversive, yet to me his styles always felt familiar, vaguely comforting, coming from roots that I know. If fashion has historically been a way to enhance and solidify social status—at least, that's what we hoped for in our household—Versace changed the game; he internalized the taste of the poor, drawing on the influences of southern Italy to create a multimillion-dollar empire. Perhaps that's the subversion, the fact that he had turned haute couture on its head with designs that might be called couture.

IN THE 1970S, THE ONLY designers my mother and I knew were those who mass-marketed clothes, attaching their fussy initials to T-shirts, ties, and sheets. My mother, however, could have used some Armani-like help now that my aunt had closed her chapter in my fashion story. With my mother in charge of my wardrobe, she had to ensure that her daughter wouldn't look *gavone*. Luckily, she had a convenient means of protection: we lived within walking distance of a branch of Saks Fifth Avenue. Once my mother decided that we would shop at Saks, I'm sure she also experienced the satisfaction of one-upping my aunt. Haynes was a middle-class New Jersey store; Saks symbolized the epitome of upper-crust taste.

My mother still knew that there were mistakes to be made among the assorted racks of the preteen department, and she was worried about having the time to shop for me because she worked as a secretary to help pay college tuition bills for my brother Bob. She befriended an elderly woman named Mrs. Smith who managed the preteen department, and my mother asked her to be in charge of shopping for my clothes. We worked out an arrangement: I would walk to Saks after school carrying my mother's charge card, and would find Mrs. Smith. Because children usually adapt to the circumstances they're presented with, it never struck me as odd that my mother didn't take me shopping; her excuses about time pressures seemed to make sense.

Mrs. Smith, a small woman with powder white hair and a face mapped with wrinkles, might have been more comfortable pointing a ruler at a blackboard filled with English grammar than lifting plastic hangers and prodding me toward the dressing room, which she did as we solemnly approached each fitting. I was uncomfortable with this little woman standing next to me while I undressed, nodding, judging, surveying my body from head to toe, but my mother seemed to have supreme confidence in her choice of Mrs. Smith as the new designee to mold my fashion taste. It was as if she had found the perfect headmistress and had just enrolled me in boarding school at Saks.

The few times a year that I bought school clothes became a chore because I now had to please Mrs. Smith as well as my mother, and as an adolescent I had exuberant taste, preferring crayon-box colors (an incipient Versaceite?) to the muted shades my mother had in mind. And we made a few mistakes, Mrs. Smith and I, with some major purchases, like the winter coat debacle. We picked out a long, powder blue coat with a curly white wool collar and two large pockets embroidered in iridescent swirls of pink, blue, and purple that resembled a butterfly fluttering through a bad trip. Mrs. Smith thought it was marvelous, this coat dubbed "the Butterfly" by my brother Bob. My mother hated it, but what could she say—Mrs. Smith had helped choose the woolly wonder and she couldn't insult her taste. Although I insisted I loved the coat, after two winter seasons I began to feel like a ripe caterpillar that wanted to touch the sky but forever was a chrysalis trapped inside its neon cocoon.

WALKING INTO THE VERSACE BOUTIQUE, I feel relaxed and amused. I pass the glossy vinyl pants and dazzling striped tops, and pick up a scanty red shift decorated with three-inch metal zippers at the chest and longer zippers that serve as front pockets. The shift looks like a racy version of the housedresses my mother wore, except it's thirteen hundred dollars. I can imagine older women buying the cashmere sweaters in argyle pastels with gold lamé running through the wool, crowned with Medusa-head buttons. I notice the sharp stare of a saleswoman; I am an intruder with no intention to buy, and feel superior rejecting overdone, overpriced clothes.

In the Armani shop, I am tense looking at clothes that I find beautiful, racks of long beige jackets and slim-cut pants as delicately varied in shade as grains of sand, and gauzy blouses that move effortlessly, like a calm breeze. I feel out of place, self-conscious; I am among people with whom I don't belong, next to clothes that I cannot afford. His is a fairy-tale world of clothes, a kingdom that I could pretend to live in as a child, and still long for as an adult.

The styles of these two men were the yin and yang of my youth: clothes could make you look southern Italian or Anglo-Saxon, extravagant or refined, sexy or powerful. In choosing either style, I had something to lose.

FOR MY MOM AND ME, clothes were the purest comfort. Clothes formed one of our strongest and, for a time, it seemed, least threatening bonds, giving us a lasting topic of conversation, a point of mutual interest compared to schoolwork, which failed to hold my mother's attention, or cooking, which was solely her domain, her short body and sturdy legs positioned by the electric stove, where she stirred and I sat a few feet away. We could talk about clothes as we watched TV, discussing the latest styles or reminiscing about memorable looks, like the tight black leggings that Mary Tyler Moore wore on *The Dick Van Dyke Show* long before anyone else.

My mother didn't realize that when she cut the umbilical cord so young, teaching me the importance of fashion and yet using intermediaries to send me out in style, there would be a natural yet unforeseen result. I would develop my own taste, which I would use to place myself in the world. The rift between us grew after I left home for college.

One summer, my application for a saleswoman's job at our favorite spot, the local Saks, was accepted. About a month into my summer job, the personnel director stopped by my department to tell me about a "Fashion Board" for college students that I might like to join, which would include an end-of-the-summer fashion show. She told me to see a woman named Maureen who was running the board. My conversation with the personnel director led me to believe that I had already been selected, and I didn't realize that Maureen was judging each girl.

The look on Maureen's face when I entered her small corner office in the back of the store told me that my future modeling career was not yet assured. "I'm just not sure you're right for us," she said, looking me up and down and acting as if the "us" were the Ford modeling agency and she were choreographing the next shoot in Milan. I was probably ten pounds heavier than Maureen desired, and I was darker than the rest of the girls I would meet, most of whom had blond or sandy brown hair.

My confidence withered, and I felt like a character out of *The Adventures of Augie March*, a book I quoted often during those years, returning to Bellow's words of wisdom on my dog-eared green index cards attached to a spiral wire. Like Augie, I decided that I was powerless in the face of all those who misunderstand "how you're liked for what you're not, disliked for what you're not, both from error and laziness. The way must be not to care, but in that case you must know how really to care and understand what's pleasing or displeasing in yourself."

Those words, mouthed over and over, were little solace to a youthful ego that shifted between miserable self-pity and angry self-righteousness. Eventually I was accepted to the board; each girl had to submit an essay about fashion, and Maureen, who circled the Saks parking lot in a red Mercedes with a personalized license plate that read "Moo-reen," seemed to enjoy the name-dropping piece that I wrote. The prospect of the fashion show kept my attention during the tedious hours of a sales day. But my head buzzed with alarms from all those years of shopping: Don't look cheesy, don't look *gavone*—you must have good taste. What clothes would my aunt have liked? What would Mrs. Smith have chosen? Would my mother approve?

As the show approached, we were told to choose sporty outfits, except for our last walk down the runway, which called for an elegant dress. I wasn't entirely pleased with the selection of clothes before me, but I picked out checked and solid wool pants and blazers that I could imagine wearing in school. For my last dress I decided to have some fun with a slinky, bright purple silk sheath.

The night of the show, the main floor of Saks was temporarily rearranged for the evening, filled with little wooden folding chairs and bright-colored balloons that surrounded a makeshift catwalk installed between the handbag and blouse departments. The personnel director took aside our groups of jittery girls about to face a handful of people and a horde of balloons and gave some last-minute advice: Smile, she said. Look like you're having a good time. And when you're on the runway, dance to the music.

All of us exchanged complaints to forget about the stage fright. We lined up, single file, in the hallway of the dressing rooms, giggling and primping, complimenting each other, forgetting that we had barely exchanged a word during the previous weeks together in the department store. Perhaps because girls are dressed up, and dress up dolls so young, bonding can be simple and pure when zippers and buttons get fastened.

Soon the music played and, following our cue, we began an odd-looking prance, each unsure of how to walk and dance down the runway. Skipping, walking, running, I was through most of my wools and still didn't see my mother, who I knew would be detained by her after-dinner cleanup. By the time I entered the dressing room to slip into my last outfit, the sleeveless purple silk, I had begun to relax. Feeling elegant and happy, I added a little extra jump to my step as I started down the runway. Completing a twirl, I noticed that my mother had arrived; already she looked displeased by what she saw.

Back in the dressing room, I received polite but tepid enthusiasm, with no suggestion of a budding modeling career. My mother and I walked home together, a sullen and silent ten-minute trip. Knowing what was bothering her and in a bald search for approval, I asked how I looked.

As soon as we reached our house, she unleashed her fury: my little dance on the runway was embarrassing. Why wasn't I walking in a sophisticated way? Why had I picked that purple dress? I tried to explain that we were told to dance and look happy, but soon my eyes filled with tears and words poured out of my mouth in a pathetic attempt at self-defense. Screaming in the hallway, I hardly noticed that my mother, seated on our worn blue couch with her head bowed, had started to cry. I was stunned by the rare sight of my mother crying but furious that she had the power to make me feel so awful.

It was dark in the upstairs of our house; my father and brother were watching television on the floor below, pretending to be oblivious to the mother-and-teenage-daughter battle that raged above them. We screamed into the night without bothering even to turn on a light, as if the darkness could absorb our wounds. I had betrayed my mother's sense of good taste; she had betrayed my hope for approval. I knew the argument was ludicrous, my offense minor, but still I couldn't stop the shouting or the tears. Clothes were supposed to make me accepted, serious, responsible. Instead, I had picked a bright purple sheath and frivolously danced down the runway.

That night the wounds of many years reopened. My mother never had the pleasure of dressing her child, handing over that responsibility first to my aunt and then to a stranger at Saks. That night we shared a mutual anger; we each had a story about the other that we wished we could erase. As I couldn't imagine the sweaters she had chosen that won another man's admiration, she couldn't accept me wearing a close-fitting silk dress that outlined my young body. The purpose of good clothes was to make us Americans, not to heighten our Mediterranean sexuality; to tamper with the power of clothes, to allow them to seduce, could cause an explosion like the one I witnessed that night.

My clothes memories always bring me back to the early moments of painful separation, the night of the fashion show when I watched my mother reduced to tears as she sat on a torn and faded couch. Her hopes had been put into clothes, into the illusion that a beautiful, tasteful dress could provide the wearer with the necessary confidence to meet the world. I'm sure she believed that she could have saved me that night, that another dress would have shaped me into a prettier, better person. If only she hadn't had to rely on others for judgment or for money; if she could have picked out clothes for both of us with the same confidence that she had had in the sweater shop, receiving praise for those luxurious, creamy wools that she alone had chosen.

WHEN I WAS IN MY late twenties, my mother continued to walk to Saks several times a month in a faded raincoat, once a handsome purchase from the store, and flat shoes with worn heels. She would pick out clothes for me as soon as they were marked down, proud of the savings. For the first time in my life, my mother actually dressed me, and her shopping lasted until I got married, ending the irreplaceable comfort of my mother taking care of my needs.

Maybe because I no longer lived at home, dressing me proved to be the best connection between us, and she could ensure that in my nascent working life I looked good. And it embarrassed me that I only received compliments on the clothes she had picked out—elegant tailored skirts and jackets, thick cowl-neck sweaters and silk blouses—but never on my own choices. "Let her shop for me," "Give me that jacket when you're tired of it," my friends would say. (What was equally surprising was that I worked at the *Village Voice*, and all the clothes my colleagues liked came from the haut bourgeois Saks.)

Today my wardrobe consists mainly of black and beige, with an occasional touch of bright red. My bland color scheme may be the product of putting on the monochrome mask that many New Yorkers choose to wear, as well as my internal check not to look too Italian-American. I have inherited my mother's taste, and have become even more conservative in my choices, seeking comfort in quiet shades when a little color would serve me well.

"WHO WAS HE?" MY MOTHER asks me on the phone after reports about the Versace murder blare on CNN night after night. "Your brother said his clothes were *gavone*. Is that right?"

I avoided a direct answer, wanting to pay Versace homage with a small tribute, not a sarcastic quip. Afterward, I thought about what Versace had achieved with his look of elegant whimsy. I thought about the endurance of his media legend, how Versace, too, would be liked for what he was not, disliked for what he was not; how we all weave myths in fabric, create a self in the clothes we wear; how my impulse to reject his fanciful palette and Versace's desire to color his background had a similar beginning: the self-consciousness of a southern Italian past. So as I considered my mother's question, I realized that the man who wished to be a Medici was also due a peasant elegy. Yes, his clothes were *gavone*, and the world rightly proclaimed them chic.

LUCIA PERILLO

The Sweaters

Used to be, fellows would ask if you were married—
now they just want to know what kind of diseases
you've got. Mother, what did they teach you of the future
in those nun-tended schoolrooms of the Sacred Heart?

Nobody kept cars in the city. Maybe you'd snuggle
when the subway went dark, or take walks
down Castle Hill Avenue, until it ran into the Sound—
the place you called "The End": where, in late summer,

the weeds were rife with burrs, and tomatoes ripened
behind the sheds of the Italians, beside their half-built
skiffs. Out on the water,
bare-legged boys balanced on the gunwales
of those wooden boats, reeling in the silver-bellied fish
that twitched and flickered while the evening dimmed to purple.

What sweater did you wear to keep you from the chill wind
blowing down at The End, that evening you consented
to marry Father? The plain white mohair, or the gray
angora stitched with pearls around the collar?
Or the black cashmere, scoop-necked
and trimmed with golden braid, stored in a box below the bed
to keep it hidden from Grandma? Each one prized,
like a husband in those lean years during the war.

I see him resting his face against whichever wool it was,
a pearl or a cable or braid imprinting his cheek
while the Sound washed in, crying *again, again*.

Mother, we've abandoned all our treasured things, your sweaters
long since fallen to the moths of bitter days. And what
will I inherit to soften this hard skin, to make love tender?

Afterwards, Elsa said, "You know, Garibaldi"—

sometimes she calls me Garibaldi—"you're a good lay."

SEX, LOVE, AND GOOD LOOKS

KIM ADDONIZIO

For Desire

Give me the strongest cheese, the one that stinks best;
and I want the good wine, the swirl in crystal
surrendering the bruised scent of blackberries,
or cherries, the rich spurt in the back
of the throat, the holding it there before swallowing.
Give me the lover who yanks open the door
of his house and presses me to the wall
in the dim hallway, and keeps me there until I'm drenched
and shaking, whose kisses arrive by the boatload
and begin their delicious diaspora
through the cities and small towns of my body.
To hell with the saints, with the martyrs
of my childhood meant to instruct me
in the power of endurance and faith,
to hell with the next world and its pallid angels
swooning and sighing like Victorian girls.
I want this world. I want to walk into
the ocean and feel it trying to drag me along
like I'm nothing but a broken bit of scratched glass,
and I want to resist it. I want to go
staggering and flailing my way
through the bars and back rooms,
through the gleaming hotels and the weedy
lots of abandoned sunflowers and the parks
where dogs are let off their leashes
in spite of the signs, where they sniff each
other and roll together in the grass, I want to
lie down somewhere and suffer for love until

it nearly kills me, and then I want to get up again
and put on that little black dress and wait
for you, yes you, to come over here
and get down on your knees and tell me
just how fucking good I look.

TOM PERROTTA

Joe College

∽◠◡◠∾

M Y CONCENTRATION WAS FURTHER DISRUPTED BY guilty thoughts of Cindy, whose calls I'd been dodging for the past several weeks. I knew we needed to talk, but I figured that if I avoided her long enough, she'd get tired of waiting and supply my half of the conversation on her own, thereby sparing me the unpleasantness of having to be the bad guy. She wasn't getting the message, though, and her persistence was starting to worry me.

Cindy was a girl from home. We hadn't moved in the same circles in high school, hadn't been well-enough acquainted even to sign each other's yearbooks. I had forgotten all about her until my first day of work the previous summer.

God knows I hadn't wanted to spend the summer riding shotgun in the Roach Coach, selling plastic-wrapped Danishes to tired-looking factory workers. I would much rather have been in Manhattan or Washington, D.C., interning for a magazine or a congressman, but nothing had come through that paid enough to make either plan even remotely plausible. In the end, it had come down to the Roach Coach or the forklift for me, and the Roach Coach at least offered the promise of novelty, as well as a boss who wasn't going to address me as "Joe College" and reserve the shit jobs especially for me.

I met her outside a small manufacturing plant in Union Village that looked like a scale model of our high school. I'd already made change for her dollar before I paid enough attention to her face to realize that I knew her.

"Cindy, right?"

She gave me back the same squinty look. I raised the bill of my baseball cap to help her out.

"Danny? What are you doing here?"

"Helping my dad."

"Dante's your father?"

I hesitated a second before saying yes, not because I was embarrassed or anything, but simply because it was hard for me to get used to hearing my father referred to as "Dante." Like me, he normally went by "Danny" or "Dan," but for some reason had decided to use his given name on the truck.

"He's a trip." She shook her head in cheerful reminiscence, as if she and my father were the ones who'd gone to school together.

I took a moment to really look at her. At Harding, she'd always just faded into the background, but out there, in that sunstruck Monday morning industrial nowhere land, she seemed mysteriously vivid, a person worth getting to know.

"Aren't you at Harvard or something?" she asked.

"Yale."

"Wow." She shook her head in sincere wonderment and glanced down at the coins in her hand. "I guess I don't have to count my change."

"You better," I told her. "I'm an English major."

CINDY WAS A RELIGIOUS COFFEE drinker and made it a point to stand on my line instead of my father's. From our brief exchanges, I learned that she worked full-time in the office of Re-Coil Industries, a company that manufactured a revolutionary kind of nylon hose for use in a highly specialized machine whose name she could never remember. During the school year, she took night classes in accounting and marketing at Kean College. She still hung out with her high school crowd, but said it was getting boring. She went to the gym whenever she could and was thinking about buying a new car.

At the beginning of the summer, my attraction to her was tainted by doubt and disapproval. I was dismayed by her hair, the outdated *Charlie's Angels* thing she was still doing with the curling iron and blow-dryer. She was big on pastels and had a weakness for matching culottes and blouses, an ensemble my mother referred to as a "short set." She chewed Juicy Fruit, painted her nails, and didn't skimp on the eye shadow. The girls I liked in college favored baggy sweaters and objected to makeup on political grounds. On special occasions they wore thrift-store dresses and cowboy boots. They didn't devote a lot of time to their nails, and a surprising number of them had mixed feelings about shaving their legs. I had the feeling they wouldn't have approved of Cindy.

As the weeks went by, though, my reservations began to crumble. Who was I to be a snob about hairstyles and nail polish? Maybe I went to Yale nine months of the year, but right now I was back home in New Jersey, spending my days speeding from one godforsaken industrial park to another in a truck with a cockroach painted on the front doors, trading stale quips about Jodie Foster with guys who wore their names on their shirts, and cultivating an impressive tan on the lower two thirds of my right arm. What did I care what the girls I went to school with—girls I hardly knew, from places like Park Avenue and Scarsdale and Bethesda and Newton and Buckhead and Sausalito and Saratoga Springs and Basel frigging Switzerland—what did I care what they would think about someone like Cindy, whom they were never going to lay eyes on or have a conversation with anyway?

I was lonely that summer, and her face lit up every time she saw me. She complimented me on my new glasses, asked what I did to stay in such good shape, made frequent comments about what a jerk her ex-boyfriend had been and how she hadn't had a date for the past eight months.

Sometimes she wore a tight denim dress that buttoned down the front, and she always smelled like she'd just stepped out of the shower. Even in that little candy-striped jumper I hated, you could see what a nice body she had, that she worked out but wasn't a fanatic about it, not like some of the girls I knew at school, girls who ran so much their bodies were just bones and angles. Cindy smiled a lot and had a distracting habit of touching me ever-so-lightly on the wrist as she talked, maintaining the contact for just so long, but not a fraction of a second longer. I'd spent my entire high school career pining for girls like her. Two years of college had changed me in a thousand ways, but not so much that I didn't get a little dizzy every time she uncapped her cherry Chapstick and ran it lovingly over her dry, puckered lips.

MY MOTHER HAD BEEN TELLING me all year that my father needed a rest, but I hadn't realized how badly he needed one until I'd spent a few weeks on the job. He looked like he'd aged ten years in a matter of months. He had indigestion from too much coffee, hemorrhoids from driving all day, and the haunted, jittery look of a fugitive from justice. He talked to himself more or less incessantly, often in a hostile tone of voice: "You idiot!" he'd say, slapping himself in the head the way they did on those V-8 commercials, "you forgot to refill the cup holders!" A slow driver in our path could trigger a rage in him that was frightening to behold, a teeth-grinding, horn-pressing, dashboard-pounding fury that made me thing he was just a couple of red lights away from a massive heart attack or a full-scale nervous breakdown.

It was painful to compare the frayed version of my father with the optimistic, rejuvenated man he'd been the summer before, the risk taker who'd chucked his job as assistant manager of a Pathmark and gone deep into debt to buy the lunch truck and route from a guy who was calling it quits after thirty years in the business. You could see how excited he was by the uncharacteristic boldness of his decision, how proud he was to finally be his own boss, to own a truck with his name on it. He spent entire weekend afternoons washing and polishing it in our driveway, making that black-and-silver lunch wagon shine. His high spirits manifested themselves in the very name of the truck, which had previously gone by the more prosaic moniker of Eddie's Breakmobile. If people were going to call you the Roach Coach anyway, he'd reasoned, why not beat them to the punch?

It wasn't hard to see what had defeated him. Running a lunch truck is grueling, thankless work, marked by long hours, low profit margins, and constant time pressures. If a company's coffee break is at 10:15, you'd better be out in the parking lot at 10:14, open for business. Nobody wants to hear about the traffic jam or the flat tire that held you up, though they're more than happy to give you an earful about the sludgy coffee or how you supposedly shorted them on the ham in yesterday's sandwich. It starts to grind you down after a while.

By late June I knew the ropes well enough for my father to start taking Fridays off, leaving my parents free to spend long weekends relaxing at their campground near the Delaware River. (They loved it there, though Camp Leisure-Tyme always struck me as a grim parody of the suburban life they were supposedly getting away from, trailers lined up one after the other like dominoes, all these middle-aged couples watching portable TVs inside their little screen houses.)

My first day in charge, hustling from one stop to the next, singlehandedly taking care of the customers we usually split between us, I carried in my mind a comforting image of my father crashed out on his hammock in the shade of a tall tree, empty beer cans littering the grass below. The following Monday, though, he confessed that he'd been a nervous wreck the whole day, unable to do anything but deal out one hand of solitaire after another, mechanically flipping the cards as he tormented himself with elaborate disaster scenarios involving me and his precious truck.

Cindy asked me out on a Friday morning in early August, the third day of what turned out to be the worst heat wave of the summer. It was only ten o'clock, but already the thermometer was well into the nineties. I felt wilted and cranky, having awakened at four in the morning in a puddle of my own sweat. She worked in an air-conditioned office, and I could almost feel the coolness radiating off her skin.

"Poor guy," she said. "Looks like you could use a cold one."

"A cold two or three sounds more like it."

"Why don't you come to the Stock Exchange tonight? A bunch of us hang out there after work on Fridays."

"I just might take you up on that."

"Great." She smiled as though she had a question for me, but then decided to keep it to herself. "I'll keep an eye out for you. Come anytime after six."

I drove through the day in a miserable heat daze, stopping every now and then to soak my head in the spray from someone's lawn sprinkler. When it was finally over, I took a shower and fell asleep on the living room couch for a couple of hours. It was close to eight by the time I finally made it to the restaurant, and Cindy was alone at the bar.

"I thought you stood me up," she said, not even bothering with hello.

"Where's everyone else?" I asked. "Wasn't there supposed to be a bunch of you?"

"They left about an hour ago. Jill's brother invited us to a party down the shore."

"You could have gone. It wasn't like we had a date or anything."

She nodded slowly, trying to look thoughtful instead of hurt.

"I see them all the time. I thought it might be nice to be with someone different for a change."

I climbed onto the stool next to hers and played a little drumroll on the bar, feeling unexpectedly calm and in control.

"It is nice. How come we didn't think of this a month ago?"

She reached down and squeezed my leg just above the knee. It was a ticklish spot, and I jumped in my seat.

"I've been waiting for this all summer," she said. "I can't believe you're really here."

I WOULDN'T HAVE PREDICTED IT, but Cindy turned out to be a talker. She drank three glasses of rosé with dinner and held forth on whatever popped into her head—her indecision about buying a car, her crush on

Bruce Springsteen, a bad experience she once had eating a lobster. She had so many opinions my head got tired from nodding in real or feigned agreement with them. She believed it was better to die in a hospice than a hospital and thought tollbooths should be abolished on the parkway. She disapproved of abortion, loved trashy novels, and was angered by the possibility that rich people might be able to freeze their bodies immediately after death, remaining in a state of suspended animation until a cure was found for whatever had killed them.

"It doesn't seem fair," she said. "When you're dead you should just be dead."

"That's right. It should be available to everyone or not at all."

"I want to travel," she blurted out. "I don't just want to rot around here for the rest of my life."

I looked up from my Mexi-burger, startled by the pleading in her voice. She smiled sheepishly.

"I don't know what's gotten into me. I'm not usually such a chatterbox. I hope I'm not boring you to death."

"Not at all. I'm happy to listen."

And I was, too, at least most of the time. Even when she recounted in minute detail a complex dispute her mother had had with the cable company, or tried to convince me that I needed to read *The Late, Great Planet Earth*, I still found myself diverted by the unexpectedness of Cindy and touched by her need for my approval. I wasn't used to thinking of myself as someone other people needed to impress. Until quite recently, in fact, I had generally felt the obligation moving in the opposite direction.

"Do I sound stupid to you?" she asked.

"What makes you think that?"

"I'm just going on and on. I'm not even sure if I'm making sense."

"It's nice," I said. "I'm having a good time."

She stuck one finger into her wineglass, stirring the pink liquid into a lazy whirlpool. Then she transferred her finger from the glass to her mouth, sucking contemplatively for a few seconds.

"You're sweet," she said finally, as if pronouncing a verdict. "You're sweet to even put up with me."

SHE DECIDED SHE WAS TOO tipsy to drive and happily accepted my offer of a ride home. We maneuvered our way through the crowded parking lot, bodies brushing together accidentally on purpose as we walked. It was still muggy, but the night had cooled down just enough to be merciful. I reached into my pocket and fished around for the keys.

"Oh my God," she said, grabbing me roughly by the wrist. "You're driving me home in this?"

I had spent so much of my summer in and around the Roach Coach I didn't really notice it anymore. But her startled laughter made me look at it as if for the first time: the gleaming silver storage compartment with its odd, quilted texture, the old-fashioned cab, the grinning cockroach on the passenger door, emblem of my father's rapidly fading dream. The roach was a friendly looking, spindly legged fellow, as much person as bug, walking more or less upright, with white gloves on his hands and white high-top sneakers on his feet. He seemed to be in a big hurry to get wherever it was he was going. DANTE'S ROACH COACH, said the bold yellow letters arching over his head. Beneath his feet, a caption read, COMIN' ATCHA!

"It's all I have," I said. "My parents took the station wagon to the campground. We can take your car if you want."

"That's okay," she said cheerfully. "How often does a girl get to ride in a lunch truck?"

I opened the door and helped her up into the cab. Then I circled around to the driver's side, climbing in beside her. An open box of Snickers bars rested on the seat between us, along with a parking ticket and a stack of coffee cups decorated with a Greek-column motif. Cindy helped herself to a candy bar. I started the truck.

"Kinda melted," she informed me, struggling with the taffylike strand of caramel produced by her first bite. "You should keep these things out of the sun."

FIVE MINUTES LATER WE PULLED up in front of her house. I shut off the ignition and headlights, turning to her with one of those dopey whatnow shrugs that was the best I could muster in the way of a suave opening gambit. She nodded yes, sliding toward me on the seat. I moved the candy bars and coffee cups on top of the dashboard, out of harm's way.

I hadn't been kissed all summer, and the first touch of her tongue on mine released me from a prison I hadn't even known I was in. All at once, the boundary between myself and the rest of the world disappeared; a sudden weightlessness took hold of me, as though I were no longer a body, just a mouth filled with tastes and sensations. For some unidentifiable period of time, I lost track of who and where I was.

When I could think again, my first thought was, *This is amazing!* My second was, *She's a secretary!* The thought was so jarring, so ridiculous and uncalled-for, it made me pull away in confusion. We sat there in the humid cab, separated by a distance of maybe a foot, breathing so hard we might as well have just delivered a refrigerator. She ran one hand through her formerly neat hair and looked at me as if I'd said something peculiar.

"What do you want?" she asked, her voice low and urgent.

"Want?" I said.

"Why are you even with me?"

Instead of answering—or maybe by way of answering—I kissed her again. This time it felt more like real life, two bodies, two separate agendas. I put my hand on her breast. She removed it. I groaned with disappointment and tried again, with the same result. Instead of backing off, though, she kissed me even harder, as if to reward my persistence. I wrenched my mouth away from hers.

"My parents are away for the weekend," I whispered. "We'd have the whole house to ourselves."

She ignored the invitation. Her face tightened into a squint of pained concentration.

"Tell me what it's like," she said.

I didn't bother to pretend I didn't know what she was talking about. In some strange way, we'd been talking about it all night.

"It's just college," I told her, leaning back against the door, trying to calm my breathing.

"How'd you get in?"

"I applied."

"Yeah, but—"

"I don't know," I said. "I did really good on the SATs. Much better than I expected."

This was my standard answer whenever anyone at home asked me how I'd gotten into Yale. It was easier to write it off as a fluke than to go into all the other stuff, the AP classes I'd taken, the papers I'd written for extra credit, the stupid clubs I'd joined just so I could list them on my application, all the nights I'd stayed up late reading books like *Moby Dick* and *The Magic Mountain* with a dictionary beside me, the endless lists of vocabulary words I'd memorized, the feeling I'd had ever since I was a little kid that I was headed out of town, on to bigger and better things.

"But it's hard, right? They give you a lot of homework?"

The word "homework" seemed jarring to me; it had dropped out of my vocabulary the day I graduated from high school.

"I didn't know what homework was," I admitted. "High school's a joke in comparison."

"It must be fun, though. Living in a dorm and everything."

"It's okay. The food's a little scary."

"I did really bad in high school," she said. "My mother was sick a lot. Then I got involved with this older guy. Before I knew it, the four years were gone and I hadn't really learned anything. Now I feel so stupid all the time."

"An older guy?" Just the phrase made me a little queasy.

"I was a cashier at Medi-Mart. He was one of the supervisors."

I remembered seeing her a lot at Medi-Mart back when we were in high school, thinking she seemed more at home behind the register than she did walking the halls of Harding.

"How long'd you go out?"

"Two years." She looked away; all the life seemed to have drained out of her. "He was married and everything. You must think I'm horrible."

I reached for her face, gently steering it in my direction. She was teary-eyed, but happy to be kissed again. This time I tried some new strategies, nibbling on her lips and licking up and down the salty length of her neck. Within minutes she was breathing in quick, trembly gasps, murmuring encouragement. When she seemed ready, I tried maneuvering her onto her back, but she went rigid, not resisting exactly, but certainly not cooperating.

"What's the matter?"

She gave me a glassy-eyed smile of incomprehension.

"Nothing."

"Are you sure?"

"I love this," she said, running her tongue around her chapped and swollen-looking lips. "I could kiss you forever."

THREE WEEKS LATER, I WAS starting to believe her. All we ever did was kiss. Nearly a month of heavy making out, and I hadn't even succeeded in getting my hand up her shirt. I couldn't figure out what I was doing wrong.

Other than that, we had a pretty good time together. Sometimes we went to the movies or out to dinner, but mainly we just shopped for cars. It was the consuming quest of her life. We read the stickers, quizzed the salesmen, took demos out for drives—Civics and Corollas, Escorts and Omnis, K-cars and Firebirds, Mustangs and Rabbits. But despite all our work, she seemed no closer to making a decision. New or used? Automatic or stick? Foreign or American? Hatchback or sedan? Every night we started from scratch. There was always another dealership, new variables to ponder. I started to wonder if she saw car shopping and kissing as ends in themselves—wholly satisfying, self-contained events—rather than starting points on the road to bigger things.

I think I would have lost patience with her a lot sooner if the end of the summer hadn't been looming over us from the start. Every day, in some process of withdrawal that was as subtle as it was relentless, I looked upon her less and less as my actual girlfriend and more and more as a potential anecdote, a puzzling and amusing story I would share with my roommates in one of those hilarious late-night conversations that I missed so much when I was away from college.

Cindy saw it differently. As I retreated, her attachment to me intensified. She hated the idea that I was just going to pack my bags and disappear, leaving her right where she was at the beginning of the summer. The average night ended with her in tears, me awkwardly trying to comfort her. Shyly at first, then more insistently, she began to explore the possibility of continuing our relationship after I returned to school. We could write and talk on the phone, couldn't we? I could come home for occasional weekends and vacations. It was do-able, wasn't it? Then she brought up the idea of visiting me in New Haven.

"It's not far, right? And I'll probably have my new car by then." I saw how excited she was by this prospect, and how hard she was trying not to show it. "It'll be really cool, don't you think?"

I didn't think it would be cool at all, but it seemed even more uncool to say so.

"Where would you sleep?" I asked, in a tone that suggested simple curiosity.

"Where would you want me to?" she asked, her excitement tempered by caution.

"What I want doesn't seem to matter."

"What do you mean?" Her voice was quiet now, a little defensive.

"What do you think I mean?"

"Tell me." Even in the darkness of the Roach Coach, I could see that she was getting ready to cry again. I hated it when she cried, hated how guilty it made me feel, and how manipulative she seemed in her misery.

"My parents are away," I told her. "We can do anything we want to. So why are we sitting here arguing about nothing?"

Something suddenly seemed very interesting to her outside the passenger window. I let her stare at it for as long as she needed to.

SHE CAME OVER THE FOLLOWING night. It happened to be the Saturday before I left for school, our last chance to take advantage of the empty house. She made the decision herself, after I made it clear that I wasn't much feeling like going anywhere.

I had everything ready when she arrived. Hall and Oates on the record player, Mateus in the refrigerator, candles in the bedroom. In my pocket I carried two Fourex lambskin condoms. (Fourex were my condoms of choice in those days. They came in little blue plastic capsules, which, though inconveniently bulky and difficult to open, seemed infinitely classier than the little foil pouches that housed less exotic rubbers. I used the brand for several years, right up to the day someone explained to me that "lambskin" was not, in fact, a euphemism.)

We drank a glass of wine and went upstairs. I lit the candles. We kissed for a while and started taking off our clothes. Her body was everything I'd hoped for, and I would have been ecstatic if Cindy hadn't seemed so subdued and defeated in her nakedness. She sat on the bed, knees drawn to her chest, and watched me fumble with my blue capsule, her expression suggesting resignation rather than arousal. Finally the top popped off.

"There!" I said, triumphantly producing the condom.

She watched with grim curiosity as I began unfurling it over the tip of my erection, which already seemed decidedly more tentative than it had just seconds earlier.

"This is all you wanted," she said. She stated it as a fact, not a question.

"Don't be ridiculous," I muttered. I found it hard enough to put on a condom in the best of circumstances, and almost impossible while conducting a serious conversation.

"I should've known," she said. "This is all it ever comes down to, isn't it?"

The condom was only halfway on, and I could feel the opportunity slipping away. I tried to save it with a speech, telling her that sex between two people who liked and respected each other was a natural and beautiful thing, a cause for celebration, and certainly nothing for anyone to be ashamed of, but by the time I got to that part the whole issue was moot anyway. I watched her blank gaze travel down to the deflated balloon dangling between my legs and then back up to my face.

"There," I told her. "You happy now?"

CRIS MAZZA

In Six Short Lessons

⌒〜⌒

1. Meet class

Who says meeting new people is difficult? Plenty of people will always need dog-training classes. Twenty students per class, four classes per week, roughly six sessions per year, that's 480 new people I've met this year. I would tell them about it in divorce therapy group, if I were still going—what a hostile crowd, glad I never opened my mouth.

2. Introduce the first cardinal rule: Never accept undesirable
behavior. Always reward only desirable behavior. Be 100%
consistent.

I'll have to tell them what happens when undesirable behavior is rewarded even if unintentionally. I have to give an example. The illustration I always use is when you attempt to get a dog to let go of a sock he's been chewing by trying to pull it out of his mouth: Dogs love tug-of-war; you're giving him a great time; his favorite reward is a great time; so you've taught him to never let you have anything he's got because you've been rewarding him for hanging on to it. One time I had enough courage to tell Derek I was going to use him as an example of this. Luckily he decided not to listen so I didn't elaborate. I could imagine it, though, calmly telling them that Derek thoroughly enjoyed each sweaty, aching, sometimes bloody, shattering moment— especially if I was fighting back, he loved it more. Maybe in a way I was being rewarded too: a dumpy girl like me with a guy like him? It should've been the same as every other time I've walked past a construction site, someone (this time Derek) shouts, "Hey, my friend here says you got nothing to offer!" Except this time I smiled at him. He looked so much like those advertisements where a job in a generic form of manual labor looks like a romantic, patriotic, religious experience: silhouetted guys in slow motion with showers of sparks behind them. He didn't have a pot gut, his hair was clean, his teeth were all there, his jeans fit, it was just around sunset. Halfway on my way to becoming a feminist lawyer and wound up married to an illiterate laborer. As though all the cardinal rules ceased to exist. Quit school when my nose was broken. His forehead in the dark. Didn't he say it was an accident? But he also took the closet door off its hinges, his voice coming from between clenched teeth, "That was the best yet," snarled into my ear, already full of blood running from my broken nose. Behavior rewarded will be behavior repeated. I can't count the number of times, the number of different ways I've said that. But with dogs some things are easier: Take a firm stand, be the alpha, the pack leader; then instead of winding up with a broken nose or a few loose teeth, you'll win his undying respect and loyalty. Maybe if I hadn't left school. Derek celebrated with a six-pack the night I quit. I stopped bothering to flinch. Didn't even duck. And look what that got me: Held a bottle of Sominex in one fist for three days after he packed some clothes in a grocery bag, called me a cold fish and moved out.

3. *The second cardinal rule: Expect your dog to behave properly.*
You'll almost always get exactly what you expect of your dog, if you work at it. If you expect it consistently. Ask them: Where else in life does that ever work? Don't wait for an answer. The first few weeks are more to retrain the people than their dogs. In six short weeks I try to teach these people how to live with their animals. Actually the animals had also better be learning to live with their people. One or the other will have to be broken.

Or I could say it this way: Expect what you know you'll get, you'll always get what you expect. Is that the same thing?

4. *How Dogs Learn*
Just like people, dogs have enough memory to avoid what is unpleasant and repeat only what is pleasant. Tell them to think of the things they've learned without realizing. I never go to double features anymore because of the headaches I used to get, even my old broken nose throbbed. And I've learned to hate certain foods; if I've ever thrown it up, I hate it. (I also got

nauseated once while doing yoga. Maybe it was because Derek had hit me in the solar plexus with a law book. I thought the lotus position would calm me down. I've never done any yoga since.) I love to play board games—complicated ones with lots of rules—but hate two-person-only games and hate to play with people who get silly and play wrong then say "It's only a game," or "Let's change the rules." Every time Derek missed a question in Trivial Pursuit, he tore the card in half. I never told him, but there were a few other things I didn't care for about him: he was fascinated by the sound of his tires burning rubber; he thought it was funny to make mooing noises at overweight girls; he wouldn't admit to being ticklish; he seemed to live by a rule that fast-n-loud is required in everything from music to cars to TV shows to eating. Aren't I better off? I'm always where I expect to be any time during the day. I always know what I'll be doing next. (I never suddenly find myself shoved face-first against a wall, breaking a tooth, one arm twisted behind my back.) The people I see and talk to are always those I expect to see and talk to. And they say the types of things you expect to hear. (Never "Get your ass back here, we're going to fuck.") I also know what to expect from these classes, so I don't know why I'm bothering to update my lesson plans. There's nothing new to say. I know every class will be the same grace-less people tripping over or being dragged around by their wolfish mongrels. Even the application forms are the same; when I ask if the dog is aggressive, I want to know if I'm going to get bitten, but half of them answer as though it's shameful to admit their dog *isn't* aggressive. They'll write, "We're working on it," or "Not enough, that's why I'm taking this class." This one will be no different.

5. *Praise your dog*

WEEK #2

1. *Review praise*

I always have to review this several times. Why am I still thinking about the guy who stayed after class last week to ask how to praise his dog. He has a silky black-and-white mongrel bitch named Tanya. I usually learn the dog names. (But guys like this one seldom have bitches and usually use names like Magnum or Corvet, Dinger, Suds or Max.) He waited patiently while some blowhard told me all the things his hippy-dog (neckkerchief) could do already, like open doors and fill his own water dish. The guy with the bitch was listening and I saw him smile. I'm not sure if he smiled because the blowhard was the kind of guy he'd like to listen to while having a beer in the parking lot at the beach, or if he was laughing because the blowhard was an asshole. I didn't care. I'd seen him smile during class at all my old built-in jokes. One of those flash-of-lightning smiles—electrical current and all— made me almost start to laugh when I looked at him, so I sputtered and choked while explaining leash corrections or how to control barking. Don't even remember what I was talking about, yet I can remember the smile in detail. And his dog sits there looking up at him the whole time—all through class and all the time he waited afterward to talk to me. Finally the blowhard left and the guy, Tanya's guy, said he needed advice about how to talk to his dog. His dog who obviously adores him. He said, "I was a Marine sharp-shooting instructor for ten years and I was trained to speak differently to different types of people. There's one way to talk to recruits, another way to speak to an officer, and, I know you won't like this, a different way to speak to a woman." Was he speaking to me in the way he'd learned to speak to a woman? Little Tanya just sat there gazing up at him, waving her tail slightly every time he glanced down at her. I could picture them together out at the shooting range, him squeezing off shots at a human-shaped cutout, the bitch licking his ear for every fatal hit.

He said, "So I don't really know the best way to talk to my dog. I guess I'm a little inhibited, but I want to make sure I communicate with her the right way. Do I have to talk in a high squealy voice?"

"Talk to her like you would talk to yourself," I said, which is (I didn't say) like thinking out loud—just be careful. A comment made to myself or the wall, but spoken carelessly in plural pronouns, "We should maybe do the laundry more often. It reeks." Later on or the next day—nothing on his face, no hint in his voice—Derek said, "Get outside and do your laundry." All of my dirty underwear scattered on the sidewalk and lawn in front of the apartment—and some were quite old with stains in the crotches—I've done the laundry once a week ever since.

Tanya gently stood and put her front feet on the guy's leg. He held her head for a moment and she shut her eyes. I said, "There's nothing wrong with your relationship with her, so you must be doing something right. She'll know when you're being phony, so don't be. Don't be a Marine when you talk to her."

He laughed, said thanks, and left. Maybe he'll stay after every class to ask something. But then he'll leave for good and never realize I occasionally think about his dusty, sweat-streaked face, nose-to-nose with a fuzzy-headed recruit, screaming "You stupid fucking asshole." And the flip side, in dress uniform and white gloves, holding a woman and drying her tears, saying something that seems uncharacteristic, like "I'll take care of you." Then the combination: field fatigues, dirt and sweat, oiled rifle; deep, ardent voice— not screaming—saying, "Don't worry about these fucking assholes, I won't let them hurt you."

Week #3

1. One more way to say what I've been saying all along: your dog doesn't care if he's the low man on the pecking order. All he wants is to know for sure. Be consistent in your treatment of him.

They should know this already after last week's demonstration of the alpha roll. Grabbed the biggest, huskiest male mutt, didn't even wait for him to display aggression—had him on his back before he could think, then strad-dled him, lowered my weight slowly over him, holding the skin on the sides of his face in both fists. We were motionless. Then I looked up. I looked up and our eyes immediately met, Tanya's guy. Maybe it was the position the dog and I were in, I remembered Derek's little motto: you can't fight city hall when you have your legs spread and city hall's on top. Yet even though you know it's wrong, you can't argue because you don't know how it could possi-bly be wrong. What is that different way Tanya's guy speaks to women? He stroked her back through the whole alpha demonstration. Maybe in ten years of sharpshooting, he never killed anyone, never pointed the gun at anyone—turned it into an artform, lovingly perfected, masculinely precise.

2. Getting the dog to come when called

This can be a big help if your dog is on the verge of getting into a fight. Once the fight starts, though, it's too late, no dog is going to turn tail and come back to his hysterical owner. I should know. In the middle of it, the phone rang—how I managed to answer it I'll never know (one arm must have been free somehow); it was Derek's boss. I don't know if his boss heard him say "Go to hell," the phone was already flying across the room, broke a mirror, lay there beeping and whining until it was all over.

Wouldn't this be a better lesson in class with a real illustration. Two dogs could get into it. The real thing, serious dog business, pull the leashes out of their frantic owners' hands. I always picture a dogfight as a twisting, upright tornado of two dogs and a powerful roar in the air. So it could happen in class, before anyone can move there's a cloud of dust and the blood-quickening sounds of a fight-to-the-death. Because of my insurance, I'll have to stop it, so I have to move in and get a hold of one (or both) by the skin on the backs of their necks. This, I know, is an incredibly stupid thing to try to do. But there's only one thing that can save me now: a soldier. Without a gun, he shields me, throws himself over me. But he's smart enough to realize even he can't stop the fight—all he does is get out of the middle. One of the dogs would eventually have enough and start to run, the other on his heels, the owners all giving chase. The class doesn't end nor is dismissed, it just disintegrates. So only he and I (and Tanya) are left in the dimly lit parking lot. He touches a wound on my arm, but there's nothing to say, so I still don't hear him speak to a woman.

It would seem a contradiction, though, since I saw him leave class last week in a battered yellow Subaru BRAT, stereo blaring, MARINES bumper sticker on the back. Tanya shared the front seat.

WEEK #4

It's more than half over. Still feels like it's waiting to start. He hasn't stayed after class to ask a question since that first time. When I say, "That's all for tonight unless you have questions," I see him head for the Subaru with Tanya just before I'm surrounded by the inevitable half-dozen with problems. During the times when I'm explaining something and the whole class gathers around, he wears glasses—not sunglasses. He takes them off during training activities. A Marine in glasses. It seems like I have to keep watching him so I can figure out what's so fascinating about it. Does he look at me that way because it's the way good Marines listen to instructions, or does he maybe want to talk to me differently than the way a Marine talks to an officer? Differently than the way he talks to just anyone. Except maybe Tanya.

What's on for tonight . . .

1. Rudiments of protection training
Teach your dog to bark at people outside the house. Have a friend walk around while you stay inside with the dog encouraging him to bark, barking with him, exciting him to bark.

Might be interesting if I hint or insinuate that there have been several burglaries in my neighborhood, or that I hear noises in the bushes at night, or there's a Peeping Tom. His shadow flickers outside my windows. It couldn't be Derek again; Derek doesn't know where I live anymore; I won't even mention Derek. Then I'll say, "In this instance you'd want a dog who knows what to bark at." I don't want anyone encouraging their dogs to attack. They may be friendly pets now but with the wrong handling could be turned into dangerous weapons. Then maybe after class Tanya's guy will stay with all the question-askers. As soon as one is satisfied and leaves, the others turn questioningly to each other to see who's next. Tanya's guy always indicates "you go next" and he continues to wait. When the last problem-digger, problem-chewer, problem-licker has finished trying to convince me their problem is impossible to solve—they don't want answers, they want me to agree nothing can be done—when they're all gone, Tanya's guy is still there to say, "No dogs to protect you?" Dogs aren't always enough. "Maybe I could stay with you tonight and scare him off," he'll say.

I should bring an airline crate to class tonight. Tanya will have to have one so she can ride in the bed of the Subaru when her guy gives me a ride home after my '64 Rambler finally chokes out a death rattle. Amazing that it lived this long—Derek got it for a couple hundred, took it apart three times, cursing at me because he said I didn't deserve my brand-new Toyota. A great day when he finally got the motorcycle he wanted so badly. I gave him the down payment. I only got one ride before he cracked it up; even helmetless he was unscratched, as though his skin—the same color all over—was protection enough, the beauty completely invulnerable, all that construction work and his hands still lovely. But the ruined motorcycle—I couldn't afford to replace it. My fault, he said, he'd had to buy such a cheap one. And I had only one ride. Maybe I'll remember it forever: Taking a turn without slowing down, leaning into it like one body, twenty miles later your heart's kicking you as though you ran the whole way. A ride in a Subaru can't be anything like that. But I wasn't given a choice. I'll let him kneel by the window all night with a rifle, although he never has to aim it at anything. In the morning we'll have to decide whether he should come to stand guard every night until the prowler returns. But maybe once will be enough.

Luckily I can teach this class by rote, just go on with saying the things I've said a thousand times before, hardly hear myself saying them.

WEEK #5

How far have we come? Looked around the class last week—they are actually improving. Big dogs sitting, waiting for a command; walking relaxed beside their owners on a loose lead; staying when told. But I don't remember teaching any of it—describing technique, giving individual help and advice, explaining canine learning patterns . . . when was I doing all that? I stand there talking, watching Tanya's guy fondle the inside of her ear with his thumb which makes her lean against him with her head tilted back, her legs relaxed, her belly showing, and I don't know what I've been talking about. Can't even pay attention to myself, I must not be a very good instructor. Derek used to say only assholes were teachers. I prefer to call myself a *trainer*. He thought I should get a job as a cocktail waitress so he and his friends could go out and not have to waste so much money on tips. Locked me out of the house when I was fired. Screamed out the window, "What kind of a worthless bitch can't even serve beer!" Said I was a snot, that I thought I was too good, a spoiled-little-rich-girl. So I gave him my Toyota for his birthday. I was left with the Rambler, but he never *gave* it to me. He said I'd gotten too much for Christmas and my birthday when I was younger, so it was his job to straighten me out by not giving me presents. Also called me a spoiled brat every time I suggested I could quit punching the cash register at Kmart and go back to school. There's nothing stopping me now from going back. Derek predicted I would. But maybe I'll do something he couldn't predict so easily. Join the Marines. Tanya's guy will talk to me like a recruit, our faces less than an inch apart as he screams about what a stupid-fucking-asshole-with-maggots-for-brains I am. I'll smell his skin—sweat and mud and canvas and gunpowder. My knees may weaken, but I'll stand stiffly at attention, maintaining that half-inch of space between us consistently from head to foot, quivering but not touching anywhere. Then after the formation has gone trotting double-time down the dusty road, after "chow," I'll come back to the range, alone, and he'll be there to lie beside me, show me how to aim the gun, put his cheek beside mine as I glare down the barrel. That's when he'll talk to me as a woman.

WEEK #6

1. Ask Tanya's guy where I could get a gun, could I borrow his?
I know how to find Derek. That little bar where I was a waitress for two weeks. Follow him home. He won't recognize the yellow Subaru trailing him. Derek steps out of the Toyota. His hair is a little longer, a little blonder. He hasn't shaved since yesterday morning. Tanya's guy is quiet and still beside me in the Subaru, parked across the street from Derek's apartment. Derek puts his six-pack under one arm and unlocks his mailbox. I'm moving

now—I know Derek won't pause to read the return addresses. The Subaru door blows open, I somersault out, like I learned . . . somewhere. Crawl on my belly across the asphalt, crouch behind the Toyota, set myself, brace the rifle over the fender. In my sights, his blue eye—but before firing, I shout. I want him to know it's me. I want to see his eyes terrified.

Derek screams like a girl and runs into the bushes, thrashing around, the mail like large white snowflakes on the lawn. I'm still shouting. I don't know what I'm shouting, just my voice, harsh and wild. Mid-word, I'm hit from behind, slamming my gut and chest into the car's fender, the gun flies out of my hand, skids over the car's hood and rattles into the gutter while I am wrestled to the street, Tanya's guy smothering me between himself and the pavement, the force of his body all over me, and the force of his voice, talking to me like he would talk to himself, "No, no, no, no . . ." But I'll have to fight him off so I can run to Derek, to hold him until he's no longer trembling, stroke his hair and mumble so low that the only way he can hear me is through his ear pressed against my chest. Tanya's guy is watching, holding the gun, muzzle to the ground, and our eyes meet. Which one should I love, since both are neither real nor imaginary?

WEEK #7

Graduation
After I hand him his little certificate and he smiles without really looking at me, not even wearing his glasses, and he starts to walk away with Tanya swishing her fanny—maybe like an unanticipated gunshot, like sniper fire, I'll call out his name, which I don't even know.

GREGORY CORSO

Hair

My beautiful hair is dead
Now I am the rawhead
O when I look in the mirror
the bald I see is balder still
When I sleep the sleep I sleep
is not at will
And when I dream I dream children waving goodbye—
It was lovely hair once
it was
Hours before shop windows   gum-machine mirrors   with great
   combs

pockets filled with jars of lanolin
Washed hair I hated
With dirt the waves came easier and stayed
Yet nothing would rid me of dandruff
Vitalis Lucky-Tiger Wildroot Brilliantine   nothing—
To lie in bed and be hairless is a blunder only God could allow—
The bumps on my head—I wouldn't mind being bald
if the bumps on my head made people sorry—
Careless God! Now how can old ladies cookie me?
How to stand thunderous on an English cliff
a hectic Heathcliff?
O my lovely stained-glass hair is dry   dark   invisible
not there!
Sun! it is you who are to blame!
And to think I once held my hair to you
like a rich proud silk merchant—
Bald! I'm bald!

Best now to get a pipe
and forget girls.

Subways take me one of your own
seat me anybody
let me off any station anyman
What use my walking up Fifth Ave.
or going to theatre for intermission
or standing in front of girls schools
when there is nothing left for me to show—
Wrestlers are bald
And though I'm thin O God give me chance now to wrestle
or even be a Greek wrestler with a bad heart
and make that heart make me sweat
—my head swathed in towels in an old locker room
that I speak good English before I die—
Barbers are murdered in the night!
Razors and scissors are left in rain!
No hairdresser dare scheme a new shampoo!
No premature hair on the babe's pubis!
Wigmaker! help me! my fingernails are knived in your door!
I want a wig of winter's vast network!
A beard of hogs snouting acorns!
Samson bear with me! Just a moustache
and I'd surmount governance over Borneo!
O even a nose hair, an ingrown hair,
and I'd tread beauty a wicked foot, ah victory!
Useless   useless
I must move away from sun
Live elsewhere
—a bald body dressed in old lady cloth.
O the fuzzy wuzzy grief!
Mercy, wreathed this coldly lonely head a crowning glory!
I stand in darkness
weeping to angels washing their oceans of hair.
There goes my hair! shackled to a clumping wind!

Come back, hair, come back!
I want to grow sideburns!

I want to wash you, comb you, sun you, love you!
as I ran from you wild before—
I thought surely this nineteen hundred and fifty nine of now
that I need no longer bite my fingernails
but have handsome gray hair
to show how profoundly nervous I am.

Damned be hair!
Hair that must be plucked from soup!
Hair that clogs the bathtub!
Hair that costs a dollar fifty to be murdered!
Disgusting hair! eater of peroxide! dye! sand!
Monks and their bagel heads!
Ancient Egypt and their mops!
Negroes and their stocking caps!
Armies! Universities! Industries! and their branded crews!
Antoinette Du Barry Pompadour and their platinum cakes!
Veronica Lake   Truman Capote   Ishka Bibble   Messiahs   Paganinis
Bohemians   Hawaiians   poodles

Richard Russo

The Farther You Go

I'VE CUT ONLY A COUPLE OF SWATHS when I have to shut the damn thing down because of the pain. It's not dagger pain, but deep, rumbling, nausea pain, the sort that seems to radiate in waves from the center of my being. There are those who think that a man's phallus *is* the center of his being, but I have not been among them until now.

From inside the house Faye heard me shut off the mower, and now she's come out onto the deck to see why. She shades her eyes with a small hand, scout fashion, to see me better, though the sun is behind her. Ours is a large yard and I'm a long way off. "What's wrong?" she calls.

I'd like to tell her. It's a question she's asked on and off for thirty years, and just once I'd like to answer it. *My dick is throbbing*, I'd like to call out, and if we had any neighbors within hearing, I believe I would, so help me. But to prevent that we've bought two adjacent lots. Regrets? I've had a few. I mow their yards and my own.

"Nothing," I call to Faye. It's my standard line. Nothing is wrong. Go ahead, just try to find something that's wrong. If something were wrong, I constantly assure her, I'd say so, always amazed at how readily this lie springs to my lips. I've never in my life told her when anything was wrong, and I have no intention of telling her about my throbbing groin now. She already spent a thousand dollars we didn't really have on a riding mower simply because the doctor insisted I not "overdo it" so soon after the operation. It didn't occur to her that for a man recovering from prostate surgery, sitting on top of a vibrating engine might not be preferable to gently guiding a self-propelled mower. I can hardly blame her for this failure of imagination, since it didn't occur to me either until I was aboard and in gear.

I start up the mower again and cut a long loop back to the base of the deck, stopping directly below her and turning the engine off for good.

"You're finished?"

"You can't tell?" I say, looking back over the yard. I appear to have cut a warning track around a fenceless outfield, and am now sitting on home plate.

"Why are you perspiring?"

It's true. There is autumn in the air, and no reason whatsoever to be sweating, cast about as I might. "It's a beauty," I say, slapping the steering wheel affectionately. "Worth every penny. How much was it again?"

"I just got off the phone with Julie," she says.

This does not sound good to me. Our daughter seldom calls without a reason. She and her husband, Russell, owe us too much money to enjoy casual conversation. They're building a house half a mile up the road from our own. "Where?" I asked last year after Faye broke the news that they'd purchased a lot. "Here? In Connecticut? In *Durham*?" I was certain that some kind of trust had been violated. Could it be that we'd loaned them the money without a distance clause in the contract? We'd been prudent enough to ensure against neighbors on either side, but we were so focused on the threat of strangers that we failed to take family into account. Another failure of imagination.

Faye bends over the railing and holds out a delicate hand for me—half grateful, half suspicious—to take. "I know this is the last thing in the world you need, but I think you should go over there. Today," she adds, in case there's a shred of doubt in my mind that whatever this is about, it's serious.

"What," I say.

Now that she has my attention, she seems reluctant to do anything with it. She's looking for the right way to say it, and there is no right way. I can tell that much by looking at her.

"Julie says . . . Russell hit her."

I am shocked, though I've known for some time that their marriage was in trouble. To make matters worse, Russell has recently quit a good job for what he thought would be a better one, only to find that several large loans needed to start up the project he's to direct have not, as promised, been approved. It could be weeks, he admits. Months.

"I'm not sure I believe Russell would hit Julie," I tell Faye.

"I do," she says in a way that makes me believe it too. When my wife is dead sure, she's seldom wrong, except where I'm concerned.

"What am *I* supposed to do? Hit *him*?"

"She just wants to see you."

"I'm right here."

"She thinks you'll be angry."

"I *am* angry."

"No, that she didn't come to see you in the hospital. She feels guilty."

"She didn't know I'd be grateful?"

"She thought you'd be hurt. Like you were. Like I was."

"Thirty years we've been married and you still confuse me with yourself," I tell her. "I didn't want Julie at the hospital. I didn't want *you* at the hospital. Heart surgery would've been a different story."

"There are times I think you could use heart surgery. A transplant, maybe. This is our daughter we're talking about."

"One of our daughters," I correct her. "The other one is fine. So's our son."

"So is Julie."

I would like to believe her, but I'm not so sure. Before the wedding, I'd wanted to take Russell aside and ask him if he knew what he was doing. In time Julie might turn out fine, as well as the other two, but she somehow wasn't quite ripe yet. Not for the colleges she'd been in and out of. Not for a husband. Not for adult life.

As I am not ripe for intervention. My daughter may not be an adult, but she's acting like one—getting married, having houses built, borrowing money. And I don't, on general principle, like the idea of trespassing once people have slept together, because they know things about each other that you can't, and if you think you're ever going to understand what's eating them, you're a fool, even if one of them happens to be your own daughter. Especially if one of them happens to be your own daughter.

"We cannot tolerate physical abuse," Faye says. "You know I'm fond of Russell, and it may not be all his fault, but if they're out of control, we have to do something. We could end up wishing we had."

I would still like to debate the point. Even as Faye has been speaking, I've been marshaling semivalid reasons for butting out of our daughter's marriage. There are half a dozen pretty good ones, but I'd be wasting my breath.

"Julie thinks they should separate. For a while, anyway," Faye says. "That makes sense to me. She wants to insist, and she wants you to be there."

I'm not thinking of Julie now but of my own parents. If I want your help, I'll call you in, I remember telling my father during the early days of my own marriage when we had no money and things seemed worse than they really were. Maybe it's that way with Julie and Russell. Maybe things seem worse than they are. I wish for that to be the case, almost as fervently as I wish I hadn't been called in. But I have been.

I start out on foot, explaining to Faye the exercise will do me good, though in truth I just don't want to sit on top of another motor. Julie and Russell's house is only a half mile up the road, and up until the operation I'd been running two miles a day—usually in the opposite direction. Seeing their house rise up out of the ground has been an unsettling experience, though for some time it did not occur to me why, even when I saw the frame. Only when the two decks were complete—front and back—did it dawn on me why they'd wanted to use my contractor. My daughter is building my house.

"Well of course they are," Faye said when I voiced this suspicion. "You should be flattered."

"I should?" I said, wondering exactly when it was that I'd stopped being the one who saw things first. "Theft being the sincerest form of flattery. Besides, they're a mile away. It's not like people are going to think it's a subdivision."

"Half a mile," I said. "And what bothers me is that Julie would *want* to build our house."

Their mission tile is already visible, but halfway up the hill I have to stop and let the nausea pass. Off to the side of the road there's a big flat rock that looks like a feather bed, so I go over and stretch out. It takes every bit of willpower I can muster not to unzip and check things out. Instead, I lie still and watch the moving sky. When I finally stand up again, I'm not sure I can make it the rest of the way, though this is the same hill I was running up a few months ago when I was fifty-one. Now I'm fifty-two and scared that maybe I won't be running up that many more hills. The doctors have told me they got what they were after, but I'm aware of just how little the same assurances meant in my father's case. After the chemotherapy, they sent him home with a clean bill of health and he was dead in two months.

Nevertheless, I do make the top of the hill. Up close, the house looks like a parody, but that's not Julie and Russell's fault. They simply ran out of money—their own, ours, the bank's. The grounds aren't landscaped and the winding drive is unpaved. There are patches of grass and larger patches of dirt. Not wanting to ring the doorbell, I go around back, hoping to catch sight of Julie in the kitchen. I want to talk to her first, before Russell, though I have no idea what I will say. I'm hoping that in the past half hour she will have changed her mind about inviting me into their lives. Maybe I'll see her at the window and she'll flash me a sign. I'm willing to interpret almost any gesture as meaning that I should go straight back home.

Around back, I remember there are no steps up to the deck, which is uniformly three feet off the ground on all sides. I'm looking around for a makeshift ladder when Julie comes out onto the deck, sliding the glass door shut behind her. Except for not knowing how I might join her up there, my plan seems to be working.

"I didn't think you were coming," she says.

"Hand me one of those deck chairs," I tell her.

She does, and I step up onto it. When she offers a hand, I take that too, putting my other one on the rail to heave myself up. Julie is wearing a peasant blouse, and when she leans over I see that she is wearing no brassiere. There have been other times when, against my will, I have been subjected to the sight of my daughter's bare breasts, and I wonder if this casual attitude of hers might be one of the problems she has with Russell. He might not like the idea of his friends becoming so intimately acquainted with her person over the onion dip. According to Faye, Karen, our oldest, has always kept one lone brassiere handy around the house for our visits. There is much to be said for hypocrisy.

"He's asleep on the sofa," Julie says. "Neither of us slept much last night. He finally zonked." She smiles weakly, and when she turns full-face, I get a better view of her eye, which sports a mouse. The cheek beneath is swollen, but so is the other, perhaps from crying. Her complexion, which a year ago had finally begun to clear up, is bad again. Then, suddenly, she's in my arms and I can't think about anything but the fact that she is my daughter. If I'm not going to be much good at blaming Russell, at least I'm certain where my loyalties must be, where they have always been.

Finally, she snuffs her nose and steps back. "I've gotten some of his things together. He can pack them himself."

"You're sure about this?"

"I know I should be the one to tell him—"

"But you want me to," I finish for her. "Stay out here then."

She promises, snuffs again. I go in through the sliding door.

I know right where to find Russell. It's my house they're living in, after all, and their sofa is right where ours is. Russell, in jeans and a sweatshirt, is sitting up and rubbing his eyes when I come in. Oddly enough, he looks glad to see me.

"Hank," he says. "You don't look so hot."

"You're the first to notice," I tell him. He wants to shake hands and I see no reason not to.

"I shouldn't be sleeping in the daytime," he says, with what sounds like real guilt.

Or punching my daughter, I consider saying. But there's no need, because it's beginning to dawn on him that my unexpected appearance in his living room is not mere happenstance. He peers out through the kitchen window. Only Julie's blond head is visible on the deck outside.

"So," he says, "you're here to read me the riot act."

"Russell," I say, suddenly aware of how absurd this situation is. "I'm here to run you out of town."

"What do you mean?"

"I mean I'm going to give you a lift to the airport."

"You can't mean that."

"Russell, I do."

A car pulls up outside, and we both look to see who it is, probably because whoever it is will upset the balance of our conflict. One of us will have an ally. I do not expect it to be Faye, but that's who it is, and when Russell sees this, his face falls, as if my wife's mere presence has convinced him that I am fully vested and authorized to banish him from his own property.

When Faye rings the bell, I open the door and tell her to go around back and join Julie. She wants to know how things are going. I say I just got here. How could I have just got here, she wants to know. I tell her to go around back.

"This is nuts," Russell says.

There's nothing to do but agree, so I do, and then I tell him that Julie has gathered a few of his belongings and he should get packing. Russell looks like he can't decide whether to cry or fly into a rage, but to my surprise he does as he's told.

Once he's gone off down the hall, I realize that with Julie and Faye out back, I have no one to talk to and nothing to do. It seems wrong to turn on the TV or browse through their books. I can hear Russell in the closet of one of their bedrooms, and I figure he's looking for either a suitcase or a gun. I sit down to wait, then remember something and get up. Julie has helped her mother up onto the deck and is crying again. I study the pair of them before stepping back outside. From the rear they look remarkably similar, almost like sisters. I look for something of myself in Julie and find precious little. When Faye notices me standing there at the window, I join them on the deck.

"How much do you have in your checking account?" I ask our daughter.

She blinks.

"How much?" I say.

"Not a lot," she says. "There's never much. A couple hundred dollars maybe."

"Write me a check," I say. "I'll take him to the airport."

"You want me to pay for it?" Julie says.

"You want *me* to?"

"Hank—" Faye starts.

But I'm not about to budge on this one. I'll loan her money later, or give it to her if I have to, but if she wants Russell on a plane, she's going to experience at least the appearance of paying for it. Julie fetches the checkbook from the drawer in the kitchen. Though she hates the idea, she writes the check anyway. I look it over, then slip it in my pocket.

"He's at the bedroom window, staring at us," Julie whispers. "Don't look."

I don't intend to.

IT'S FORTY-FIVE MINUTES TO BRADLEY International. I tell Russell to take it easy. After all, it's not like we're trying to catch any particular flight. Where I will send Russell is one of the many things we have not discussed. Why he has struck my daughter is another. More than anything, I'm afraid he'll tell me what's wrong with my daughter, and why their lives together went wrong.

I know too much already. Knew, in fact, as soon as I saw my house taking shape on their lot, knowing that this wasn't Russell's idea, that if Russell had his way they'd be living in New Haven in an apartment, spending their money in restaurants, on the occasional train into New York, the theater, maybe, or a cruise around the island. The sort of things you have a ticket stub to show for when you're finished. It would take him a decade or so to want something more permanent, and even then it would be against his better instincts. He didn't need a house right now and he certainly didn't need a replica of mine. When we drove away, he hadn't even looked back at it.

I know all this better than he does. He probably imagines that whatever it is that's between him and Julie is more immediate. He may even think he's a bad lover or a bad person. I doubt he likes what he's thinking as the Connecticut countryside flies by and recedes behind us liked a welshed promise. I'd asked if he minded driving, and he said why should he. Why indeed? It's his car.

"It's funny," he finally says when we hit I-91.

"Please, Russell," I beg him. "Don't tell me what's funny."

"Why not?"

"Because it won't be."

"What's funny is . . . I'm relieved."

"See what I mean?"

"No, seriously," he says. I suspect he doesn't know what serious means, though he's learning. "Ever since last night I've been trying to figure out some way to punish myself. Now I can leave the whole thing in your capable hands. You're about the most capable man I've ever known, Hank. I don't mind saying it's been a bitch competing with you."

I can't think what to say to this, but I have to admit, now that I've heard him out, that it *is* funny. "I hope you won't misconstrue my running you out of town as not liking you, Russell."

We both smile at that.

"Were you and Faye ever unhappy?" he asks.

"Together or separately?"

"Together."

"Sure."

He thinks about this for a minute. "I bet that's not true," he says. "I bet you're just saying it for one of your famous philosophical reasons, like happiness just isn't in the cards for human beings, the sort of thing guys like you say to college students in your late afternoon classes before you go home and spend a happy evening in front of the television."

There is a curious mixture of wisdom and naïveté in this observation, and it makes me even sadder to be putting Russell on a plane. "Julie always says that's what she had in mind for us. To be as happy as you guys."

Once again I am aghast at how little my daughter knows me, at what a desert her imagination must be. What does she see when she looks at me? When I look at myself, the evidence is everywhere. I know now why she didn't come to see me at the hospital. It was the nature of my operation. It wasn't that she couldn't imagine me with cancer. She couldn't imagine me with a dick. That I am a man has somehow escaped her, which is why she doesn't think twice about bending over in front of me in her peasant blouse. And maybe it's even worse than that. If she has never thought of her father as a man, can she imagine herself as a woman?

Russell's car rides smoothly enough, but like most small Japanese models there is a low-level vibration that comes from being close to the earth and the buzzing engine. When the nausea I felt atop the lawn mower returns, I close my eyes and will it away, hoping that Russell will conclude I've fallen asleep.

"The good thing is I know now that I can't make her happy. That's what hitting her meant, I think. It was what I was thinking when I hit her. That I'd never make her happy. It pissed me off, because I always thought that was something I *could* do."

"You're very young, Russell," I tell him.

For some reason this observation also pisses him off and he looks over as if he's thinking about hitting *me*. "You can be one cold son of a bitch, you know that, Hank? You're just the kind of guy who'd kick a man out of his own house, take him to the airport in his own car, put him on a plane, and figure he had a right to. The only reason I'm going along with this shit is because you look half dead. One little poke in the stones and I could leave you alongside the road for the undertaker."

"There," I say after a respectful moment of silence. "I guess you told me."

BRADLEY IS CROWDED, SO WE have to take the shuttle from a distant parking lot to the terminal. Then we walk a little and I begin to feel better again, waiting in line at the ticket counter, Russell behind me with his two suitcases.

When it's my turn, an earnest young woman wants to know how she may serve me. How do people keep such straight faces, I wonder. "Where can you go for two hundred dollars?" I ask her. "One way."

"Sir?"

I repeat my question.

"Lots of places. Boston. New York. Philadelphia . . ."

"Nothing west of the Mississippi?" Russell asks.

She shakes her pretty head. The farther you go, the more expensive it gets. Such is life, she seems to imply.

"Tough luck, Hank," Russell says.

"How about Pittsburgh?" I suggest, noticing that a flight's leaving in half an hour. I think of a woman I know who lives there, or did once. We met at a convention a dozen or so years into my marriage. My one infidelity. She had recently been divorced, and we made love more or less constantly for three days. Then she returned to Pittsburgh as I did to Faye, and I'd never heard from her again. For several years I stopped going to academic conventions, afraid that she would be there and I would prove faithless a critical second time. Lately, though I feel no real desire for her, she's been on my mind.

"Pittsburgh." Russell shrugs. "Why not."

There are only twenty-five minutes to departure, so we head for the gate.

"You can split if you like," Russell says. "You have my word I'll get on the plane."

In fact, I don't trust him. In his shoes, I would not get on the plane. Or maybe I'd get on and then off again, circling back to the departure lounge to watch whoever was seeing me off wave as the plane taxis down the runway. No, I intend to see him onto the plane, and then see it airborne. After that, if he wants to get off it's his business.

Blessedly, the gate is not far. I'm not looking forward to driving back home. I almost asked Faye to come with us, but that would've left Julie home alone. It occurs to me it's not just the drive I'm dreading.

"When you get there," I say, facing Russell, "let me know how to contact you. We'll need your signature to get you and Julie out from under the house."

"Sometimes I think it's the house that killed us," he admits without much conviction, as if it's one of a dozen equally plausible explanations he's considered in the last twenty-four hours.

"At least you don't have to go back to it," I say.

He gives a rueful laugh, then turns somber. "I wish you'd let me take the car," he says suddenly. "It's really not fair that I should end up in a strange city and not even have a way of looking for a job. I mean, I've been a shit and everything, but—"

In truth, I hadn't thought of this. Failures of imagination abound. And now that he's brought the unfairness of it to my attention, I know I can't put him on that plane.

"I swear to Christ," he says. "If you let me take my car, I'll go far away. Farther than Pittsburgh."

Right now, he seems about the most generous person I've ever known. After all, he doesn't need my permission. The keys I'm holding are his keys. They fit the ignition to his car. Only a combination of generosity and scalding guilt can account for the fact that he hasn't put up a fuss. By hitting Julie he has unmanned himself, losing everything but kindness. And I am suddenly sure he'll do as he says.

A voice comes over the intercom announcing that those needing assistance will be boarded first, then passengers traveling with small children. I hand Russell his keys.

"I didn't mean that about you being a cold son of a bitch, Hank," he says as we start back to the terminal.

"And you'd never poke me in the stones," I add, smiling.

At the sliding doors we shake hands, and I watch him lug his two suitcases across the huge parking lot. I don't feel too bad about him. Almost anyplace he ends up will be better than where he is now.

I'm left standing there holding an airline ticket to Pittsburgh that will need to be cashed in. Then I'll have to call Faye and admit to her what I've done. She will have to come collect me. It seems too much to ask—of either of us, so instead I head back to the gate. I arrive just in time to see the Pittsburgh flight airborne. "You're too late," says a young man in an official airline blazer.

"I guess so," I tell him. In fact there's no doubt about it. Odds are that she's no longer in Pittsburgh. She's probably married again by now, not that it matters, really. I only wanted to see her at some restaurant with half-moon booths where I might tell her about my surgery. For some reason I'm convinced that my brush with mortality would matter to her, and that I'd feel better after confessing to someone that I fear the nausea, that I consider it prophetic, a sign that some terrible malignancy remains. I remember her body and the way we made love, and I guess I was hoping that she would remember my body too. Maybe she would be afraid for me in the way I want someone to be afraid.

Back in the terminal I feed coins into the pay phone, dial, and let it ring a dozen times before hanging up and trying Julie's number, which does the same thing. I'm too tired to be sure what this means. Probably Faye has given our daughter a sedative. Perhaps I have caught my wife in transit between houses. I wait a few minutes and try my house again, wondering if I've forgotten our number.

Whoever I'm dialing is not home. I go outside onto the terminal ramp and am about to ask a taxi driver how much it would cost to take me to Durham when Faye pulls up right in front of me, so I get in.

"I got to thinking about it," she says, "and realized you'd give him the car."

I just look at her, wondering if she might also have intuited that I just missed getting on a plane to Pittsburgh, that I had a lover fifteen long years ago who I want to tell things I can't tell my wife.

"You think I don't know you after thirty years?" she says, as if in answer to my unspoken question.

"Not intimately," I tell her.

"Hurry up and mend then," she says.

Night is coming and most of the trip back will be in the dark, but the car is warm and there will be no harm if I fall asleep. Faye knows how to get us home.

MARY CAPONEGRO

The Star Café

⌒⌒⌒

C AROL HEARD A NOISE AS SHE undressed for bed; it frightened her—she'd actually been half undressing for bed and half searching for the book she had intended to read in bed, but after she heard the noise she was only a third involved with each of these tasks and a third involved in trying to figure out where the noise had come from—though of course these things could not be measured like sugar or flour; in fact, it would be more than a third of trying to determine the source of the sound anyway, because there was fear attached to that fraction, and fear has a way of dispossessing its neighbors. Carol checked the living room, bathroom and kitchen, and found nothing out of order.

The sound seemed to have come from below her apartment; the more she thought about it the more right that seemed, and since she couldn't stop worrying about it, she went back into the bedroom and slipped into the skirt she'd just taken off, rebuttoned the blouse she'd never gotten around to removing, was thankful she hadn't yet taken off underwear, considered putting back on her shoes but rejected that idea, and walked into the living room again, toward the door.

As she was undoing the latch, she saw on the small table between door and sofa the book she'd been looking for; it must have been there all along. She picked it up so as not to misplace it again, and opened the door. On the landing she heard the noise a second time. Though she'd been expecting it, it startled her anew, so much so that she dropped the book, then watched it tumble to the second-to-last step.

The hallway was dark and the darkness had intensified the sound. It was dark because the light switch was located on the wall opposite the banister at the bottom of the stairs, and she hadn't gotten there yet because she'd been interrupted by the sound; she was still standing there at fearful attention, like a deer with a flashlight shining in its eyes, as if stillness were some kind of defense instead of vulnerability.

Carol wondered why there wasn't a switch at the top landing as well as at the bottom. Perhaps the architect was biased toward those ascending? Or would it be the electrician? She knew so little about these practical matters; she knew so little about this building she lived in. If she had to guess when it had been built, she might have erred in the region of decades rather than single years. What she did know was that there was far too little light for a building with so many windows, all located on its tree-blocked western exposure.

The noise had stopped but Carol couldn't get it out of her head. It seemed to become clearer rather than less clear in proportion to time elapsed since its occurrence. But how could someone really know if the hold she had on what had been heard or seen or felt was really becoming clearer, that is, truer, or more distorted? Was intensity a proper gauge? Wasn't it often the case that those who felt most enlightened were in fact most deluded?

Then she heard it again, not memory or imagination. It had to be coming from somewhere downstairs, and she had to go downstairs, if only to retrieve her book, so she slowly descended, thinking that it was really the simplest sound, so why so difficult to characterize? It only seemed eerie because she didn't know the source, she kept telling herself.

When she reached the bottom of the staircase, Carol stood a moment, then sat down on the penultimate step, next to her book, listening to the sound that still hadn't stopped—its duration was the longest of the three occurrences—trying to get up the courage to go open the door that led to the little restaurant she'd lived above for all these months but never entered. The mixture of curiosity and fright had led her this far, she could hardly give up now; the noise might stop again any second and then it would be harder to trace. She walked down the hall and stood against the door with her hand curled on the knob, as if she were holding a piece of fruit still attached to a branch.

She placed the sound the instant she opened the door. The first time she heard it she should have known what it was. Who would have thought an innocent little blender—well, not so little, really, larger, in fact, than any she'd ever seen; she guessed it could hold several gallons—but who would have thought it could make such a queer noise, an innocent if somewhat oversized blender, making what looked like banana daiquiris? She giggled, and suddenly realized she wasn't alone, that she was being scrutinized by a man—a waiter?—more likely the owner, an extremely handsome man in all the conventional ways: dark and tall, both noble and rugged. He switched off the mighty appliance, poured a fraction of its contents into a long-stemmed glass, held that out to her and smiled.

"Hello, Carol," he said.

She was so relieved by the release of all that tension that she suddenly wanted, urgently, to talk to him, though it could have been to anyone, any sympathetic ear into which she could expel what had been building up inside her. She found herself babbling about how pleased she was to have the mystery solved; she was glad it was only that. He listened attentively, but rarely responded. Perhaps she didn't give him much chance.

He was looking at her intently from behind the counter, and when she felt too uncomfortable to confront his gaze directly she stared at the travel posters that adorned the wall behind him. She must have imagined that his eyes were unusually bright; it was her weariness, it was the candlelight, but for some reason she felt compelled. She was telling him all these things about herself, all the silly thoughts, the things about the architect and the light fixture, how they'd been so long next door to each other and never known each other better, and really she'd never done anything like this before but she was letting him hold her; first he had held her hand and then suddenly she was in his arms, he was murmuring softly, "yes, yes," consoling her, reassuring her, stroking her hair, and then other parts of her, and before she knew it she found herself in bed with him, in the back room, which was not so sordid as it might sound. There was a bed and all the accoutrements of civilized sexuality, of comfort; it wasn't after all a closet, but she wondered what he would do if a customer came in, and then she began to wonder why there weren't customers out there. There hadn't been any when she came in, nor all the time they'd been, or she'd been, talking; she'd run on so about up and down the stairs and light; she'd been overwhelmed, full of herself in a way quite foreign to her, though there was also the sense that she was acting out a role that came very naturally, almost as if she'd rehearsed it, and she wondered if all this was the thing people always meant by the term "attraction," "I'm so attracted to you," as if people were magnets, which would be at least somewhat specific, or if she was just needy because of the fright, and lonely, lonely for a long time now, which would be at least not entirely, merely physical.

In either case she wasn't proud of herself; it was strange to be in bed with a man she barely knew, though in those minutes of talking it seemed there was some intense acquaintanceship occurring. It was strange to be in bed with someone at all, she'd been alone so long, almost out of habit; the "with" of "in bed with" was the important part of the construction, to be in the presence of another human being, because the sex came naturally enough; the angels never really withheld that.

Awkwardness granted, the motions materialized, to such a degree, in fact, that she felt she was experiencing far more than just going through them. She couldn't remember such satisfying sex; was it just the novelty? But everything clicked. She felt that they'd held each other's bodies for years and every gesture had the right timbre and timing, but with none of the staleness that might characterize the context. It was perfect but also felt, not slick. She certainly felt, and it seemed the kind of feeling that could not exist except reciprocally. It was as if they were lovers reunited after a long separation, fitting easily into place again. What was passion if not this? She slept a blissful, sated sleep.

When she woke up, she was alone. Everywhere around her were mirrors. The way school buses have mirrors to cover every possible vantage, this room, from her position on the bed, allowed her to see her body from every angle. She was fascinated by this, and distracted for quite a while, but then began to be afraid. She couldn't find her way past the immediate space around her. It reminded her of fancy New York stores in which it is difficult to find one's way because the different departments are separated by walls of mirrors.

Suddenly he was there in the mirrors. She was extremely moved that he'd come to be with her there, to rescue her; for some reason she was certain that he wasn't trapped by the situation, but had purposefully navigated to it, to get to her. Her first impulse was to take his hand and run with him out of this world of reflection, but he didn't lead her out; instead, to her shock, he climbed on top of her—what could be less appropriate?—at least out of sequence; that came after the rescue, in the gratitude and relief stage, while here she was, still a captive of this reflective dragon. But as the weight of his body pressed against her, she decided she'd been wrong; it was completely appropriate. She was so tied to her sense of propriety. There was no need to leave the place right now; no exits would seal while he entered—which happened so quickly she was startled, but startled at how *un*startled her body was, unkindled but still receptive—he taught her so much by his body.

He was thrusting in her so energetically it should have hurt, but it didn't, or if it did, the hurt was subsumed in the intensity of pleasure and excitement she felt. She had an orgasm as intense as any she had ever experienced, and felt after as if she could never have another, intense or otherwise, but just as she was thinking that he turned her over onto her belly and came into her from behind, and she heard herself make sounds she had never heard from her own mouth, in response to this pleasure on the crest of saturation.

She made them all the way to her second orgasm, not a very long way, in fact, and then there were others; she'd always thought that a myth. Only as she was coming did she remember the erotic potential of this room or space she was in—she'd been so overwhelmed with sensations and feeling that it hadn't occurred to her to heighten the effect with the visual; she was angry at herself to have missed out on that; when would she ever have such an opportunity again.

She loved the idea of watching their bodies in conjunction with each other, of him pressing into her. She turned to look back over her shoulder so that she could see him disappearing into her, and then turned her head in order to be able to see without straining, in all the mirrors. Her orgasm, at its most intense point, was retracted. The cry that rose from her throat continued, though perhaps the pitch changed just slightly, or the quality of the sound; maybe only she could hear the difference, that it wasn't from pleasure or surfeit anymore but from shock and bewilderment, because in all the mirrors she was there writhing—she could see her breasts and belly and legs, all from underneath, as if there were no bed obstructing; she could also see herself from his vantage; she could see what someone opening a door, if there were a door, would see, from far away, with the head prominent and the hair draped over the bed; she could see her shoulders and back, but he was not depicted in any of these images. She lay on the bed without partner. She felt humiliated and horrified, and guilty too, though she couldn't have said why.

She had no idea how to attack this problem with relation to the other person who might or might not be present. It was an extreme case of some kind of sexual etiquette. The problem was, she didn't know this man, the café owner, at all; she knew him no better than she'd know a blind date, and yet they were sharing, weren't they, this intimate circumstance. Everything had felt so natural before; she'd let the sensation absorb any uncomfortableness, but now she was too disturbed by his absence from the mirror to retrieve her passion, and she felt too silly or shy to inquire about it directly.

Would he think she was crazy, or was he somehow manipulating his own image for some sinister reasons she had no idea of? Oh, why did she ever with this perfect stranger, and hadn't he seemed it in both senses of the term, but now she would pay. What would her mother say, who'd always been so cautiously liberal . . . "Carol, if you don't know a man's last name, you don't know him well enough to . . ." Thus what had seemed the most natural thing in the world suddenly de-naturalized and was transformed into the most awkward. How could she carry on this charade, when she possessed private knowledge that her partner was missing? It was just ludicrous to continue and at the same time witness the bleak absurdity of her body making love to the atmosphere. The postures could be made to look ridiculous enough even with both parties attending, but then at least they were salvaged by familiarity. Maybe the act itself was unnatural, maybe this was some elaborate lesson for her. She could be alone the rest of her life; she knew how.

She couldn't ask him what he saw in the mirror; she wished she could be so direct, but they hadn't spoken since that initial conversation, which might as well have taken place in some other world. She could feel the motions going on in some removed physical dimension, but to a very different effect. She was numb now, throughout her body; she wondered if he'd notice; he must notice. Was he intending all this, and should she then try her best to play along to try to countertrick—how appalling to have to think in terms of strategy in such circumstances—pretending she really did see him in the mirror? Or was this some entirely different conspiracy of the elements in which he was as innocent as she? But was she? How could she be in such a terrible predicament if she hadn't done something terribly wrong; yes, it was repression and all the rest, but really, this kind of thing didn't happen to the average person. Confront, evade, despair? She didn't know which to do.

She'd never in her life faked an orgasm, as women were supposed to be notorious for, and she hadn't had so many either; in fact these recent ones constituted more than a small percentage of the total, but to do precisely that suddenly seemed the best plan, to get it all over with, so that this beginning-to-be-very-oppressive weight would be removed, and she wouldn't have to continue doing this thing, performing these movements, which are by definition directed toward another, to no one. She even managed to make some noise; she was surprised at how convincing it sounded, having expected the artificiality to be glaring. The trouble was, he took no notice; she might have spared herself the trouble—he wasn't through. Then she realized that she hadn't noticed if he had yet had one to her many, how selfish of her; she'd been caught up in the intensity of her own pleasure. But he seemed insatiable. It felt so odd, and now it was the etiquette thing amplified thousands of times, because she wanted to say, "Excuse me, do you think you'll be through soon?" as if to someone at a pay phone, except she had made all her calls and just wanted to hear the receiver click.

As she looked at her body now, it was limp and tense at once, receiving the invisible—less absurd than what she'd seen in the heat of her solitary passion, but still pathetic. Maybe there was a device analogous to the one-way mirror: a half-mirror, in which only one party at a time was visible. Such a thing could exist. So now the big question was, did he see only himself, the same way she saw only herself? How simple it all was; she was immensely relieved for the second time in—how many hours had this been going on?—she had no idea, but was overjoyed to realize that the sum of their perceptions would yield a complete lovemaking couple; she thought she might cry with the relief of it. Suddenly it was as it had been back in the café; she had invented all the problems; she was ashamed at having suspected him. She wanted to tell him everything and have him say, "Silly thing," and stroke her, make it all better.

But he didn't say that and she was still trapped underneath him: this man she was not with despite his presence. It was happening to someone else; he was inside someone else, who only happened to be Carol. Who cared about sex? She'd give up sex forever; just get her out of here. She yearned for nothing so much as the removal of this corporeal hook whose eye she was. Oh, give her the pain; she'd rather that, to feel her body affirming the wrongness of what was being done to/in it, the participation that pain was, rather than this numbness, distance, this irrevocable breach with the action she was party to.

She was exhausted now. Maybe she could cry so much that her body would force itself to sleep and when she woke up it would be normal, because that was the way things had worked till now; why shouldn't it solve itself so simply? But how could it when the situation had changed so drastically? She had not chosen this. Everything was different; he wasn't the same he; she herself—oh, was she also different, not just in the sense of having learned something, but substantially altered? Could she not go home again even to the home of her being? Was it going to prove that large a crime she'd committed, to herself, or invited if not committed: some psychic leaving of the keys in the car, or the house unlocked? Take from me; violate me? But no, how could she have known that the locks would not only be changed by the time she got home, but in her impotent presence the lock, the whole house changed, the door, the windows, the stairs (how long ago it seemed she'd stood at the top of her stairway) all turned inside out and impossible to put back in order.

That's when he stopped. Vision was the only sense that informed her, because feeling had long since been used up. The point was that nothing was different after he stopped, the same way on a long trip you feel like you're driving even after you get out of the car. She wanted to know what it was that made that particular point the one he'd selected as enough. Maybe he'd climaxed. But she suspected he had a completely different kind of sexuality, not based on that system. Even if it was the same system it was different, because no man ever took that long to get to the point conventionally regarded as completion; no ordinary man. Or had she drawn it out in her mind because she was so uncomfortable? No, there couldn't be that much disparity.

He was leaving. He had dismounted and left the bed. It seemed that he didn't need any time to recover from his own experience. He was walking away and she was free, no longer oppressed by that weight, that invasion; she'd been granted just what she pleaded for. But what would she do, if he left her all alone in the room again, with no one and no way out and no way of knowing where? She was more afraid than ever.

"Oh please don't go," she said. "Don't leave me alone. I'm afraid to be alone here."

Her request wasn't on the order of begging the lover to linger a little longer, wanting to draw out his sweet company, not Juliet bemoaning the lark song; it was simply preferring any risk to the risk of solitude, the way someone you're suspicious of suddenly seems harmless when you see the real villain. But she was only half involved with this anxiety about his departure, probably more than half, that is, not entirely consumed by the fear, because she was partly caught up in watching him begin to dress, seeing his body for the first time from a distance, with perspective. And she was also ashamed at feeling renewed attraction for this man whom she'd minutes ago felt utterly victimized by. But she couldn't get over his beauty; at this moment she wasn't so much aroused by the sight of him naked as interested in his body aesthetically.

She dwelled upon the refined features: cheekbones, throat, his beautiful hands. Her own hands had felt the softness of his dark hair, from that of his head to the field that pooled below his navel. He was fuzzy and nice down there, she remembered the feeling of that against her. Before she had only seen him hard, now she found it just as appealing soft; she supposed he wouldn't appreciate that sentiment, he would surely not deviate from the norm in that respect. She also wondered if it was abnormal of her to feel as she did, not to prefer it hard.

They had been united by that organ; now it was just a part of him again; perhaps it had its own little memory, its own will, and was choosing now to disassociate itself from the warm surround she had provided. And how she had soared in the first stages of that providing. She'd never had such a strong sense of being with a man: that she was the feminine to his masculine. He elicited from her a quality of her own femaleness that she'd never before experienced on that physical plane—a response she realized might be hopelessly bound up in the conditioning of role, but was nonetheless immensely powerful. It was getting clear again, with the distance, with his going, the power of the sensation that had made her respond in a way she never had: totally. She'd come outside herself to meet him through the medium of body, through the act of letting him inside her, and yet never felt so fully in her body, in her self, as when she had.

HE WAS WORKING NOW TOWARD his clothes: a neat pile contrasting with her own things, scattered around it. She didn't remember him taking off what he was now putting on; she thought they were the same clothes he'd been wearing when they first met and talked. It was a button-down shirt, that much she remembered, but the color looked a little different than it had in the candlelight: pale pink oxford cloth; it might look effeminate on most men but on him it was just right, perfect for his blend of beauty and masculinity, his refined masculinity.

As she was observing him in the act of dressing, deep in her own reflections, she felt quite spontaneously in her genitals the muscular contractions of orgasm. She'd been concentrating on the pinkness of the shirt, and watching him put his firm, muscular—first right, then left—legs into his gray flannel trousers in a businesslike manner, when out of nowhere her body had produced this gratuitous release to no accumulated tension, in an instant of incredible intensity that left her completely drained, as if she'd been building up to it for some time. She'd often wished she could speed up that process but this was a most undesirable other extreme, this joyless, arbitrary orgasm; it was in no way satisfying. If anything, scary. This very strange ventriloquism made her furious. For the first time toward him she felt her emotions focus as unmitigated, almost violent anger. She felt used, much more so even than when he had been doing to her what technically could be considered rape. But to do this intimate thing from across the room! How cowardly of him; that's what it was, truly unmanly, that he wouldn't even face her with his body to manipulate her, though in a way it was honest, to be so blatant.

A marvelous thing indeed it would be if she could think her way to orgasm, or come just by watching him, but this was quite different, as removed a process as artificial insemination, this artificial climax for which she had been just the vehicle. She wanted to hit him but she was practically incapacitated as a result of her climax. She wanted to hit him because she felt stunned as if she had been struck; she had fallen back from an upright position, and as she'd fallen back, her peripheral vision had received the mirror's version of that moment. It contained two genders; a man's reflection had been for that instant there: a single thrust by all the reflected men in all the mirrors: multiple petals around her lonely, central, actual pistil, from which no bee sucked nectar. Why was she surprised, that they would contradict no matter what, turn appearances around as a matter of course? She should have the pattern down by now.

A few minutes later she had her strength back, but since immediacy would have been the point, there was no use in striking him now. It would probably only end up hurting her anyway. Alternatively she decided to maintain utter dignity, which was difficult because she needed to go to the bathroom and there wasn't a chance she'd be able to divine the whereabouts of the ladies' room. She got off the bed in as stately a manner as she could accomplish and walked slowly but deliberately to where he stood. She tried not to feel vulnerable despite the fact that she was naked and he now completely clothed.

"There's a matter of some urgency," she said.

He looked up at her. "If you want to leave," he said, "all you have to do is figure it out. No one will stop you. I certainly won't."

After she had held her breath a minute, determined not to start crying, she tried again. "That's not the matter I had in mind—something much more mundane. You see, I have to, I need to [he was no help] find a bathroom."

"There aren't any." He wasn't very gracious.

"Oh," she said, at a loss. Then she found courage.

"Look, you have to help me."

She was afraid he wouldn't answer, and was thankful when he finally said, as if he'd been thinking about it all the while rather than ignoring her as she'd thought, "In fact, there is something," and hastened to add, "but it's only meant to be decoration. It was part of the architect's design."

Since her urgency was not decreasing she couldn't afford to be choosy. Responding to her expectant look, he led her to an alcove she could have sworn had not existed, but then it was hard to tell because of all the reflection. In any case she hadn't noticed this place before. Somehow the mirrors masked the contours. It was hard to tell how far the room extended, hard to distinguish what was reflection from what was actual space.

"This is all I have," he said (what a funny salesman he'd make, she thought), gesturing toward two gleaming urinals, affixed to the wall at waist height, totally out of place though in another way consistent with the atmosphere.

"Are you going to watch?" she asked in an injured tone, and he accommodatingly turned to walk away, but then she called him back and asked him to give her a hand, being pragmatic rather than proud.

"Help me," she said, but it was a question rather than a statement because she didn't know exactly what she wanted him to do for her, or whether he would even know how to help her. She had in mind a position that would somehow enable her to put feminine function into masculine form. She stood on tiptoe and stepped backward, facing him—she did not want to have her back to him—until she straddled the fixture. It was difficult to do this, but not impossible because she, although not tall, had fairly long legs, and the thing itself was not all that high. The insides of her thighs made contact with the porcelain rim; it was cold, but she couldn't raise herself high enough to avoid it.

She was still looking at him for some kind of assistance, and he, regarding her now as if she were truly demented, approached her, reaching his hand out hesitantly, as if he felt obliged to offer it but didn't know quite where to touch her, how to hold or support her. Finally he squatted in front of her and the urinal, and grasped her legs just above the knee, as one might hold a ladder someone else is standing on, to make it secure. This was no help. It was so strange to have him touching her in this functional way; she realized she didn't want him to touch her at all. Certainly she didn't want him to witness her in the actual act of urinating, especially in this awkward posture, and she couldn't wait much longer. Perhaps realizing that he was making no contribution, he rose, but kept standing there, out of malice or ignorance she wasn't sure: his face was blank.

"Thanks for the help," she said, hoping he would take that as dismissal.

He looked mesmerized by her sustained acrobatic—an expression foreign to his face as she knew it: being in the power of something rather than being in power over something, someone. Then he snapped out of it, looked normal again, and said, "The needs of his guest are a host's first priority." Was he sneering, or was it her own distortion of his smile? Then he turned quickly away. They seemed far from anything sexual now, poles apart from each other's sexuality. It was as if her nakedness were the most ordinary thing in the world to him now. At least he was gone and she could urinate in peace, if not exactly comfort, since relief was thwarted by the awkwardness of posture. There was so little space between her and the fixture that she got splashed by little droplets. Well, it's sterile anyway, she thought. Of course there was nothing to wipe herself with; there were no accessories to this monstrosity. It vaguely resembled a baptismal font.

She eased herself off, gripping the sides for support; this time she didn't have to worry about looking dignified. Once on land again, dry, flat land, she spread her legs, planting her feet far apart, and waved her hand rapidly between her thighs to speed up the air-drying process, as she leaned against the cold porcelain, too cold to keep contact with for any longer than neces- sary. She was tired of being in discomfort. Hadn't she suffered enough? She stopped leaning and tried fanning with no support but found her legs still too unstable, so she compromised by kneeling, though that didn't leave much space in which to wave her hand. All her muscles ached now; she wanted to find the bed again and lie down, but she couldn't summon the energy. Fatigue overcame any squeamishness she had about lying on the floor near the urinals: he had said they were only used as a decoration. She lay on her back, at first with her legs up, positioned like an open scissor, as in one of the exercises she did, to facilitate fanning, which her left hand had taken over. The absurdity of the whole endeavor suddenly struck her; she dropped her legs to the floor, exhaled, and closed her eyes, vowing she would allow herself the luxury for only a minute. It might have been several minutes, because she was seized by panic. Where had he gone when she'd sent him away? She forgot about her fatigue and ran into the main part of the room, trying not to bump into glass. He was nowhere. As she was about to call him she realized she had no name for him. Oh, what a fool she was, alone just as she'd feared, and all her own fault. How useless everything was.

But she wouldn't let herself cry—no more despair. It was time to be practi- cal, at least to go through the motions of being practical, for her own sake, to try to create some sense, even a contrived one, of order, in this most peculiar, relentless universe. So she began to dress, even though there was no rational reason to do so, except to feel dignified, and what else was there to do? She looked fondly at her scattered clothes. She regarded them as a soldier might some article that had been with him through numerous battles. And who knew what battles were yet to come, she thought, almost saying it out loud to her faithful skirt and blouse, the ones she'd been in the process of removing when she left her bedroom to investigate, the thing that got her into this night- mare: her fear of the sound, followed by her—feeling—for the café owner.

On some level she knew she was an intuitive person, but she hadn't learned to trust herself, too cautious, as if there were a very strong force at work inside her all the time that wasn't allowed to come to expression, like all that sun missing her house, all this foliage in her head, that was so pretty and interesting and alive, but how much it got in the way. She suspected that her mind had evolved in some distorted fashion, different from the rest of the world. And now here she was, trapped in this stagnancy of glass, that had become by all its clarity a blur, itself a distortion. She couldn't forgive herself, though she supposed she'd suffered enough to be redeemed of any number of sins or crimes. She cursed her intuition, because she'd never have stayed with him if she'd weighed, considered, evaluated. On the other hand, she'd never do anything if she always weighed, considered, evaluated; that was precisely what so often kept her from doing any number of things, things she felt a genuine desire to do, but couldn't get over this habit or obsession of getting stuck, nothing resolving itself. She felt the irony of the whole thing as deeply, as physically, as a metallic taste in her mouth: that the only time she'd ever felt not removed from her body, when will and act had meshed, was with him; it had felt so right, but clearly had been wrong, as wrong as anything could be. She slid the tab of the zipper all the way up and fastened the button of the waistband of her skirt, then leaned against one of the mirrors as she dreamily repeated the motion of button through opening, gentle grasps and pulls, all the way up her blouse. If only there were as simple a motion to secure her exit. He had said she had only to figure it out. And there had to be a door, somewhere there had to be. She thrust her weight hard against the mirror as she leaned, then moved forward to tuck in her blouse. Had the mirror seemed to give a little as she had pressed? She must be imagining it. Perhaps if she pushed against every mirror, one of them might yield.

IN THE CAFÉ, HE POURED her a drink, yellow, creamy stuff from the blender into a large, stemmed glass. He held it high as he poured, the way waiters had poured milk for her in restaurants when she'd been young; she'd been impressed at how high they could go and still not spill. She fumbled in her pocket for change, feeling stupid, not knowing where she stood. He put his hands over hers and said, "On the house."

"Oh," she said softly. "Thank you."

She had no idea what role she was playing. Was she customer, or worse, had he been hers? It was so different, he was nice again. His demeanor toward her suggested that they were only now about to be lovers, romantic, but she knew they'd already been, and what had gone on had had little to do with romance. She wasn't making much progress with the daiquiri, taking occasional nervous gulps, clutching the glass.

"It's different now," she said with desperate bravery.

"Same ingredients as always," he replied. "Are you sure you've had one before?" The way he smiled made her nervous. This was more confusing than ever.

Too uncomfortable to look at him, she kept surveying the room and its contents: the candles, the fancy Breuer chairs, all the bottles and glasses lined along shelves on the mirrored wall of the bar, a large quilt that somehow fit in with the rest of the decor; the central part of its design was a large star—it took her a minute to realize it was there because of the name of the place: the Star Café. The quilt took up almost all of one wall; the other walls were decorated with posters, mostly from museum exhibits. There were the travel posters as well, one a sophisticated montage of tourists and countryside in Greece, each scene in a separate little box. On the bottom was Greek lettering. She had always wanted to go there; it seemed like such a magical place, not just in some superficial sense of island and sun (one of the little boxes showed tourists lying on a beach) though that was appealing, and not just in the sense of the magic of the past either, being surrounded by ancient history; her sense was of a magic that was also chthonic. That was the world of myth, of gods and goddesses, of honor and heroism, justice, revenge. That was a much larger world than her own, she felt, that company of furies and sirens in which choice was fate, and fate was really everything, but no matter what brutality caused by what whim of some god's arbitrary favoritism, reliable rosy-fingered dawn was always waiting in the wings to make it all into poetry. She was enamored of that civilization which was a celebration of the splendor of form. She thought of the perfection of body that lived in those white marble statues, the strength and grace which rhymed for her with his body, the body that had mingled with her own, but was now so distant. She needed to know that it had.

"Were you ever there?" she asked him, not even asking for understanding so much as simple information.

"Once, years ago," he said, "but it's too dirty and the food's too greasy. I like a more antiseptic atmosphere; Scandinavia's more to my taste."

Willfully or inadvertently he had taken her to be referring to the travel poster. She resented this glib distortion of her meaning. He had no right to be so evasive. Or had he just misunderstood? He had no right not to understand. Anger supplanted her nervousness so that now she had no trouble looking directly at him. But he wasn't looking at her; he was eyeing the blender, and before she could challenge him he was onto that as the new topic, as if his little remark had been an adequate response to her searching question, and no more need be said about it. What nearly disarmed her was the tenderness with which he said, when he looked back at her, "How sweet that you were afraid of my blender, silly thing."

That was just what she would have wanted to hear before, but not now that she'd been through what she'd been through, an experience of suffering so vivid that it created a landscape in her mind as powerful as the mythical one in which she had just been lost. In fact they became one for her at this moment; she could envision her own story painted across some urn, the woman whose lover wasn't there, in little scenes that reminded her of the travel poster, except that they weren't photographed and weren't in boxes, little red figures depicted on the urn. Carol in her apartment, then going downstairs, then in the bar, Carol in bed, then in the mirrored room, Carol looking in the mirrors, him there, him not there, but Carol crouching in the urinal was really too squalid for the likes of any Grecian urn, and now, with her imagination engrossed in this world that did not take passion lightly, that addressed mortality and immortality as real concerns rather than abstractions, and raised to the highest pitch the difference and link between the two—now, it was grossly inadequate, even pathetic.

"I'm not your silly thing," she blurted out, and he seemed taken aback by her anger.

"What's got into you?" he asked.

"Stop pretending you don't know," she said. "You know what I'm talking about. Tell me if you were there or not."

"I've already told you—" he began, but she cut him off. She was very worked up now.

"When I ask if you were there, I mean were you with me, in the room? I mean I know you were with me, but what I'm asking is . . . why are you trying to make me think I was imagining you?" This speech was delivered *crescendo ed accelerando*. "You owe it to me to tell me!" She was very excited and annoyed to realize she had to urinate again. She must have managed to get down more of that daiquiri than she thought.

"Yes," he said quietly.

"What do you mean yes? You can't say yes or no if I ask you, was it a, b, or c. I need a specific answer. Was it real or my imagination?"

"Yes!" This time it wasn't quiet.

He didn't look like someone playing games; he looked tortured himself, but she was sure he must be trying to get away with something.

"You're being cryptic again," she said. "You're trying to confuse me. And I need the ladies' room; does that ring a bell? I may as well tell you that it's illegal not to have one in a public eating place, so don't try to tell me there isn't any."

"You think you're so smart," he raised his voice to match hers. "I have something to tell you too. There is, technically speaking, no ladies' room. There is, however, one rest room, androgynous, past the bar and to your right."

She began the journey immediately. When she'd taken only a few steps he called to her, by name, for the first time since that very first time.

"Carol!"

She turned around.

"We're through."

That was fine with her; she turned away again directly and continued on the prescribed route. Once through a corridor she found the door immediately to her right, marked simply "rest." She opened it, entered, and shut it behind her, pushing in the little circle in the middle of the knob to lock it, then tried to jiggle the knob to make sure. She realized how silly that was; who was she locking out? The man who had seen and known her body to the full extent of possibility between human beings? But locking it made her feel better. The interior was clean enough; she would have tried to hold out if it hadn't been. This bathroom was extremely clean, in fact, so she didn't feel the need to get in and out as quickly as possible. It was mirrored, of course, mirrored tiles on the walls and floor. Also the ceiling. The toilet and sink were ordinary. A fresh bar of soap lay in the dish on the arm of the sink—so much nicer than powdery stuff out of a dispenser, she thought. How good it would feel to have clean hands. She rubbed the soap between her palms for a long time, working up a rich lather with warm water from the faucet. She decided to wash her face as well; she hadn't had the opportunity in so long. She held her hair with one hand but couldn't completely avoid getting it wet. She didn't mind; she would happily have dunked her whole head into the basin for the feel of this welcome refreshment.

In fact, why stop there, she thought, and pulled her blouse off over her head. She felt sweaty and horrible; scrubbing some soap under her arms would make her feel a little better, since she couldn't shower. She unhooked the closure in front of her bra and slipped the straps down her arms one at a time with her wet hand. In the mirror she stared at her small breasts, and was pleased with them. Her nipples were hard. She rubbed the soap vigorously under her arms, then rinsed, trying to stand over the sink in such a way that the least water would spill on the floor.

She had forgotten to check for a towel before she started; there was none, so she dabbed herself dry with pieces of toilet paper. She'd almost forgotten about her urgency; she'd make some superficial attempt at washing of genitalia after. She pulled down her panties, stepped out of them and hung them on a hook she'd just noticed protruding from the door. She rescued her blouse from where it had fallen and hung that too. She gathered up her skirt with her right hand, intending to sit on the toilet, but was distracted by suddenly seeing herself in the mirrored wall, as if seeing another person. She looked at this person who held her skirt in her arms so that it draped her hips but revealed her belly, fur and thighs. Her breasts were still uncovered also, and just as she had found them adequate, satisfying, she now found this lower region of her body, in fact the whole body, cut off as it was at the waist—she found the entire image attractive.

She stood transfixed by this lovely landscape under canopy of skirt. Her flesh seemed firmer than she remembered, more muscle tone, maybe the exercises she'd been doing in the morning and before bedtime had finally paid off. It had been hard to motivate herself to do them, with no prospect of anyone to appreciate the results, since she'd had no way of knowing about the café owner. She couldn't have predicted that, though as it was happening, there had been, in the midst of all that anguish and terror and pleasure, a tiny seed of déjà vu; that was a common phenomenon, of course.

Well, it didn't make much difference in the end, did it? She knew that she often allowed herself to become the victim of her own speculations, reflections. Now it all seemed unimportant compared to the immediacy of the woman in the mirror, the urgency of that woman's sexuality or physicality. Strange to feel genuinely aroused by this image of herself. She amused herself with the idea that it was perfectly logical for her to associate her unaccompanied reflection with arousal, since that had been the consistent image during her definitive sexual experience.

Now the woman in the mirror was touching herself, sliding her palm up her thigh, transferring the skirt to the guardianship of the left hand. Then she left skin to approach her breasts. She caressed them fervently, then left skin again to return below the skirt, lingering for a long time when the hand met flesh again, languidly rubbing the soft pubic hair, just a shade darker than the honey-colored hair of her head, which fell away from her shoulders, skimming the floor as she bent low for the mirror.

The mirror-woman did a seductive dance, holding the skirt tight across her hips, swaying; she watched the curve of her calves as she gracefully inscribed the area of the bathroom floor, often lifting her leg so high that her lips were visible.

She was extremely aroused by this time, and not ashamed of it; she wanted to possess this beautiful moving image. She felt a fullness in her groin, decided it was her old need to urinate, which seemed less and less urgent; she couldn't be bothered with addressing that now—it was confusing how similar that feeling was with that of being sexually excited. She was rubbing herself, much more vigorously than was her habit; she let the skirt drop to have both hands. She tried to put one finger of her free hand inside herself but couldn't gain entry, despite the fact that she was very wet by now. It wasn't necessary anyway, and she was happy enough to have access to both hands for rubbing.

She was so tensed and excited that her vision was blurred; she'd lost the mirror's reflection, but it was firmly fixed in her mind; she dwelled on all the postures, the confronting gaze, the beauty and sensuality of that body. She needed some kind of support, weak from so much excitement. When leaning against the sink proved insufficient she quickly closed the lid of the toilet and sat there.

Under the skirt she rubbed so fast that her hand was tiring, so she supported the right with the left, cupped the two and stroked, leaning back against the tank. She recalled there must be semen in her still, if he had come, that is, but he must have come, at least once, and probably generously, he had to have, it just wasn't possible—she felt it coming out of her, not just dribbling but in spurts, as she herself climaxed. She cried out with the new pleasure of it, an intense, confined pleasure, as she felt suddenly claustrophobic; she needed air, even if it was just the air of the corridor. She rose and unlocked the door by turning the knob hard, opened it and stuck her head out, like a seasick traveler leaning out a porthole; she saw down the length of the corridor into the room with the bar, where it had all begun. Directly in the line of her vision was the poster of Greece; it was far away, and the contents of the little boxes were fuzzy, like the last letters of the eye doctor's chart, but she could see rocks and white sand, and tall, white columns. She was drawn toward them, she wanted to see every box clearly; her nakedness did not inhibit her for some reason. He didn't matter so much anymore; she wouldn't let him keep her from exploring. There was nothing to be embarrassed about. No one was there.

ANTHONY VALERIO

Frank Sinatra

ოოი

ICOME TO FRANK SINATRA MIDWAY through my life when I'm happy
with my woman, when I've learned to dance the tango and when I dis-
cover that Frank Sinatra lost his mother in a plane crash, depriving him of
the opportunity to kiss her forehead one last time, run his fingers through
her hair. Italian boys are not accustomed to their mothers flying. We see
them in the kitchen shuffling from the sink to the stove, retrieving grocery
bags from the trunk of a car, driving off to the bank. Mrs. Natalie Sinatra
loved her son so much that she was willing to fly to California just to visit
with him. She was also unusual in that she came from Genoa instead of
Naples or Sicily. In Hoboken she settled for a Sicilian, a good man named
Martin who fought fires and ran a tavern and was so beleaguered by the Irish
that he boxed under the name of Marty O'Brien. Harry James once advised
Frank Sinatra to change his name. What's Harry James's real name, Betty
Grable's? Frank Sinatra had a cousin who with his real name, Ray Sinatra,
was doing well behind the scenes of a radio show. Also, Frank Sinatra never
thought he would leave the neighborhood let alone hit the big time, and so it
didn't pay singing in roadhouses under an assumed name. Up in Canada
after my father finished postgraduate work in dentistry, his prosthetics pro-
fessor offered him a job.

"My brother has a flourishing practice in New York, on Park Avenue. He's
getting on in years and could use a fine young dentist like you, but first you'll
have to change your name."

My father belted the professor in the mouth, kept his name and opened a
neighborhood practice in Bensonhurst.

Natalie Sinatra was gregarious and full of life, and she went out to work in order to contribute her share. She developed a facility for dialects, not only her husband's but also those of the Irish and Poles and Ukrainians. She was made Democratic ward captain. She was invited to join the Hoboken branch of the Sicilian Cultural League. Some parasites have said that Frank Sinatra's link with organized crime stems from this time, but Waxey Gordon was Hoboken's *capo di tutti capi*—what's a Gordon going to do for a Sinatra? One of Waxey Gordon's descendants became a jeweler and opened a shop in Bensonhurst in the shadows of the New Utrecht Avenue El. He became our jeweler. The watches he sold us didn't work and his gold was bogus. A priest affiliated with a Bay Ridge parish supposedly launched Vic Damone, about whom Frank Sinatra once said, "First there's Vic Damone and then there's everybody else." I'm happy to hear that Vic Damone recently found happiness with Diahann Carroll and that he took the time to help his friend Fugazy launch his fleet of limousines. My parish priest now is Father Bill. He's known as the Priest to the Stars. The stars come back to Father Bill to confess and marry discreetly. If they do not find him in the church, they look for him across the street in Arturo's. Recently, I came upon him sitting at an outdoor table, wearing a Hawaiian shirt and nursing a medicinal libation before evening vespers.

"Father Bill, I'd like to talk to you."

"Sit down, sit down. Waiter, a drink for this fine young man! Now shoot!"

"I'm having a lot of trouble with my girlfriend. She comes from Argentina and has had most everything taken from her by men, beginning with her father and then her husband and then a procession of lovers down there and up here. We live in separate studios, they're very small, and I don't have the money to get us a place. I scrimped and saved and bought her a piano and paid for our round-trip tickets, New York–Buenos Aires–New York. I bought her a king-size Castro convertible so that we could sleep together once in a while. We're two horses, and when we made love our bodies pressed against the cold steel of the frame. I bought her a high rise at Kleinsleep. Then I bought her a regular bed with a futon mattress and she's content and so am I, sleeping with her wonderful body in my arms, but I inherited a chronic disease from my maternal grandfather, excessive flatulence, it's uncontrollable and escapes me while I sleep. Elsa lies awake, waiting, listening, and when I explode she scurries to the bathroom, takes up the aerosol can and returns with it behind her back, then sprays me all over like I'm some kind of insect. No matter what I do she says she's alone, and now she's thinking of going out with other men."

"How old is she, my son?"

"Fifty."

"Be her friend," said Father Bill. "Go to that phone over there and call her and tell her that no matter what she does you love her and want to be her friend."

I got up and hurried blindly to the phone booth on the corner of Houston and Thompson. "No matter what you do," I told Elsa, "including go out with other men, I love you and want to be your friend."

"Me, too," Elsa said, and everything has been fine since then.

At the end of the day when the Sinatras convened for supper, all dialects were left outside on the doorstep. Feelings were communicated with a glance, a meeting of the eyes, a gesture. Words now were simple and clear and true. In his house Frank Sinatra heard most every word he would sing in his songs. The attention he pays to lyrics is in harmony with Enrico Caruso's attitude toward them: "I think to the words of my aria, not to the music, because first is written the libretto and is the reason of the composer to put the music, like the foundation of a house."

For half a century Frank Sinatra has been tough enough to withstand the bloodsucking of a million leeches, mainly male journalists. Ed Sullivan, who I believe married an Italian, was consistently fair with him, as were Sidney Skolsky and Louella Parsons, Sheilah Graham and Dorothy Kilgallen. Some male journalists have said that Frank Sinatra's tumultuous personal life stems from a neglected childhood. Nonsense! His cheeks were hollow early on, it's true, but they've filled out. Latent or full our cheeks are always there, for we need them to eat properly. It was a godsend that Frank Sinatra was at times left to himself. He stood outside his house with his foot up against the door and listened to the roar of the Erie Lackawanna trains. He was given the time and peace for his feelings to flood his heart, and then they rose to his throat and a song was born. There are prominent Italians in their forties whose mothers were always in the house who still bring home the laundry. Would it have been better for Frank Sinatra to follow in his father's footsteps, like Ray Mancini, who on behalf of his father gets his brains knocked in, losing himself in the process? Natalie Sinatra wanted her son to be an engineer, but at the same time she scrimped and saved and bought him a p.a. system, mike and loudspeaker. They came through to her as she disappeared into the sunset. I see her now saying good-bye. She turns on the top step and smiles and waves to her son on the observation deck. He snaps down the brim of his hat and waves.

On this the forty-sixth celebration of my name day, St. Anthony of Padua,

I would like to send Frank Sinatra my condolences. Now I am able to commiserate with him when on entering *his* forty-sixth year he sought to settle down with a good woman, too. His friends were married: there was a Mrs. Martin, a Mrs. Bishop, a Mrs. Davis and a Mrs. Lawford. And so while Frank Sinatra was out driving and happened to pass Juliet Prowse's legs, I fully understand how he hit upon the idea of taking them for a ride, and if Miss Prowse consented, taking them home so that they could do a little dance. Juliet Prowse had been born in India, Bombay, and she stopped dancing only to whip up a few dishes Frank Sinatra was not accustomed to, like curries and yogurt.

Italian boys are usually named after their paternal grandfather or the saint of that day. On the day we're born a family member approaches the religious calendar hanging in the kitchen and with an open mouth, biting the tongue, searches with a forefinger and then stops and reads in small print the name of the saint. "Hey, everybody, here it is: Louie or Tony or Jimmy or Frankie!"

A name day is a day of truth. Just as on their daughters' wedding days all Dons grant any wish whatever, on their name day they are obliged to tell the truth. The truth is that St. Anthony was not born in Padua, he performed his miracles there. He was born in Portugal. As an infant he was sickly and was transported with care to Africa. He gained strength and on the way back to Portugal stopped off in Padua and stayed.

The truth: is it possible for one man, even an Italian one, to romance the likes of the following women, with prime time taken out for a marriage to his first and eternal love, his Italian sweetheart: Lana Turner, Jill St. John, Princess Soraya, Ava Gardner, Lady Beatty, Marilyn Monroe, Kim Novak, Lauren Bacall, Marilyn Maxwell, Gloria Vanderbilt, Linda Christian, Anita Ekberg, Juliet Prowse, Dorothy Provine, Mia Farrow?

A name day is also a festive one, but the truth is I've been alone all day with northerly gales blowing pollen in through my window. Dark clouds are rolling over. My door is kept open a body's width by a dagger. Not a real one, as the blade is made of wood, but the sheath is real, strong Argentine hemp, and so it disguises the nature of the blade enough to keep out prowlers and the neighbors. Elsa gave it to me. Frank Sinatra is singing tunes written by Antônio Carlos Jobim, the great Brazilian composer. Elsa introduced me to his music as well as to the music of all of South America and to musical instruments I had never heard before like the *bandoneón* and the *charango*. Last night she played disc jockey and I was the audience. I asked her, "Would you say it's a reflection of Frank Sinatra's taste that he sings Tom Jobim's music?"

"Oh, definitely and nobody sings it better. Agh!" and she swooned.

"Can you dance to this music, the rumba, merengue?"

"No, no."

"Does Tom Jobim write his own lyrics?"

"No. Vinicius de Moraes wrote them."

"Isn't that the guy who you told me sings with a bottle of Johnnie Walker in front of him and fucks anything that walks?"

"That's him, the old fucker."

"He still alive?"

"Yup."

"Got anything with him singin'?"

"Yes."

She puts on Vinicius de Moraes.

"Please translate."

"You can't really."

"Try."

I am going to love you in every goodbye.

I am going to love you desperately.

I know I am going to love you—

"That's enough. They're very nice, thank you," I said, and then we made love.

Afterward, Elsa said, "You know, Garibaldi"—sometimes she calls me Garibaldi—"you're a good lay."

"*Gracias,*" I said.

The truth is that I fear for those of us named after our fathers, who become known in the neighborhood as "Junior." They spend their childhoods in confusion, forever shouting nervously, "Which one!" They become practitioners of the double take, and by the time they reach puberty they don't know if they have their own dick. Frank Sinatra named his son Franklin after President Roosevelt but it was inevitable that when the boy opened his mouth to sing, he would become known as Frank Sinatra, Jr. He's a loving son and an accomplished musician, plays several instruments, the flute in addition to the piano, and he's composed piano concertos. Frank Sinatra had no way of knowing that many of his contemporaries who went on to become doctors and dentists and lawyers blamed Franklin Roosevelt for letting all the Puerto Ricans into New York. They had not as yet spread to God's country, Bensonhurst, but one day a Chinese couple was seen walking hand in hand to the train. They had moved surreptitiously into the multiple dwelling up near Fifteenth Avenue where the ailanthus trees are older and taller, casting the houses in shadows. Every morning and every evening the couple walked to and from the West End line, on tiptoes, silent, nodding to each and every neighbor they passed. They passed Mr. Rosa's Lincoln Continental parked in his driveway. They had never seen such a car and marveled at how he traded it in every year for a new model. Unfortunately, Mr. Rosa couldn't trade in his wife, and by the time their Junior reached the age of eleven it was too late to give him his own name. When Mr. Rosa married Nellie, he had no way of knowing that after she gave birth to their son, she would refuse to leave the house. She didn't have to leave, everything was brought to her. There was a continuous procession of grocery boys and hairstylists, and then around four o'clock Nellie emerged from the darkness inside her house and stood in the sunlight behind her screen door. She smiled and waved to those of us curious about what she was like. At times she had red hair and at times blond. She always dressed nicely. Occasionally, her adventurous spirit broke through and she opened her door a crack, stuck out her head and spoke to us. She was bright and gay and sounded like our mothers, except that Nellie's voice was many decibels higher. Everything was normal. A crime had not as yet been committed in Bensonhurst and so the doors were always open. Mr. Rosa's door was always open, and I figured if the grocery boy could go in unannounced, so could I. Besides, Junior was my friend, and so at eight o'clock during the summer months I went in holding my ball.

"Junior! Junior!" I called from the parlor. When no one answered, I thought that maybe Junior was still asleep and I sliced through the parlor feeling like an intruder in a room full of phantoms, phantoms who when they materialized would have to sit on plastic, but there was a couch and a coffee table and wing chairs and a big TV console just like in everybody else's parlor. I made a sharp right into Junior's bedroom, stood at the threshold and looked around. Every morning I looked around until my eyes lit upon Junior's bed, and every morning my dream of an all-day ball game was snatched away and was replaced by the vision of Junior lying in his bed in his mother's arms, his head on her breast, and she was stroking his hair.

"Ready to go, Juney?"

Nellie's blond hair rested against the headboard. She turned her head slowly and looked at me. She said nothing, then turned away. Junior raised his head and looked back at me, too. His hair was rumpled, his eyes glassy. He didn't say anything either and then returned to his mother's arms. I wish I could have said what I thought, that though what they were doing was unusual, it was a wonderful way to start the day. I had never been held by my mother in bed; I had never so much as seen her there. And the only time I had glimpsed her naked had been when she thought I was half asleep, when I called her in the middle of the night to bring me a glass of water.

Sooner or later Junior joined us in our play, but he was too gentle to make a first-rate ballplayer. In his frustration of competing with kids with their own names who were also bigger and stronger and whose mothers had kicked them out with the arrival on the block of the sun, Junior often picked a fight rather than play harder. He stammered and cried, and when he was getting the worst of it, he ran away. He ran into his house. If he had picked a fight with me, I ran right after him, mother or no mother, threw open the screen door and flew through the parlor all in a rage, sweating, sniveling. I slowed down a step to make my sharp right into the bedroom. My eyes searched wildly for Junior and found him but to get at him I would first have to fight Nellie. They were in his bed and Junior was once again in his mother's arms, calm, and Nellie was stroking his hair.

Junior didn't join us for our daily predinner orgy. Around four o'clock the girls put away their dolls and jump ropes and chalk, the boys put away their bats and balls, and we all naturally gravitated to the alley between my uncle's office and our garage. There was a wood-slatted door which we could close. By now the sun had traveled all the way to Shore Road. My house was tall, three stories high, and cast us deep in its shadows. We had to be quiet because my uncle was a cardiologist and he needed silence in order to hear his patients' heartbeats. Maryanne, Nicky, Theresa, Albee, me— whoever was around—we formed a circle, alternating girl-boy-girl-boy. We held hands, felt our warm willing flesh. We let go, and the girls reached right and left, lowered our zippers, then they snaked their fingers under our pants and touched our little dicks. The boys in turn reached right and left, and our fingers crawled under the girls' pants and touched their smooth skin. We touched the crack. Silent, still, we explored with our fingertips, our lips parted, our faces beaming and turned toward the sky. There were two older girls, sisters, who lived around the corner. They were like night and day in that one had blond hair and her sister's hair was black as night. I liked them, they were beautiful and they were kind to me, but I didn't think of touching them because they were always laughing and talking and forever putting the question to me, "Who do you like better: Bing Crosby or Frank Sinatra?"

I thought hard, every day I tried to conjure up the idols' faces, their voices, the heart of the contest. I went alone to the Hollywood Theater under the El and saw *The Kissing Bandit*. Still I could offer no intelligent opinion. I had Maryanne Volpi and Theresa Mineo on my fingertips. I still have them on my fingertips. When Elsa shaved her mons and I ate it anyway, I found that I didn't like it and requested that she let her hair grow. What happened during the intervening years?

THE TROUBLE WITH FRANK SINATRA started when my father was ten years old and his mother took him shopping in New York. She lost her pocketbook, so now she had to find a way to get home without money. In her black coat, biting her lip and holding her son's hand, she approached a policeman and said in good English, as she had been raised in a convent in Brooklyn, "Officer, I lost my pocketbook, and my son and I have no way to get home. We live in Brooklyn. Would you please lend us the money? I promise to pay you back."

"Get lost!" snapped the policeman, waving his arm.

Maria and her son took half a day to walk home. They walked across the bridge, and my father would never forget the policeman's accent or his big red lipless face or his uniform. Every day after school he fought the Irish in civilian clothes. He broke two knuckles on his left hand, but he didn't need his knuckles to shoot crap on the New Utrecht High School roof. In the classroom below, the great baritone Robert Merrill prepared to graduate. Robert Merrill sings the National Anthem before the ball games, and Frank Sinatra sings "New York, New York" during the games—why hasn't anyone questioned Robert Merrill's ties with the underworld, *his* political leanings? Across the river in Hoboken, Frank Sinatra also fought the Irish, he has a scar on his neck to prove it, but he was a skinny little kid and got his lumps while my father had a powerful left arm, and so it was inconceivable how his poor opinion of Frank Sinatra was formed for life merely on the hearsay of a patient who had gone to Las Vegas on a junket. Back in the office the patient reported that around a crowded gaming table he saw Frank Sinatra jostle this guy and say some real nasty things. An ordinary-looking guy but one who wasn't about to take any shit from Frank Sinatra or anybody else. He stood his ground, cocked his arm but before he could let one fly was jumped by five goons. At twelve o'clock my father runs up the stairs in his white gown, his hair in front of his wild eyes.

"That punk, Sinatra—he picked on the wrong guy this time!"

"Don't believe it, Pa. If the powers that be didn't know that Frank Sinatra had a mouth, a way with words, American words, if they didn't know he could talk turkey and pay off, he would have been jailed a dozen times. Pa, Enrico Caruso was put in jail. That's right, the greatest voice the world has ever known was convicted of molesting a woman! At first he didn't even understand the charges. At his trial the interpreter got it all wrong and translated a confession instead of a denial."

It happened in the monkey house at the Central Park zoo. A cold January morning in 1906, one year before my father was born, Caruso takes a leisurely stroll through the zoo, which is near his hotel. He suddenly feels chilled and seeks refuge in the monkey house. It's empty except for a proper-looking woman who is watching two chimpanzees beg for food, stretching their hairy arms through the bars, entreating her with their human eyes. Caruso stands beside the woman and watches, too, as one enjoys company in a zoo.

"Mornin'," Caruso says, doffing his hat.

He had bought some fruit, oranges, grapes and bananas. He loved the bananas of America. They were huge and yellow and meaty. Italian bananas were imported from Africa and were green and small, hardly a mouthful. Caruso tosses the bananas into the cage. Pleased, he looks at the woman. She smiles and moves over to the orangutans, who are playing tag in their tree house. Caruso follows, as it's natural in a zoo to progress from one cage to the next. When the woman moves over to the spider monkeys and Caruso follows her this time, she screams, "Help! Help! He rubbed against me!"

Caruso grasps her arm with concern and says, *"Che c'è, signora?"*

"Help! He touched my side!"

Her partner in crime was a plainclothes policeman named Kulhane. Dressed as a zookeeper, he pounces on Caruso, cuffs him and hauls him off to the Sixty-ninth Precinct station house. Caruso is fingerprinted and arraigned for molesting a woman. He didn't understand the charges, but he understood ignorance and maltreatment. He bellowed to the booking lieutenant, "I'm Enrico Caruso!"

"And I'm Garibaldi!" the lieutenant cried.

"Yeah, and I'm Machiavelli!" said a detective who happened to pass by.

Caruso filled his great lungs and let out a B-flat natural that shook the chandelier.

"All these ginneys think they can sing," said Officer Kulhane.

"Lock him up!"

Caruso tried to put two and two together and in the process suffered the first of a series of fatal headaches. As he was being led away, he offered in his best English the following explanation:

"How I poke from behind when I wore heavy coat and wool suit which I keep buttoned because of cold? I go to monkey house because of cold. I have hands behind back all the time and for nothin' she says I go, 'Whoop! Whoop!'"—and then as a way of simulating the trumped-up charge, Caruso projected his abdomen and took several stutter steps forward.

He was kept in jail overnight, and the next day bail of five hundred dollars was posted. When he arrived at his hotel, he heard the doorman singing "That Funny Feeling." Caruso had him fired. A painting hanging in the lobby was entitled "The Friars of St. Simian." Caruso had it taken down. His next performance was as Rodolfo in *La Bohème*. In the Fourth Act, Musetta hands the dying Mimi a muff. Caruso insisted that it be made of rabbit fur. The great Polish soprano Marcella Sembrich refused to sing with him. Officer Kulhane moonlighted in front of the monkey house, charging admission to hear Caruso sing to the monkeys. Business was brisk. On the other side, the head of the Comédie-Française wrote: "If D'Artagnan were alive today and traveled to New York, he would be locked up, too."

Puccini himself wrote: "It's a tragic misunderstanding. Caruso knows that Italian women love to be rubbed up against by tenors, midgets, too—they bring good luck."

My father says, "Go on, Anthony. Remember that time in the Garden? It was a disgrace!"

Joe Freeze had given the whole neighborhood free tickets to an Italian rally in Madison Square Garden. Frank Sinatra would be presiding and providing the entertainment, including a young singer named Aretha Franklin. We packed the front car, and during the ride my father kept asking, "Who's this Aretha Franklin?"

"Wait till you hear her—she's terrific!"

Ten thousand bleached blondes wrapped in millions of dead minks accompanied by ten thousand short squat men with bald spots and wearing dark suits descended upon Madison Square Garden. The orchestra, composed mainly of strings, warmed us up with "O Sole Mio" and "Come Back to Sorrento," and then the evening's festivities got under way. There must be a secret tunnel under Madison Square Garden, because the first speaker suddenly appeared at the microphone. His skin was pink and he spoke with a kind of brogue and wore a suit one size too small. He clasped his hands and said, "Good evening, ladies and gentlemen, I'm Ed McMahon."

He paused, looked around, expecting a smattering of applause, but you couldn't hear a pin drop and so he went on with a tremulous voice, "Frank Sinatra couldn't make it tonight, but he's sent along one of the world's finest entertainers, Mr. Sammy Davis Jr. H-e-e-e-e-r's Sammy!"

The olive of twenty thousand Italian faces grew bright yellow. Insulted faces simultaneously turned right and left in search of corroboration. The men straightened their ties. The women tugged at their skirts, pulling them tight over their knees. The same thought entered twenty thousand dark mysterious minds: "For an ugly little black guy he's got a helluva lot of nerve."

Sammy Davis Jr. conducted himself royally. He sang and danced and played the drums. He introduced the Italian guest speakers with the required amount of respect, a lot. Scholarships were handed out, and the future of our country ran up and accepted them. Aretha Franklin was being saved for the end, when the momentum of the evening had grown favorable in that everybody was a little tired. But then Sammy Davis Jr. announced, "Miss Aretha Franklin is ill but her younger sister has agreed to sing in her place. She's never sung before such a large audience, so let's hear it!"

She emerged amid silence from an exit ramp, made her way through an aisle between wooden folding chairs and mounted the stage. The Italians waited until she had sung a few bars, then en masse they got up and made for the exits, creating a racket. The courageous young woman kept singing. She looked around. No one gave her a glance. Sammy Davis Jr. hopped onto the stage, stopped the song and said with a mixture of outrage and disgust, "Please return to your seats! This is a travesty, the worst display of manners I've ever seen! Never again will I do one of these things!"

Good! thought the Italians still in the Garden.

THE COUP DE GRÂCE OCCURRED in 1947 when the papers reported that Frank Sinatra was seen in Havana in the company of Lucky Luciano, Al Capone's brother Ralph, and the Fischetti brothers of Brooklyn, Miami and Chicago. Frank Sinatra had begun his holiday in Mexico. Nothing untoward happened there, but then he flies to Miami to play a benefit and bumps into Joe Fischetti and his brothers. They persuade him to join them on a junket to Havana. Frank Sinatra gets off the plane in Havana carrying a small suitcase. He had never been seen carrying his own suitcase, and neither Joe Fischetti nor his brothers are carrying one, and they do not offer to carry Frank Sinatra's. Packed neatly in the suitcase is six million dollars in small bills destined for the deep, wide pockets of Lucky Luciano, who is vacationing in Havana. The Fischetti brothers, Ralph Capone, Lucky Luciano and Frank Sinatra meet at a bar, then they go to the races together, jai alai games, dine and spend relaxed evenings of craps and baccarat at the Havana Casino.

I know the truth about all this. I got it from the horse's mouth, from Lucky Luciano himself! A female friend of his was a patient of my father's. She came for bridges, full uppers and lowers, and as such work takes time, my father got to know her. Over dinner he said that she was lovely, had a gay spirit and was respectful, and though he had never heard her sing, he imagined she had a fine soprano voice "because she studies hard and dresses nice." Lucky Luciano drove her to the office, then waited outside. He sat in his car awhile, parked out front in the shade of our tree. He got out, paced and smoked. From our living-room window I watched him walk back and forth in front of our garden of honeysuckle vines and snowballs. He wore the first full-length camel's hair coat I had ever seen. When he removed his hat to wipe his brow, I saw that his hair was silver and wiry and not a strand was out of place. Sunlight bounced off his full cheeks. He put out his cigarette in the patch of dirt around the tree. Sometimes he stayed under there, and sometimes he kept walking up toward Fifteenth Avenue. I'd lose him in the shadows, but he always came back.

One day while Lucky Luciano's friend was in the chair, I went down to the office through the house. I loved to visit my father while he worked. He was happy in his office, and he greeted me in his white gown with a smile and a genuine salutation. He called me champ and mootzie, short for mozzarella. I surprised him through a door which only he used, the one in the narrow, sunless corridor between his operating room and his darkroom, where he developed his impressions and spent many, many hours in peaceful reverie. In the silent darkness he daydreamed about his one chance at happiness with a woman. Ruby was her name, and he had met her in Canada, Halifax. I got to know her through the photographs Don Antonio showed me. He didn't like my mother, she had a strain of Neapolitan, and so while we were playing *scoppa* on his porch, he fetched some photographs from the bottom drawer of the chest in his dining room. If I was old enough to play Italian cards, I was old enough to know about the woman my father should have married. I remember only that she had blond hair. Maybe Lucky Luciano's friend reminded my father of his Ruby, because when I opened the door a crack, poked in my head and said, "Hi, Pa," I saw that his left arm was around the patient's hair and it was blond and long, extending from the headrest to the motor on the floor which my father kicked to set off his drill. His face was so close to hers that it was practically inside her mouth. He withdrew his exploratory mirror, released her from his grip.

"Hey, champ—what are you doing down here?"

"Thought I'd say hello."

The woman turned and smiled. Her hair was rumpled, and around her neck was a white towel stained with blood. She unclipped it, revealing a peasant's blouse. I stared at the fair hide of her chest. She spoke with cotton in her mouth.

"So this is little Anthony—how are you?"

"Fine."

"You're looking trim and fit."

"Well, you know, I play ball all day."

"I'd like you to go outside and say hello to Mr. Lucania. He's heard a lot about you." She giggled. "He doesn't like to come in here. He says dentists' offices make him nervous."

I go outside through the waiting room. Patients hold their swollen jaws, tears in their eyes. Up the short stairwell deep as a moat then out into the sun and around the hedges to the tree. Lucky Luciano is in his car, behind the wheel, and he's gazing up the avenue. Soft knocks at the window on the passenger side. I mouth very clearly, "I'm the doc's son."

He unlocks the door and I hop in.

"Lock it."

"Oh, sure . . ." When I turn from locking the door, I see a gun glide from his palm into his jacket pocket. "Mr. Lucania," I begin, "I'd like the truth about Frank Sinatra in Havana, but first I want to thank you for helping us win the war." He had aided the Allies in the invasion of Sicily. "You know, I was with my mother when the news came. She was hanging out clothes to dry and I was beside her, teetering on the sill. Suddenly, people down on the street start screaming. I look at my mother and she's screaming. Mrs. Ernesto comes to her window and she screams. I almost fell onto the garage."

Lucky Luciano muses, "We had a good thing going for a while, selling partisan flags."

He had been in partnership with Don Antonio's brother, Santo, who came to America in 1943 with a trunkful of partisan flags. Don Antonio had come with his tool kit in 1915, and his arrival coincided with the widespread use of stainless steel. The huge kitchens in our schools, hospitals, airports— Don Antonio supervised building them. He made good money and invested in real estate. He lived in a house around the corner from us, and walking there in the dark beside my father was an adventure. It was the first thing we did together as men. With my father as guardian, holding my hand, I could look up at the black sky filled with stars and appreciate its immensity, its grandeur. Don Antonio's house had a garden in front and a yard with a garage where as a boy my father kept his pigeons. The house had a cellar, a deep cellar, a hundred steps straight down. After dinner I followed Don Antonio down. We knew our way through the darkness to his workbench. He snapped on the naked light bulb, and I sat beside him on my stool. We didn't talk. He lived in the United States sixty years and didn't learn English. He worked naked from the waist up and wore a hat to keep in the heat. He made shovels and wrenches and pots, all out of stainless steel. I still have a few of his knives. He also made locks. He was Frank Uale's private locksmith. Mr. Uale, also known as Frankie Yale, invented the Sicilian hand-shake and the Sicilian bullet.

"How do you do?" he would say.

You offer your hand, he takes it, pulls you off balance, then blows your brains out with the gun in his left hand. He killed Dion O'Banion this way in his flower shop in Chicago. Frankie Yale didn't trust his eye, he trusted his bullets. "With my bullets," he used to say, "you pump in a case of gangrene. First you boil onions in water, then take out the onions. Toss ordinary bullets into the onion water and while they boil, peel a few cloves of garlic and chop to a paste. Rub the bullets all over with the garlic. You're ready to load."

Don Antonio and Frankie Yale fed the poor of the neighborhood during the Depression. They drove around in Mr. Yale's bulletproof car. He gave Al Capone a short count on some bootleg liquor around the time the Thompson submachine gun was introduced in Chicago. It made its debut in Brooklyn on Frankie Yale alone in his bulletproof car.

Don Antonio also made his own banister: two long solid rods of gleaming stainless steel. His brother Santo found it easily and settled into the house with his flags. He walked around in his shorts. Don Antonio told him, "Please wear your pants."

Santo explained that in Messina he always walked around in his shorts.

"You're in Brooklyn now," said Don Antonio. "Besides, my daughter Anna is pregnant. *Para brutto.*"

The next morning Santo came to the breakfast table in his shorts and Don Antonio kicked him out.

Anna had married a Sicilian named Joseph Garaffa, and it was through Uncle Joseph that Lucky Luciano entered our lives. They had grown up together on the Lower East Side of New York. Joseph liked to gamble and was in a crap game that was raided. His watch was taken. His mother goes to the Lucanias: "I saved my whole life for that watch . . ." Joseph got his watch back. In turn he bought Lucky Luciano his first pair of silk underwear. Joseph became a cutter for Lily of Saks and cut Lucky Luciano a few suits.

"Tell me, how's your uncle, Joey Gaff?" Lucky Luciano asks me in the car.

"He passed on."

"What a guy, Joey Gaff: flashy dresser, great driver. He was the best driver I ever had. In the old days we were tough, it's true, but, you know, we loved to dance. Joey, me, George Raft, we'd dress to the teeth and go uptown and dance. George, he was the best of us."

"Where did you learn the tango, do you know?"

"The tango was the rage. It was a new import from France. Valentino had danced it in *The Four Horsemen.*"

"Did my father hang around with you guys?"

"Later on. He used to come along with Joey."

"Did my father dance the tango?"

A big smile breaks on his face. "He liked to fox-trot. Let me tell you something about your father: he was so handsome that all the girls flocked around him. We had to dance with ourselves. Once in Havana he was at the bar surrounded by these beautiful hookers, you know, and he puts his arms around them and says with tears in his eyes, 'Now what are nice girls like you doing in a place like this?' "

"My father was in Havana?"

"Your father was anywhere where there was a big crap game: Nassau, San Juan, Mar del Plata, Havana, Monte Carlo—you name it, he was there."

"He did disappear the month of August. Was he in Havana when Frank Sinatra was there?"

"Look, I read the papers. We don't take a roll call. In a foreign country, especially a small one like Cuba, Americans tend to stay together. We meet at the bar—your father, me, Joey Gaff, Ed Sullivan, Frank Sinatra, whoever's down—and, yeah, we eat together and go to the races and jai alai and gamble! Who do you think can afford the best hotels and restaurants and patronize the gambling establishments? The journalists? The Cubans? Puerto Ricans?"

"Ralph Capone?"

"He was in Chicago. I remember for a fact because I called his cousins Charlie and Rocco Fischetti and asked them why they hadn't come down. They said that Ralph needed help in the jukebox end of business. Crooners like the Eberle Brothers, Dick Haymes and Frank Sinatra were breaking away from the big bands. There were a lot of new singles to put in the jukeboxes. It's a cash business, and you should know that when it comes to cash, Italians call on their family."

"So Frank Sinatra wasn't in Florida with the Fischetti brothers."

"Only Joe, and he was legit, in real estate. Frank didn't want to go to Havana with Joe because of his brothers, but what was he supposed to do? Tell Joe he couldn't fly on the same plane? You'll have to talk to the ticket agent."

"This business about a valise with six million in small bills . . ."

He pulls up his coat, reaches into his back pocket, withdraws his wallet and hands it to me.

"It's heavy."

"There's ten thousand in C-notes in there. Six million in *twenties* would fill your father's office. You'd need ten longshoremen to carry it. Besides, would I have an entertainer in the public eye bring me money?"

"We all went out in a boat to welcome Uncle Joseph home from the war. I got lost in a sea of legs, but the thing to watch for was a bridge over the water. As we approached it, I looked up and saw hundreds of sailors in white uniform. Joseph was among them, and they cheered and waved and tossed their white hats. Joseph came home with every inch of his arms covered with tattoos. They set him apart for me. I didn't ask where he had gotten them, what port, what battle, what woman, or what had entered his mind that would make him the only tattooed Sicilian in the family, if they made his skin feel any different or his blood. I preferred that the world of Joseph's tattoos remain a mystery even as the years passed, saying only, "Gee, you gotta lot of tattoos."

"I liked to sit next to him at the table because he showed me things he had learned in the Navy, like salt brings out the flavor of watermelon and lemon brings out the flavor of cantaloupe and honeydew. I sat close beside him when he drove and couldn't take my eyes off his tattooed hand working the tall shaft. As I grew older we drifted apart. His role in the family was impermeable to the admiration of a nonblood nephew. He was the husband of the younger sister, the brother-in-law who goes through life unappreciated. He is quiet, respectful, always ready with a smile. He drives you anywhere at any hour of the day and night. He knows how to fix things and does so without complaint. He has a job, a boss, and keeps them for life. He calls home at noon to say hello. His children don't go to the best of schools. They're the apple of his eye. He cares for them when their spouses die and when they divorce. He is an usher in church. Despite illness and inclement weather he shows up on Sunday to pass around the basket. He goes to the barber once a week for a shave and haircut. He numbers the barber among his friends. He suffers one heart attack after another but still smiles and struts like a king, lighting up a Camel."

I say to Lucky Luciano, "Thanks a lot, and I'd like to leave you with a nice little story. When Don Antonio told his brother Santo to wear pants because Anna was pregnant, he was telling the truth. Your old friend Joey Gaff and Anna had a daughter, Alice, and she's had a hard life. Her husband died in an accident at an early age. She raised two children on her own, tried this man and that one. Out of spite she married a cop who on his wedding night turned out to be a virgin. She got cancer and beat it. Then she married a good man named Jake. They're in their sixties now, and recently went to Atlantic City to see Frank Sinatra. Alice called me.

"'When he was just about to sing, holding the mike, he dropped his shoulder and I couldn't help myself—I got up and screamed "Frankie! Frankie!"'"

RITA CIRESI

Sometimes I Dream in Italian

∽∾∾

T HE MINUTE I STEPPED INSIDE THE South Seas Restaurant, I knew my sister had invited me there just to be facetious. The lobby was so red it hurt my eyes, and the gold plastic dragon on the wall looked more like a deranged poodle than some fierce mythological animal. The menu posted on the cash register boasted authentic Polynesian and Chinese cuisine, but the man behind the counter obviously was Vietnamese. His name tag read: YOUR HOST MR. V. TRAN.

Inside, Lina waited by the back wall, at a tiny bentwood table for two that was topped by a red and black umbrella. The fabric on the umbrella looked spray-painted, and I suspected that if we stripped it we would find the tricolors used to decorate pizza patios, and maybe even a bold advertisement for CINZANO.

"Where in the world did you find this place?" I whispered.

Lina smoothed a lock of her shellacked black hair. "Bob used to take me here."

Bob was Lina's old lover. He had given her genital warts, a topic I didn't care to discuss just before lunch. I sat down and opened the red laminated menu.

"Forget the food," Lina said. "This joint is known for the drinks."

I looked at my watch.

"It's Saturday," she reminded me. "Besides, if you eat a lot of rice, it'll wear off by one-thirty."

When our waiter—a Mr. T. Tran—appeared, Lina felt compelled to state her order twice, in the loud exaggerated tones our parents used to use whenever they spoke English to someone who wasn't Italian. To make up for Lina's condescension, I mumbled my order and had to repeat it twice.

Lina got a mai tai. I got a frothy drink called a grasshopper, which reminded me of the seafoam green punch my aunts had served after my mother's funeral.

Lina reached over and stole the tiny paper umbrella out of my glass. "Pammy loves these things," she said. "I'll save it for next time she starts whining. Did you know Pammy's a whiner?"

"Yes," I reminded her. "I've baby-sat."

"Phil sends his love," Lina said. "To you."

"My love also," I said, sipping the grasshopper.

Lina's plum-colored lips raised slightly, as if she had just confirmed what she had suspected for years: that I once had harbored a strange crush on her husband. "You've got a foam mustache," she said, and I wiped my lips with a red paper napkin.

Lina took a long drink of her mai tai, folded her plum-tipped fingers together, and leaned across the table. "All right, let's get down to business."

Ostensibly Lina and I were meeting to settle the question of what to do with our father. For months now, Babbo had let everything go. The house was draped with cobwebs; the car growled because it needed a new muffler; the laundry sat gray and stiff in the corner; and Babbo, who refused to bathe, smelled gamy as a stuffed skin that the taxidermist hadn't treated quite right.

"He's a mess," Lina said. "The other day I went over and the faucet in the kitchen sink was streaming water because he forgot to turn it off. The toilet was clogged with poop—"

"Spare me the details."

"—and Babbo started talking at me in Italian."

"What did he say?" I asked.

"How the hell should I know?" And when I frowned at her, Lina said, "Like I'm supposed to remember? Use it or lose it, as they say. Anyway, I kept yelling at him, *Non capisco, I don't kabeesh you, Daddy,* and I kept on repeating it until a mouse—a real live mouse—zoomed out from under the couch, looked at me, and then zoomed back in."

I shuddered. "I hope he's not home when I get there—"

"Oh, Babbo never goes anywhere—"

"No, the *topolino.*"

Lina wrinkled her nose. "You could feed him the three-month-old *formaggio* that's been sitting in the fridge."

"Stop. I'll be sick."

Lina straightened her silverware on the table. "Phil says we should put Babbo in a home."

I hesitated. Then I said, "All right. Keep on talking."

"But the whole thing gets me depressed. It's like Mama all over again." She swallowed the last of her mai tai. "Do you ever think about Mama?"

I felt like telling Lina, *I dream she's coming at me with her fingers pinched together, ready to pick the nits out of my hair. I dream someone opens her coffin and her face instantly caves in, like a jack-o'-lantern melted by a candle—*

"Oh goody," Lina said. "Here comes the pu-pu platter." She pushed her glass across the table at the waiter. "I need a refill," she said. "Another mai tai."

Mr. T. Tran nodded and took the glass. He pointed at mine—still half-full—and I shook my head.

"Watch, he'll come back with a Coke or something," Lina said.

"Be quiet," I said, and selected a pu-pu, or whatever one of the individual things on the plate was called. Grease dribbled down my chin.

"What about a home nurse?" I asked.

"Too expensive," Lina said.

"What's the other going to cost?"

"Big bucks too," Lina said. "But thank God for Medicare. And Phil's big fat salary. Phil can pay for anything. Mmm, try one of these rolled-up things; they're actually edible. Do you know why Connecticut is called the Nutmeg State? Pammy has to write a report for school."

I shook my head. "Babbo's never even been in the hospital," I said. "I wonder how he'll react when you tell him."

Lina tapped the table with her red plastic swizzle stick. "What do you mean, *me* tell him? You're not getting off easy on this one, pal."

I gave her what I hoped was a frosty look. "Of course I'll be there to tell him," I said. "Just give me the date."

Lina took her calendar out of her purse and turned to her *To Do* list. "I'll start calling around on Monday," she said, writing a note to remind herself. "It's probably just like day care—you have to get on a waiting list for something decent."

I thought about Saint Ronan's, where Mama had lived for three years after her stroke. "All those homes are horrible," I said. "Full of construction paper cutouts and Lawrence Welk on big-screen TV."

"High-school glee clubs in to sing Christmas carols," Lina added.

"Little children marching around in Batman and Barney costumes on Halloween," I said.

"Talk about hell on earth!" Lina finished the last pu-pu and licked the grease off her well-manicured fingers. "Thank God you could come today. I couldn't wait to ditch Pammy and Richie with the baby-sitter. They love the baby-sitter. They hate me." She paused. "Do you think Phil hates me?"

"Of course not," I said.

"Sometimes I wonder," Lina said, smiling, as if the very idea gave her satisfaction.

LINA GOT THE HAPPY FAMILY, which she hardly touched. I got the Perfect Match with white rice, cold sesame noodles, and a spring roll. I tried not to think about Mama and mice and Babbo babbling in Italian as I glumly ate my sour, salty main dish, half-listening as Lina gave me the rundown on the doings at her house.

"Pammy plays 'Frère Jacques'—with two hands—on the piano," she said. "Richie's still padding around in those Big Bird slippers that make his feet stink. Every day when I drop him off at day care I tell the teacher, *Have a good day*. Notice I don't say *nice*. And she says, *Every day is good when you wake up alive*. Like you're gonna wake up dead? I feel like asking her. But I keep my mouth shut because she's still Pollyanna-izing. *Every morning when the alarm clock rings*, she says, *I thank God for another day*. Oh yeah? I feel like saying. Well I think: *Fuck, six-thirty already?* But like I said, I don't breathe a word of this. I keep my mouth shut because I'm afraid if I'm rude they'll molest my kid or cheat him out of his goddamn graham crackers for snack. I mean, once I told Pammy's teacher I didn't have time to sell candy bars. For weeks afterward Pammy complained about how she always got stuck playing with the bald-headed doll during recess." Lina paused. "So what do you think of my exciting life?"

She looked around the restaurant, which was empty except for an older couple sitting in a booth toward the front. Her eyes looked vacant, and the deep plum color of her lips seemed to tremble.

"Bob just wanted me because I looked different," she finally said.

I nodded.

"He wanted me to talk in Italian to him," Lina said. "Like I know more than four or five things to say. I mean, he'd be fucking me and I'd be telling him, *Fish on Fridays*, or *Shut the hell up!* Then he'd come with these great big groans and I'd be saying, *Hey thanks, paesano, you're a real goomba, how goes it?*"

I laughed. Lina shrugged and looked across the table at me. I knew she was evaluating, with dissatisfaction, my green turtleneck and navy sweater.

"Do you ever feel like waltzing into a bar, leading some guy on, and then giving him the wrong phone number?" she asked.

"Nope," I said, using my fork to stab a scallop.

She took another drink. "The minute that mouse looked at me, I knew I needed a face-lift," she said. "I'm getting a face-lift."

"Don't," I warned. "You'll end up looking like Liberace."

Lina sucked on her swizzle stick. "How could we have watched Liberace for all those years and not realized he was the gayest blade on earth? God, wouldn't it be great to be a kid again and not realize anything?" She looked intently at me. "You know, Pammy's got those two black girls in her class. The other day when I pick her up she whispers in my ear, *Daniella and Nicole are different.* So I get all set to roll out the Sesame Street we-are-the-world minilecture when Pammy leans over with a devilish look on her face and says, *They've both got beads in their hair.* Isn't that something? Out of the mouths of babes—"

"Ofttimes come burps," I finished for her. It was a line Phil had coined when Pammy was a colicky infant and screamed herself red in the face until she belched herself out of her indigestion.

The waiter came over and pointed to my empty spring-roll plate. I nodded and he cleared it away. After he was halfway to the kitchen, Lina said, "God, to think I have to pay fifty bucks a month for gloss to get that kind of shine in my hair."

I sighed. I picked a little bit more at my rice, while Lina sat back and opened and closed the tiny umbrella that had been in my drink. She had a dreamy look on her face. All of a sudden I was afraid she might be remembering her days in the high-school drama club. I was scared she might break out into "Shall We Dance?" from *The King and I* or "Happy Talk" from *South Pacific*. To head off trouble, I blurted out, "I'm seeing someone."

Lina dropped the toy umbrella. She leaned forward, her hands pressed flat on the table, and in an exaggerated ladies-lunch voice she said, "Do tell."

I paused, twirling my sesame noodles around my fork. "He's German."

"No way! What's his name?"

I paused. "Dirk Diederhoff."

"Can he change it?"

"I doubt he's ever even considered it."

"Where'd you two hook up?" Lina asked.

"He's from Minnesota," I said, evasively.

"I guess you didn't meet him in a bar, then."

"I don't do bars," I said. "Anymore."

"So where—?"

"I answered his ad," I said. "In the newspaper."

"Oh my God!" Lina said. "My little sister answers dirty ads."

"They're not dirty."

"I can't believe it. What did the ad say?"

I pressed my lips together.

"God," Lina said, "I can imagine the kind you'd answer. *Long walks at Grant's Tomb—*"

"That's full of crack addicts now," I said.

"Evenings listening to chamber music. Saturday afternoons in the stacks of the New York Public Library."

"So what kind would you answer?" I asked.

"I wouldn't answer," Lina said. "I'd *advertise*." She laughed ruefully. *"Bored housewife needs something to keep her out of the mall."* She sucked wistfully on her discarded straw. "I've seen those ads in the paper. I've read them. Do you notice how the men always want a photo?"

"And the women always want a man who can bench-press three hundred but isn't afraid to cry," I said.

"What gets me are the euphemisms for *fat*," Lina said.

"Zaftig."

"Rubenesque," Lina said.

"Statuesque."

"Does he fuck you in German?" Lina asked loudly.

I looked over at the cash register, where Misters V. and T. Tran were conferring. Lina impatiently said, "I'm telling you, they don't get English. One day I ordered the moo shu and they brought the chow mein. Do I look like someone who orders chow mein?"

I shook my head. "Dirk doesn't talk much," I lied.

Lina laughed triumphantly. "Neither does Phil. Bob never did either. It's a male thing. It's like they're afraid their dicks will fall off if they open their mouths." She leaned back in her chair. "The other day Richie pulls down the fly on his jeans—did I tell you how much I hate the way his Big Bird slippers make his feet stink?—and he goes to me, *Mommy, Mommy, I've got a peenie. Great*, says I. *Now you can go out and rob a bank*." She sucked in her cheeks and pursed her lips at me. "Did I tell you I'm going out for Halloween as a dominatrix?"

I looked at her empty mai tai glass. "You're acting like an asshole."

Lina sighed. "I should have been a man," she said. Then she pulled her ear to indicate she was joking. "So this relationship, is it serious?"

I shrugged. "I think so. Yes."

Lina turned and craned her neck. "Where's the waiter? We need our fortune cookies right now. Chop chop."

"Stop it," I told her.

"What's Kirk—I mean Dick's—I mean Dirk's astrological sign?"

"Aries, I think."

"The ram. Great. He'll never be impotent." She took a cup and poured some of the tea that had been sitting in the stainless-steel pot since the beginning of the meal. "I'm going to read your tea leaves."

"That's the Gypsies, Lina."

Lina stared down into the cup. "Ah . . . I see . . . I see . . . life full of great fortune and profound sorrow." She stifled a burp. "Not-so-happy family comes back to haunt you. New family of many blond daughters. One son, strong as ginseng root. But beware the evil tuna fish—"

"Lina, stop it," I hissed as the waiter came over and silently gathered our dishes.

"Do you think I should leave Phil?" Lina asked, watching the waiter stack the plates.

"For who?" I asked, no longer caring about decorum.

"For myself," she said, and then asked the waiter, "Could you wrap this? I want to feed it to my dog."

I got up without excusing myself and disappeared for three or four minutes into the ladies' room. It was a single-stall bathroom, cold and not very clean, and after I had gotten over some of my shame at being related to someone like Lina, I went back into the dining room. Lina was bent over her compact mirror, reapplying her lipstick. She had coated only her bottom lip when Mr. T. Tran came back carrying the check and two fortune cookies wrapped in cellophane on a black lacquer tray.

"You choose," Lina told me, her top lip pale and cracked compared to her coated bottom lip. "You first. You have a future. I only have fate."

I selected the cookie on the left. Lina put down her lipstick and seized her own cookie, as if certain it would contain some secret as to how she should live her life.

We hesitated, then ripped the cellophane and gingerly broke our cookies in half. I thought about how different we were in our approach from Phil and Dirk, both of whom extracted their fortunes by breaking the cookie in half with their teeth.

I looked at Lina expectantly.

"Do not purchase any items from the Home Shopping Channel," she pretended to read from her fortune. "All that glitters is not gold."

I leaned over, took the scrap of white paper out of her hand, and read the real message: *Good friends stick by your side.*

Lina took mine and read aloud, *"Be confident."* Then she tossed it down to the table. "Have you noticed how shitty these fortunes have been lately? They used to sound like Confucius. Now they sound like your local Girl Scout leader." She looked back toward the kitchen door. "I feel cheated. I demand a refund."

"Lina," I said warningly.

She clenched her fists on the table. "I swear to God, if you marry him—"

"I'm just going out with him," I said.

"You said it was serious, and serious means marriage. Which really means jail."

"You're a sour person, Lina," I said.

"I know," she said. "I'm just like the eggplant Mama used to pickle in vinegar." Lina looked around the restaurant. "Bob used to take me here," she said, as if she hadn't told me that already. Then she told me something I hadn't heard before. "I stole money from Phil to get an abortion."

I sucked in some breath. "How could you?"

"How could I not?" Lina pursed her crooked lips together. She looked all lopsided as she said, "Now when I fall asleep—God, I have so much trouble going to sleep—I dream about tidal waves. I read about them in the *Reader's Digest* in the clinic. They're called nightmare waves. They rush out of nowhere onto the shores of South Sea islands. They're supposed to be sent by a hostile god. Whole families, entire villages, get swept away."

I felt the sharp corners of my fortune cookie melting in my mouth.

"Do you ever have weird dreams?" Lina asked.

"Sometimes I dream in Italian," I told her. "I'm talking, but I don't have the least idea what I mean to say."

I sighed. I reached over for the check, but Lina grabbed it first. "I'll pay," she said. "You know I like to pay."

NICK TOSCHES

My Kind of Loving

What is it with you people who don't understand
the senseless slaughter of animals?
What is it with you people
who don't want to wear fur?
I want to fuck you in fur.
Kill me a Kennedy;
that's my idea of foreplay.
Bring me his fucking pig-faced mick head
on a silver platter—
No, better yet: Aynsley makes these plates,
22-karat gold and blue Cobalt—
Fuck the silver; bring me his head on one of those.
Wear your diamond-seamed stockings,
special shoes from Brazil.
I'll see you there.
I'll see you there.

"The kind of woman your mother is," my uncle Pat
once said to me, *"is the kind of woman who serves one*
pork chop per customer for dinner."

FOOD

BARBARA GRIZZUTI HARRISON

An Accidental Autobiography

I LOVE FOOD. I ALSO SEE it as the agent of my destruction.

When my lover and I separated I bought a bread-making machine. It was such a comfort to me, having something I could feed and control so that it would feed me, knowing that if I pushed all the right buttons I would get all the right results.

Food is good, the source of immediate sensual pleasure, gratification, gain . . . which is what makes it bad: food is bad, it's the source of gain. Fat. Which we all hate.

But it's perfectly possible to hate one's fat and to love one's body at the same time. I'm fat. I love my body when I'm having sex, nice body, so obedient, so capable . . . I rise, like yeast . . . so beautifully able to give and to take.

I DON'T THINK I KNOW a single woman who knows what she looks like.

Mirrors notwithstanding, and in spite of the fact that we're invited, from the time we approach puberty, to take stock of our physical assets (and maximize them), and of our deficiencies (so as to minimize or mask them), I can't think of anybody who sees her body in a clear and dispassionate light, of anyone who doesn't center her anguished attention on an imperceptible flaw, or, on the other hand, perversely see as lovely that which others perceive to be flawed and love herself exactly for those physical attributes others have chosen tactfully to overlook. Make the most of what you've got, Mama says; but she looks so hopeless and sounds so exasperated when she says it ("your *hair*, dear . . ."), preparing us all for lives of trembling narcissism.

I thought I was fat when I was in junior high school. I wasn't fat. My breasts were developed—my first bra was size 32B. I didn't wear the trainer bras girls wore in those days, the point of which eludes me: Were they meant to coax nonexistent breasts into being? buds into flower? Were they supposed to make girls feel that they were northerly endowed so as to reduce the envy they presumably felt for their southerly endowed brothers? Were they a way (like dollhouse tea parties) to ape Mommy? Were they a transition between playing dress-up and being real women?

So much attention given to what wasn't there. In my case, however, what wasn't there *was* there, prematurely. I was unconcerned until Aunt Angie presented me with that size 32B from Macy's, to the accompaniment of female family laughter; and after that I was painfully aware of my breasts when I played punchball in the school gym in my horrid pea green standard-issue middy suit, unable to absorb the principle of running around bases, so terrified was I of exposing my busty difference. I was more keenly aware of them when I was issued a freshman's drab tank swim suit in New Utrecht High School. (Every week I told the phys ed teacher I had my period, so as not to have to get into that suit; it was months before it dawned on her that if I were telling the truth, I was a medical anomaly if not a freak.) I was the champion roller skater of West Ninth Street because skating was something you could do alone, in the dark, with no one to regard your breasts jumping up and down like independent creatures. Skating was like levitating, almost: one flew, and executed daring turns and stops, and, in the swimmy light of streetlamps filtered through maple leaves, one imagined one had auburn hair and green eyes. Nobody could touch me then.

"Barbara is water-retentive," my mother said (it was one of her ritual proclamations), as if I needed any more proof that I was fat. Which I was not.

When I was seventeen I sat with my teacher Arnold Horowitz (the thrilling proximity of beloved flesh!) on the window seat of his living room (the gross inadequacy of my flesh!) regarding, with the heart-stopping mingled terror and joy of first love, the winy maple tree that perfumed his room; we listened to a record of Kathleen Ferrier singing a folksong one line of which was about the "soft brown down" on someone's white arms in the moonlight. I took that as a coded direction to visit the electrologist. Can you imagine? I peer at my arms now and wonder what I could have been thinking of, what I could have been agonizing over. What on earth, except a totally crazy relationship to my own body, could have caused me to regard the hair (such as it was) on my body as a problem? In fact (I know now) I had beautiful hair, and negligible body hair. One school day when I was fifteen, teaching us to parse a sentence, Arnold wrote on the blackboard *The girl with hair the color of sun-warmed wheat* . . . , and then he passed my desk and smiled and mouthed *you*. What, I wonder now, would it have taken to reconcile me to myself in those sad and tingling days?

. . . In those days when I had gonorrhea. How I might have gotten a vene-real disease was a mystery to me, but I had learned, from reading *Dr. Fish-bein's Medical Home Examiner*, a staple tome in those households for which I baby-sat, that a spur on the heel was an indication of that disease. I also had, according to the evidentiary tables of *Dr. Fishbein's Medical Home Examiner*, pleurisy and rheumatic fever; but I chose, not insignificantly or inconsequen-tially, to worry only about gonorrhea. I didn't wear sandals for years.

Whenever I see and am tempted to envy a pretty teenager striding along in apparent possession of her beauty and in disregard of approval or con-demnation, I remind myself to think: The chances are she hates her flesh.

Once from the window of a moving car I saw a young girl sitting at a soda counter, penny loafers dangling from her toes. For a long time I saw her image—her bare feet, the daring of exposure—as the perfect image of freedom.

I despised my fat. I weighed 110 pounds; I was five foot two ("Short legs, dear, are not American"—guess who said that).

I was thinking about this the other day as I ate the fruit-jelly slices I'd ordered from the Vermont Country Store catalogue. I was eating the sugared fruit-jelly slices—semicircles of lime green and orange and lemon yellow and pink with crescent candied rinds marginally more chewy than the jellied flesh of the sugared fruit—because I wanted to eat the sugared fruit-jelly slices, in defiance of the fact that I am fat. (Perhaps this doesn't explain why I ate two pounds of them. Moderation was another of those Mama-speak virtues I seemed incapable of exercising.) I happened to be nostalgic for jelly slices (also for sourballs) at the time I ordered; how was I to know that my latest diet would coincide with their arrival?

Nostalgia, for me, often takes the shape of food. When I think of my old neighborhood, I think of the corner candy store: jelly beans in a sack, and "dots"—little sugary pastilles of pale yellow and pink and blue, stuck on long strips of virginal white paper; black and red licorice sticks, and jawbreakers and candied "lips"—rubbery gummy things you attached to your own lips and ate from the inside out (a satisfying sort of cannibalism); and malted-milk balls and Sugar Babies and candy cigarettes, red at the tip. I think of the ice cream truck: it had a little picket-fence swinging door and a gabled roof with fake windows, so sweet and small-town-like—Icicles and Fudgsicles and Creamsicles and chocolate-almond bars, Dixie cups and sugar cones and plain cones: abundance. If you were good, your mother let you have one. (But it had to be from the Good Humor man; the other brands were, in some indecipherable way, bad for you.) Lemon and chocolate ices from the Italian bakery, charlotte russes—goodness, I long for them—in summer season: sponge cake in a ruffled paper cup and a layer of mashed fresh strawberries and whipped cream with a cherry on top, the bliss. When I think of home I think of Grandma cooking the Sunday gravy—the tomato sauce for "macaronies"—on the big black stove in the kitchen. When I was a good girl, Grandma let me dip a piece of bread in the thick sauce, which bubbled for hours.

I can't remember a time when the words *good* and *bad* didn't attach to food. *Mangia, mangia, it's good for you. . . . Don't eat that, you naughty girl, it's bad for you.*

I went with Grandma to the kosher livestock market and watched chickens being ritually slaughtered, blooded, their necks slashed. Grandma collected the blood in a tin bucket, and she went home and made blood pudding of it, blood thickened with sugar and flour, blood punctuated by raisins. . . . I went home and sat beneath the mulberry tree, which formed a circle around me, hiding me, protecting me; I ate the ripe purple berries, staining my lips, my face, my hands, my starched white blouse with the blood of the sweet and delicate fruit. . . . When I lived in India with Mr. Harrison for four years, I missed (in addition to the love I did not feel for my husband) only one thing: dark red cherries.

I measure generosity and I measure meanness in terms of food. "The kind of woman your mother is," my uncle Pat once said to me, "is the kind of woman who serves one pork chop per customer for dinner." This was a summary of her character as far as he was concerned, and with it I secretly concurred.

"Barbara has a weight problem," my mother used to say, a kind of mantra when she was mad at me. I wouldn't have minded so much except that she said it in front of my beaus, or, lacking that opportunity, when she was in the process of devouring a whole huckleberry pie and (life being unfair) not gaining an ounce as a consequence. "Barbara is water-retentive." Jesus, what a judgment.

I was a slender young woman. Sometime in my late twenties (when my poor grandmother, who regarded me as maritally retarded, was making novenas for me to marry) I grew, imperceptibly to me, into my early image of myself: I became slightly overweight . . . and, later—now—frankly fat.

("Why are you fat?" a colleague asks. "Don't you like men?" People are idiots.)

ONCE, IN LIBYA, THE SHEIK of a pre-Islamic oasis called Gadames told me Sophia Loren had slept in the bed I was about to sleep in (the sheets, apparently, hadn't been changed since she made a moving picture in the hotel four years earlier); he told me I was more beautiful than she, and I allowed myself to feel flattered until he added this codicil: "Because you're fatter." (He'd weighed me on the barley scale.)

The miraculous meal we had that night had been prepared by a Neapolitan couple who led an odd kind of improvised life in the desert, this little patch of which they had made to blossom like the rose . . . and the fig tree, and the mulberry tree. They squabbled incessantly—their contentious syllables the music of their lost home. The old man shot pigeons for us and cooked them; we had rough red wine of his making; and his wife served the olives she had cured, and the pasta she made, and a sauce composed of tinned tomatoes and fresh cactus pulp. The sheik, as we stood on a windswept dune surrounded by oceans of sand where Tunisia, Libya, and Algeria conjoined (and where French military planes swooped like desert hawks), told us he'd met Josephine Baker once in Paris, and spoke of steak and *pommes frites* as if they were foods fit for gods; he was sad and glad in equal measure—glad because he had seen the wide world, and sad because he never would again. (He didn't whine.) There were seashells buried in that sand—and water nowhere to be seen. In that surreal wilderness of stingy sand, only the food was real.

I HAVE GIVEN MUCH THOUGHT to food, and to the flesh in which I live, and have entertained much conjecture on the subject of fat. I have learned that almost anybody can sound authoritative on this subject, in spite of the fact that the theories, the analyses, the prescriptions are mutually contradictory. It's almost as if anything one says about food and flesh is capable of reflecting truth—or the truth of the moment.

Is overindulgence a form of self-medication for pain or a frank urge to self-destruction? Is it neither? Is it sensuality pure and simple? Is fat a matter of genes, or of character and will, of discipline and sloth? of mommies? Is gluttony a mortal sin or is overeating a disease or disorder? And do the answers lie in our culture or in our poor selves (if indeed there are any definitive answers)?

When I am at the supermarket, are people "reading" my food cart in order to read my character?

Sometimes I want a boy's body—I want, when I swim, to enter the water like a sword. I do not want the impediment of breasts.

Do we really look to drag queens the way they look to us?

What has happened to the civilized, simple pleasures of the table?

In 1936, the satirical essayist Rose Macaulay was able to speak of food as pleasure and perishable art: "Here is a wonderful and delightful thing, that we should have furnished ourselves with orifices, with traps that open and shut, through which to push and pour alien objects that give us such pleasurable, such delicious sensations, and at the same time sustain us. A simple pleasure."

A simple pleasure, however, that led to the downfall of the human race ("every pleasure has also its reverse side, in brief, its pain . . . [all pleasures have] the little flavor of bitterness, the flaw in their perfections . . . which tang their sweetness and remind us of their mortality and our own, and that nothing in this world is perfect"): "The vice of gluttony was in Paradise, most deplorably mistimed." It was through gluttony "that our first parents fell." *Macaulay* took the fruit-and-downfall business with a dollop of wit: "The only fruit that has ever seemed to me to be worthy of the magnificently inebriating effects wrought by its consumption on both our parents is the mango. [How many calories in a mango, I wonder.] When I have eaten mangoes, I have felt like Eve."

Somehow one knew Eve, mother and sister of us all, ultimate troublemaker, twin and dangerous friend, was at the bottom of all this. Haven't we always been told so?

"It scarcely bears thinking about, the time and labour that man and womankind has devoted to the preparation of dishes that are to melt and vanish in a moment like smoke or a dream, like a shadow, . . . and afterwards no sign where they went is to be found."

Oh yes, there's a sign. The stigmata we bear are called cellulite.

Even Macaulay, frank and free in her appetites, expressed a degree of aristocratic disgust for food: Bread, sausage, jam, veal, "Better see no food prepared. Close the eyes, open the mouth, and say a grace that you were not there at the making of the pleasant finished product that slips so agreeably down your throat and into your system. And, if you come to that, what would your system look like, do you suppose, if you should have the misfortune to see *that?* It ill behooves us, with our insides, to be dainty about looking upon the manufacture of anything that goes into them; at its worst stage the object to be consumed can scarcely have presented so ill an appearance as does the place prepared for its reception."

Poor Macaulay, she starts off singing the uncomplicated praise of food and winds up describing the human body that consumes it as a sewer.

I read Sartre in my late teens and made the mistake of taking him seriously. He told me that if one really loved another human being, one had to set oneself the imaginative task of loving every orifice, every inch of intestine, everything the loved body contained, enveloped, or expelled: gall and mucus, shit and spit. I gave this imperative grave consideration, never for a moment understanding that Sartre might have loathed flesh—particularly if it was female flesh—and was himself incapable of human love. . . . Men are afraid of women's bodies (their secret interior plumbing); women exude so much, not the least of which is blood. (Unclean! An Arab text tells us that breast milk is menstrual blood "twice-boiled.") Men are bound both to love and to hate the bodies they exited from and from which they must separate so completely in order to be distinguishably male. And women read men's self-centered words and wonder why the world seems off center. We are both erotic and motherly, and as a consequence, alas, threatening. We don't mind nearly as much as they do that men, who have exited from us, also enter us. We don't mind at all.

We are heir to the imperatives and the contradictions of decades, of centuries. A less kind way of saying this is that we are slaves of fashion. (The first time I saw the expression *fashion slaves* was in 1983, in the window of Milan's Rinascente: stylishly dressed mannequins held the banner— FASHION SLAVES—aloft. The Milanese are a realistic people and are capable of singing in their chains.)

In the fifteenth century the ideal beauty had narrow shoulders, small breasts, a large rounded belly, wide hips, great big thighs, short legs, and a small head—she was a perfect embodied Botticelli. (Also she wore a permanent half-smile akin to a simper.) In the 1880s women were obliged to have hourglass figures to satisfy the demands of fashion, the ideal measurements being 38-18-38, which means that their waists were smaller, even, than Scarlett O'Hara's, around which Rhett Butler could join his two hands. In the 1920s fashion dictated no tits, no hips; women were fashionable ironing boards around which to drape cloth. The 1940s were complicated, as, from my mother's wardrobe, I remember: Women worked in war factories, so they had to look strong and capable; they also, poor things, had to look soft (like Betty Grable), as if on call for the men who flew the planes they built. They had somehow to give the illusion that if you ripped off their clothes you'd find pink candy underneath. Stand-ins for the men at the front, they had to be women (unmanned) underneath. I rather like the fashions of the 1940s, and I do think women have a shoulder-pad fantasy—*undress me and I'm ready to service and to serve.* In the 1950s, when I grew up, a moderate hourglass figure was called for, à la Monroe and Loren. Simultaneously, adorable Audrey Hepburn, coltish and elegant, offered us fashion lessons (as if anyone in the world could ever look like more than a pale caricature of her, so *sui generis* was she; an actress who worked with Hepburn told me that during the filming of *A Nun's Story* she lived on apples, mineral water, and vitamin shots, a penance worse than that which the nun suffered).

Women are offered alternative visions or versions of beauty upon which to model themselves. Paradoxically, the fact that idealization of female beauty takes different forms results not in the perception of choice but in a multiplication of bondage. "Throughout the nineteenth century," writes Lawrence Venuti, the translator of I. U. Tarchetti's nineteenth-century novel *Passion* (which provided the inspiration for Sondheim's musical), "romantic writers and painters challenged the dominant concept of female beauty by associating the erotic with illness. In opposition to the fleshy, salubrious ideal of femininity that characterized bourgeois culture, a consumptive thinness was construed as the sign of a heightened sensibility, both passionate and spiritual. The title character of Jules Barbey d'Aurevilly's *Lea* (1832) possesses a more than angelic beauty precisely because she suffers from tuberculosis. Her lover, Reginald, waxes rhapsodic: 'You are the most beautiful woman in creation! I shall never give you up, not you, nor your sunken eyes, your pallor, your sick body.' Their first kiss turns out to be their last. At that very moment she succumbs to the disease, and love and death are grotesquely linked in her bloody vomit: 'Her heart's blood flooded her lungs and rose to her mouth,' leaving her 'no more than a corpse.'" In *Passion*, the hero's carnal infatuation with a woman of abundant physical charms is revivifying; his later obsession with the tubercular Fosca, on the other hand, "is marked by a rapid physical decline that implicitly depicts her as a vampire-like femme fatale, sustaining her own life at the expense of her lover's."

. . . I am hopelessly retro, I love the 1950s. . . . I am strolling down a Brooklyn street; honeysuckle; and I am holding Arnold Horowitz's hand. I am dressed in a flared, quilted skirt, bright flowers splashed on a field of black satin, that reaches in provocative waves to my calves, and a silky wraparound black blouse, and black Capezio ballet slippers, I am wearing Shalimar because it smells like vanilla and Arnold loves it. I am loving myself, feet skimming the ground, loving the way I look. . . .

A brown shirtwaist dress with faint yellow and orange stripes and pearly buttons that emphasized my hourglass à la mode figure; a body-clinging dress of lamb's wool, soft as a cloud, for which my own curves provided the only ornamentation; an olive green dress, black checks, high at the neck, tight to the waist, flared in inverted pleats to midcalf; a shaggy pink angora sweater that cinched my waist and a thin black silk moiré skirt—how I loved those clothes. Why did I abandon the body I loved, the clothes I loved? By insidious degrees. And sometimes I allow myself to think that this body, which, after all, men have loved, is fine, capable, and beautiful. The theories I entertain are contradictory; so are my own.

Toward the end of the 1950s, lots of us who believed ourselves to be free spirits took to wearing a beatnik-type uniform: black. Black skirt, black blouse, black leotards. The head of the secretarial pool at Macmillan, where I worked, sent out memo after memo: Wear nylons! she said. We ignored her. (She was Steichen's daughter and Sandburg's niece—*and don't you forget it!*) We thought she was old. Old and fey. We knew we'd get old someday, but we didn't *know* we'd get old. (It's interesting how knowing one will die—and I did know that—is quite different from knowing that one will grow old.) Dan Wakefield asked me to go with him to a fashion show given by Jimmy Baldwin's sister. "I can't go," I said, "I've been wearing the same black blouse and skirt all summer." "All the more reason," he said. "Anyway, I'm getting married that day," I said. Which was true. I curled my hair for my wedding; I cut my long brown hair and curled it. I agonized over whether to wear gloves. I carried white gloves. I didn't wear them. I couldn't decide whether to let the neckline of my hastily bought white dress plummet to reveal the curve of my breasts, or to modify the neckline with a pin. At this time I weighed 130 pounds and considered myself—except when making love (but not to my future husband)—grotesque. I was not grotesque. I was not skinny, either. I'm fatter now.

RAYMOND DeCAPITE

The Coming of Fabrizze

❧

ALL DAY THE STORE WAS PACKED. Igino stayed outside and played the harmonica under a rainbow of balloons tied to his shoulder. It seemed he had dropped in from a land of song and play. Inside Tony strummed the guitar to set a furious pace. Bassetti and Mancini were trapped behind the counter. Rumbone carried olives and candy to people waiting at the trolley stop. Poggio kept soaring up the ladder out of the crowd to pluck down cheese and ham from the ceiling. Once he was sent up for provolone.

"How's this one?" he said.

"No, no, no," said the customer. "I don't want it!"

"They're all the same," said Poggio.

"Don't tell me about it!" shouted the customer.

"A little louder," said Poggio. "I can't hear you."

"I want the one in the corner! The one out of the light! That one or nothing!"

For a moment the crowd was breathless as Poggio held a salami and reached far into the corner. Gasping, he called for a knife.

"Why doesn't he come down and move the ladder?" said a voice.

"Be quiet," said another.

"Where are you?" said Poggio, straining. "Let me hear your voice again. Is this the cheese you want?"

"That's the one!"

"Come over here," said Poggio. "One more step. One more step. Stand still. Hold your hands out."

Poggio slashed the string and the provolone fell on the man's head. He buckled there.

"Is that the one?" said Poggio.

"I'm not so sure," said the customer, rubbing his head.

"How about a ham?" said Poggio.

"You'll finish me on the spot, eh?"

A man called Ravello was charmed off the trolley by the song of the harmonica. He came over to investigate. He peered through the door. People swept him in from behind. He was trapped there in the crowd. Fabrizze appeared six inches away with a smile so engaging and eyes so clear that Ravello smiled back with all his heart. He felt like a child. Fabrizze put cheese and bread in his left hand while pinching his arm in sudden affection. Fabrizze was swallowed by the crowd. Ravello went after him. An elbow was driven into his neck. His hat was knocked off. He retrieved it and here was Fabrizze with flaming hair and deep soft eyes and that nose like a command. Ravello was longing to be pinched. Fabrizze put salami on his bread and vanished. Someone filled his right hand with wet olives. He wound up in the corner with Tony Cucuzza who whispered and smiled in a way that sent him back into the crowd.

"You there," he said. "Are you Rumbone? The man with the guitar says you'll take care of me. I want a quarter of a pound of Romano cheese. And that's all."

"A quarter of a pound?" said Rumbone. "You have mice?"

"Where are you going?" said Ravello.

"Come with me," said Rumbone.

Rumbone led him back to the storeroom and gave him a glass of wine. They drank several toasts and then came out. Rumbone caught sight of a girl filling the doorway with light and beauty.

"Mendone," he said. "Take care of Ravello here. He's waiting an hour for a quarter pound of Romano."

"Not a quarter of a pound," said Mendone.

"Are you a clerk?" said Ravello, following him.

Mendone poured wine in the storeroom. He was wearing a white apron. A yellow pencil was behind his ear.

"It's a good thing I came into your hands," said Ravello.

"Have another glass then," said Mendone.

"I saw this face in the crowd," said Ravello. "I was feeling reckless out there."

Fabrizze slipped in for a glass of wine.

"Look who's here," he said.

"I saw you out there," said Ravello.

"I remember you," said Fabrizze, pinching him. "Did you taste the figs from Sicily?"

"Where are the figs?" said Ravello, helplessly.

"Look for me before you leave," said Fabrizze. "Let me thank you for stopping in. I'll have something for you."

"What is it?" said Ravello.

"A surprise," said Fabrizze.

"Really? Will you show me the figs?"

Rumbone had pounced on the girl.

"I want some olives," she said.

"How easy to please," said Rumbone, bowing and smiling. "This way, my dear. Make room there. Let's taste them."

Rumbone plunged into a barrel and came up with a shining black olive. He held it like a pearl and then insisted on popping it into her mouth.

"A pound of the black?" he said. "You make up your mind in a flash! And what else? Say the word. Come closer."

The girl blushed and turned away.

"But I think I know," said Rumbone. "You'd like to taste the other olives, eh? You're ashamed to say it. How sweet."

Twice more he popped olives into her mouth.

"And what else?" he said. "Come closer. I can't hear a thing with this crowd. Such beautiful eyes. What an idea I have! It's for a summer afternoon, my dear. A barrel of olives and a bit of wine. And you. And nothing more."

"I want bay leaf, if you please."

"So polite," said Rumbone. "And she wants bay leaf. But what will you do with bay leaf?"

"We put it in spaghetti sauce," said the girl, softly.

"It sweetens the sauce, eh? How she takes hold of things. And what else? Come closer, my dear. This crowd, this crowd."

"Fennel?" said the girl, afraid to risk it.

"Fennel, fennel," said Rumbone, delighted. "But what are your plans with this fennel?"

"My father makes sausage."

"He makes sausage!" cried Rumbone. "Benedico! As though he hadn't done enough!"

Ravello was being served. His voice boomed through the store.

"Cheese, cheese," he said, pounding the counter. "Give me a pound of Romano then! How much is that piece?"

"Over a pound," said Mendone.

"Over a pound?"

"Almost two pounds," said Mendone.

"Almost two."

"Exactly two and one quarter," said Mendone. "It's just right for you. The other piece is too much. It's almost three pounds."

"But it may be five after all," said Ravello. "Make an end of this. Give me the small one."

Carrying two great bags Ravello struggled out to the sidewalk. Rumbone was telling the girl about Augustine.

"A famous watchman," said Rumbone. "We must watch for love, he says, and take it where we find it. How he watches us!"

Ravello set his bags down and mopped his brow.

"Here is Ravello," said Rumbone. "Did you get the balloons for your children?"

"Balloons?" said Ravello.

"Let me light your cigar," said Rumbone.

"It never ends," said Ravello, half to himself. "I had music. I had wine. I was leaving when the man with the gold hair gave me a box of torrone candy. We went back and took a few glasses to my health. He put a cigar in my mouth. He invited me to his house for supper. Now it's balloons. Give me the red and the blue then. And put me back on the trolley. I started out to buy a hat."

MICHAEL PATERNITI

The Last Meal

⌘

T HE NIGHT BEFORE THE LAST MEAL, I visit a stone church where
mass is being said. In the back row, a retarded boy sits with his mother,
his head tilting heavenward, watching, in an unfocused way, the trapped
birds that flutter and spin in the height of the church vault. About a hundred
yards away, in the immense holy hangar, tulips bloom on the altar. It's the
end of December—gray has fallen over Paris—and the tulips are lurid-red,
gathered in four vases, two to a side. A priest stands among them and raises
his arms as if to fly.

Last I remember, I was on a plane, in a cab, in a hotel room—fluish, jet-
lagged, snoozing. Then, by some Ouija force, some coincidence of foot on
cobblestone, I came to a huge wrought-iron door. What brought me to
France in the first place was a story I'd heard about François Mitterand, the
former French president, who two years ago had gorged himself on one last
orgiastic feast before he'd died. For his last meal he'd eaten oysters and foie
gras and capon—all in copious quantities—the succulent, tender, sweet
tastes flooding his parched mouth. And then there was the meal's ultimate
course, a small, yellow-throated songbird that was illegal to eat. Rare and
seductive, the bird—ortolan—supposedly represented the French soul. And
this old man, this ravenous president, had taken it whole—wings, feet, liver,
heart. Swallowed it, bones and all. Consumed it beneath a white cloth so
that God Himself couldn't witness the barbaric act.

I wondered then what a soul might taste like.

Now I find myself standing among clusters of sinners, all of them lined in
pews, their repentant heads bent like serious hens. When the priest's quav-

ery monotone comes from a staticky speaker, cutting the damp cold, it is full of tulips and birds.

Somewhere, a long time ago, religion let me down. And somehow, on this night before the last meal, before I don a white hood, I've ended up here, reliving the Last Meal, passing my hand unconsciously from my forehead to my heart to either shoulder—no—yes, astonishingly pantomiming the pantomime of blessing myself.

Why?

When it comes time for communion, why do I find myself floating up the aisle? Why, after more than a decade, do I offer my tongue with the joy of a boggled dog and accept His supposed body, the tasteless paper wafer, from the priest's notched, furry fingers? Why do I sip His supposed blood, the same blood that leaves a psychedelic stain on the white cloth that the priest uses to wipe my lip? Why am I suddenly this giddy Christ cannibal?

At the end of mass, the priest raises his arms again—and the retarded boy suddenly raises his, too, and we are released.

Then I find the hotel again. I lie awake until dawn. Fighting down my hunger.

That's what I do the night before the last meal.

ON HIS GOOD DAYS, THE president imagined there was a lemon in his gut; on bad days, an overripe grapefruit, spilling its juices. He had reduced his affliction—cancer—to a problem of citrus. Big citrus and little citrus. The metaphor was comforting, for at least his body was a place where things still grew.

And yet each passing day subtracted more substance, brought up the points of his skeleton against the pale, bluish skin, he spent much of his waking hours remembering his life—the white river that ran through his hometown of Jarnac, the purple shadows of the womblike childhood attic where he had delivered speeches to a roomful of cornhusks. He sat, robed and blanketed now, studying how great men of ancient civilizations had left the earth, their final gestures in the space between life and death. Seneca and Hannibal went out as beautiful, swan-dive suicides; even the comical, licentious Nero fell gloriously on his own sword.

Yes, the gesture was everything. Important to go with dignity, to control your fate, not like the sad poet Aeschylus, who died when an eagle, looking to crack the shell of a tortoise in his beak, mistook his bald head for a rock. Or the Chinese poet Li Po, who drowned trying to embrace the full moon on the water's surface. Yes, the gesture was immortal. It would be insufferable to go out like a clown.

So what gesture would suit him? The president was a strange, contradictory man. Even at the height of his powers, he often seemed laconic and dreamy, more like a librarian than a world leader, with a strong, papal nose, glittering, beady eyes, and ears like the halved cap of a portobello mushroom. He valued loyalty, then wrathfully sacked his most devoted lieutenants. He railed against the corruptions of money, though his fourteen-year reign was shot through with financial scandals. A close friend, caught in the double-dealing, killed himself out of apparent disgust for the president's style of government. "Money and death," the friend angrily said shortly before the end. "That's all that interests him anymore."

And yet as others fell, the president survived—by tricks of agility and acumen, patrician charm and warthog ferocity. Now this last intruder hulked toward him. He shuffled with a cane, stooped and frosted silver like a gnarled tree in a wintry place. It took him an eternity to accomplish the most minor things: buttoning a shirt, bathing, walking the neighborhood, a simple crap.

And what would become of the universe he'd created? What would become of his citizens? And then his children and grandchildren, his wife and mistress? Was this the fate of all aged leaders when they were stripped of their magic: to sit like vegetables, shrivel-dicked, surrounded by photographs and tokens of appreciation, by knickknacks and artifacts?

When he slept, he dreamed of living. When he ate, he ate the foods he would miss. But even then, somewhere in his mind, he began to prepare his ceremony des adieux.

I'M GOING TO TELL YOU what happened next—the day of the last meal—for everything during this time in December shaped itself around the specter of eating the meal.

That morning, I pick up my girlfriend, Sara, at Orly airport. I've prevailed on her to come, as any meal shared around a table—the life lived inside each course—is only as good as the intimacies among people there. Through customs, she's alive with the first adrenaline rush of landing in a new country. But then, as we begin driving southwest toward the coast and Bordeaux, she falls fast asleep. It's gray and raining, and ocean wind sweeps inland and lashes the car. The trees have been scoured lifeless. Little men in little caps drive by our windows, undoubtedly hoarding bags of cheese in their little cars. And then a huge nuclear power plant looms on the horizon, its cooling towers billowing thick, moiling clouds over a lone cow grazing in a fallow pasture.

There is something in the French countryside, with its flat, anytime light, that demands melancholy. And I wonder what it means to knowingly eat a last meal. It means knowing you're going to die, right? It means that you've been living under a long-held delusion that the world is infinite and you are immortal. So it means saying sayonara to everything, including the delusions that sustain you, at the same time that you've gained a deeper feeling about those delusions and how you might have lived with more passion and love and generosity.

And then the most difficult part: You must imagine yourself as a memory, laid out and naked and no longer yourself, no longer you, the remarkable Someone who chose a last meal. Rather, you're just a body full of that meal. So you have to imagine yourself gone—first as a pale figure in the basement of a funeral home, then as the lead in a eulogy about how remarkable you were, and then as a bunch of photographs and stories.

And that's when you must imagine one more time what you most need to eat, what last taste must rise to meet your hunger and thirst and linger awhile on your tongue even as, before dessert, you're lowered into the grave.

IT WAS JUST BEFORE CHRISTMAS 1995, the shortest days of the year. The president's doctor slept on the cold floor in Latche while the president slept nearby in his bed, snoring lightly, looked down upon by a photograph of his deceased parents. He was seventy-nine, and the doctor could still feel the fight in him, even as he slept—the vain, beautiful little man punching back. In conversation with the president's friends, the doctor had given him about a 30 percent chance of making it to December. And he had. "The only interesting thing is to live," said the president bluntly.

So there were lemon days and grapefruit days and this constant banter with the tumor: *How are you today? What can I get you today? Another dose of free radicals? Enough radiation to kill the rats of Paris? Please go away now.* There was also a holy trinity of drugs—like blessed Dilaudid, merciful Demerol, and beatific Elavil—that kept the pain at a blurry remove, convinced him in his soaring mind that perhaps this was happening to someone else and he was only bearing witness. Yes, could it be that his powers of empathy—for all his countrymen—were so strong that he'd taken on the burden of someone else's disease and then, at the last moment, would be gloriously released back into his own life again?

With the reprieve, he would walk the countryside near Latche, naming the birds and trees again, read his beloved Voltaire, compose, as he had thousands of times before, love letters to his wife.

He planned his annual pilgrimage to Egypt—with his mistress and their daughter—to see the Pyramids, the monumental tombs of the pharaohs, and the eroded Sphinx. That's what his countrymen called him, the Sphinx, for no one really knew for sure who he was—aesthete or whoremonger, Catholic or atheist, fascist or socialist, anti-Semite or humanist, likable or despicable. And then there was his aloof imperial power. Later, his supporters simply called him Dieu—God.

He had come here for this final dialogue with the pharaohs—to mingle with their ghosts and look one last time upon their tombs. The cancer was moving to his head now, and each day that passed brought him closer to his own vanishing, a crystal point of pain that would subsume all the other pains. It would be so much easier . . . but then no. He made a phone call back to France. He asked that the rest of his family and friends be summoned to Latche and that a meal be prepared for New Year's Eve. He gave a precise account of what would be eaten at the table, a feast for thirty people, for he had decided that afterward, he would not eat again.

"I am fed up with myself," he told a friend.

AND SO WE'VE COME TO a table set with a white cloth. An armada of floating wine goblets, the blinding weaponry of knives and forks and spoons. Two windows, shaded purple, stung by bullets of cold rain, lashed by the hurricane winds of an ocean storm.

The chef is a dark-haired man, fiftyish, with a bowling-ball belly. He stands in front of orange flames in his great stone chimney hung with stewpots, finely orchestrating each octave of taste, occasionally sipping his broths and various chorded concoctions with a miffed expression. In breaking the law to serve us ortolan, he gruffly claims that it is his duty, as a Frenchman, to serve the food of his region. He thinks the law against serving ortolan is stupid. And yet he had to call forty of his friends in search of the bird, for there were none to be found and almost everyone feared getting caught, risking fines and possible imprisonment.

But then another man, his forty-first friend, arrived an hour ago with three live ortolans in a small pouch—worth up to a hundred dollars each and each no bigger than a thumb. They're brown-backed, with pinkish bellies, part of the yellowhammer family, and when they fly, they tend to keep low to the ground and, when the wind is high, swoop crazily for lack of weight. In all the world, they're really caught only in the pine forests of the southwestern Landes region of France, by about twenty families who lay in wait for the birds each fall as they fly from Europe to Africa. Once caught—they're literally snatched out of the air in traps called *matoles*—they're locked away in a dark room and fattened on millet; to achieve the same effect, French kings and Roman emperors once blinded the bird with a knife so, lost in the darkness, it would eat twenty-four hours a day.

And so, a short time ago, these three ortolans—*our* three ortolans—were dunked and drowned in a glass of Armagnac and then plucked of their feathers. Now they lie delicately on their backs in three cassoulets, wings and legs tucked to their tiny, bloated bodies, skin the color of pale autumn corn, their eyes small, purple bruises and—here's the thing—wide open.

When we're invited back to the kitchen, that's what I notice, the open eyes of these already peppered, palsied birds and the gold glow of their skin. The kitchen staff crowds around, craning to see, and when we ask one of the dishwashers if he's ever tried ortolan, he looks scandalized, then looks back at the birds. "I'm too young, and now it's against the law," he says longingly. "But someday, when I can afford one . . ." Meanwhile, Sara has gone silent, looks pale looking at the birds.

Back at the chimney, the chef reiterates the menu for Mitterand's last meal, including the last course, as he puts it, "the birdies." Perhaps he reads our uncertainty, a simultaneous flicker of doubt that passes over our respective faces. "It takes a culture of very good to appreciate the very good," the chef says, nosing the clear juices of the capon rotating in the fire. "And ortolan is beyond even the very good."

THE GUESTS HAD BEEN TOLD to hide their shock. They'd been warned that the president looked bad, but then there were such fine gradations. He already looked bad—could he look worse?

It seemed he could. On his return from Egypt, he'd kept mostly to himself, out of sight of others; his doctor still attended to him, but they had begun to quarrel. The president's stubbornness, his fits, and his silences—all of them seemed more acute now. When he entered the room, dressed in baggy pants and a peasant coat, he was colorless and stiff-legged. He was supported by two bodyguards, and part of him seemed lost in dialogue with the thing sucking him from earth—with his own history, which was fast becoming the sum of his life. He was only half physical now and half spirit.

When the dying are present among the living, it creates an imbalance, for they randomly go through any number of dress rehearsals for death—nodding off at any time, slackening into a meaningful drool. They ebb and flow with each labored breath. Meanwhile, we hide our own panic by acting as if we were simply sitting in the company of a mannequin. It's a rule: In the vicinity of the dying, the inanity of conversation heightens while what's underneath—the thrumming of red tulips on the table and the lap of purple light on the windowpane, the oysters on crushed ice and the birds on the table, the wisp of errant hair drawn behind an ear and the shape of a lip—takes on a fantastic, last-time quality, slowly pulling everything under, to silence.

The president was carried to a reclining chair and table apart from the huge table where the guests sat. He was covered with blankets, seemed gone already. And yet when they brought the oysters—Marennes oysters, his favorite, harvested from the waters of this region—he summoned his energies, rose up in his chair, and began sucking them, the full flesh of them, from their half shells. He'd habitually eaten a hundred a week throughout his life and had been betrayed by bad oysters before, but, oh no, not these! Hydrogen, nitrogen, phosphorous—a dozen, two dozen, and then astonishingly, more. He couldn't help it, his ravenous attack. It was brain food, and he seemed to slurp them against the cancer, let the saltwater juices flow to the back of his throat, change champagne-sweet, and then disappear in a flood before he started on the oyster itself. And that was another sublimity. The delicate tearing of a thing so full of ocean. Better than a paper wafer—heaven. When he was done, he lay back in his chair, oblivious to everyone else in the room, and fell fast asleep.

NOW I HAVE COME TO France, to the region of François Mitterand's birth and his final resting place, and on this night, perhaps looking a bit wan myself, I began by eating the Marennes oysters—round, fat, luscious oysters split open and peeled back to show their delicate green lungs. Shimmering pendulums of translucent meat, they weigh more than the heavy, carbuncled shells in which they lie. When you lift the shell to your mouth and suck, it's like the first time your tongue ever touched another tongue. The oysters are cool inside, then warm. Everything becomes heightened and alive. Nibbling turns to hormone-humming mastication. Your mouth swims with sensation: sugary, then salty, then again with Atlantic Ocean sweetness. And you try, as best you can, to prolong it. When they're gone, you taste the ghost of them.

These are the oysters.

And then the foie gras, smooth and surprisingly buttery, a light-brown pâté swirled with faint greens, pinks, and yellows and glittering slightly, tasting not so much of animal but of earth. Accompanied by fresh, rough-crusted, homemade bread and the sweet sauternes we drink (which itself is made from shriveled grapes of noble rot), the foie gras dissolves with the faint, rich sparkle of fresh-picked corn. It doesn't matter that it's fattened goose liver. It doesn't matter what time it is. Time slows for it.

This is the foie gras.

The capon is superb—not too gamey or stringy—furiously basted to a high state of tenderness in which the meat falls cleanly from the bone with only the help of gravity. In its mildness, in its hint of olive oil and rosemary, it readies the tongue and its several thousand taste buds for the experience of what's coming next.

This is the capon.

And then the wines. Besides the sauternes (a 1995 Les Remparts de Bastor, a 1995 Doisy-Daëne), which we drink with the oysters and the foie gras, there are simple, full-bodied reds, for that's how Mitterand liked them, simple and full-bodied: a 1990 Château Lestage Simon, a 1994 Château Poujeaux. They are long, old, and dark. Complicated potions of flower and fruit. Faint cherry on a tongue tip, the tingle of tannin along the gums. While one bottle is being imbibed, another is being decanted, and all the while there are certain chemical changes taking place between the wine and its new atmosphere and then finally between the changed wine and the atmosphere of your mouth.

This is the wine.

And so, on this evening in Bordeaux, in the region where Mitterand was born and buried, the eating and drinking of these courses takes us four hours, but then time has spread out and dissipated, woodsmoke up the chimney. Mitterand, who was famous for outwaiting his opponents, for always playing the long, patient game, once said, "You have to give time time."

And so we have, and time's time is nearing midnight, and there are three as-yet unclaimed ortolans, back in the kitchen, that have just been placed in the oven. They will be cooked for seven minutes in their own fat—cooked, as it's gently put, until they sing.

WITH EACH COURSE, THE PRESIDENT had rallied from sleep, from his oyster dreams, from fever or arctic chill, not daring to miss the next to come: the foie gras slathered over homemade bread or the capon and then, of course, the wines. But what brought him to full attention was a commotion: Some of the guests were confused when a man brought in a large platter of tiny, cooked ortolans laid out in rows. The president closely regarded his guests' dismayed expressions, for it gave him quiet satisfaction—between jabs of pain—to realize that he still had the power to surprise.

The ortolans were offered to the table, but not everyone accepted. Those who did draped large, white cloth napkins over their heads, took the ortolans in their fingertips, and disappeared. The room shortly filled with wet noises and chewing. The bones and intestines turned to paste, swallowed eventually in one gulp. Some reveled in it; others spat it out.

When they were through, one by one they reappeared from beneath their hoods, slightly dazed. The president himself took a long sip of wine, let it play in his mouth. After nearly three dozen oysters and several courses, he seemed insatiable, and there was one bird left. He took the ortolan in his fingers, then dove again beneath the hood, the bony impress of his skull against the white cloth—the guests in silence and the self-pleasing, pornographic slurps of the president filling the room like a dirge.

AT THE TABLE NOW, THREE ortolans, singing in their own fat. We'll eat the birds because the ocean storm is at the purple windows; because this man, our chef, has gone to great lengths to honor us at his table; because we're finishers; because it's too late and too far—the clock is literally striking midnight—to turn back.

We offer the third bird to the chef.

And so he's the first to go. An atheist, he doesn't take his beneath the napkin. He just pops the bird in his mouth, bites off the head with his incisors, and holds a thickly bundled napkin over his lips, occasionally slipping it from side to side to sop up the overflowing juices. Slowly, deliberately, he begins to chew. As he does, he locks eyes with Sara. For long, painful minutes during which we can hear the crunch and pop of bone and tendon, he stares deeply across the table at her, with the napkin to his mouth.

I believe the chef is trying to seduce my girlfriend, a scene mirrored by ortolan-eating lovers in Proust, Colette, and Fielding. But then I realize that he's not so much trying to take something from her as trying to find a still point from which he can focus on the chaos in his mouth. He's chewing, sucking, slobbering, savoring. And he's trying to manage all of the various, wild announcements of taste.

After he swallows and dabs his napkin daintily at the corners of his mouth, it's our turn. We raise our birds and place them in our mouths. I can't tell you what happens next in the outside world because, like Mitterand, I go beneath the hood, which is meant to heighten the sensual experience by enveloping you in the aroma of ortolan. And the hood itself, with its intimation of Klan-like activity, might trouble me more if not for the sizzling bird on its back in my mouth, burning my tongue. The trick is to cool it by creating convections around it, by simply breathing. But, even then, my mouth has gone on full alert. Some taste buds are scorched and half-functioning, while others bloom for the first time and still others signal the sprinkler system of salivary glands.

And now, the hardest part: the first bite.

Like the chef, I sever the head and put it on the plate, where it lies in its own oil slick, then tentatively I try the body with bicuspids. The bird is surprisingly soft, gives completely, and then explodes with juices—liver, kidneys, lungs. Chestnut, corn, salt—all mix in an extraordinary current, the same warm, comforting food as finely evolved consommé.

And so I begin chewing.

Here's what I taste: Yes, quidbits of meat and organs, the succulent, tiny strands of flesh between the ribs and tail. I put inside myself the last flowered bit of air and Armagnac in its lungs, the body of rainwater and berries. In there, too, is the ocean and Africa and the dip and plunge in a high wind. And the heart that bursts between my teeth.

It takes time. I'm forced to chew and chew again and again, for what seems like three days. And what happens after chewing for this long—as the mouth full of taste buds and glands does its work—is that I fall into a trance. I don't taste anything anymore, cease to exist as anything but taste itself.

And that's where I want to stay—but then can't because the sweetness of the bird is turning slightly bitter and the bones have announced themselves. When I think about forcing them down my throat, a wave of nausea passes through me. And that's when, with great difficulty, I swallow everything.

Afterward, I hold still for a moment, head bowed and hooded. I can feel my heart racing. Slowly, the sounds of the room filter back—the ting of wineglasses against plates, a shout back in the kitchen, laughter from another place. And then, underneath it, something soft and moving. Lungs filling and emptying. I can hear people breathing.

AFTER THE PRESIDENT'S SECOND ORTOLAN—he had appeared from beneath the hood wide-eyed, ecstatic, staring into a dark corner of the room—the guests approached him in groups of two and three and made brief small talk about the affairs of the country or Zola or the weather. They knew this was adieu, and yet they hid their sadness; they acted as if in a month's time he would still be among them.

And what about him? There was nothing left to subtract now. What of the white river that flowed through his childhood, the purple attic full of corn-husks? And then his beautiful books—Dostoyevsky, Voltaire, Camus? How would the world continue without him in it?

He tried to flail one last time against the proof of his death. But then he had no energy left. Just an unhappy body weighted with grapefruits, curving earthward. Everything moving toward the center and one final point of pain. Soon after, he refused food and medicine; death took eight days.

"I'm eaten up inside," he said before he was carried from the room.

WE WAKE LATE AND SENSELESS, hungover from food and wine, alone with our thoughts, feeling guilty and elated, sated and empty.

The day after Mitterand's last meal seems to have no end. Huddled together, we wander the streets of Bordeaux, everyone on the sidewalks turning silver in the half-light. And then we drive out toward Jarnac, the village where Mitterand is buried—through winding miles of gnarled grape trees in the gray gloom. We visit Mitterand's tomb, a simple family sarcoph-agus in a thickly populated graveyard, and stand on the banks of his child-hood river.

If I could, I would stay right here and describe the exact details of that next day. I would describe how we watched children riding a carousel until twilight, all of their heads tilting upward, hands fluttering and reaching for a brass ring that the ride master manipulated on a wire, how the stone village looked barbaric in the rain, with its demented buildings blackened by soot from the cognac distilleries.

We just seemed to be sleepwalking. Or vanishing. Until later. Until we were lost and the streets had emptied. Until night came and the wind car-ried with it the taste of saltwater and the warm light in the *boulangerie* win-dow shone on loaves of bread just drawn from the oven. And we were hungry again.

TONY ARDIZZONE

Cavadduzzo's of Cicero

W E U S E O N L Y T H E F I N E S T I N G R E D I E N T S, everything top of the line. No shortcuts. Nothing fake or artificial, imitation or second-rate. Our sugar is only the purest granulated. Our salt is the very best from the sea. You can sift through any barrel of our flour and see not one single gnat! Hey, there's a shop I won't name two blocks south of here they use a flour so full of flies the customers think the bread is poppy seed! Another shop I know cuts its flour with sawdust. In the name of Saint Rosalie, it's true.

Our flour is pure, 100 percent wheat. Our milk and cream only yesterday were still part of the cow. That's one of the reasons why we moved out here to Cicero from the city, to be closer to the farmer. Our honeys—both dark and light—are so sweet that the beehives that produced them don't *zzzzz*, they *mmmmm*.

Our almonds—the taste floats on the tip of the tongue! Now, you don't want an almond that bites the tongue back. An almond should caress the mouth delicately, like a breeze swaying a new leaf on a tree. The same is true of cinnamon. There you aim for an elegant pungency, a somewhat sharper taste that also arouses the nose. A nut, bark, or bean should persuade and seduce the taste buds, never dominate or overwhelm. We select all our spices and flavorings with the utmost care. My Carla and I search constantly for new combinations. If only the mouth had time enough to sample them all!

Our vanilla is so silky that just its smell makes you think you're floating away on a cloud. Our cocoa bursts warmly across the tongue with an assurance as complete as an embrace. You know the three wise men who brought baby Jesù gold, frankincense, and myrrh? I think much better gifts would have been vanilla and almond, cinnamon and cocoa. What else, other than the Madonna's most sweet and holy milk, could have given the Child more delight?

We use only the purest butter, never oleo or lard. Even a goat's tongue can tell the difference. Butter lends a lightness to the dough that its greasy impersonators can't possibly match. We spare no expense.

Our eggs, they're so fresh we crack them when they're still warm from the hen. And clean! I scrub each egg with a little brush until its shell is so shiny it hurts my heart to have to break it. Of course, with food you can never be too sanitary. You're right, we could eat off the floor we're standing on. And your kitchen floor, too, I bet.

Here, have a taste. *Biscotti*, just five minutes out of the oven. Yes, yes, of course it's free. Free taste, the *Americani* way. Try it and believe me. You like? Isn't that one of the most delicious things you ever put in your mouth?

A dozen? Sure. Or maybe you'd like two dozen? This bag can hold two dozen, easy. Our *biscotti* never go stale, though your family will eat them up too fast to find that out.

Two dozen it is, and for your hardworking husband I'll throw in two extra. No husband? Go on! Not married? A knockout like you? I can't believe it! You're pulling my leg!

THESE DAYS, IT PAYS TO advertise. I talk to everybody who walks in, though the *mugghieri* don't let me go on a tenth as long. They know me well and have heard it all before.

"Cavadduzzo, Cavadduzzo," they say with a laugh, "you allow your tongue to gallop around too many words."

It's a joke on my name. I laugh along with them.

"If I wanted to hear a sermon," they tell me, "I'd go to church. For a speech I'd visit the alderman or drop by Bughouse Square!"

They're entitled to a smile after working all day: the women at home with their kids doing the cooking and washing and ironing, the men shoulder to shoulder in the factories, operating the complex machines of American industry.

Factory, home, shop—the difference is small. Work is work. Every shoulder drags a cross. Each head bleeds beneath its own crown of thorns. Everyone labors on one type of assembly line or another, doing the same things over and over every day, all day long, sunrise to sunset, day after day after day.

I remind myself of this whenever I grow weary, when it's four in the morning in the dead of winter and I want to remain curled in bed beside Carla's dark warmth, when it's summer—ninety-five-degrees—and the temperature of my kitchen becomes so high I swear I'm baking, too, when I see a short-cut in a recipe and the devil whispers, hey, Cavadduzzo, listen to me, I know an easier way, no one will ever know, Cavadduzzo. In these moments when I'm tempted to make not the best loaf of bread I can but something merely passable, something the mouth will not too strenuously object to, I think of what it means that working people eat and depend on me. I pretend that my dear mother and father will break the next loaf, and then I think the same of their parents, then their parents. And when I'm so tired that even my great-grandmother Crucifissa's face doesn't encourage me, I make believe I've been selected as the baker for the Last Supper, and Jesù Cristu will hold my bread up in his hands.

"*Mangiate,*" he'll say to the apostles.

Taking his example, I draw the next breath and continue.

STILL, MOST PEOPLE DON'T KNOW quality unless you smack them with it in the face. They don't know what they want until you convince them that they want it. A man doesn't crave his own candle before God has sug-gested that he can be a saint. For the sake of the bacon, sometimes you have to tickle the pig's ass.

During our first months here we kept the front door open so as to lure any passers-by with the smell of our bread. I waited patiently by the cash regis-ter and watched. The people of Cicero walked down the street, head down, most of them fast, like busy people with a purpose, intent on getting where they wanted to go. You could see that their heads were full of this and that. Some mouths would mumble a steady intonation to the sidewalk. Other mouths would smile or frown, as if remembering better times. Then they'd get a whiff of my bread and hesitate, head whirling about, nose uncon-sciously sniffing the air. The nose would then compel the brain to order the feet to turn into Cavadduzzo's bakery, *now.*

Then they'd walk through our doorway, and even if they'd just left the eve-ning table their mouth couldn't help but begin to water. Usually they'd over-hear me talking to somebody as if the person was my best friend—and how will people ever become my friend if I don't treat them as one?—and then I'd see the stranger's mouth drooling and I'd offer the tempted soul a free taste, a sweet piece of whatever just came out of the oven, and three times out of five they'd walk out with not just a loaf of bread but a bag full of *bis-cotti* or perhaps a cake or pie or both.

People make a habit of buying from our shop. They learn the times of day when our breads emerge hot from our ovens. They assume a fresh loaf will always be waiting for them. In this business, timing is everything. You don't tell a woman with three kids at her ankles and a fourth in her arms rushing home to cook her husband's dinner to wait. We strive to match supply to their demand. By day's end when we've guessed right we have five or six loaves remaining, just like Jesù Cristu with the loaves and fishes. As you know, after his sermon in the desert the apostles gathered up twelve baskets of leftovers. Not too bad when feeding thousands. The wise baker always ends his day with a little left over, and never disappoints by selling out.

After a while many form a favorite weakness, something special, for their sweet tooth, whenever they have an extra nickel. For many it's our *cannoli,* which I make two or three times a week.

Everybody wants me to tell them its secret.

"Cavadduzzo, Cavadduzzo," they implore, "every Christmas, Easter, and Saint Joseph's Day my dear wife makes *cannoli,* but hers are never quite this good. Do you have any hints for her?"

"Tell her not to go to all the trouble," I answer, "when she can always find them here."

"Cavadduzzo, Cavadduzzo," others continue, "you know I respect your privacy and in my wildest of dreams would never intrude, but please, tell me one thing. What sweetener do you use? And how much sugar and bitter chocolate do you blend into the cream?"

"Precisely the right amounts," I respond.

Sometimes they plead, wringing their hands. They fall down before me on their knees. They kiss my hands, feet, the hem of my apron. "Cavadduzzo, Cavadduzzo, trust me! I'll do anything on earth for you, please! I'll even name you godfather to my firstborn son! Just tell me the sweet secret to your *cannoli!*"

I make a big show of looking around, shushing them quiet with a finger to my lips, shutting the light, locking the front door, bringing them back into my kitchen by my ovens, clearing my throat, sipping a glass of cool water so as to facilitate movement of my vocal cords as well as lubricate my powers of memory, and then I have them place one hand over their heart as they swear never to tell anyone what I am about to say.

"My secret," I then whisper into their ear, "is use only fresh."

One man told me that as his great-uncle Federico lay on his deathbed he waved away the monsignor and in the delirium of his fever asked instead for my *cannoli.* No sooner had word of this request reached my ears than I had a boy in the neighborhood deliver to the unfortunate man a dozen of our

finest cannoli in a paper box. The next morning I was informed by the griev-
ing nephew that as the angels came down for the old man's soul he was pol-
ishing off the eighth *cannoli* and had bitten into a ninth!

Here was a priest offering a dying man Holy Communion, and he wanted
instead just one more taste of the creamy sweetness that comes only from
the kitchen of Cavadduzzo!

Perhaps I blaspheme. May God forgive me. But between you and me, the
pews at Sunday mass would be infinitely more crowded if the pope used a
crispier wafer and a sweet ricotta filling!

LET ME TELL YOU HOW Cavadduzzo's of Cicero began.

One day in our former shop, down on Chicago Avenue just west of Hud-
son Street, near Saint Philip Benizi's in Chicago's Little Italy, a man stopping
by for a loaf of bread told me that he was moving to Cicero to work at a new
factory being built there, Western Electric. Line work, he said, acceptable
pay, assembling the earpieces of telephones.

Make mine loud, I said. The one we got here on the wall—I pointed to
our shop's pay telephone—its receiver is way too low. Oh, he said, I can fix
that easy. As I made change for his coin, he unscrewed all our phone's
screws and was disconnecting the various different wires inside the piece
you hold up to your ear. Of course we never heard one sound out of that
telephone again, but in passing the man did say how much he'd miss eating
our bread.

So I said, don't they have bakeries where you're going? And he said, what
do you think, there's a Sicilian bakery on every street corner in *La Merica?* I
said, perhaps not Sicilian but maybe Neapolitan. And he said, what do you
think, there's a Neapolitan bakery on every corner? So I said, perhaps not
Neapolitan but maybe Genovese. And he said, do you think there's even a
Genovese bakery on every corner? Even every other corner? So I said, well,
perhaps not Genovese, but maybe Tuscan. I hear the Toscani don't make too
bad a loaf of bread. But not sweet, he said, with a sad shake of his head, not
sweet like your Sicilian bread.

In truth there's no bread on earth as good or sweet as Sicilian, no higher
compliment you can pay a person—living or dead—than to say that he or
she's as good as bread.

I reached for a loaf and gave it a kiss as he again said, you know, I'll really
miss this. Here, my friend, I said, breaking off the loaf's end, breaking off a
piece for me, then pouring two glasses of chianti.

Any crust of bread, I said, is good if nourishment you lack. He knocked back his glass and said, maybe if you're sick or cold and dead, but since I'm still alive and hot I'll say there are some breads I would not want to put too near my face, and so I said, in this new place is there really no good bread? Go on, I said, you're pulling my leg.

He said, I beg you, listen, there's not even a Tuscan bakery there, and I said that the Toscani bake their share of decent bread. But not fair, he said, not rich and sweet like this!

God blessed this wheat himself!

Eat, I said, breaking off another piece.

At least today, he said, I'll feast and end up full. He pulled my sleeve and said, I grieve to think of the thousand and one *cristiani* just like me who'll work all day long in the hot factory in Cicero and trudge home to a table empty of good bread.

He sighed, then with his fingertip wiped away a tear.

"What I eat today," he cried, "may I eat next year!"

LATER IT BECAME CLEAR TO me that he was no ordinary man. Undoubtedly he was a messenger from God himself, most likely an angel or archangel whose earthly assignment was to get my feet moving down the path of my destiny. So of course I concluded that I had no choice but to journey to Cicero.

Then all at once the place's name hit me. "Cicero!" I shouted. I threw my apron to the floor. With the heel of my hand, I gave my forehead a loud whack. The name itself seemed like a sign from God. I ran to the back of the shop to find Carla, who sat beside our warm ovens, sewing. "Can you believe it," I shouted, "here in the prairies of *La Merica* there's a town named for the famous Roman orator, statesman, and philosopher Marcus Tullius Cicero!"

Carla looked up calmly from her needle and thread. "Living all these years with you, Gerlando, I've come to believe even in green mice."

I paid her no mind. "Cicero!" I cried. "Known the world over for the rhythm and cadence of his sentences, his elegant diction, his skillful balance of antithesis, and several other oratorical qualities too numerous to recount or remember!" I'd always been a firm believer in the powers of oration, so I was careful to enunciate each of my consonants and vowels, creating a firm yet flexible hollow of my mouth, pushing breath up from my diaphragm while simultaneously gesturing with both hands and arms.

"See-sah-rro!" I sang, a cappella. Like cookie dough in sugar, my tongue happily rolled the *r*. "Carrr-lah," I crooned, "too-morrr-ow we jourrr-nee to See-sah-rrro!"

WEARING OUR FINEST CLOTHES, WE began at the Hawthorne Works gate and walked wherever our feet carried us, finding one less than adequate Czechoslovakian bakery and a pair of general groceries run respectively by a German and a Pole with rheumy eyes. None of these storekeepers comprehended the melodious tongue of Marcus Tullius nor any of its more muscular southern dialects. Ergo, Carla and I returned to the main plant, where we waited outside the gates until a squadron of whistles shrieked a somewhat less than ceremonious ending to the day shift. Then we let our ears be our guide, listening for the least scrap of Italian, until we found and then followed a pack of several young *cristiani* smoking twisted black cigars as they trudged home.

The men entered their doorways breadless, having stopped along the way home at no bakeries.

I asked Carla for her thoughts. She said she was still quite displeased that the angelic visitor had broken our telephone, and at the same time happy that this morning she'd thought to wear comfortable shoes.

"No," I said, "I mean about this place."

"I'd forgotten just how bad those cheap cigars stink," she replied. She waved a hand before her nose. "Gerlando, I'm so very glad you don't smoke."

"I leave that for my ovens," I said with a wink.

Once again we traced our steps back to the factory. In the meadows alongside the road, a hundred thousand grasshoppers soliloquized noisily, clinging to the swaying blades of wild grasses and weeds. "No bread," the chorus of grasshoppers sang. "No bread, no bread, no bread!"

"Maybe the broken telephone is a sign, too," I said. "Taken literally, it suggests that we should make no more calls from that box. At least here in the village of Marcus Tullius Cicero"—I pointed to Western Electric's huge Hawthorne Works complex—"if our telephone ever breaks again we'll know where to get it fixed!"

In the end Carla had to admit that the angel had been right about one thing. There was no place anywhere, no matter what direction you walked in, for the workers to buy a decent loaf of bread.

That is, until Cavadduzzo rode to the rescue!

"I hate you, I hate you," he cried at his father before running out of the apartment, and then down the side staircase to the first landing, where he grabbed his roller skates.

POP

꙳

Gay Talese

Unto the Sons

∽✍∾

Throughout the winter of 1944, Joseph prayed several times each day in the living room of his home, kneeling on the red velvet of the prie-dieu under the portrait of the saint, ignoring the store bell below and leaving the operation of his business largely to his wife. He did this at Catherine's suggestion, for he had been hospitalized after the Christmas holidays with appendicitis, and after returning to work he had become so uncharacteristically curt with the customers that he realized the business would be better served by his absence. A high percentage of the clientele now were American servicemen on shore leave, young men demanding quick service, often insisting that their uniforms be pressed or their newly earned chevrons be sewn on while they waited; and among such customers, many of whom had returned from triumphant tours in Sicily and Italy, Joseph could not always conceal the humiliation and divided loyalty he felt as an emotional double agent.

He had dutifully attended the memorial service for the town's first war victim—Lieutenant Edgar Ferguson, a customer's son who had died in Italy (Joseph had hesitated only briefly before approaching the victim's family to express his condolences)—and Joseph had punctually participated in his daily shore patrol assignments along the boardwalk, on the lookout for German submarines with his fellow Rotarians, until his hospitalization had interfered; but since his release from the hospital in early February 1944, he had tried to isolate himself from his friends and business associates on this island that had become increasingly jingoistic as the war's end seemed to be nearing and victory for the Allies seemed inevitable. He had stopped having lunch as usual at the corner restaurant near his shop because he was weary of the war talk at the counter, and tired of hearing such tunes on the jukebox as "Praise the Lord and Pass the Ammunition." He ceased attending the ten-fifteen mass on Sunday mornings and went instead to an earlier one, at seven, which was less crowded and fifteen minutes shorter; it came without the sermon, which tended to be patriotic, and without the priest's public prayers that singled out for blessing only the servicemen of the Allies.

Joseph continued to keep up with the war news in the daily press, but now he bought the papers at a newsstand beyond the business district, a six-block trip instead of the short walk to the corner cigar store, because he wanted to avoid the neighborhood merchants and his other acquaintances who lingered there and might try to draw him into their discussions about the war in Italy. The last time he had gone there, during the summer before his illness, Mussolini had dominated the headlines (he had just been imprisoned by the Italian king) and as Joseph left with his papers underarm, he heard a familiar voice calling out from the rear of the store: "Hey, Joe, what's gonna happen to your friend now?"

Joseph glared at the men gathered around the soft-drink stand, and spotted his questioner—a thin, elderly man named Pat Malloy, who wore a white shirt and black bow tie and had worked for years behind the counter of the corner restaurant.

"He's no friend of mine!" Joseph shouted, feeling his anger rise as he stepped down to the sidewalk and went quickly up the avenue with his papers folded inward so that the headlines and the photographs of the jowly-faced interned dictator were covered. Joseph did not make eye contact with the soldiers and sailors he saw among the strollers, although he could hardly avoid the American flags that flapped across the sidewalk in front of every shop on Asbury Avenue, including his own; and it was never possible at night to forget the ongoing war: the town was completely blacked out—all the streetlamps were painted black; lowered shades and drawn curtains hid the lighted rooms within houses; and few people drove their automobiles after dark, not only because there was a gas shortage but also because the required black paint on their headlights induced automobile accidents and collisions with pedestrians and wandering dogs.

Although there had been no new German submarine attacks in the area since an American tanker had been torpedoed ten miles south of Ocean City a year before, the island's continuing blackout had introduced new problems: gangs of hoodlums from the mainland regularly ransacked vacant summer homes during the winter months; they also operated a flourishing trade in pilfered cars, having an abundance of parked vehicles to choose from during the nocturnal hours, when it was more difficult to drive cars than to steal them.

Joseph secured his dry-cleaning trucks each night in a garage, and he chained the bumper of his 1941 Buick to a stone wall in the lot behind his shop. Before driving it he often had to hammer the ice off the lock, but he accepted such delays as by-products of the war and the blackout—a blackout which, in his case, extended well beyond the boundaries of his island. He had been cut off from communication with his family in Italy, and his cousin in Paris, for many months. Antonio's last letter, received in the spring of 1943, before the Allies had attacked Sicily, described the Maida relatives as sustaining themselves but expecting the worst, and added that the POW husband of Joseph's sister (captured by the British in North Africa) might have been shot while trying to escape; in any case, no official word of his whereabouts had been received. Whether Joseph's brother Domenico was dead or alive was also questionable; he had not been heard from in more than a year. Antonio had passed on the report that Domenico was possibly with a German-led Italian infantry division near the Russian front— Antonio had received this information from a contact in the Italian Foreign Ministry—but he had emphasized to Joseph that the report was unsubstantiated. Since the arrival of Antonio's last letter, the Allied invasion of southern Italy had begun; Mussolini had been rescued from prison by Germans to serve as Hitler's puppet; and Joseph was now trying to recuperate on this island where he had lived compatibly for almost twenty-two years but on which he currently felt estranged as never before.

While his withdrawal was voluntary, having not been prompted by flagrant personal slights or expressions of ostracism toward his business, Joseph felt powerless to free himself from his remoteness and the hostile emotion that too often erupted within him after such remarks as Pat Malloy's. It was possible that Malloy's referring to Mussolini as Joseph's "friend" was a casual remark, made without ill intent. Joseph was, after all, the town's most prominent Italian-born resident, one who had delivered lectures on Italian history and politics to community groups on the island and the mainland; and there had also been no derisive tone in Pat Malloy's voice, to say nothing of the cordial informality he had always shown toward Joseph in the restaurant. Furthermore, to be linked with Mussolini in Ocean City was not necessarily insulting, for the antiunion, Communist-baiting policies of the Duce had long been popular among the staunch Republicans who governed the island; and even in recent years, as the Fascist and Nazi regimes had closed ranks, Mussolini gained from whatever was to be gained in the United States by being identified as less odious and murderous than Hitler.

Still, during this winter, Joseph dwelled in a state of exile, adrift between the currents of two warring countries; he would read the newspapers at the breakfast table until nearly 10 A.M., his children having already left for school and his wife gone down into the shop, and would then exit down the side stairwell of the building and out the back door, wearing his overcoat and homburg and with a heavy woolen scarf wrapped around his neck, and proceed across the lot to the railroad tracks, and then onward through the black ghetto toward the bay—in the opposite direction from the ocean and his binoculared submarine-searching friends and acquaintances who were lined up with their feet on the lower railings of the boardwalk and their eyes squinting toward the sea. The bayfront district was the most desolate section of town during the winter months; a few black men and women ambled through the bungalow- and shack-lined streets and the weedy fields cluttered with rusting car parts and other rubble, but there was no other sign of human life back here, save for the motorists driving along Bay Avenue, and the white workmen who sometimes scraped the bottoms of overturned dinghies and sloops in the boatyards, and repaired the docks in front of the vacated yacht club. There were hardly any seagulls around the bay, where the scavenging possibilities could not compare with those offered by the ocean; and never during Joseph's excursions did he meet pedestrians whom he knew well enough to feel obliged to pause and converse with, and explain why he was off by himself traipsing about on the broken concrete sidewalks and frosty fields of this black, backwater part of town. His doctor had not suggested that daily walks would be beneficial to the restoration of his health, although Joseph had said so in explaining to his employees his comings and goings from the store; and it also became the excuse his wife gave to those regular customers who inquired, as some did, why he was constantly out of the shop and spotted frequently by them as they motored along Bay Avenue. Joseph had full confidence in Catherine's ability to make whatever he did seem plausible and proper, and meanwhile to carry on the business without him. She was assisted of course by her saleswomen, and by the old retired tailor from Philadelphia, who now worked a six-day week on the island; and she was supported as well by the reliable Mister Bossum, the black deacon and bootlegger who supervised the dry-cleaning plant and had taken over the responsibilities for the punctuality of the irresponsible pressers, especially the one presser everybody called Jet, the flat-footed, carbuncled ex-jazz musician who even now on snowy days arrived for work wearing sandals and short-sleeved silk Hawaiian shirts.

Joseph passed close to Jet's boardinghouse each morning en route to the bayfront, and he was sometimes tempted to stop in and see if Jet had left for work yet; but Joseph resisted, having more urgent concerns. His mother was rarely out of his thoughts during his walks, although he found himself chiding her as much as praying for her. If only she had followed his father to America, Joseph told himself again and again, all the family would now be better off. They would be living with Joseph, or near him, somewhere in America, sparing him his present anxieties about their welfare, and his nagging suspicion that he had somehow abandoned them. If only he had some confirmation that his mother and the rest of his family were alive, that the Allied troops had skirted Maida and left the village undestroyed, he believed, he would no longer be the reclusive and petulant man he had become.

But the war news from southern Italy was scant and inconclusive as far as Maida was concerned. From the Philadelphia and Atlantic City papers he purchased each morning, and from the *New York Times* he received each afternoon in the mail, sometimes two days late, he knew only that the Allies were pushing back the Germans from several locations in the general vicinity of Naples. But Maida was too small, or too insignificant militarily, to warrant mention in the reports; and whatever damage had occurred there, or was occurring now, was left to Joseph's ever-darkening imagination.

When he returned from his walk, by noon if not sooner, he would unlock the rear door on the north side of the building and ascend to the apartment by the walled-in staircase without being seen by anyone in the shop. He would then press once on the wall buzzer near the living room door, signaling to his wife at her desk downstairs that he was home; and usually within seconds she would acknowledge his message with a return signal, and would press twice if she wanted him to pick up the phone extension to discuss something she thought he should know before she closed the shop at five-thirty and came up for the evening. Only on rare occasions did Catherine press twice, however, for there was hardly anything about the business that she could not handle at least as well as he could—a fact that they were both aware of, but that neither discussed. Catherine felt herself sensitive to his every mood and vulnerability, particularly at this point in the war, and in the aftermath of his illness. Having lived under the same roof with him virtually every hour of their almost fifteen years of marriage, except for the recent fortnight of his hospitalization, she thought she knew his strengths, his weaknesses, and his daily routine perhaps better than she knew her own. She knew that when he returned from the bayfront walk, he would first hang up his coat and hat in their bedroom closet in the rear of the apartment, then walk through the corridor back into the living room to kneel briefly at the prie-dieu. A quick lunch would follow in the kitchen, invariably consisting of a plain omelet with crisp unbuttered toast, and a cup of reheated coffee left over from breakfast. He ate little during the day and preferred eating alone. He washed and dried his dishes, but never put them away, leaving this chore for his daughter, Marian, when she came home from school.

Catherine did not leave the shop at lunchtime; instead she had the saleswomen who had their lunches at the nearby five-and-ten soda fountain bring back a milk shake for her. If it was relatively quiet in the shop at midday, as it nearly always was in wintertime, Catherine could hear her husband walking through the corridor after lunch to the mahogany Stromberg-Carlson console in the far corner of the living room, near his record collection. By this time she had already turned off the two particular neon lights in the front of the shop that caused most of the static upstairs on the radio; and if she did not hear him pacing the floor as he listened to the war news, she assumed Joseph was seated in the faded velvet armchair next to the set, leaning forward while twirling his steel-rimmed glasses. He would usually switch stations every three or four minutes, turning the console's large brown asbestos knob slowly and cautiously, as if fearing what the next broadcast might bring. At night she had often observed the intensity with which he listened to the news, awaiting each battlefront bulletin with his face so close to the set that his soulful expression varied in color as the console's green "eye" fluttered in and out of frequency. The children were asleep at this time, these nightly reports often being broadcast well beyond midnight; Catherine herself usually retired shortly after closing the children's bedroom doors, having earlier helped them with their homework. But for hours afterward she lay awake restlessly, not because of the softly tuned radio that continued to absorb her husband's attentions in the living room, nor because of the pink light from the corridor torchère that was reflected forty feet away on the ceiling above the L-shaped ten-foot-high mirror-faced divider that masked the marital bedroom. She was disturbed instead by her husband's pacing back and forth in the living room *after* he had turned off the set, pacing that continued sometimes until dawn, to end only when he had fallen asleep on the sofa, fully clothed. In the morning, hoping not to wake him, Catherine would whisper as she alerted the children for school; but he was always up before they had finished breakfast, and before shaving he would come into the kitchen in his rumpled suit to greet the children formally and then address his wife more gently, usually speaking to her in Italian so the children would not understand.

Except when disciplining them, Joseph paid a minimum of attention to the children during this troublesome winter. Each had been assigned daily chores, both in the apartment and in the store. Even when the chores were performed punctually and competently, Joseph regularly found things to criticize. His complaints were expressed as assertively to eight-year-old Marian as to twelve-year-old Gay. Of the two, only Marian was bold enough to defend herself against his accusations; she alone had the nerve to defy him. While she agreeably carried her mother's shopping list to the neighborhood grocery store, where the family had a charge account—it was actually a barter arrangement dating back to the Depression, when her father and the grocer began exchanging goods and services, making up the difference with gifts at Christmastime after the annual tallying—Marian was far less cooperative in her parents' store. She dusted the glass cases carelessly, swept the floors of the fitting rooms grudgingly when she did so at all, and reacted to her father's reprimands sometimes by dropping the broom or dustpan and stomping out of the shop, ignoring her father's promises of punishment.

"You're more stubborn than my mother," he once shouted at Marian, whom he had named in honor of his mother, although physically she clearly favored his wife's side of the family. Marian had her mother's fair complexion and the red hair of her mother's father, Rosso. She did not appear to be the sibling of her olive-skinned, dark-haired brother, who, while more tractable and less defiant than she, was also more capable of remaining out of their father's sight. Only during his father's illness and self-imposed exile from the shop did Gay enter it without feeling tense and apprehensive—and return to it after school without fear of being late, for his mother was not a clockwatcher; and thus in the winter of 1944 he began taking a more leisurely route home each afternoon, stopping first at the Russell Bakery Shop on Asbury Avenue, where a friend, the baker's grandson, could be counted on to bring a few éclairs out to the alley for a delicious, hastily consumed treat, and then play catch for a few minutes with the rubber ball that Gay always carried in his schoolbag.

Later, in the pressing room, after delivering to Jet and the other presser, Al, enough hangers-with-guards to fulfill their needs for at least a half-hour, Gay had the option of exiting through the back door via the steam screen provided by the pressers, and practicing his pitching form in the lot behind the shop—hurling the rubber ball against the brick wall of the neighboring hardware store's annex, and at times letting it carom off the roof of his father's chained Buick before catching it. He was secure in the knowledge that his father spent the afternoons up in the apartment on his knees, or sitting in the living room listening to operas or news broadcasts, and so he was stunned one afternoon to hear the thumping sounds of his ball punctuated by the urgent rapping of his father's knuckles against the rear window that overlooked the lot.

Gay ran back into the safety of the pressers' steam and quickly resumed the task of affixing guards to hangers, and also sandpapering and unbending those rusty and crooked hangers that customers had provided in response to the store's advertised appeal, and its promise to pay half a penny for each wire hanger, because of the wartime metal shortage. As he worked, he feared the appearance of his father and some form of retribution that might well be overdue. In recent weeks, he had received a failing report card after the midterm examinations; and he had been warned repeatedly by his father to discontinue making his prized model airplanes, for the glue used in sealing their parts cast a hypnotic and possibly toxic odor throughout the apartment. His father had furthermore charged that the glue was most likely the cause of his son's daydreaming and general dim-wittedness in school, the lack of scholarship that had been noted, in kinder terms, by the Mother Superior on the bottom of the recently received report card.

Gay anxiously worked at the hangers, still awaiting his father's arrival in the workroom, knowing that he could expect no protection from Mister Bossum, or Jet, or Al, or the old tailor. But as the minutes continued to register on the misty-faced clock that hung on the workroom wall, and he sandpapered one hanger after another without interruption, he lost track of the time until he saw in front of him his mother's high-heeled shoes and heard her consoling voice suggesting that he was working too hard. It was also closing time, she said, as she extended a hand to help him up from his crouched position.

He was surprised to see that the tailor and the pressers had already left; now only slight sizzling sounds rose from the valves of the machines. Marian also stood waiting, holding a light bundle of groceries in the cloth sack their mother had made because of the paper scarcity. Gay walked up the interior staircase behind his mother and sister, then entered the living room and saw his father seated near the console with his back turned, leaning forward with his head in his hands. The radio was off. He could hear his father softly crying.

His sister, who seemed unaware of it, headed toward the kitchen with the groceries. Gay followed her. Catherine hastened toward her husband and placed a hand on his shoulder. For several minutes they could be heard speaking quietly in Italian. Then she left him and went into the kitchen to prepare the children's dinner; she explained to them that their father was feeling worse than usual, and added that after they had finished dinner they were to go to their rooms and close their doors, and, as long as they kept down the volume, they could listen to their radios. There was no homework to worry about. It was Friday night. Tomorrow a more leisurely day was in the offing, the always welcomed Saturday that brought no school bus or any chores in the shop until after ten A.M.

JOSEPH SPENT FRIDAY NIGHT ON the sofa, having hardly touched the dinner on the tray Catherine had placed on the coffee table in front of him. She had remained in the living room with him until midnight, continuing to speak in Italian. English was heard only when Catherine went to warn Marian that her radio was too loud, and to remind her that she should soon turn off the bed lamp because the following morning she would be picked up by the parents of one of her classmates, with whom she would be attending a birthday party on the mainland.

On Saturday morning after nine, when Gay got up, he saw that his sister had already left. Her door was open, her bed unmade. His parents' bedroom door was shut, as usual, but he knew his mother was downstairs, opening the store for the busy Saturday trade. He could hear the bell downstairs as customers opened and closed the shop's main door on Asbury Avenue. It was a sound he associated with Saturdays, and he always found the tones reassuring, signals of his family's financial stability. In the kitchen, as he poured himself some orange juice, he noticed that there were newspapers on the table that had not been there the night before. Returning to the front of the apartment, he saw no sign of his father. He found it odd to be in the apartment by himself and uniquely exhilarating to be able to walk around freely and privately, answerable to no one. As he approached the console, he noted that its usual gleaming mahogany exterior was now smudgy with fingerprints. He then saw his father's bathrobe lying on the floor behind the sofa, and the ashtray filled with cigarette butts, and sections of newspapers that had been crumpled up and hurled in the other corner, and had come to rest near the piano. Since his father had always been the family's enforcer of tidiness and order, Gay could not even venture a guess as to the cause of this laxity.

Back in the kitchen, sitting in front of a bowl of dry cereal that his mother had left for him, he looked at the headlines and photographs on the front pages of the newspapers. One was an Italian-language paper that he of course could not read; another was the *New York Times*, which he refused to read because it did not have comics. But on this day he was drawn to the front pages of these and other papers because most of them displayed pictures of the devastation left after recent air raids—smoke was rising out of a large hilltop building that American bombers had attacked in Italy, and had completely destroyed. The headlines identified the ruins as the Abbey of Monte Cassino, located in southern Italy, northwest of Naples. The articles described the abbey as very old, dating back to the sixth century. They called it a cradle of learning throughout the Dark Ages, a scholarly center for Benedictine monks, who had occupied it for fourteen centuries; it was built on a hill that Nazi soldiers had taken over during the winter of 1943–1944. The raid on February 15, 1944, had involved more than 140 of America's heaviest bombers, the B-17 Flying Fortresses; these, together with the medium-sized bombers that followed, released nearly six hundred tons of bombs on the abbey and its grounds. It was the first time the Allies had deliberately made a target of a religious building.

After breakfast, while brushing his teeth in the bathroom, dressed and ready to go down to the store, Gay heard strange noises in the apartment, a pounding on the walls and the cursing of an angry male voice. When he opened the door, he saw his father, in overcoat and hat, swatting down the model airplanes suspended from Gay's bedroom ceiling by almost invisible threads.

"Stop it, they're mine!" Gay screamed, horrified at the sight of his carefully crafted American bombers and fighter planes, framed with balsa wood and covered with crisp paper, being smashed into smithereens by his father. *"Stop, stop, stop—they're mine, get out of my room, get out!"* Joseph did not seem to hear, but kept swinging wildly with both hands until he had knocked out of the air and crushed with his feet every single plane that his son had for more than a year taken countless evening hours to make. They were two dozen in number—exact replicas of the United States' most famous fighter planes and bombers—the B-17 Flying Fortress, the B-26 Marauder, the B-25 Mitchell, the Bell P-39 Airacobra fighter plane, the P-38 Lockheed Lightning, the P-40 Kittyhawk; Britain's renowned Spitfire, Hurricane, Lancaster; and other Allied models that until this moment had been the proudest achievement of Gay's boyhood.

"I hate you, I hate you," he cried at his father before running out of the apartment, and then down the side staircase to the first landing, where he grabbed his roller skates. "I hate you!" he yelled again, looking up toward the living room door, but seeing no sign of his father. Crying, he continued to the bottom of the staircase and out onto the avenue, then thrust his skates around his shoe tops without bothering to tighten them; and as quickly as he could, he headed up Asbury Avenue, thrashing his arms through the cold wind and sobbing as he sped between several bewildered people who suddenly stepped aside. As he passed the Russell Bakery Shop, he lost his balance and swerved toward the plate-glass window. People were lined up in front of the pastry counter, and two women screamed as they saw the boy, his hands outstretched, crash into the window and then fall bleeding with glass cascading down on his head.

Unconscious until the ambulance arrived, and then embarrassed by the crowds staring silently behind the ropes that the police held in front of the bakery's broken window, he turned toward his father, who was embracing him in bloody towels, crying and saying something in Italian that the boy did not understand.

"Non ti spagnare," Joseph said, over and over—don't be afraid—using the old dialect of southern Italians who had lived in fear of the Spanish monarchy. *"Non ti spagnare,"* Joseph went on, cradling his son's head with his bloody hands, and closing his eyes as he heard his son repeating, tearfully, "I hate you."

Joseph then became silent, watching the ambulance crew arrive with a stretcher as the police ordered the people in the crowd to keep their distance. When Joseph next spoke, he did so in English, although his son found him no less bewildering than before, even as Joseph repeated: "Those who love you, make you cry. . . ."

DAN LEONE

Chicken

A BOY WAS LEARNING HOW TO LIVE. He wet his pants and wet his bed. He spent hours staring into his mom's underwear drawer, wondering what it was like to be a grown-up, or a chicken, or soap.

He was down in the basement, in the laundry room, trying on the laundry, when he suddenly heard a dog barking upstairs. The boy didn't have a dog. He had a bird. Then his dad opened the basement door and hollered down, "You have a dog. I got you one. What should we name it?"

"Barky," the boy said. He put his own clean clothes back on and went upstairs to meet the new dog.

The dog licked the boy's face. The boy rolled with the dog.

"It's a dog," the boy's dad said.

THE BOY'S UNCLE, UNCLE ROSIE, ran a pet shop. That's where the dog came from, and where the bird had come from, and where the cat would eventually come from.

The boy's dad, on the other hand, was an airplane mechanic.

The boy's mom was studying to be a hypnotist. She would practice on his dad, who was acting like a chicken one day when the boy came down for breakfast. His dad had his thumbs tucked into his armpits and was walking around with his knees bent, flapping his elbows and clucking.

"I did it!" said the boy's mom, laughing.

His dad was laughing too. The boy was happy for his dad. It looked like a lot of fun, being a chicken. The boy had never been hypnotized. His mom always practiced on his dad.

Now it was time to hypnotize the dog, who had been around for a month or two, by then, and was still getting into trouble with the boy's mom. "You will not poop in the house," she said to the dog. "You will never poop in the house. You will always poop outside."

Later that day, the dog ran away.

A WEEK AFTER THAT IT was Christmas Eve. The dog still hadn't come back. None of the neighbors had seen it. The boy was confused. He wondered if maybe Barky had died, if his parents were just pretending Barky ran away because they didn't think the boy was old enough to understand about death.

But he knew that if the dog was still alive, he would eventually come back. The boy's dad, who didn't know this, went to Uncle Rosie's pet shop on Christmas Eve and came home with a cat. They named it Chestnut. The boy's dad meant well, but the cat did not. That night, the cat's first night in their house—Christmas Eve night—Chestnut got into the birdcage and bit the head off the boy's bird, Chirpy.

THE BOY'S DAD FOUND THE headless bird, Chirpy, very early on Christmas morning. He didn't think the boy was old enough to understand about death, so he called and woke up Uncle Rosie.

"Oh God, what is it?" Uncle Rosie said, thinking someone had died.

"It's me," whispered the boy's dad.

"*What's* you?" Uncle Rosie said. Uncle Rosie was not entirely awake, and was afraid it was his younger brother who had died, and who was somehow calling to let him know firsthand.

"Are you awake, Rosie?"

"Okay, yes," Rosie said.

The brothers discussed the situation quietly over the phone, quietly agreeing that Chirpy's untimely death, especially on top of Barky's disappearance, might ruin the magic of Christmas for the boy for the rest of his life. They had both heard about that kind of thing happening.

So the two men met at the pet shop before it was light out, and while the boy still slept, they picked out the bird that seemed most like Chirpy before Chirpy got his head bit off. And they picked out a new cage for the new Chirpy, a cage that Chestnut, the new cat, would never be able to get into.

This accomplished, they wished each other a Merry Christmas, hugged, then went outside into their separate cars and drove back to their separate homes through the dawning holiday.

I would like to say that it was snowing out, but it wasn't. This happened in Santa Barbara.

THE BOY, WHO WAS STILL learning how to live, woke up on Christmas morning having dreamed a huge glass of ice cold water as big as a swimming pool. He woke up thirsty and wet. It was Christmas!

He believed in Santa Claus, this boy, more than he believed in Jesus. Sometimes he couldn't wait to be older and religious, like his dad, and important. He couldn't wait to be smart and sad, like his mom. But he was easily distracted by other things, such as presents. He never even noticed, opening them that morning, any small changes there may have been in the bird Chirpy. Chirpy was Chirpy, and he was there in the background, as always, singing his same old birdsongs.

For Christmas, the boy got army guys and everything else he'd asked for. There was even something for Chirpy: a new birdcage!

WITHOUT EVER KNOWING THAT CHESTNUT, the cat, had bit the head off Chirpy, the bird, the boy instinctively hated Chestnut, the cat. He didn't want a cat. He didn't say anything because he loved his dad and didn't want to hurt his dad's feelings and maybe even ruin his dad's Christmas, but he hated *hated* *HATED* Chestnut from the moment he saw him. In fact, that first night in bed—Christmas Eve night—before falling asleep, the boy wished that his new cat would get run over by a car.

And he came down with the giggles the next day after dinner when carolers came to their door and sang, "Chestnut's roasting on an open fire. . . ."

His mom made him go to his room.

HIS DAD CAME UP AND sat on the boy's bed next to the boy, who was trying to remember what cardboard was.

"Did you have a good Christmas?" his dad said.

"Yes."

"Did you get everything you wanted?" he said.

"Yes."

His dad put his big hand on the boy's knee. "Do you miss Barky?" he said.
"Yes."

"Me too," his dad said.

There was a moment of silence between them.

"At least we still have Chirpy," the boy said.

THE BOY WAS WATCHING CARTOONS when Barky came back. It was the Saturday after Christmas. The boy heard the dog-door open and close in the kitchen and then Barky was there going straight for Chestnut's throat. The boy heard cat-bones snap. He jumped up and down. Just like on TV, things could change!

Barky was back. Chestnut was dead. His mom was in the basement, doing laundry. His dad was in the garage, fixing the boy's bike.

Barky licked the boy's face.

"He's back!" the boy yelled, but his mom couldn't hear him for the washing machine, and his dad had the college football game on the radio in the garage.

"Mom! Dad! Chirpy!" the boy was saying. "Look who's here! And look what he did!"

The evil cat Chestnut was dead, just exactly like a cartoon, with Xs for eyes and his long, pink tongue hanging out. It was a beautiful thing.

The boy's dad had warned the boy not to let Chirpy out of his new cage because of how Chestnut was a cat and how cats would sometimes eat birds. But Chestnut was dead now and Barky was back, and Chirpy and Barky were great friends, so the boy went and opened Chirpy's cage.

Barky didn't notice any difference in his friend Chirpy, either. He wagged his tail and barked and Chirpy flew straight out the kitchen window.

It wasn't like Chirpy to do that.

The boy screamed and then his mom and dad were both suddenly there; and the boy was pointing toward the open window.

"Chirpy," he said.

THIS IS AN EXAMPLE OF how much a father loves his son:

He didn't ask how Chirpy got out of the cage in the first place, or where did Barky come from, or what, for that matter, was Chestnut doing dead. The scene certainly begged for an explanation, but the boy's dad didn't even ask for one. He didn't say anything. He just grabbed a paper bag and ran out the back door after Chirpy.

The mom put her arm around the boy's shoulders and they watched together out the kitchen window while the dad chased Chirpy all over the neighborhood. The boy knew his dad would get the bird. His dad was great.

His mom had bleach and laundry detergent on her fingers. She asked the boy why he had let the bird out of the cage, but the boy didn't answer.

Chirpy was so small and yellow that they could hardly even see him from inside the house. They could always tell where he was, though, by which tree the dad was climbing, or whose house he was leaning a ladder up against, or whose roof he was running around on. The dad could see Chirpy.

All their neighbors either came outside or came to their windows to watch. Some of them were trying to help, keeping track of the bird, running and pointing. Some were just watching.

The boy was proud of his dad. He thought that his dad was the most important person in the neighborhood, if not the whole world. His dad would definitely bring Chirpy back, and in fact he was *this* close to having him, on the Richardsons' roof. Chirpy was just sitting there on one end of it, tired out and waiting to be caught, it looked like, except at the last second, when the boy's dad was just about to bag him, Chirpy flew and his dad— what a guy!—flew after him.

For one moment the boy was so proud of his dad he thought he would burst, and then the next moment he was totally blind. His mom's hands slapped over his eyes and locked the boy inside himself; her voice rang and retreated outside of him, like a rapidly fading nightmare, replaced by the harsh, real smell of bleach, which confused the boy so much that he was sure he must have been hypnotized by his mom and turned into a chicken, and that this was what it was like.

J. T. BARBARESE

Our Fathers

Our fathers stole useless supplies
from Westinghouse and Bruders
where they worked third shift and always felt
like shiftless wops, intruders,

so they walked off with tools,
rivet guns, calipers, gauges
fine enough to measure steel
thinner than these pages,

built boxes for the tools they stole,
tool-boxes shaped from steel
they milled during their lunch-breaks.
They stole things just to steal,

graphite powder, vises, paints,
mounts and sticks for mixing,
rivet guns, rivets, bolts and lines
to lash down everything

they stole in case of apocalypse
to the roofs of the used cars
we helped them wax on Saturday.
They were the great martyrs

of the immigrant religion
whose eucharist was loot,
they lived in borrowed overalls,
they're buried in borrowed suits.

Victoria Gotti

Superstar

⤞⤝

He dropped her off near dawn in front of the Beverly Wilshire, where she was staying. Temporarily, Chelsea reminded herself. She'd have to get out of here soon. It was just a matter of time before the manager would ask for payment. But she had some calls to make.

From the moment Chelsea saw the newspaper headline, she was able to think of nothing else. She decided to blow off the "audition" her agent had scheduled with the casting director of a pilot and make some calls instead. Her thinking was twisted—a sure sign, her psychopharmacologist had warned her, to take it easy, take the tranqs along with the Depakote for a few days. This new mood stabilizer she was taking was easier on the organs, but it didn't seem to work as well on her mood swings as some of the other medicines she'd used.

When she started going into a high, she no longer felt human, but rather supernatural. She could paint pictures, write songs, devour novels, and work nonstop at the studio for days on end. She forgot to eat. Sleep was not a requirement. The higher her illness took her, the more her body and brain called out—*More, let's do more*—and drugs were but one of the things she indulged in. When a high took her away, she'd buy—it didn't matter what— jewelry, clothing, shoes, CDs. When she eventually crashed, she would have to drag her ass back to the stores to return everything. It was amazing that salespeople hadn't figured her out yet, but then, even when her soul was black, her heart on the floor, Chelsea knew how to manipulate.

She was particularly adept at maneuvering things her way when she was on a high cycle. Mostly she manipulated men. During those times, she couldn't get enough sex, often juggling two, maybe three men in a day.

Sometimes she heard her mother's voice, shrilly reminding her that she was the child of the devil, that she was damned, possessed by evil. But most of the time she remained detached. She even kept a list of men she partied with—her slumming list. These were always younger men, of many backgrounds, each with his own style. Where they came from didn't matter. Sex was sex. Men were to be used.

Sometimes the sensations intensified beyond what she considered her usual mania. She'd begin to see things, hallucinate. She would make up entire scenarios that involved imaginary people. Sometimes these scenes included torture or murder, and she'd cower under her blanket, paralyzed by her own fantasy. Often to "protect herself," she'd break out of this mode and become violent—harming herself or even threatening strangers once she got out on the street. Inevitably she would go into a manic psychosis, needing help and medication to bring her back to reality.

Sometimes she'd end up in the emergency room on her way to the psych ward at Cedars-Sinai. When this happened, her on-and-off psychiatrist would be called in. Then he'd start up with the same conversation. "You must go on Lithonate or Haldol," he would say. The hip, new generation of mood stabilizers were less toxic than lithium. But Chelsea would not take the medication. If she lost her highs, she'd have nothing: Life would be gray; she wouldn't be unique; her sexuality would diminish—no way.

Today she was on the high end of her emotional spectrum. The news about Roger Turmaine screamed out to her—an invitation to finish the "conversation" she'd started a few months ago in his office. She'd waited for a sign of when to put the rest of her plan into action, and this, indeed, was her sign: He was about to die. It was time to get her just deserts. No more B movies for her. Especially now that Edward had left her with nothing but debt.

Hollywood, the land of dreams and promise, had, in reality, been her personal hell. Chelsea thought of all the ways in which she'd compromised her dignity since leaving Maria and East L.A. How full of plans that little girl had been, how big her dreams. Step by step, the ceaseless striving to be noticed, to have impact in this unreal town had worn her down like a file gnawing away at steel. When was it she'd become a whore—no, she corrected herself: a courtesan. She knew the difference between the two. Whores rarely got ahead. They spent their money on drugs and alcohol, they hung out in seedy nightclubs, and they belonged to greasy, greedy pimps. Courtesans slept with wealthy, influential men, used their money wisely, and played and lived by their own rules. Courtesans were not abused or degraded, and throughout the years, some had even changed the course of history.

Chelsea reasoned that her fate had been sealed the day she was born, the moment someone switched her, the daughter of Hollywood royalty, with the bastard baby of Maria Hutton. She had no choice; the years devoted to lowering herself had been preordained. But now the end was in sight.

Chelsea knew her own downfall, the insanity she'd been born with, ruled her, but she resisted—denying, lying about it, going from shrink to shrink, waiting for the one who would corroborate her belief that her emotional disorder fueled her talent. It was necessary for her to succeed. The doctor had not come along yet, but the chaos about to descend on Roger Turmaine's dynasty offered, she was certain, one opportunity. She didn't know what exactly, but there was a chink in the Turmaine wall and she was going to slip through it.

Chelsea went into the bedroom, locked the door, and took the newspaper clipping out of a manila envelope. She spread it out on the bed and studied it. She remembered the day she figured it all out. It was only a few months ago, right after her mother finally died. It had taken Maria months, years to die. She had chosen to torture Chelsea right up until the last moment of her poor, miserable life, coughing her way through middle age, dying a slow, deliberate death from emphysema.

Father Tom said mass for Maria and officiated at the burial ceremony that no one had cared to attend. All these years later, he still gave Chelsea the creeps.

Afterward, Chelsea returned to her mother's squalid apartment, where she had lived as a child. She wanted to simply burn the entire contents but thought better of it, hoping against hope that Maria had a life insurance policy buried in all the mounds of papers in her bedroom.

Chelsea didn't find an insurance policy. But she found something better.

February 18, 1987
TO: *Lawrence Hibbel, Esq.*

REGARDING: *Maria Hutton vs. Lebanon Hospital*

Careful investigation of birth records for April 1966 indicate there is only one individual who could be the biological match for Chelsea Hutton. Her biological mother is Mrs. Lana Turmaine, now deceased.
Her attorney would like very much to settle this matter out of court. Please contact my office as soon as possible.

Sincerely,
Charles Kaplan
Attorney for Lebanon Hospital

Chelsea leafed through the other correspondence and documents in the box. She came upon another letter from the hospital suggesting the case be settled for $750,000. As Chelsea dug deeper into her mother's files, she found more than twenty-five uncashed checks accompanied by letters from Turmaine's attorney, each memo indicating that the check was "for the child's welfare."

Chelsea flashed on her dismal childhood—the thrift-shop clothes and donated toys, her mother's vicious accusations. When pictures of Cassidy Turmaine's sixth birthday party were in the newspaper, Chelsea was fascinated by the carousel right beside her house. Maria had taunted her mercilessly. "So, missy. You think you should have been invited just because you were born on the same day. Do you really think the little Fairy Princess of Hollywood would have anything to do with you?"

Three-quarters of a million dollars would have made life much easier for Chelsea.

Chelsea studied the letter from the hospital and began to put the pieces together. Hah—the checks were to shut her mother up. But these people hadn't counted on Maria Hutton's God—or her incredible capacity for denial.

Chelsea felt the adrenaline rush, knowing this would tip her body's balance despite the lithium. She sat back on her heels, papers strewn around her on the bed, and considered her options. Soon ideas were flitting through her brain. Hadn't Lana Turmaine been married to Roger Turmaine, the famous director? Obviously he would want this little mistake buried. And he was still alive.

Chelsea was transported to the fantasies of her youth, when she would try to wish away the poverty and squalor of her surroundings, when she imagined herself a little rich girl. And to think she was really Lana Turmaine's daughter!

Hours later, just before midnight, Chelsea fell asleep on Maria Hutton's decrepit bed, papers and checks strewn around her. And by the next evening, Chelsea had come up with a plan.

It was after hours—eight o'clock, to be exact—and Century City Towers, L.A.'s monolith, was nearly empty. Few of the office windows were lit. Chelsea could discern the random pattern the cleaning crew followed by noting which floors were lit versus which were dark. Roger Turmaine's business address was no secret. She entered the lobby and told the guard she had an appointment with Roger Turmaine. "I'm his daughter," she said, not giving her name. The guard spoke briefly into the security phone and Chelsea could hear Turmaine's exclamation. All of Hollywood knew Turmaine and his daughter were estranged.

Before the guard could stop her, Chelsea jumped into the elevator.

So far, so good. The Haldol she'd taken worked very quickly. Chelsea had started back on lithium, determined to stay level-headed and keep her manic mood swings at bay.

The Desmond Films logo, an elegant castle against a backdrop evoking ancestral Ireland, was painted in gold lettering on the heavy glass doors. As soon as Chelsea approached, a buzzer sounded and the security lock released. She opened the door and followed the corridor lights to the north-west corner of the floor.

"Cassidy!" Turmaine spoke sternly from his office before she reached it. "What—" Chelsea heard wheels of a chair quietly turning. She sensed Turmaine walking toward the door. Steeling herself, Chelsea closed her eyes and in that brief moment visualized all the things she wanted for herself.

"What the hell!"

Chelsea opened her eyes to find the man in all the newspaper clippings and magazine pieces facing her. He had removed his suit jacket; the pale pink-toned dress shirt was starched to perfection. His gray pants fit his slim waist and fell precisely in a very slight bell-bottom to the tips of his tasseled black loafers. There was no more time to study the man's clothing because his black eyes pulled hers to look at his. We look alike, she thought, but he left her no time to speak.

"Who are you?" he growled, taking a step toward her. Instinctively she stepped back.

"I'm your daughter." Chelsea fumbled with the clasp of her knockoff Chanel tote, where the papers to prove her paternity were stashed. But her hands were sweaty.

"Get out of here, young lady. I'll have you arrested immediately," Turmaine said, already behind the reception desk, obviously about to call security. Chelsea reached down inside herself for every ounce of courage, strength, and drive she had.

"Please, listen to me." Strands of her honey-blond, straight, shoulder-length hair were glued to her face with perspiration.

Turmaine hesitated. Then, more calmly, he said, "Please take a seat while I make a call."

Chelsea watched as the powerful man sat down and spoke quietly and quickly into the telephone. She couldn't hear a word, yet she sat across from him not five feet away.

"I'm afraid I don't know your name," he said, getting off the phone.

"I'm Chelsea Hutton," she said. She reached to shake his hand and he complied. Chelsea sat in a red buckskin chair with brass bolts, the soft fabric whispering against her stockings as she crossed one leg over the other.

"Ms. Hutton"—Turmaine's voice was calm, quiet—"my attorney is on his way. But I'd rather straighten this out between the two of us." He paused.

Chelsea thought how smooth he was—how persuasive, even charming. It was no wonder Lana fell for him. Lana Turmaine, her mother; Chelsea felt herself awash in heat at the very thought of it.

Roger leaned his elbows on the massive redwood desk as two phones rang at once. The fax machine spewed paper into its tray. "What I'm trying to say, Ms. Hutton, is just tell me what you want and let me see if I can make some sense of this unfortunate . . ." He fumbled for the right word. "This mishap."

"Would you like to answer that?" Chelsea nodded toward the one line that was still ringing. It was making her head throb. It was time for another tranquilizer and probably the last three capsules of today's lithium. For a moment she considered excusing herself but decided to stay with Turmaine right here, in this moment.

"No, they'll stop. Could you answer me?"

Chelsea forced herself to ignore the anxiety in her solar plexus, collecting like dirty water in a still, quiet pond. "I guess I'm here to meet you, first of all, and then to . . ." Chelsea noticed Turmaine's silver hair had no dark roots—there was nothing artificial about his handsome features. He was drop-dead gorgeous. Chelsea felt proud. Here was a man she'd always dreamed of as a father—rich, successful, handsome, famous—and now her dream had materialized. It was a miracle. Suddenly she heard Roger's words pierce her cascading thoughts.

"You are not my daughter. If you continue this charade, this obvious con game, I'll press charges."

"But you don't understand," Chelsea said as she pulled the papers from her bag. This time she extracted the file, but the man stood, pounded his fist on his desktop, and then waved his finger in her face.

"Who put you up to this?" She assumed that Roger, like all successful men, had made many enemies. It was within the realm of possibility that someone might try to set him up, extort from him, plant a scandal—any number of things.

"You don't understand—" Father, she wanted to add, but she checked herself. No, he wasn't ready to accept her yet. She'd have to help him arrive at the truth gradually.

Footsteps padded quickly down the gray carpeted corridor. A man around

Roger's age pushed aside the lock of brown hair mixed with gray that had fallen over his eyes.

"What's going on here?"

"Thanks for coming so quickly. Ms. Hutton, this is my attorney, James Renthrew. James, maybe you could take over this . . . disaster."

"Take it easy, Roger," the lawyer interrupted. "Get a bottle of water from Miriam's refrigerator. I'll handle Ms. Hutton."

Chelsea recognized his name as the signer of the checks she had found. She cringed at the way this man said her name. His words felt like talons digging into her shoulder. The attorney was tall and handsome, in a dark, Mediterranean way. Still, unlike Roger, he did seem soft, approachable.

As Chelsea was trying to stay focused, Renthrew took a large check recorder from his briefcase. He scribbled a check and threw it at her. She saw it was for one hundred thousand dollars. He handed her a handwritten letter, which she recognized immediately as some form of agreement. Some legal deal to get rid of her.

A foggy feeling was beginning to take over her, and Chelsea realized she wasn't going to get anywhere this way. She ripped up the check and the letter. Standing, she leaned over the desk, allowing her salon-tanned, perfect apple-shaped breasts to spill from her blouse.

"Keep it, Mr. Attorney. I'm not going to be bought." And I'm not going away, she thought to herself.

"Just out of curiosity," she said pointedly, throwing her tote bag over her shoulder, a gesture that spoke of more confidence than she really felt, "if Roger Turmaine has nothing to hide, why would you try to pay me one hundred thousand dollars? And why did he—you—send seven hundred and fifty thousand to my mother?"

Not waiting for a response, knowing deep inside Turmaine would never listen to her, that she'd never know her father, Chelsea turned her back, posing just long enough to give the lawyer a good glimpse of her ass. "She never cashed them, you know."

Then she left, closing the heavy glass door with its gold-leafed logo behind her.

PAT JORDAN

A Nice Tuesday

ᴄᴡᴀᴇᴡ

I TOLD MY FATHER A MAGAZINE would pay for us to go gambling at the Foxwoods Casino near Ledyard, Connecticut. He didn't act thrilled. He knew I'd never been much enamored of his gambling. I never saw it like my brother did, as Dad's personal idiosyncrasy that made him so amusing, a character out of Damon Runyon. I saw it as a debilitating vice that almost destroyed us all.

We left Bridgeport for Ledyard, a two-hour ride, in a driving snowstorm at five o'clock on a Saturday morning—Dad and I going to gamble together for the first time in our lives. He was eighty-two, an old man by some standards, but as young, vigorous, and quick-witted as always. I hated to admit it, but it was gambling that kept him young.

"We've got three hundred dollars to gamble with," I said.

"Well, then we'll go right down the line like Maggie Kline."

I looked across at him. "Now what the hell does that mean?"

"It's a Prohibition expression." He smiled. "It means we'll shoot it all."

Jeez, I thought. The old man will never change. Just a few weeks ago he'd shot pool with his sixteen-year-old great-grandson. It inspired him to go to a pool hall in Bridgeport to hustle up a game. He found a black guy named James. Well dressed, Dad said, whatever that meant.

"He was a pretty good shooter," Dad said. "So I made him spot me the eight and nine in nine-ball. He said, 'You may be an old man, but you might make me stand up and take notice. How do I know you ain't hustlin' me?'" Dad just lowered his head, fingering the fedora in his pudgy hands, trying to look as pitiful and harmless as he could. James bought it. "I guess I'll take a chance," he said.

Dad let him win five dollars. "The setup," Dad said. "Next time we'll play for more money." I couldn't help but laugh. The old man was still hustling. That's what he loved about gambling—the hustle.

He began hustling pool when he was discharged from the orphanage at fifteen. He played nine-ball for $100 a game. A fifteen-year-old kid. But he was so good at it, the balls dropping with a thudding monotony, game after game. I should know. I spent most of my adult life trying to beat him at his game. But I never could, except once.

My parents had visited us in Florida when they were in their late seventies. They had only been with us for two days when I had my first argument with Dad. We had been arguing constantly, it seemed, for over forty years. That's why I had invited them to come visit Susan and me. To make my peace, finally, with the old man. But it wouldn't be easy.

After the argument, I called my brother back in Connecticut. "Jeez," I said, "the old man's still a pain in the ass."

"Why can't you just get along with him?" my brother said.

"I'm trying! I'm trying! But he drives me nuts!"

"Forget it, already. Listen, why don't you take the old man out? Just you and him. Go shoot some pool. You know how you used to love to shoot pool with him."

"All right."

I took Dad out to a bar–pool hall out on Dixie Highway, near the body shops and the auto-parts stores. A redneck sort of place just over the railroad tracks. I parked in a gravel lot between a pickup truck that looked like it had been repainted with a brush and an orange Chevelle Super Sport with racing slicks and rusted mag wheels. I heard country and western music through the open door. It was dark inside. It smelled of urine and baby powder and stale beer. I went over to the barmaid, who was talking to a fat, bearded guy with a clip of keys hanging from the belt loop of his oil-stained jeans. She seemed deliberately not to notice me and Dad. I waited at the bar. Dad stood by the door, a small, tentative old man fingering his hat in his hands. Finally, the barmaid came over to me. I asked for a rack of balls.

She gestured with her head toward Dad. "For you and pops, huh?" She had teased hair like straw, dyed black.

"Yeah," I said with a smile. "The old man shoots a pretty mean stick."

"I'll bet, honey." She handed me the balls. "Take your pick." She gestured toward the six deserted Brunswick tables.

My father and I went over to one of the tables and turned on the conical light over it. Dad ran the flat of his hand over the green felt. He shook his head. We got two pool cues from racks along the walls. Dad laid his cue stick flat on the table and rolled it over the felt. It wobbled. He got another. That one wobbled too. He got another and another until finally he got one that didn't wobble. I racked the balls.

"A game of straight, Dad?" I said. He nodded. I played a safety. The cue ball stopped at one end of the table, and only one ball broke free from the rack at the other end. I'd left him a long, straight-in shot. It was a tough shot, but it could be made. Dad went over to the barmaid and said something. She handed him a can of Johnson's baby powder. He sprinkled it on his hands and returned to the table. He examined the balls quickly, bent low over the cue ball, and sighted his shot.

He had short, fat fingers. Not a pool shooter's hands. My mother called them "sausage fingers." Like she threw in the spaghetti sauce, she said. I watched Dad grip the stick. He still had that firm left-hander's bridge, even at seventy-six, and that smooth stroke that I always tried to copy, but never could. Dad shot and missed. The cue ball broke into the rack and scattered the balls. I had a dozen easy shots to choose from. I remembered what Dad had told me once. "The eyes go before the stroke," he had said. "When you play an old man, always leave him long." That was almost twenty years ago. I was a pretty fair shooter then. I had picked up the game during all that dead time I had in the minor leagues. But I could never beat Dad. We would play for hours. I would get sweaty and hot-tempered while he, cool-eyed, with that maddeningly methodical stroke, pocketed ball after ball without missing. The other players stood around and watched my father shoot. I was both proud of Dad's talent and furious that I could not beat him. More than anything then, I wanted to beat him in pool. My father's game.

After only a few racks it became obvious that Dad's eyes were gone. I had built up a big lead, playing hard and ruthless. The way Dad had played me when I was in college. He never let up on me. Never gave me a break, the way some fathers do. I wouldn't have had it any other way. The thought of seeing him deliberately miss a shot so that I could win would have made me sick. It was a good lesson. But it never really took. I could play Dad hard and ruthless for a while. But it was an act I could never sustain. I didn't feel it. The hardness.

I stepped back from the pool table and blinked. I shook my head to clear it. I was ahead by over twenty balls. Dad was standing there, leaning on his stick, an old man with a gray fringe of hair at his temples, waiting for me to shoot. I leaned over the table, took an almost impossible shot, and missed. The balls scattered over the green felt.

"What the hell's a matter with you?" he said. "You know better than that." I shrugged, shook my head as if disgusted with myself. Dad leaned over the table and ran out the rack. I racked the balls again. "That's what happens when you get careless."

I missed my next shot by hitting the object ball just hard enough to make it pop back out of the pocket after it had dropped in. "You've got a touch like a blacksmith," Dad said.

I lost the game to my father by three balls. I threw my arm over the old man's shoulders and said, "Dad, you're still the best."

"You shoulda beat me," he said. "You got careless." He looked up at me and shook his head as if truly sad. "As usual."

I returned the balls to the barmaid and paid the bill. She smiled at me. "The old man took you to the cleaners, huh?" she said.

I looked around for Dad. He was over by the door, out of earshot. "I let him win," I said.

"Sure you did. Sure you did."

I smiled.

That night my parents and my wife and I ate dinner on the deck outside our apartment that overlooked the Intracoastal Waterway. It was a warm, soft, Florida night in February. My wife had lit candles enclosed in glass. The sky was the color of purple plums, dotted here and there with white stars. A breeze blew upon the water while we ate. Boats rocked in the water. I raised a glass of red wine and said, "A toast! To Mom and Dad!" Their faces were illuminated by the flickering lights of the candles. We all clicked our glasses over the table heaped with food. Me. My wife. My mother. My father.

"Who won, son?" my mother said. I looked at her as we all began to eat. "In pool," she added. "Did you beat Dad?"

I smiled. "Are you kidding, Ma? You know I can't beat the old man."

Dad stopped eating. "He got careless, Florence," he said. "He had me beat and then he began taking these crazy shots."

"Oh," she said. "You mean Patty let you win." My father looked at her and then looked at me.

"You sunuvabitch!" he said to me. "You *did* let me win."

"Come on, Dad. I've been trying to beat you for years. You think I finally get you on the ropes I'm gonna go in the tank?" I shook my head.

"You sunuvabitch!" he said. He was furious. Not that I'd let him win. But that he didn't pick up that I was letting him win. I had outhustled him.

RAY ROMANO

—

Dad

‿⁂‿

I'VE ALWAYS SAID THAT IF MY father had hugged me once, I would never be in show business.

My theory has always been that everyone in show business is there because they were deprived of some attention as a child.

Every performer. Every singer, every dancer, every movie and TV star. If these people got their required attention as a child, there'd be no entertainers at all. Nothing for us to sing, watch, or read.

Thank God for undemonstrative parents, or we'd all be bowling.

On the upside, there'd be no karaoke.

To be fair to my father, he did hug me once on my twenty-first birthday. It was very awkward, and I think I know what it was that made me feel so uncomfortable.

The nudity.

To be honest, my father is probably the person that I got my sense of humor from. I'm not saying I got *his* sense of humor. I'm saying I got *a* sense of humor.

His sense of humor I don't think anybody has. I can't quite describe it. He's got a very bizarre, dry way of *trying* to be funny, a very slow, droll manner of speaking, so it's hard to detect that he's joking at all. Very subtle.

And it's dangerous, because if you don't know he's trying to be funny, you could take him the wrong way.

Unfortunately, to this day my wife is taking him the wrong way.

I'm kind of stuck in the middle. I can't tell you how many times I've tried to calm my wife down with the same pleas.

"He's *joking!* He's making a *joke!*"

"*Well, I'm sorry! I don't see how it's funny when he says he thinks one of our two-year-old twins has 'homosexual tendencies.'*"

I've tried to explain my father's sense of humor to my wife countless times, but she just doesn't get him.

The dangerous thing is, I find him funny. I'm not condoning his actions. Look, he's a pain in the ass to me too. But even though he drives my wife crazy, I have to laugh sometimes. Quietly. To myself.

Of course, his comic masterpiece—or as we refer to it, the "Answering Machine Incident"—almost broke up our marriage.

Don't get me wrong. The Answering Machine Incident was not without comedic merit. The timing was bad, though; my wife was still alive.

My dad figured out—I don't know how, I don't know why—how to call into our answering machine and retrieve our messages. He cracked our answering machine code.

He'd listen to our messages, then call back and leave us a message advising us what to do about the *other* messages.

"Ray, the guy from the gas station called, your car's gonna be ready tomorrow. What'd you do to it? I told you to check the oil, ya dummy. And why did Anna's gyno call? Is she pregnant again?"

Three, two, one . . .

"*What the hell is he doing? That's like reading our mail, Ray. Don't tell me you think* this *is funny.*"

I thought it was kind of funny.

I talked her down, she got over it, life returned to normal.

Until the next day, when my father figured out how to change our *outgoing* message. My wife and I were at a friend's house and we called our machine. Instead of hearing my voice on the outgoing message, we heard my father's.

"Uh, hi . . . ! You've reached Ray and Anna. If you want them, leave a message at the beep. If you want me, Al Romano, I'm at 555-2006."

I want to thank my father, because without him I would never have had the pleasure of hearing my wife say the word "cocksucker."

I don't want to paint the wrong picture of my father. His pranks may sound mean-spirited, but let me tell you something. I grew up with him, and believe me, it's a lot better now than forty years ago when he was, shall we say, *prankless.*

Back then, all I remember is him being a guy who had a little bit of a temper. Certain things would just set him off.

One place I never wanted to be with my father was in the car while he was driving, stuck in traffic. I know no one likes traffic and we're all frustrated when we're in it, but my dad had a particularly low tolerance for people when he was on the road.

Everyone around us became a "hump."

"Look at this hump, tryin' to squeeze in on me. I see ya! You're not going anywhere, ya *hump*."

My mother would always try to contain his anger. "Albert, please, you're scaring the children. Just calm down . . . and let the fire truck go by."

"Fire my *ass!* It's lunchtime for these humps! There's always a fire at lunchtime, right? Go ahead, ya hump!"

One time when I was older I made the mistake of actually saying something to him while he was in "hump" mode.

"Dad, you're right on this guy's bumper. Pull back a little."

"Ohhhhh . . . look at Mr. Know-It-All! Mr. College Boy. Mr. Philosophy Major. Hey, why don't you go back to school and waste another twenty thousand dollars of my life with that 'tree falls in the forest' *bullcrap*. 'I hump, therefore I am,' okay? Or how about this: 'I hump, therefore *you* am.' How's that sound, Socrates?"

"All right, Dad, relax."

Wherever we had to be, we were usually late because he was always implementing some plan or theory to avoid the traffic.

"If we leave now it'll be rush hour and it'll take an hour to get there. But if we leave in a half hour, there'll be no traffic and it'll only take fifteen minutes to get there. We'll actually pass ourselves had we left right now."

MY FATHER WAS THE DISCIPLINARIAN of the house. He didn't go overboard, but he was from the old school, and if we did something wrong, he wasn't above a little smack on the butt.

I remember once when I was about nine, I was riding bikes with my brother Richard, and I almost got hit by a car. I wasn't looking, but luckily the car stopped short and the only thing that got scratched was my bike.

On our way home, Richard said he was going to tell my father what happened unless I gave him a dime.

Now, like I say, Dad was the discipline guy, so this kind of "gimme a dime" blackmail went on all the time between me and my brothers. You didn't want Dad to find out if you screwed up in any way.

"I'll give you a nickel."

"No. A dime."

"No, no way. What did I do wrong? I'll give you a nickel."

"Sorry, a dime or nothing."

"Then nothing . . . idiot."

"Dickhead."

"Pimpleface."

Okay, you get the picture. We called each other names for the whole ride home, and needless to say, we never struck a deal.

When we got in the house, my brother told my dad. Guess what happened? Let's just say that would have been a dime well spent.

On its face, there seems to be no logic getting a spanking for almost being hit by a car. What was my dad thinking? "Thank God you're not hurt, so *I* can hurt you."

But now that I'm a parent, I understand where that comes from. When your kids do something careless that puts them in danger, it scares you so much, you want to teach them a lesson so they'll never do it again.

The weird part is, if I had been even slightly hurt by the car, I would never have gotten the spanking.

So, basically, one of two things could have happened:

1. The car hits me, I get hurt.
2. The car misses me, I get spanked.

Obviously, the moral to the story is "Don't lowball."

IRONICALLY, LOWBALLING WAS MY FATHER'S specialty. He was a man obsessed with haggling. As I got older, whenever I paid for something, he'd always ask how much it cost, and I'd be afraid to tell him because I knew what was coming next.

"Forty dollars for that haircut? Holy Christ, you're dumber than I tell people."

When I started doing stand-up and making money, he'd always ask how much I made on every gig. It was never enough.

"That's it? That's all they gave you?"

"That's it, Dad."

"Well, can you Screw the Uncle at least?"

Let me explain "Screw the Uncle."

One of the things my father hated most—and when you're talking about things my father hated, it's a very long list—was the government. To be more specific, having to pay the government.

"They want a piece of everything you got! Bastards. You pick your nose and find a dime in there, they want some of it!"

So Screwing the Uncle—the "Uncle" being Uncle Sam—was his way of asking if I didn't have to pay taxes. That he loved.

"Can you Screw the Uncle with the money?"

"Yeah, Dad. It's off the books."

"Atta boy."

NOW THAT I'VE MOVED TO Los Angeles, I keep in contact with my parents about twice a week on the phone. But Dad's phone personality is quite the opposite of Mom's.

While my mother never lacks for something to say, when my father gets on, it's always a little awkward. Like I said, he isn't a very demonstrative guy. And probably because of that, I tend to be the same way.

We never really know what to say to each other. Sports is about the only thing we can talk about comfortably. We have that in common. So he kind of rushes through the required topics, just to get to sports.

"How are the kids?"

"Fine."

"Anna?"

"Fine."

"You?"

"Fine."

"Fuckin' Yankees!"

"Tell me about it!"

And we both relax.

ACTUALLY, NOW THAT I HAVE a TV show, we talk a little bit more. He's taken an interest.

"Hey, I saw you beat *Cosby* last week in the ratings."

"Yeah, Dad, by a little."

"So they should pay you more than they pay him."

"That's not how it works, Dad."

It's very strange to hear what he has to say about my television world. He's got a sharp business mind, but he knows nothing about show business. We're talking about a man whose last movie he saw in a theater was *Patton*.

It makes for interesting conversation. There was one week where CBS had a college basketball game that ended about a half hour early. So they ran one of our episodes to fill the time. The next day I got a call from Dad.

"Hey, Raymond? You know they ran one of your shows yesterday after the game?"

"Yeah, I know."

"They gotta pay you for that."

"They will, Dad."

My father thinks if I don't call CBS every time my show airs, I don't get paid.

"Hello, CBS? This is Ray Romano. Yeah, my dad just told me you ran one of my episodes last night."

"Oh, he did? Well, you caught us! We'll send a check right out to you. Listen, we need a one-hour rerun for tomorrow night, but we don't want to pay anyone. Do you know if Chuck Norris is out of the country?"

I MAKE MORE MONEY NOW than I used to, and last Christmas I went out and bought my parents a brand-new car.

It felt good. It was the first time in his life my dad owned a brand-new automobile. He was always good with cars, and he could fix almost anything on them. Which was fine. Although combine that with being a little frugal, and you have a guy who would never have thought he had to spend more for a car than I would for a haircut.

The car I remember most was a 1964 Falcon, which my father bought from some guy in 1974 for fifty dollars. He fixed it all up, and we had it until 1984. That's from when I was seventeen until I was twenty-seven.

Let me explain the ramifications of that. Seventeen to twenty-seven are your prime dating years. And as far as women go, they were enough of a challenge for me to begin with.

Now, throw a '64 Falcon into the mix. Do you need any more explanation, or should I show you the prom pictures with my cousin?

So Christmastime I give Mom and Dad a brand-new car. Should be a good thing, right? Seems logical.

Before: only old cars.

Now: *new* car!

Before: always pay for car.

Now: *free* car!

Everyone should be happy, right? And for one golden moment, when we gave it to them, everyone was. My mother cried, my father actually smiled. Everything was perfect. And then:

"Will I know how to drive it? It's brand-new."

"Oh Christ, what's the insurance on that?"

"I heard those air bags are dangerous."

"What made you think I like green?"

And so went Christmas Day.

The next morning, before we left for the airport, I peeked out the back window and saw an image that left a warm Hallmark feeling in my heart. There were my mom and dad, sitting in the front seat of the car, which was in the garage, with the wipers on.

Faintly I could hear them yelling.

"Albert, teach me about the intermittent."

"Read the goddamn manual."

Last time I talked to my father on the phone, I got very annoyed at him because it's been six months and the car still has its original tank of gas.

"Why don't you use it?"

"I don't want to run it into the ground. I want it to last."

"Dad, you're seventy-three, and Mom's seventy. What are you waiting for?"

"What does our age gotta do with it?"

"I'm just saying, you're seventy-three."

"Yeah?"

"I don't know. I'm just saying you're getting kinda . . ."

"What?"

"You know, I mean, just how long do you, uh . . ."

"What, what? Spit it out!"

". . . Fuckin' Yankees, huh?"

LUCIA PERILLO

The Northside at Seven

Gray sulfurous light, having risen early this morning
in the west, over the stacks of Solvay, has by now
wafted across the lake and landed here on Lodi Street,
where it anoints each particular with the general grace
of decay: the staggering row houses, the magazines flapping
from the gutters like broken skin, the red Dodge sedan
parked across the street from where I'm hunched in the pickup.
The Dodge's driver was ahead of me at the counter
in Ragusa's Bakery, making confession before an old woman
who was filling pastry shells with sweetened ricotta:

I put a new roof on her house, he was telling the woman,
but the lady don't pay me. I do a good job; she got no complaint.
But see, a man must hold his head high so I took her car.
The old woman trilled as she stuffed another log of cannoli.
Turning to me he said, *She can call the cops if she wants—*
I'll tell 'em I got kids to take care of, I got a contract.
I shrugged: all the absolution I could bring myself to deliver
before grabbing the white paper sacks the woman slapped down
and walking out the door, leaving the man in the midst
of what he needed to say. I don't know—

there was something about his Sicilian features, his accent,
his whole goddamned hard-luck story that just gnawed on me so,
like those guys who came to unload on my own old man, muttering
Bobby, Bobby, see we got a little problem here Bobby . . .
the cue for women, kids to leave the room. But since then
my father has tried to draw me back into that room,
driving me along the tattered Bronx streets of his boyhood,

sometimes lifting his hands from the steering wheel and
spreading them, saying: *Look, those people are* paesan,
you're paesan, *nothing you're ever gonna do can change that* . . .

We'd spend the rest of the day on food, eating spiedini,
the anchovy sauce quenching my chronic thirst
for salt, and shopping for the dense bread made from black
tailings of prosciutto, I forget the name of it now.
I forget so much. I even forget why tears come on the freeway,
mornings I drive by these old buildings when bread is cooking—
why? for what? Sometimes I feel history slipping from my body
like a guilty bone, & the only way to call it back
is to slump here behind the wheel, licking sugar from my chin,
right hand warmed by the semolina loaves riding shotgun,

the way my father might have spent his early mornings years ago,
before he claimed the responsibilities of manhood—of marrying
and making himself a daughter who would not be trapped, as he
felt he was, by streets washed over in the slow decay of light.
Making her different from what he was. And making her the same.

JOSEPHINE GATTUSO HENDIN

The Right Thing to Do

SHE COULD SEE HIM IN THE distance, trying to hide behind a news-paper as he sat on the bench in front of the ruins of P.S. 5. For days she had caught glimpses of him reflected in store windows. Turning suddenly she had caught sight of him limping into a doorway or stepping back deeper into a subway car. He was unmistakably there now, waiting to see where she would go. He was still at it. Once or twice you could meet Nino by chance. But this was something else. I haven't fooled him at all, she realized. How long had he been doing this, watching her drop off a weekly supply of unread books before, dressed demurely as a Catholic schoolgirl, she went to meet Alex and strip?

Gina stepped back into the library, unable to decide what to do. Should she meet Alex anyway? Should she try to lose Nino on the train? Should she call his shot and just confront him? Should she spend the evening in the library and make Nino wait for nothing? What was the right thing to do?

If he wants to follow me, I'll give him a chase he won't forget, Gina thought grimly. It came to her, the determination to make him run, run, run in the sun-light that was still hotter than kisses. It came like a fire itself, freeing and fuel-ing her rage. Who was he not to believe what she said? He wouldn't stand for the truth; he wouldn't stand for her lying. So let him not stand at all, let him exhaust himself until he couldn't tell the difference between truths and lies. A war was a war. Once he realized he wasn't going to win, he would give up.

Gina moved out onto the library steps, walking slowly so that he would be sure to see her. What if he didn't get up? What if he were only reading the paper? Geared for war, the possibility of a missed fight wasn't what she wanted. But she could tell now for sure, seeing him gathering himself together, that he was following. She moved toward the station, deliberately crossing the street so that he could climb the long staircase of the El without fear that she would see him. The shaded stairway seemed cool; out on the subway platform the sun shone down on the hot, splintering wood. She loved this platform. From the end, looking over the dome of Saint Demetrios's Church, she could see the New York skyline, suspended in the shimmering heat.

On the street below were the private houses, the six-story apartments, the little yards overpacked with rosebushes and fig trees—the vestigial village beyond which the city stood like a mirage. Were you thirsty? The city was water. Were you low? It was all height and promise. Were you lonely? There was Alex. She could hardly keep her mind on Nino. That was the trouble with Nino. When he was around, he focused everything. When he was gone, it seemed as though he didn't exist at all. I'm not, she realized, purposeful enough for a good vendetta. I don't want revenge, I want out. But there he was, committed to pursuit to the last drop of blood. She looked away, into the rosebushes pinned and pruned on their trellises.

It was the month they call in Sicily the time of the lion sun. There the heat ruled without rivals. Here in Astoria the rose-packed gardens hurled sweetness into the dust-laden air, the smells of cooking bubbled from open kitchen windows into streets pungent with car exhausts, the El rained soot on the street below; all seemed fused into a seething life that was fair match for the ravenous sun. The BMT went crashing around the curve from Hoyt Avenue, its wheels grinding to an ear-splitting stop on the hot rails. Gina got on the train. Peering through the filmy car window she saw Nino limping into the next car. She settled nervously into a seat facing the Manhattan skyline, still visible through the streaked windows as the train screeched on.

There it was. At work, every day, in the city, typing past-due bills, or letters politely requesting payment, the beauty of it receded before the familiar routine of drudge-work. But even the bills she typed sometimes seemed launched into that other world where people lived gracefully, lightly, never paying their dues. Not my lot, she thought wistfully. With Nino your bills were always due. You could meet them on the infinite installment plan. Pay-as-you-go-to-the-grave in regular portions of work, marriage, christenings, funerals. Spellbound you paid and paid. What made it all work for so long? What was the magic? The sense of fear? Just fear of Nino's rages, the wreckage he made with his words and his cane? It was part of it. You couldn't short-change his menacing voice and punishing ways. But it wasn't that alone that made it seem impossible to default on Nino. He had an air of being right. Nino! she wanted to scream. You can't collect from me! But his air of certainty made her feel doubtful, confused. And so she felt only a sense of faint dread, a sudden exhaustion that paralyzed the will to cross him. Her weariness came before the fight, making it all seem hopeless before it had begun.

The train plunged into the tunnel that brought not a darkness but only a harsher light. The fluorescent rods, exposed through the broken shields, showed the ragged papers and soot swirling slowly as the train lumbered under the river. The thought of the river overhead, the oily surface stained by chaotically moving tides, pressing its weight year after year against the concrete and steel, never failed to bring the question to mind: When would it give? When would it break, when would the barricade yield passage beneath the surface, finally giving way to the tides? It was a kid's thought. It should have passed long ago. But it didn't. In Sicily, near Amerina, there was a lake, Pergusa, where Hades was supposed to have risen to go foraging for a woman. When he kidnapped Persephone, he took her back through the milky water to the underground place, the hell that was his to rule. Her trip through the water—suspended, airless in alien hands—must have been terrifying. It was just a story, a story without a place in a subway car inscribed with graffiti. Yet it stayed in her mind like the image of Nino in the next car.

The train was really speeding now, rocking into the bright blue bulbs that lit the tunnel's sides. She could see herself moving toward the door that led to his car, forcing it open, feeling the hot wind between the cars, standing before him, screaming hello over the noise. Maybe that would be the best. The train lurched violently to one side, hurling her against the seat. It hadn't been much of an idea, anyway. Whatever she said, he would refuse to acknowledge; he wouldn't seem even slightly surprised. That would end the ride, but he'd take it as her capitulation, her recognition that he had found her out.

By now, Nino had read the sports news so many times he remembered it even better than usual, and he usually remembered it all. After the train had passed Bloomingdale's, his curiosity and suspicion rose. He hadn't thought she was going shopping, but still, he nodded, fanning himself with the *News*, you never know. She was, he could see, leaning forward and stretching by the window, arching back in her seat, staring at the lights in the tunnel. When Union Square came and went, he saw her rise.

Eighth Street, he thought. She could catch him on that stop easily, if she hesitated after getting out. He would have to move quickly to avoid getting caught in the door. The absence of a crowd, the midday silence of the station, all gave him pause. He was so easy to spot, a crippled old man. But she moved very quickly, without looking back when she left the station. Heading west, she stopped at the corner, waiting for the light to change. She walked slowly, glancing in store windows. She stopped near University Place, studying the display carefully. He ducked into a doorway of a butcher shop, watching her through a rack of prime rib roasts until she finished window-shopping and went on, turning down University Place. Hobbling quickly, he glanced into the window to see what had made her stop so long. Red lace bras with feathers sprouting from the top, transparent bikini underpants with little red lips embroidered on them, black see-through camisoles, some with cutouts where the nipples would be— Nino clenched his teeth, dug his cane into the sidewalk, and marched on.

She was heading into Washington Square Park. In the heat, only the elegant mansions on the north side seemed to remain intact. Everything else seethed, bubbled. Once, Nino thought, peering at her from behind a tree, this was a potter's field, just a burying ground for the poor. Now, he thought disgustedly, looking at the addicts, winos, and stoned drifters lying on the grass, it looks as though the bodies have surfaced again. There she was in the middle of it all, buying a soda from a vendor, drinking on a bench in the blistering sun. You could barely see south to Judson Church, the fog of marijuana was so dense. The noise of conga drums, rude and numbing, thudded through the heat. She sipped her diet soda, taking it all in. He edged behind her, moving behind a tree so that even if she turned she couldn't spot him.

Glancing up, Nino met Garibaldi's eye. There the statue was, newly whitewashed in its frozen stride. Garibaldi stood balanced on his right foot, his left leg about to move forward; his right hand was poised on the sword strapped to his left side. Was he taking it out of the sheath, or putting it in? Politics aside, that was the kind of man you could see would use his sword to defend the right things. But the question came back. Was he drawing his sword against some tyrant, or was he putting it away because he had already won? The face, whitewashed of its lines, smoothed by rains and snows, couldn't tell you much anymore. But the stance was proud, a gentleman's stance without being showy. There he was, after all these years, a warrior with a paunch, not too proud when he had to leave Italy to help out Meucci, the inventor, in his candle factory in Staten Island. And then even after going back to Italy to lead victorious armies, to keep writing to Meucci as "Dear Boss"!

Nino shook his head. There was a man for you. And people say Italians are lousy fighters, never able to go the distance.

Gina's hands held the can of soda like a chalice. She had the mentality of a three-year-old, Nino thought, shaking his head. He had taken her here through the park so many times on the way to Aunt Tonetta's. They had even sat on the bench where she sat now. In those days he didn't have to hide behind her! He had bought the ice cream pop, the soda, the lemon ice she had held so solemnly. He had sat with her, telling her stories, or rushing her along so they wouldn't be late. The new playground on the south side, with its fancy swings and fake hills, hadn't been there.

Rising, turning, Gina glimpsed Nino's face, darkened with sentiment, still turned toward the statue. Garibaldi again, she thought disgustedly. The white-washed statue was already flecked and pitted with soot, chips had fallen from the pedestal where skateboards had crashed into it. Yet the sight of him had always made Nino gab. What hypocrisy, a petty tyrant like him talking about a liberator. She stuffed the straw into the soda can with her right fist. Striding toward a garbage basket, she hurled the soda into it through a mass of bees hunting for sugar. She had to walk slowly, she realized, or he would lose her, fall too far behind in the winding streets that he used to take her through on the way to visit relatives whose hearts and mouths were always open. By now, each had had his appointed funeral and gone on.

Nino moved after her as she walked south, ambling across West Third, he only dimly realizing they were on their way past Aunt Tonetta's on Thompson Street. How he remembered the wine she used to make, thick as chocolate and half as sweet, bubbling in soda glasses a third full of 7UP. Past the lemon ice stand, past the old playground, she crossed Houston, pausing by Saint Anthony's Church. She was moving south. Where was she going? But the question faded as memories hit, as his shirt dampened and ran with sweat in the heat, his neatly knotted tie under the starched collar wet as a marathon runner's sweatband. No more village now. No hotpants, no sera-pes. The little boys of six and seven in shorts, squatting to draw circles for games of war on the sidewalk, older boys wrapping tape on a broomstick, kids playing boxball, seemed like new versions of old snapshots of himself. His glasses steamed. His rage faded; he kept on, propelled as much by his past as by her. So many mirrors in so many strange faces. Now she was moving east, backtracking, weaving between Spring Street and Houston.

Suddenly she was gone. On the right an empty lot studded with refuse, wild grass, old bottles. On the left an almost unbroken row of tenements. He knew she hadn't reached the corner. He covered the block again. There it was, a narrow alley. Jersey Street? Maybe through here. As he went in, it widened to almost six feet, cutting through the center of the block, virtually paved with broken glass. Green beer-bottle glass, brown glass from other beers, and clear long shards lay shining on the cobblestones in patches where the sun knifed through the alley, all gleaming, even in the shadows. He dragged his left foot gingerly, afraid of falling into the shimmering, cutting edges. Halfway through he realized where he was. He was moving toward the old cathedral on Prince and Mott. He could see ahead of him the chin-high wall of rust-colored brick, the sagging wooden door painted shut to the rectory's back entrance. In the old country the priests could confuse you. There was an old saying: The hand raised in benediction was also the hand that took bread from your mouth. Here in the old days the Irish priests just drenched you with contempt. He grasped the cool, shaded brick wall of the alley. The alley, he remembered, had always been here. Once it had a street sign—Jersey Street? Maybe not. Anyway, it was long gone. He was losing his balance, leaning against the wall as his bad leg, numbed, came to rest. Without going farther, he could picture what was outside. The sagging wooden door would blend into the old brick wall continuing the length of Prince Street, turning the corner at Mott and circling the block, enclosing the old garden cemetery of Saint Patrick's. He forced himself onward, spotting Gina as she slowly reached the corner, letting her hand drift along the hot brick wall. Her dark hair, brushed back by the hot breeze, her white skirt flaring over curving hips, her bare brown legs, sandaled feet—she looked achingly familiar, one of the girls he would have watched forty years ago, leaning against the hot brick wall with his friends. Teasing, cajoling, from the safety of the gang they would call, entice, never getting a response.

He was never very good at it. He was much too shy for even the most promiscuous to pay any attention to him. Yet, in the end, it had paid off. Meeting Mariana, the baker's daughter, on the subway, she had trusted him. For days and evenings after that, they met out of the neighborhood, touched in alleys they didn't know. He could almost feel her soft cotton blouse, smell her rosewatered body, feel the beads of wetness on her arms in the summer heat, in the sun that was hotter than caresses. He grasped the rough brick wall. Mariana that night, that last night when they had gone to Coney Island and stayed, walking under the boardwalk at nightfall. He swallowed painfully. How silky her breasts, her belly had been against the cooling, grainy sand.

This was ridiculous. He forced himself to move against the dizziness, the blinding dizziness of the yellow sun, the rods of light forcing their way between the tenements across the street into his eyes. They were tearing now. Suddenly the air seemed to be thickening. To move was to move against a vapor-wall filled with ghosts, ghost smells, ghost memories rising from the cemetery like the scent of dreams and nightmares. The DelMonte funeral home, still there—a good business, death!—the grocer with his cheeses and salamis—the store that had sold espresso pots and china had given way to dry goods. But nowhere was Gina to be seen.

Nino circled the block, moving toward the main entrance of Saint Patrick's. How many years since he had been inside! His eyes raked the cemetery. She wasn't there, browsing among the tombstones or the ill-kept grass. How nice it had once been, with sprinklers going all the time and Father Montale planting herbs to border the path. He had a regular collection: thyme, sweet basil, dill; and even, hidden away from view, so nobody would get the wrong idea, a grape arbor concealed behind a ramshackle fence at the corner.

Nino fell back quickly against the wall as he opened the door. So there she was. She was reading the names of people who had donated stained-glass windows to the church. The yellow light, pouring through the brilliant blue and red glass, lit the interior in an odd, garish way. How dusty it seemed inside. The cream-colored walls and painted spindle fences around the altar somehow looked out of place. There was not enough marble in this country to make a proper show when they built this, Nino thought. He edged back out the door, hiding behind it, waiting for her to leave.

In the chapel in back of the church he had married Laura. He swallowed; his throat felt painfully parched. How different his life might have been if he had married Mariana. He had been young and a great dancer. And she was luscious, sweet, voluptuous. It was the summer. The New York summer sweated sex even out of a dead man. He sighed, looking up when the church door slammed. Gina was striding down the walk leading to Mott Street. He rose, limping after her. In the old days he could have outsprinted her for miles, miles, miles. If he had married Mariana, she wouldn't be here at all, he mused. Mariana. It was better not to wonder what had happened to her. How could he have married her, after all? She had let him have his way with her without being married. If she was willing to do that, she could have done it with someone else while married to him. Once you cross a line, you keep crossing. That was human nature.

Nino limped forward. The air was almost unbreathable. All the exhausts of the city, the basements exhaling roach poisons, the fumes of cars, the light pollen of surviving grasses, the rolling dust and soot flurries, were crashing in his lungs. And look at her, that bitch. His suit jacket too was drenched now, sopping and stuck to his body on the shadeless street. And she, running on, gliding over the sidewalks in bare legs and sandals, her white dress still white.

He began to cough, a slow wracking cough, spewing out the city vapors, the memories that stuck like tar in his throat. She moved down Mott past the pork butcher's store on Spring Street, where hams and sausages hung from rope over the white porcelain display; on she went past Kenmare Street, past the liquor shop on Broome with a window full of Mondavi reds,

Zinfandel in blackish letters on a paper banner. There, she was slowing, finally slowing, standing in front of the Villa Pensa, looking across the street. His tired eyes followed her glance. Ferrara's. How large it had become. She crossed in the middle of the street, not bothering about the desultory traffic, and strolled under the Pasticceria sign into the store.

Nino waited for the light to change and dragged himself across the street. How flashy Ferrara's had gotten. The window was full of packaged boxed candies with fancy Ferrara labels; coffee cans in red and green blared the name again. Sleek display cases showed the pastries. Shiny black-lacquer ice cream parlor chairs; yellow Formica tables. Where were the little wooden chairs, the chipped Carrara marble tables, the cozy friendliness of the old place with its trays of pastries? The young waiters, each trying to look like Valentino, had waltzed them around when they felt like it. He leaned against the window and felt its coolness. Now there was even air-conditioning. He could see her at a table near the door, ordering. Dizziness and exhaustion rolled over him in waves. His good leg was throbbing horribly, pain working itself up from his toes, through his arch, past the ankle ringed with popping blue veins.

"Come and have some iced coffee," Gina said, reaching uncertainly for his arm. How could she have done it, she thought, looking at his thin hair matted with sweat, the lines deepening in his face, the heightened color in cheeks that seemed to burn with fever. She began to feel remorse. No, she couldn't be drawn that way into regret. If she didn't harden herself against him, she would always be bound to him. She had had her revenge. It wasn't sweet; but it had made the point, all the same.

Nino, sunk in his dizziness, looked at her without recognition, or even, for a moment, surprise. Leaning on her arm, he moved with her into the coolness, the dry frigid air sending a shiver through his body, shocking him into humiliation and sorrow.

"What's this?" he asked, sitting at the chair she held out for him.

"Iced espresso. Better than amphetamines," she joked, adding cream to her huge goblet filled with coffee. "All you have to do is sip, and it sends"—she groped—"a rush of energy into your veins."

She was looking at him steadily, her clear dark eyes probing his. When had she seen him? he wondered. How long had she known he was following her? It was incredible.

"I'm always willing to try something new," he said, aiming for a casual tone. He took a long drink. The black coffee, slightly bitter, smoothed the lump in his throat. The coolness of the place was steadying. To be cool! That it should seem like such a luxury to sit down, to rest, to drink. He should throw it in her face for humiliating him like this. She knew he had nearly killed himself for her; because of her he was dizzy, weak. The waiter was putting another iced coffee in front of him. She must have signaled for it. How self-possessed she was, the little bitch. He watched her, adding sugar and cream to the coffee.

"Why don't you save yourself the trouble and just order coffee ice cream?" he asked her mildly.

"This way it comes out just the way I want," Gina said. The waiter brought them two sfogliatelli. She was really doing it up, he thought. He should crack her across the face with his cane. It would serve her right! But you only did that to a girl her age for one reason, and he wasn't about to do that in public. Not in this neighborhood, where everyone would know what it meant.

I've got him now, Gina thought. He looked awful. It ought to teach him a lesson, not to try to follow me. It was one thing to demand you acted a certain way at home. It was his, after all, rotten as it was. But quite another to think you could dictate everything else. It was a question of freedom. She hated him when he was dictatorial; but now she realized she found him more troublesome when he was pathetic. Since she felt she had won, she was prepared to be kind. Up to a point.

"What a coincidence that we decided to go for a walk in the same place at the same time," Gina said, smiling sweetly and touching his hand.

"Not really," Nino said smoothly. "You've already made it clear it was no coincidence at all."

He was turning it all around; never say die, Nino, right? Her resolve against him was so saturated with shame and wariness it was rapidly retreating to diplomacy. "I was looking for Columbus Park," she lied.

"But you didn't find it," he pointed out.

"No," she agreed. "I didn't."

"You didn't find it because it isn't here," he pointed out. "It's been west and south of here—between Baxter and Mulberry—since the 1890s, when they leveled the ragpicker settlement to build it." My God, would she have been willing to walk all the way past Canal?

"Amazing how many slums and cemeteries have been turned into parks," she choked out.

"Amazing how many parks are turning into slums and cemeteries," he countered.

"Oh, sure. It's one big burial ground." So he wasn't willing to give up. What a dope she had been to think he might.

"Not really," he said. "Not really. What makes you say that? Do you feel ready to go? Is this your idea of putting your life in order?"

She ignored him and sipped her coffee.

"Where were you going?" he demanded softly, gripping her arm.

Gina tightened her face into a smile. "It's just what you said, Nino. I was just going out with you, in my own way." She looked him in the eye.

He looked at her coldly. The enormity of her gall was hard to take in. To think that she could do this to him—drag him around by the nose, and then, when he was exhausted, humiliate him with kindness! She was forcing his hand. He shook his head. If she could do this, she could do anything. He would have to assume that she had. He had no choice.

"Finish your pastry," he ordered. "It's time to go."

"Go where? You're not going to run my life."

"Home," Nino said. "I've had enough walking." He signaled for the check and paid it. "Thanks for your hospitality." He grinned.

He held the door open, ushering her into the street. The thickening evening air, rising from the hot street in steamy fumes, enfolded them.

MICHAEL DECAPITE

Sitting Pretty

ৎৡৎ

IT'S A BRIGHT MORNING IN AUGUST, I'm riding with my father to the track. We're rolling down Pearl in traffic, bumper to bumper, every surface aglare—outside it's a big hot kaleidoscope: strip mall on shopping center, shoe store on auto parts on fast food . . . blinding in the heat . . . the deepest wilds of the suburbs, and everybody's out. It's too much, I search myself for cigarettes, headache and all.

"Doesn't anybody work in this town? Where they all going?"

"Well, they're relentless shoppers, here," he says.

The match-flame's invisible, just a sizzle at the cigarette-end, adding more heat to the day. I'm laughing . . . one franchise collapses into another . . .

We get stuck at a light.

"Car holding up okay?" he asks.

"Yeah."

"Isn't it a lot of trouble to keep a car up there?"

"Yeah, it's a pain in the ass."

"Mm."

"I was up there without it, but I gotta have a car, I've always had a car. Without it I just . . . I mean you gotta be able to get out, otherwise you're sunk. It raises you up, having a car. Gives you some control."

He nods. I feel like I've been talking for five minutes.

"I dunno. When I don't have a car I'm at a loss. It's part of my identity. I mean I think of myself as ah . . . as a uh—"

"As a motorist."

"Exactly."

Another light. They've moved to Parma Heights, he and my mother. My Buick's back at their building, fresh from a 500-mile haul. With its busted grille and never-washed flanks—its no backseat and NY plates—it's an insult to the other cars in the lot. Yesterday I was sailing through traffic and a van roared up beside me—at a red light—the guy leaned over. "Hey, we don't *drive* like that here!" The words sounded strange to me: "we" and "here." Now I'm hungover from a late night on the Southside. I slept at Al's and got up early to catch my dad. His Impala's old too, but clean. The tidy black interior is everywhere hot to touch. I feel dishonest sitting in it, wondering if he can smell the alcohol off me. By the bank sign it's 87 degrees at 12:13.

"You see your friends last night?"

"Yeah, I was at the Lit. Bunch of people there."

We hit the freeway ramp at a crawl. He gets it up to 55 and merges left, holding his lane.

Post time's an hour away and we've been out in the heat for an hour already. Two supermarkets, a bakery, and a newsstand for the *Form*. His days are long and he's restless. He gets up in the dark, before the birds. By 6 A.M. dinner and a salad are ready in the fridge. My mother gets up, he serves her half a grapefruit and coffee and toast, she goes off to work. By eight o'clock he's done with the paper and there's nothing to stand between him and time.

He doesn't care to be distracted, he's taking time on the chin. His life seems to be mostly about satisfying a duty toward time. Keeping an eye on it, for one thing. Monitoring its passage. He occupies himself with bare, well-worn activities which don't interfere much with that. He's concerned with trying to satisfy certain necessities—cooking or eating or errands—with care, and a kind of dogged finesse. He pats his pockets for keys and glasses before leaving the apartment, he handles produce on his shopping rounds, or money at the counter . . . His movements have acquired the easy weight of rite and memory. He handles the world the way you'd play with an old dog: rough, familiar, preoccupied . . .

Going to the track is a way for me to take part in his routine. The track is mostly about sitting around, it's a place to go. You find your bench and get to work dealing with time. You figure it down to fifths of seconds and then wait twenty-five minutes for the race to go off. For a student of time like my father, it's perfect.

"Let me have one puff of that, Danny."

I gave him my cigarette. He takes a hit and hands it back. I take a last burnt drag and flick it into the hot windroar.

ACROSS FROM THISTLEDOWN, PARKING'S FREE at the mall . . .
packed with cars already—a shimmering expanse . . . trackrats are filtering
through it toward the road, like refugees . . . It's so bright my soul squints—
asphalt . . . metal, glass . . . My father beats a path. We hurry across Emery
Road—halfway—stranded in traffic. Others are ranged along the median—
some won't make it to safety . . . the brick fortress with its flags . . . you can
hear a bugle from over the walls. The traffic thins out—we make a break for
it—my father's headlong and bowlegged, it's every man for himself . . .
through the lot, valet parking . . . I catch up but it's too hot to talk. He hands
me a couple dollars to pay my way in. I knock his hand away, it comes back,
insisting. We pass under a brick wall to the dim cool interior—he's through
the turnstile . . . an old bit-player . . . his understudy behind him . . . toward
a guy at a wooden lectern selling programs . . . I buy my own . . .

"We'll go upstairs," he says.

"Why? Who's there?"

"Oh, Mel and Dino, Nick Stavros. Lefty and Paul."

"Really? Paul's here?"

"Yeah, Lefty brings him out."

Paul—I see a snapshot taken at a birthday party—my fourth or fifth. Paul's
in the picture, a bigger kid than I was. He's hovering behind me . . . with
curly black hair . . . dressed up for the occasion in a blue double-breasted
sportjacket. He's smiling at the camera in a private sweet way, as though pro-
tective of me. He's aware he's not the subject of the photograph—I'm look-
ing down at my cake—and he's careful not to intrude . . .

Growing up I was aware of him. Now and then his name came up. First
he was "slow," and then "troubled," and then "in trouble." I haven't seen him
since that party so I don't know what to expect. A boy in a blue double-
breasted jacket, somewhat disheveled.

"I'm gonna get a coffee. You want one?"

"No. I'll meet you on the second floor."

I walk over to a concession, it's early.

"Small coffee."

The woman brings it. Tearing open cuplets of half-and-half . . . one . . .
two . . . I'm grateful for these moments alone inside the low swarm of my
hangover . . . two sugars. I always need moments alone, for punctuation. It's
good to be away from my wife, out here in the world. And it's good to be
away from my father for a few minutes. Same as he does, I need to be
away—it's a continual preoccupation, like smoking.

I ride the escalator and scout around. They're in back, behind the line of cashier windows—the group of them. They meet on Fridays as though by accident . . . cautious of commitment—a weekly coincidence they're all in the same remote corner of the second floor. Away from the general population, they watch the races on a TV screen. Two Italians, two Greeks, and a Pole—a delegation from the Old Southside. Mel says "Hey, Danny"—He's the successful one, an ad exec with a country estate—a heavy sports bettor by phone who drops in here once a week. He's confidential, as though speaking in mixed company. He asks about NYC and jokes about the price of his last breakfast at the Plaza. Nick Stavros is a real gentleman in a white shirt and summer hat, a retired Pinkerton agent, always courteous. He asks after my wife. Dino works for a bookie, I don't know him so well. Paul is watchful as I shake hands all around. Lefty, a little guy, is leaning forward like a bullpen manager . . . the same half-specs as my father . . .

He looks up from his studies. "How you doing, Danny?"

The crow's-feet deepen—now I remember his smile—he reaches a hand up. His grip is strong. The doctors have given him a year to live. But there's nothing of the hospital about him. He's right here.

Paul's waiting to be spoken to—his eyes are back and forth between us.

"Good to see ya, Lefty."

He holds me with that rascal grin . . . goes back to the *Form* . . .

There's room on the bench—"Hi Paul, how's it going?" . . . I take a seat . . .

"Yeah, hi. Hi Danny. Nice to see ya. Yeah, I got this shirt at Goodwill—five bucks, brand new. I—"

"It's good."

"Yeah, thanks. It's Ban-Lon. I used to have five of 'em at home, pure Ban-Lon, with a stripe, like Martin Landau in *Space 1999?* I had five of these, in perfect condition. But they're really flammable, this's the only one I got left."

Just like that he launches in, no one else is listening. He's unreadable—tossing side glances to make sure I'm with him . . .

"Huh."

"Yeah. I talked to the woman at Goodwill to ask her where she got them—I want her to order me a whole case of them, she's supposed to let me know. That'd be great: a whole box of them, brown cardboard, maybe ten or twelve to a box, maybe two dozen, all completely sealed—airtight."

"Uh-huh."

"She's supposed to get back to me, I gave her my number. She was totally helpful."

"Well, that's great."

"Yeah. Thanks."

He thanks me for seeing it his way.

"I remember that party. You had a Batman cake, it was beautiful. I hear you're married now."

"Yeah, I am."

I fish my cigarettes out—offer him one . . .

"Huh? No thanks, I had one at twelve o'clock. I'm supposed to have one every two hours. I'll have one at two o'clock. Hour and twenty-three minutes to go."

"You tryna quit?"

"No. My doctor said I should have one every two hours. Twelve, two, four, six, eight, ten. Save money too. I've had this pack since Wednesday. I buy a carton at Speedway—$13.90. It lasts me twenty-five days. So there's five days left over per month, sometimes six, unless it's February—then it's only three days left over except for Leap Year, then it's four. So that's like an extra carton per year, yeah, thirteen cartons per year, total. But I get a carton for my birthday. So that's twelve cartons per year I have to buy."

"You got this all worked out."

"Yeah, thanks."

"How long you been on this program?"

"'Bout a week."

He takes a breath, his belly rising beneath the Ban-Lon shirt. The guys are talking about splitting a few doubles.

He said, "Is your wife a blonde?"

"No, she got brown hair."

"Oh, a brunette—brown hair, dark brown hair, yeah. That's good. Good for you, Danny. Like Erin Gray, she's a brunette, she's beautiful. She's hot."

"Who's that?"

"Erin Gray—*Buck Rogers in the 25th Century*, yeah. I've got a whole scrapbook on her full of pictures, some black-and-white, some full-color. I've got an eight-by-ten glossy she sent me, autographed Best of luck, and ten pictures I took from the TV, totally rare, full-color."

"Really?"

"My mom helped me put 'em in the scrapbook, she mounted 'em perfectly. They're sealed behind clear sheets of plastic: nothing can touch 'em, they'll never decay. I've even got the bathing suit picture, in mint. Yeah. The scrapbook's got a red cover. Looks like leather but it's vinyl—that thing'll last forever—impervious to wear and tear, waterproof, stain-resistant. I'm not worried about it."

Okay. I get up, drop my cigarette and step on it. I set the empty cup on the floor.

"Done with that, Danny?"

"Wha— Yeah."

"Thanks."

He retrieves the plastic stirring stick and flicks it free of moisture, drops it into a shirtpocket.

"Still good," he says.

It's five minutes to post, I gravitate toward my old man.

"Who you got?"

He and Lefty have bet Foreclosure, with Wiley While in the second race. I bet the same ticket. The Southside delegation trickles in: Mel's tasseled slippers and polo shirt, Nick's black gumshoes and straw fedora, Dino's Kmart slacks. The race goes off, we watch it on TV.

Foreclosure wins it.

The men rustle around rehashing it, bitching or pacified according to their bets. Paul has watched the race without flinching.

He says, "How'd we do, Dad? Did we win it?"

"Not yet, Paul. We had him in the double. We gotta win the second race too."

He and my father are busy in their *Forms*.

"Then how much do I win?"

"I dunno yet. Depends on what the second horse pays. I'll let you know, buddy."

Paul puts himself on hold.

MY OLD MAN AND LEFTY convene, the others mill around. They lean in, they move off . . . Paul's a few feet away, moonfaced, sitting apart. Mel, Nick, and Dino give him a wide berth.

I wander off, there's plenty of time before the next race. I move through the loose crowd . . . I'm abstracted, hungover . . . the bar catches my eye . . . a drink? . . . or not . . . maybe? . . . too early . . .

Back at the bench, Paul's talking about music—Mel has strayed too near and gotten caught. Paul asks him if he's heard Tangerine Dream.

"Tangerine Dream, Paul?" He's looking at his program. "Is that a rock band or a dessert?"

"Yeah, Tangerine Dream—*Force Majeure*. You'd like it, Mel."

Mel's unsure. "Would I?"

I sit down, get him off the hook. Paul turns to me . . .

"*Force Majeure?* Tangerine Dream?"

"Yeah."

That does it.

"Yeah, thanks. I've got that on LP and CD. The first side is all one song, eighteen minutes, it's an electronic symphony. And then side two. 'Cloudburst Flight' and 'Thru Metamorphic Rocks.'"

"Yeah, I don't really—"

"Nothing could be better than their music."

He hums a few bars . . . And then he's off. Since I'm such a Tangerine Dream fan—what about Jean-Michel Jarre? *Equinoxe?* Or Jean-Luc Ponty, his electric violin? "The Struggle of the Turtle to the Sea." Sweeps you right along—into the waves—Majestic.

The names come spilling out of him. Vangelis? A genius. Very serious, always frowning. How about Nektar? "Burn Out My Eyes"—in four parts, including "Void of Vision" . . . "Pupil of the Eye" . . . "Look Inside Yourself," and "Death of the Mind."

I nod my head, I'd like to agree but he's lost me now.

Lapidary? "And The Mage Disdains the Oracle." Their two-album set— with 3-D cover, long out of print—*Execration of the Masses*.

"I bought two copies at a garage sale. Oh it's wonderful, it's like glory hallelujah. Get it, Danny."

"Okay."

He's deadpan but he's talking fast. ELP—I must know them.

"'Karn Evil No. 9.' Their music is classical. Keith Emerson's the mastermind behind it all. When he plays the piano the whole platform lifts up, right off the stage. And then it starts to spin! Revolve! He wears a seat belt. He goes end over end—with a grand piano! He's just a blur! Doesn't miss a note."

"Now, Paul, does he do that in concert, or does he do it in the studio too?"

He looks over.

"I don't know, I've got the live album, three-record set. But I'm gonna get the album *Tarkus*. I saw it once at Record Exchange, still sealed in shrink wrap, never opened, perfect mint condition. It was beautiful, the cover's a work of art. The painting of Tarkus? I cut that picture out of a book. Laminated it. I'd like to get a poster of that for my room, five or eight feet tall. If I had that . . . I'd listen to the record and stare at the poster."

I remember the picture—he excites himself talking about it: Tarkus himself: part armadillo, part tank. Invincible. Roll on, big armadillo.

"And the last movement—the finale. 'Aquatarkus.'"

Part armadillo . . . part tank . . . part submarine.

"Yeah, Paul, I definitely remember that cover."

That's all he needs, he's rolling now. Hawkwind's *Hall of the Mountain Grill* . . . Lothario's Peril—their first record—*Memories of the Dugong*—a hundred percent electronic . . . synthesizers, Moogs, mellotrons . . . Dybbuk—"Anamorphic Warlord"—all keyboards—layers and layers of them, all playing at warp speed . . .

Lefty overhears him and leans over, lowering his voice.

"Hey, Paulie, whyncha give Danny a little break now, withthese bands."

"No, Lefty, it's fine."

"Sorry, Dad, yeah. Sorry, Danny."

Paul clams up. He shoots me a side glance, a little spooked . . . he's sorry he got us in trouble. I was ready to get up but I stay put. Paul's alert . . . silenced . . . he's biding his time . . . another countdown. It's embarrassing.

"So, Paul, uh . . . What you been doing lately?"

"The usual. Thanks."

"Uh-huh."

We sit there a minute quiet.

"Well, I'm gonna bet this race. I'll see you in a bit."

"See ya, Danny."

I leave him sitting there.

DO I LIKE BEING HUNGOVER, enclosed within it? Or is it just being alone, away from Paul talking, conversation in general, people's expectations? Why's it so hard to be around other people? It's like I have to reformulate myself to become tangible. Someone's talking, I have to concentrate on being a person there to listen. I've got to pretend to be human. It's so much easier to be just thoughts. Being alive involves pretense. You have to pretend to be a point of view. How's my old man do it? The pensive gaze, the enigmatic understanding smile. He's a point of view. Is he really here, the hard bone of his red forehead above reading glasses, or does he feel the same as I do? A definite entity? Or a gas of escaping possibilities? He once cautioned me about judging myself against him, an accomplished fact. Do you eventually become an Old Master at being alive or are you always a set of diminishing perceptions? Do you finally attain the present by default? Do you finally attain the present by accepting one narrow way of being? Do you finally attain the present?

I've drifted toward the bar and I veer away from it. I wander up a ramp and out to the grandstand and lean on the metal railing. Through the sunlight the lay of the track describes itself. Three seagulls are perched on the white wooden rail of the home stretch. Far across the infield the horses are movement, moving toward the gate . . .

BACK AT THE BENCH, THE race goes off onscreen. The colors are sharp: a condensed version of something furious happening nearby. There's bitter excitement among the Southside Gang—it looks good, it looks bad, there's a chance . . . Experience is easier to read on a small screen. Wiley While wins it.

Again, Paul's watched the race as though waiting for the news. Lefty with that smile leans toward my father saying something out of the corner of his mouth and Mel smacks his program and smiles are all around . . . even my old man allows himself one . . . Paul's at attention, still furtive—he's beginning to understand . . . like the moon beside the sun . . . he catches a bit of a smile off his old man, he tries it out . . . brightens up . . . it vanishes quickly, he's wary . . . His father flicks him in the leg with the program, says "We hit it, Paulie."

"We did? Oh. Thanks, Dad."

"That'll pay forty-eight and change."

"That's great, yeah. How much do I win, Dad?"

"I'm splitting it with Ray, but I'll slip you a few bucks."

"Yeah. Oh, great, Dad. I can use it."

I'M AT THE WINDOW WHEN the bell goes off. I slide the guy my ticket. The double pays $48.40. Just like that. I fold the cash into pocket, suddenly missing my wife. I wish she were here . . . that we had more of a life together . . . more than the shared aggravations of living in New York . . . more than fights in common. Why didn't she come with me? Busy in New York. Fifty's a lot of money to me, but I'll blow it all while I'm here, and drive back with enough for gas and the Holland Tunnel. I can already feel the jolting ride along Canal Street, the dips and fast bumps, the potholes . . . the padlocked metal fronts and signs lit down sidestreets . . . jewelry stores and China joints, a closed-up news shack . . . that party's-over feel, with the roaring garbage trucks at work . . . left on Center Street, right on Kenmare . . . Delancey toward the bridge . . . back to my life . . .

BACK AT HEADQUARTERS I GET the *Form* from my old man and pretend to concentrate. Mel's telling Dino about some black pitcher who betrayed him the other night. Nick's gone and Lefty comes back counting money. He gives my father half and my father leans back, straightening a leg and pushing the money into a pants pocket. Paul's not watching the transaction. But he's at the edge of his seat.

"Here you go, Paul."

"Oh. Thanks, Dad."

Three singles. He smoothes them on his leg.

"Three up," Paul says.

"Yeah, good."

"I never bring any money. I come with nothing so I can tell how much I win."

"Uh-huh . . ." I'm scanning the *Form*, I've got the third race narrowed down . . .

"I've got $3,017 saved now."

I look at him.

"Really?"

"Yeah, $3,017. It's in my savings account, for my future. I got a blue passbook in a clear plastic slipcover, it's safe, totally secure. Even if you spill something on it."

"Wow. I can never save any money."

"Thanks. I get disability checks, I can't work anymore. My dad says I gotta put half in the bank. It gets interest, it keeps getting more and more. Someday I'll be living like a king. I'll be sitting pretty."

I lift my eyes from the *Form*, deciphering a place in the air . . .

"Danny, lemme see the *Form*."

I hand it over.

Paul says, "That leaves me half for expenses. Cigarettes, postage, records. I don't spend money on beer anymore."

"No?"

"No. I'm not supposed to have any. I'd like one now, I love Miller, they have it here, yeah. That's the best beer, it's delicious . . . tastes good cold. No thanks, Danny."

"Okay."

"It's not good for me. That's the best though. Miller beer and smoke a bowl. Ride around. My friend had a Camaro, candy blue."

"Mm-hm."

"Nineteen minutes to go."

I keep an eye on the odds, my father not so much. His stock is up among the guys for picking the double—they're consulting him . . . they'll all bet differently. An excellent handicapper who loses according to his own lights, he pans across *Form* and program and toteboard for the glint of a logic to conform with his natural bias. His choices tend toward the longshot, the secret outsider. Maybe betting is his final real form of expression . . .

He and the guys are putting together a trifecta. I stay out of it, seems like more than someone should ask, to hit a trifecta. It's outside the laws of noth-ingness by which I try to live. I wait in line and make a different bet.

We all lose.

"How'd we do, Dad? Did we win it?"

"Not this time, Paul."

A setback. Paul sits there buzzing with anxiety and faith. I move off.

WHEN I GET BACK, MEL'S bitching about the Democrats. Lefty takes issue. He and Mel are from different worlds, politically. Lefty's a dyed-in-the-wool liberal, he and my father are in quiet agreement about that. Nick and Dino stay out of it, they're gamblers first and conservatives when pressed. Paul and I are apolitical. Mel uses the word *democrat* sarcastically—with a small *d,* meaning a black. Lefty sticks to his guns, dis-missing Mel's wisecracks. His voice lowers. Mel doesn't press it. Instead he tells a joke about a black, a Jew, and a Pole—it's funny—by way of changing the subject and getting the last word in . . .

Paul senses tension and gets up, trolls off to a concession stand.

I'm sitting next to Lefty, his forearm's on his knee. He's worked for years as a maintenance painter at Ford. His forearm is thin and corded with mus-cle, the skin of it relaxed with age and illness under short dark hairs, down to a thick wrist and a big strong hand holding the flimsy newsprint of the *Form.* At home he paints oils with small brushes. Landscapes, faces. I watch him and the word *darkness* registers. Greek. The thin black hair slicked back and gray at the temple, the impossible hooked nose, which is the whole meaning of his face . . . a born profile . . . the face hard on facts and worry and expe-rience, the crow's-feet like scars of laughter . . .

Paul comes back with more stirring sticks and three crisp singles—he's exchanged his old ones—brand-new bills . . .

"Here comes my two o'clock smoke," he says, taking out a pack of Merits. He offers them around, he wants everyone to be friends now.

"No thanks, Paul, I got some."

"Ray?" He leans forward—offers the pack to my father. "Cigarette?"

"No, Paul. Thanks though."

"Why not? Have one, Ray. They're good."

"All right, I'll take it for later." My father reaches across Lefty and takes one from the pack . . . puts it behind his ear.

Lefty, dying of cancer, sits in the middle of this.

I light Paul's cigarette and one of my own.

"Mel? Cigarette, Mel?"

"No, kid."

"Dino? How about it, Dino?"

"Okay. Thanks." Dino takes one and lights it with a plastic lighter and forgets it in the same gesture.

Paul's happy now, we're smoking . . . he feels expansive . . .

Nick lifts his hat and wipes a line of sweat with a hanky.

"Nick, did you ever hear Tomita's *Firebird Suite?*"

"No I didn't, Paul."

"You'd like it, Nick."

"Really?"

"Yeah. He can play any instrument. He plays extended range fixed filter band, voltage controlled lowpass filter, oscillator—"

"Yeah?"

"Yeah. Bode ring modulator, Roland phase shifter, random signal generator . . ."

"Yeah? Well . . . That sounds nice."

"It is. You'll like it, Nick. Thanks."

MY FATHER SITS BY LEFTY and the guys politely steer clear of Paul. They form a loose crescent in front of him while treating Lefty deferentially. They're hoping Lefty enjoys himself. They want him to win every race, at least when he's not betting against them. They go out of their way to include him in their exactas and trifectas. Dino, the dark horse of the group, brings him a coffee. They ask his opinion of this horse or that, they get him into conversation. So-and-so from the old days comes up.

"Roxie, always on the corner? Hah?"

"Remember Benny, when he got outta the service?"

"That time they come looking for Ray, when he's AWOL?"

Lefty enjoys it, he listens with one ear. He's got a lot on his mind, trying to win this race, for himself and for Paul, trying to get ahead of the game and wondering what's going to happen with his son and his wife.

Even so he can't help getting sucked into it . . . the memories. My father, who's been circumspect so far, mentions a job they had mopping floors at the Federal Reserve Bank, eighteen dollars a week, after which they'd go shoot craps on Euclid Avenue. One night they won twelve hundred dollars. Lefty starts to laugh. When he does, lines around his eyes draw back as though pulled by the same string which reveals his incisors. It happens slowly. First a smile, savoring laughter to come. His eyes are watching a story take shape in front of them. And then the soundless laughter, even glee. It's a dark and welcome laughter, telescoped backward to boyhood.

Everyone but Paul seems to know Lefty is dying. He's locked out, sitting on the edge of the bench, hands on his knees, with the wide rolled gaze of a killer whale.

He says, "Those doctors know what they're doing, they're scientists. My dad was sick but he went to see the doctor. They can do anything. The doctor gave him some pills, he's better now. Aren't you, Dad? Hey, Dad, you're my sunshine, right?"

He puts an arm around Lefty and pulls him over, kisses him on the cheek.

"That's right, Paulie." Lefty smiles . . .

Paul's thinking it over.

He says, "There's a God, right? There has to be."

It's gotten quiet, everybody's heard him. Nick and Mel and Dino are busy with *Forms* and programs—they're doing some serious handicapping now, staying out of this one.

"There must be a God, up in Heaven, right, Danny?"

"Yeah."

"Ray? There's a God, Ray."

"Yeah, Paul. Of course there is."

"I'm sure there's a God. He's watching over us."

I get up and wander off, I come back, and each time Paul is sitting there, a big boy grown old overnight—institutions, medications—dumped on that bench by a long rolling wave of bad nights . . . quiet now . . . outwardly placid . . . sitting beside his father, his thick hair combed over and thinning already in his early thirties, alert, like a player who's been benched. He's a mascot now, trapped inside there, watching you from behind his eyes, watching himself talk, sensitive to your reaction.

I'm his age so he fastens onto me whenever I sit down, trying to make me understand . . .

"*I, Robot?* Alan Parsons Project—*I, Robot?* Oh, it's nice, Danny . . ."

"Yeah, I dunno about that, Paul."

Lefty says, "Danny, lemme see your program a minute."

I hand it over.

"On the way home we stop at Coconuts. Right, Dad?"

"We'll see."

"I gotta stop there, Dad. It's a *must*."

"What're you getting?" I ask him.

"Isotope. If I saw that, I'd buy four of 'em."

"Why?"

"'Cause they're beautiful. Yeah. They're nice to have."

PAUL'S A FAT SPIDER DRAINING my blood and wrapping me up in words till all I can move is my cigarette hand. Tickets and cigarette butts collect on the floor. The track is happening while he spins his web of non sequiturs—I phase out and back in time to hear him going on about a View-Master slide he once saw—

"Thor was there. His ray goes right through a pole and into the gargoyle. Turns him into protoplasm."

"Uh-huh."

"Yeah."

He waits a moment.

We sit there.

Just when I'm starting to breathe again, he says, "I took pictures out of my yearbook, four girls, I cut 'em out. Then I took photos of 'em with my camera. Julie Skur, Becka Gravenstein, Jill Hrvatski and Jonna Stockdale. They're beautiful. Jonna Stockdale was the Homecoming Queen. My mother's taking them in today to get 'em developed—she says she's positive they'll all come out."

"Good."

"Yeah, thanks."

"Then what?"

"She's gonna mount 'em for me under a thick sheet of Mylar, right on top of my desk. It'll be perfect."

The other guys—each takes a turn slipping away . . . wandering off . . . to bet . . . to breathe . . . and longer . . . gone until post time. Paul accepts Lefty's losses, knowing it'll get better. When it does, and Lefty slips him a few singles, Paul takes them straight to a concession to exchange them for new bills. Lefty's aware of Paul but doesn't interfere with him. Speculating with my father, figuring the odds, he allows the others their unspoken irritation and lets Paul be.

Then Paul gets on the subject of some movie . . . *East of Eden*—he saw it on TV. He's talking about Jo Van Fleet, he's captivated . . . Jo Van Fleet . . . she's struck a chord with him. He goes on about her. Finally even Lefty gets annoyed.

"Who you talking about?"

"Jo Van Fleet, she's beautiful."

"She's *not* beautiful."

Paul flares up. "She *is* beautiful! She's a great actress!"

"Goddamn it," Lefty says. He can't help himself. "Jo Van Fleet wasn't even pretty. In fact she was ugly!"

"Jo Van Fleet?" says my father. "She was always playing an older woman, wasn't she? Even when she was young . . ."

"That's her," says Lefty.

"She was pretty good. She's good in *Wild River*."

"She's beautiful," Paul asserts. He's emphatic.

Lefty spits, he's shaking his head, goes back to the *Form*.

There's an uncomfortable lull, the announcements are audible, Paul and Lefty are brooding . . .

I wonder how someone could watch *East of Eden* and overlook James Dean for Jo Van Fleet—Paul turns on me—

"I went to Unique Thrift Store the other day, I got a roll of wallpaper— green-and-white checkers, it's plastic! Plastic wallpaper—I got it for a dollar!"

"Good work."

"Thanks."

Lefty gets up and goes off to bet. Paul and I watch him go.

Paul says "We're having pork chops for dinner tonight. Breaded pork chops, mashed potatoes, green beans, rye bread and butter, and salad with Italian dressing. Double fudge chunk ice cream for dessert. Coffee. What're you having, Mel?"

Mel, standing nearby, folds up his *Form* and sticks his program in a back pocket. "What's that?"

"What're you having for dinner tonight, Mel?"

"I'm having pasta."

"Oh, that's good. Spaghetti and meatballs, I like that, yeah."

"You know what I had last night?"

"No."

"Pasta."

Paul is watching him.

"You know what I had the night before?"

"No."

"I had pasta."

"Yeah?"

"Yeah. You know what I had the night before that?"

"No."

"Pasta. And you know what I had the night before that?"

"Pasta?"

"No, I had steak."

Paul nods.

He says, "My mother makes steak in the frying pan, she fries it in olive oil with onions. Home fries."

He doesn't have a sense of humor, Paul. He's intense and spooked and humorless, like someone on cocaine. Life is serious. He spots my father's blue windbreaker on the bench. Cautiously he reaches out and touches it. He rolls a bit of the fabric between thumb and fingers.

"That's nice, Ray. Is it nylon?"

My father looks at the jacket, noticing it himself.

"I don't know. It might be."

Paul fingers a frayed cotton elastic cuff.

"That's nice, that's a find," he says. "Did it come like this?"

"No, Paul, it's just worn . . ."

"I really like this jacket, Ray. It's a beaut. Where'd you get it?"

"I don't remember. Maybe from Penney's."

"Oh yeah, JC Penney, we got Penney's near us, at the mall. I'll go there, Ray."

Lefty reappears and before sitting down he stops behind the bench. He runs a hand down the back of Paul's head, over his son's wiry black hair. He rests his hand there, above the acned neck . . .

"How we doing, Dad?"

"A-okay, buddy boy," Lefty says.

Paul's okay, he's got the go-ahead. He starts up with the music again.

"Allan Holdsworth, 'The Un-Merry-Go-Round'?"

"What's it called?"

"'Un-Merry-Go-Round.'"

"Wow. No, I don't—"

"'Oneiric Moor.'"

The litany begins again. Tangerine Dream, "The Mysterious Semblance at the Strand of Nightmares." His hands ripple in the air. Vangelis— *Pulstar*—the hands plunge down on dark chords. His face doesn't change. He's talking fast and shooting me glances. An offhand drumroll, then *whew*—he's winded. He catches his breath—close call—he sobers up.

Andreas Vollenweider—"Steam Forest" . . . virtuoso of the moon harp. Paul's pudgy hands pick out delicate harp notes. He reminds me that Momus recorded one song in a former cathedral. "Chimerical Underling." Then there's Yes—"Topographical Oceans." He's a DJ of the imagination. Fantasy landscapes upheave inside his head—I can see them: ledges, waterfalls, plateaus . . . mossy asteroids . . . gatefold sleeves and CD covers, you get lost in them . . . underwear scenes, lonely Edens . . . He puts in a word for Katharsis and their epic-length "Opus 1," including "Cavern of Disappointment," "Straits of Disenchantment," "Kathartic Vista," and "Latitudes of Despairing Transcendence"—purely instrumental, no lyrics . . .

I'm out of breath, filling up with warm sand. I'm suffocating . . . drowning from inside . . . A race goes by, I don't even bet. Sunk beside Paul. The others ignore us, they've cut me loose.

"Estuaries of the Pagan Incubi"—a mood piece, only two minutes long—by Druid's Uncle. "Egregious Dudgeon of High Winds" . . .

Suddenly I want to kill him. I take slow measured breaths, looking for something organic to rest my eyes on. They land on his black polyester slacks, his black plastic workboots.

"The Witch's Umbrage"—he's just rattling off names now—"A Beldam's Regrets" . . .

"A *Belgian's* Regrets?"

"Beldam's."

"Oh."

"Yeah. Thanks."

Paul, mental voyager and master of fantasy, gets up and toddles off to the men's room.

He comes back with a few more titles, his fly unzipped . . .

"Senate of Stones" . . . by Zeitgeist . . . played on three pipe organs and recorded in a cistern. "Gossamer Headwings" by Middle Earth, complete with strings and choir and chanting. "The Sombre March of the Grampians"—recorded in a grain silo. "Wrath of the Obelisk" . . .

"Hang on a minute, Paul." I get up to keep from hollering. I've got to get away from him. The seventh race is about to go. I drift into line, the tote reads 0 to post and I step up . . .

I'm about to bet Beldam's Regrets and can't find it in the program. The cashier's looking at me, I step aside, the next guy lurches forward . . .

The bell goes off and people move toward the grandstand. Others cluster below the TV screens. I walk to the bar. A bartender in a black vest comes over.

"Shot of Jim Beam, straight."

He pours me a neat regulated shot in a plastic cup. I slide him a five and drink the shot and light a cigarette and then lean there, my back against the counter, looking around at everyone focused on the race. The bar counter is a makeshift representation of my world, the bartender, in his silly vest, is a representative of that world. At six he'll take off the vest and go to a bar himself, or home to a room or a woman. The bourbon feels good, it hits me right away. The rest of the day is changed. It's been channeled into one of the few streams a day can go to, it's familiar, a relief.

Back at the bench, Paul is talking to my old man. His shirtpocket bulges with plastic forks and spoons. I mill around beside Nick and Mel . . .

Paul says "How come Danny lives in New York?"

"Well, Paul—" He's stumped. "That's where he lives. He likes the city."

"You love him, don't you?"

"Yes, I do."

"No questions asked, right?"

"That's right, Paul." He smiles.

"No questions asked."

My father's smile fades to introspection. He catches my eye, says, "Well? Should we go?"

"Okay."

He stands up. I shake hands with the guys, I'll see them next time around. Paul is visibly nervous, like when I showed up. He doesn't like it when things change. Lefty's looking up from the bench, our hands are clasped. His hand is warm and hard.

"Take care, Danny," he says.

He hits me with that grin. It's the last time I'll see him.

"Take care, Lefty. . . . Okay, Paul."

"Yeah, okay, Danny. My friend just bought a new Ford. Fourteen thousand dollars, yeah. He said he'll drive me around in it, no charge. Thanks."

WE TAKE THE STAIRS AND hand our programs to men waiting at the bottom and head into the heat. The brightness is impossible: all you can do is watch the ground at your feet. Other trackrats are filtering out through the cars. We cross Emery, unlock the Impala and step away from the shimmering heat inside it . . .

First thing we're rolling I light a cigarette. In heavy traffic, Firestone on donut shop, we creep toward the freeway. The summer haze stands in the air. The car radio—has it ever been turned on? Does he know it's here?

Probably my mother turns it on. He's never seemed like a married man to me. In a sense he isn't, he's always been solitary. I see him moving away . . . advancing . . . contracting toward the horizon. A little bowlegged . . . he moves like an old hand . . . on Earth, in time. Which he is.

"Lemme have one puff of that, Danny."

I hand it over, he takes a puff and hands it back.

From childhood, I was accustomed not only to seeing the dead laid out in open caskets but also to kissing the corpse's chilly forehead on the morning of burial.

DEATH

∽∂∽

LUCIA PERILLO

Outtake: Canticle from the Book of Bob

We hired the men to carry the coffin,
we hired a woman to sing in our stead.
We hired a limo, we hired a driver,
we hired each lily to stand with its head

held up and held open while scripture was read.
We hired a dustpan, we hired a broom
to sweep up the pollen that fell in the room
where we'd hired some air

to draw out the stale chord
from the organ we hired.
And we hired some tears because our own eyes were tired.

The pulpit we hired, we hired the priest
to say few words about the deceased,

and money changed hands
and the process was brief.
We said, "Body of Christ."
Then we hired our grief.

We hired some young men to carry the coffin,
we hired a woman to sing for his soul—
we hired the limo, we hired the driver,
then we hired the ground and we hired the hole.

CAMILLE PAGLIA

The Italian Way of Death

ᨀᨆᨆᨆ

I TALIANS ARE MASTERS OF THE CONCRETE, from the vast engineering projects of the Roman Empire to the gritty manual labor of Renaissance painting and sculpture to our domination of the trade in paving, masonry, ironwork, garden ornaments, and gravestones in modern America. We specialize in the markers and monuments of the messy human transit of birth and death.

Italians view death in simple, pragmatic terms, as a physical process to be efficiently planned and managed. Our culture is strongly ritualistic, with the public theatricality of early tribalism. Italian funerals are major events where, despite our reputation for histrionics, extreme emotion is strictly limited. The gravity and dignity of Italian funerals predate Catholic ceremonialism and probably originate in the Etruscan death cult, whose inspiration may have been Egyptian.

As an Italian-American, I was raised with respect for but not fear of death. Italians dread incapacity and dependency, not extinction. Since the dead are always remembered, they are never really gone. In rural Italy, cemeteries are like parks where the survivors picnic and tend the graves. In America, family plots are purchased like vacation condos; one knows one's future address decades in advance.

An education in death is part of the Italian facts of life. From childhood, I was accustomed not only to seeing the dead laid out in open caskets but also to kissing the corpse's chilly forehead on the morning of burial. At home, elderly relatives burned votive candles before framed photographs of the deceased. Anniversaries of the date of death, recorded on plasticized saints' cards, are still marked by special Masses and devotions.

The Italian realism about death was formed by the primitive harshness of agricultural life, where food, water, shelter, and sex were crucial to survival. Country people are notoriously blunt and unsentimental about accidents and disasters, which tend to traumatize today's pampered, squeamish middle-class professionals. Bobbie Gentry's 1967 hit song, "Ode to Billie Joe," preserves something of that premodern flavor when a crusty Mississippi farmer, indifferent to his daughter's feelings, reacts to the news of a young man's fatal plunge off a bridge by remarking, "Well, Billie Joe never had a lick of sense. Pass the biscuits, please."

The steely Italian stoicism and even irreverence about death have often gotten me into trouble in American academe, where bourgeois pieties reign supreme. Hamlet's black humor about Polonios's corpse—"I'll lug the guts into the neighbor room"—is very Italian. Informed of a death, we shun the usual polite, unctuous hush and take great interest instead in the technicalities: "How did it happen?" Italians recognize both the inevitability of death and its unique grisly signature, which seems fascinating to us in a way that strikes other people as morbid or insensitive. And as in TV soap operas, we like prolonged debate about how a death will affect others—pathos and voyeurism as mass entertainment.

Movies about Italian-Americans have rarely caught our essence. We are, after blacks, the most defamed and stereotyped minority group. The over-praised *Prizzi's Honor* (1985) and *Moonstruck* (1987), for example, are grotesquely bad, with all the ethnic verisimilitude of a minstrel show. Woody Allen's films, in contrast, convey a keen sense of America's social codes as perceived by an anxious, alienated Jew. Allen's *Broadway Danny Rose* (1984) deserves more attention for its comparison study of Italian and Jewish style and thought, notably in regard to death.

Allen's preoccupation with death is well-known, a haunted pessimism partly produced by the persecutions of Jewish history. But Allen turns his terrors into candidly self-revealing comedy, which is why I prefer his work to that of overly ironic literary modernists like T. S. Eliot and Samuel Beckett. In *Annie Hall* (1977), his alter ego, Alvy Singer (played by himself), announces "I'm obsessed with death" as he presents two books as love gifts to the perky, ultra-WASPy Annie (Diane Keaton) after their first sexual encounter—*The Denial of Death* and *Death and Western Thought*. The film's amusing refrain is Alvy's attempt to reeducate Annie by repeatedly taking her to Marcel Ophuls's dour, four-hour epic on Nazism, *The Sorrow and the Pity*. Busily packing boxes after their breakup, she reminds him, "All the books on death and dying are yours."

In *Broadway Danny Rose,* Allen plays a compassionate, ethical Jew for whom suffering and death define the human condition. He belongs to an exquisitely internalized guilt culture: "I'm guilty all the time, and I never did anything," he sighs. Danny has a madcap adventure with a tough New Jersey broad, Tina (brilliantly played by Mia Farrow), whose honor-based, vendetta-filled shame culture is completely Italian: "I never feel guilty. You gotta do what you gotta do," she proclaims. Her slangy speech has an aggressive Mediterranean flamboyance: "You're lucky I don't stick an ice pick in your goddamned chest!" she yells at her lover as she trashes the apartment. "Drop dead!"

Allen wonderfully catches the brusquely routine Italian attitude toward death when Danny drives Tina away from a (somewhat caricatured) Mafia lawn party. He asks if she and her husband are divorced. "Some guy shot him in the eyes," she says casually. "Really," says Danny, horrified. "He's blind?" "Dead," she flatly replies. Danny cringes with pained, nauseated empathy: "Dead? Of course—because the bullets go right through—[gestures behind his glasses]. Oh, my God! You must have been in shock!" "Nah," she replies, "he had it coming." Ethnicity has reversed the sex roles here, with a man about to faint from a woman's bloodthirsty bluster.

That the Italian directness about death is part of a more general worldview is clear in the first two parts of Francis Ford Coppola's *The Godfather* (1972, 1974), based on Mario Puzo's best-selling novel. True masterpieces of our time, they dramatically demonstrate the residual paganism of Italian culture, with its energy, passion, clannishness, and implacable willfulness. The stunning, choreographic violence of these films is like a sacrificial slaughter where blood flows as freely as the waters of life. Coppola constantly juxtaposes and intercuts images of food and death to suggest the archaic Italian, or rather pre-Christian, cycle of fertility, destruction, and rebirth.

Don Corleone's right-hand man, Peter Clemenza (Richard Castellano), is the primary vehicle of this theme. "Don't forget the cannolis!" his wife calls out to him from the front porch. On an airy highway in the New Jersey marshlands, he says, "Hey, pull over, will ya—I gotta take a leak." While his back is turned, three shots blast into the driver's skull from the shadowy backseat. Ambling back to the car, Clemenza curtly tells his henchman, "Leave the gun. Take the cannolis." The white pastry box is tenderly lifted from its place next to the corpse bloodily jammed against the steering wheel, and burly Clemenza primly carries the pastries away. Now, that's Italian!

In another scene, the don's inner circle hangs out, tensely waiting for news of his condition after an assassination attempt. Clemenza is happily making tomato sauce. "Hey, come over here, kid," he calls to the don's youngest son, Michael (Al Pacino). "Learn sumpin'. You never know, you might have to cook for twenty guys someday!" Instructions follow about olive oil, garlic, tomato paste. "You shove in all your sausage and your meatballs": as Clemenza's big, hammy hand slides the gray meats into the pot, we can't help thinking of the corpses piling up in the plot. And indeed his next remark is a cheerful aside about the roadside execution: "Oh, Paulie—you won't see him no more!" Cooking and killing are as intimately related as in the Stone Age, with past guests easily ending up on the menu.

One of *The Godfather*'s most gruesome rubouts occurs at Louis's Restaurant, "a small family place" in the Bronx where a drug kingpin advises his crony, a corrupt police captain, "Try the veal—it's the best in the city." Moments later, their dinner companion, Michael Corleone, shoots them both in the face with a pistol. The astonished captain, laden fork raised over his bib, gurgles and chokes as if still chewing, then slams headfirst on the table, bringing everything to the floor with a crash. As Michael flees, we can see the overturned table stained with red splotches that could be wine, tomato sauce, or blood—or perhaps, in the Italian way, all three. Coppola then inserts a montage of headlines with real police photos of gory gangland hits, followed by a staged shot of a big bowl of leftover spaghetti being dumped into a garbage can. *Sic transit gloria mundi.*

The Godfather is full of these vivid visual effects that show death as a barbarically sensual experience, integrated with the body's normal and abnormal functions and spasms. For example, in his famous final scene as Don Corleone, Marlon Brando, cutting monster teeth out of an orange peel, frolics with his grandson among his tomato plants in his arbor, a re-created patch of Italy. Death comes quickly but subtly: The don's steps turn to a stagger and his laughter to gasps for breath, until his heavy form topples and sprawls on the ground. Or death can be a terrible explosion of the nerves, as when the don's disloyal, pretty boy son-in-law, Carlo, is garroted from behind by Clemenza and convulsively kicks out the windshield of a moving car.

My favorite scene in *The Godfather* (sometimes censored for TV broadcast) shows the Italian cultivation of death as an artistic strategy, an operatic spectacle of hands-on activism. Vito Corleone (played as a young adult by Robert De Niro) revisits Sicily to settle an old score—the murder of his parents decades before by the ruthless Don Ciccio. Vito and his local business partner, bearing a gallon of olive oil, respectfully approach the feeble and nearly deaf don, who genially asks, "What was your father's name?" Leaning in close on the sunny veranda, Vito softly replies, "His name was Antonio Andolini, and this is for you"—as he jams the don with a knife, ripping his gut crosswise to the top of his chest. Magnificent and inspiring, in my Homeric view. "Turn the other cheek" has never made much of a dent in Italian consciousness. Death Italian style is a luscious banquet, a bruising game of chance, or crime and punishment as pagan survival of the fittest.

DANA GIOIA

Planting a Sequoia

All afternoon my brothers and I have worked in the orchard,
Digging this hole, laying you into it, carefully packing the soil.
Rain blackened the horizon, but cold winds kept it over the Pacific,
And the sky above us stayed the dull gray
Of an old year coming to an end.

In Sicily a father plants a tree to celebrate his first son's birth—
An olive or a fig tree—a sign that the earth has one more life to bear.
I would have done the same, proudly laying new stock into my father's
     orchard,
A green sapling rising among the twisted apple boughs,
A promise of new fruit in other autumns.

But today we kneel in the cold planting you, our native giant,
Defying the practical custom of our fathers,
Wrapping in your roots a lock of hair, a piece of an infant's birth cord,
All that remains above earth of a first-born son,
A few stray atoms brought back to the elements.

We will give you what we can—our labor and our soil,
Water drawn from the earth when the skies fail,
Nights scented with the ocean fog, days softened by the circuit of bees.
We plant you in the corner of the grove, bathed in western light,
A slender shoot against the sunset.

And when our family is no more, all of his unborn brothers dead,
Every niece and nephew scattered, the house torn down,
His mother's beauty ashes in the air,
I want you to stand among strangers, all young and ephemeral to you,
Silently keeping the secret of your birth.

MARIANNA DE MARCO TORGOVNICK

FOR MY FATHER, SALVATORE DE MARCO SR. 1912–1992

Crossing Back

∽∾∾

I

WHEN I WAS A CHILD, I thought of my father as connected to the larger world—the glittering "City." Every day, my tall, slim father dressed in a dark suit and tie, combed his brown hair with a pronounced part to the side, groomed his thin Don Ameche mustache and headed for "the City"—a Rudolph Valentino look-alike, very Italian. My father knew "the City" and it was a point of pride for him; the "King of New York," my husband called him recently. My father was born in Manhattan, on the Lower East Side, and the New York of his youth was his private heartland. He boasted about having been rough in school and being kicked out in the eighth grade after a fight in which his nose was broken into an exaggerated Roman beak. He would tell again and again how he was expelled; bored with the story, my mother would murmur with vague disapproval, "Oh yeah, a tough guy."

For most of the years I was growing up, my father had a job that put him in touch with "the City." He was a messenger for a large bank—First National City, now Citibank; actually, he was what was called an armed guard, delivering stocks, bonds, and cash from office to office and for a while collecting payments in Harlem with a black partner he liked named Oscar Joseph. Later, he worked in the mail room of an insurance company and he liked this job too. But my father loved best his bank job, and the gun he carried as an armed messenger added a certain jauntiness to his image.

At the bank, the city was his beat. It was the equivalent of the police route he always coveted but couldn't get. My father was six feet tall—unusual among second-generation Sicilian Americans—but he was too thin for his height to pass the physical examination for the Police Department. He took the physical three times; it was part of the family lore that he gulped malteds several times a day before the last examination. But although he always had a hearty appetite, he just couldn't gain enough weight—and it was a profound disappointment. All his life, my father would say of certain acquaintances, with admiration and a kind of hush in his voice, "He's a cop." He kept track of raises in policemen's pay scales; he loved detective shows on TV. I think he always felt he had missed out on a certain level of excitement, missed out as well on the financial security of being a policeman for the city.

Still, at the bank, Manhattan was his beat and he took personal responsibility for knowing it. My father could reel off the exact location of everything—hotels, movie theaters, even stores and restaurants. He knew the subway and bus routes by heart. He never wanted to leave New York and would tell people again and again when he visited us in North Carolina that he was a New Yorker and that outside of New York everything was "boring." Later in life, after he had retired and stopped going into Manhattan regularly, one of his most annoying habits was continuing to give directions to places that had changed, especially driving directions, since he never drove.

But when I was young, my father's intimacy with the city was his special charm. He took me on excursions that must have been on his vacations, since my mother was never there and was probably working. We went to out-of-the-way museums, like the Museum of the City of New York; to zoos and parks for sledding; to Wall Street (where he worked). To Radio City Music Hall or the old Roxy (these with my mother) every birthday, to see the movie and stage shows. These were places that made me feel the pulse of life beyond Brooklyn—and my father was, at first, the key.

He also introduced me to the world of reading. Until he needed glasses, my father was an avid reader. He would pass along the newspaper every day after work and sometimes paperbacks he got from friends. Once, via Oscar Joseph, I got the autobiography of Althea Gibson, an African American female tennis player. It was typical of my father that he was friendly toward blacks in a general way, despite sharing some of the prejudices of our neighborhood: without really thinking about it, he taught me tolerance by little things like his stories about his buddy Oscar Joseph and the book about Gibson. But my father always claimed he could not read using glasses—and so he simply stopped reading once and for all when he was in his fifties and had to use them. In later years, I would sometimes buy him books I thought he might like about the Mafia or mysteries but he never read them—because of the glasses.

My father smoked exactly a pack a day between the ages of ten and sixty and then gave up cigarettes cold turkey—as firmly and definitely as he gave up reading. He also never ate cake after dinner, just at breakfast, and never used more than one slice of cold cuts in his sandwiches. He was a man with many rules—some of them nonsensical—which he would proclaim repeatedly as simple matters of fact: "Nope. I don't eat cake at night" or "That's right, just one slice of provolone." As he aged, I saw the rigidity in his life but forgot the younger man, the reader, the adventurer who took me all over town. I needed to forget in order to become myself. For if adolescents need rebellion, female adolescents in Bensonhurst need it even more. Now I am free to remember.

II

My father, who always liked above all things to walk, got lung cancer. Within two months of the diagnosis, he could only walk a half block at a time. On a good day—a very good day—he walked five short blocks and felt euphoric. All his life he had been prone to exaggerate minor illnesses. After he retired, he paced the floor, restlessly, and jingled change in his pockets. He lost interest in almost everything but a few weekly TV shows. He became irritable over nothing. I thought he might fall apart at the lung cancer. Instead, he pulled together. Now that he had something real to worry about, he was able to act brave. Bringing up the subject of a living will and signing one frankly. "I don't want to be a guinea pig," he said. "You have to help me get the words right"—but his own words were pretty good. He made calls to see if any social agency would provide help for him and my mother. Being brave. Taking charge.

In the months after I learned he had lung cancer, I was bombarded with memories. Once, when I was about five, my father was reading the *Daily News*. On the front page was a picture of Marilyn Monroe during her marriage to Joe DiMaggio. The headline was about a miscarriage (not, I think, her first). "What a shame," my father said. "Such a beautiful woman, so famous, and she just can't do what a woman is supposed to do." The very things that would so frustrate me about Italian Americans were all there in his remark—the narrow aspirations for women, the expectation that they must bear children, the disregard for things other than family—but at the time I didn't have a single feminist hackle to raise and I'm sure as sure that this remark lodged firmly in my subconscious.

So firmly that I connect this memory seamlessly with one from twenty years later, sitting with my father on my front porch the week my own baby died. He didn't know that I felt I had failed, just like Marilyn. Without a hint of the bravado that might accompany such a remark, just matter of factly, my father said, "It should have been me instead of that baby. I would have been happy to die instead." These were his only words to me on the subject, ever, and somehow they were enough since I knew what he meant. A pragmatic man, he wanted to keep the generations straight and spare me improper pain: he should have died, not the baby.

My other, strongest, memory of my father comes from when I was about ten. He had just gotten off the phone with his brother, talking about his niece, my cousin Marion, much older than me and the mother of my playmate Patricia. Marion had cancer. They weren't sure yet how bad. "It's spread through her body. She's going to die." His voice croaked, his eyes were red, and there were tears beginning to roll down his face. Then he wiped his eyes heartily with a handkerchief, and that was all. Marion was his favorite niece—fat and always jolly. But there was no helping a bad situation, and no privacy for expressing grief in our small apartment. I think my father didn't want to scare me, who was watching. But it did scare me—especially since, after Marion died, he sometimes accidentally called me by her name, so close to mine, a momentary confusion that I understand now, when I sometimes call one daughter by the other's name. "Oh, Mom!" they say, exasperated. But when my father called me Marion it made me shiver—his calling me by my dead cousin's name.

There's a way to see these memories as about Italian-American contempt for females. My father telling me early that women were valuable only as reproducers. My father crying at my female cousin's death but not wanting to make too big a deal of it. My father confusing my name with his niece's. But these readings would be wrong.

My father was not a philosophical man, not able to or even interested in expressing what he felt. Nor was he an especially sensitive or demonstrable man, emotionally. He was a family man, devoted to custom because in his experience custom was what kept families going. People had children because people loved their children and took care of them: nothing in life was more basic than that to my father. You didn't make a big deal of things or fall apart because that would make it harder to keep going: that was basic too. Even as a child, I understood the way he reacted to Marilyn, Marion, and me, Marianna, to show that I was important to him, that my mother's life would have been—from his point of view, and hers—incomplete without my being born. My mother was thirty when she married and thirty-six when she had me: a career woman's pattern today. But back then she had no career and was in danger of spending her life as a maiden aunt, caring for her sister's family. My father had saved her from what would have been in his terms a "waste," even a "disgrace." So he was not devaluing females; he was valuing them in the way he knew best.

In fact, my father loved his female relatives intensely. He adored his mother, who lived with my parents after their marriage and died a few months before I was born and given her name. In her last illness, some kind of pneumonia, he tried to give her mouth-to-mouth resuscitation when she stopped breathing. He wondered aloud, sometimes, if he had killed her; my mother always said quickly, "No, don't think it. She was dead already." He was extremely close to his sister, Minnie, visiting her several times every week until she died in 1982.

My father was unusual among Italian men in that he was always involved with running the house. He did housework—perhaps because my mother worked, perhaps because he liked it, but I suspect because he remembered his own mother as tired. Each time, he would draw the blinds and instruct us not to tell the neighbors that he was ironing, doing the dishes, whatever it happened to be. I didn't understand his concern, since it didn't seem shameful to me that a man should do chores. I can still see him wearing what we agreed to call my mother's aprons or, more often, a dish towel tucked into his belt. When he was young, he was a painter and also finished furniture (breathing every day, I realize now, fumes and asbestos); so he did traditional men's work too, like painting and putting up wallpaper. Until he was into his seventies, he could be counted on to do repairs well—it was part of his public image. After that, he became a little obsessive about the details, scrubbing pots for hours (his tongue protruding as it always did when he concentrated) and he sometimes broke what he tried to fix.

LOOKING BACK, PUTTING TOGETHER THE pieces, I understand my father to have been my ally in crossing Ocean Parkway. He was pulling for me underneath—though not always and not uniformly. He was proud of my bookishness and sensitivity. But he was an Italian-American male—so he worried about them too. At times, he could be macho and even cruel in attempts to "toughen me up" and teach me to follow orders. Some of what I learned was useful later in life; but even now I feel ambivalent about the lessons.

Once, for example, when I was about five, I cried hard at a Jerry Lewis skit on TV and my father banished me in a rage from the living room. In the skit, Jerry was a poor kid in a rich community who had worked hard all summer to buy a lottery ticket for a bicycle; he won, but couldn't make it through the crowd in time to claim his prize. I still think it wasn't funny, it was sad—though I probably overreacted. My father couldn't understand why I would cry over something that happened on TV. Television was background noise or entertainment and neither he nor my mother would ever take it to heart. My father got mad and wouldn't let me watch television for a week until I learned to "control myself and not spoil things for other people."

Similar things happened when I just couldn't sit at the table when a Sicilian delicacy called what sounded like "capuzeddu" (*capozella*) was served—a whole, baked sheep's head with gaping eyes and exposed larynx. "She's too soft; she's got to learn," he would say to my mother—and he'd make me eat in the bathroom, sitting on the washing machine. At first, being sent off alone made me feel sad and rejected; I wanted to control myself, to be part of the family circle. But gradually something else took shape—a feeling of pride in being different. At school, teachers praised me for empathizing with books and having strong opinions; I was appointed "school librarian," so that I could spend several hours each day alone, reading or doing whatever I wanted. I think I came to associate being on my own with being special. So by the time I was ten or eleven, I began to rather like these scenes of banishment at home.

At other times, my father could be patient and supportive. When I was put ahead from second to third grade in the middle of the school year, he sat with me for hours, teaching me cursive writing, making the transition work. "A Philadelphia lawyer!" he would joke when I said something clever. He was hostile to the Church for reasons he never revealed—and that made it easier for me to break away when I was fourteen. Once he had started me on going to "the City," I kept going and I always had money for things like movies and plays. I suspect now, in retrospect, that these kinds of luxuries were my father's doing, just as it was my mother who provided extra money for clothes.

My mother sewed dresses in a factory near our apartment and only went to Manhattan for Radio City to see the shows or, sometimes, to shop with me. She was smart and strong, the kind of woman who could have been a CEO in a different life. But if she had been making decisions about me alone I suspect I would have been confined more to "the neighborhood." My father did not dream wild dreams but he definitely saw me in the world of "the City." He wavered just enough in his opposition to my ambitions (letting me go to college, for example, but not out of town) so that while I did not exactly get what I wanted, I got what I would need.

III

During my father's illness my visits to Bensonhurst grew more frequent. I saw different sides of the neighborhood from those I saw as a child and teenager. My father had always been faithful in visiting people in hospitals or attending funerals. This is an important part of Italian-American life and one reason why my father was so familiar with sickness and death—much more so than I am, his Americanized daughter. Now people returned the "respect" he had shown. The neighbors didn't desert my parents or avert their eyes politely. People visited, some every day, some more than once a day. Food arrived. Connie next door delivered grapefruits, apples, eggs, bread, cakes. She offered the extra room in her apartment if I needed to stay overnight. Sometimes I did stay, surrounded by statues of the Virgin Mary and Saint Teresa, and by numerous pictures of Il Papa, Pope Paul. The barber across the street volunteered his services for both parents. The community drew together, as it always has done best, in times of trouble.

Back in Bensonhurst, I felt observed and shut in, as usual. But there was something else taking shape as I contrasted the neighborhood's reaction to my father's illness with the college town where I had last experienced grief: there was no embarrassment here, no shunning. Some of the aloofness and reserve I had cultivated toward the neighbors began to change. I was grateful for their help, willing to listen politely to their stories in exchange, giving the ritual kisses and hugs sincerely.

In the same way, I felt close to my brother in a way I had not for years, even decades, as our politics and ways of life grew apart. Again and again, I was surprised at how little we had to say to understand what the other was thinking—and at how much we thought alike. Once, when my father suddenly seemed worse, I asked my brother if I should come to New York immediately. "I can't say, Marianna," he responded. "That's for you to decide." My parents and brother had always been bossy. So while it sounds like a small thing, this comment was golden.

MY FATHER HUNG ON TO life, tenaciously. His fingers clawed the blanket, searching for texture. He concentrated, hard, at hearing conversations from the rooms adjacent to the bedroom, where he was now confined. He talked over, again and again, every detail of where things should be placed in his sickroom—the bed, the clock, his eyeglasses. He was proud of lucid moments when he recognized everyone and everything clearly and could participate in conversation. I was proud too that he retained minutes of lucidity until the end—eating some breakfast and talking to his nurse the very day he died.

More and more, his body gave way on an alert mind. Teeth getting loose; limbs sticklike; jaw swollen grotesquely with a new cancer. A merciless disease that extracted every ounce of strength from my father, still struggling, still brave. And I can't say that there was not some quality of life until the very end: enjoyment of the visits, of the food, of the holidays, even, though it's not clear at all that one day was very different from another. On one visit, I bought a portable television for the bedroom, distressed at the silence in which my father spent his days and nights—so different from the radio and television noise he had always seemed to like. I had always hated the soundtracks of the police shows he preferred, but now I flipped eagerly through the channels, glad when I found one with the right jarring and staccato notes. On that visit, my next to last, my father seemed to be permanently bedridden. I was surprised the next week when he was up once more and I heard him over the phone joking with his visiting nurse at the kitchen table. "It often happens," the nurse said when I called the hospice. "We don't know why but some people get a burst of energy before they go back to bed for good."

As he neared death, he didn't pay attention to petty things—the rules about cake, the glasses, the TV. When he was not lucid he talked to himself, or perhaps (as he made caressing gestures) to his dead mother or sister. When he was alert, my father talked directly about his illness, his coming death. He wanted no nonsense and got none. "I always thought of myself as a tough guy," my father said, "but I'm sure scared now." Near the end, when I asked whether he wanted me to keep talking or just to be silent, he said, "Really, what is there to say?" So I stayed quiet. The day before he died, he said, "This is too much now." So I was glad when it stopped.

IV

At the funeral, it was my father's jolliness people remembered—his sense of humor, his participation in life. Funerals are like résumés—only the good survives—but it pleased me to hear these things from family and my parents' friends.

I had dreaded the Italian funeral, even before I knew it would fall on New Year's Eve, then New Year's Day, cold and windy. Lots of people were away for the holidays and could not be reached; to my other fears was added the fear that too few people would come. Still, people did come, drifting in and out—relatives (some of whom I had never met), people from the Senior Citizens' Center, neighbors alone or in groups of two and three—talking, remembering, even laughing. Some of them had known my father for fifty, even seventy or more years, and I heard about him as a boy, a teenager, a young man.

The number of flowers in the room grew and grew as the contributions of friends and neighbors arrived. The stands erected for mass cards began to fill. We reached a decent number of visitors, flowers, and cards and I began to feel better. I thought of the irony: this man, who never went to church, will have many masses. I, who thought the cards and flowers meaningless, am keeping tabs.

Before my father died, my mother talked about how she wanted to give the money people might spend on flowers to the hospice that cared for my father near the end. Then, the day he died, she amazed me by reciting a list of flower arrangements she wanted me to order—specific, with names, colors, and sizes: a "Bleeding Heart" for her, three feet across and all made of roses; a carnation "Rosary" for the grandchildren, to hang in the coffin. This woman, who would walk miles to save a dollar on a can of coffee, spent over a thousand dollars on flowers. My brother and I followed her orders unthinkingly. But even we were surprised by the lavishness of the "Gate of Paradise" she had ordered for us. Over five hundred dollars of orchids, roses, and lilies densely woven in a six-foot arch—a real fantasy, "what children give their parents." In the funeral home, looking for hours at these flowers, I thought about how much more useful the money would have been at the hospice; later, we made a contribution in my father's name. But I cannot deny it, I was comforted by the flowers and the funeral cards—so wasteful but so necessary for the occasion.

At first, I found the traditional Italian funeral creepy: people swooping in, making my mother tell the story of the last weeks again and again, making her cry, sometimes outdoing her themselves in tears and drama. Then, everybody settled in. There were fewer new arrivals, and fewer scenes. We were, as is the Italian custom, sitting and keeping watch over the body in the open coffin. My father's body became a comfortable presence in the room. He was wearing a new suit (my mother's preference), and he had been made up skillfully so that he looked healthy and years younger. By the end of the second day, the day before the burial, looking at him, I even wondered why he had to die, though that had been so vivid just days before in the hospice, as he struggled painfully for air.

The familiar rhythm of Italian gossip got going. The funeral "home" is, or so the relatives whispered, favored by the Mafia. Signing some papers, I looked up to see a man with a face so coldblooded and heartless—pocked, stretched, and rubbery like old Silly Putty, like a cartoon gangster—that it took my breath away. He was wearing a long leather coat, an expensive suit, and gold and diamond rings on every finger. A mafioso, or so it seemed, who became a family joke for the rest of the funeral. I never thought that I identified with the Mafia, or, rather, with Italian-Americans' fascination with the Mafia—yet here I was, joining in. It was a bond with my family and my father.

When I was a child I suspected that my missing paternal grandfather, a union organizer for barbers, had had Mafia connections. Then, when I was married and deemed ready for such news, I was told he had been a bad husband, a womanizer, and that was why he was missing from my family's life. My father had stood up for my grandmother, rebelled against his father, and his father had left the house. It turns out I was right as a child—even though what I was told later on was also true. During the funeral, my brother recalled how my father always said that Lucky Luciano had been his godfather. Among Sicilians, so celebrated a godfather is a real distinction—and no accident. Although he was not a mafioso, my father's father must have needed to have, at the very least, the connivance of the Mafia to run his union. He must have done certain favors and handled himself in a way that won Luciano's "respect." I understand now my father's tacit pride in the Mafia, though the family has been out of the business for two generations and he himself always wanted to be a policeman.

The last stop before the cemetery at an Italian funeral is the church, and here too there were surprises. I had not been in church for years and there were many changes. The priest went about his business energetically and impressively. He minced no words: if we are believing Catholics, there can be no absolute sadness in the face of death. He wafted his incense, controlled his altar. It was an impersonal service, as is typical of Catholic masses. Nothing was said about my father but his name; no space was provided for eulogies, so the one my husband wrote stayed in his pocket unread. Then—I realized too late—the priest offered communion. The entire neighborhood rose and moved to the altar. So did my mother and my brother, although my brother (I could tell from his face and the way he held his body) expected just to escort her to the altar, not to take communion himself.

I had not been to confession, had not fasted, was in a state of mortal sin. I remembered all the warnings of the nuns from my childhood, and feared committing blasphemy at my father's funeral. I stayed seated. So did my husband and daughters, who are not Catholic. I thought it would be a bad moment, but no one, not even the neighbors, seemed to mind. The priest handed my brother a host, unexpectedly. His face showed confused feelings; then he swallowed it, glaring at me to say absolutely nothing. After mass, people told me that now they decide whether they are ready to take communion—no confession or fasting are needed. I was back in Bensonhurst, and making peace; but I no longer knew all the rules.

V

When a parent dies, you are freed from images of the last few years, from the physical form in which you knew them then. Until a few months before he died, my father was a handsome man of eighty, with abundant silver hair still mixed with black, tall and slim and elegant. His hair would jut forward over his forehead while he worked, making him look almost boyish. He had relatively few wrinkles. The only real signs of his advanced age were his thick glasses and an occasional wobble from an inner ear condition. He was always neatly dressed and never really informal. He looked odd in shorts, which he wore only at the beach. When he lacked a tie or a jacket, he often wore a vest or cardigan. He always wore polished or suede shoes, never sneakers, even to take his long daily walks.

But now, in my imagination, my father has floated free of the physical images from his last years. He is the dark-haired, slim man (almost always wearing a dark suit) from the photographs. My father on the subway, holding the straps, teaching me the ropes of going into "the City." My father flying kites at my cousin's country house, helping me chase a kite down a road for miles and miles. I remember still how that kite looked, finally trapped in some telephone wires, as we turned and walked away. I remember the gold tooth he hasn't had since his late fifties, when he got false teeth. There it is in my mind. It's as much a part of my father now as anything else. Then, as I am waking up one morning, I see my eighty-year-old father on the inside of my eyelids—his beaked nose, his thin mustache, his crooked smile. He starts to speak, but it's too late—I'm fully awake. It's so vivid that I need a few seconds to remind myself that he is recently dead.

When a parent dies, you also cross from one state to another. All my life I have defined myself by rebellion against Bensonhurst. But the grounds for rebellion are running out.

W. S. Di Piero

Cheap Gold Flats

1. "Philly Babylon"

The bartender tossing cans, carton to cooler,
hand to hand with silky, mortal ease,
while the 4 P.M. beer and shot standees
study the voiceless TV above our heads.
The worst and longest storm on record.
Iceworks canal the pavements, power lines down,
cars pillowed helpless in the snow.
Bus fumes vulcanize the twilight's
911 sirens. Enter HOTSPUR, with alarums,
enter HAZEL, touching my elbow at the bar.
My staticky *Daily News* breaks in the draft.
"What's my horoscope say today, honey?"
Dear Hazel, dear Pisces, don't be hurt,
leave me alone a while, my mother's dying,
I've been beside her for several days,
today she had an extremer monkey look,
her forehead shrunk down to the bucky jaw,
and when she looks above her head, she groans
to see whatever it is she sees, so here,
take my paper, go home, forgive me.

2. Finished Basement

Tonight's big question: What will she
be laid out in? Disco tracks
jump inside the paneling.

Rita loved to dance and so do I.
The sisters, Rachel and Jeanette,
and nieces coming straight from work,
shout across her bed, voicing with
our faithful music in the walls.
Charm bracelet, definitely, the one
she hardly wore, and cheap gold flats
that made her look young and men look twice.
Yackety-yak. The unconscious bone
doesn't miss a thing we say,
its used-up flesh helpless
on the pillow. Later, alone with her,
the only noise near me is this new rattle
in her throat. I hear it behind me, too,
the disposal upstairs, a drainpipe clearing,
whatever it is, I feel it coming closer
to finger my hair and stroke my neck.

MIKE LUPICA

A Brother's Keeper

ᔆᔆᔆ

T HE SUN THROWS A MORNING LIGHT that covers the Atlantic like a blanket both soft and warm. Out the back window you can see Egg Rock sitting in the middle of the water like a piece of God's sculpture, and beyond that, on Massachusetts's North Shore, Lynn Harbor and Marblehead. Fresh cookies are on the kitchen table. There is the smell of coffee.

And suddenly, from another part of the house, like thunder signaling the coming of a storm and a darkening morning, there is the terrible sound of the coughing.

"That's him," Billy Conigliaro, the middle brother, says at the kitchen table. He stares out at the water and clasps his fingers tightly.

"He can't keep his lungs clear. The threat of pneumonia is something we fight continually."

He gets up from the table. "C'mon," he says. "I'll show you around." We go into the bar area of the beautiful house in Nahant. Here, on the walls, are the plaques and photographs that tell of the brief, shining career of Billy's older brother, Tony Conigliaro. Tony C.

Here is Tony C., young and lean and dark and handsome, with Willie Mays. Here is Tony with his two brothers, Billy and Richie. Tony was in the big leagues by then, with the Red Sox. Billy and Richie were still kids. But they were ballplayers, too. Here is Tony C. in a Red Sox uniform, crossing home plate. He was the youngest American League home-run champ in history. Even after a terrible beaning in 1967 that took a season and two months out of his career and nearly cost him the sight in his left eye, Tony C. had 164 home runs by the time he was twenty-six.

Those of us who grew up in New England in the 1960s and loved baseball thought that even with all the bad luck he had seen—two broken arms with the Sox, a fractured wrist, the eye—he still was going to hit 600 home runs for the Boston Red Sox. That was long before Tony C. and everybody found out he didn't know anything about bad luck, anything at all.

Down the hall from the plaques and the pictures, a woman is chattering on, almost musically, nonstop.

"You just a big phony." She laughs. There is more coughing, a man's coughing. "You wanna go out in the car today? Maybe we'll go to the mall. Dress you right up and take you to the mall."

Billy Conigliaro says, "That's Yvonne Baker. We call her the Big E. She's one of his nurses. We gotta go around the clock with him."

Then from down the hall comes Yvonne Baker, a pretty, wide-faced black woman pushing a wheelchair into the morning.

Seated in the wheelchair, hands forgotten in his lap, wearing a white T-shirt, the pants from a red jogging suit, and white sneakers, no longer the boy from Swampscott who hit those balls over the wall at Fenway, a forty-three-year-old man trapped in his own body since his heart stopped beating in Billy's car for several terrible minutes seven years ago, unable to feed himself or walk without help or say more than a couple of words, too much of his brain lost for good, is Tony Conigliaro, Tony C.

Billy squeezes his brother's hand and kneels in front of him. "Hey, pal," he says. "How're you doin' today?"

"HE WAS A NATURAL HOME-RUN hitter," Billy Conigliaro says. Billy's own big-league career, which began with the Red Sox, was cut short by a knee injury. "Tony grew up with one dream: hitting home runs for the Boston Red Sox."

He was doing it by the age of nineteen. He hit twenty-four home runs in 1964, in just 111 games; he had broken his arm in the spring and gotten a late start. In 1965 he hit thirty-two and won the home-run title. By August 1967, more than halfway through the Red Sox's Impossible Dream season, when magic came back into the storied little ballpark, Tony had twenty more.

He was twenty-two years and seven months old on the August night at Fenway in '67 when a Jack Hamilton fastball hit him in the temple and shattered his cheekbone. The Red Sox's dream continued, but Tony C.'s abruptly halted.

"He had been in a little slump before that," Billy remembers. "Before the game that night he told me, 'You gotta get up on the plate to hit home runs. I'm gonna stand a little closer and stand in a little longer.'"

He did not play again in 1967. The damage to the retina was worse than the doctors had originally thought. They told Tony C. the headaches would go away eventually, but he would never see well especially to hit a baseball again.

But he came back. He hit twenty homers in 1969 and was Comeback Player of the Year. In 1970 it was as if Tony, still only twenty-five, had never been away. He hit thirty-six home runs and knocked in 116. Billy was a rookie center fielder with the Red Sox that season. Richie was playing a hot shortstop at Swampscott High.

But Tony still had some trouble seeing the ball in the outfield as late afternoon became night. This he confided to coaches late in the season. Billy believes it got Tony traded to the California Angels. "After everything, they decided to get as much for him as they could before the eye went bad," Billy says today. "Nice business, huh?"

The eye did get worse; he hit four home runs for the Angels in 1971 and retired. He made one more comeback with the Red Sox, in 1975. Only the Conigliaro family and the most lunatic of trivia buffs know that he opened that World Series season as the Red Sox's designated hitter, and even hit his last two home runs. But, really, the vision was no better. It was Conigliaro's heart that kept bringing him back.

The Red Sox sent him to the minor leagues. The last time I saw him in a baseball uniform was at McCoy Stadium in Pawtucket, Rhode Island, in his final baseball summer. After he retired for good, he drifted into television work.

"He never once said, 'Why me?'" Billy Conigliaro says. "He never once complained about his luck."

YVONNE BAKER, THE BIG E, helps Tony C. into the red jacket that goes with the red pants. She positions the wheelchair in front of the large Panasonic television screen. Geraldo Rivera's talk show comes on.

Billy returns to the kitchen. He stares through the doorway at his brother, who stares at Geraldo Rivera. "You can't even ask him how's he feeling," Billy says. "He can't respond."

Yvonne Baker goes over to the kitchen counter and makes fresh coffee. In the living room, Tony Conigliaro's head has dropped to his shoulder in front of the screen. He is asleep.

"It's not Tony," Billy says. "If he could fight, he would fight, because he fought his whole life. Tony could overcome anything, if he just had the chance."

ON JANUARY 9, 1982, BILLY was driving Tony to Logan Airport, only fifteen minutes away from their Nahant home. Tony had been home for the Christmas holidays and stayed to audition for a job as the Red Sox's TV analyst on Boston's Channel 38. According to Billy Conigliaro, Tony had been told the night before that the job was his. "He said, 'I'm finally coming home,'" Billy remembers. It was two days after Tony Conigliaro's thirty-seventh birthday. He still looked like a movie star. He was going to be very big on Channel 38.

In a voice made of stone, Billy Conigliaro says, "We were just talking about the new job and how great it was that he was coming home. We were about two miles from the airport when it happened. A girl had called looking for him a few days before, and I said, 'You ever think of who that girl was that called?' And he didn't answer me right away. So I looked over. And his face was twitching. I thought he was fooling, making fun of the girl or something. He was a great mimic. Now I said, 'Tony, what are you doing?' He didn't answer me. Then his head fell to the side, and tears started coming out of his eyes. I thought to myself, Geez, he's passed out. But he was breathing still, so I didn't think he was having a heart attack. I thought about pulling over to the side and calling for help. But Mass General was close by, so I pushed down on the gas and started goin' about eighty for the emergency entrance. It couldn't have taken me more than five minutes. But it seemed like an hour. By the time we got there, he had no pulse."

Billy Conigliaro stops here, remembering again what he cannot forget. There is just the sound of the television from the other room. Then he tells of the doctors performing the tracheotomy, and getting the heartbeat back, and how he, Billy, had to go fetch his father, Sal, from the Suffolk Downs racetrack nearby. Sal Conigliaro, dead now, had just had a bypass operation himself. Billy Conigliaro got nitroglycerin pills for his father before leaving Mass General and made him take the pills at Suffolk Downs before telling him about Tony.

They drove back to the hospital. Tony Conigliaro was in the coma from which he would not emerge for three weeks. The sudden cardiopulmonary arrest had cut off oxygen to the brain's cells. The brain damage, of course, was irreversible.

"My brother was dead for five minutes," Billy says. "How was he going to be normal after that?"

IN THE ROOM WHERE TONY C. does physical therapy, there is an elevated exercise mat as big as a queen-size bed. There is a table, to which he is attached and turned upside down to help his blood circulate. With the help of a walker, his feet being picked up and laid down by the nurses, Tony C. can be taken outside to walk around the swimming pool that overlooks the Atlantic.

"Sometimes," Billy says, "in the summer, I'll come by and they'll have him lying out by the pool and he'll look, in that split second, like . . . Tony."

A few friends still come by to see him. Tony Athanas, who owns the famous Anthony's Pier 4 restaurant in Boston, comes by, and so does Bill Bates, another friend, and Ben Davidson, the former Oakland Raider whom Tony met in California, will call from a trip to Maine and say he is driving down. Baseball teammates like Rico Petrocelli and Mike Andrews used to come by, but not so much lately, as the years move everybody except his family and closest friends away from the Tony Conigliaro everybody remembers.

"You have to prod him," Billy says. "But sometimes if you give him the first name of a teammate, he'll give you the last. You say 'Rico' and he'll say 'Petrocelli.' If somebody he knows comes over, he'll look up and laugh. Or cry. Really, not many people come by anymore. It's been so long. I think they feel funny."

Billy Conigliaro shrugs.

"Don't you?" he says.

In the living room, Yvonne Baker talks Tony C. awake and tells him they're going to the mall soon. Above him, over the fireplace, is a portrait, a lovely portrait, of Tony C. swinging a bat, done by his cousin.

"I just keep pushing him," Billy says. "But it's not even like teaching someone how to talk, because he can't retain anything." He walks into the living room and kneels in front of his brother. He says, "Where you going with the Big E? C'mon. Talk to me. You're going for a . . ." Tony C. says, "Ride." With love that the house can barely contain, Billy, his brother, touches him on the cheek.

TERESA CONIGLIARO, THE MOTHER, HAS come back from morning errands and immediately offers a plate of cookies. She is sixty-eight years old. She lost her husband to his bad heart in 1987. Half an hour with her tells you she has had a certain marvelous strength her whole life. We have been talking at her kitchen table about this passage in the Bible, from First Corinthians, one promising that God will give no person more burden than he or she can bear.

"I used to believe that," she says. "And the part about seek and you shall find, and ask and you shall receive. I've been asking for five years."

She takes a breath and tries building another smile. "There I go. You can't look back. If I did, I'd cry all the time."

YVONNE BAKER COMES INTO THE kitchen for another cup of coffee. Tony C. has gone back to sleep. At forty-three, going on forty-four, he has gray hair and is quite skinny; you already see what he will look like at sixty-four.

In the kitchen, I tell the Big E she has a lot of energy. "It doesn't help if I come in every day with a sad face," she says. "All I do then is drag him down."

In the living room she shuts off the television and pokes Tony C. on the shoulder.

"C'mon fella," the Big E says, "we've got interesting things to do today."

NICHOLAS A. VIRGILIO

Six Haikus

deep in rank grass,
through a bullet-riddled helmet:
an unknown flower
IN MEMORY OF LAWRENCE J. VIRGILIO

flag-covered coffin:
the shadow of the bugler
slips into the grave

my gold star mother
and father hold each other
and the folded flag

removing the shroud:
mother and father alone
step out of the crowd

beneath the coffin
at the edge of the open grave:
the crushed young grass

lily:
out of the water . . .
out of itself

FELIX STEFANILE

FORT DEVENS, MASSACHUSETTS

Elegy, 1942

Dowd was the old man of the company,
the one we listened to. He taught us tricks,
like sewing, or he showed us how to roll
a cigarette, or how to take stove black
and cover over cracks in a worn locker
and make it shine. Whenever he got drunk
he'd sing, in a low whisper, some old tune,
"An Orphan and in love," and go to sleep.
He cowed those blackjack players in the back
who liked to stay up late, and swear and smoke,
and keep us all awake, night after night.
When Dowd was by, we slept like innocents.

He heard Cerruti swearing once, and ribbed him,
told him that was some prayer the seminary
was teaching all the boys. Cerruti blinked,
and kept on blinking, searching for the words.
"That seminary is none of your business."
We all knew that Cerruti had washed out
of the seminary, and gone home. In shame
he left home then—imagine—for the Army.
Big Dowd leaned over him, grinned, shook his head:
"It's guys like me who swear. We don't know words.
That leaves holes in the head we paper over
with swear-words. You have learning. You should read,
and study things, not try to be like us."
He walked away. Cerruti blinked again,
and lowered his head to buff his combat boots.

Dowd was shipped out. It was for convoy duty,
an anti-aircraft crew. His empty cot
was taken over soon by someone else,
and that was that. We all forgot about him
except Cerruti; they kept in touch with cards,
and then the cards stopped coming. Came a day,
months later, Nally told us Dowd got his
in the North Sea. The whole convoy went down.

Cerruti dropped his boots, and walked outside;
I watched him through the window, pacing, blinking,
kicking at gravel, searching for the words,
until like death-besotted Lear he shouted
fuck it fuck it fuck it fuck it fuck it.

"Blessings to Thee, O Jesus. I have fought winds and cold. Hand to hand I have locked dumb stones in place and the great building rises. I have earned a bit of bread for me and mine."

WORK

JOHN FANTE

Ask the Dust

ᔟᔟ

ONE NIGHT I WAS SITTING ON the bed in my hotel room on Bunker Hill, down in the very middle of Los Angeles. It was an important night in my life, because I had to make a decision about the hotel. Either I paid up or I got out: that was what the note said, the note the landlady had put under my door. A great problem, deserving acute attention. I solved it by turning out the lights and going to bed.

In the morning I awoke, decided that I should do more physical exercise, and began at once. I did several bending exercises. Then I washed my teeth, tasted blood, saw pink on the toothbrush, remembered the advertisements, and decided to go out and get some coffee.

I went to the restaurant where I always went to the restaurant and I sat down on the stool before the long counter and ordered coffee. It tasted pretty much like coffee, but it wasn't worth the nickel. Sitting there I smoked a couple of cigarettes, read the box scores of the American League games, scrupulously avoided the box scores of National League games, and noted with satisfaction that Joe DiMaggio was still a credit to the Italian people, because he was leading the league in batting.

A great hitter, that DiMaggio. I walked out of the restaurant, stood before an imaginary pitcher, and swatted a home run over the fence. Then I walked down the street toward Angel's Flight, wondering what I would do that day. But there was nothing to do, and so I decided to walk around the town.

I walked down Olive Street past a dirty yellow apartment house that was still wet like a blotter from last night's fog, and I thought of my friends Ethie and Carl, who were from Detroit and had lived there, and I remembered the night Carl hit Ethie because she was going to have a baby, and he didn't want a baby. But they had the baby and that's all there was to that. And I remembered the inside of that apartment, how it smelled of mice and dust, and the old women who sat in the lobby on hot afternoons, and the old woman with the pretty legs. Then there was the elevator man, a broken man from Milwaukee, who seemed to sneer every time you called your floor, as though you were such a fool for choosing that particular floor, the elevator man who always had a tray of sandwiches in the elevator, and a pulp magazine.

Then I went down the hill on Olive Street, past the horrible frame houses reeking with murder stories, and on down Olive to the Philharmonic Auditorium, and I remembered how I'd gone there with Helen to listen to the Don Cossack Choral Group, and how I got bored and we had a fight because of it, and I remembered what Helen wore that day—a white dress, and how it made me sing at the loins when I touched it. Oh that Helen—but not here.

And so I was down on Fifth and Olive, where the big streetcars chewed your ears with their noise, and the smell of gasoline made the sight of the palm trees seem sad, and the black pavement still wet from the fog of the night before.

So now I was in front of the Biltmore Hotel, walking along the line of yellow cabs, with all the cabdrivers asleep except the driver near the main door, and I wondered about these fellows and their fund of information, and I remembered the time Ross and I got an address from one of them, how he leered salaciously and then took us to Temple Street, of all places, and whom did we see but two very unattractive ones, and Ross went all the way, but I sat in the parlor and played the phonograph and was scared and lonely.

I was passing the doorman of the Biltmore, and I hated him at once, with his yellow braids and six feet of height and all that dignity, and now a black automobile drove to the curb, and a man got out. He looked rich; and then a woman got out, and she was beautiful, her fur was silver fox, and she was a song across the sidewalk and inside the swinging doors, and I thought oh boy for a little of that, just a day and a night of that, and she was a dream as I walked along, her perfume still in the wet morning air.

Then a great deal of time passed as I stood in front of a pipe shop and looked, and the whole world faded except that window and I stood and smoked them all, and saw myself a great author with that natty Italian briar, and a cane, stepping out of a big black car, and she was there too, proud as hell of me, the lady in the silver fox fur. We registered and then we had cocktails and then we danced awhile, and then we had another cocktail and I recited some lines from Sanskrit, and the world was so wonderful, because every two minutes some gorgeous one gazed at me, the great author, and nothing would do but I had to autograph her menu, and the silver fox girl was very jealous.

Los Angeles, give me some of you! Los Angeles come to me the way I came to you, my feet over your streets, you pretty town I loved you so much, you sad flower in the sand, you pretty town.

A day and another day and the day before, and the library with the big boys in the shelves, old Dreiser, old Mencken, all the boys down there, and I went to see them. Hya Dreiser, Hya Mencken, Hya, hya: there's a place for me, too, and it begins with B, in the B shelf, Arturo Bandini, make way for Arturo Bandini, his slot for his book, and I sat at the table and just looked at the place where my book would be, right there close to Arnold Bennett; not much that Arnold Bennett, but I'd be there to sort of bolster up the B's, old Arturo Bandini, one of the boys, until some girl came along, some scent of perfume through the fiction room, some click of high heels to break up the monotony of my fame. Gala day, gala dream!

But the landlady, the white-haired landlady kept writing those notes: she was from Bridgeport, Connecticut, her husband had died and she was all alone in the world and she didn't trust anybody, she couldn't afford to, she told me so, and she told me I'd have to pay. It was mounting like the national debt, I'd have to pay or leave, every cent of it—five weeks overdue, twenty dollars, and if I didn't she'd hold my trunks; only I didn't have any trunks, I only had a suitcase and it was cardboard without even a strap, because the strap was around my belly holding up my pants, and that wasn't much of a job, because there wasn't much left of my pants.

"I just got a letter from my agent," I told her. "My agent in New York. He says I sold another one; he doesn't say where, but he says he's got one sold. So don't worry Mrs. Hargraves, don't you fret, I'll have it in a day or so."

But she couldn't believe a liar like me. It wasn't really a lie; it was a wish, not a lie, and maybe it wasn't even a wish, maybe it was a fact, and the only way to find out was watch the mailman, watch him closely, check his mail as he laid it on the desk in the lobby, ask him point-blank if he had anything for Bandini. But I didn't have to ask after six months at that hotel. He saw me coming and he always nodded yes or no before I asked: no, three million times; yes, once.

One day a beautiful letter came. Oh, I got a lot of letters, but this was the only beautiful letter, and it came in the morning, and it said (he was talking about *The Little Dog Laughed*) he had read *The Little Dog Laughed* and liked it; he said, Mr. Bandini, if ever I saw a genius, you are it. His name was Leonardo, a great Italian critic, only he was not known as a critic, he was just a man in West Virginia, but he was great and he was a critic, and he died. He was dead when my airmail letter got to West Virginia, and his sister sent my letter back. She wrote a beautiful letter too, she was a pretty good critic too, telling me Leonardo had died of consumption but he was happy to the end, and one of the last things he did was sit up in bed and write me about *The Little Dog Laughed*: a dream out of life, but very important; Leonardo, dead now, a saint in heaven, equal to any apostle of the twelve.

Everybody in the hotel read *The Little Dog Laughed*, everybody: a story to make you die holding the page, and it wasn't about a dog, either: a clever story, screaming poetry. And the great editor, none but J. C. Hackmuth with his name signed like Chinese said in a letter: a great story and I'm proud to print it. Mrs. Hargraves read it and I was a different man in her eyes thereafter. I got to stay on in that hotel, not shoved out in the cold, only often it was in the heat, on account of *The Little Dog Laughed*. Mrs. Grainger in 345, a Christian Scientist (wonderful hips, but kinda old) from Battle Creek, Michigan, sitting in the lobby waiting to die, and *The Little Dog Laughed* brought her back to the earth, and that look in her eyes made me know it was right and I was right, but I was hoping she would ask about my finances, how I was getting along, and then I thought why not ask her to lend you a five spot, but I didn't and I walked away snapping my fingers in disgust.

The hotel was called the Alta Loma. It was built on a hillside in reverse, there on the crest of Bunker Hill, built against the decline of the hill, so that the main floor was on the level with the street but the tenth floor was downstairs ten levels. If you had room 862, you got in the elevator and went down eight floors, and if you wanted to go down in the truck room, you didn't go down but up to the attic, one floor above the main floor.

OH, FOR A MEXICAN GIRL! I used to think of her all the time, my Mexican girl. I didn't have one, but the streets were full of them, the Plaza and Chinatown were afire with them, and in my fashion they were mine, this one and that one, and someday when another check came it would be a fact. Meanwhile it was free and they were Aztec princesses and Mayan princesses, the peon girls in the Grand Central Market, in the Church of Our Lady, and I even went to mass to look at them. That was sacrilegious conduct but it was better than not going to mass at all, so that when I wrote home to Colorado to my mother I could write with truth. Dear Mother: I went to mass last Sunday. Down in the Grand Central Market I bumped into the princesses accidentally on purpose. It gave me a chance to speak to them, and I smiled and said excuse me. Those beautiful girls, so happy when you acted like a gentleman and all of that, just to touch them and carry the memory of it back to my room, where dust gathered upon my typewriter and Pedro the mouse sat in his hole, his black eyes watching me through that time of dream and reverie.

Pedro the mouse, a good mouse but never domesticated, refusing to be petted or housebroken. I saw him the first time I walked into my room, and that was during my heyday, when *The Little Dog Laughed* was in the current August issue. It was five months ago, the day I got to town by bus from Colorado with a hundred and fifty dollars in my pocket and big plans in my head. I had a philosophy in those days. I was a lover of man and beast alike, and Pedro was no exception; but cheese got expensive, Pedro called all his friends, the room swarmed with them, and I had to quit it and feed them bread. They didn't like bread. I had spoiled them and they went elsewhere, all but Pedro the ascetic who was content to eat the pages of an old Gideon Bible.

Ah, that first day! Mrs. Hargraves opened the door to my room, and there it was, with a red carpet on the floor, pictures of the English countryside on the walls, and a shower adjoining. The room was down on the sixth floor, room 678, up near the front of the hill, so that my window was on a level with the green hillside and there was no need for a key, for the window was always open. Through that window I saw my first palm tree, not six feet away, and sure enough I thought of Palm Sunday and Egypt and Cleopatra, but the palm was blackish at its branches, stained by carbon monoxide coming out of the Third Street Tunnel, its crusted trunk choked with dust and sand that blew in from the Mojave and Santa Ana deserts.

Dear Mother, I used to write home to Colorado, Dear Mother, things are definitely looking up. A big editor was in town and I had lunch with him and we have signed a contract for a number of short stories, but I won't try to bore you with all the details, dear Mother, because I know you're not interested in writing, and I know Papa isn't, but it levels down to a swell contract, only it doesn't begin for a couple of months. So send me ten dollars, Mother, send me five, mother dear, because the editor (I'd tell you his name only I know you're not interested in such things) is all set to start me out on the biggest project he's got.

Dear Mother, and Dear Hackmuth, the great editor—they got most of my mail, practically all of my mail. Old Hackmuth with his scowl and his hair parted in the middle, great Hackmuth with a pen like a sword, his picture was on my wall autographed with his signature that looked Chinese. Hya Hackmuth, I used to say, Jesus how you can write! Then the lean days came, and Hackmuth got big letters from me. My God, Mr. Hackmuth, something's wrong with me: the old zip is gone and I can't write anymore. Do you think, Mr. Hackmuth, that the climate here has anything to do with it?

Please advise. Do you think, Mr. Hackmuth, that I write as well as William Faulkner? Please advise. Do you think, Mr. Hackmuth, that sex has anything to do with it, because, Mr. Hackmuth, because, because, and I told Hackmuth everything. I told him about the blonde girl I met in the park. I told him how I worked it, how the blonde girl tumbled. I told him the whole story, only it wasn't true, it was a crazy lie—but it was something. It was writing, keeping in touch with the great, and he always answered. Oh boy, he was swell! He answered right off, a great man responding to the problems of a man of talent. Nobody got that many letters from Hackmuth, nobody but me, and I used to take them out and read them over, and kiss them. I'd stand before Hackmuth's picture crying out of both eyes, telling him he picked a good one this time, a great one, a Bandini, Arturo Bandini, me.

The lean days of determination. That was the word for it, determination: Arturo Bandini in front of his typewriter two full days in succession, determined to succeed; but it didn't work, the longest siege of hard and fast determination in his life, and not one line done, only two words written over and over across the page, up and down, the same words: palm tree, palm tree, palm tree, a battle to the death between the palm tree and me, and the palm tree won: see it out there swaying in the blue air, creaking sweetly in the blue air. The palm tree won after two fighting days, and I crawled out of the window and sat at the foot of the tree. Time passed, a moment or two, and I slept, little brown ants carousing in the hair on my legs.

I WAS TWENTY THEN. What the hell, I used to say, take your time, Bandini. You got ten years to write a book, so take it easy, get out and learn about life, walk the streets. That's your trouble: your ignorance of life. Why, my God, man, do you realize you've never had any experience with a woman? Oh yes I have, oh I've had plenty. Oh no you haven't. You need a woman, you need a bath, you need a good swift kick, you need money. They say it's a dollar, they say it's two dollars in the swell places, but down on the Plaza it's a dollar; swell, only you haven't got a dollar, and another thing, you coward, even if you had a dollar you wouldn't go, because you had a chance to go once in Denver and you didn't. No, you coward, you were afraid, and you're still afraid, and you're glad you haven't got a dollar.

Afraid of a woman! Ha, great writer this! How can he write about women, when he's never had a woman? Oh, you lousy fake, you phony, no wonder you can't write! No wonder there wasn't a woman in *The Little Dog Laughed*. No wonder it wasn't a love story, you fool, you dirty little schoolboy.

To write a love story, to learn about life.

Money arrived in the mail. Not a check from the mighty Hackmuth, not an acceptance from *The Atlantic Monthly* or *The Saturday Evening Post*. Only ten dollars, only a fortune. My mother sent it: some dime insurance policies, Arturo, I had them taken up for their cash value, and this is your share. But it was ten dollars; one manuscript or another, at least something had been sold.

Put it in your pocket, Arturo. Wash your face, comb your hair, put some stuff on to make you smell good while you stare into the mirror looking for gray hairs; because you're worried Arturo, you're worried, and that brings gray hair. But there was none, not a strand. Yeah, but what of that left eye? It looked discolored. Careful, Arturo Bandini: don't strain your eyesight, remember what happened to Tarkington, remember what happened to James Joyce.

Not bad, standing in the middle of the room, talking to Hackmuth's picture, not bad, Hackmuth, you'll get a story out of this. How do I look, Hackmuth? Do you sometimes wonder, Herr Hackmuth, what I look like? Do you sometimes say to yourself, I wonder if he's handsome, that Bandini fellow, author of that brilliant *Little Dog Laughed?*

Once in Denver there was another night like this, only I was not an author in Denver, but I stood in a room like this and made these plans, and it was disastrous because all the time in that place I thought about the Blessed Virgin and *thou shalt not commit adultery* and the hardworking girl shook her head sadly and had to give it up, but that was a long time ago and tonight it will be changed.

I climbed out the window and scaled the incline to the top of Bunker Hill. A night for my nose, a feast for my nose, smelling the stars, smelling the flowers, smelling the desert, and the dust asleep, across the top of Bunker Hill. The city spread out like a Christmas tree, red and green and blue. Hello, old houses, beautiful hamburgers singing in cheap cafés. Bing Crosby singing too. She'll treat me gently. Not those girls of my childhood, those girls of my boyhood, those girls of my university days. They frightened me, they were diffident, they refused me; but not my princess, because she will understand. She, too, has been scorned.

Bandini, walking along, not tall but solid, proud of his muscles, squeezing his fist to revel in the hard delight of his biceps, absurdly fearless Bandini, fearing nothing but the unknown in a world of mysterious wonder. Are the dead restored? The books say no, the night shouts yes. I am twenty, I have reached the age of reason, I am about to wander the streets below, seeking a woman. Is my soul already smirched, should I turn back, does an angel watch over me, do the prayers of my mother allay my fears, do the prayers of my mother annoy me?

Ten dollars: it will pay the rent for two and a half weeks, it will buy me three pairs of shoes, two pair of pants, or one thousand postage stamps to send material to the editors; indeed! But you haven't any material, your talent is dubious, your talent is pitiful, you haven't any talent, and stop lying to yourself day after day because you know *The Little Dog Laughed* is no good, and it will always be no good.

So you walk along Bunker Hill, and you shake your fist at the sky, and I know what you're thinking, Bandini. The thoughts of your father before you, lash across your back, hot fire in your skull, that you are not to blame: this is your thought, that you were born poor, son of miseried peasants, driven because you were poor, fled from your Colorado town because you were poor, rambling the gutters of Los Angeles because you are poor, hoping to write a book to get rich, because those who hated you back there in Colorado will not hate you if you write a book. You are a coward, Bandini, a traitor to your soul, a feeble liar before your weeping Christ. This is why you write, this is why it would be better if you died.

Yes, it's true: but I have seen houses in Bel-Air with cool lawns and green swimming pools. I have wanted women whose very shoes are worth all I have ever possessed. I have seen golf clubs on Sixth Street in the Spalding window that make me hungry just to grip them. I have grieved for a necktie like a holy man for indulgences. I have admired hats in Robinson's the way critics gasp at Michelangelo.

I took the steps down Angel's Flight to Hill Street: 140 steps, with tight fists, frightened of no man, but scared of the Third Street Tunnel, scared to walk through it—claustrophobia. Scared of high places, too, and of blood, and of earthquakes; otherwise, quite fearless, excepting death, except the fear I'll scream in a crowd, except the fear of appendicitis, except the fear of heart trouble, even that, sitting in his room holding the clock and pressing his jugular vein, counting out his heartbeats, listening to the weird purr and whirr of his stomach. Otherwise, quite fearless.

Here is an idea with money: these steps, the city below, the stars within throwing distance: boy meets girl idea, good setup, big money idea. Girl lives in that gray apartment house, boy is a wanderer. Boy—he's me. Girl's hungry. Rich Pasadena girl hates money. Deliberately left Pasadena millions 'cause of ennui, weariness with money. Beautiful girl, gorgeous. Great story, pathological conflict. Girl with money phobia: Freudian setup. Another guy loves her, rich guy. I'm poor. I meet rival. Beat him to death with caustic wit and also lick him with fists. Girl impressed, falls for me. Offers me millions. I marry her on condition she'll stay poor. Agrees. But ending happy: girl tricks me with huge trust fund day we get married. I'm indignant but I forgive her 'cause I love her. Good idea, but something missing: *Collier's* story.

Dearest Mother, thanks for the ten-dollar bill. My agent announces the sale of another story, this time to a great magazine in London, but it seems they do not pay until publication, and so your little sum will come in handy for various odds and ends.

I went to the burlesque show. I had the best seat possible, a dollar and ten cents, right under a chorus of forty frayed bottoms: someday all of these will be mine: I will own a yacht and we will go on South Sea cruises. On warm afternoons they will dance for me on the sundeck. But mine will be beautiful women, selections from the cream of society, rivals for the joys of my stateroom. Well, this is good for me, this is experience, I am here for a reason, these moments run into pages, the seamy side of life.

Then Lola Linton came on, slithering like a satin snake amid the tumult of whistling and pounding feet, Lola Linton lascivious, slithering and looting my body, and when she was through, my teeth ached from my clamped jaws and I hated the dirty lowbrow swine around me, shouting their share of a sick joy that belonged to me.

If Mamma sold the policies things must be tough for the Old Man and I shouldn't be here. When I was a kid pictures of Lola Lintons used to come my way, and I used to get so impatient with the slow crawl of time and boyhood, longing for this very moment, and here I am, and I have not changed nor have the Lola Lintons, but I fashioned myself rich and I am poor.

Main Street after the show, midnight: neon tubes and a light fog, honky tonks and all-night picture houses. Secondhand stores and Filipino dance halls, cocktails 15¢, continuous entertainment, but I had seen them all, so many times, spent so much Colorado money in them. It left me lonely like a thirsty man holding a cup, and I walked toward the Mexican Quarter with a feeling of sickness without pain. Here was the Church of Our Lady, very old, the adobe blackened with age. For sentimental reasons I will go inside. For sentimental reasons only. I have not read Lenin, but I have heard him quoted, religion is the opium of the people. Talking to myself on the church steps: yeah, the opium of the people. Myself, I am an atheist: I have read *The Anti-Christ* and I regard it as a capital piece of work. I believe in the transvaluation of values, Sir. The Church must go, it is the haven of the booboisie, of boobs and bounders and all brummagem mountebanks.

I pulled the huge door open and it gave a little cry like weeping. Above the altar sputtered the blood-red eternal light, illuminating in crimson shadow the quiet of almost two thousand years. It was like death, but I could remember screaming infants at baptism too. I knelt. This was habit, this kneeling. I sat down. Better to kneel, for the sharp bite at the knees was a distraction from the awful quiet. A prayer. Sure, one prayer: for sentimental reasons. Almighty God, I am sorry I am now an atheist, but have You read Nietzsche? Ah, such a book! Almighty God, I will play fair in this. I will make You a proposition. You make a great writer out of me, and I will return to the Church. And please, dear God, one more favor: make my mother happy. I don't care about the Old Man; he's got his wine and his health, but my mother worries so. Amen.

I closed the weeping door and stood on the steps, the fog like a huge white animal everywhere, the Plaza like our courthouse back home, snow-bound in white silence. But all sounds traveled swift and sure through the heaviness, and the sound I heard was the click of high heels. A girl appeared. She wore an old green coat, her face molded in a green scarf tied under the chin. On the stairs stood Bandini.

"Hello, honey," she said, smiling, as though Bandini were her husband, or her lover. Then she came to the first step and looked up at him. "How about it, honey? Want me to show you a good time?"

Bold lover, bold and brazen Bandini.

"Nah," he said. "No thanks. Not tonight."

He hurried away, leaving her looking after him, speaking words he lost in flight. He walked half a block. He was pleased. At least she had asked him. At least she had identified him as a man. He whistled a tune from sheer pleasure. Man about town has universal experience. Noted writer tells of night with woman of the streets. Arturo Bandini, famous writer, reveals experience with Los Angeles prostitute. Critics acclaim book finest written.

Bandini (being interviewed prior to departure for Sweden): "My advice to all young writers is quite simple. I would caution them never to evade a new experience. I would urge them to live life in the raw, to grapple with it bravely, to attack it with naked fists."

Reporter: "Mr. Bandini, how did you come to write this book which won you the Nobel Award?"

Bandini: "The book is based on a true experience which happened to me one night in Los Angeles. Every word of that book is true. I lived that book, I experienced it."

Enough. I saw it all. I turned and walked back toward the church. The fog was impenetrable. The girl was gone. I walked on: perhaps I could catch up with her. At the corner I saw her again. She stood talking to a tall Mexican. They walked, crossed the street and entered the Plaza. I followed. My God, a Mexican! Women like that should draw the color line. I hated him, the

Spick, the Greaser. They walked under the banana tree in the Plaza, their feet echoing in the fog. I heard the Mexican laugh. Then the girl laughed. They crossed the street and walked down an alley that was the entrance to Chinatown. The oriental neon signs made the fog pinkish. At a rooming house next door to a chop suey restaurant they turned and climbed the stairs. Across the street upstairs a dance was in progress. Along the little street on both sides yellow cabs were parked. I leaned against the front fender of the cab in front of the rooming house and waited. I lit a cigarette and waited. Until hell freezes over, I will wait. Until God strikes me dead, I will wait.

A half hour passed. There were sounds on the steps. The door opened. The Mexican appeared. He stood in the fog, lit a cigarette, and yawned. Then he smiled absently, shrugged, and walked away, the fog swooping upon him. Go ahead and smile. You stinking Greaser—what have you got to smile about? You come from a bashed and a busted race, and just because you went to the room with one of our white girls, you smile. Do you think you would have had a chance, had I accepted on the church steps?

A moment later the steps sounded to the slick of her heels, and the girl stepped into the fog. The same girl, the same green coat, the same scarf. She saw me and smiled. "Hello, honey. Wanna have a good time?"

Easy now, Bandini.

"Oh," I said. "Maybe. And maybe not. Whatcha got?"

"Come up and see, honey."

Stop sniggering, Arturo. Be suave.

"I might come up," I said. "And then, I might not."

"Aw honey, come on." The thin bones of her face, the odor of sour wine from her mouth, the awful hypocrisy of her sweetness, the hunger for money in her eyes.

Bandini speaking: "What's the price these days?"

She took my arm, pulled me toward the door, but gently.

"You come on up, honey. We'll talk about it up there."

"I'm really not hot," said Bandini. "I—I just came from a wild party."

Hail Mary full of grace, walking up the stairs, I can't go through with it. I've got to get out of it. The halls smelling of cockroaches, a yellow light at the ceiling, you're too aesthetic for all this, the girl holding my arm, there's something wrong with you, Arturo Bandini, you're a misanthrope, your whole life is doomed to celibacy, you should have been a priest, Father O'Leary talking that afternoon, telling us the joys of denial, and my own mother's money too, Oh Mary conceived without sin, pray for us who have recourse to thee—until we got to the top of the stairs and walked down a dusty dark hall to a room at the end, where she turned out the light and we were inside.

A room smaller than mine, carpetless, without pictures, a bed, a table, a washstand. She took off her coat. There was a blue print dress underneath. She was bare-legged. She took off the scarf. She was not a real blonde. Black hair grew at the roots. Her nose was crooked slightly. Bandini on the bed, put himself there with an air of casualness, like a man who knew how to sit on a bed.

Bandini: "Nice place you got here."

My God I got to get out of here, this is terrible.

The girl sat beside me, put her arms around me, pushed her breasts against me, kissed me, flecked my teeth with a cold tongue. I jumped to my feet. Oh think fast, my mind, dear mind of mine please get me out of this and it will never happen again. From now on I will return to my Church. Beginning this day my life shall run like sweet water.

The girl lay back, her hands behind her neck, her legs over the bed. I shall smell lilacs in Connecticut, no doubt, before I die, and see the clean white small reticent churches of my youth, the pasture bars I broke to run away.

"Look," I said. "I want to talk to you."

She crossed her legs.

"I'm a writer," I said. "I'm gathering material for a book."

"I knew you were a writer," she said. "Or a businessman, or something. You look spiritual, honey."

"I'm a writer, see. I like you and all that. You're okay, I like you. But I want to talk to you first."

She sat up.

"Haven't you any money, honey?"

Money—ho. And I pulled it out, a small thick roll of dollar bills. Sure I got money, plenty of money, this is a drop in the bucket, money is no object, money means nothing to me.

"What do you charge?"

"It's two dollars, honey."

Then give her three, peel it off easily, like it was nothing at all, smile and hand it to her because money is no object, there's more where this came from, at this moment Mamma sits by the window holding her rosary, waiting for the Old Man to come home, but there's money, there's always money.

She took the money and slipped it under the pillow. She was grateful and her smile was different now. The writer wanted to talk. How were conditions these days? How did she like this kind of life? Oh, come on honey, let's not talk, let's get down to business. No, I want to talk to you, this is important, new book, material. I do this often. How did you ever get into this racket. Oh honey, Chrissakes, you going to ask me that too? But money is no object, I tell you. But my time is valuable, honey. Then here's a couple more bucks. That makes five, my God, five bucks and I'm not out of here yet, how I hate you, you filthy. But you're cleaner than me because you've got no mind to sell, just that poor flesh.

She was overwhelmed, she would do anything. I could have it any way I wanted it, and she tried to pull me to her, but no, let's wait awhile. I tell you I want to talk to you, I tell you money is no object, here's three more, that makes eight dollars, but it doesn't matter. You just keep that eight bucks and buy yourself something nice. And then I snapped my fingers like a man remembering something, something important, an engagement.

"Say!" I said. "That reminds me. What time is it?"

Her chin was at my neck, stroking it. "Don't you worry about the time, honey. You can stay all night."

A man of importance, ah yes, now I remembered, my publisher, he was getting in tonight by plane. Out at Burbank, away out in Burbank. Have to grab a cab and taxi out there, have to hurry. Goodbye, goodbye, you keep that eight bucks, you buy yourself something nice, goodbye, goodbye, running down the stairs, running away, the welcome fog in the doorway below, you keep that eight bucks, oh sweet fog I see you and I'm coming, you clean air, you wonderful world, I'm coming to you, goodbye, yelling up the stairs, I'll see you again, you keep that eight dollars and buy yourself something nice. Eight dollars pouring out of my eyes, Oh Jesus kill me dead and ship my body home, kill me dead and make me die like a pagan fool with no priest to absolve me, no Extreme Unction, eight dollars, eight dollars. . . .

PHILIP CAPUTO

A Rumor of War

᠃᠊᠌᠊᠃

AT THE AGE OF TWENTY-FOUR, I was more prepared for death than I was for life. My first experience of the world outside the classroom had been war. I went straight from school into the Marine Corps, from Shakespeare to the *Manual of Small-Unit Tactics,* from the campus to the drill field and finally Vietnam. I learned the murderous trade at Quantico, Virginia, practiced it in the rice paddies and jungles around Danang, and then taught it to others at Camp Geiger, a training base in North Carolina.

When my three-year enlistment expired in 1967, I was almost completely ignorant about the stuff of ordinary life, about marriage, mortgages, and building a career. I had a degree, but no skills. I had never run an office, taught a class, built a bridge, welded, laid bricks, sold anything, or operated a lathe.

But I had acquired some expertise in the art of killing. I knew how to face death and how to cause it, with everything on the evolutionary scale of weapons from the knife to the 3.5-inch rocket launcher. The simplest repairs on an automobile engine were beyond me, but I was able to field-strip and assemble an M-14 rifle blindfolded. I could call in artillery, set up an ambush, rig a booby trap, lead a night raid.

Simply by speaking a few words into a two-way radio, I had performed magical feats of destruction. Summoned by my voice, jet fighters appeared in the sky to loose their lethal droppings on villages and men. High-explosive bombs blasted houses to fragments, napalm sucked air from lungs and turned human flesh to ashes. All this just by saying a few words into a radio transmitter. Like magic.

I came home from the war with the curious feeling that I had grown older than my father, who was then fifty-one. It was as if a lifetime of experience had been compressed into a year and a half. A man saw the heights and depths of human behavior in Vietnam, all manner of violence and horrors so grotesque that they evoked more fascination than disgust. Once I had seen pigs eating napalm-charred corpses—a memorable sight, pigs eating roast people.

I was left with none of the optimism and ambition a young American is supposed to have, only a desire to catch up on sixteen months of missed sleep and an old man's conviction that the future would hold no further surprises, good or bad.

I *hoped* there would be no more surprises. I had survived enough ambushes and doubted my capacity to endure many more physical or emotional shocks. I had all the symptoms of *combat veteranitis:* an inability to concentrate, a childlike fear of darkness, a tendency to tire easily, chronic nightmares, an intolerance of loud noises—especially doors slamming and cars backfiring—and alternating moods of depression and rage that came over me for no apparent reason. Recovery has been less than total.

I JOINED THE MARINES IN 1960, partly because I got swept up in the patriotic tide of the Kennedy era but mostly because I was sick of the safe, suburban existence I had known most of my life.

I was raised in Westchester, Illinois, one of the towns that rose from the prairies around Chicago as a result of postwar affluence, VA mortgage loans, and the migratory urge and housing shortage that sent millions of people out of the cities in the years following World War II. It had everything a suburb is supposed to have: sleek, new schools smelling of fresh plaster and floor wax; supermarkets full of Wonder Bread and Bird's Eye frozen peas; rows of centrally heated split-levels that lined dirtless streets on which nothing ever happened.

It was pleasant enough at first, but by the time I entered my late teens I could not stand the place, the dullness of it, the summer barbecues eaten to the lulling drone of power mowers. During the years I grew up there, Westchester stood on or near the edge of the built-up area. Beyond stretched the Illinois farm and pasturelands, where I used to hunt on weekends. I remember the fields as they were in the late fall: the corn stubble brown against the snow, dead husks rasping dryly in the wind; abandoned farmhouses waiting for the bulldozers that would tear them down to clear space for a new subdivision; and off on the horizon, a few stripped sycamores silhouetted against a bleak November sky. I can still see myself roaming around out there, scaring rabbits from the brambles, the tract houses a few miles behind me, the vast, vacant prairies in front, a restless boy caught between suburban boredom and rural desolation.

The only thing I really liked about my boyhood surroundings were the Cook and DuPage County forest preserves, a belt of virgin woodland through which flowed a muddy stream called Salt Creek. It was not too polluted then, and its sluggish waters yielded bullhead, catfish, carp, and a rare bass. There was small game in the woods, sometimes a deer or two, but most of all a hint of the wild past, when moccasined feet trod the forest paths and fur trappers cruised the rivers in bark canoes. Once in a while I found flint arrowheads in the muddy creek bank. Looking at them, I would dream of that savage, heroic time and wish I had lived then, before America became a land of salesmen and shopping centers.

That is what I wanted, to find in a commonplace world a chance to live heroically. Having known nothing but security, comfort, and peace, I hungered for danger, challenges, and violence.

I had no clear idea of how to fulfill this peculiar ambition until the day a Marine recruiting team set up a stand in the student union at Loyola University. They were on a talent hunt for officer material and displayed a poster of a trim lieutenant who had one of those athletic, slightly cruel-looking faces considered handsome in the military. He looked like a cross between an all-American halfback and a Nazi tank commander. Clear and resolute, his blue eyes seemed to stare at me in challenge. JOIN THE MARINES, read the slogan above his white cap. BE A LEADER OF MEN.

I rummaged through the propaganda material, picking out one pamphlet whose cover listed every battle the Marines had fought, from Trenton to Inchon. Reading down that list, I had one of those rare flashes of insight: the heroic experience I sought was war; war, the ultimate adventure; war, the ordinary man's most convenient means of escaping from the ordinary. The country was at peace then, but the early 1960s were years of almost constant tension and crisis; if a conflict did break out, the Marines would be certain to fight in it and I could be there with them. Actually *there*. Not watching it on a movie or TV screen, not reading about it in a book, but *there,* living out a fantasy. Already I saw myself charging up some distant beachhead, like John Wayne in *Sands of Iwo Jima,* and then coming home a suntanned warrior with medals on my chest. The recruiters started giving me the usual sales pitch, but I hardly needed to be persuaded. I decided to enlist.

I had another motive for volunteering, one that has pushed young men into armies ever since armies were invented: I needed to prove something—my courage, my toughness, my manhood, call it whatever you like. I had spent my freshman year at Purdue, freed from the confinements of suburban home and family. But a slump in the economy prevented me from finding a job that summer. Unable to afford the expense of living on campus (and almost flunking out anyway, having spent half my first year drinking and the other half in fraternity antics), I had to transfer to Loyola, a commuter college in Chicago. As a result, at the age of nineteen, I found myself again living with my parents.

It was a depressing situation. In my adolescent mind, I felt that my parents regarded me as an irresponsible boy who still needed their guidance. I wanted to prove them wrong. I had to get away. It was not just a question of physical separation, although that was important; it was more a matter of doing something that would demonstrate to them, and to myself as well, that I was a man after all, like the steely-eyed figure in the recruiting poster. THE MARINE CORPS BUILDS MEN was another slogan current at the time, and on November 28 I became one of its construction projects.

I joined the Platoon Leaders' Class, the Marines' version of ROTC. I was to attend six weeks of basic training the following summer and then an advanced course during the summer before I graduated from college. Completion of Officer Candidate School and a bachelor's degree would entitle me to a commission, after which I would be required to serve three years on active duty.

I was not really ambitious to become an officer. I would have dropped out of school and gone in immediately as an enlisted man had it not been for my parents' unflinching determination to have a college graduate for a son. As it was, they were unhappy. Their vision of my future did not include uniforms and drums, but consisted of my finding a respectable job after school, marrying a respectable girl, and then settling down in a respectable suburb.

For my part, I was elated the moment I signed up and swore to defend the United States "against all enemies foreign and domestic." I had done something important on my own; that it was something which opposed my parents' wishes made it all the more savory. And I was excited by the idea that I would be sailing off to dangerous and exotic places after college instead of riding the 7:45 to some office. It is odd when I look back on it. Most of my friends at school thought of joining the army as the most conformist thing anyone could do, and of the service itself as a form of slavery. But for me, enlisting was an act of rebellion, and the Marine Corps symbolized an opportunity for personal freedom and independence.

Officer Candidate School was at Quantico, a vast reservation in the piny Virginia woods near Fredericksburg, where the Army of the Potomac had been futilely slaughtered a century before. There, in the summer of 1961, along with several hundred other aspiring lieutenants, I was introduced to military life and began training for war. We ranged in age from nineteen to twenty-one, and those of us who survived OCS would lead the first American troops sent to Vietnam four years later. Of course, we did not know that at the time: we hardly knew where Vietnam was.

The first six weeks, roughly the equivalent of enlisted boot camp, were spent at Camp Upshur, a cluster of Quonset huts and tin-walled buildings set deep in the woods. The monastic isolation was appropriate because the Marine Corps, as we quickly learned, was more than a branch of the armed services. It was a society unto itself, demanding total commitment to its doctrines and values, rather like one of those quasi-religious military orders of ancient times, the Teutonic Knights or the Theban Band. We were novitiates, and the rigorous training, administered by high priests called drill instructors, was to be our ordeal of initiation.

And ordeal it was, physically and psychologically. From four in the morning until nine at night we were marched and drilled, sent sprawling over obstacle courses and put through punishing conditioning hikes in ninety-degree heat. We were shouted at, kicked, humiliated and harassed constantly. We were no longer known by our names, but called "shitbird," "scumbag," or "numbnuts" by the DIs. In my platoon, they were a corporal, a small man who was cruel in the way only small men can be, and a sergeant, a nervously energetic black named McClellan, whose muscles looked as hard and wiry as underground telephone cables.

What I recall most vividly is close-order drill: the hours we spent marching in a sun so hot it turned the asphalt field into a viscous mass that stuck to our boots; the endless hours of being driven and scourged by McClellan's voice—relentless, compelling obedience, a voice that embedded itself in our minds until we could not walk anywhere without hearing it, counting a rhythmic cadence.

Wan-tup-threep-fo, threep-fo-your-lef, lef-rye-lef, hada-lef-rye-lef, your-lef . . . your-lef . . . your-lef.
Dress it up dress it up keep your interval.
Thirty-inches-back-to-breast-forty-inches-shoulder-to-shoulder.
Lef-rye-lef.
TothereAH HARCH . . . reAH HARCH . . . bydalef-flank HARCH!
Dress it up keep your dress DRESS IT UP SCUMBAGS.
Lef-rye-lef. Dig those heels in dig 'em in.
Pick-'em-up-and-put-'em-down DIG 'EM IN threep-fo-your-lef.
DIG 'EM IN LET'S HEAR IT DIG 'EM IN.
Threep-fo-your-lef, lef-rye-lef.

Square those pieces away SQUARE 'EM AWAY GIRLS. YOU, SHIT-
  HEAD FOURTH MAN IN THE FRONT RANK I SAID SQUARE
  THAT FUCKIN' PIECE, SQUARE IT AWAY Wan-tup-threep-fo.
YOU DON'T SQUARE THAT PIECE I GONNA MALTREAT YOU
  BOY KNOCK YOU UP THE SIDE O' THE HEAD three-fo-your-lef
  SQUARE THAT PIECE! YOU FUCKIN' DEAF? EYES FRONT!
  DON'T LOOK AT ME NUMBNUTS! EYES FRONT! SQUARE
  YOUR PIECE! Now you got the idea, nummie. Wan-tup-threep-fo.
Threep-fo-your-lef, lef-rye-lef, hadalef-rye-lef, lef-rye-lef. Lef-rye-lef, lef-
  rye-lef, your-lef, your-lef, YOUR OTHER LEF SHITHEAD. Lef-rye-
  lef, lef . . . lef . . .
Lef-rye-lef.

The purpose of drill was to instill discipline and teamwork, two of the
Corps' cardinal virtues. And by the third week, we had learned to obey
orders instantly and in unison, without thinking. Each platoon had been
transformed from a group of individuals into one thing: a machine of which
we were merely parts.

The mental and physical abuse had several objectives. They were calcu-
lated first to eliminate the weak, who were collectively known as "unsats,"
for unsatisfactory. The reasoning was that anyone who could not take being
shouted at and kicked in the ass once in a while could never withstand the
rigors of combat. But such abuse was also designed to destroy each man's
sense of self-worth, to make him feel worthless until he proved himself
equal to the Corps' exacting standards.

And we worked hard to prove that, submitted to all sorts of indignities
just to demonstrate that we could take it. We said, "Thank you, sir" when the
drill sergeant rapped us in the back of the head for having a dirty rifle. Night
after night, without complaint, we did Chinese push-ups for our sins (Chi-
nese push-ups are performed in a bent position in which only the head and
toes touch the floor). After ten or fifteen seconds, it felt as if your skull was
being crushed in a vise. We had to do them for as long as several minutes,
until we were at the point of blacking out.

I don't know about the others, but I endured these tortures because I was
driven by an overwhelming desire to succeed, no matter what. That awful
word—*unsat*—haunted me. I was more afraid of it than I was of Sergeant
McClellan. Nothing he could do could be as bad as having to return home
and admit to my family that I had failed. It was not their criticism I dreaded,
but the emasculating affection and understanding they would be sure to

show me. I could hear my mother saying, "That's all right, son. You didn't belong in the Marines but here with us. It's good to have you back. Your father needs help with the lawn." I was so terrified of being found wanting that I even avoided getting near the candidates who were borderline cases—the "marginals," as they were known in the lexicon of that strange world. They carried the virus of weakness.

Most of the marginals eventually fell into the unsat category and were sent home. Others dropped out. Two or three had nervous breakdowns; a few more nearly died of heatstroke on forced marches and were given medical discharges.

The rest of us, about seventy percent of the original class, came through. At the end of the course, the DIs honored our survival by informing us that we had earned the right to be called Marines. We were proud of ourselves, but were not likely to forget the things we endured to claim that title. To this day, the smell of woods in the early morning reminds me of those long-ago dawns at Camp Upshur, with their shrill reveilles and screaming sergeants and dazed recruits stumbling out of bed.

Those who passed the initial trial went back to Quantico two years later for the advanced course, which was even more grueling. Much of it was familiar stuff: more close-order drill, bayonet practice, and hand-to-hand combat. But there were additional refinements. One of these was a fiendish device of physical torture called the Hill Trail, so named, with typical military unimaginativeness, because it was a trail that ran over a range of hills, seven of them. And what hills—steep as roller coasters and ten times as high. We had to run over them at least twice a week wearing full pack and equipment. Softened by the intervening two years of campus life, dozens of men collapsed on these excursions. The victims were shown no mercy by the DIs. I remember one overweight boy lying unconscious against a tree stump while a sergeant shook him by the collar and shouted into his blanched face: "On your feet, you sackashit. Off your fat ass and on your feet."

Recreation consisted of obstacle-course races or pugil-stick fights. The pugil-stick, a thick, wooden staff, padded at each end, was supposed to instill "the spirit of bayonet"; that is, the savage fury necessary to ram cold steel into another man's guts. Two men would square off and bash each other with these clubs, urged on by some bloodthirsty instructor. "Parry that one, now slash, SLASH! Vertical butt stroke. C'mon, kill the sonuvabitch, kill 'im. Thrust. Jab. That's it, jab. JAB! KILL 'IM."

Throughout, we were subjected to intense indoctrination, which seemed to borrow from Communist brainwashing techniques. We had to chant slogans while running: "Hut-two-three-four, I love the Marine Corps." And before meals: "Sir, the United States Marines; since 1775, the most invincible fighting force in the history of man. Gung ho! Gung ho! Gung ho! Pray for war!" Like the slogans of revolutionaries, these look ludicrous in print, but when recited in unison by a hundred voices, they have a weird, hypnotic effect on a man. The psychology of the mob, of the *Bund* rally, takes command of his will and he finds himself shouting that nonsense even though he knows it is nonsense. In time, he begins to believe that he really does love the Marine Corps, that it is invincible, and that there is nothing improper in praying for war, the event in which the Corps periodically has justified its existence and achieved its apotheosis.

We were lectured on the codes Marines are expected to live by: they never leave their casualties on the battlefield, never retreat, and never surrender so long as they have the means to resist. "And the only time a Marine doesn't have the means to resist," one instructor told us, "is when he's dead." There were classes on Marine Corps history, or, I should say, mythology. We learned of Lieutenant Presley O'Bannon storming the fort of the Barbary corsairs at Tripoli, of Captain Travis seizing the fortress of Chapultepec— "the halls of Montezuma"—during the Mexican War, of the 5th and 6th Regiments' bayonet charge at Belleau Wood, of Chesty Puller whipping the rebels in Nicaragua and the Japanese on Guadalcanal.

Around seven hundred and fifty men began the advanced course; only five hundred finished. The graduation ceremony took place on a scalding August afternoon in 1963. We stood at attention on the liquefying asphalt of the parade field on which we had spent countless hours drilling.

A squad of field grade officers began taking their places in the reviewing stand, campaign ribbons adding a splash of color to their khaki shirts. The sun glinted off their brass rank insignia and the polished instruments of the band. There was a small crowd of civilians, mostly parents who had come to watch their sons take part in this martial rite of passage. Awards were presented, the usual messages of congratulation read, and someone made a brief duty-honor-country valedictory speech. We stood patiently, sweat trickling from our noses and onto our ties, the heat wilting the creases in our shirts.

Finally, the order to pass in review rippled down the line. We marched past the stand, snapping our heads at the command "Eyes right" while the gold and scarlet guidons fluttered in the breeze and drums rolled and the band played the Marine Corps Hymn. It was glorious and grand, like an old-fashioned Fourth of July. Bugles, drums, and flags. Marching across the field in battalion mass, with that stirring, soaring hymn blaring in our ears, we felt invincible, boys of twenty-one and twenty-two, all cheerfully unaware that some of us would not grow much older.

NICHOLAS PILEGGI

Wiseguy

〜∽∾〜

HENRY HILL WAS INTRODUCED TO LIFE in the mob almost by accident. In 1955, when he was eleven years old, he wandered into a drab, paint-flecked cabstand at 391 Pine Street, near Pitkin Avenue, in the Brownsville–East New York section of Brooklyn, looking for a part-time, after-school job. The one-story, storefront cabstand and dispatch office was directly across the street from where he lived with his mother, father, four older sisters, and two brothers, and Henry had been intrigued by the place almost as far back as he could remember. Even before he went to work there Henry had seen the long black Cadillacs and Lincolns glide into the block. He had watched the expressionless faces of the cabstand visitors, and he always remembered their huge, wide coats. Some of the visitors were so large that when they hauled themselves out of their cars, the vehicles rose by inches. He saw glittering rings and jewel-studded belt buckles and thick gold wrist bands holding wafer-thin platinum watches.

The men at the cabstand were not like anyone else from the neighborhood. They wore silk suits in the morning and would drape the fenders of their cars with handkerchiefs before leaning back for a talk. He had watched them double-park their cars and never get tickets, even when they parked smack in front of a fire hydrant. In the winter he had seen the city's sanitation trucks plow the snow from the cabstand's parking lot before getting around to cleaning the school yard and hospital grounds. In the summer he could hear the noisy all-night card games, and he knew that no one—not even Mr. Mancuso, who lived down the block and groused about everything—would dare to complain. And the men at the cabstand were rich. They flashed wads of twenty-dollar bills as round as softballs and they sported diamond pinky rings the size of walnuts. The sight of all that wealth, and power, and girth was intoxicating.

At first Henry's parents were delighted that their energetic young son had found a job just across the street. Henry's father, Henry Hill Sr., a hardworking construction company electrician, always felt youngsters should work and learn the value of the money they were forever demanding. He had seven children to support on an electrical worker's salary, so any additional income was welcome. Since he was twelve years old, when he had come to the United States from Ireland shortly after his own father died, Henry Hill Sr. had had to support his mother and three younger brothers. It was work at an early age, he insisted, that taught young people the value of money. American youngsters, unlike the children of his native Ireland, seemed to dawdle about in their adolescence much longer than necessary.

Henry's mother, Carmela Costa Hill, was also delighted that her son had found a job nearby but for different reasons. First, she knew that her son's job would please his father. Second, she hoped that the after-school job might get her feisty young son out of the house long enough to keep him from bickering incessantly with his sisters. Also, with young Henry working, she would have more time to spend with Michael, her youngest son, who had been born with a spinal defect and was confined to either his bed or a wheelchair. Carmela Hill was further pleased—almost ecstatic, really—when she found that the Varios, the family who owned the cabstand, came from the same part of Sicily where she had been born. Carmela Costa had been brought to the United States as a small child, and she had married the tall, handsome, black-haired young Irish lad she had met in the neighborhood at the age of seventeen, but she never lost her ties to the country of her birth. She always maintained a Sicilian kitchen, for instance, making her own pasta and introducing her young husband to anchovy sauce and *calamari* after throwing out his catsup bottle. She still believed in the religious powers of certain western Sicilian saints, such as Santa Pantaleone, the patron saint of toothaches. And like many members of immigrant groups, she felt that people with ties to her old country somehow had ties with her. The idea of her son's getting his first job with *paesani* was the answer to Carmela's prayers.

It wasn't too long, however, before Henry's parents began to change their minds about their son's after-school job. After the first couple of months they found that what had started out as a part-time job for their son had become a full-time compulsion. Henry Junior was always at the cabstand. If his mother had an errand for him to run, he was at the cabstand. He was at the cabstand in the morning before going to school and he was at the cabstand in the afternoon when school let out. His father asked about his homework. "I do it at the cabstand," he said. His mother noticed that he was no longer playing with youngsters his own age. "We play at the cabstand," he said.

"My father was always angry. He was born angry. He was angry that he had to work so hard for next to nothing. Electricians, even union electricians, didn't earn much in those days. He was angry that the three-bedroom house was so noisy, with my four sisters and two brothers and me. He used to scream that all he wanted was peace and quiet, but by then we'd all be like mice and he'd be the only one screaming and yelling and banging dishes against the wall. He was angry that my brother Michael should have been born paralyzed from the waist down. But mostly he was angry about me hanging around the cabstand. 'They're bums!' he used to scream. 'You're gonna get in trouble!' he'd yell. But I'd just pretend I didn't know what he was talking about and say that all I was doing was running errands after school instead of running bets, and I'd swear that I was going to school when I hadn't been near the place in weeks. But he never bought it. He knew what really went on at the cabstand, and every once in a while, usually after he got his load on, I'd have to take a beating. But by then I didn't care. Everybody has to take a beating sometime."

Back in 1955 the Euclid Avenue Taxicab and Limousine Service in the Brownsville–East New York section of Brooklyn was more than just a dispatch center for neighborhood cabs. It was a gathering place for horse-players, lawyers, bookies, handicappers, ex-jockeys, parole violators, construction workers, union officials, local politicians, truck drivers, bookmakers, policy runners, bail bondsmen, out-of-work waiters, loan sharks, off-duty cops, and even a couple of retired hit men from the old Murder Incorporated days. It was also the unofficial headquarters for Paul Vario, a rising star in one of the city's five organized-crime families and the man who ran most of the rackets in the area at the time. Vario had been in and out of jail all his life. In 1921, at the age of eleven, he had served a seven-month stretch for truancy, and over the years he had been arrested for loan-sharking, burglary, tax evasion, bribery, bookmaking, contempt, and assorted assaults and misdemeanors. As he got older and more powerful, most of the charges brought against him were dismissed, either because witnesses failed to appear or because very generous judges chose to fine rather than jail him. (Brooklyn Supreme Court Judge Dominic Rinaldi, for instance, once fined him $250 on bribery and conspiracy charges that could have sent him away for fifteen years.) Vario tried to maintain a modest amount of decorum in a neighborhood known for mayhem. He abhorred unnecessary violence (the kind he hadn't ordered), mainly because it was bad for business. Bodies deposited haphazardly on the streets always made trouble and annoyed the police, who at that time could generally be relied upon to be reasonably complacent about most mob matters.

Paul Vario was a large man, standing six feet tall and weighing over 240 pounds, and appeared even larger than he was. He had the thick arms and chest of a sumo wrestler and moved in the lumbering manner of a big man who knew that people and events would wait for him. He was impervious to fear, impossible to surprise. If a car backfired or someone called his name, Paul Vario's head would turn, but slowly. He seemed invulnerable. Deliberate. He exuded the sort of lethargy that sometimes accompanies absolute power. It wasn't that Vario couldn't move swiftly if he wanted to. Henry had once seen him grab a sawed-off baseball bat from his car and chase a nimbler man up five flights of stairs to collect a loan-shark debt. But usually Vario was reluctant to exert himself. At twelve Henry began running Paul Vario's errands. Soon he was getting Vario his Chesterfield cigarettes and coffee— black, no cream, no sugar—and delivering his messages. Henry got in and out of Paulie's black Impala two dozen times a day when they made their rounds of meetings throughout the city. While Vario waited behind the wheel Henry would bring supplicants and peers to the car for their conversations.

"On 114th Street in East Harlem, where the old guys were suspicious of their own noses, they used to look at me through their slit eyes whenever Paulie brought me into the clubs. I was a little kid and they acted like I was a cop. Finally, when one of them asked Paulie who I was, he looked back at them like they were nuts. 'Who is he?' Paulie said. 'He's a cousin. He's blood.' From then on even the mummies smiled.

"I was learning things and I was making money. When I'd clean out Paulie's boat I'd not only get paid but I'd also get to spend the rest of the day fishing. All I had to do was keep Paulie and the rest of the guys aboard supplied with cold beer and wine. Paulie had the only boat in Sheepshead Bay without a name. Paulie never had his name on anything. He never even had his name on a doorbell. He never had a telephone. He hated phones. Whenever he was arrested he always gave his mother's Hemlock Street address. He had boats his whole life and he never named one of them. He always told me, 'Never put your name on anything!' I never did.

"I got to know what Paul wanted even before he did. I knew how to be there and how to disappear. It was just inside me. Nobody taught me anything. Nobody ever said, 'Do this,' 'Don't do that.' I just knew. Even at twelve I knew. After a couple of months, I remember, Paul was in the cabstand and some guys from out of the neighborhood came for a talk. I got up to walk away. I didn't have to be told. There were other guys hanging around too, and we all got up to leave. But just then Paulie looks up. He sees that I'm leaving. 'It's okay,' he says, smiling at me, 'you can stay.' The other guys kept walking. I could see that they were afraid to even look around, but I stayed. I stayed for the next twenty-five years."

When Henry started working at the cabstand, Paul Vario ruled over Brownsville–East New York like an urban rajah. Vario controlled almost all of the illegal gambling, loan-sharking, labor rackets, and extortion games in the area. As a ranking member of the Lucchese crime family Vario had the responsibility for maintaining order among some of the city's most disorderly men. He assuaged grievances, defused ancient vendettas, and settled disputes between the stubborn and the pigheaded. Using his four brothers as his emissaries and partners, Vario secretly controlled several legitimate businesses in the area, including the cabstand. He owned the Presto Pizzeria, a cavernous restaurant and pizza stand on Pitkin Avenue, around the corner from the cabstand. There Henry first learned to cook; there he learned how to tot up a comptroller's ribbon for the Vario policy bank that used the pizzeria's basement as its accounting room. Vario also owned the Fountainbleu Florist, on Fulton Street, about six blocks from the cabstand. There Henry learned to twist wires onto the flowers of elaborate funeral wreaths ordered for departed members of the city's unions.

Vario's older brother, Lenny, was a construction union official and ex-bootlegger who had the distinction of once having been arrested with Lucky Luciano. Lenny, who was partial to wraparound sunglasses and highly buffed nails, was Paul's liaison to local building contractors and construction company managers, all of whom paid tribute in either cash or no-show jobs to guarantee that their building sites would remain free of both strikes and fires. Paul Vario was the next oldest. Tommy Vario, who was the third oldest in the family, was also a union delegate for construction workers and had a record of several arrests for running illegal gambling operations. Tommy oversaw Vario's bookmaking and loan-sharking operations at dozens of construction sites. The next in order, Vito Vario, also known as "Tuddy," ran the cabstand where Henry first went to work. It was Tuddy Vario who hired Henry the day the youngster walked into the cabstand. Salvatore "Babe" Vario, the youngest of the brothers, ran the floating card and dice games in apartments, school basements, and the backs of garages every night and twice a day on weekends. Babe was also in charge of accommodating, or paying off, the local cops to guarantee peaceful games.

All the Vario brothers were married and lived in the neighborhood, and they all had children, some of them Henry's age. On weekends the Vario brothers and their families usually gathered at their mother's house (their father, a building superintendent, had died when they were young), where raucous afternoons of card games and an ongoing banquet of pasta, veal, and chicken dishes emerged from the senior Mrs. Vario's kitchen. For Henry there was nothing as exciting or as much fun as the noise and games and food on those afternoons. There was an endless procession of Vario friends and relatives who came marching through his life, most of them stuffing folded dollar bills inside his shirt. There were pinball machines in the cellar and pigeons on the roof. There were trays of *cannoli*, the cream-filled Italian pastries, sent over as gifts, and tubs of lemon ice and *gelato*.

"From the first day I walked into the cabstand I knew I had found my home—especially after they found out that I was half Sicilian. Looking back, I can see that everything changed when they found out about my mother. I wasn't just another kid from the neighborhood helping out around the stand. I was suddenly in their houses. I was in their refrigerators. I was running errands for the Vario wives and playing with their kids. They gave me anything I wanted.

"Even before going to work at the cabstand I was fascinated by the police. I used to watch them from my window, and I dreamed of being like them. At the age of twelve my ambition was to be a gangster. To be a wiseguy. To me being a wiseguy was better than being president of the United States. It meant power among people who had no power. It meant perks in a working-class neighborhood that had no privileges. To be a wiseguy was to own the world. I dreamed about being a wiseguy the way other kids dreamed about being doctors or movie stars or firemen or ballplayers."

Suddenly, Henry found, he could go anywhere. He no longer had to wait in line at the local Italian bakery for fresh bread on Sunday mornings. The owner would just come from around the counter and tuck the warmest loaves under his arm and wave him home. People no longer parked in the Hill driveway, although his father never had a car. One day neighborhood youngsters even carried his mother's groceries home. As far as Henry could see there was no world like it, certainly no world he could ever have entered.

Tuddy (Vito) Vario, who ran the cabstand, had been looking for a sharp and speedy kid for weeks. Tuddy had lost his left leg in the Korean War, and even though he had adapted to his disability, he still couldn't move about as swiftly as he wished. Tuddy needed someone to help clean out the cabs and limos. He needed someone who could run around to the Presto Pizzeria in a pinch and deliver pies. He needed someone whom he could send to the tiny four-stool bar and grill he owned two blocks away to clean out the register, and he needed someone smart enough to get sandwich orders straight and fast enough to bring the coffee back hot and the beer cold. Other young-sters, including his own son, Vito Junior, had been hopeless. They dawdled. They moped. They lived in a fog. Sometimes one would take an order and disappear. Tuddy needed a sharp kid who knew his way around. A kid who wanted to hustle. A kid who could be trusted.

Henry Hill was ideal. He was quick and he was smart. He ran errands faster than anyone had ever run errands before, and he got the orders right. For a buck apiece he cleaned out the taxicabs and limousines (the limos were used for local funerals, weddings, and delivering high rollers to Vario card and dice games), and then he cleaned them out again for free. Tuddy was so pleased with Henry's seriousness and dispatch that after Henry's first two months at the cabstand he began teaching him how to jockey the cabs and limos around the cabstand's parking lot. It was a glorious moment—Tuddy walking out of the cabstand carrying a phone book so Henry could see over the dashboard, determined that the twelve-year-old would be driving cars at the end of the day. It actually took four days, but by the end of the week, Henry was tentatively edging the cabs and limousines between the water hose and the gas pumps. After six months Henry Hill was backing limos with inch-clearing accuracy and tire-squealing aplomb around the lot while his schoolmates watched in awe and envy from behind the battered wooden fence. Once Henry spotted his father, who had never learned to drive, spying on him from behind the fence. That night Henry waited for his father to mention his skill in driving, but the senior Hill ate dinner in silence. Henry of course knew better than to bring up the subject. The less said about his job at the cabstand the better.

"I was the luckiest kid in the world. People like my father couldn't under-stand, but I was part of something. I belonged. I was treated like I was a grown-up. I was living a fantasy. Wiseguys would pull up and toss me their keys and let me park their Caddies. I couldn't see over the steering wheel and I'm parking Caddies."

At twelve Henry Hill was making more money than he could spend. At first he would treat his classmates to galloping horse rides along the bridle paths of the Canarsie marshes. Sometimes he would pay for their day at Steeplechase Amusement Park, topping off the treat with a 260-foot para-chute drop. In time, though, Henry grew bored with his schoolmates and tired of his own largesse. He soon learned that there were no heady rides on sweaty horses and no amusement parks he had ever seen that could match the adventures he encountered at the cabstand.

"My father was the kind of guy who worked hard his whole life and was never there for the payday. When I was a kid he used to say he was a 'subway-man,' and it made me want to cry. He helped organize the electrical workers' union, Local Three, and got flowers for his funeral. He worked on skyscrapers in Manhattan and housing projects in Queens, and we could never move out of our crummy three-bedroom house jammed with seven kids, one of them stuck in his bed with a bum spine. We had money to eat, but we never had extras. And every day I saw everyone else, not just the wiseguys, making a buck. My old man's life wasn't going to be my life. No matter how much he yelled at me, no matter how many beatings I took, I wouldn't listen to what he said. I don't think I even heard him. I was too busy learning about paydays. I was learning how to earn.

"And every day I was learning something. Every day I was making a dollar here and a dollar there. I'd listen to schemes and I watched guys score. It was natural. I was in the middle of the cabstand every day. Swag came in and out of that place all day long. There'd be a crate of stolen toasters to be fenced, hot cashmeres right off a truck, cartons of untaxed cigarettes hijacked off some cowboy truckers, who couldn't even complain to the cops. Pretty soon I was delivering policy slips to apartments and houses all over the neighborhood, where the Varios had guys with adding machines counting up the day's take. People used to rent a room in their apartment to the Varios for $150 a week and a free phone. It was a good deal. The wiseguys took only two or three hours in the late afternoon to add up the policy bets on the adding machine tape and circle all the winners. Lots of times the places Paulie and the numbers guys rented belonged to the parents of the kids I went to school with. At first they were surprised to see me coming in with a shopping bag full of slips. They thought I was coming to play with their kids. But pretty soon they knew who I was. They could see I was growing up different.

"After I got my first few bucks and the nerve to go shopping without my mother, I went to Benny Field's on Pitkin Avenue. That's where the wiseguys bought their clothes. I came out wearing a dark-blue pinstriped, double-breasted suit with lapels so sharp you could get arrested just for flashing them. I was a kid. I was so proud. When I got home my mother took one look at me and screamed, 'You look just like a gangster!' I felt even better."

At thirteen, Henry had worked a year at the cabstand. He was a handsome youngster with a bright, open face and a dazzling smile. His thick black hair was combed straight back. His dark-brown eyes were so sharp and bright that they glittered with excitement. He was slick. He had learned how to duck under his father's angry swats, and he was a master at slipping away from the racetrack security guards, who insisted he was too young to hang around the clubhouse, especially on school days. From a distance he almost looked like a miniature of the men he so admired. He wore an approximation of their clothes, he tried to use their street-corner hand gestures, he ate their kind of *scungilli* and squid dishes though they made him retch, and he used to sip containers of boiling, bitter black coffee even though it tasted awful and burned his lips so badly he wanted to cry. He was a cardboard wiseguy, a youngster dressed up for the mob. But he was also learning about that world, and there were no adolescent aspiring samurai or teenage Buddhist monks who took their indoctrination and apprenticeship more seriously.

Rachel Guido DeVries

Italian Grocer

꩜

After he was produce manager for the A & P,
Pop opened his own store. He polished apples
to lay alongside sweet Jersey peaches all
fuzzy and gold, and sometimes got figs which he
held up like gems. Bread and baccala, olives
in a big brown barrel. Provolone, locatelli,
Genoa salami, prosciutto behind a gleaming
case. Each morning he donned a white coat
like a doctor, marched the aisles, and watched.

He hired Angie the dyke to keep things neat.
She fed me cherries when I was three. Mamma
worried I'd choke. Pop and Angie laughed
and Angie said I'd learn what to do
with those pits.

When the store burned, Pop went mad and wept
all over the street. Angie vanished from me, and
the queer man upstairs lost all of his drag. White
people in the neighborhood said Pop the Wop
torched his own store for insurance. He had none.
His white coat, smelling of cheese and fish,
was gone.

NICK TOSCHES

Cut Numbers

∽⧿∾

THE MORNING HAD TURNED INTO A day that was blue and clear and breezy. Louie walked downtown to the bar where those who sought him knew to find him. It was an old, out-of-the-way place called Mona's, owned by a Brooklyn man known as Mr. Joe, a cousin of Il Capraio's, who crossed the river only rarely.

The daytime bartender, a middle-aged man reputed to have been a master forger, spoke even less than Louie and, while otherwise highly professional in his service, he was adamant in his reluctance to foster business or wheedle tips by stooping to engage in the amenities of casual intercourse or illusory bonhomie, all of which he dismissed generally as "pulling these monkeys' pricks to shake a dime out of their assholes." This attitude, which would have made it impossible for him to tend bar most anywhere else, seemed not to bother Mr. Joe.

He brought Louie a glass of club soda with a piece of lemon in it and put two envelopes before him, each bearing the name of the man who had left it. Louie looked at the names, then removed the money, counted it, and stuck it in his left pocket.

A garbageman entered in a green garbageman suit with an orange garbageman stripe across his back.

"Put out your can, here comes the garbageman," Louie intoned.

"It's sanitation. *Sanitation*. How many times I gotta tell you? I'm a sanitation man."

The garbageman took out money and counted it while the bartender put a V.O. on the rocks in front of him.

"Garbage is garbage," Louie said. He reached out and took the garbage-man's money; then he counted it and put it away.

The garbageman finished his drink and gathered his change slowly, hop-ing that Louie might buy him a shot. Leaving two quarters on the bar, he stood there, lingering, still hoping. Louie looked at him. "What are you wait-ing for? A receipt?"

"Just thinkin'," the garbageman muttered, then walked out.

"I hate garbagemen," Louie said.

"The only thing cheaper than a fuckin' garbageman is a fuckin' cabdriver," the bartender said.

That was their conversation for the day.

A short black man wearing a hat made out of a paper bag ambled in and patted Louie on the back.

"Here's my friend." He grinned.

The bartender held up a bottle of Myers's Rum, and the black man nod-ded eagerly.

"Got a hundred for me, Lou?"

"For you, Pete? Anything."

The black man nodded happily and drank his drink. As Louie counted out five twenties, he looked into the mirror and adjusted his paper hat.

"How you want to pay this time?" Louie held the money just beyond the black man's reach.

"Pay? I don't want to pay. I always light a candle and pray you'll get run over and die. It's a long shot, but, then again, a candle's only a dime."

"That's nice to know, Pete. But, just in case you get a dud candle or some shit, how do you want to pay?"

"Let's see. How about two weeks? What's that come out to?"

"Two weeks, twenty percent. Sixty dollars a week."

"How about three weeks?"

"Three weeks, twenty-five percent. Forty-two dollars a week."

"How about a month?"

The bartender, looking away, raised his eyes to heaven.

"A month, thirty percent. Thirty-two dollars and fifty cents a week. I'll give you a break, you can forget about the fifty cents."

"That sounds good. I'll take the month."

"That's what you always say."

"Yeah, but I like to hear them numbers."

Louie gave him the hundred dollars, and he began to spend it immedi-ately, joining customers at the other end of the bar, buying them drinks, and feeding dollars into the jukebox. When the single-action runner came in, he gave him five dollars on the two, five on the two-one bleeder. Then he bought more drinks for those around him. He was their favorite Negro.

The man whom Louie next received had been his first customer, years ago. Known as George the Polack—so much of dignity, and no more, had he wrestled from life—he was a fat, woebegone longshoreman who was well past the age of retirement but who traveled by bus to Port Newark for work whenever there was work to be had. He had borrowed against his pension to pay off his gambling debts but had gambled away that money, too. He would die a debtor. He knew that. And, until then, he would eat cheap meat and drink cheap beer, and even go without, just to pay the vig of his doom. His sad and bleary sunken eyes seemed to see nothing but that doom. He was cursed that way—born a fool, but not fool enough to hope.

"They garnisheed my pay," he said.

Louie looked at him, at those eyes of martyrdom in that big, drooping, ham-colored face.

"The union rep said it wouldn't happen, but it did."

"Sit down, George."

George sat down.

"You're a nice guy, George, but you're a fuckin' idiot. You're an old fuckin' idiot, and if you had any brains, you'd blow 'em out. That would be the best thing, George. I mean that sincerely, as a friend."

Louie enjoyed this. George did not.

"Three weeks ago, you said you wanted five hundred dollars. I asked you if you wanted it on points. That way you could take forever to pay. No, you said, you'd pay me in five weeklies, thirty percent straight, a hundred and thirty a week. That's what you wanted, right, George?"

George nodded disgustedly.

"So, that's what you got. And what happens? Last week, you give me a hundred, you're thirty dollars short. What was it again?"

"The vet."

"Right, the vet. I sympathized with you, George, right? I understood. A guy like you—old, alone, no friends, so ugly he probably never even got to eat pussy without payin'—a guy like that, he needs a dog, I told myself. A guy like that, his dog gets sick, it's a big deal. You see, George, I care. All my life, that's been my ruin. People walk on me, people take advantage of me—people like you, people who walk around bent over picking up dogshit, people nobody cares about but me. If it wasn't for me, your dog could be dead right now. Then where would you be? You're already a man without love, a man without reason to live. You'd be a man without dogshit, too. A decent person, a human being, would show up today with a hundred and eighty, maybe two hundred—the hundred-thirty for this week, the thirty from last week, plus a few pounds extra—'Here,' a decent person would say, 'buy yourself a little dog of your own. I appreciate what you did for'—what's that mutt's name?"

"Cynthia," the Polack mumbled.

"'I appreciate what you did for Cynthia.' That's what I was hoping to hear. Instead, I get fucked."

"Nobody's fuckin' you."

"No, huh?" Louie's voice was different then. There was neither humor nor cruelty in it. "You're an old pro at this, George. You been in the hole, borrowin' and dodgin' since before I was born. You know the routine, and I know you. So let's cut the shit. When are you gonna make good?"

"Next week," George said wearily. In the sound of his words, there was as much loathing for himself as for Louie. "If the union don't help me, I'll figure out somethin' else."

The door opened, and in came two tiny men of obscure ethnic origin. One wore a double-knit suit the color of pale tubercular phlegm. The other, the younger and jauntier of the two, wore stiff, oversized designer jeans, turned up a good four inches at the cuffs, and a black T-shirt emblazoned with the words SEX MACHINE in bold shocking pink. Each of the little men gave Louie a ten-dollar bill. He winked at them, in the American way, bringing expressions of giddy purblind deference to their faces.

"Decent people," Louie told the Polack as they swaggered out in miniature.

As the afternoon wore on, Louie entered into two new loans: one for two hundred at thirty percent, to be paid off in a month at sixty-five dollars a week; the other for a thousand at ten points a week, every week, for as long as it would take the borrower to repay the thousand in one single, full payment. Louie knew that both men were good payers, in different senses of the term. He knew that the one would pay on schedule, and that the other would take at least two months to pay, thus assuring Louie of a minimum return of eighty percent on the principal.

It was a good day for Louie. But when the spring light began to dwindle with the paling of the sun, the world through dirty windows seemed to darken and assume the colors of some awful thing just beyond remembrance, something that brought with it a chill. It came slowly then to his mind, the picture of foreboding and gloom at the foot of his uncle's stairs; and then the breeze at his neck seemed to be the very breath of that gloom and that foreboding. It rose, it fell. Then suddenly it swelled, gusted from behind black curtains by a brooding that was darker still. He inhaled that breath and that brooding, as if to seek in their mingled scents the trace of a more elusive scent, the scent of his own errant fate. But, in the end, it all smelled alike: spilled booze and smoke.

RALPH LOMBREGLIA

Somebody Up There Likes Me

ᑛᔆᕈ

I LOGGED ON AND GOT A Network fortune cookie, followed by E-mail from my distant wife.

> Afternoon favorable for romance. Try a single person for a change.
> DATE: Mon, 12 Apr 99 14:27 GMT
> FROM: Snookie Lee Ludlow
> TO: Dante Allegro Annunziata
> SUBJECT: RE: For your delectation
>
> Dante,
>   Your last missive was so cold, I thought somebody sent me an Alaskan sockeye salmon. Then I saw on TV where the sockeye's extinct, so now I don't know what your problem is.
>   Stop hurting people, you monster.
>
> Snooks

I was on the old mainframe terminal in my office at school, surrounded by cinder-block walls and shelves stuffed chaotically with tapes and disks. I hadn't seen a friendly face in a week. Sometimes when I was down, the random-sentence generator cheered me up, so I knocked off a few new ones.

The president's unlikely urchin is tripping.
The awful dogs are howling.

Couldn't robots dine on jurisprudence?
And why shouldn't buildings puzzle over people?

You could feed the generator your own personal glossary of terms.

Vengeful Snookie bubbles San Antone into flames while academic
watchmen practice celestial sloth in bed.

In my last mail to Snookie Lee, I had sent some morsels like these—affectionately, to make her smile—and she'd taken them all wrong: the whole story of Snooks and me. She was in San Antonio and I was in San Jose, and some people say that when a woman moves 1,500 miles from her mate to get a Ph.D. in women's studies, it's the beginning of the end, if not the end of the end, and refuting those prophets of woe is not easy. Yes, we had taken some bad falls, Snookie Lee and I. We were edging into Humpty Dumpty zone. But I thought we could put it together again, and I was doing my best to convince Snookie of that.

MY letter was cold! Ha! You've been like ice! Maybe *my* feelings are hurt! I'm the loyal and true one! I'm the one who acts like he cares! You're the one who's trying to dump the whole thing down the sewer!

I made my computer do anagrams of your sweet name, Snooks—about 100,000 before I pulled the plug. Then I spent a whole day picking my favorites when I was supposed to be grading papers. Do men do this if they're not in love?

Like, elude solo now. Loud, sleek loin woe. Look, we use old line. Woo skill elude one. I use lone lewd look. Look, Lee, we sin loud. Oil noose well, Duke. Look, Lee, widen soul. Would Snook Lee lie? Look, slow Lee due in.

Do lie low, keen soul,
Dante

Besides Snookie's letter I had four from Mary Beth—three from last week, which I had not read, and a new one posted early this morning, all bearing the subject line "Your position here"—and I could have gone on to read them now, but I wasn't in the mood. Mary Beth was the chair of language and media studies at San Jose College of the Mind, where I was a junior professor. She was also out to get me. Indeed, Mary Beth's machinations were part of the reason that Snookie was gone. Snooks had wanted to teach, too, to chisel those young minds, and she deserved her chance. Not only did

she have sufficient credentials, but she had more heart than the whole Col-
lege of the Mind put together. But Mary Beth wouldn't give her even a sec-
tion of Mastering Capitalistic Prose. I volunteered to give her a section of
mine, and Mary Beth said no. When they offered me the position, they said
I'd come up for tenure in three or four years; after Snooks applied to teach,
Mary Beth took me off the tenure track.

I MET SNOOKS AT A poetry slam in 1995, when I was finishing my gradu-
ate media degree at MIT. She was up from Alabama to show them a thing or
two at Harvard, where she had made it all the way to her senior year. Some-
how we never crossed paths in Cambridge, though she was all over town and
hard to miss. We slammed, finally, in the bowels of Boston, in a basement
bookstore on Newbury Street, where Snookie Lee declaimed verses of out-
rage and indignation while shaking her spiky hair and waving Simone Weil at
the audience. They loved her. I had to follow her on with my sheaf of tech-
nological rhapsodies. They hated me. But the opinion I cared about was
Snookie Lee's. I sidled up to her after the gig and asked what she thought of
my stuff. She hated it, but she loved my name. On the strength of that, I
asked her out. "I've got a date with Dante!" she said, laughing, to one of her
girlfriends.

She was all bluff and flying feathers, and then she was my everything.
We graduated and I got the offer from College of the Mind, and since my
fellow Ph.D.s seemed ready to slit my throat for the job, I took it. Snookie
said she would follow me if I promised it was nice. My best childhood
friend, Boyce Hoodington, had lived twenty miles north, in Palo Alto, for
years, and he loved it out there. He was a project leader for a company try-
ing to simulate human consciousness with a computer. Many California
outfits were trying to do that, without much luck, but Boyce's firm had
achieved a few small, sexy triumphs that kept the investors turned on. The
firm's computer now recognized specific people when they walked into the
room, greeted them, and commented on the clothes they were wearing. It
could do other things, Boyce had told me—things he wasn't allowed to talk
about.

So I promised Snookie she'd like California, and we lived there for three
incredibly crummy years—crummy for me, the indentured professor in the
house, thermonuclear for Snooks. Our problems went beyond Mary Beth.
We experienced other disillusionments, too, such as the discovery that cer-
tain faculty couples masquerading as our friends were doing us dirty behind

the scenes. Looking back on it, trying to fix the damage by getting married was not the best idea. Snookie said so at the time. I won't say that in those dark days when she didn't get out of bed till 4:00 P.M., and never took off her robe, and College of the Mind was leaking its acid into my brain, I was Jovian about it. But I still think that in the disappointing run of men I'm a prize.

I told all this to Snookie Lee as we stood on the dead lawn of our rented bungalow, her ancient, eggplant-colored Le Car parked halfway up on the sidewalk, stuffed full of her things. She was going to San Antonio to get her own Ph.D. In the last year of our three Snooks ended up as a night-shift checkout girl at a discount drug superstore, and the worst thing was, she liked it. She stopped blaming me for ruining her life. She now said that I'd inadvertently brought about her rebirth. She'd made a lot of new girlfriends at the store, muscular young women who weren't ever going to College of the Mind or college of the anything, and Snooks would go aerobic dancing and skating with them. She decided that the best thing in life was sisterhood. I hardly ever saw her anymore. On our separation day her friends spun over on their blades to bid Snookie Lee good-bye. They stood wobbling on the brown grass in their colorful tights and kneepads, saying supportive things to Snooks and giving bad looks to me.

I said, "Sisterhood means a lot to me, too, you know." The women had a good guffaw over that. I told Snooks she was breaking my heart.

She said, "You know those plastic ant-farm things? How you buy one, and then later decide you don't really want ants after all, and you empty the whole thing out on the ground? That's heartbreak, Dante. For the ants, I mean. You're not heartbroken. You don't even look sad."

"I'm very goddamn heartbroken," I said. "Don't tell me how heartbroken I am." The girlfriends rolled closer to Snookie Lee. I *was* heartbroken, but Snookie and I had beaten each other down so badly that our parting scene was playing like dinner theater. "And that analogy's no good," I told her. "Those ant-farm ants are an exotic breed that can't live in the wild. Otherwise they wouldn't *be* heartbroken. They'd be happy. They'd be free."

"You're free," Snookie Lee said.

"I never asked to be free! I'm exotic!" I exclaimed, but I got nowhere. Snookie Lee drove away.

I was about to log off when my terminal chirped and said, in its silly voice, *"You have new mail."* I hoped the message was from her. If she was on-line, maybe I could ping her for a real-time chat. But the letter turned out to be from Boyce. I punched it up.

DATE: Mon, 12 Apr 99 20:53 GMT
FROM: Boyce P. Hoodington
TO: Dante Allegro Annunziata
SUBJECT: Death and pasta

Would have got back to you sooner, but I died. Have not logged on in days, and now speak to you from the beyond. My #*^!%!* computer went down like the Hindenburg—cellular port hosed, motherboard toasted. I'm on the dusty laptop now, shades of Orville Wright. It periodically stalls out and drops through the clouds of our thrilling but turbulent present-day network. If I suddenly disappear, that's why.

I must have a new box, Dante! Let's shop for it together! Tonight, after partaking of a momentous baked ziti. Mounds of baby peas, asparagus, and musky salad greens from the garden have turned our kitchen into a Tuscan stone cottage. I may videodisk it, it's so beautiful. But Janet regards me strangely when I videodisk food. And wait till you taste this fresh-faced fumé with overtones of apple and pear. Spanking beverage. Bought a case. Snatched a spicy zinfandel, too. Come on up!—BPH

P.S. I'll tell my sad corporate story. Slithering beast of commerce, it's a snakepit out there. Be thankful you chose the cloistered life.

P.P.S. We must talk about Snookie. You don't sound good, my brother. Janet has thoughts for you. Never mind free enterprise, Dante; women are the great challenge of our lives, the parabolic arena where we Rollerblade like angels at the speed of light, and where, I fear, we are destined to wipe out grotesquely. Yet we skate on blindly into the night. Why? Because of love, that hot transistor smoking within us.

My office hours at College of the Mind had another hour to run, but not a single student had come to see me so far. True, my door was closed and locked, and I was being very quiet. My lights were off. If I left now, I could go home and take a shower, change into my jeans (Mary Beth forbade teaching in jeans), and still make it to Boyce's for happy hour. I blowgunned my answer into the bitstream—

I Brake for Baked Ziti

—and was yet again on the cusp of logging off when I remembered the text-dissociation software they had on the server. It could sometimes ease the misery inflicted upon people by words. I gave it Snookie's letter to eat.

St. Dante,

I, thou monster. I saw on Sockeye TV where the salmon is cold. Cold, cold, cold. I thought somebody sent me an Alaskan Salmonster, but now I don't know what your last missive was. Your problem's extinct, you hurting salmon.

You, monstero, the Sockeye Salmolast.

Salmonstop,

Snooksego

It didn't kill much pain, but I sent it to her anyway.

I DROVE MY FUJI CHROMA up 280 from San Jose to Palo Alto amid contorted oaks on hilltops, like bonsai trees in amber waves of grain, except the waves weren't grain, they were dead meadow grass, two or three feet high and browned-out from drought, emblem of our republic. Also a fire hazard that should have been mowed down. A red-tailed hawk sailed from a knobby tree, plunged to the undulating grass, and flapped back to its branch with mythic pumps of the wings, taking a field mouse on a commuter hop to God.

The foothills reminded me of Hobbit-land, furry café-au-lait knolls where Frodo, Gandalf, et al., would have felt at home. Zipping up the artery in my tiny car, I succumbed to a conviction that Hobbits were living there now, in burrows beneath the gnomish topography. The old Tolkien books—the interactive laser-disk versions—had lately made a great comeback with students, and I'd been using them in my classes at College of the Mind. For doing that and certain other groovy things, I was considered a cool professor, and my sections never failed to fill up. I got glowing reviews in the campus electronic magazine, to the profound irritation of Mary Beth, whose classes the students routinely panned. And yet educating endless waves of the young had begun to unnerve me. The act of teaching unnerved everyone eventually, but usually because your students were always nineteen while you withered into your grave before their eyes. My problem was different—I remained the same while they mutated into a different species. My students implanted digital watches in the skin of their wrists, tattooed and barbered themselves so as not to appear human, took personalized drugs made from their own DNA, and danced epileptically to industrial noise. I fantasized about taking them on a field trip to the foothills for the semester-wrap picnic and then, in the thick of the Hobbit hunt, vanishing—never to be seen again. Perhaps they'd start a religion based on the mystery of my disappearance. Perhaps spirituality would flower on earth once more.

When I pulled up to Boyce's, his front lawn was preternaturally thick and green, like a gigantic flattop haircut for St. Patrick's Day. He and Janet loved landscaping and were always ministering to their lawn. I wished I had a nice house and yard like theirs. Actually, I wished I had anything. It hit me that I should enter the private sector, like Boyce, where your bosses didn't punish you for doing your job. I found him in his modern, shiny kitchen at the back of the house, assembling a fine baked ziti in a big casserole dish. He was a North Carolina Methodist, supposedly, but some Mediterranean blood had got in there somehow. The man could cook. "Romano!" he said in greeting, pointing to a quarter wheel of the stuff.

"I got E-mail from Snookie today," I said, grating the cheese.

"Excellent!" Boyce said. "You're talking! What did she say?"

"That I was a monster."

"All women say that about men, Dante. It's a figure of speech."

"What does it mean?"

"It means we're monsters."

We built the ziti and slid it into the oven. Boyce poured us big goblets of fumé. "To a new life for us all."

We clinked and sipped. "What do you want a new life for?" I asked.

"I meant the new one we're all getting, want it or not."

"What happened?"

"Tell you outside. Where nature can absorb the toxins."

We took our glasses to the verdant backyard. Boyce and Janet had a triple-depth lot—150 feet of Palo Alto crust in which Boyce had laid drip-irrigation lines, so that now it looked like the Garden of Eden back there. Lemons and limes and oranges hung over our heads at the round terrace table. Zippy the hummingbird was doing his air-and-space show, flashing in from nowhere to sip at his feeder, and then buzzing our heads before zinging back to the treetop where he lived. The little nugget of his beelike body stood in relief against the sky, microscopic stud on a eucalyptus branch.

"You can't see the knife?" Boyce said, twisting to show me his back.

I looked around him. "You've got it hidden pretty well."

"I'm out."

"Of what?"

"SoftBrain Technologies."

"What? You were in charge of the whole project. It was your division."

"The division they lopped off in the corporate downsizing."

"They lop off whole divisions?"

"That was the normal part. The stinky part was tricking me into lopping it for them."

And then Boyce told his tale. Nearly a year before, without telling him, his bosses had cut a deal to sell the consciousness-emulation division. The buyers thought they were paying too much and wanted something extra thrown in, something big and sweet. Boyce was assigned a strange and urgent top-secret task, on which he worked his heart out until just the week before—working, though he didn't know it, for his own extinction. I demanded that he tell me this top-secret thing.

"Oh, it was so typical. So depressingly superficial. Nothing. They wanted to see the computer hold a credible conversation."

"But it's been doing that for years."

"Not with its lips."

"*Lips!* It has *lips?* I didn't know it had lips!"

"I just violated my nondisclosure agreement. Don't spread that around."

"Lips!"

Monday of the previous week, at 9:00 A.M., Boyce had demoed the lips for the company brass and some invited guests with English accents. The lips were gorgeous. Everybody loved the lips. The brass congratulated Boyce in a way that implied a promotion and a load of stock. He returned to his office to pop corks with the team, though it was only coffee-break time. He felt the burgeoning glory of his division, soon to be the company jewel. At 3:00 P.M. he got the call to close it down. The British guests were the buyers. They were taking the sucker to England, lips and all.

It took me a minute to absorb this slimy information. "But they *liked* you," I said at last.

"Oh, they still do," Boyce said. "They love me. I'm a great guy."

In the week since his severance he'd been home in seclusion, drinking boutique wine and having his spine realigned by a private masseuse. Only this morning had Boyce awakened with a craving to reenter the world.

"How's Janet taking it?"

"Overjoyed. She thinks I've been miraculously spared from my own worst tendencies. She thinks I was going corporate—me, of all people."

"Were you?"

"Of course I wasn't! I thought the lips were stupid. Here we were on the trail of consciousness itself, and all the managers cared about was lips."

"Humanity's signal-to-noise ratio isn't so hot, is it?"

"Worst in the animal kingdom. By a mile."

"But we've put out some pretty clean signal, too," I said reflectively. "Over the years. Down through the centuries. It adds up."

Boyce slapped my arm. "That's what I woke up this morning thinking!" he exclaimed. "That's what I've learned from all this!"

"What?"

"That everything we've done with computers until now is totally trivial and wrong! Why have we not yet created a fantastic, free, self-reflective knowledge base of every good thing humanity has ever thought or dreamed? Not just consciousness, Dante. *Cosmic* consciousness! That's what I want to build now. The computerized mind of the world!"

"And you say Janet's not worried about you?"

"She doesn't know yet. She'll love it when I explain it. I kind of got the idea from her, in fact. But since you mention it, it's you she's worried about."

Fumé went up my nose and fizzed my sinuses. "*Me?*"

"She wants me to watch you very closely. She thinks you may do some harm to yourself."

One is rarely prepared to meet the shabby figure one actually cuts in the world, even if one already has a pretty clear mental image of the wretch. "You don't think that, do you, Boyce?"

"Would it make you feel better or worse if I did?"

"Worse. Definitely worse."

"Then I don't."

My harming myself was a silly idea, but it was nice to have friends who considered me a walking pipe bomb and yet continued to care. True, that was practically Janet's job: she was a Jungian therapist, not to mention a splendid woman at whose sagacious feet I should probably throw myself for guidance. She was certainly the best thing that ever happened to Boyce, and her wonderfulness made me wish that I had a wife too. Then I remembered—I did.

"Can I use your Chokecherry to check my mail?" I asked Boyce.

"Be my guest, but it might not even get you on. I had a hell of a time with it today. A few keys are falling off, too."

"I'll nurse it along."

"Try slapping it."

I ducked the pendulous oranges and crossed the backyard beneath fantastical shapes in the California clouds, smiling at the idea of Boyce's still using the old Chokecherry 100. The kitchen was like a lung filled with baked ziti's life-affirming breath. I walked through it and on into the darkened living and dining rooms, where the recently restuccoed walls were already cracked again from tremors. In Boyce's study the big computer lay dead on its table, the little Chokecherry sleeping beside it and waking up reluctantly when I touched its wobbly keys. Once, people had thrilled to own this little appliance of the brain. True to its name, it choked when I logged on, but I lashed it forward with repeated jabs of the Escape key. It tried to read me the fortune cookie that appeared on the screen, but the loudspeaker was broken and the latest assessment of my destiny sounded like a faltering Bronx cheer.

It may be that your whole purpose in life is simply to serve as a warning to others.

And then my one new letter flashed onto the gray wafer of screen. It was from Snookie Lee.

DATE: Mon, 12 Apr 99 21:09 GMT
FROM: Snookie Lee Ludlow
TO: Dante Allegro Annunziata
SUBJECT: RE: Dissociated Love

Dante,

I'm going nuts and you're helping me do it. You're helping quite nicely.

What was that stuff you sent? "Salmonstop" and all that. "Snooksego." What was that supposed to be? I don't understand your problem anymore. I used to think I did. I'm not studying to be a shrink. I'm studying to be a scholar, which I now realize means I need a shrink myself. Maybe yours would take me on; she's used to people with bullet holes in their feet AND their heads.

Would Snook Lee lie? No, she wouldn't. I'm taking my orals an hour from now. You'll claim you didn't know, though I've told you numerous times. You don't listen when I talk. I'm not nervous. Nerves are not why I feel like barfing. I feel like Polly, the girl who wanted a cracker. They've stuffed me full of their theories, and now they want me to spit them back. But I don't even believe in half that stuff. More than half. My professors aren't bad people, they just turn their students into apes. No, they don't do it, this system does it! This rotten system! I hate it!

But why am I telling you this? You're an ape yourself!

This is what I've been living with. I would've told you before, but I, for one, don't believe in throwing up on people. I gotta go.

Snooks

P.S. Get help.

From the time-stamp on Snookie's letter, I figured her orals were over by now. I clacked out my answer on Boyce's broken keys.

I'm up at Boyce's for dinner. I'm sorry you're not getting this before your exams. I would have wished you luck. You never told me they were today! You didn't! This is something you're always doing, telling me you told me things when you didn't tell me.

You were having preexam hysteria, Snooks—all that stuff about spitting back theories and whatnot. Classic symptoms. Just calm down and be yourself and you'll do fine. God, what saccharine advice. Fortunately, you didn't get it. If you're reading this, it's all over, and you did just fine, didn't you? Academia does this to people, Snooks. I, for one, am getting out.

When you have your Ph.D., I'll work in the drugstore and you can teach college! I can't wait!

I am not an ape and you know it.

Love, love, love,

Dante

P.S. Remember Boyce's incredible baked ziti? It's in the oven right now. And then we're going computer shopping for him. I'm gonna call you later.

I shot my letter into the colossal web of the Net. When I looked up, Janet was standing in the door. "Fixing Boyce's computer?" she said.

"Hi. No, I was just saying something to Snookie Lee."

Janet looked around. "Snookie's here?"

"I meant I was E-mailing her."

"Oh, E-mail. Not talking on the videophone?" We giggled over that for a second. Janet famously loathed all technology after the fountain pen. "Boyce thought the little computer was broken too," she said.

"It is, Janet. Just because you can answer your mail doesn't mean a computer works. See?" I picked up the Chokecherry and turned it upside down. Five or six keys fell off and a guitar pick dropped out. "He needs a new computer."

"I've heard. Well, you're communicating, at least."

"Of course we're communicating," I said, skeptical that Janet really considered Boyce's layoff a great development. "I'm here, aren't I? But it would be a hell of a lot easier with a better computer."

"Oh, I'm sure a better computer would help immensely. When was the last time you told her you loved her?"

"I thought we were talking about Boyce."

"We were clearly talking about Snookie Lee."

"We were talking about Boyce and computers! You shrinks always do that."

"What?"

"That! Ambush people."

"Have you told Snookie you loved her any time in the past two years?"

"Of course I have."

"She says you haven't."

"Goddamn gossip!" I cried, and threw the Chokecherry onto Boyce's desk. It broke in two pieces. "When did she tell you that? You two have been talking? What else did she say?"

"Plenty."

IN BOYCE'S ZITI THE ASPARAGUS had given itself to the pasta like a submissive lover. The food was so ambrosial that we didn't even need the spicy zin, though we drank it anyway. My own baked ziti never came out nearly this good, and I was the Italian one. In my present frame of mind I could take a thing like that hard, as a comment on my general integrity.

"Did you know that Janet has serious misgivings about us, Dante?" Boyce asked. "About our relentless fascination with technological goods, the way machines work, what's the latest thing." We were having dinner outside, at the round redwood table, where I sat between Boyce and Janet, opposite the empty fourth chair. "Something about it is fishy, she thinks."

"I didn't know that," I said.

"Yes, I may start studying you two," Janet said. "I may write a book on this phenomenon."

Janet had her own private practice full of wealthy clients. She wasn't jumping through flaming tenure hoops under the stony gaze of some Mary Beth, and yet she still had thoughts of writing books. What pluck!

"Why do you know so much about computers?" she asked me. "Him I can understand. But you're supposed to be a humanities guy."

"Fear of death," I said. "Sexual terror."

"Nice try."

"Because he knew I'd need a new one someday," Boyce said, "and he wanted to help me pick it out."

"Good, Boyce," I said. "Right. But follow through. What kind of computer would you like? You haven't told us."

"A Revelation 2000."

This magical product name buzzed past my ear with such an unreal twang that I looked around to see if little Zippy had just gone by again. The Revelation 2000 was the first microcomputer with a holographic screen, 1,000-bit audio/video, three billion instructions per second, and direct wireless uplink to geosynchronous satellites. It was the sexiest hardware you could put on a desk. And though I personally subscribed to the old chestnut about buying computers—get the most iron they'll let you charge on your card, and if you can't use all the power, you're doing something wrong—I couldn't believe Boyce was talking about a Rev 2K. "Revelations cost a fortune," I said.

"I've got one lined up for three thousand bucks."

"Bull, Boyce! They're twenty times that."

"My man has one for three."

"What man?"

"This guy Mickey. I've never met him. He's a friend of Brubaker's."

"Oh, no, Boyce. No."

"Honey," Janet said, "I don't think 'Brubaker' was the correct magic word."

"You said you were never dealing with Brubaker again."

"It's a *friend* of his, Dante. Plus, I'm a big boy now."

"He's saying I'm being too protective," I said to Janet.

"That seems to be it," she said.

Brubaker was an avatar of free enterprise who'd been in bed at one time or another with almost every breathing being doing business in the Valley. Like countless others, Boyce had worked for the mythical Bru. Unlike most, he remained on friendly terms with Brubaker after the experience, but then, Boyce was friends with everybody. Brubaker had seen the high times, and now he was researching the lows. He'd been charged with various white-collar crimes in recent years, wriggling off every time except the last, when they popped him for soliciting capital investment without a prospectus. He got a hefty fine and sixty days of community service—which he discharged by teaching street youths to set up their own "S" corporations.

"Stolen goods," I said to Boyce. "Hijacked tractor-trailer."

"You know I wouldn't do that."

"How does Brubaker meet these people?"

"I don't ask."

"That's the understanding you have?"

"No, I don't ask because he'd tell me."

"Since when is three thousand dollars cheap?" Janet said.

"Last computer I'll ever buy, honey," Boyce told her. "Cross my heart."

"Are you going to use it to change the world?"

"You're reading my mind."

"All right, then, you can have it," she said, sipping her zinfandel and staring into the reddening California sky. "I think I'll call my book *Modern Man in Search of a Dumpster for His Soul*."

Boyce turned to me. "And you were upset about being called a monster."

I WAS HALFWAY TO THE street when I realized that Boyce wasn't behind me. He was standing on his Crayola-green lawn, under the lady's-slipper–colored dome of California sky, staring at my cerulean vehicle parked at the curb in the striated shadow of a mimosa tree. "Do I look like I can ride in a Chroma?" he said. I was forgetting that Boyce, six foot four, couldn't even get into the freeway bubble I drove. I joined him on the lawn leading to his car. The sprinklers popped up and sprayed our legs like mechanical cats. "The downside of homeownership," Boyce called out, as we dashed off his effervescing grass.

"You finally got a pot to pee in, and it pees on you." We made it back to the sidewalk and shook our ankles. "Still, I wouldn't mind. A little pot to pee in with Snookie Lee. But I guess SoftBrain Technologies won't have a gig for me now."

"I guess not, cowboy. You wanted one?"

"I was thinking maybe technical writer."

"Impeccable sense of timing, Dante."

His silver Kodak Image hulked in the transcendental light. The automobile was so large it seemed designed to lure Japan into the quicksand with us once and for all—the two rivals going down in a cruise-controlled death embrace. When we approached it, the driver's door slid open, but not mine. "Look at that," I said. "It didn't do my side. A snoutful of microchips and it can't even open the door."

"You have to stand where it can see you, dude."

I walked to the passenger side, and the door retracted with an overdesigned hermetic suck. "My Chroma sees me no matter where I am," I said. When we were gliding through the peaceful streets, pastel homes clicking by like Necco wafers, I said, "So. Mickey."

"Brubaker says the overall impression is of an alienated vet. But in fact Mickey is not a vet. Not of any actual war."

"He's in a private militia?"

"No, just the opposite. Mickey wouldn't join any organized anything. He's a loner. He's this guy who came out the other side of the Valley dream."

"He went in the front?"

"Wrote system code in the glory days, burned out on that, went independent, specialized in lockout software. He's into hardware now."

"Designing it?"

"Testing it, more like."

Offices and malls and taco stands swept by on El Camino. We arrived at the outskirts of Palo Alto, where start-ups roiled in every dingy industrial park, in the bedrooms of brick apartment buildings, at the whittled wooden tables of the old hamburger bars. Nothing could kill the entrepreneurial spirit, not even the 1990s in California. Everybody had an angle, everybody had a scheme. It was endless, and now Boyce was one of them. He parked in front of a run-down hacienda with silver Quonset huts on either side. Night had nearly fallen. The air was acrid with the resins of burning electronics.

"You guys seen Mickey?" somebody asked when we got out of the car. A tall black man in rags had stepped out of the bushes.

"No, we haven't," Boyce said.

The guy took a step back into the light, and I saw that his clothes weren't rags. They were expensive designer things with all kinds of shapes and flaps cut into them.

"We just got here," Boyce said. "Where is he?"

"Didn't I clearly imply that I do not know where Mickey is?" the guy said, and went back into the shadows.

Then a white guy dressed in rags approached us from the opposite direction. "You guys seen Mickey?" he said.

"Would you mind stepping into the light?" I said, leading him underneath the lamp at the curb. This guy was really in rags, actual rags.

Boyce said, "What's with all you cats asking if we've seen Mickey?"

"All us cats?" the guy said. "Do I know you guys? Have I ever, like, *seen* you guys?"

"I just told the other dude. No, we have not seen Mickey."

"What other dude?"

I pointed at the bushes. "Over there somewhere. Wearing real fancy clothes. He's looking for Mickey too."

"He didn't actually say he was looking for Mickey," Boyce said. "He wanted to know if *we'd* seen Mickey. Just like you."

"That's true," I said. "Maybe you guys don't want to see Mickey at all."

"I see Mickey all the time," the guy said, and walked off into the darkness.

A small Filipino woman answered the door when we rang the bell. She seemed surprised to see us. "Isn't Mickey expecting us?" Boyce said.

"You're different," the woman said, and led us into her dwelling, where furniture and clothing and plastic media trash tumbled together indistinguishably in every room. We wound up in a wood-paneled den where two children played on shag carpeting in the blue glow of a sexual-hygiene program on the big TV. They looked a lot like their mother—for that was who she had to be. The kids were no more interested in us than in the blurry sex on the tube. I thought of my students, aliens whose human parents paid my bills, and I understood them better now. This was where they'd grown up. The house was from the 1960s, when people put wet bars in their recreation rooms. On the dusty surface of a side table lay two handguns and a rifle—not toys, not dusty.

Mrs. Mickey walked us along a breezeway to one of the Quonset huts we'd seen from the street. At the entrance, midway along the metal pod's fuselage, she left us staring inside from the threshold. The shape and corrugation made it feel like an aircraft hangar—one in which had taken place, for some reason, the Battle of Silicon Valley. Mutilated corpses of computers from the past ten years lay in heaps around the cylindrical room, most horribly crushed or burned or melted. At a workbench in the midst of this wreckage, surrounded by banks of test equipment, a large bearded man in sleeveless fatigues was blowing a heat gun at a computer in a plain black box and laughing. Text and a picture were bending like taffy on the screen. A high-pitched squeal was emerging from the thing. An oscilloscope portrayed the computer's demise in ghostly green wiggles—lots of waves, lines with some waves, nothing but lines. Finally the screen crackled violently and then went blank. Blue-black smoke twirled from the computer's vents into an exhaust hood above the bench.

"He's an *abuse tester*," I whispered to Boyce. "You didn't tell me that. He kills computers for a living."

"Don't say 'kills,'" Boyce said. "*Stresses.*"

"Piece of crap!" the man barked at the melting computer, and then he looked up and saw us standing there. He stood very still, staring at us, breathing deeply, with the heat gun still in his hand.

"Mickey?" Boyce said. "Are you Mickey? Hi, I'm Boyce. You were expecting us, right? Brubaker said we were coming?"

The man said nothing. Boyce looked worried, and worry was not a Boycean trait. It made me worried myself. But then, staring into this situation, I realized something about Mickey. He had just completed a kill and he wouldn't want to fight. He'd feel unthreatened and kingly. Unless overtly attacked, he'd be docile. He might even let smaller creatures pick at the edges of his prey. I pointed to the smoking prototype on his bench. "Did you drop it on the floor yet? I hear that's the first thing you're supposed to do. Drop it on the floor."

These words revived his inner animal. "You hear that 'cause that's what I do! *I* developed the protocol. *Me!*" He slapped himself on the chest. "Damn right I dropped it on the floor. I dropped it on the floor several times!" And then he laughed uproariously.

We were all right. He was verbalizing. Brubaker had told Boyce to expect a bearlike creature who communicated mainly by snuffling in his sinus passages, scratching himself, and emitting inexplicable giggles or guffaws.

Suddenly Mickey stopped laughing. "Brubaker told me one guy."

"That's me. Boyce. I just brought my friend along. Dante."

"*Dante?*" Mickey said, his face clouding over as he pronounced my name. He stared across the hut at old Fillmore West posters taped to the rippling metal walls. "The tomato family? Don't tell me this is the ketchup heir, the little tomato-paste trust-fund boy."

"Not *Del Monte,*" Boyce said. "Dante. He's not from ketchup money."

"They're all related," Mickey said.

"The Del Montes maybe, but he's not a Del Monte."

Mickey cackled again, but he put his heat gun down, and though he didn't explicitly invite us in, he didn't not invite us either, so we picked our way through the technological waste. "The Revelation brothers," Mickey said.

"That's us," Boyce said.

A color TV in Mickey's lair was tuned to a news story about the thousands of people living at Moffett Air Field now that NASA's demise had left the old base free to become a homeless shelter. It was an election year, and a local politician came on to gas a few bites about the looting of taxpayer coffers.

"Bring out the old rockets," Mickey said. "Ship 'em to Mars!"

"What are you saying that for?" I said. "You have homeless friends yourself. We saw a homeless guy right here in front of your house."

Mickey peeped out a small window. "Where?"

"Right out front, man. He was asking for you too. 'You guys seen Mickey?' he said."

"That's no homeless guy!"

"He looked homeless," Boyce said.

"They just dress up like that."

Our deal seemed on the verge of going bad, so I said, "Hey, let's see this great computer."

"Hey, let's see this great computer," Mickey said.

"Well, if you don't mind."

He opened a door in an unpainted plasterboard wall and rolled the Revelation in on a cart. It wasn't burned or smashed or even dented. It maybe had a few scratches on it. He plugged it into the wall and flipped the switch. "Come on, sport," he said to me. "Let's see you do your stuff."

I'D NEVER ACTUALLY SEEN A 2000 in person before. Holographic software objects floated in the space between the computer and me, one of them announcing the machine's readiness for telephony in any form. I sat down and logged onto my account, bracing myself for power and speed. Even so I wasn't ready. The thing whomped me onto the Network like a jujitsu flip.

Hanlon's Razor:

Never attribute to malice that which is adequately explained by stupidity. You have new mail.

from: marybeth@media.sjcm.edu
"Your position here"

from: marybeth@media.sjcm.edu
Re(1) "Your position here"

from: marybeth@media.sjcm.edu
Re(2) "Your position here"

from: marybeth@media.sjcm.edu
Re(3) "Your position here"

from: marybeth@media.sjcm.edu
Re(4) "Your position here"

"You got mail, dude," Mickey said.
"I see that, Mickey."
"Who's marybeth?"
"My boss."
"How come she's writing you so much? You two into something? You got something going with the boss lady, Don?"
"Dante, Mickey. Don Tay." The thought of having something going with

Mary Beth was so ludicrous I forgot what I was doing. I sat there like an idiot who didn't know what a computer was for.

"Don't know how to read mail?" Mickey said. "No problem on a Revelation. Just tell it what you want it to do."

"I don't want to read that mail right now. I'll read it some other time."

"But then how are you gonna know how blazing the Revelation is at your daily tasks? *Read the mail*," he barked at the box.

My first letter from Mary Beth joined us in the room as though we were reading the woman's mind. You couldn't describe the 2000 as "fast"—reality and the Revelation were basically indistinguishable. Everything just *was*, and in 3-D it all seemed almost edible besides. It was an amazing hardware experience. The message content was kind of a downer, though.

DATE: Mon, 5 Apr 99 20:23 GMT
FROM: Mary Beth Hinckley
TO: Dante Allegro Annunziata
SUBJECT: Your position here

My dear Dante,

 I assume some awareness on your part, however dim, of your contract's impending expiration, and of your ongoing evaluation for renewal in this department.

"What's this 'my dear' crap?" Mickey said.
"Scorn."
"Is she like this in person?" Boyce asked.
"No, she's more relaxed in the mail."

 I—all of us, actually—have been reading your student evaluations. They make a most striking collection of documents. Indeed, we've never seen anything quite like it. The students are deliriously uncritical of you, Dante. It seems you can do no wrong. Are you, perhaps, being uncritical of them? There is no learning without criticism, mon cher. We're not here to have the children like us. We're here to teach, to mold, to impart.

 More than being peculiar—nay, unprecedented—I'm afraid such student reaction to a professor raises serious questions. We must talk.

 MBH

"You poor bastard," Boyce said. "Why didn't you share it with us? You didn't have to bear it alone."

"I've always told you I hated the place."

"That's true, you have."

"You put some major mojo on this chick," Mickey said. "She wants you, Don. She wants you bad."

"I don't think so, Mickey. For one thing, she's not a chick."

"Listen to me, dude. I know. *Next*," he said, and Mary Beth's next letter materialized in our midst, followed by the others in succession as Mickey said "Next" again and again, each letter more aggrieved than its predecessor, until finally her last message bodied forth from the screen, dated this afternoon.

Signor Annunziata:

Your silence is rude and mystifying, but I'll say no more about it here. Indeed, I'll say no more here at all, since this is the last mail you'll receive from me.

The formal hearing into your future will be held tomorrow, Tuesday, 13 April, at 9 AM, in the Provost's office. Feel free to join us, in the flesh or via video, though the proceedings will be conducted in absentia in any event. If you're feeling pressed for time, I expect a very brief session.

What happened, Dante? You seemed so promising at first. And with that lovely name. I hoped you'd join our little family. But not as the Prodigal Son.

MBH

"I like how they're doing it in absentia whether you're there or not," Boyce said.

"That captures it, doesn't it? But I'll hack on your Revelation till dawn, shave and shower, drag myself in there, plead for my job. It's all I have. I'll say I've been sick. I'll get some students to claim they don't like me."

"*Reply*," Mickey said, causing an empty text-window to appear, at which he recited an incantation that scrolled obediently up the screen as he spoke. Mickey was one of those holdovers from the early days of computers, people who type everything with Caps Lock on, and he must have trained the Revelation to do the same whenever it heard his voice.

STUCK UP BITCH
DON'T MESS WITH DONNY
HE COULD OF BEEN YOURS
BUT YOU WERE HOTTY
NOW SUFFER

"Hotty?" Boyce said.

"Yeah. Stuck up. Superior. *Hotty.*"

"Oh. I see."

"That's great, Mickey," I said. "Thank you for coming to my defense. I'm touched, really I am. Now erase it, please."

"*Send,*" he said, and his voodoo poem-curse to Mary Beth vanished from the screen, sucked away by the Network's solar wind.

Sometimes you don't know how close you are to flaming out till it happens, and this was the case with me. I sat down on a deformed plastic chair in this computer criminal's Quonset hut, and I began to cry. Not big out-and-out boohooing, but there's crying and there's not crying, and I was crying.

"What's he doing?" Mickey asked Boyce, backing away from me.

"He seems to be crying," Boyce said. "You okay, pal?"

"Well, make him stop," Mickey said.

"How am I gonna do that? You just got him fired from his job, man."

"She was messing with his mind. What does he wanna work there for anyway?"

"What does anybody want to work anywhere for, Mickey? Plus, things aren't going real well with his wife right now."

"What's the problem?"

"She left."

My weeping did become out-and-out boohooing at this point.

"He's a total loss, isn't he?" Mickey said, gazing down at me. "But he likes computers, right? Computers make him happy, it seems like."

"They always do seem to cheer him up," Boyce said.

Mickey went into his secret room and wheeled out another cart.

"What's that?" I said, sniffling. "That looks like another Revelation."

"I was gonna keep it for parts, but you seem so sad, dude. I don't like people feeling sad. It makes me feel weird. You want it?"

"How much?"

"Same as for him."

"Three thousand bucks? Where are you getting these?"

"Don't ask questions like that, Don. You want it, I take cash. You don't want it, you never saw it."

I had thirty-five hundred bucks in my savings account, and after that it was the graveyard shift at Drugs 'n' Such. "I'll take it." I turned to Boyce. "Get me to a bank machine."

Mickey put his huge, heavy arm on my shoulder. "Then you're feelin' better about things?"

"Yeah, I am, Mickey, thanks. Can I ask you a question, though? I'm just curious. What's in the other Quonset hut? The one on the other side of the house?"

"What's in it? My in-laws. You want one of them, too? We could work something out. Can't do better than a nice Filipino girl."

WE DROVE OUT ONTO THE strip to look for an ATM. As the owner of a Revelation 2000, I could network with Boyce's machine and be part of his new venture, the construction of humanity's electronic mind. He offered me a job. I accepted. Then he revealed the identity of his major investor. I worked for Brubaker now.

Alongside a taco stand we found a riotously bright bank machine, its colored panels burning like gas in the California night. It sucked my card and started beeping at me.

> **Greetings, valued customer Dante Allegro Annunziata!**
> **You have new Network mail! Read it now at your Mitsubishi ATM!**
> **(Small service charge applies.)**
> **(Reminder: your credit account is past due.)**

I pushed the button and they dropped me right into my mail, no list of letters received, no fortune cookie, no nothing. They literally didn't give me the time of day. What did I expect? It was a bank. I had only one new letter anyway, from Snookie Lee.

DATE: Tue, 13 Apr 99 02:03 GMT
FROM: Snookie Lee Ludlow
TO: Dante Allegro Annunziata
SUBJECT: I did a wild thing

Dante,

I went kind of crazy. I did a wild thing.

They asked me their parrot questions, like I knew they would. No big surprise. But when I actually heard it happen, something inside me plopped. I refused to answer. I refused to say anything at all. I just sat there doing a Bartleby in my oral exams. It was so weird. I couldn't believe it. They couldn't believe it either. Surely you're going to say something, they said. I'd prefer not to, I said. This can't be happening, said my adviser. It's happening, I said. I can't believe you're not finishing this degree, she said. I'd prefer not to, I said.

There's a blank place after that. Somebody drove me home. I called Janet. She's picking me up at the airport in San Jose. I'm flying in at 10 PM. I sold my Le Car about a month ago. I guess I never told you that. Got five hundred bucks for it. We have to talk. This does not mean I'm staying. I'm on my way home to Alabama. Well, the long way. If I did stay, it would be because I had seen a goddamn miracle walking around in your pants, I'll tell you that.

Oil noose well, you said. Oil well indeed. I slipped out. But how did you know that? You are one spooky cat.

Snooks

P.S. Lie low, keen soul, you said. Slow Lee due in. How did you *know* that? I've been having some bourbon. It reminds me of my lost home in the South. Been looking at your pictures too. You were always so cute, you Italian thing.

P.P.S. That doesn't necessarily mean anything.

"This is incredible," Boyce said. He'd been reading over my shoulder. "She wouldn't speak in her oral exams? She sat there in silence?"

"Yes, and what a woman she is!" I exclaimed, dropping into savings for my three thousand bucks, full of hope and dreams beyond reckoning, even by a Revelation 2000. A gigantic flashing jet was crossing the sky, coming in for a landing at San Jose. I checked my watch. It was tomorrow morning, Greenwich Mean Time. "Snookie's on that plane!" I cried, and with my life's liquid assets wadded up in my hand, I dashed for Boyce's Kodak Image and the golden future of knowledge and love.

PIETRO DiDonato

Christ in Concrete

M ARCH WHISTLED STINGING SNOW AGAINST THE brick walls and up the gaunt girders. Geremio, the foreman, swung his arms about, and gaffed the men on.

Old Nick, the "Lean," stood up from over a dust-flying brick pile, tapped the side of his nose and sent an oyster directly to the ground. "Master Geremio, the Devil himself could not break his tail any harder than we here."

Burly Julio of the walrus mustache and known as the "Snoutnose" let fall the chute door of the concrete hopper and sang over in the Lean's direction: "Mari-Annina's belly and the burning night will make me once more a milk-mouthed stripling lad . . ."

The Lean loaded his wheelbarrow and spat furiously. "Sons of two-legged dogs . . . despised of even the Devil himself! Work! Sure! For America beautiful will eat you and spit your bones into the earth's hole! Work!" And with that his wiry frame pitched the barrow violently over the rough floor.

Snoutnose waved his head to and fro and with mock pathos wailed, "Sing on, O guitar of mine . . ."

Short, cheery-faced Tomas, the scaffoldman, paused with hatchet in hand and tenpenny spike sticking out from small dicelike teeth to tell the Lean as he went by, in a voice that all could hear, "Ah, father of countless chicks, the old age is a carrion!"

Geremio chuckled and called to him. "Hey, little Tomas, who are you to talk? You and big-titted Cola can't even hatch an egg, whereas the Lean has just to turn the doorknob of his bedroom and old Philomena becomes a balloon!"

Coarse throats tickled and mouths opened wide in laughter.

The Lean pushed his barrow on, his face cruelly furrowed with time and struggle. Syrupy sweat seeped from beneath his cap, down his bony nose and turned icy at its end. He muttered to himself. "Saints up, down, sideways and inside out! How many more stones must I carry before I'm overstuffed with the light of day! I don't understand . . . blood of the Virgin, I don't understand!"

Mike the "Barrel-mouth" pretended he was talking to himself and yelled out in his best English . . . he was always speaking English while the rest carried on in their native Italian. "I don't know myself, but somebodys whose gotta bigga buncha keeds and he alla times talka from somebodys elsa!"

Geremio knew it was meant for him and laughed. "On the tomb of Saint Pimple-legs, this little boy my wife is giving me next week shall be the last! Eight hungry little Christians to feed is enough for any man."

Tomas nodded to the rest. "Sure, Master Geremio had a telephone call from the next bambino. Yes, it told him it had a little bell between instead of a rosebush. . . . It even told him its name!"

"Laugh, laugh all of you," returned Geremio, "but I tell you that all my kids must be boys so that they someday will be big American builders. And then I'll help them to put the gold away in the basements!"

A great din of riveting shattered the talk among the fast-moving men. Geremio added a handful of Honest tobacco to his corncob, puffed strongly, and cupped his hands around the bowl for a bit of warmth. The chill day caused him to shiver, and he thought to himself: Yes, the day is cold, cold . . . but who am I to complain when the good Christ Himself was crucified?

Pushing the job is all right (when has it been otherwise in my life?), but this job frightens me. I feel the building wants to tell me something; just as one Christian to another. Or perhaps the Easter week is making of me a spirit-seeing pregnant woman. I don't like this. Mr. Murdin tells me, Push it up! That's all he knows. I keep telling him that the underpinning should be doubled and the old material removed from the floors, but he keeps the inspector drunk and . . . "Hey, Ashes-ass! Get away from under that pilaster! Don't pull the old work. Push it away from you or you'll have a nice present for Easter if the wall falls on you" . . . Well, with the help of God I'll see this job through. It's not my first, nor the . . . "Hey, Patsy number two! Put more cement in that concrete; we're putting up a building, not an Easter cake!"

Patsy hurled his shovel to the floor and gesticulated madly. "The padrone

Murdin-sa tells me, 'Too much, too much! Lil' bit is plenty!' And you tell me I'm stingy! The rotten building can fall after I leave!"

Six floors below, the contractor called, "Hey, Geremio! Is your gang of dagos dead?"

Geremio cautioned the men. "On your toes, boys. If he writes out slips, someone won't have big eels on the Easter table."

The Lean cursed that the padrone could take the job and all the Saints for that matter and shove it . . . !

Curly-headed Lazarene, the roguish, pigeon-toed scaffoldman, spat a cloud of tobacco juice and hummed to his own music . . . "Yes, certainly yes to your face, master padrone . . . and behind, This to you and all your kind!"

The day, like all days, came to an end. Calloused and bruised bodies sighed, and numb legs shuffled toward shabby railroad flats . . .

"Ah, *bella casa mio*. Where my little freshets of blood and my good woman await me. Home where my broken back will not ache so. Home where midst the monkey chatter of my piccolinos I will float off to blessed slumber with my feet on the chair and the head on the wife's soft full breast."

These great child-hearted ones leave one another without words or ceremony, and as they ride and walk home, a great pride swells the breast . . .

"Blessings to Thee, O Jesus. I have fought winds and cold. Hand to hand I have locked dumb stones in place and the great building rises. I have earned a bit of bread for me and mine."

The mad day's brutal conflict is forgiven, and strained limbs prostrate themselves so that swollen veins can send the yearning blood coursing and pulsating deliciously as though the body mountained leaping streams.

The job alone remained behind . . . and yet, they also, having left the bigger part of their lives with it. The cold ghastly beast, the Job, stood stark, the eerie March wind wrapping it in sharp shadows of falling dusk.

That night was a crowning point in the life of Geremio. He bought a house! Twenty years he had helped to mold the New World. And now he was to have a house of his own! What mattered that it was no more than a wooden shack? It was his own!

He had proudly signed his name and helped Annunziata to make her X on the wonderful contract that proved them owners. And she was happy to think that her next child, soon to come, would be born under their own rooftree. She heard the church chimes, and cried to the children, "Children, to bed! It is near midnight. And remember, shut-mouth to the paesanos! Or they will send the evil eye to our new home even before we put foot."

The children scampered off to the icy yellow bedroom where three slept in one bed and three in the other. Coltishly and friskily they kicked about under the covers; their black iron-cotton stockings not removed . . . what! and freeze the peanut-little toes?

Said Annunziata, "The children are so happy, Geremio; let them be, for even I would dance a tarantella." And with that she turned blushing. He wanted to take her on her word. She patted his hands, kissed them, and whispered. "Our children will dance for us . . . in the American style someday."

Geremio cleared his throat and wanted to sing. "Yes, with joy I could sing in a richer feeling than the great Caruso." He babbled little old-country couplets and circled the room until the tenant below tapped the ceiling.

Annunziata whispered, "Geremio, to bed and rest. Tomorrow is a day for great things . . . and the day on which our Lord died for us."

The children were now hard asleep. Heads under the cover, over . . . snotty noses whistling, and little damp legs entwined.

In bed Geremio and Annunziata clung closely to each other. They mumbled figures and dates until fatigue stilled their thoughts. And with chubby Johnny clutching fast his bottle and warmed between them . . . life breathed heavily, and dreams entertained in far, far worlds, the nation-builder's brood.

But Geremio and Annunziata remained for a long while staring into the darkness . . . silently.

At last Annunziata spoke. "Geremio?"

"Yes?"

"This job you are now working . . ."

"So?"

"You used always to tell me about what happened on the jobs . . . who was jealous, and who praised . . ."

"You should know by now that all work is the same . . ."

"Geremio. The month you have been on this job, you have not spoken a word about the work . . . And I have felt that I am walking into a dream. Is the work dangerous? Why don't you answer . . . ?"

JOB LOOMED UP DAMP, SHIVERY gray. Its giant members waiting.

Builders donned their coarse robes, and waited.

Geremio's whistle rolled back into his pocket and the symphony of struggle began.

Trowel rang through brick and slashed mortar rivets were machine-gunned fast with angry grind Patsy number one check Patsy number two check the Lean three check Julio four steel bellowed back at hammer donkey engines coughed purple Ashes-ass Pietro fifteen chisel point intoned stone thin steel whirred and wailed through wood liquid stone flowed with dull rasp through iron veins and hoist screamed through space Rosario the Fat twenty-four and Giacomo Sangini check . . . The multitudinous voices of a civilization rose from the surroundings and melted with the efforts of the Job.

The Lean as he fought his burden on looked forward to only one goal, the end. The barrow he pushed, he did not love. The stones that brutalized his palms, he did not love. The great God Job, he did not love. He felt a searing bitterness and a fathomless consternation at the queer consciousness that inflicted the ever mounting weight of structures that he *had to! had to!* raise above his shoulders! When, when and where would the last stone be? Never . . . did he bear his toil with the rhythm of song! Never . . . did his gasping heart knead the heavy mortar with lilting melody! A voice within him spoke in wordless language.

The language of worn oppression and the despair of realizing that his life had been left on brick piles. And always, there had been hunger and her bastard, the fear of hunger.

Murdin bore down upon Geremio from behind and shouted:

"Goddammit, Geremio, if you're givin' the men two hours off today with pay, why the hell are they draggin' their tails? And why don't you turn that skinny old Nick loose, and put a young wop in his place?"

"Now listen-a to me, Mister Murdin—"

"Don't give me that! And bear in mind that there are plenty of good barefoot men in the streets who'll jump for a day's pay!"

"Padrone—padrone, the underpinning gotta be make safe and . . ."

"Lissenyawopbastard! if you don't like it, you know what you can do!" And with that he swung swaggering away.

The men had heard, and those who hadn't knew instinctively.

The new home, the coming baby, and his whole background, kept the fire from Geremio's mouth and bowed his head. "Annunziata speaks of scouring the ashcans for the children's bread in case I don't want to work on a job where. . . . But am I not a man, to feed my own with these hands? Ah, but day will end and no boss in the world can then rob me the joy of my home!"

Murdin paused for a moment before descending the ladder.

Geremio caught his meaning and jumped to, nervously directing the rush of work. . . . No longer Geremio, but a machinelike entity.

The men were transformed into single, silent beasts. Snoutnose steamed through ragged mustache whip-lashing sand into mixer Ashes-ass dragged under four-by-twelve beam Lean clawed wall knots jumping in jaws masonry crumbled dust billowed thundered choked . . .

At noon, dripping noses were blown, old coats thrown over shoulders, and foot-long sandwiches were toasted at the end of wire over the flames. Shadows were once again personalities. Laughter added warmth.

Geremio drank his wine from an old-fashioned magnesia bottle and munched a great pepper sandwich . . . no meat on Good Friday.

Said one, "Are some of us to be laid off? Easter is upon us and communion dresses are needed and . . ."

That, while Geremio was dreaming of the new house and the joys he could almost taste. Said he, "Worry not. You should know Geremio." It then all came out. He regaled them with his wonderful joy of the new house. He praised his wife and children one by one. They listened respectfully and returned him well wishes and blessings. He went on and on. . . . "Paul made a radio—all by himself, mind you! One can hear *Barney Google* and many American songs!"

"A radio!"

"An electric machine like magic—yes."

"With music and Christian voices?"

"That is nothing to what he shall someday accomplish!"

"Who knows," suggested Giacomo amazed, "but that Dio has deigned to gift you with a Marconi . . ."

"I tell you, son of Geremio shall never never lay bricks! Paulie mine will study from books—he will be the great builder! This very moment I can see him . . . How proud he!"

Said they in turn: "Master Geremio, in my province it is told that for good luck in a new home, one is to sprinkle well with salt . . . especially the corners, and on moving day sweep with a new broom to the center and pick all up—but do not sweep it out over the threshold!"

"That may be, Pietro. But, Master Geremio, it would be better in my mind that holy water should bless. And also a holy picture of Saint Joseph guarding the door."

"The Americans use the shoe of a horse . . . there must be something in that. One may try . . ."

Snoutnose knew a better way. "You know, you know." He ogled his eyes and smacked his lips. Then, reaching out his hands over the hot embers . . . "To embrace a goose-fat breast and bless the house with the fresh milk. And one that does not belong to the wife . . . that is the way!"

Acid-smelling di Nobilis were lit. Geremio preferred his corncob. And

Lazarene "tobacco-eater" proudly chawed his quid . . . in the American style.

The ascent to labor was made, and as they trod the ladder, heads turned and eyes communed with the mute flames of the brazier whose warmth they were leaving, not with willing heart, and in that fleeting moment the breast wanted much to speak of hungers that never reached the tongue.

About an hour later, Geremio called over to Pietro, "Pietro, see if Mister Murdin is in the shanty and tell him I must see him! I will convince him that the work must not go on like this . . . just for the sake of a little more profit!"

Pietro came up soon. "The padrone is not coming up. He was drinking from a large bottle of whiskey and cursed in American words that if you did not carry out his orders—"

Geremio turned away disconcerted, stared dumbly at the structure and mechanically listed in his mind's eye the various violations of construction safety. An uneasy sensation hollowed him. The Lean brought down an old piece of wall and the structure palsied. Geremio's heart broke loose and out-thumped the floor's vibrations, a rapid wave of heat swept him and left a chill touch in its wake. He looked about to the men, a bit frightened. They seemed usual, life-size, and moved about with the methodical deftness that made the moment then appear no different than the task of toil had ever been.

Snoutnose's voice boomed into him. "Master Geremio, the concrete is re-ady!"

"Oh yes, yes, Julio." And he walked gingerly toward the chute, but not without leaving behind some part of his strength, sending out his soul to wrestle with the limbs of Job, who threatened in stiff silence. He talked and joked with Snoutnose. Nothing said anything, nor seemed wrong. Yet a vague uneasiness was to him as certain as the foggy murk that floated about Job's stone and steel.

"Shall I let the concrete down now, Master Geremio?"

"Well, let me see—no, hold it a minute. Hey, Lazarene! Tighten the chute cables!"

Snoutnose straightened, looked about, and instinctively rubbed the sore small of his spine. "Ah," sighed he, "all the men feel as I—yes, I can tell. They are tired but happy that today is Good Friday and we quit at three o'clock—" And he swelled in human ecstasy at the anticipation of food, drink and the hairy flesh-tingling warmth of wife, and then, extravagant rest.

Geremio gazed about and was conscious of seeming to understand many things. He marveled at the strange feeling which permitted him to sense the familiarity of life. And yet—all appeared unreal, a dream pungent and nostalgic.

Life, dream, reality, unreality, spiraling ever about each other. "Ha," he chuckled, "how and from where do these thoughts come?"

Snoutnose had his hand on the hopper latch and was awaiting the word from Geremio. "Did you say something, Master Geremio?"

"Why yes, Julio, I was thinking—funny! A—yes, what is the time—yes, that is what I was thinking."

"My American can of tomatoes says ten minutes from two o'clock. It won't be long now, Master Geremio."

Geremio smiled. "No, about an hour . . . and then, home."

"Oh, but first we stop at Mulberry Street, to buy their biggest eels, and the other finger-licking stuffs."

Geremio was looking far off, and for a moment happiness came to his heart without words, a warm hand stealing over. Snoutnose's words sang to him pleasantly, and he nodded.

"And Master Geremio, we ought really to buy the sea-fruits with the shells—you know, for the much needed steam they put into the—"

He flushed despite himself and continued, "It is true, I know it—especially the juicy clams . . . uhmn, my mouth waters like a pump."

Geremio drew on his unlit pipe and smiled acquiescence. The men around him were moving to their tasks silently, feeling of their fatigue, but absorbed in contemplations the very same as Snoutnose's. The noise of labor seemed not to be noise, and as Geremio looked about, life settled over him a gray concert—gray forms, atmosphere and gray notes. . . . Yet his off-tone world felt so near, and familiar.

"Five minutes from two," swished through Snoutnose's mustache.

Geremio automatically took out his watch, rewound and set it. Lazarene had done with the cables. The tone and movement of the scene seemed to Geremio strange, differently strange, and yet, a dream familiar from a time-less date. His hand went up in motion to Julio. The molten stone gurgled low, and then with heightening rasp. His eyes followed the stone-cementy pudding, and to his ears there was no other sound than its flow. From over the roofs somewhere, the tinny voice of *Barney Google* whined its way, hooked into his consciousness and kept itself a revolving record beneath his skullplate.

"Ah, yes, *Barney Google*, my son's wonderful radio machine . . . wonderful Paul." His train of thought quickly took in his family, home and hopes. And with hope came fear. Something within asked, "Is it not possible to breathe God's air without fear dominating with the pall of unemployment? And the terror of production for Boss, Boss and Job? To rebel is to lose all of the very little. To be obedient is to choke. O dear Lord, guide my path."

Just then, the floor lurched and swayed under his feet. The slipping of the underpinning below rumbled up through the undetermined floors.

Was he faint or dizzy? Was it part of the dreamy afternoon? He put his hands in front of him and stepped back, and looked up wildly. "No! No!"

The men poised stricken. Their throats wanted to cry out and scream but didn't dare. For a moment they were a petrified and straining pageant. Then the bottom of their world gave way. The building shuddered violently, her supports burst with the crackling slap of wooden gunfire. The floor vomited upward. Geremio clutched at the air and shrieked agonizingly. "Brothers, what have we done? Ahhh-h, children of ours!" With the speed of light, balance went sickeningly awry and frozen men went flying explosively. Job tore down upon them madly. Walls, floors, beams became whirling, solid, splintering waves crashing with detonations that ground man and material in bonds of death.

The strongly shaped body that slept with Annunziata nights and was perfect in all the limitless physical quantities thudded as a worthless sack amongst the giant débris that crushed fragile flesh and bone with centrifugal intensity.

Darkness blotted out his terror and the resistless form twisted, catapulted insanely in its directionless flight, and shot down neatly and deliberately between the empty wooden forms of a foundation wall pilaster in upright position, his blue swollen face pressed against the form and his arms outstretched, caught securely through the meat by the thin round bars of reinforcing steel.

The huge concrete hopper that was sustained by an independent structure of thick timber wavered a breath or so, its heavy concrete rolling uneasily until a great sixteen-inch wall caught it squarely with all the terrific verdict of its dead weight and impelled it downward through joists, beams and masonry until it stopped short, arrested by two girders, an arm's length above Geremio's head; the gray concrete gushing from the hopper mouth, and sealing up the mute figure.

Giacomo had been thrown clear of the building and dropped six floors to the street gutter, where he lay writhing.

The Lean had evinced no emotion. When the walls descended, he did not move. He lowered his head. One minute later he was hanging in midair, his chin on his chest, his eyes tearing loose from their sockets, a green foam bubbling from his mouth and his body spasming, suspended by the shreds left of his mashed arms, pinned between a wall and a girder.

A two-by-four hooked little Tomas up under the back of his jumper and swung him around in a circle to meet a careening I beam. In the flash that he lifted his cherubic face, its shearing edge sliced through the top of his skull.

When Snoutnose cried beseechingly, "Saint Michael!" blackness enveloped him. He came to in a world of horror. A steady stream, warm, thick, and sickening as hot wine, bathed his face and clogged his nose, mouth, and eyes. The nauseous syrup that pumped over his face clotted his mustache red and drained into his mouth. He gulped for air and swallowed blood. As he breathed, the pain shocked him to oppressive semiconsciousness. The air was wormingly alive with cries, screams, moans, and dust, and his crushed chest seared him with a thousand fires. He couldn't see, nor breathe enough to cry. His right hand moved to his face and wiped at the gelatinizing substance, but it kept coming on, and a heartbreaking moan wavered about him, not far. He wiped his eyes in subconscious despair. Where was he? What kind of a dream was he having? Perhaps he wouldn't wake up in time for work, and then what? But how queer; his stomach beating him, his chest on fire, he sees nothing but dull red, only one hand moving about, and a moaning in his face!

The sound and clamor of the rescue squads called to him from far off.

Ah, yes, he's dreaming in bed, and, far out in the streets, engines are going to a fire. Oh, poor devils! Suppose his house were on fire? With the children scattered about in the rooms he could not remember! He must do his utmost to break out of this dream! He's swimming under water, not able to raise his head and get to the air. He must get back to consciousness to save his children!

He swam frantically with his one right hand, and then felt a face beneath his touch. A face! It's Angelina alongside of him! Thank God, he's awake! He tapped her face. It moved. It felt cold, bristly and wet. "It moves so. What is this?" His fingers slithered about grisly sharp bones and in a gluey, stringy, hollow mass, yielding as wet macaroni. Gray light brought sight, and hysteria punctured his heart. A girder lay across his chest, his right hand clutched a grotesque human mask, and suspended almost on top of him was the twitching, faceless body of Tomas. Julio fainted with an inarticulate sigh. His fingers loosed and the bodiless headless face dropped and fitted to the side of his face while the drippings above came slower and slower.

The rescue men cleaved grimly with pick and ax.

Geremio came to with a start . . . far from their efforts. His brain told him instantly what had happened and where he was. He shouted wildly. "Save me! Save me! I'm being buried alive!"

He paused exhausted. His genitals convulsed. The cold steel rod upon which they were impaled froze his spine. He shouted louder and louder.

"Save me! I am hurt badly! I can be saved I can—save me before it's too late!" But the cries went no farther than his own ears. The icy wet concrete reached his chin. His heart appalled. "In a few seconds I will be entombed. If I can only breathe, they will reach me. Surely, they will!" His face was quickly covered, its flesh yielding to the solid sharp-cut stones. "Air! Air!" screamed his lungs as he was completely sealed. Savagely he bit into the wooden form pressed upon his mouth. An eighth of an inch of its surface splintered off. Oh, if he could only hold out long enough to bite even the smallest hole through to air! He must! There can be no other way! He must! There can be no other way! He is responsible for his family! He cannot leave them like this! He didn't want to die. This could not be the answer to life! He had bitten halfway through when his teeth snapped off to the gums in the uneven conflict. The pressure of the concrete was such, and its effectiveness so thorough, that the wooden splinters, stumps of teeth, and blood never left the choking mouth.

Why couldn't he go any farther?

Air! Quick! He dug his lower jaw into the little hollowed space and gnashed in choking agonized fury. Why doesn't it go through! Mother of Christ, why doesn't it give? Can there be a notch, or two-by-four stud behind it? Sweet Jesu! No! No! Make it give . . . Air! Air!

He pushed the bone-bare jaw maniacally; it splintered, cracked, and a jagged fleshless edge cut through the form, opening a small hole to air. With a desperate burst the lung-prisoned air blew an opening through the shredded mouth and whistled back greedily a gasp of fresh air. He tried to breathe, but it was impossible. The heavy concrete was settling immutably and its rich cement-laden grout ran into his pierced face. His lungs would not expand and were crushing in tighter and tighter under the settling concrete.

"Mother mine—mother of Jesu—Annunziata—children of mine—dear, dear, for mercy, Jesu-Giuseppe e' Mari," his blue foamed tongue called. It then distorted in a shuddering coil and mad blood vomited forth. Chills and fire played through him and his tortured tongue stuttered, "Mercy, blessed Father—salvation, most kind Father—Saviour—Saviour of His children, help me—adored Saviour—I kiss your feet eternally—you are my Lord—there is but one God—you are my God of infinite mercy—Hail Mary divine Virgin—our Father who art in heaven hallowed be thy—name—our Father—my Father," and the agony excruciated with never-ending mount, "our Father—Jesu, Jesu, soon Jesu, hurry dear Jesu Jesu! Je-sssu . . . !" His mangled voice trebled hideously, and hung in jerky whimperings. Blood vessels burst like mashed flower stems. He screamed. "Show yourself now, Jesu! Now is the time! Save me! Why don't you come! Are you there! I cannot stand it—ohhh, why do you let it happen—where are you? Hurry hurry hurry!"

His bones cracked mutely and his sanity went sailing distorted in the limbo of the subconscious. With the throbbing tones of an organ in the hollow background, the fighting brain disintegrated and the memories of a baffled lifetime sought outlet.

He moaned the simple songs of barefoot childhood, scenes flashed desperately on and off, and words and parts of words came pitifully high and low from his inaudible lips.

Paul's crystal-set earphones pressed the sides of his head tighter and tighter, the organ boomed the mad dance of the tarantella, and the hysterical mind sang cringingly and breathlessly, "Jesu my Lord my God my all Jesu my Lord my God my all Jesu my Lord my God my all Jesu my Lord my God my all."

Nuns circulated among the cripples, touching their limbs kindly and reverently, telling them how blessed they were, and how wonderful.

GOD

BEVERLY DONOFRIO

Looking for Mary

◦~◦◦

I AM LYING IN BED SHIVERING under the covers in a small Bosnian village where millions, maybe even billions, believe the Virgin Mary has been appearing for the past sixteen years. The recurring apparitions have become a magnet for believers from around the world. I, too, am here to see. I am on a silent fasting retreat with forty-nine zealous Catholics and haven't spoken or eaten anything besides bread and tea for days with the hope that if we are hungry enough, we will fill with God. And now, I guess because those deprivations are not enough, the wind just blew out the lights, and I'm stunned by the appropriateness of the symbolism: I may be on a religious retreat, but I am left in the dark.

I've come as a writer and have been going to chapel and lectures and church every day as part of the job, but I've also been praying to Mary, hundreds of Hail Marys, which is not part of the job. Then, to see how confession would feel, I made an appointment with the priest and have been lying in bed dreading what I will say. "Forgive me, Father, for I have sinned; it has been thirty-five years since my last confession. I have slept with more men than I care to remember; I'm a selfish daughter and lousy mother whose grown son was damaged by neglect; and my default reaction to disappointment is despair." It seems impossible to actually say this.

I slink farther down under the covers and hear the line of a hymn, "Do not be afraid, I am with you," and break into tears. I weep when the wind screeching at the window wakes me in the middle of the night; I weep in the morning as I sit up in bed and stare at the rain dribbling down the glass; and I cry again in the little chapel where we meet for mass at noon every day when the lady with the doily on her head says, "For the poor and the lonely and the lost, let us pray." As the tears fall, I know I did not come here only to write about the experience; I came because I want Mary to mother me and teach me mother things, like how to love.

That evening I traipse through the gusting winds, praying on my rosary beads, then kneel in the village church with all the pilgrims. I wish and I hope and I pray for a little mustard seed of faith to move the mountain that is me out of the dark and into the light.

If you told me a year ago that this person looking for Mary and paraphrasing Christ was me, I would have fallen off my chair laughing.

SIX YEARS BEFORE I LANDED in Bosnia, the Virgin Mary was no more than a dim memory, another fairy tale from my childhood as I sat in my rocker day after day, heartbroken over a man, but really over my life, which I thought of as pathetically impoverished. I was forty and alone and had just moved to a tiny village by the sea called Orient, where I knew nobody. I rocked and stared at the bay, which changed from midnight blue to battleship gray; then when I turned on the light I was horrified, and mesmerized, by my own reflection: my gray roots were an inch long (vanity hadn't fled with the onslaught of depression, just the energy to keep up any semblance of a beauty regimen); the creases that ran from the sides of my nose to the sides of my mouth made me look like a puppet; my eyes were hollow and sad. The man I was mourning, Kip, had insisted he still loved me, but he was a coward and he was lying. It wasn't only the physical that had repulsed him. It was the cold hard heart in the middle of me: too defended, too brittle, too pockmarked by life. There'd been no soft pillow of comfort for him to sink into. No motherliness in me.

In the end, I'd been the one to leave, the way I'd left so many men, pridefully. Yet when I dropped Kip at Bradley International Airport, there'd been no pride left. I'd sobbed and gasped for breath. Kip's face was shiny with tears, too; both of us crying for the sweet promise we had and the sweet promise we had broken. He walked around to my side of the car and kissed me through the window; our faces were slippery with tears. Then, as he slung his backpack onto his shoulder, I took one last look at the familiar tilt of his neck, the loveliness of his body as he walked away, and my heart cracked, not like an egg but like a dried-up riverbed.

And so I rocked and I hugged myself as though the hypnotic rhythm, the pressure on my chest, would soothe away the hole of longing, coddle the ache in my heart, make me feel like a baby in the cradle of her mother's arms. Then I shut off the light and drifted to bed without brushing my teeth, or washing my face, or looking in a mirror, or doing anything with my hands besides squeeze them between my knees.

I'd been depressed before and was afraid if I didn't end it some way, this dark night of the soul could stretch on for years. A walk off a dock with rocks in my pockets seemed a good idea; but instead, for the New Year, I plunged into therapy—again.

"You have to learn to love yourself," said my new therapist, Eileen.

I needed to pay money to hear this? "And how do I do that?"

"Sometimes people find another person who loves them unconditionally, and then, because they feel loved, they can love themselves."

I'd say I'd been looking for that about half of the days of my life—okay, maybe a third; writing took up a lot of my time. I figured Kip was as close as I was going to get, and he'd kicked me in the heart. "Don't you have to love yourself before anyone's going to love you?" I asked rhetorically.

Eileen sidestepped the question. "Sometimes people find love through God."

"God?" Great—I'd signed on with an evangelist. "I hate God!" I almost yelled. "I grew up Catholic. Every time I stubbed my toe I had to figure out what I'd done wrong to deserve it. I spent five years in my first therapy trying to get rid of the guilt the church put there. Oh, really." I shuddered. "I would just love to try to be perfect and beat myself up every night before bed, not only for the things I did but for the things I didn't do—and what I thought in my head. No thank you."

"A holy person," she redefined. "Spirit, Buddha, whatever you want to call it. And you reach them through meditating. Meditation works."

I'd always meant to meditate. I'd done affirmations till I was blue in the face, and I did believe that if somehow you could be given the unconditional love you didn't get when you really needed it, as a child, then you could heal. For me a holy person might be the only way, a last-ditch effort.

And so I began to meditate. I started with five minutes and did guided meditations, encouraged by Eileen, who'd suggested I try to imagine a spirit or a holy person. Mary? I thought about her. But she was too removed and sterile, too far away up in the virginal Catholic clouds. I couldn't sense her, or touch her. An embroidered Virgin of Guadalupe throw had, however, made it back with me from Mexico, where I'd lived with Kip. It was colorful with accents of gold and covered my computer like a good-luck charm. For a time, I pictured a young Persian-looking woman on a flying carpet who flew me around and bathed me in rivers. Eventually I settled on a little Buddha. I am a stone-cold statue abandoned in the woods and tangled in vines, and this little Buddha finds me there, loads me onto his cart, and wheels me into the sunshine in the middle of a beautiful garden. Then he begins chipping away the stone. First I feel the heat of the sun on my skin, then the breeze, which is fragrant with flowers. Very slowly I open my eyes, and the first thing I see is an emerald green garden and, at its edge, purple flowers shaped like little trumpets, cascading to the ground.

BY THE SPRING, I'D BEEN doing this meditation for a few months and felt adventurous enough one Saturday morning to drag myself out of bed at seven, wash my face, drink a cup of coffee, then head out for yard sales with the local paper in hand. I had only the set of table and chairs I'd dragged around with me since my teenage marriage home, the rocker I'd been glued to, a desk, a bed, a bureau, and a small advance to write a novel I hadn't even begun. So, I was really going on a furniture-scavenging excursion. My first stop was a contents-of-house sale, which usually means the owner has died. The place was a homely little aluminum-sided, post–Korean War affair, which I almost drove right by; but I made the decision to be open and not pass judgments. It was only seven-thirty and the sign said No Early Birds, but the husky little boy guarding the back door let me in. There were a few others already milling around the kitchen, whose cupboard contents had been piled onto the Formica table. I picked up a few shot glasses, because I had none, then walked into the living room.

The furniture was fake Colonial and identical to my parents'. I pressed my hand to my chest to protect my heart. Would my siblings and I sell my mother's department-store dishes, my father's woodworking tools, virtually none of which we'd want for ourselves? Would we stand guard as people snatched the crocheted afghan from their couch, then watch it disappear out the door?

My parents were almost seventy; both of them smoked; and they were not in good health. Yet, with his chronically aching back, that fall my father had driven all the way from Connecticut to Vermont in his pickup truck to help me move. In New London we'd taken the ferry across Long Island Sound and had eaten grilled-cheese sandwiches, then strolled outside on the deck. My father's thick silver hair rippled in the breeze as he jangled the change in his pocket and we leaned on the rail, gazing out over the sound. "I always liked the water," he said.

"Me, too. I always wanted to live by the sea one day, and now I will."

"Atta girl."

When my father and I pulled up to my spindly old rented Victorian in Orient, a village on the northeasternmost tip of Long Island, my son, Jason, who'd come from New York City to help us, was sitting on the step waiting. Jason had graduated college and was living in our old apartment on Avenue A. He was always on time and absolutely dependable, a good boy who'd never given me a moment's trouble. His hair, platinum and straight when he was a child, had been brown and wavy since high school. He was now twenty-three years old, over six feet tall, and, as a few of my younger women friends had let me know, a babe. My father and he patted each other's shoulders as they shook hands; then Jason kissed me on the cheek. "Hey, Mama."

I cupped my hand to his face, then kissed him, too. "Hey, Jase."

We unloaded my few pieces of furniture, my boxes of dishes and linens, and my thirty-two boxes of books. I made us ham-and-cheese sandwiches with mustard, which we ate at the table in my new kitchen, followed by slices of the apple-walnut cake my mother had sent. I looked at them gratefully, the two men in my life. There were no others. My father had brought his toolbox, just in case, and it was a good thing. The wood around the hinges on my cellar hatchway had rotted, so my father moved them a few inches farther apart. He removed a door I didn't want between the kitchen and the dining room, and then at dusk I kissed them both good-bye in my driveway. "You take care now," my father said.

"Bye, Ma," my son said, looking worried.

This was the first time in my life I'd lived without my son or a man. The next morning, I'd headed for the rocker.

At the yard sale, I did not want to imagine how desperately alone I'd feel when my parents passed away, and nearly ran from that Colonial furniture and up the stairs to the second floor, where, in a small bedroom on a nightstand next to a single bed, the Virgin Mary took my breath away. She was in a framed postcard as Our Lady of Fatima, dressed in a white luminescent gown, floating peacefully in a powdery gray, star-twinkled sky. Glitter graced her veil, and a single white rose sat on each foot as three little kids in babushkas knelt on a grassy hill, looking adoringly up at her, and I was struck by a powerful urge—the same feeling I get when I'm handed a furry kitten or an adorable baby: I just wanted to eat her up. Another shopper walked in and I grabbed that picture so fast you'd have thought I was a starving street dog who'd just been thrown a T-bone steak.

I hung that little picture in my bedroom next to the light switch; and the next Mary—a crosscut of a tree on which Mary in a varnished print looks concerned for *you* as she points to her own stabbed heart—I hung next to the mirror in the bathroom. A Rubenesque Mary looking knowingly at a chubby baby Jesus on her lap found a place above my bed.

I did feel love for Mary every time I looked at the paintings I'd begun to collect, but I was in love with my other yard-sale paintings, too. I had no idea that before long the Blessed Mother would multiply all over my house like Richard Dreyfuss's little mud mountains in *Close Encounters of the Third Kind*.

But I get ahead of myself. As that little Mary postcard entered my house that first spring in Orient, Mary planted one little hook in my heart that let in one little ray of light, and Nancy Sawastynovicz, my new best friend, came in.

I'd seen a big blond woman with braids, digging across the road that spring; then, a few days after I found my first Mary, on my way home from buying coffee around the corner at the general store, the woman stabbed her spade in the earth, stood, and offered her hand. "I'm Nancy Sawastynovicz McCarthy," she said. "That's my son, Seth." She indicated a little boy on a tricycle down the road. "I had him late in life. I'm forty-one. I'm never having another." Her eyes sparked and I thought she might be looking for a joke, but I was still depressed and not in the mood.

I did, however, notice the coincidence. Nancy and I had both said, "I'm never having another," even though we'd had kids at the opposite ends of our lives. But I was still feeling separate and looking for differences, not similarities. I smiled and excused myself.

But blessings can be as persistent as curses, and Nancy refused to be discouraged. She knocked at my door later in the day, carrying a shovel and a shoebox. "I brought you some flowers from my mother's yard. You could plant them out back."

"They'll probably die."

"Nah. All they need's water and food."

She carried them through my kitchen and out the back door, so I followed her. "You got a spade?"

I shook my head.

"That's okay." She stabbed her shovel into the ground near the back fence. "I got an extra. You could have it."

"I couldn't."

"Why not?" She pulled two baby plants, joined at their roots, apart. "These are sweet williams. They'll do good here. Look, you got evening primrose coming up." She brushed some leaves away and I could see pale green shoots poking through the earth. I ran my hand over the little nubs. Had they been growing all through the winter in the dark and the cold? Nancy brushed away more leaves and began yanking out clumps of dead stalks. I'd had unremarkable vegetable gardens a few times, but I'd never grown flowers and wasn't sure I wanted to start. But I knelt beside Nancy and yanked, too. Then, as she patted the sweet williams in the ground and watered them in, she said, "Did you read all those books I saw you carrying when you moved in?"

"Hell, no."

"I should have helped you."

"Why?"

" 'Cause you needed it? I'm a DP—dumb Polack. I stayed back in the third grade. I can't spell."

"Spelling's overrated." I remembered from our earlier conversation that Nancy was a year older than I. Because she'd stayed back we probably had graduated high school in the same year. "I graduated in '68, too."

"Queen of the Prom." She jabbed her thumb at her chest.

"The Girl Who Got Pregnant." I jabbed my thumb at mine.

She howled. "You want a margarita?"

Nancy stopped by every day just to check in. If my dishes were dirty, she did them. She swept the floor; she watered my plants. "Sit down," I'd say. "I don't want to," she'd say back.

We made dump runs together, waded into the bay to clam, and rowed a boat out to scallop. We pedaled on our bikes by the light of the moon, through bulrushes rustling by our ears, past newly plowed fields that smelled of damp earth, by choppy inlets we could hear lapping in the distance. When the moon was full, we pedaled harder, and Nancy repeated every few minutes, "I'm mooning, man." Back home we were too stirred up to sleep, so we sipped tea in my kitchen and told stories. Nancy had played piano and guitar when she was younger and told me how she used to perform at teen mass. "It was All Saints' Day; I play 'When the Saints Come Marching In,' and they kick me out. It was All Saint's Day! The morons. I never went back, not even when my cousin Sissy got married; I stood outside the door."

The sky that winter could be overcast for weeks, allowing not even a glimpse of the moon; but Nancy and I could tell when the moon was waxing or waning by the tone of our moods. The sea, the moon, the earth are all feminine, and perhaps because you couldn't walk from your house to your car without smelling or feeling them, there was a tradition of powerful women in Orient. When whale oil still lit the lamps of the world, the men left for long, two-year stretches to hunt the seas for whales. The women worked the land; they grew the food, raised the children, chopped the wood to heat their houses. I had heard rumors that there was a coven of witches in Orient, which I tended not to believe, especially once I heard the same rumor about Nancy and me. I knew for certain, though, that there was an enclave of lesbians. Half of the land was still farmed in Orient, and from the time the asparagus appeared early in the spring till the pumpkins and squash came late in the fall, stands dotted the roads "manned" by women. In this woman-dominated world, the very air I breathed made me feel planted, grounded, rooted, sane.

WHILE MY HOUSE CONTINUED TO fill with Marys (on a felt banner as the Virgin of Guadalupe, she stood at the top of the stairs; in a small bedroom I planned to turn into my shrine room, she was a regal queen wearing a jeweled crown, with all of humanity nestled in her cape), I went outside my third spring in Orient and started to dig. I dug a garden along the back fence and a plot twenty feet by six in the lawn. I pulled onion grass for so many hours that when I closed my eyes at night I saw the white bulbs traveling through the earth like sperm. The sun warmed the back of my neck as my fingers reached into the damp earth like they were roots themselves. I stayed out in the rain. I kneeled in the mud; I didn't answer the phone. I had new deadlines: a bed to dig, seedlings to transplant, mulching, watering, feeding to do.

One day late that third spring, when the chestnut blossoms on the trees had already faded, I came in at sunset after a full day's gardening and stood at the bathroom sink to wash my hands. I glanced at my face in the mirror and noticed for the first time that it was next to Mary's face on the varnished print. It looked like we were standing next to each other. Mary wore a mysterious half-smile as her hand gently pointed to the red heart on her sky-blue dress; flames shot out the top (passion); a sword went right through it (pain); tears dripped down (sorrow); but beautiful pink roses made a ring around it, too (joy, celebration, beauty, grace, redemption).

That heart told a story like a novel. It was just like life: complicated, changing, never the same. And Mary was showing this to me. I started to weep and didn't know why. But I think it was from gratefulness. My heart wasn't feeling so cracked anymore. It was feeling like one of Mary's hearts: a sword had pierced it, but roses encircled it, too.

MARY CAPPELLO

Nothing to Confess

⌒⌒⌒

IN THE SAME ATTITUDE AND AROUND the same age in which I'd cut my curls, adaze and adoze before the TV set, I lay belly to rug with one hand down the front of my pedal pushers, the other twirling a stray coil of hair round and round my fingertips, when my mother happened upon me and said: "Mary! What are you doing? Have you ever seen me doing that?" I don't think I realized how ludicrous the question was until I was an adult. No, I hadn't ever seen Mom masturbating, but then masturbation was something one did in the self-enclosed, lambent space of television-gazing, and my mother rarely watched TV. My third-grade teacher, Sister Mary Conrad, spoke as though masturbation was only something men and boys, who were barbarians, did, and she'd rap each boy's hand while screeching disgustedly about his "sticky fingers." She had a special preoccupation with conjuring for us the image of female prostitutes—she'd ask us to picture their halter tops, miniskirts, and high-heeled shoes. Then, just as I was imagining riding off with them on the back of my motorcycle, a sound, like a cannon blast would issue from Sister's yardstick hitting the desk as she tried to convince us that if we ourselves wanted to join God and his heavenly angels in the next life, we would do best to wear our woolen school uniforms round the clock.

From about age eight to age sixteen, in those perilously "formative" years, when vampirism and werewolfism threaten to suit the face of one's emerging id just so, I was a supplicant at the altar of two major icons: the Blessed Virgin Mary and Batman and Robin. The figures who won my gaze were elaborately robed but mournful religious heroes, and stalwart men in tights, saviors in disguise, fairies.

Recently I rediscovered the three-volume gold Naugahyde-covered *Lives of the Saints* whose stories, names, and pictures gave shape to my childhood fantasies and fears. I shared with a friend some of the images that most obsessed me as a child: "Saint John in Boiling Oil": a naked John seated in a life-sized cauldron underscored by raging flames, turns his head to one side as a man with a pointed beard, pointed nose, pointed ears, pointed hair, and bulging buttocks pours a pot of hot oil on his head. "St. Engracia": in one hand she holds a spike—emblem of her torture—like a pencil; the other hand holds both of her breasts between the span of her thumb and pinky, while those same fingers press into the respective nipples. Her eyes roll heavenward; a translucent scarf like a death shroud dances around her neck. "The Devil and St. Wolfgang": the devil appears as a Martian (he's green), or, if you will, as a cross between a mammal and reptile (he has both hooves and scales, gills and lungs). Last but not least, a photograph, "the Severed Arm of St. Francis": mightily decayed flesh clings to the bones of what once were a living hand and forearm, now displayed in a specially shaped and specially lined casket made just for it. Though the art in the book was almost uniformly drawn from the oeuvre of accomplished painters—from Botticelli to Raphael, from El Greco to Velázquez—the images of the saints appear to me now as grotesque cartoons, and *The Lives of the Saints,* a comic book tabloid of bad art through the ages, an encyclopedia of suffering.

Talking with my friend about the television shows we consumed most heartily or dreamily as children, I mention that my mother forbade certain ones like *Gilligan's Island, The Brady Bunch,* and *The Partridge Family.* Though she did not censor TV outright, she made me feel that such shows were only amusing to the brain-dead, and to watch them was to enroll oneself willingly in the universal club of morons. *Star Trek,* I recall, was allowed because it resembled the parables of Jesus and *Lives of the Saints:* every episode had a moral. I don't recall my mother's assessment of *Batman and Robin.* That was a show that I seemed to indulge in secret, unbeknownst to all. To my friend who has just toured *The Lives of the Saints* with me, my story is absurd: "So you weren't allowed to watch *The Brady Bunch,* but this book was deemed appropriate for children?!"

Within the domain of faith, anything goes. The Confirmation ritual (one of the Seven Blessed Sacraments) trained me at age eight to think of myself as a transgressor. I whispered my sins into the priest's ear, but more important, I did penance for my sins, said my prayers, and asked forgiveness before the statue of the Blessed Virgin Mary. Mary stands, palms open to me, feet bared, body robed, head veiled, eyes sullen, in the left transept of our parish church—B.V.M.—so that if I stand in front of her, I can see the altar in a blurred periphery. I know that my head should bow in humility before this great woman, but I always find myself searching out her eyes. When I don't turn into a pillar of salt (my confusion of the act of curiosity with another biblical story), I continue to gaze. Her hands say I can come to her, her feet say she can get down and dirty, but her eyes report a mystery of sadness. None of the saints in this church ever smiles, and she is no exception. In fact, she's the model saint, the Saint of Saints.

Sometimes when I lift my unknowing eyes to her sad face, I read her sadness as a sign of the pity she feels for me for being yoked to her daughters' tutelage: the punishing Sisters of the Immaculate Heart. I think they are nothing like her, and I remark to myself even at this young age the contradictions between the way the sisters treat us—often via bodily harm—and the precepts of a faith based on forgiveness.

"Every day's a holiday with Mary," Dick Van Dyke had sung in a Disney musical I knew, and though he'd been singing of a real woman whom he loved, I applied the song to my Mary, the Blessed Virgin. The candles that were forever lit before her in our church led me to think of birthday parties, and I knew she was connected to a special, a "miraculous" birth. A consummation larger than life, one that did not require a man, marked her. And yet the celebration was tainted. On a walk to the candy store with my cousin, I whistle my heart out, until she tells me that, according to our grandmother Rose, "girls who whistle make the Blessed Mother cry." That the Blessed Mother *can't* cry, I always thought, was precisely the problem, or my problem with her statue. Her hurt remains as remote and as incurable (by me) as my mother's. The celebration is tainted because the real-life female followers of this woman lack significant power within the church. From a very young age I was aware of the nuns' diminished worth in the eyes of the church and in the eyes of their "brethren," the priests. The hierarchy was clear: the nuns punished us because the priests devalued them. But Mary again remained a mysterious alternative, and I couldn't believe that she cried when little girls whistled, that little tomboys made her sad.

There must be a link between prohibited sexuality and Catholicism because to be Catholic is to be defined by a coming-out story. Every ex-, lapsed, or still-practicing Catholic has one to tell, and I have seen such stories, however devoid of poetry, however banal, typically tinged with horror and humor, bind a group of strangers together like a charm. The Catholic coming-out story is characteristically one of humiliation and abjection; it is the storyteller's share in the cultivation of self-loathing and fear that his religious training bequeathed him. The Catholic coming-out story is equivalent to a sharing of stigmata: "Here's my wound, my battle scar, my badge," we seem to say. "Can you imagine that? Can you imagine I survived to tell the tale?"

It's the day after Halloween, All Saints' Day, a Catholic holy day, and I have gorged myself the preceding night with one too many Reese's Peanut Butter Cups. I'm in sixth grade, which means I am enduring the rite of passage through the disciplinary hoops of one of the harshest sisters, Sister Bernice. Sister Bernice has already drawn blood from me when, one day, making her rounds to inspect our math problems, she decides to poke the point of her pen into the top of my scalp in time with the rhythm of her sentence. Each jab is equivalent to a word: "I (jab) told (jab) you (jab) to (jab) write (jab) the (jab) problem (jab) out (jab) first (jab) before (jab) solving (jab) it (jab)."

"But I did, Sister! Here it is on the other page," and I show her through my crossed brow.

"Sorry," she says. "Sorry," and I remember bringing my hand to my head, and the horror and anger and fear when I see the blood from my head on my hands, the blood she has made me bleed. Wincing with pain, I cry silently as I continue to add the table of numbers on my page using the method she has taught me: "Six plus 7 equals 13, write the 3, carry the 1."

I didn't tell my mother because I was afraid she would complain, and I was convinced this would only make my life with Sister Bernice more miserable—she'd punish me more harshly for exposing her. I saw what happened when people's parents got involved—the child's life with Sister became a living hell. It was maybe one or two o'clock in the afternoon in Sister Bernice's class on All Saints' Day and she was going over a catechism lesson. I remember we were learning the words for the various church dignitaries, constituencies, and hierarchies. The pope was different from a bishop who was different from a cardinal who was different from a priest, and the range of their jurisdiction had separate names. I felt a sick, gassy, diarrhealike feeling, but I knew that lavatory time had already passed, and I knew we were expected "to go" only during designated times of the day. If you raised your hand in the middle of a lesson to ask to go (which I never, ever did), Sister would yell at or thrash you before letting you go, and sometimes she wouldn't let you go at all. Diarrhea doesn't allow for laborious decision making. Every now and then I looked in the direction of my best friend, and she looked back as if to say, "What? What is it?" I wanted to tell her how I felt, and to consult with her about whether I should ask to go to the bathroom, but before I knew it, all such agonizing was over and I had shit in spite of my best efforts at self-control. Horrified, I continued to pretend that nothing was wrong as Sister Bernice announced we should report to homeroom, pack our bags, and file into line for church. Today, a holy day, would be concluded with a visit to church. The stench emanating from the back of my wool uniform was unbearable; my homeroom classmates could smell it now, but the teacher distracted them from their search for the source by giving us instructions on the church service that was to follow.

Once in church, Sister Bernice somehow ended up sitting next to me. I could keep the smell under control so long as I didn't move, but moving from sitting to kneeling and from kneeling to standing unleashed a scent that "stunk to the high heavens," as Sister Mary Conrad used to say of marigolds. And with each movement, I looked either at Sister Bernice's face or at Eileen Hogan's, who sat on the other side of me. Eileen looked as though she wanted to vomit into her prayer book, but I could see that "Bernice," as we called her, had been more deeply affected. She looked woozy and gray, her senses were askew, the words of her prayer were a jumble, her ears hurt (she kept covering them). Every now and then, she would, wincingly, get out of the pew and walk a lap around the church. Secretly I thought I had achieved a small triumph, I had been getting back at her. I don't know what kept her from humiliating me further—she must not have been able to truly tell where the smell was coming from, and at the end of the longest church service of my life, I ran all the way home, crying all the way, home to my mother who showered and bathed me and helped me to feel less desperately alone.

I think that I came to believe after that incident that I had paid for the sin of overindulgence. It was the kind of warped stranglehold that Catholicism applied to desire. But Catholic ritual, its forms, its rhetorics, its images, visages, scents, and artifacts, its inability to console, even its punishing face *produced* sensuality and made certain powerful feelings emerge in bold relief. My teachers' presumably nondescript and generalized garb, for example, actually encouraged me to think more than I otherwise might about their bodies. I fantasized about the color of each sister's head of hair. Did her hair match her eyes? Was it long or short? Did she allow herself to see it for herself, or did she wear her veil round the clock? Did she stroke or comb it, or had she shaved her head bald? Later I discovered that truly beautiful women didn't need hair as a beautifying prop. This I learned when I saw on a talk show my heartthrob, Lynda Carter—who played (rather poorly, but who cared?) Wonder Woman in the TV series—in a guise that had her hair plastered to her head. Her face was so strong and purely gorgeous, I thought she didn't need a fancy hairstyle. Or maybe I could see her face now, just as I contemplated my sisters', because she had downplayed her hair. And the sisters' wimples made me wonder if it hurt their jaws to chew or talk; and a wisp of hair escaping from their veils onto their necks made me want to touch their necks; and the heavy cross that left an indentation on the part of their uniform that covered their breasts made me wish to lift the cross to kiss it. One nun had the habit of running her thumb and index finger inside the elastic cummerbund that was part of her uniform. Could I slip my hand inside and feel her stomach? Did her hand inside her waistband feel to her the way, on a winter's day, through a marble cold church service, I found my hands inside my muff?

No matter with what conviction I tell myself that I have left the precepts of Catholicism behind—for they were more harmful than helpful to me—Catholicism still asserts itself as the bedrock, perhaps the major tableau vivant of my desiring, and Christianity's visage seems ever to mediate my most intimate relationships with other people, and even my means of communicating with myself. It has left its indelible mark, and on some level I will never fully own the power and magic of its traces.

ROBERT A. ORSI

"Mildred, Is It Fun to Be a Cripple?"

∽∾∾

O<small>N THE FIRST SATURDAY OF EVERY</small> month in the 1960s my Uncle Sally, who has cerebral palsy, used to go to a different parish in New York City or its suburbs for mass and devotions in honor of Our Lady of Fatima and then afterward to a Communion breakfast sponsored by that month's host church. These special outings for "shut-ins" and "cripples" were organized by the Blue Army of Mary, an association of men and women dedicated to spreading the messages of apocalyptic anti-Communism and personal repentance delivered by Mary at Fatima in 1971. My uncle would be waiting for me and my father in the hallway of his mother's apartment, dressed in a jacket and tie and smoking cigarettes in a long, imitation tortoiseshell holder that my grandmother fitted between the knotted fingers of his left hand. He smoked by holding his hand stiff on the green leatherette armrest of his wheelchair, then bending his torso forward and bringing his legs up until his lips reached the burning cigarette. He was always afraid that my father wouldn't show up, and as his anxiety mounted my uncle clenched again and again over his cigarettes so that by the time we got there—always early—the foyer was dense with smoke.

We laid Sally down on his back on the front seat of the car. My grandmother, in an uncharacteristic moment of hope and trust, had taken my uncle as a boy to a mysterious doctor on the Lower East Side who said he could make him walk; instead, he had locked Sally's legs at the knees, sticking straight out in front of him, fusing him into a ninety-degree angle, and then had vanished. Sally reached back, hooked his right wrist into the steering wheel, and pulled himself in while we pushed. When he was in the car up to his legs, my father leaned in over him and drew him up. He angled my uncle's stiff limbs under the dashboard and wedged them in.

My father went around the car and dropped into the other side. He looked over at his brother-in-law, the two of them sweating and panting. "Okay?" he asked. My uncle nodded back.

We drove to a designated meeting place, usually another church's parking lot, where members of the Blue Army, wearing sky-blue armbands printed with an image of the Virgin of Fatima and the legend "Legion of Mary," helped us pull my uncle out of the car. Other cripples were arriving. The members of the Blue Army knew who wanted to sit next to each other, and they wheeled my uncle's friends over to him, locking them in place beside him. He greeted them solemnly, not saying very much. From here a big yellow school bus would take the cripples out to the church; we'd follow in the car. My uncle was anxious to get going.

The wheelers teased him in loud voices whenever they brought a woman over. "Here's your girlfriend!" they shouted. "I saw her talking to So-and-So yesterday! Aren't you jealous?! You're gonna lose this beautiful girl! Come on, Sal, wake up." They pounded my uncle on the back. "Don't you know a good thing when you got it?" Their voices and gestures were exaggerated, as if they were speaking to someone who couldn't understand their language.

The women rolled their heads back and laughed with bright, moaning sounds, while their mothers fussed at their open mouths with little embroidered handkerchiefs, dabbing at saliva. "Calm down, calm down," they admonished their daughters, "don't get so excited."

My uncle laughed too, but he always looked over at me and shook his head.

THERE WAS A STATUE OF San Rocco on a side altar of the Franciscan church of my childhood. The saint's body was covered with open, purple sores; tending to the bodies of plague victims, he had been infected himself. A small dog licked the sores on his hands. The Franciscans told us that St. Francis kissed a leper's sores; once he drank the water he had just used to bathe a leper.

ONE WOMAN, A REGULAR OF the First Saturday outings, came on a stretcher covered with clean sheets in pale pastel colors; her body was immobile. She twisted her eyes up and looked out at us through a mirror fixed to the side of the stretcher, while her mother tugged at her dress to make sure it stayed down around her thin ankles.

These were special people, God's children, chosen by him for a special destiny. Innocent victims, cheerful sufferers, God's most beloved—this was the litany of the handicapped on these First Saturdays. Finding themselves in front of an unusual congregation, priests were moved to say from the pulpit at mass that the prayers of cripples were more powerful than anyone else's because God listened most attentively to these, his special children. Nuns circulated among the cripples, touching their limbs kindly and reverently, telling them how blessed they were, and how wonderful. To be standing these mornings in a parking lot or church basement was to be on ground made holy by the presence of beds and wheelchairs and twisted bodies.

At breakfast, the mothers of the cripples hovered over them. They held plastic straws, bent in the middle like my uncle, while their children drank coffee or juice; they cut Danishes into bite-sized pieces; they cleaned up spills. Volunteers from the parish and members of the Blue Army brought out plates of eggs and sausage.

"You have such a big appetite this morning!"

"Can you eat all that? God bless you!"

"If I ate like you I'd be even fatter than I am!"

But why had God done this to his most beloved children? What kind of love was this? What kind of God?

When he was done with his coffee, my uncle cupped himself around his cigarette.

PHYSICAL DISTRESS OF ALL SORTS, from congenital conditions like cerebral palsy to the unexpected agonies of accidents and illness, was understood by American Catholics in the middle years of the twentieth century as an individual's main opportunity for spiritual growth. Pain purged and disciplined the ego, stripping it of pride and self-love; it disclosed the emptiness of the world. Without it, human beings remained pagans; in physical distress, they might find their way back to the Church, and to sanctity. "Suffering makes saints," one hospital chaplain told his congregation of sick people, "of many who in health were indifferent to the practices of their holy religion." Pain was a ladder to Heaven; the saints were unhappy unless they were in physical distress of some sort. Catholic nurses were encouraged to watch for opportunities on their rounds to help lapsed Catholics renew their faith and even to convert non-Catholics in the promising circumstances of physical distress.

Pain was always the thoughtful prescription of the Divine Physician. Thomas Dooley's cancer was celebrated in Catholic popular culture as a grace, a mark of divine favor. Dooley himself wrote, "God has been good to me. He has given me the most hideous, painful cancer at an extremely young age." So central was pain to the American Catholic ethos that devotional writers sometimes went so far as to equate it with life itself—"The good days are a respite," declared a laywoman writing in a devotional magazine in 1950, "granted to us so that we can endure the bad days."

Catholics thrilled to describe the body in pain. Devotional prose was generally overwrought, but on this subject it exceeded itself. A dying man is presented in a story in a 1937 issue of the devotional magazine *Ave Maria* as having "lain [for twenty-one years] on the broad of his back, suffering from arthritis . . . his hands and fingers so distorted that he could not raise them more than an inch . . . his teeth set . . . so physically handicapped that in summer he could not brush away a fly or mosquito from his face because of his condition." It was never enough in this aesthetic to say simply "cancer," stark as that word is; instead, it had to be the "cancer that is all pain." Wounds always "throbbed," suffering was always "untold," pain invariably took its victims to the very limits of endurance.

The body-in-pain was itself thrilling: flushed, feverish, and beautiful— "The sick room is rather a unique beauty shop," one priest mused, where "pain has worked more wonders than cosmetics"—it awaited its lover. A woman visiting a Catholic hospital in 1929 came upon a little Protestant girl who was dying and reported:

He has set His mark upon her. Somehow you guess; those frail little shoulders are shaped for a cross, those eyes are amber chalices deep enough for pain, that grave little courteous heart is big enough to hold Him! He will yet be her tremendous lover, drawing her gently into His white embrace, bestowing on her the sparkling, priceless pledge of His love—suffering.

This was a darkly erotic aesthetic of pain, one expression of the wider romanticism of American Catholicism in this period; but for all this culture's fascination with physical distress, the sensual pleasure it took in feverish descriptions of suffering, it was also deeply resentful and suspicious of sick persons—a nasty edge of retribution and revenge is evident in these accounts. In one priest's typical cautionary tale of pain, "a young woman of Dallas, Texas, a scandal to her friends for having given up her faith because it interfered with her sinful life, was severely burned in an explosion. Before her death, through the grace of God, she returned to the Church." According to a nursing sister, writing in the leading American Catholic journal for hospital professionals, *Hospital Progress,* in 1952: "Physical disability wears off the veneer of sophistication and forces the acceptance of reality. It is difficult for a patient imprisoned for weeks in a traction apparatus to live in a state of illusion." Pain gives people their comeuppance; it serves as chastisement and judgment.

As American Catholics interpreted an ancient tradition in their contemporary circumstances, the idea that sickness was punishment for something the sufferer had done took deeper hold. The more sentimental view of sickness as the training ground for saintliness was commonly reserved for people with congenital conditions, such as Sal and his friends; their suffering, at least, could not be attributed to any moral failure since they were born this way. The innocence of handicapped people made them central to the elaboration of the gothic romance of suffering; because they were "innocent," unalloyed spiritual pleasure could be taken in the brokenness of their bodies. There was a cult of the "shut-in" among American Catholics in the middle years of the twentieth century, a fascination with "cripples" and a desire to be in some relation to them, which was thought to carry spiritual advantages. In the summer of 1939, *Catholic Women's World,* one of the most modern and upbeat of the Catholic magazines, set up a pen-pal system so that readers going away on vacation could write to shut-ins about their trips; the project was so popular that "many readers have written to us requesting that we put them in touch not only with one, but as many as three or four shut-ins." There were a number of organizations dedicated to harnessing the spiritual power of shut-ins and putting it to work for the rest of the Church, such as the Catholic Union of the Sick in America (CUSA), which formed small cells of isolated handicapped persons who communicated through a round-robin letter and whose assignment was to direct their petitions, more powerful by virtue of their pain, toward some specific social good. The spiritual pleasure taken by the volunteers on the First Saturdays in their proximity to the handicapped was a reflection of this cult as well.

ONE SATURDAY THE BUS DIDN'T come. Something had happened somewhere along its route. The hot summer's morning dragged on; the sidewalk around Sal's chair was littered with cigarette butts; and the garbled messages—there'd been a crash, no, it was just a flat tire, he'll be here any minute, he's upstate—from the people in charge of the outing, meant to be reassuring, just made the confusion and anxiety worse.

A man I didn't recognize, not one of the Blue Army regulars, strolled over to the back of Sal's chair and gripped its rubber handles as if he were going to push my uncle off someplace. He winked at me and my father. Maybe Sal knew him from someplace. "So, Sal," he boomed at the back of my uncle's head, sounding pleased with his own cheerfulness, "looks like you're gonna have to spend the night in this parking lot, hunh?"

My uncle gave an angry wave of dismissal, but the man behind him, comfortably resting his weight on the chair, went on, "Hey, Sal, you hear what I said? You're gonna have to spend the night out here in the parking lot! I hope you got your blankets! Maybe we can get the girls over there to sing you a lullaby."

My uncle rocked himself from side to side in his seat, as if he wanted to dislodge the man's grip on his chair and move him out from behind his back. Bored with the game, the man let go. "Jesus, I hope we get the hell out of here soon," he said to my father, and walked away.

Sal smacked the brakes off his chair with his hard, calloused hands and began to spin himself around in circles. My father tried to calm him down. "Sally," he said, "the bus'll be here any minute, I know it. It's probably just a flat tire. Come on, don't get like this, you're gonna make yourself sick." But my uncle went on spinning. "Ahhhhhh," he roared, "ahhhhhh."

EVERYONE TEASED THE CRIPPLES, JOKED with them and needled them almost all the time; this may have been what the man behind Sal's chair was doing, but I don't think so. He was sweaty and angry. Maybe he was only there that morning because of his wife's devotion to Our Lady of Fatima; maybe he hated cripples and the stories they told about the human body, of all that could and did go wrong with it. He had bent forward over the back of Sally's head and stared down at his bald crown and coarse gray hair. Maybe he hated the way the cripples drooled when they sucked up their coffee and juice on these Saturday mornings, the mess they made of Communion breakfast.

My uncle began to push himself along the parking lot's chain-link fence, hitting the wheels of his chair with hard shoves; when he got to the end of the fence, where it connected with the church, he spun himself around and began pounding his way back.

Maybe the man found it hard to sustain the idea that Sal and his friends were holier than he was, closer to Heaven, when they sprayed him with saliva and bits of egg.

My uncle wheeled around again and started back along the fence.

"This is the only guy I know," my father said to me, "who can pace in a wheelchair."

Someone came over and demanded that Sal stop. "Control yourself! These things happen, Sal," she yelled at him, bending to lock his chair in place, but my uncle pushed her hand away and kept moving.

The morning wore on, and the fortunate unfortunates, disappointed and upset, got on everybody's nerves.

THERE WAS ONLY ONE OFFICIALLY sanctioned way to suffer even the most excruciating distress: with bright, upbeat, uncomplaining, submissive endurance. A woman dying horribly of an unspecified cancer was commended by *Ave Maria* for having written "cheerful newsy notes" home from the hospital, with "only casual references to her illness." In the spirit of a fashion editor, one devotional writer counseled the chronically ill to "learn to wear [your] sickness becomingly. It can be done. It has been done. Put a blue ribbon bow on your bedjacket and smile." Visitors were instructed to urge their sick friends and kin to make the best use of their time; the sick should be happily busy and productive even in the most extreme pain. "Only two percent of the various types of pain are permanent and continual," wrote Mary O'Connor in an *Ave Maria* article for the sick in 1951. She was onto their games; she knew they were likely to "wallow in the muck of self-pity or sympathy": "[I]f the sieges of pain let up a little now and then, take up an interesting hobby and throw yourself into it with all you've got. You'll be delighted to find that your pain is lessening as a result." Her own experience was exemplary in this regard: since the onset of her pain a decade earlier, she had written over two thousand poems, articles, and stories.

If such pitiless badgering failed to arouse the sick, against their sinful inclinations, to saintliness, there was always the scourge of the suffering of Jesus and Mary: no matter how severe your suffering, the sick were told, Jesus' and Mary's were worse, and *they* never complained. What is a migraine compared to the crown of thorns?

The language used against people in pain was harsh and cruel, devoid of compassion or understanding, and dismissive of their experience. As one priest demanded, if a child spends "seven or nine years" in an iron lung, "what of it?" There was only scorn, never sympathy, for the sick who failed to become saintly through pain. Bending the images and idioms of popular religion against them so that even the suffering Christ emerged as a reproach, devotional writers crafted a rhetoric of mortification and denial for the sick. This was particularly cruel since they were doing so in the language and venues of popular devotionalism, to which sick people customarily turned for spiritual and emotional comfort.

The consequence of this rhetoric was that pain itself—the awful, frightening reality of something going wrong in the body—disappeared. It was hidden behind the insistence that the sick be cheerful, productive, orderly; it was masked by the condescending assurances offered to the shut-in handicapped by those who were not that it was better to be a cripple; it was occluded by the shimmering, overheated prose, the excited fascination with physical torment, and the scorn and contempt for the sick. There is not nearly as much suffering in the world as people complain of, chided a writer in the pages of *Ave Maria*—two years after the end of the First World War. "I enjoyed my week with the lepers of Molokai," a traveler exclaimed as if he had not been sojourning among people he had just described as looking "more like corpses than human beings." Chronic illness brought families together in special joy and intimacy, according to these writers. Even Jesus' pain could be denied: lest they find in his Passion an expression of the reality of their own experience, the sick were occasionally reminded that, since he had been conceived without Original Sin, Jesus himself was never sick—the risk of Docetism apparently less troubling than that of compassion. It was in this spirit that William P. McCahill, executive secretary of the President's Committee on National Employ the Physically Handicapped Week, could report with approval a child's question to a handicapped person: "Mildred, is it fun to be a cripple?" Yes, it is! McCahill assured his readers.

Physical distress that had been thus purged of its everyday messiness, of the limitations it imposed on the body, and of the dreariness of its persistence could be transmuted into its opposite: "pain" became a "harvest" ripe for the gathering, a spiritual "powerhouse" that could light the church, a vein of gold to be mined, minted, and spent. "It isn't suffering that's the tragedy," one of CUSA's mottoes proclaims, "only wasted suffering."

Since all pain was God-sent and good, and since it was never in any case as bitter as weak, whining sick people made it out to be, there was no need to account for its place in the universe, to respond to the spiritual and intellectual distress it might have occasioned. Protestants required this, perhaps, but not Catholics, who knew that God sent pain always for a purpose; and priests, who might have been expected to sympathize most compassionately with the spiritual and physical dilemmas of the sick, were said to be always cheerful in the presence of suffering because, unlike their counterparts in other faiths, they knew that the problem of pain had been "solved." In any case, as American devotional writers reminded the sick, comprehensible suffering was not real suffering. Catholics were said to prefer to suffer humbly and submissively, in recognition of their own guilt, rather than attempting to lessen the sting of it through understanding. Only spoiled children required such reassurance.

"THEY HID US AWAY," MY uncle shouted at me one afternoon on the back porch of the home. He lifted himself off his chair by his elbows and rasped at me, "You don't know what it was like!"

We were in the middle of a conversation—an "interview," I was calling it— about Sal's favorite saints for a new project of mine when he began telling me how the families of his friends, ashamed of them, hid them away in back rooms so that their neighbors wouldn't see them. "We talk to each other about these things," Sal said over and over to me, and, "You don't know what I know."

My grandmother never hid Sal away. Before the operation on his knees, he used to crawl out of the apartment and slide down the building's steps on his rear end, then sit on the stoop watching over First Avenue. Later on, his brothers carried him downstairs or he would lean sideways out his bedroom window on a pillow. But not all the neighbors were comfortable with the sight of him. One crazy woman taunted my grandmother constantly about Sal. She called him "a diseased piece of meat." "May the doors of Calvary"— a cemetery in Queens—"close behind you," she screamed at my grand- mother on the street, announcing to the stoops and sidewalks that Sally was a judgment on his family.

"They left them alone all day in dark rooms. I know these things—they told me about them—you don't know."

Sal has always had many friends, male and female, all over the city, and he's had a number of extended, monogamous, romantic engagements over time, as have most of his acquaintances. Sal's closest friends belong to the United Cerebral Palsy Federation, which has a large, modern building on Twenty-third Street between Lexington and Park Avenues where Sal and the others go for classes and social events. This is where Sal said he'd heard stories of people being abandoned in back rooms, left all day without even water to drink.

"YOU CAN GET UP AND go get yourself a glass of water," Sally was saying to me in a tense, hoarse voice, "whenever you want. You can get up and walk out of here today, but I can't!" He waved his arm in the direction of the front door.

First the stories of friends hidden in back rooms, and now this; Sally had never been so angry with me before. In between his accusations and challenges my uncle took deep breaths and held himself rigidly against the back of his chair with his long arms, looking away from me, shaking his head.

A new holy figure had recently entered Sal's customary pantheon of saints: Blessed Margaret of Castello. Sal kept an image of her propped up on his messy, cluttered desk alongside holy cards of St. Francis and St. Anthony and pictures of his girlfriend, his nieces and nephews, and himself with various camp counselors and UCP staff. I'd never heard of her before or seen her image anywhere else. The holy card showed a small, bent figure leaning on a rough wooden staff; her eyes are closed, and her feet are turned in. A pamphlet from Margaret's shrine in Philadelphia describes her as "A PATRON OF THE UNWANTED . . . A SAINT FOR OUR TIMES . . . BLIND . . . CRIPPLED . . . HUNCHBACKED . . . DWARF."

Sal had heard about Margaret at one of the First Saturday gatherings he still attended occasionally; a Dominican priest talked to the group about her. "If she'd been born today," Sally said to me, "she'd 'a been an abortion." Margaret's father was Captain of the People of the Umbrian city-state of Metola; his thirteenth-century victory over the neighboring Republic of Gubbio had brought him great fame and wealth. The captain hoped that his first child would be a son to carry on the family's name and increase its glory, but his wife had given birth instead to a tiny girl, blind and horribly misshapen, in 1287. The bitterly disappointed couple hid the infant away in the castle, refusing even to give her a name. A gentle servingwoman called the baby "Margarita." The child was not only blind, but had a twisted foot and a hunchback; she was also a dwarf.

When Margaret was six years old, her father, terrified that the lively child would wander out of the castle's shadows and be seen by someone, to the disgrace of his name, had her walled up in a room. The child was fed through a small window. She remained in this cell for seven years, and it was here that Margaret, cheerful and forgiving even in these circumstances, according to her biographers, began experiencing Jesus' presence in an unusually vivid way. She fasted continually from the age of seven on and mortified her flesh by wearing a hairshirt to increase her discomfort in the cell, which was hot in the summer and freezing in the winter. (It was also here that Margaret, as an adolescent, began struggling with temptations against her purity, as most popular biographies of her say. Sally must have known about this, although he didn't mention it to me.)

When she was thirteen years old, Margaret was taken by her mother to the nearby town of Città di Castello and abandoned there in a church. Her devout vividly imagine the little girl groping her way along the cold walls of the sanctuary, calling out for her mother, with the church bell marking the hours of the day's passing as she gradually realizes what has happened to her. Margaret lived on the streets for a while, begging for her food, until the townspeople became aware of her sanctity and took her into their homes. She eventually entered a Dominican order of laywomen and died in 1320, when she was thirty-three years old.

"YOU KNOW WHAT I LIKE about her?" my uncle asked me at the end of the story. "I like it that there's somebody up there"—he glanced Heavenward—"like us."

Old Bronx joke: What did Washington say when he was crossing the Delaware? "Fá 'no cazzo di freddo qui!"

EACH OTHER

⌒⊶⌒

Evan Hunter

Streets of Gold

ⱦⱦⱦ

I'VE BEEN BLIND SINCE BIRTH. THIS means that much of what I am
about to tell you is based upon the subjective descriptions or faulty memories of others, blended with an empirical knowledge of my own—forty-eight years of touching, hearing, and smelling. But paintings, rooms with objects in them, lawns of bright green, crashing seascapes, contrails across the sky, the Empire State Building, women in lace, a Japanese fan, Rebecca's eyes—I have never seen any of these things. They come to me secondhand.

I sometimes believe, and I have no foundation of fact upon which to base this premise, that *all* experience is secondhand, anyway. Even my grandfather's arrival in America must have been colored beforehand by the things he had heard about this country, the things that had been described to him in Italy before he decided to come. Was he truly seeing the new land with his own eyes? Or was that first glimpse of the lady in the harbor—he has never mentioned her to me, I only assume that the first thing all arriving immigrants saw was the Statue of Liberty—was that initial sighting his *own,* or was there a sculptured image already in his head, chiseled there by Pietro Bardoni in his expensive American clothes, enthusiastically selling the land of opportunities where gold was in the streets to be picked up by any man willing to work, himself talced and splendored evidence of the riches to be mined.

The villagers of Fiormonte, in the fifth year of their misery since *la fillossera* struck the grape, must have listened in awestruck wonder as Bardoni used his hands and his deep Italian baritone voice to describe New York, with its magnificent buildings and esplanades, food to be had for pennies a day (food!), and gold in the streets, gold to shovel up with your own two hands. He was speaking figuratively, of course. My grandfather later told me no one believed there was *really* gold in the streets, not gold to be mined, at least. The translation they made was that the streets were *paved* with gold; they had, some of them, been to Pompeii—or most certainly to Naples, which lay only 125 kilometers due west—and they knew of the treasures of ancient Rome, knew that the statues had been covered with gold leaf, knew that even common hairpins had been fashioned of gold, so why not streets paved with gold in a nation that surely rivaled the Roman Empire so far as riches were concerned? It was entirely conceivable. Besides, when a man is starving, he is willing to believe anything that costs him nothing.

Geography is not one of my strongest subjects. I have been to Italy many times, the last time in 1970, on a joint pilgrimage—to visit the town where my grandfather was born and to visit the grave where my brother is buried. I know that Italy is shaped like a boot; I have traced its outline often enough on Braille maps. And I know what a boot looks like. That is to say, I have lingeringly passed my hands over the configurations of a boot, and I have formed an image of it inside my head, tactile, reinforced by the rich scent of the leather and the tiny squeaking sounds it made when I tested the flexibility of this thing I held, this object to be cataloged in my brain file along with hundreds and thousands of other objects I had never seen—and will never see. The way to madness is entering the echo chamber that repeatedly resonates with doubt: is the image in my mind the *true* image? Or am I feeling the elephant's trunk and believing it looks like a snake? And anyway, what does a snake look like? I believe I know. I am never quite sure. I am not quite sure of anything I describe because there is no basis for comparison, except in the fantasy catalog of my mind's eye. I am not even sure what I myself look like.

Rebecca once told me, "You just miss looking dignified, Ike."

And a woman I met in Los Angeles said, "You just miss looking shabby."

Rebecca's words were spoken in anger. The Los Angeles lady, I suppose, was putting me down—though God knows why she felt any need to denigrate a blind man, who would seem vulnerable enough to even the mildest form of attack and therefore hardly a worthy victim. We later went to bed together in a Malibu motel-cum-Chinese restaurant, where the aftertaste of moo goo gai pan blended with the scent of her perfumed breasts and the waves of the Pacific crashed in against the pilings and shook the room and shook the bed. She wore a tiny gold cross around her neck, a gift from a former lover; she would not take it off.

For the record (who's counting?), my eyes are blue. I am told. But what is blue? Blue is the color of the sky. Yes, but *what* is blue? It is a cool color. Ah, yes, we are getting closer. The radiators in the apartment we lived in on 120th Street were usually cool if not downright frigid. Were the radiators blue? But sometimes they became sizzling hot, and red has been described to me as a hot color, so were the radiators red when they got hot? Rebecca has red hair and green eyes. Green is a cool color also. Are green and blue identical? If not, how do they differ? I know the smell of a banana, and I know the shape of it, but when it was described to me as yellow, I had no concept of yellow, could form no clear color image. The sun is yellow, I was told. But the sun is hot; doesn't that make it red? No, yellow is a much cooler color. Oh. Then is it like blue? Impossible. The only color I know is black. I do not have to have that described to me. It sits behind my dead blue eyes.

My hair is blond. Yellow, they say. Like a banana. (Forget it.) I can only imagine that centuries back, a Milanese merchant (must have been a Milanese, don't you think? it couldn't have been a *Viking*) wandered down into southern Italy and displayed his silks and brocades to the gathered wide-eyed peasants, perhaps hawking a bit more than his cloth, Milanese privates securely and bulgingly contained in northern codpiece; the girls must have giggled. And one of them, dark-eyed, black-haired, heavily breasted, short and squat, perhaps later wandered off behind the grapes with this tall, handsome northern con man, where he lifted her skirts, yanked down her knickers, explored the black and hairy bush promised by her armpits, and probed with northern vigor the southern ripeness of her quim, thereupon planting within her a few thousand blond, blue-eyed (blind?) genes that blossomed centuries later in the form of yours truly, Dwight Jamison.

My maiden name is Ignazio Silvio Di Palermo.

Di Palermo means *of* Palermo or *from* Palermo, which is where my father's ancestors worked and died. All except my father's father, who came to America to dig out some of the gold in them thar streets, and ended up as a street cleaner instead, pushing his cart and shoveling up the golden nuggets dropped by horses pulling streetcars along First Avenue. Ironically, he was eventually run over by a streetcar. It was said he was drunk at the time, but a man who comes to shovel gold and ends up shoveling shit is entitled to a drink or two every now and then. I never met the man. He was killed long before I was born. The grandfather I speak of in these pages was my mother's father. From my father's father, I inherited only my name, identical to his, Ignazio Silvio Di Palermo. Or, if you prefer, Dwight Jamison.

My father's name is Jimmy, actually Giacomo, which means James in Italian; are you getting the drift? Jamison, James's son. That's where I got the last name when I changed it legally in 1955. The first name I got from Dwight D. Eisenhower, who became president of these United States in 1953. The Dwight isn't as far-fetched as it may seem at first blush. I have never been called Ignazio by anyone but my grandfather. As a child, I was called Iggie. When I first began playing piano professionally, I called myself Blind Ike. My father liked the final name I picked for myself, Dwight Jamison. When I told him I was planning to change my name, he came up with a long list of his own, each name carefully and beautifully hand lettered, even though he realized I would not be able to see his handiwork. He was no stranger to name changes. When he had his own band back in the 1920s, 1930s, and 1940s, he called himself Jimmy Palmer.

There is in America the persistent suspicion that if a person changes his name, he is most certainly a wanted desperado. And nowhere is there greater suspicion of, or outright animosity for, the name-changers than among those who steadfastly *refuse* to change their names. Meet a Lipschitz or a Mangiacavallo, a Schliephake or a Trzebiatowski who have stood by those hot ancestral guns, and they will immediately consider the name-changer a deserter at best or a traitor at worst. I say fuck you, Mr Trzebiatowski. Better you should change it to Trevor. Or better you should mind your own business.

For reasons I can never fathom, the fact that I've changed my name is of more fascination to anyone who's ever interviewed me (I am too modest to call myself famous, but whenever I play someplace, it's a matter of at least some interest, and if you don't know who I am, what can I tell you?)—a subject more infinitely fascinating than the fact that I'm a blind man who happens to be the best jazz pianist who ever lived, he said modestly and self-effacingly, and not without a touch of shabby dignity. No one ever asks me how it feels to be blind. I would be happy to tell them. I am an expert on being blind. But always, without fail, The Name.

"How did you happen upon the name Dwight Jamison?"

"Well, actually, I wanted to use another name, but someone already had it."

"Ah, yes? What *was* the other name?"

"Groucho Marx."

The faint uncertain smile (I can sense it, but not see it), the moment where the interviewer considers the possibility that this wop entertainer—talented, yes, but only a wop, and only an entertainer—may somehow be blessed with a sense of humor. But is it possible he really considered calling himself Groucho Marx?

"No, seriously, Ike, tell me"—the voice confidential now—"*why* did you decide on Dwight Jamison?"

"It had good texture. Like an augmented eleventh."

"Oh. I see, I see. And what is your *real* name?"

"My real name has been Dwight Jamison since 1955. That's a long, long time."

"Yes, yes, of course, but what is your *real* name?" (Never "was," notice. In America, you can never lose your real name. It "is" always your real name.) "What is your real name? The name you were born with?"

"Friend," I say, "I was born with yellow hair and blue eyes that cannot see. Why is it of any interest to you that my real name was Ignazio Silvio Di Palermo?"

"Ah, yes, yes. Would you spell that for me, please?"

I changed my name because I no longer wished to belong to that great brotherhood of *compaesani* whose sole occupation seemed to be searching out names ending in vowels. (Old Bronx joke: What did Washington say when he was crossing the Delaware? *"Fá 'no cazzo di freddo qui!"* And what did his boatman reply? *"Pure tu sei italiano?"* Translated freely, Washington purportedly said, "Fucking-A cold around here," and his boatman replied, *"You're* Italian, too?") My mother always told me I was a Yankee, her definition of Yankee being a third-generation American, her arithmetic bolstered by the undeniable fact that *her* mother (but not her father) was born here, and she herself was born here, and I was certainly born here, ergo Ignazio Silvio Di Palermo, third-generation Yankee Doodle Dandy. My mother was always quick to remind me that *she* was American. "I'm American, don't forget." How *could* I forget, Mama darling, when you told me three and four times a day? "I'm American, don't forget."

In Sicily, where I went to find my brother's grave, your first son's grave, Mom, the cabdriver told me how good things were in Italy these days, and then he said to me, "America is *here* now."

Maybe it *is* there.

One thing I'm sure of.

It isn't *here*.

And maybe it never was.

Joseph Tusiani

Antonin Scalia

❦

ASSOCIATE JUSTICE, U.S. SUPREME COURT

Allow my vision not to see in you
Astraea with a pair of scales in hand
or crowned with stars above man's iron age.
Rightly, so long as golden times endured,
she dwelt on earth with lavish gifts of grace,
but sped immortal to immortal light
as soon as men to other men made war.
If I see less in you, then I see more—
a multitude of laborers that land,
lonesome and longing, on a dreamed-of shore
where soon bread turns into affright and woe;
but on they tread from mine to railroad, on
from tunnel to skyscraper, weary, wan,
yet dauntless still through decades of despair;
and when all spit upon them with contempt
and all their hopes are dashed against the sky
and, far from their ignoring native land,
they are ignored and jailed and lashed and lynched
where liberty and justice should be one,
oh, with no weeping (tears have long been shed)
and without talking (words have not been learned)
they stare into the future, not yet theirs,
and see one of them there, one of them there,
where now you sit, Sir, speaking for them all.

HELEN BAROLINI

How I Learned to Speak Italian

He was a patient man. His sloping shoulders curved with a bearing that spoke more of resistance and steadfastness than of resignation; his ruffled hair was graying, his eyes were mild and gray behind the glasses that were the badge of his work—he set type and proofread for *La Gazzetta*. It was because of his job at that weekly Italian-language newspaper in Syracuse that I met Mr. de Mascoli. In my last year at the university I determined it wasn't Spanish that interested me, after all, but Italian. However, at that point I couldn't switch my language requirement; I would have to keep Spanish and do Italian on my own. I went to the *Gazzetta* to put in a want ad for a tutor. Instead I found Mr. de Mascoli willing to teach me.

And why Italian? Because during that last year before graduation I had met an Italian student who had come over on a Fulbright grant to study at Syracuse University. Knowing him awakened in me unsuspected longings for that Mediterranean world of his which I suddenly, belatedly, realized could also be mine. I became conscious of an Italian background that had been left deliberately vague and in abeyance by my parents who, though children of Italian immigrants, had so homogenized into standard American that their only trace of identity was an Italian surname, often misspelled and always mispronounced.

I knew nothing of Italian. It was not a popular subject at home. We had just come out of World War II in which Italy had been our enemy, and my father was at once scornful and touchy about Italy's role in that conflict. And even before that we had never been part of the Italian community of the North Side, my parents having selected their first, then second, homes on

James Street, a thoroughfare of great mansions receding eastward into large, comfortable homes, then more modest two-families until, finally, it became the commercial area of Eastwood. I would not learn until recently that I had grown up on the street named for Henry James's grandfather, an early developer of the barren tracts from which Syracuse grew and from which Henry enjoyed his income.

My parents' aspirations were away from the old Italian neighborhoods and into something better. My father made a significant leap into the American mainstream when he became a member of both the Rotary Club and the Syracuse Yacht and Country Club where he and my mother golfed and I spent aimless summers.

It never occurred to my father to speak his own father's language to my two brothers or to me, and so we grew up never conversing with our only two living grandparents, my father's father and my mother's mother, and so never knowing them. My grandfather came to call each Christmas, my father's birthday; he sat uneasily in the sunroom with his overcoat on, took the shot of Scotch he was offered, and addressed the same phrase to me each year: "Youa gooda gehl?" Then he'd hand me a nickel. There was a feeling of strain in the performance. My father was a man of substance, his was not.

With my grandmother there was a brief ritual phrase in her dialect mouthed by us children when we went to the old Queen Anne–style house in Utica where my mother and all her brothers and sisters grew up. My grandmother was always in the kitchen, dressed in black, standing at a large black coal range stirring soup or something. My brothers and I, awkward in the presence of her foreignness, would be pushed in her direction by our mother during those holiday visits, and told "Go say hello to Gramma."

We'd go to the strange old woman who didn't look like any of the grandmothers of our friends or like any of those on the covers of *Saturday Evening Post* around Thanksgiving time. Gramma didn't stuff a turkey or make candied sweet potatoes and pumpkin pies. She made chicken soup filled with tiny pale meatballs and a bitter green she grew in her backyard along with broad beans and basil, things that were definitely un-American in those days. Her smell was like that of the cedar closet in our attic. She spoke strange words with a raspy sound.

When we stepped into her kitchen to greet he she smiled broadly and tweaked our cheeks. We said in a rush the phrase our mother taught us. We didn't know what it meant. I think we never asked. And if we were to know it meant "how are you?" what difference would it have made? What further knowledge would we have had of the old woman in the shapeless black garment, with her wisps of gray hair falling out of the thick knob crammed with large old-fashioned tortoiseshell hairpins? None. We were strangers.

When, on a visit upstate I had occasion to drive through Cazenovia, a village on the shores of Lake Cazenovia, it appeared to me as if in a dream. I saw again the lakeshore meadow that has always remained indelibly imprinted on my mind from childhood, but which I had thought must, by now, have vanished from the real world. That meadow, now called Gypsy Bay Park, was the site of family picnics to which we and Aunt Mary's family proceeded from Syracuse, while the other contingent (which was by far the greater number—my mother's three brothers, two other sisters and all their families plus our grandmother) came from Utica. Cazenovia was the approximate halfway point, and there in the meadow on the lake the cars would all pull up and baskets of food would be unloaded for the great summer reunion.

My father drove a car that had a front fold-up seat which I was allowed to stand at and hold on to while looking straight out the window at the roadway, pretending that I was the driver guiding us all to the lake. I always made it, and the weather was always fine.

And so we met in a landscape which, today, I would never have expected to glimpse again in its original state. Whenever, over the years, I would think back to the picnics in Cazenovia, I would imagine the locale filled with new housing developments or fast-food chains on the lakeshore. But no, the meadow was still green with grass, still fringed with trees bending toward the water, still free of picnic tables, barbecue grills on metal stands, and overflowing trash cans. It was the same as when I was five years old and the gathering took on the mythic quality that it still retains for me.

It was Gramma who had decreed this annual outing. When two of her daughters married and moved from Utica, she had made known her wish: that the family should meet each summer when travel was easier and eat together *al fresco*. It was her pleasure to have all her children, and their children, convene in the meadow, and spend the day eating, singing, playing cards, gossiping, throwing ball, making jokes and toasts. It was a celebration of her progeny of which she, long widowed, was the visible head, the venerable ancestor, the symbol of the strong-willed adventurer who had come from the Old World to make a new life and to prosper.

She was monumental. I can see her still, an imposing figure, still dressed in black although it was summer, seated on a folding camp chair (just for her) under the shade of a large, leafy elm tree. She sat there as silently as a

Sioux chief and was served food, given babies to kiss, and paid homage to all day. The others spread around her, sitting on blankets on the grass, or on the running boards of their Oldsmobiles and Buicks. What made my grand-mother so intriguing was the mystery of her. For, despite its gaiety, the family picnic was also a time of puzzlement for me. Who was this stranger in black with whom I could not speak? What was her story? What did she know?

What I knew of my grandmother, I heard from my mother: she believed in good food on the table and good linen on the bed. Everything else was frip-peries and she had the greatest scorn for those who dieted or got their nour-ishment through pills and potions. She knew you are what you eat and she loved America for the great range of foods that it provided to people like her, used to so little, used to making do. She could not tolerate stinginess; she lived with her eldest son and his family of eleven and did all the gardening and cooking, providing a generous table.

She founded the family well-being on food. She had gotten up early, baked bread, or used the dough for a crusty white pizza sprinkled with oil, oregano, and red pepper or with onions and potatoes, olives and anchovies—but never with tomato sauce for that disguised the taste of good bread dough and made it soggy and soft. She provided these pizzas, or *panini,* to the mill workers whose wives were too lazy or too improvident to do it themselves. She kept the men's orders all in her mind; she had great powers of concentration and her memory took the place of jotted-down notes. She never got an order wrong. From workers' lunches, she expanded into a small grocery store. Soon she was importing foodstuffs from Italy. Eventually, what she turned over to her sons was one of the largest wholesale food companies in central New York.

At those picnics my cousins were older than I, mostly young people in their teens and twenties. The boys wore knickerbockers and played banjos or ukeleles and the girls wore white stockings and sleeveless frocks. My uncles played cards and joked among themselves; the women arranged and served endless platters of food. Somebody was always taking snapshots, and I have many of them in a large album that has survived a dozen moves.

My grandmother stayed regally under her tree like a tribal queen, and mounds of food were placed around her like offerings. Her daughters and daughters-in-law kept up a steady parade of passing the foods they had been preparing all week: fried chicken, salames, prosciutto, roasted sweet pep-pers, fresh tomatoes sliced with mozzarella and basil, eggplant fritters, *zuc-chini imbottiti,* platters of corn, huge tubs of fresh salad greens, caciotto cheese, rounds of fresh, crusty bread, every kind of fruit, and biscotti galore. It was as if my grandmother's Thanksgiving took place not in bleak November, but on a summer day when there would be sun on her shoulders, flowers blooming and cool breezes off the lake, blue skies above and the produce of her backyard garden abundantly present. She lived with the memory of the picnic through the long upstate winter and by the time spring had come, she would go out to plant the salad greens and put in the stakes for the broad beans and tomatoes, planting and planning for the coming picnic.

We were about fifty kin gathered in that meadow, living proof of the family progress. Gramma's sons and daughters vied to offer her their services, goods, and offspring—all that food, those cars, the well-dressed young men who would go to college. And Butch, an older cousin, would take me by the hand to the water's edge and I'd be allowed to wade in Cazenovia's waters which were always tingling cold and made me squeal with delicious shock.

And yet with all that, for all the good times and good food and the happy chattering people who fussed over me and my brothers, I still felt a sense of strangeness, a sense of my parents' tolerating with an edge of disdain this old world *festa* only for the sake of the old lady. When I asked my mother why Gramma looked so strange and never spoke to us, I was told, she came from the old country . . . she doesn't speak our language. She might as well have been from Mars.

I never remember hearing our own mother speak to her mother, although she must have, however briefly. I only recall my astonishment at mother's grief when Gramma died and we went to Utica for the funeral. How could mother really feel so bad about someone she had never really talked to? Was it just because she was expected to cry? Or was she crying for the silence that had lain like a chasm between them?

Mother was a smartly dressed, very American lady, who played golf and bridge and went to dances. She seemed to us to have nothing to do with the old woman in a kitchen where, at one time, a dozen and more people had sat around the long, linoleum-covered table. Nor did my father, with his downtown meetings and busy manner seem to have any connection with his own father, who was called the Old Man and wore baggy pants and shuffled like a movie comedian.

There was no reason for me or my brothers to think, as we were growing up, that we were missing anything by not speaking Italian. We knew that our father spoke it, because at Christmas when the Old Man came to call, we'd overhear long streams of it and laugh at the queerness of it in our home. My mother, no, could never have been said to speak or know Italian, only some dialect phrases. But in my father reposed the tongue of his fathers; and it hadn't been important to him (or to us) that we have it.

Once, in my convent school history class, Sister Matilda asked me to pronounce Marconi's first name for her. I should know, she said, because I was Italian. No, I don't know, I answered proudly (even though I could correctly picture it, written out, in my mind). I was not Italian, I was American. And I flushed with shame at the nun's having singled me out like that.

What had I to do with Marconi or Mussolini or any of those funny types I'd see on the North Side the few times I accompanied my mother there for shopping? We didn't speak or eat Italian at home with the exception of the loaf of Italian bread my father brought home every day from the Columbus Bakery. Occasionally my mother would prepare an Italian dinner for her mostly Irish friends and then she'd have to go to the North Side where the Italians lived and had their own pungent grocery stores to find the pasta or the imported cheese and oil she needed. I hated to accompany her; the smell from barrels of dried and salted *baccalà* or of ripe provolone hanging by cords from the ceiling was as great an affront to my nose as the sound of the raspy Italian dialect spoken in the store was to my ears. That it all seemed crude and degrading was something I had absorbed from my parents in their zeal to advance themselves. It was the rather touching snobbery of second-generation Italian Americans toward those who were, in their view, "just off the boat."

But it was on the North Side that the *Gazzetta* offices were located, so I had to go there. And there I met Mr. de Mascoli. I could have grown up in Syracuse and lived there all my life without ever knowing that the *Gazzetta* existed. It took the Italian student to make me aware of the Italian paper, the beauty of Italian, and a lot of other things, too.

My father, as a Rotary project, had invited the Italian student (and a Colombian and a Venezuelan, also) home for Thanksgiving dinner to give them a taste of real America. What happened during that curious cultural exchange was not so much a forging of ties with America for the Italian and the South Americans, as an awareness in myself of my own Latin bloodline and a longing to see from where and what I originated. At Thanksgiving dinner it wasn't pilgrims and Plymouth I thought of but Catullus. The Latin poets I read in my college courses connected to the Italian student who was already a *dottore* from an Italian university and was saying things in a sharply funny, ironic way—a way no American spoke. It was strange that my awakening came at an all-American celebration through the medium of a tall, lean-faced student of forestry who was relating to my father in good English his experience during the war as an interpreter for the British troops pushing up through the Gothic Line to Florence.

Florence! I had never given thought to that fabled place, but in that instant

I longed to see it. In my immediate conversion, I who knew nothing of Italy or Italians, not even how to pronounce Marconi's first name, became aligned forever to the Italianness that had lain unplumbed and inert in me. My die was cast, over crammed turkey *gigante,* Yankee creamed onions and Hubbard squash, across from parents who would have been horrified to know it.

I was attracted to the Italian student, and he to me. When we started seeing each other, he was critical of my not knowing his language. "I know French and Spanish," I said. He was not impressed.

"Your language should have been Italian," he said sternly.

"I've had Latin, so it shouldn't be so hard to learn," I replied.

"Try this." He handed me his copy of the *Gazzetta.* It was the first time I had seen the paper, seen Italian. I couldn't make any sense of unfamiliar formations like *gli* and *sgombero,* the double zs and the verb endings. I was filled with dismay, but I decided to learn and I thought it could be done easily, right at home. After all, my father knew Italian.

"No use in learning a language like that," my father said dismissively when I approached him. "Spanish is more useful. Even Portuguese will get you further than Italian."

Further where? Toward the foreign service in Brazil? But that was not my direction.

Learning Italian became something stronger than just pleasing the Italian student. I began to recall things like my mother saying that just before her death Gramma had called for a sip of the mountain spring water near her Calabrian village. That was her last wish, her last memory; she had left Calabria at the age of seventeen with a husband of almost forty and had never gone back. But sixty years later as she lay dying in Utica it was only the water of her native hills that she wanted and called for.

I wanted to go see where she came from. I wanted to be able to talk to the Old Man who still came each Christmas, and to tell him who I really was besides a gooda gehl and to find out who he was.

I went deliberately to the *Gazzetta* on the North Side to find an Italian teacher rather than to the university's Italian department because, when I called the department, I was answered by a professor who said, giving his name twice, "Pah-chay or Pace speaking." As if one could choose between the Italian name and the anglicized version. For me, even then, there was only one way he could have said his name and if he didn't understand that, he was not the teacher I wanted. Mr. de Mascoli was.

He was like Pinocchio's stepfather, a gentle Geppetto. And he was genuinely pleased that I should want to learn Italian. He would give me lessons in his home each evening after supper, he said. He wanted no payment. He had come from the hard, mountainous, central part of Italy called the Abruzzo. He arrived in America in the late 1920s, not as an illiterate laborer, but as an idealist, a political emigré out of sympathy with the fascist regime. And he had been educated. He had a profound love for his homeland, and it was that love which made him want to give me its language.

I accepted his offer. And I thought of all the fine things I would send him in return when I got to Italy—the finest olive oil and parmesan cheese for his wife; the nougat candy called *torrone* for his children; and for him an elegantly bound volume of Dante. I would send him copies of Italian newspapers and magazines because he had told me confidentially that, yes, *La Gazzetta* was really the *porcheria* everyone said it was. But bad as it was, it kept the language alive among the people on the North Side. When it was gone, what would they have?

I went to Mr. de Mascoli's home each night in the faded old Chevy my father had passed on to me for getting to the university. The first night I arrived for my lessons I wore a full-skirted, almost ankle-length black watch tartan skirt my father had brought me from a trip to Chicago. It was topped by a wasp-waisted buttoned-to-the-neck lime green jacket. It was the New Look that Dior had just introduced to signal the end of wartime restrictions on fabric and style and I felt very elegant, then too elegant as Mr. de Mascoli led me down a hall to his kitchen. We sat at the table in the clean white kitchen which showed no sign of the meal he and his wife and children had just eaten. Mrs. de Mascoli, a short, pudgy, youngish woman, made a brief appearance and greeted me cordially. I could hear she was American, but had neither the education nor the ascetic and dedicated air of her husband. She spoke the kind of rough-hewn English one heard on the North Side. In her simple, friendly way she, too, was pleased that I was coming for Italian lessons.

In their clean white kitchen I spent a whole winter conjugating verbs, learning the impure s and the polite form of address. I began to speak Mr. de Mascoli's native language. I learned with a startled discomfit that my surname had a meaning and could be declined. *Mollica* was not only a family name but a noun of the feminine gender meaning crumb, or the soft inner part of the loaf as distinct from the good, hard outer crust. The name had always been a bane to me since teachers, salesgirls, or camp counselors were never able to say it. I would always have to repeat it and spell it as they stuttered and stumbled, mangling and mouthing it in ludicrous ways. It was my cross, and then I learned it meant crumb.

I began to fantasize: what if, like the draught that changed Alice's size, I could find a DRINK ME! that would switch me from a hard-to-pronounce crumb to something fine like Miller? Daisy Miller, Maud Miller. Even Henry. I'd be a different person immediately. In fact, for the first time I'd be a person in my own right, not just a target for discriminatory labels and jokes.

From years of Latin I could see how my name was related to all those words meaning "soft": *mollify, mollescent* (the down side of tumescent), *mollusk.* (A moll, as in Moll Flanders, was something else!)

The Italian minces no meanings: *mollare,* the verb, means to slacken; from that, the adjective *molle* means not only soft or limber, but flabby, pliant, even wanton. From *molle* comes *mollica,* and then, *mollizia,* that intriguing word meaning effeminancy and suggesting its counterpart, *malizia,* which signifies cunning malice. But I was marked from the start by softness not cunning.

My mother could have been Mrs. Mollifiable, so thoroughly had she taken on the meaning of her married name. Her maiden name, Cardamone, derived either from an Eastern spice plant called *kardamon* in Greek (the Calabria of her family origins had been the ancient Greek dominated Magna Graecia), or from one who cards wool, and, if this last, in Italian one who is a carder is a tease (a "card"?) and, worse, a backbiter. This meaning derives from the Latin *cardus,* thistle, whose prickles were used to card wool; then, figuratively, the meaning extends to include the prickles of a verbal barb, as in bad-mouthing. Which might have given my mother a certain luster that her soft Mollica weepiness did not.

And what must have been the lewd cracks my father was party to with a name from which so many allusions to soft and limp could be made?

A molleton, or *molletone* in Italian, is literally a swanskin, or a soft skin. Is this, I asked myself, why I was so hyper-sensitive, and thin-skinned? Because I came from a genetic line that was so incongruously delicate among the smoldering emotions of south Italy that they became identified forever after by a surname that told all? Were my forebears a soft touch, too soft for their own good in a place where basic fiber and guts would have been more pressingly urgent than skin like a swan?

What if I had been not Miss Softbread but, say, Sally Smith of the hard edge, a name evoking the manly English smithy at his forge with all the honorable tradition and advantage *that* entailed? How my life might have advanced! I wondered about translating my name to Krumm; being female had an advantage—I could marry a right-sounding name. But then I'd have to abandon my Italian lessons and the plan to go to Italy and the Italian student.

I continued my lessons. At home I practiced singing in Italian with my opera records as I followed words in the *libretti*. In the high-flown phrases of operatic lingo I began to form myself a language as remote as could be from my grandmother's dialect on the North Side, but, I thought with satisfaction, very grand and eloquent.

"Ardo per voi, forestier innamorato," I sang in the sunroom along with Ezio Pinza. *"Ma perchè così straziarmi,"* I said to Mr. de Mascoli one night, right out of Rossini's *Mosè*, when he plied me with verbs. Or, rhetorically, *"O! Qual portento è questo?"* I expressed no everyday thought but something compounded of extreme yearning, sacrifice, tribulation or joy. In the speech of grand opera everything becomes grander, and I felt so, too, as I sang all the roles. It was as if I were learning Elizabethan or Chaucerian English to visit contemporary London as I memorized my lines preparatory to leaving for Italy. I had worked and saved for a year to get there.

When I went to say good-bye to Mr. de Mascoli, he seemed sad and stooped. We had often spoken of the harshness many Italians had suffered in their own land and how they had had to emigrate, leaving with nothing, not even a proper language to bolster them. I told him I would write to him in Italian and send him news of his country. He said, "My country is a poor and beautiful place. I do not hate her."

"And I never will!" I answered.

I went to Italy thinking to rejoin the Italian student, who had already returned to his country, but that is another story: he turned out to have always been married. It wasn't the end of the world for me. I was in Italy and everything else was just beginning.

I studied in Perugia, I wrote articles for the Syracuse *Herald-Journal*, I saw Italy. I surpassed my initial Italian lessons and acquired a Veneto accent when I met and married Italian poet and journalist Antonio Barolini. He had courted me reading from a book of his poetry that included an ode to Catullus with the lovely lines (to be put on my grave marker): *ora la fanciulla è sogno, sogno il poeta e l'amore*. . . . Thus I acquired another Italian surname. Like the wine? some people inquire at introductions. Yes, I say even though they're confusing me with Bardolino. But having been born bread, I like that union with wine.

We lived some years in Italy before Antonio was sent to New York as the U.S. correspondent for *La Stampa*. We found a house outside the city and it was there, finally, that I thought again of Mr. de Mascoli. The unlikely link to the printer was a May Day pageant given at my children's country day school. As the children frolicked on the lush green lawn, they sang a medley of spring songs, ending with an English May Day carol whose refrain was:

For the Lord knows when we shall meet again
To be Maying another year.

It struck me with great sadness. I thought of the Italian student, of my grandmother and the mountain spring she had never returned to, of Mr. de Mascoli and his gentle patience, of all the lost opportunities and combinations of all our lives.

I had never written to Mr. de Mascoli from Italy or sent him the fine gifts I promised. That night I made a package of the Italian papers and magazines we had at home along with some of my husband's books that I had translated from Italian and sent them to the printer in Syracuse with a letter expressing my regret for the delay and an explanation of what had happened in my life since I last saw him more than ten years before.

The answer came from his wife. On a floral thank-you note (which I still have) with the printed message, *It was so thoughtful of you,* she had written: "It is almost three years that I lost my husband and a son a year later which I think I will never get over it. I miss them very much . . . it was our wish to go back to Italy for a trip but all in vain. The books you sent will be read by my sister-in-law who reads very good Italian, not like me, I'm trying hard to read but don't understand it as well as her, but she explains to me. Like my husband to you. . . ."

I thought of time that passed and the actions that remained forever stopped, undone. The May Day carol kept coming back to me:

For the Lord knows when we shall meet again
To be Maying another year.

And if not Maying, all the other things we'd planned to do for ourselves, for others. And then the others are no longer here. A few years after that May Day, Antonio died suddenly in Rome. He is buried far away in his Vicenza birthplace while I continue to live outside of New York, alone now, since our daughters are married and gone. Life does not permit unrelenting sadness. May goes but comes back each year. And though some shadow of regret remains for all the words left unsaid and acts left undone, there will be other words, other acts. . . .

I often think of how my life, my husband's, and the lives of our three daughters were so entwined with the language that Mr. de Mascoli set out to give me so long ago. Despite his efforts and my opera records, I still speak Italian with an upstate tonality; my daughters do much better. Though Italian couldn't root perfectly in me, it did in them: the eldest is chair of the Italian department at an Ivy League university; the middle one lives and teaches in Italy, a perfect *signora;* and the youngest has brought up her own two American daughters to speak Italian from birth.

Occasionally I visit Susanna in Italy, but it's long between trips and each visit is short. The country has changed: Mr. de Mascoli's Italy is no longer a poor country of peasants pushed into war and ruinous defeat by a dictator, but a prosperous industrial nation. Susi married an Italian artist from Urbino and they have two sons, Beniamino and Anselmo, with whom I speak Italian for they speak no English.

Now I am called *Nonna.* I never knew the word to address my own grandmother with when I was a child standing mute and embarrassed in front of her. Now, if it weren't too late, I would call her *Nonna,* too. We could speak to each other and I'd hear of the spring in Calabria.

How unexpected it all turned out . . . how long a progress as the seed of a long-ago infatuation found its right ground and produced its fruit. None of it did I foresee when I sat in his tidied white kitchen and learned with Mr. de Mascoli how to speak Italian.

LUIGI FUNARO

The B-Word

Bafongool!
It's fun to say
If you're a wop
say it every day
It's like "Fuck you!"
Or "Up your ass!"
Dagos say *coolie*
'cause we got class
Grandpop said it
so you should, too
Let him hear you yell
Bafongool!

FRED GARDAPHE

Breaking and Entering

᪥

What you carry in your head you don't have to carry on your back.
—ADVICE FROM AN OLD WORKER

I GREW UP IN A LITTLE Italy where not even the contagiously sick were left alone. To be alone is to be sick. The isolation that reading requires was rarely possible and considered a dangerous invitation to blindness and insanity. This was evidenced by my being the first American-born of the family to need glasses before the age of ten.

There was no space set aside for study. We had one of the larger homes in our extended family, and so our house was the place where the women would gather in the basement kitchen after sending their husbands off to work and their kids to school. They'd share coffee, clothes washing, and ironing; they'd collectively make daily bread, and prepare afternoon pastas, and evening pizzas and foccacie. Those without children would spend the entire day there, and so we always returned home from school to scenes that most of our classmates only knew on weekends or holidays. We were expected to come home from school, drop our books on the kitchen table, and begin our homework. It was difficult to concentrate on work with four children at the table all subjected to countless interruptions from family and friends who passed through the house regularly.

The only books that entered my family's home were those we carried home from school. Reading anything beyond newspapers and the mail required escaping from my family. I would try reading, but the noise would be so great that I'd shout out, "Shut up, I'm trying to read," to which my mother would respond, "Who you tellin' to shut up? If you want to read, go to the library." But the library was off limits to any kid who wanted to be tough. I'd leave the house with homework in hand, find a place to park my books and join in on the action in the streets. When the action didn't consist of organized play, it was made up of disorganized troublemaking.

If it were not for reading, I would have become a gangster. This I know for a fact. I grew up in the 1950s, when the only Italians you saw on television were either crooning love songs or singing like canaries in front of televised government investigations. In my Chicago neighborhood, we never played cowboys and Indians. Inspired by television programs like *The Untouchables,* we played cops and robbers, and none of us ever wanted to be the cops. While there might have been Italian-American cops in our town, there were none on television. It is no wonder then that many of us young Italian-American boys became so infatuated with the attention given to the Italian-American criminals that we found our own ways of gaining that notoriety and power.

Once, while I was being chased by the police for disturbing local merchants so my partners could shoplift, I ran into the public library. I found myself in the juvenile section and grabbed any book to hide my face. Safe from the streets, I spent the rest of the afternoon reading, believing that nobody would ever find me there. So whenever I was being chased, I'd head straight for the library. The library became my asylum, a place where I could go crazy and be myself without my family finding out.

It wasn't long before my reading habit outgrew the dimensions of the library. I had developed a chronic reading problem that identified me as the *merican* or rebel. My reading betrayed my willingness to enter mainstream American culture, and while my family tolerated this, they did little to make that move an easy one. Sometimes at night I would bring a flashlight to bed and read, but sharing a bed with my two brothers, this often ended up in a fight, as well as a reprimand from my father, telling me I was not only keeping my brothers from sleeping, but that I was also teaching my brothers bad habits. In spite of all these obstacles I managed to become quite the bookworm. I read to escape both my home and the streets and in the process entered places in my mind I had never before seen.

While my father encouraged my studies, he wanted me to know what real work was like. So whenever he'd see me reading something that was obviously not homework, he'd put me to work in the family business—a pawnshop as well as the building we owned. Only after I'd clean floors, put away stock, and run errands, would I be given some time for myself. There wasn't much to read in the store; the constant flow of customers would not allow for anything longer than a news article at one stretch, but I always managed to get through a newspaper and the *Green Sheet,* a daily horse racing newsletter. I'd return home and reenter the imaginary worlds others created through words, never thinking there could be a bridge between the two. For a long time it never occurred to me that literature was something that could or even should speak to me of my experience, especially not of my ethnicity. The worlds I entered through reading were never confused with the world in which I lived. Reading was a vacation. The books I read were written by others about experiences that were not mine; they took me places I had never been. This naive notion of reading was shattered the day my father was murdered.

When I read the news accounts, it seemed for the first time that my life had become a subject for writing. Since we share the same name, to see his name in print was to see my own name. It was especially haunting to see that name on his tombstone. I knew that a part of me had been buried with him. From that day on, I began to read in a new way. For many reasons I began to feel that my life was no longer in control; I began to think that the only way I could regain control of it was to be the one who wrote the stories. So shocked by reality was I that I began to search for a way out, and that way, I thought, would come through reading. Because my father was mur-dered in the pawnshop, my family wanted me to have nothing to do with the business, but my grandfather needed me more than ever. I returned to the store, now in my father's place, in spite of the fact that I was just a kid.

Since books were nonnegotiable items in my community, the giving of them was considered not only impractical but taboo. Sometime shortly after my father's death, my Uncle Pasquale gave me a copy of Luigi Barzini's *The Italians;* he just handed it to me, without even a word, assuming through his glance that I would know what to do with it. Back then I thought I knew too much about being Italian. But all I really knew was that being Italian meant being different from the ones I wanted to be like. The last thing in the world that I wanted at that age was to read about a group with which I no longer wished to be associated. I put the book on a shelf connected to my bed, the only shelf outside our kitchen; there it would lie unread for seven years. From then on I read nothing beyond my school assignments. One day—a day of no special occasion—one of my aunts again broke this book-as-gift taboo by giving my mother a copy of Mario Puzo's *The Godfather;* she told my mother that if her nephew was so intent on reading he might as well read a book about Italians (neither of them had read it, of course). The title of the book was quite appropriate since, due to my father's early death, I, at the age of ten, had been made godfather to one of my cousins.

The novel lay unread until I found out that there was an excellent sex scene on page twenty-six. That's where I started reading. I sped through the book, hoping to find more scenes like the one in which Sonny screws the maid of honor at his sister's wedding. Along the way I encountered men like Amerigo Bonasera, the undertaker; Luca Brasi, the street thug; and Frankie Fontaine, who were like the regulars I knew in the pawnshop. Some would come in with guns, jewelry, and golf clubs to pawn. Men like these formed alliances in order to get things done. Because of its stock of familiar characters, *The Godfather* was the first novel with which I could completely identify. The only problem I had was that this thing called Mafia was something I had never heard of. I was familiar with the word *mafioso*, which I had often heard in reference to poor troublemakers who dressed as though they were rich. But that these guys could have belonged to a master crime organization called the Mafia was something I had never fathomed. In spite of this, the world that Puzo created taught me how to read the world I was living in, not only the world of the streets, but also the world within my family, for in spite of the emphasis on crime, Puzo's use of Italian sensibilities made me realize that literature could be made out of my own experiences.

The novel came out the year after my grandfather was killed in a hold-up at the pawnshop. With him gone, the business was sold and I was free to find my own way through the world. One of the ways I searched was crime. All throughout my high school years, I was accused of being in the Mafia. So during my senior year, I decided to investigate the subject through my semester-long thesis paper that my Irish-Catholic prep school required. One way or another I had been connected to the Mafia since I left my Italian neighborhood to attend the high school, so I decided it was time to find out what this thing called Mafia was. This was the first writing project to excite me.

The more research I did, the more I learned about the men I thought I had known. Whenever I saw familiar names I would be amazed that they had done something so important that someone had taken the time to write about them. People never talked, in public at least, about these men.

One night I was in the back room of a restaurant for a private party given by my employers. I was the youngest employee, and as we were being served, my boss turned the group's attention to me by proudly asking what I had been doing in school. I told them, quite loudly, that I was doing a research paper on the Mafia. When he asked what I was reading, I blurted out, *The Valachi Papers*. Everyone stopped talking and turned to me. I was shocked by the sudden silence; my eyes went around the table and I realized that there were men in that room who had their names in that book. Someone changed the subject and nobody said another word about my project.

When I completed the paper I was certain of an excellent grade. The grading committee decided that the paper, although well written, depended too much on Italian sources, and because I was also Italian my writing never achieved the necessary objectivity that was essential to all serious scholarship. I read the C grade as punishment for my cultural transgression and decided to stay away from anything but English and American literature in my future formal studies.

I did, however, continue to search for and read books about organized crime. The way a convict becomes a better criminal by going to prison, I became an expert in the history of Italians in organized crime by reading. I would read the books and then tell the guys about what I had read. Kids would come up to me and ask what I had read about their fathers or uncles. I was christened with the nickname "*professore*," and many were the times when local gang leaders would use my stories to help them organize their gang activities. My knowledge of Roman history and Caesar's war stories, gained through my prep school studies, helped them create organizational structures that were as sophisticated as any the FBI could imagine. I soon found myself taking in money without having to do much. Younger kids, anxious to be a part of our gang, took over the legwork at our direction. The older guys had their eyes on me, but when the draft became a threat, I disappointed them by going to college.

JERRE MANGIONE

Growing Up Sicilian

BEFORE MY PARENTS CONSIDERED ME OLD enough to go beyond the picket fence that separated me from the children on the street, I would peer through it for hours, longing to play with them and wondering what they could be saying to one another. Although I had been born in the same city as they, I spoke not their language. English was forbidden in our home—for reasons of love. Afraid of losing communication with their own flesh and blood, my parents, who spoke only Sicilian, insisted we speak their tongue, not the one foreign to them.

The feeling of being an outsider may have begun with that edict. Or it may have started when, finally allowed to go beyond the picket fence, I found myself among jeering strangers—the sons of Polish, German, and Russian Jewish immigrants who lived on the same block. Their loudest taunts were directed against my baptismal name of Gerlando, which they reduced to Jerry as soon as they had accepted me. From this action came the awareness of being doomed to lead a double life: the one I led among my drove of Sicilian relatives, the other in the street and at school.

There was also a third life, the one I lived with myself, which gradually was to dictate the secret resolve to break away from my relatives. It was largely based on para-Mitty feats of the imagination that could easily transport me into agreeable realms far removed from the harsh realities of my everyday existence. (One winter I galloped over the snow-packed sidewalks of our neighborhood in the moonlight, believing I was a god disguised as a horse; in another season I kept rescuing my beautiful third-grade teacher from the flames about to consume her while she slept.) My fantasy life was well nourished by the piles of books I brought home from the public library, most of which I read clandestinely in the bathroom or under the bed since my mother believed that too much reading could drive a person insane.

As I tried to bridge the wide gap between my Sicilian and American lives, I became increasingly resentful of my relatives for being more foreign than anyone else. It irked me that I had not been born of English-speaking parents, and I cringed with embarrassment whenever my mother would scream at me in Sicilian from an upstairs window, threatening to kill me if I didn't come home that minute. If I rushed to obey her, it was not because I was frightened by her threat (there was nothing violent about her except the sound of her anger), but because I did not want my playmates to hear her Sicilian scream a second time.

My fondness for privacy, which my relatives considered a symptom of illness, added to my feelings of incompatibility. I was offended by their incessant need to be with one another. If they could have managed it, they would probably have all lived under the same roof. Only the families of my Jewish playmates approached their gregariousness, but they were recluses by comparison. My relatives were never at a loss for finding reasons for being together. In addition to parties for birthdays, weddings, anniversaries, and saint days, there were also parties when a child was baptized, when he was confirmed, and when he got a diploma. The arrival of another relative from Sicily or the opening of a new barrel of wine was still another pretext for another gathering of the clan.

Pretext or not, on any Sunday or holiday a score of relatives would crowd into our tiny house at the invitation of my father, whose capacity for hospitality far exceeded his income, to partake of a Lucullan banquet consisting of at least three meat courses and, at Christmas and Easter, *cannoli*, the masterpiece of his art as a pastrymaker, his original trade in Sicily. As long as the celebrations were held indoors away from public scrutiny, I could enjoy them, especially when my relatives were swapping stories about Sicily. But in the summer months, when they took to serenading one another in the dead of night, waking up their non-Sicilian neighbors with their songs and mandolins, or when they invaded the public parks with their exuberant festivals, I would be tormented with the worry that they were making a bad impression on the Americans around us. The most excruciating moments came when the Sicilian mothers in our party, not caring how many Americans might be watching, bared their breasts to feed their infants.

A mindless conformist like most children, I was incapable of appreciating my relatives' insistence on being themselves, or realizing that this was their way of coping with an alien world that was generally hostile. Nor was I aware of how much antagonism they had endured and how much they had been slandered. I learned long afterward (not from them) that at one point the public's image of Sicilians in Rochester was so sinister that the immigrants had felt compelled to prove they were a civilized and moral people, not criminals involved with the Mafia or the Black Hand, as the press would have the community believe. As evidence of their good character, the Sicilian community decided to enact the Passion Play. Included in the large cast were milkmen, masons, ditchdiggers, shoemakers, bakers, tailors, and factory hands, among them some of my relatives. The date set for the elaborate production was Columbus Day, 1908. Although invitations were mailed to hundreds of American community leaders and their spouses, only a few showed up. Fortunately, their enthusiasm for the quality of the production generated such excitement that the Sicilians were encouraged to stage a second performance. This time the auditorium was packed with both Americans and Italians, among them my father and my mother and to some degree, myself, for I would be born in a month's time. The lines in the drama were spoken in Italian but the Americans were as deeply moved by the performance as the rest of the audience and joined in the prolonged applause. The next day came the big payoff: the same newspapers that had been headlining Sicilian crime on their front pages devoted the same kind of space to praising the Sicilian community for making such an impressive contribution to the city's cultural life.

But it takes more than a play to change public opinion. Within a year the press was back to its old routine of unduly emphasizing crimes that involved Sicilians.

Of all our relatives my father was the most sensitive about the honor of Sicilians. So much so that on learning that Boy Scouts carry knives, the weapon that was commonly associated with Italian homicide, he forbade his sons to become Scouts. Not understanding his concern, the image of Sicilians as knife-wielding criminals rather appealed to our Hollywood-nurtured love of melodrama, but we saw no evidence of it among our relatives. Although there were about a hundred of them, only two ever came to the attention of the police, and in both instances they were victims rather than culprits. The most tragic was my mother's favorite brother Calogero, a gentle, dreamy-eyed father of two young children, who was killed at a wedding party when he tried to stop a fight between two guests, one of whom had a revolver. The killer was sent to the electric chair but this did not diminish the grief of my relatives, especially of my mother, who all of her life spoke of the murder as though it had just happened.

The second victim was my Uncle Stefano who, abhorring manual labor, had been operating a small jewelry business from his living room which catered to a clientele of Sicilian immigrants about to be married or engaged. The business was beginning to prosper when two of his *paesani* invaded his apartment one morning and, after tying him to a chair and threatening to blow off his head if he did not reveal the combination of his safe, took all of his jewelry including the wedding ring he wore. He was untied by a Jewish neighbor who heard his cries. The neighbor, without consulting him, then telephoned for the police.

The arrival of the police officers horrified Uncle Stefano as much as the robbery itself. Eventually he and the rest of my relatives were to make a distinction between the American police and the blatantly corrupt police system they had known in Sicily. But at the time all policemen were regarded as obstacles to justice. When questioned, Uncle Stefano gave the police a vague account of the robbery and refused to guess at the identity of the thieves. As a result, the newspaper accounts broadly hinted that he himself may have plotted the robbery in order to collect the insurance. No one had bothered to check out the fact that there was no insurance. My uncle was completely wiped out.

In an attempt to recover the stolen jewelry, Uncle Stefano visited a *paesano* who was reputed to be a power in the Rochester underworld, and gave him all the information he had withheld from the police. The *paesano* expressed horror that "a gentleman as honest and as respected" as my uncle would be robbed by two of his compatriots and promised on his honor to do everything possible to restore the jewelry. A few days later, with much apologizing, he reported that the thieves, on seeing the newspaper accounts of the robbery, had taken fright and left for Sicily. Unless they returned, which was unlikely, there was nothing he could do.

None of my relatives considered it strange that Uncle Stefano should have gone to a *mafioso* for help; nor did they doubt that if the police and the press had not interfered, he would have recovered the jewelry. While they did not condone *mafiosi*, they held that when you could not trust the police to deal with you with enough respect, you placed your trust in those who could enforce your rights as a respected person. In the vocabulary of my relatives the words *respect* and *honor* were interchangeable and sacred.

Convinced that our teachers made no effort to teach us the meaning of respect, my father distrusted American schools even more than the police.

He held them responsible for promoting such shocking customs as that of boys and girls dating without a chaperon or young people marrying without their parents' consent. The American school system, for him, symbolized everything that outraged him about his adopted country. His diatribes on the subject were of such eloquence as to make us feel guilty for daring to like any of our teachers. Beneath his fury was the conviction that they were encouraging immorality, disrupting family life, and undermining his position as the head of his family.

Like other Sicilian fathers, he never permitted his children to forget that they were living under a dictatorship, albeit, in his case, a loving one. In the eyes of his Sicilian peers, he was regarded as a maverick. He allowed his children to address their parents with the familiar *tu*, a concession rarely granted to children of Sicilians. And instead of spending his leisure time with his cronies drinking and playing cards, as was the habit of most Sicilian fathers, he preferred the company of his immediate family and would seldom go anywhere without them. He differed from the others in still another significant respect: despite his easily triggered hot temper, he never lifted a hand against his wife or his children.

Although he was of small stature, he conveyed the authority of a giant as he exhorted us to disregard the "nonsense" that the teachers stuffed into our skulls. Repeatedly we were reminded never to succumb to teachings that would cause us to disobey our parents. One evening, in a voice pregnant with moral significance, he read aloud to us the newspaper account of a Sicilian neighbor who had caught his daughter secretly dating an American; the neighbor had trailed the couple and, while they were kissing each other good night, pounced on the young man and bitten off part of his ear. "The teachers of that girl are to blame," my father told us, "for not teaching her to respect the wishes of a father."

Later, when my father discovered that his own daughter was seeing an American medical student on the sly, I expected a burst of temper that would badly scald my sister. But nothing of the kind happened. He simply asked her to invite the young man to the house. Then almost as soon as they were introduced, my father asked him point-blank whether he intended to marry his daughter. The bewildered young man paled and stuttered, trying to explain he was too young to think of marriage. In that case, my father told him, he was also too young to court his daughter. And that was the end of the romance.

As much as my father ranted against American schools, he and my mother yearned to send one of their sons to college, something which, they reminded each other, only the rich could afford to do in Sicily. Here it was not such an impossible dream. They chose me since I was the eldest and also because of my passion for reading, which they mistook for scholarly aptitude. I disappointed them at once by refusing to become either a doctor or a lawyer which, like most immigrants, they considered the only truly prestigious professions. Uncle Stefano urged that I become a pharmacist and presented me, on my next birthday, with an elaborate chemistry set. Because I was fond of him, I managed to show some interest in the possibility, but it literally went up in smoke when I almost set the house on fire while tinkering with hot test tubes.

My true ambition, which I tried to keep secret from my parents as long as possible, was to be a writer. It seemed to me that I had no talent for anything else; that, moreover, it offered the fastest avenue of escape to the world outside that of my relatives. The hope of becoming a writer was easily nurtured by my addiction to reading, but it may have first taken root at the age of ten when Uncle Peppino, who had a penchant for non-Italian widows, wealthy ones especially, began commissioning me to ghostwrite his love letters. The first of the letters, for which I received a dime, must have been a disaster. In my vast ignorance of women, I had stressed my uncle's passion for the widow's properties rather than his passion for her. When there was no reply to the letter, my uncle attributed the woman's silence to her cold Anglo-Saxon nature and addressed himself to other widows. There were some responses, enough to encourage both of us, but nothing much came of them. However, another correspondence I undertook for an immigrant cousin who had fallen in love with a Polish-American girl proved quite effective. After the third letter, they eloped, and my dreams for a writing career went soaring.

Apart from the dimes he paid me, I felt a special affinity for Uncle Peppino, mainly because he was an iconoclast by nature constantly at odds with his relatives for his un-Sicilian behavior. It delighted me to learn that shortly after his arrival in the United States he declared the Catholic Church a force for evil and joined the Baptist Church, which he found far more cheerful and where, as he put it, he could concentrate on his worship of God without having to ration it among a large roster of saints, whom he dismissed as superfluous intermediaries. He remained in the Baptist Church only long enough to make certain that all of his children became Baptists. After that he explored various religious sects, finally settling for the Holy Rollers, whom he came to regard as God's solace for widowers.

His relatives could not take his church life seriously; sooner or later, they predicted, he would return to the arms of the Mother Church. They attributed his flirtations with religious sects to an American "madness" which they were confident would pass as soon as he found a good Sicilian wife to care for him and his six children. What they failed to understand was his craving for venturing beyond his Sicilian world and exposing himself to new ideas and customs. Since I shared the same craving I could understand it. Yet I perceived that, except to take on a new religion or a new American mistress, he would not venture far. Although he had the brains and brawn to surmount the barriers of his environment, even to become a Moses of his people, his lack of English, together with his lack of interest in improving his status, would prevent him from developing into anything more than a gadfly philosopher content with being a bricklayer, playing a noisy game of poker and *briscola,* and taunting his relatives with the unorthodoxies of his not-so-private life.

Unlike Uncle Peppino, who relished publicizing his experiences with "Americans" (that is, non-Italians), I instinctively became closemouthed on the subject, fearing perhaps that my mother or my father might detect my scheme to put my Sicilian life behind me as soon as it became feasible. Except for whatever Italian girls came my way who would let me kiss and pet them, I usually gravitated to contemporaries who were not Italian. Throughout most of my teens my closest friend was Mitch Rappaport. He was nearby, minutes away from our home and seconds away from St. Bridget's, the church my mother ordered her children to attend every Sunday. Mitch, a burgeoning skeptic like myself, was my savior. When I began secretly boycotting St. Bridget's because the priest who listened to my confessions had taken to castigating me for reading the novels of Anatole France, I would take refuge at Mitch's house and stay there until mass was over. On such occasions Mitch, the brightest of my contemporaries and the valedictorian of the two schools we attended, would regale me with outrageous parodies of biblical stories which he invented on the spot. A few minutes before mass was finished, I would dash from his house to the church, just in time to intermingle with the congregation as it poured out of its doors, making certain I was seen by relatives who would be likely to tell my mother what a fine, churchgoing son she had.

Mitch and I were kindred spirits yet quite different. While I churned with anxieties that kept me lacking in confidence, he was consistently calm and self-assured. Yet his parents were immigrants with as little education as mine. They spoke Yiddish to each other and broken English to their five children. I marveled that Mitch, unlike myself, accepted their foreign mannerisms with no embarrassment; he was obviously content with his lot.

The fear of being discriminated against was prevalent among the children of Italians I knew. Some pretended their parents were French or anglicized their names when they applied for jobs at factories like Eastman Kodak and Bausch and Lomb, which then favored anyone else but Italians, Jews, and blacks. Others followed the example of their parents and rarely made friends outside their own ethnic group. My own inclination was to associate mainly with Jews, who stimulated my intellect more than the Italians I knew. Mitch was not my first Jewish friend. Before him came a freckled redhead named Morrie Levenberg who tutored me in math and Latin (my weakest subjects) and got me a part-time job hawking newspapers at a Main Street newsstand which he and his brother operated.

At Morrie's suggestion I joined a boys' club called the "Aurorans," which consisted of fourteen Jews and me, in a neighborhood settlement house. Financed by funds contributed to the city for charitable causes, the club was my first inkling that our neighborhood was officially regarded as a slum inhabited by disadvantaged families. The extent to which we were disadvantaged did not occur to any of us until our director, a volunteer social worker who was an affluent WASP, took us to his exclusive country club one evening and treated us to a sampling of how the rich spend some of their leisure: a tobogganing party in the moonlight followed by the most luxurious repast we had ever seen. It was enough to make us feel disadvantaged the rest of our lives, especially after we learned that no Jew or Italian was ever permitted to join the club.

KEN AULETTA

Hard Feelings

⌒⌒

W ITH THE AID OF A RAZOR strap, my father was very persuasive. "Don't go near the mobsters who hang out on Mermaid Avenue," he warned me at an age when I still looked up to tough guys. "You see them, you walk across the street."

I listened. In the late 1960s, when the Justice Department reported that Anthony Scotto was a *capo* in the mob, when the press printed tales of Scotto's alleged waterfront perfidies, I walked across the street. I worked in politics, where Scotto was important, but I kept my distance.

In 1971, when I worked for OTB, one of Scotto's close friends was recommended for a job. I took the application to an expert on organized crime. He said he did not know whether it was true or false that Scotto was a *capo*, or even whether he worked for the mob. "But I'm sure of one thing," he said. "The mob controls the waterfront, and Tony Scotto would not have been made head of the longshoremen's union at such a young age unless he at least played ball with them."

It may have been unfair, but Scotto's friend did not get the job.

I didn't know Scotto, but I was always struck by the gap between his appearance and his reputation. He dressed and talked like a banker, not a racketeer. Since I also sported a vowel at the end of my name, I sometimes wondered whether he was not a victim of vicious innuendo, of ethnic stereotyping.

Still, I stayed across the street. We shook hands once in an elevator on the way to a press conference I was covering. Last Christmas I talked with

Scotto and his wife, Marion, at a party. She wore a bright smile and asked to be remembered to my dad, whom she knew from her work in the Brooklyn borough president's office. A nice gesture, I thought.

At a friend's wedding this spring I again ran into Marion and Anthony Scotto. We talked briefly, exchanging a few jokes and pleasantries. "How's your father?" Marion asked, aware that cancer had recently plundered our family. I noticed that when the Scottos talked to you, they didn't look around the room. They seemed like nice, sincere people.

I stayed away from Scotto's trial, although I followed every word of it in the newspapers. Scotto sounded guilty. The prosecutors' evidence—the tape-recorded conversations of Scotto retreating to bathrooms to accept cash-filled envelopes, his whispering to an associate of a "kitty" that "we'll split up"—seemed devastating.

I remembered the advice of my dad and of the OTB crime adviser, thought not of the good deeds Anthony Scotto performed for the port of New York but of the workers and businesses and consumers who have been bled or bludgeoned by the mob's control of the waterfront. Once again I became stern. Anger swelled as I read some of our favorite columnists. If Scotto was guilty, they said, then all blue-collar workers—indeed, society, the system, the world—were guilty. They blamed the prosecution for using tapes, not Scotto for what he said on those tapes.

They sounded mushy-minded, too emotionally involved. To excuse Scotto by claiming that everyone who lives in a blue-collar world practices a little extortion is not only insulting to honest men and women but is akin to saying the law should apply only to those we don't care for. Like the Gulf executive who makes illegal cash contributions to win foreign contracts, for instance.

SUFFUSED WITH MORE THAN MY usual high quotient of self-righteousness, I went to the federal courthouse early Wednesday. Once in the seventh-floor courtroom, I briskly asked, "Could I please have the complete transcript of the trial summations?" Heading toward a rear bench, several pounds of paper in tow, I was stopped by a pretty blonde with a rainbow for a smile who asked, "How's your father?"

Marion Scotto's shower of kindness momentarily washed away my journalistic edge. Here, on the fourth day of this wake, waiting nervously for the jury to return with a verdict that could send one father to jail for twenty years, Marion Scotto asked about another father. I didn't think it was an act. Torn between what I felt and what I thought, I wanted to offer sympathy, a word of encouragement. Coolly, I kept my distance.

Escaping to the rear of the courtroom, I busied myself reading the final arguments of the defense and prosecution. James LaRossa, Scotto's able attorney, stuck to two basic themes. Instead of laboring over a detailed factual rebuttal to the charge that his client extorted and pocketed $300,000 from waterfront firms, he went on the offensive, attacking the credibility of the prosecution's principal witnesses. They were people who had pleaded guilty to crimes, LaRossa said, and in a desperate attempt to bargain for leniency, had offered Scotto's head.

The second major defense thrust was one of innocence by association. "The sitting governor of the state of New York doesn't walk into a criminal trial and testify for everybody," LaRossa said. "Two prior mayors, a future president of the AFL-CIO, and on and on and on. Could have brought a hundred of them in . . . This whole town would have come in for Anthony Scotto."

"You know, a lot of lawyers will do all kinds of sympathetic things and suggest that his family is sitting in a certain place in the courtroom, that he has four children, or anything like that," he declared. "Let me tell you something, folks. I am not doing that, and I'm not getting on my knees to you. He doesn't need it."

This seemed very clever of LaRossa, especially since Marion and her four children—Elaina, Rosanna, John, and Anthony Jr.—appeared daily in the first two rows to the right of the jury. Each day as the jurors filed in or out, they brushed past the Scotto family. LaRossa ended by asking the jurors to say, "Anthony Scotto, go home. Keep up the work."

LOOKING UP, I SAW MARION Scotto embrace one of their many friends and relatives who joined her daily vigil. Anthony Scotto, hands in his pocket, glided in and out of the courtroom, good-naturedly joked with reporters, studied the caricatures of his family drawn by the press artists, instinctively touched friends, refusing to permit their pity.

A friend of the Scotto family, Marion's gynecologist, introduced himself. "Isn't it terrible what the prosecution has done," he told me. "I reread 1984 the other day. The police state that George Orwell wrote about we're seeing here in this courtroom." He complained of how Scotto was bugged, tailed, how his kids saw planes swoop so low overhead to snap pictures they feared the planes would crash into the house. To the good doctor, Scotto was a victim.

To U.S. Attorney Robert Fiske, the prosecutor, he was a villain. Relying on tape recordings, Fiske peppered the jury with the alleged facts—Scotto's collecting regular envelopes, Scotto's telling an associate to burn the books if the federal government subpoenaed them.

He dismissed Scotto's impressive character witnesses because "they were not there when any of those things happened." The issue, Fiske stated, was not whether Scotto was a good labor leader or a friend of the famous. Nor whether he served his city and state well. The issue was extortion for personal gain.

I glared at Scotto. Even if the jury found him innocent of the legal charges, surely the moral bias of Scotto's defense was weak. LaRossa conceded that Scotto took $75,000 in cash from the waterfront firms (not the $300,000 charged). He said he took it for political campaigns, not personal gain. The cash went to Mario Cuomo's 1977 mayoral effort and Hugh Carey's 1978 reelection, he said. Since such cash contributions are illegal, LaRossa was implicitly pleading guilty to a state misdemeanor in order to avoid a federal felony charge.

Scotto admitted he gave expensive dinner tickets to the city commissioner of ports and terminals, the agency that supervises the waterfront; that an employee of the Waterfront Commission, which polices the port, was encouraged to smuggle to Scotto confidential information concerning investigations; that he knowingly approved "phony disability" payments to his workers. Above all, Scotto used reported political contributions, totaling $1.3 million in 1977 and 1978, to purchase political power.

Scotto dealt from one reality, the prosecutors from another. Scotto's world is peopled by practical "business" transactions. I walked over and asked Scotto about this. Raising funds from waterfront businesses is not extortion, he said evenly, looking me squarely in the eye and leaning back against the rail behind the defendant's table, his arms folded. "It is no different than what the AFL-CIO or maritime interests do nationally. The maritime industry puts together maritime funds. You see it on the state level where contractors get together with the building trade unions . . . There's no question that unless you're strong in the state legislatures and the Congress, you can lose what you won at the bargaining table."

A moment later, just a few feet away from Scotto, a prosecutor spoke of another reality. "If I accepted Scotto's own testimony as the truth—which I don't," he said, "it's one hell of an indictment of the political process." Cash contributions to campaigns may be *normal*, as politicians suggested all last week, but they are not legal.

PRIVATELY, MANY REPORTERS COVERING THIS trial believed the facts eclipsed Scotto's able defense. However, several admitted they were secretly rooting for Marion and Tony Scotto. The facts collided with their feelings.

Glancing quickly at Marion Scotto as I left the courtroom, I was determined not to let that happen. After a while the elevator came. The Scotto children got on first, trailed by relatives, friends, and Marion and Tony Scotto.

The last place in the world I wanted to be was on that elevator, but the Scottos insisted on squeezing the rest of us on. Part of me wanted to reach out and wish them luck; another insisted I keep a journalistic distance. I stared at the floor lights: 6 . . . 5 . . . 4 . . . 3 . . . 2 . . . 1.

The doors finally parted. As we walked out, a hand touched my arm. "Remember us to your father," Marion said. "And, Ken," she added, smiling but sad, "be good to us."

On Thursday the jury was not good to Marion and Anthony Scotto. I thought the jury probably made the only decision they could. Excuse me for sounding mushy-minded, but when I heard the news I felt sick.

ROBERT VISCUSI

Oration upon the Most Recent Death of Christopher Columbus

∽∾∾

1

i found christopher columbus hiding in the ash tray
what are you doing there, if you please
no one smokes, he said, leave me alone

2

we used to wear a saint christopher medal
it was for driving in the car
then they said
there is no saint christopher get rid of the medals
and we had to fly in airplanes
without the protection of this nonexistent saint
plenty of people were scared of flying without said christopher
and yet they fly

3

we will learn to get along without columbus
whom we used to love so well
there's mcdonald's in columbus
but colón has gone to hell

there's an awful smell
where he must dwell

we will live without columbus
whom we used to love so well

4

the fact is columbus day will go the way of the dinosaur
along with everything else
meanwhile what about garibaldi
who was fighting for the poor of italy
but after the revolution
lived to see the rich steal italy
and starve the poor
selling them to labor gangs in suez
shipping them to new york to dig subways
in return for cheap american grain
they brought back in the empty ships
the italians went to america in steerage
that means they slept down below
all in one room seasick for weeks
another room would carry wheat the other way
the italians didn't know where they were going
when they got there the people spit at them
and garibaldi lived to see all this begin to happen
which was his reward for helping the rich steal italy
he should have come to new york to fight in the civil war
and march in the columbus day parade

5

the americans loved columbus in those days
he was the *right* kind of italian
not like these dirty dagoes
and guineas and wops
stick you as soon as look at you
they carry shivs in their pants
the brown-eyed bastard italians
the icecream men stilettos up their sleeves

handing your daughter the big vanilla
with the handlebar moustache italians
fixing the races at the track
can get you girls
they run the numbers
and killed danny shea the dago did
for a dirty look and twenty quid
the americans preferred columbus
our man who wore a telescope in his pants
who bought america from the indians
and gave it to the bankers
they named sixty or seventy cities and towns columbus
columbia a university a country
they called a world's fair
columbian meaning *forward-looking*
inventive daring not afraid of fools and bigots

6

in those days they would sic columbus on the priests
they would have a play in which the inquisition said to columbus
the earth is flat, it says so right here in this book of theology
and columbus would stand there all smug like galileo
signifying the progress of science and the freedom of inquiry
while the priests competed to see
which of them could say the dumbest thing
people loved these plays
in a protestant country
where they were afraid of priests
because they hated them
and found they hated priests
because they were afraid of them
this particular logical slave-bracelet
often called itself the history of science

7

nowadays of course this history of science includes
a lot more chapters than it had a hundred years ago
in those days they never heard of auschwitz
they never heard of hiroshima
they never thought someone could kill lake erie
or cause the disappearance of thousands of species
the most beautiful creatures in creation
butterflies bluer than night now only memories
cats that can jump a hundred feet forgotten
except by a few historians of extinction
so of course it is no longer so wonderful
to be the patron saint of science

8

italians are a family people
not as in some political speech
but as in the caves of desolate matese
as on the frosty mountains of gran sasso
family people since the days of visigoths
and the roman legionaries
families protecting their own from the soldiers and the police
even their so-called criminals
even their real criminals
because who were the soldiers
they were worse than criminals
they were *foreigners*
they were foreign soldiers
whom no one was watching
they came where they came
and they took what they liked

9

people used to fight over columbus
the spaniards said he was spanish

in 1940 salvador de madariaga published a beautiful book
proving colón was and *had* to have been a jew
but came the quincentenary
no one wanted columbus
except the italians
they sat in their kitchens and said
he was ours when he was rich and lovely
and he has to be ours tomorrow
otherwise what are we anyway
when the foreign soldiers come back

1 0

i found christopher columbus hiding in the ash tray
what are you doing there, if you please
no one smokes, he said, leave me alone
so I brought him a little soup
i would sit next to him reading a book
until he fell asleep
it was the house arrest that befalls even good people
when they grow old and cannot do anything
he's useless now but he's still yours

The Anglo-Saxons could wear a necktie and nothing else, but somehow they would get it to match their belly button and look well-dressed.

EVERYBODY ELSE

ED McBAIN

—

Kiss

—

⤳⤳

I SEE," CARELLA SAID.

  "So if we allow this trial to become a name-calling contest . . ."

"Uh-huh."

"One minority group against another . . ."

"Uh-huh."

"An Italian-American victim versus . . ."

"I find *that* word offensive, too," Carella said.

"Which word?"

"Italian-American."

"You do?" Lowell said, surprised. "Why?"

"Because it *is*," Carella said.

He did not think that someone with a name like Lowell would ever understand that *Italian*-American was a valid label only when Carella's great-grandfather first came to this country and acquired his citizenship, but that it stopped being descriptive or even useful the moment his *grand*parents were *born* here. That was when it became *American,* period.

Nor would Lowell ever understand that when we insisted upon calling fourth-generation, native-born sons and daughters of long-ago immigrants "*Italian*-Americans" or "*Polish*-Americans" or "*Spanish*-Americans" or "*Irish*-Americans" or—worst of all—"*African*-Americans," then we were stealing from them their very American-ness, we were telling them that if their forebears came from another nation, they would never be *true* Americans here in this land of the free and home of the brave, they would forever and merely remain wops, polacks, spics, micks, or niggers.

"My father was American," Carella said.

And wondered why the hell he had to say it.

"Exactly my—"

"The man who killed him is American, too."

"That's how I'd like to keep it," Lowell said. "Exactly the point I was trying to make."

But Carella still wondered.

GEORGE PANETTA

Suit

∾⧖∾

O NE THING ABOUT THE ANGLO-SAXONS, THEY know how to dress. They could wear a necktie and nothing else, but somehow they would get it to match their belly button and look well-dressed. But not me and Joe; no matter what we wear, we always look as if we just got off the boat. And I think we worry about that; not consciously—unconsciously (I'm sure that if our conscious mind knew what was in our unconscious mind, we would've rushed to a psychiatrist). I think we just try to wear a few things that make us look like them, like the time Joe bought the suit that looked either tan or gray, but was actually white.

How Joe happened to buy the suit was we were looking at windows instead of girls. I don't know why that was, but that's what we were doing, walking down Fifth Avenue and looking in windows at everything, even dresses. We stopped at a girdle store, but only briefly, and then, in a window all by itself, we saw the suit. It was a gabardine suit, so tan it was almost white, with pearly gray buttons, and one of those all-lapel jackets which would look good on monkeys, or people built like monkeys, which was what me and Joe were.

"Nice suit," said Joe.

In the window it looked good. The more we looked at it, the more tan it became, the less white; if it had looked white to us we wouldn't've bought it because when me and Joe were kids street cleaners wore white suits, and even though the Anglo-Saxons wore a lot of white summer suits, we couldn't forget that they belonged on street cleaners. But it looked more tan than white.

"You sure?" Joe asked.

"Looks more tan," I said.

"Step back a little," said Joe. We stepped back a few feet from the window. "Sometimes you get a better idea of the color from a distance."

"More tan," I said.

"You're right," said Joe. "I'm gonna buy it. How about you?"

"I don't need a suit."

"You don't need a suit. How many you got?"

"Three."

"Three's enough?"

"Yeah, three's enough," I said, pretty sure of myself.

"I got six and I still need one."

"So buy it."

"I don't know what the hell you do with only three suits."

"I wear one every three days."

"What about the people in the office? They see you with the same suits all the time."

"They see me with only three suits, but they figure there must be three or four suits they don't see me with."

"You're wrong. They don't figure that way. What they don't see they figure you haven't got. They know every suit you got. The color. The style. They keep records in their heads."

"Okay, they know I got three suits."

"You gonna buy it?"

"I owe money to six banks. How the hell can I buy it?"

"I owe some banks too, you know. You don't have to pay cash; you charge it." Joe was really feeling bad over the thought of getting a suit while I didn't. "You charge it, they send you a bill in a month, and then you skip a couple of months before you pay it."

"I don't need a suit, Joe, honest. Go ahead, you get it."

"Three suits," said Joe, and shook his head. Then, before going into the store, he took another look in the window. "More tan," he said, and we went into the store.

It was a big store that sold women's things too, and whenever there's a store like that, the women's things are always on the ground floor, and the men's things are either up on the roof, or down in the basement, or someplace it takes a man two hours to find, and then he's lost. This time the men had the basement. There were about a million suits there, and about a million men who sold them. When we walked down the stairs, all the salesmen turned and looked at us; they didn't run at us because there must have been some rule they couldn't grab us, but they watched us go down and—I'm not sure, but I think—the suits watched too. When we reached the bottom, all the salesmen moved a step. This was something they were supposed to do, but it took me and Joe unawares, and we stopped and wanted to go upstairs again. But the one step was all they took.

"Let's pick an Italian salesman," said Joe.

We looked.

We looked for a big nose, dark eyes, and an expression that living was something wrong to do.

"How about that one?" said Joe. He pointed to one with a big nose, but red hair.

"Red hair," I said.

"You never heard of redheaded Italians?"

"Never."

"He's dark. And the hair isn't so red."

"It's your suit, get him."

"Supposing he's not Italian?"

"He has to be Italian?"

"An Italian I can talk to. I have a lot of trouble under the arms, and if I know the guy's Italian I can take my time telling him just what I want. The other guys I can't talk to."

"So let's get the manager and ask for an Italian salesman."

"No," said Joe, "that looks like we're prejudiced."

I agreed.

We looked at the redhead again.

"I know a lot of Italians got red hair."

"Let's try him."

We went up to the salesman, and besides the big nose and red hair, he had a yellow flower in his lapel, which we hadn't been able to see from where we stood, maybe because of the size of the nose. The nose was the only thing about him that looked Italian; the rest of him was all happy looking, especially his eyes, which were blue, and had a twinkle with a future in it. (Italian eyes are all dark, with a lot of yesterdays in them, and if they're not like that it's possible there was an adultery somewhere, even though the Italian wife is watched better than any other wife in the world.) When we saw the eyes, we knew we were stuck.

"Gentlemen," he said. It was a boy's voice.

"I want a suit I saw in the window," Joe said. "Tan gabardine with two buttons."

"I know," he said, and went to one of the racks.

"He's an Englishman," said Joe.

"I'm not sure—"

"Blue eyes, red hair, flower in his lapel."

"He doesn't talk like an Englishman."

"He's in New York now."

"So what?"

"You lose your accent in New York."

He came back with a suit; it looked whiter.

"Is this the one?" he said.

"Yes," said Joe.

But to me it looked whiter, much whiter.

"Beautiful gabardine," he said, and led Joe to one of the mirrors.

Joe put the jacket on; right away I saw street cleaners.

But Joe was smiling. "Nice," he said.

I nodded; it wasn't my suit.

Joe went closer to the mirror.

"A beauty," the salesman said. "A real beauty."

"What color is it?" I said.

"Gray."

"He thinks it's tan."

"Tan or gray, same thing. Gabardine you can hardly tell the difference."

"I think it's white."

"It could be white too," and he said it in a kind, unhurt way, as if he loved all the colors.

Joe was fussing under the arms, turning around, trying to see the back.

"How's it look?" said Joe.

"Okay," I said.

"Put on the pants," said the salesman.

Joe took the pants into a little room. I had nothing to do, so I took a look in the mirror. It was a three-way mirror. If you're short, with a thick neck, and a big head, don't ever look in those mirrors. The salesman came over.

"You want a suit too?"

"Not now," I said.

"Case you do," he said, and gave me his card. I looked.

His name was Anthony Montafusco.

"You Italian?" I asked.

"Yes," he said. "You?"

"Me and my friend, we're both Italians."

We shook hands.

"How come you got red hair?" I said.

"I dye it," he said.

"Why don't you dye it black?"

"Black is what I got. No good. I dye it red so everybody can see it."

I didn't know what he meant, and he saw that I didn't.

"I'm the only salesman with red hair, it's easy to see me."

That was true.

"You got blue eyes," I said.

"We all got blue eyes in my family."

"You're all Italians?"

"All."

"Full-blooded?"

"Full-blooded. My mother had blue eyes, my father, all of us."

Joe came out with the whole suit on.

"He's Italian," I said.

Joe shook hands with him. "How come you got red hair?" said Joe.

"He dyes it red," I said.

"So the people can see me. You know, attract attention."

Joe didn't understand any more than I did, but he nodded. "How's the suit look?" said Joe.

"Beautiful."

"Now look," said Joe, "I want under the arms a certain way. Thank God you're not an Englishman or one of those guys you can't talk to. I want a lot of room under the arms. I want to move this way and that way and not feel that there's something pulling me underneath, know what I mean?"

"I know what you mean," said Anthony Montafusco.

"The tailor Italian?"

"Jewish."

Joe looked at me for help. I looked at Anthony Montafusco.

Anthony said, "Whatever I tell him to do, he'll do."

"I like the Jews," Joe said. "But when it comes to fixing suits, they got their own ideas."

"Not this one," said A.M. "What we tell him to do, he does."

And he went for the tailor.

Joe said: "It looks more tan than in the window."

I nodded; a nod is less of a lie.

"You like the two-button effect?" said Joe. "Like the long lapel?"

I looked in the mirror with him, but all I could see was the Department of

Sanitation. I nodded, just a couple of times. The salesman came back with the tailor. He was about ninety years old.

"Just let him take the measurement," said Anthony. "Don't say a word."

Joe didn't.

The suit was getting whiter and whiter.

When the tailor got to the arms, Joe wanted to say something, but Anthony put his finger to his mouth. From one Italian to another, that was enough.

The tailor was making marks all over; it must've been a white suit because the chalk marks were black.

"The pants should hit the top of my shoe," said Joe.

"He knows," said the salesman.

And the poor old man looked like he knew what he was doing; he made the mark on the pants, then quietly, without saying a word, just taking the little breath he had to, he went away.

"Be ready in a week," said the salesman.

"Charge it," said Joe.

The suit was white, not tan, and if I had any brains I would've told Joe it was white. But he liked it. He liked the two buttons, which were like pearls, and the long lapels, which made him feel six feet tall. I didn't want to spoil it for him. When he was looking in the mirror, he kept standing on his toes, as if he was trying to be as tall as he felt he was. If you're five feet tall and maybe a couple of inches, you know what it is if all of a sudden you become six feet tall. I guess that's why I didn't tell him; I just didn't want to spoil it for him. But I should've. Because what happened after was much worse than if he looked as short as he actually was.

Joe picked up the suit a week after he bought it, and then, about three weeks after that, he wore it to work.

It was white, no question about it.

I got scared when I saw it. I was about to go into Joe's office, and there was the suit, as if Joe wasn't in it, and what I did was turn and go back to my office. I didn't want to be seen with Joe. I was scared—scared of what the Anglo-Saxons would say when they saw it on him, scared of what would happen to Joe's office if a Brooks Brothers suit came in and stood beside him.

I closed the door in my office: if anyone saw him, I didn't want to start any discussions about it. I wanted nothing to do with it; it was his. The phone rang, and I was afraid to answer it. Then, because I'm Italian and have a loyalty beyond reason, I began to feel sorry. Would Joe leave me alone under the same circumstances? Yes, he would. But would he hide in his office, not answer the phone, be such a lousy coward? He would. But he'd come around after a while; he'd be scared, and run away the way I did, but after a while he'd come around and help me defend the suit. So I went.

When he saw me, it was as if he weren't wearing the suit.

"Where were you?"

"I just got in."

"Weren't you here before?"

I shook my head.

"I must be seeing things."

I sat in the easy chair which he had stolen from one of the vice presidents' office so that whenever I was in his office I could sit in it.

"You wearing the suit," I said. I had to; Joe didn't know he had it on.

"Oh, yeah," he said. And stood up to show me.

I looked.

One other thing I hadn't noticed before: the pants cuffs came to a point.

"Nice," I said.

"My wife thinks it's gray."

"That's what the salesman thought it was. I think it's tan."

"It's tan. The Nut's a little color-blind."

He turned all around for me to see. I tried to think who would wear this suit, what animals in the human race? Monkeys, was all I could think.

But Joe was happy with it.

He felt the material, showed me the fine stitching all around the lapels, and then walked around the room with it, to show me how it looked while walking. It was then that an Anglo-Saxon saw him.

It was Len Cooke, who, besides going to Yale, had a dirty look in his eye. He saw the suit from the door, couldn't believe it, came into the office, took another look.

"What's the matter?" said Joe.

"New suit?"

"Yeah, new."

"My!" And before Joe had a chance to kick him or something like that, he was out of the office.

"What the hell did he mean?"

"He was jealous."

But just as Joe was trying to figure whether he was jealous because the suit cost so much or because it was so beautiful, another Anglo-Saxon came in and looked at it. This one I didn't even know, there were so many all over the place.

"New suit?" said this A-S.

Joe looked up, nodded, and this Anglo-Saxon went away.

"I guess it's attractive," Joe said.

"Yeah."

And then it happened. About fifteen of them all came into the office to look at the suit.

"What's the matter?" Joe said, as if at last the Anglo-Saxons had got together to attack us. "What're you guys doing here?"

"We just came to see the suit," someone said.

And then someone laughed; and then they were all laughing.

"Where in hell did you get that suit?" someone asked. And someone else answered: "Harlem."

And they all laughed again, big loud laughs.

Joe didn't know what to say or do; he just looked down at the suit. And now he saw what I had seen before, the Department of Sanitation.

He got as small as before he bought the suit, if not smaller.

"Wear it well," someone said.

"Good suit," said someone else.

And one by one they went out of the office; when the last one was out, I got up and closed the door.

"Put the chair under the knob," Joe said, in a very weak voice.

I put my special chair in front of the door and sat in it.

Joe said, "What's wrong with it?"

I didn't want to tell him.

"Come on, tell me." I thought he was going to cry.

"It's white."

"You said it was tan."

"It looked tan."

"You knew it was white all along."

"I wasn't sure. The salesman said it was gray."

Someone knocked at the door.

"Don't open it," said Joe. "Just sit there."

We could see the shape of the head of whoever was knocking; it was an Anglo-Saxon–shaped head.

"Why didn't you tell me it was white?"

"I wasn't sure. Besides, it's not just the color."

"What else?"

"The cuffs."

"What's the matter with them?"

"They come to a point."

The one who knocked went away. Then someone else came, knocked, went away.

"What're you gonna do?"

"I'm going home and take it off."

"You better."

Joe took another look, a last one, as if it were somebody's coffin. "It still looks tan."

"It's white. Plain white. And those buttons—how could you like those buttons?"

"The buttons too?"

"The buttons too!"

Joe felt them. He could understand the cuffs and the color, but not the buttons. They were soft, innocent; he kept feeling them with the tips of his fingers, and he got so quiet doing it I thought he was going to start crying. But he just sat quiet. I was quiet too, but not as sad, because after all it wasn't my suit: I was more like the visitor at the wake. A lot of Anglo-Saxons came knocking at the door, but I was blocking it with my big comfortable chair.

When it looked like the place had run out of Anglo-Saxons, we decided to make a break for it and get Joe home safe into another suit. I sneaked out, went down the back stairs, and got a taxi; then I made sure the coast was clear, and Joe came out with no head, just the suit walking behind me, until we got into the taxi.

THE SUIT WENT INTO JOE'S closet, and it would have stayed there forever, like something dead and buried, except one morning his wife got up with her eyes closed and went into the closet. She was afraid of closets anyway, but when she saw the suit, it was like a man was in the closet which she had thought was the bathroom. Poor Joe had to get up and tap her on the head to stop her screaming. The Nut got whiter than the suit, but when she came to she blamed the suit for putting the bathroom in the wrong place, and Joe had to get it out of the closet that very morning, or go find a new apartment where the bathroom wasn't so near the closets. He took the suit to work with him.

"What's in that box?" I asked.

"The suit."

I closed the door right away. "The suit?" I said.

"It scared the Nut."

"How?"

Joe told me.

"What're you gonna do with it?"

"I'm giving it to Frankie the shoeshine."

"You're crazy! That's a brand-new suit."

"My wife almost dropped dead."

"That doesn't mean you have to give it away. We can sell it."

"To who?"

"You can get at least fifty bucks for it."

"From who?" said Joe.

I was thinking.

"You *mind* if I give it to Frankie?"

"Why the hell should you give it away? It cost you a hundred bucks."

"Didn't cost me anything."

"Didn't cost you anything?"

"I'm not paying the bill."

"Why not?"

"They sold me the wrong suit."

"You picked it out yourself."

"They sold me the wrong color, the wrong cuffs, even the wrong buttons."

And when Joe said "buttons," there was a sad look in his eyes.

"They'll sue you."

"Let 'em."

I was still thinking about who to sell the suit to. I said, "You sell the suit you make a profit."

"Well, who, who? Tell me who to sell it to and we'll sell it."

Then it came to me. "My brother," I said.

"Which one?"

"Rocco, the one that likes a lot of suits."

"He'll like this?"

"I think so."

"All right, sell it to him."

Why I didn't think of my brother Rocco sooner, I don't know, because no matter where we were, and what suit I had on, he always wanted to buy it from me. I never gave in: it would have killed my rotation of three suits. Three suits looked like more, in spite of what Joe said; two suits always feels like one suit, and besides, there's some saint suit manufacturers must pray to who sees to it that you always meet the same people with the same suit on.

I called Rocco and told him I had this suit for him. I didn't tell him the color or the shape. I told him the price, forty dollars (discount of ten dollars from the original fifty because he was my brother) and that it cost Joe a hundred dollars. I told him Joe was selling it because somebody died on him and he was going into mourning. My brother said meet him in front of Gimbels with the suit.

We met in front of Gimbels.

"See, Joe," I said, "he's your size."

They were, just about, but my brother was handsomer.

"Joe just bought this suit," I said, "but now his sister-in-law died."

"Sorry," said my brother, well-mannered.

"I'll be in mourning at least six months," said Joe.

"Let's go in and try it on," said Rocco.

"In where?" I said, because I actually didn't know.

"In Gimbels."

"They'll let you try it on?"

"We just go stand in front of a mirror."

"They'll let you?" said Joe, because he actually didn't know.

My brother nodded, and went in. We followed him. He stopped at a mirror in the women's hat department; I guess this was where he always tried on suits he happened to buy from people. We took the suit out of the box; the women stopped trying on their hats.

My brother put the jacket on.

The women stared at him: I think they were afraid he was going to try on the pants.

"Nice," said my brother, to the mirror, "nice."

Joe had disappeared, embarrassed.

The women weren't paying any attention to the hats anymore. There were two or three other mirrors, but my brother was moving around as if he might try the pants, and if he did they didn't want to have to make up their minds about what hat to buy.

"I like it," said my brother. "How much he want for it?"

"Forty dollars," I said.

"I wanna show it to Lucy," he said.

"That's okay," I said.

He took the jacket off, put his own jacket on, put the white jacket in the box, put the box under his arm, and walked over toward Joe As soon as he was out of the way fifteen women put hats on their heads and took over the mirror.

Joe was hiding among the underwear reduced for clearance.

"I like it," said my brother.

"It's yours," said Joe.

"But first I want my wife to see it."

"Okay," said Joe.

And my brother Rocco had the suit.

He promised to call us in a couple of days but he didn't call for a week, two weeks. Joe didn't mind. He assumed the suit was sold and it was just a matter of waiting for the money. Besides, Joe was happy without the suit. His wife went into the closet two or three times by mistake, but at least she didn't see the suit there: Joe had to thank my brother for that. And he was getting revenge on the Anglo-Saxons: they came around every morning looking for the suit, figuring Joe had to wear it again sometime; when they didn't see it, they turned green and looked as if they wanted to ask Joe when he was going to wear it again. Of course they couldn't do that because it would tip Joe off and then he'd never wear the suit again.

Three weeks passed without my brother calling, then four weeks, five weeks. Finally Joe wanted me to call him, but I didn't because my brother was the kind of guy who if you called him up about something like that he wouldn't want it anymore.

One thing Joe didn't want was the suit back.

Then one day we were walking along Sixth Avenue when all of a sudden we saw the suit coming toward us with my brother in it.

It stopped right in front of Joe.

"I'm wearing it," said my brother.

"Looks good," I said.

Joe couldn't talk, couldn't see, and the only thing that could bring him back to life was the forty dollars cash.

"I wish I could keep it," said my brother.

Joe died.

"You can't keep it?" I said.

"I like it," said my brother.

"But what?"

"Lucy."

"His wife," I said to Joe, but he was beyond hearing.

"She doesn't like it," said Rocco.

"But you're wearing it," I said, but in a nice way. I didn't want to start anything with my own brother.

"I'm wearing it to prove to Lucy it's a good suit."

I understood that; if I didn't it meant we had no more hope of selling the suit.

But poor Joe. I never saw him so white-looking, and so hurt. He had a gray suit on, with a red-striped tie, but that was all right because he didn't remember he told my brother he was selling the suit to go into mourning for six months. He looked real sick. The worst thing about it was that you could see a "principle" forming in his head, the way his eyes rolled and seemed to run away from behind the glasses.

"I'll see what Lucy thinks," said my brother, and the suit went away, up Sixth Avenue.

The "principle" in Joe's head was this: a guy shouldn't wear a suit unless he's paid for it. But he remembered the store and all the letters they were sending him to hurry up and pay for the suit; then the "principle" became: a guy shouldn't wear a suit until he makes up his mind to buy it. That was a good principle, and I couldn't argue with it, even for my brother.

Then my brother sent the suit back, with a very nice note saying his wife didn't like it. Joe's only argument was he didn't know where I got that kind of a brother, but that was no argument because I didn't either.

Anyway, Frankie the shoeshine now has the suit.

JOHN D'AGATA

Round Trip

1

ISAAC, WHO IS TWELVE, HAS COME involuntarily.

"We insist he grow up cultured," his mother says, leaning over our head-rests from the seat behind. "My father brought me to Hoover Dam on a bus. There is just no other way to see it."

Hours ago, before the bus, I found the tour among the dozens of brochures in my hotel lobby. It had been typed and Xeroxed, folded three times into the form of a leaflet, and crammed into the back of a countertop rack on the bellhop's "What to Do" desk in Vegas.

Nearby my tour in the brochure rack were announcements for Colorado River raft rides that would paddle visitors upstream into the great gleaming basin of the dam.

There were ads, too, for helicopter rides—offering to fly "FOUR friends and YOU" over "CROWDS, TRAFFIC, this RIVER & MAN's MOST BEAU-TIFUL structure—all YOURS to be PHOTOGRAPHED at 10,000 FEET!"

Hot-air balloon tours.

Rides on mountain bikes.

Jaunts on donkeys through the desert, along the river, and up the dam's canyon wall.

There was even something called the Hoover Dam Shopper's Coach, whose brochure guaranteed the best mall bargains in Nevada, yet failed to mention anywhere on its itinerary Hoover Dam.

Brochure in hand, I stood in line at the tour's ticket booth behind a man haggling with a woman behind the glass. He wanted a one-way ticket to Hoover Dam.

"Impossible," the woman said. "We sell The Eleven-Dollar Tour. One tour, one price."

The one-way man went on about important business he had at the dam, things he had to see to, how the tour's schedule just wasn't time enough.

"Sir," she said, through security glass, "I'm telling you, you'll have to come back. They're not gonna let you stay out there."

He bought a ticket, moved on.

We boarded.

Like the ad said, The Eleven-Dollar Tour comes with a seat on the bus, a free hot-dog coupon, and a six-hour narrative, there and back.

Our bus is silver, round, a short, chubby thing. It is shaped like a bread box. Like a bullet. "Like they used to make them," says Isaac's mom.

I turn to Isaac, my seatmate, say, "Hi, my name is John," and he says he doesn't care, and proceeds to pluck the long blond lashes from his eyelids, one by one, standing them on his wrist, stuck there by their follicles.

It is at this point that Isaac's mom leans over our headrests and tells me that Isaac is a good boy, "talkative, really," that he just happens to be grumpy today because "Mother and Father" have insisted that he accompany them on this "educational tour." Isaac's mother tells me that to keep Isaac entertained in Las Vegas they are staying in a new hotel—the largest in the world, in fact—with five thousand guest rooms, four casinos, seventeen restaurants, a mega-musical amphitheater, a boxing ring, a monorail, and a thirty-three-acre amusement park, all inside an emerald building. She presents the brochure.

I say, "Wow."

Then Isaac's dad, looking up from another brochure he holds in his lap, says, "You know, kiddo, this Hoover Dam looks pretty special!" And then come statistics from the paragraph he's reading.

The feet high.

The feet thick.

The cubic yards of concrete.

Of water.

The three million kilowatts.

And the plaque.

"Let me see that." Isaac's mom takes the brochure and reads the plaque's inscription to herself. She shakes her head.

"Do you believe that? Isaac, honey, listen."

Isaac's eyes roll far away. His mother's voice climbs up a stage.

She is just loud enough to be overheard. Just hushed enough to silence all of us.

It is her voice, and the quiet, and the words on the plaque that I think might have made the whole trip worth it even then, even before we left the tour company's parking lot and learned there'd be no air-conditioning on the six-hour ride; even before we stood in line for two hours at the dam; before the snack bar ran out of hot dogs and the tour guide of his jokes; before the plaque was laid in 1955 by Ike; before the dam was dedicated in 1935 by FDR; before the ninety-six men died "to make the desert bloom"; or before the Colorado first flooded, before it leaked down from mountains, carved the Grand Canyon, and emptied into the ocean. Even before this plaque was cast by a father and his son in their Utah blacksmith shop, there was the anticipation of the plaque, its gold letters riding on the backs of all creators. And Isaac's mother's voice, even then, I believe, was ringing circles somewhere in the air: ". . . the American Society of Civil Engineers voted this one of the Seven Modern Wonders of the World!"

These are the seven wonders of the world: a beacon, a statue, gardens, pyr-amids, a temple, another statue, and a tomb. I have set eyes on them all— this Lofty fire of Pharos, and the statue of Zeus by Alpheus, and the Hanging Gardens, and the Colossus of the Sun, and the Huge Labor of the High Pyramids, and the Vast tomb of Mausolus, and the House of Artemis mounted to the Clouds—and I tell you, as a scholar and as a wanderer and as a man devoted to the gods, they are and always will be the Seven Greatest Liberties man will ever take with Nature.
—ANTIPATER OF SIDON, FROM HIS LOST GUIDEBOOK, C. 120 B.C.

2

Our driver maneuvers lithely through the streets filled with rental cars. I tilt my head into the aisle. There is his green-sleeved arm, his pale, pudgy hand that is dancing on the gear stick rising out of the floor. His head, bobbing above the rows of seats in front of me, seems to bounce in rhythm with his horn. He honks to *let* pedestrians cross.

He rearranges his hair.

Leans a little forward.

Fluffs a cushion at his back.

We are idling at a crosswalk. We are there seven minutes, when suddenly, out of the air, our driver's voice comes coiling.

On the right side of us is the Flamingo Hotel where Elvis Presley owned a floor of that hotel on our right side.

On the left side of us is the Mirage Hotel where Michael Jackson owns a floor of that hotel on our left side.

His words emit circles, whip bubbles around our heads. His sentences wrap around the bus and greet themselves in midair. All the way to the dam the bus rumbles inside this cloud, the date slips steadily away, the tour transforms into a silent scratchy film that is slowly flitting backward through frames of older dreams.

We sit among neo-Gothic images heaping up from the pages of a souvenir borrowed from Isaac's grandfather, a 1935 photographic essay entitled "The Last Wonder of the World: The Glory of Hoover Dam." On its brittle pages machines still throb, light still beams from the book's center spread.

A full, glossy, long-shot view of the generator room reveals round, sleek, plastic bodies lined up like an army, surrounded by looming concrete walls adorned with pipes of gleaming chrome. Everything stands at attention. Nothing but light is stirring. The whole scene is poised forever to strike against an enemy that never breached the river's shore.

Gambling wasn't legalized in our state until 1935 is when they legalized gambling in Nevada.

The patterns in these pictures are like wax dripping from candles, islands coagulating from spurts of lava, liquid steel pouring out of kettles into rifle molds, Buick frames, the skyscrapers of Chicago. The round machines spin their energy like spools, all of it rolling off their bodies, through the pages, over the slick, curved surface of the next machine, which is identical to the last: which is blinking the same, rounded the same, parodying his sentences revolving around our heads, and shielding our tour from starts and stops, from *In the beginning*, from *Ever after*, from *Now* and from *Then*, and from any time—from all time—in which this vacuous progression cannot fit, because its round body is nowhere near the right shape for the boxy borders of dates.

Just to let you know, folks, our tour company's been on the road since 1945 is how long we've been traveling this road.

I mention to Isaac that the machines resemble something I once saw in *Doctor Who,* and he says, "No they don't"—which is the first thing he has said to me in an hour.

"It's more like *Star Trek*'s Plasma Generator," he says. But when I tell him I don't quite follow him, we decide that something from *Batman* suits our conflicting descriptions best.

What we do not know at this moment, however, is that in 1935, when the dam was opened, Batman was about to make his debut in comic strips. So was Superman, and other superheroes—summoned from Krypton or Gotham City to defend our country against impending evils—their bodies toned flawlessly as turbines. They came with tales of an ideal Tomorrow. They came jostled between two wars, buffering our borders against enemies on every side, encircling the country with an impenetrable force field, and introducing at home a new architecture of resistance: round, sleek, something the old clunky world slipped off.

A lot of these trees and most of this grass is brought in from out of state.

A lot of these trees and most of this grass is brought in from Arizona.

These are the same curves I once found in my grandmother's basement. Toasters so streamlined they're liable to skid off the kitchen counter. A hair dryer filched from Frankenstein's brain-wave lab. A Philharmonic radio taller than my ten-year-old body, and reeking of Swing—leaking tinny voices, platinum songs, and the catch-me-if-you-can whorls from Benny Goodman's silvery tube.

My grandmother's is the world that dropped the bomb—itself a slick object—so elegantly smooth it managed to slip past American consciousness, past enemy lines.

Afterward, in her world, "Atomic" was the prefix attached to the coming world and all the baubles to be found there. But in that present, at the opening of Hoover Dam, the designers of the future could only have guessed what atoms looked like.

And still their imaginations leaped instantly to *round*, to fast, to *heralds of the future*.

3

During the sixth century, St. Gregory of Tours compiled a list of the seven wonders of the medieval world which demonstrates an inaccurate knowledge of history. He retained four wonders from the original list, but made three additions of his own: Noah's Ark, Solomon's Temple, and the Original Tree of Life—which, he claimed, had been discovered in the underground archives of a church in his native France. But St. Gregory, of course, was wrong. The remains of the Tree of Life were used to construct the Crucifix on which our Saviour died—now housed, of course, in the Holy Cross Church in Rome.

—FROM MY GRANDMOTHER'S LIBRARY, G. B. SMITH'S *REMEMBERING THE SAINT*

4

"There's this computer game I like so I guess that counts right? It's not the real world but it lets you do really awesome stuff that's pretty cool so you can call that a wonder I bet. But I gotta go to my friend's house to play it though 'cause my parents won't get it for me 'cause they think it's too violent. Hey you can't write this down or I'm not talking man. It's called *Civilization*. You start with two guys—a guy and a girl—and they're like at the start of the world or something. But after all the animals are made and stuff. And then—um—you have to make babies because the whole point is to you know start the civilization. So the computer keeps asking you what you want to do. Like if you want to have babies at a certain time or if you wanna be a hunter and gatherer or start farming and all that. So at the same time the computer has its own family that it's starting and you have to be in competition with them. So you start your family and all that and you become a village and . . . that's all the boring stuff. But you have to do it to start up the game. So before you know it you're like the leader and everything and people start gods and that kind of stuff and there's laws that you get to make up like if you want people to steal or how many wives you can have. And all of a sudden the computer calls war on you and you have to fight them 'cause if you don't then the game ends 'cause the computer can kill all your people. So there's whole long parts when you gotta learn how to do battle and you decide if you wanna use your metal to make weapons or not and how many people you'll make fight 'cause after you play a long time you learn that if you keep some people in the village during the war you can make them keep making weapons and stuff and help the fighters who are hurt. And usually if you make it through the war with some people left then the computer won't kill you off 'cause it'll let you try to start the village again. So all that happens and—um—every now and then the computer lets you know that someone in the village makes an invention. Like if they use the well to try to make a clock or they build a building with stones that has a roof so you can put more floors on top of it and—you know—then cities start. Then people start sailing down the river and they find other places to live and there are like whole new civilizations that the computer controls that you get to find. Now it all depends on how you act with the new people that tells whether or not you start a war or something or if you join their village and team up your forces. When that happens the computer gives you a lot more technology. So all that goes on and like thousands of years go by and pretty soon it starts looking like the modern world and you're controlling a whole country. Then your goal is to get control of the whole world which only one of my friends has done but then there's always this little place you don't know about that starts a revolution and then the whole world starts fighting and everyone ends up dead. I've never gotten that far though. I've controlled a couple countries before and I usually make them all start a colony in space and what's great is that if you tell them to fly to a planet in the solar system then the computer isn't programmed that far and it lets you do whatever you want for a little while until it just ends the game 'cause it doesn't know how to continue 'cause it can't compete with you if you just keep inventing new stuff it hasn't heard of. So sometimes I get like three countries to go up there and they start this whole new civilization and there are new animals and just the right amount of people and all the buildings are beautiful and built with this river that turns hard when you pick up the water and you can shape it how you want. So there's all this glass around and it's awesome but it only lasts like a year because the computer gets freaked out and ends up stopping the game. The game always ends up destroying the world."

5

When the Canal was being completed, the renowned sculptor Daniel Chester French and the best-known landscape architect of the day, Frederick Law Olmsted, were hired to decorate it. After a careful survey, the two artists refused the commission. So impressed were they by the beauty which the engineers had created that they declared, "For we artists to add to it now would be an impertinence."
1. THE PANAMA CANAL, 1914

MY LIST
"Hello, Joe Miller here."

"Hi, sir. I'm wondering if maybe you could help me out. I'm trying to find the American Society of Civil Engineers' list of the Seven Modern Wonders of the World. Are you the right person to talk to?"

"Yeah, yeah that's me. I think the list you're talking about is pretty old, though. We just announced a new list you might be interested in."

"A new list?"

"The 1999 Modern Wonders of the World."

"Oh. Well, actually I guess I'm interested in the old Modern list."

"Well, that's forty years old! This new one we have is a lot more impressive. I think this is what you're looking for."

"Well, could you maybe tell me about the first list anyway? I can't find it mentioned anywhere in my library. I kind of need it."

"Well, that'll take some time. . . . Let me get back to you . . ."

A common witticism on that bleak Depression day when this spectacular skyscraper opened its doors was, "The only way the landlords will ever fill that thing is if they tow it out to sea." But such pessimistic sentiments were wrong, as pessimists always have been in America. The population of the building now is that of a small city!

2. THE EMPIRE STATE BUILDING, 1931

MY GRANDFATHER'S LIST
"Just put down the Statue of Liberty.
That's all I want you to put down."

How do you dig a hole deeper than anyone has ever dug, fill it with more concrete and steel than has been used in any other public works campaign, and do it all in the middle of California's busiest harbor, swiftest current, most stormy shore? No, no! it would be sheer folly to try—but they did it anyway!

3. THE SAN FRANCISCO–OAKLAND BAY BRIDGE, 1936

MY MOTHER'S LIST
1. The Twin Towers
2. The Apollo Space Program
3. PCs
4. Cannabis
5. Picasso
6. August 9, 1974 (Richard Nixon's resignation)
7. Cape Cod

Then the fun begins. The aqueduct's route crosses two hundred forty-two miles of terrain that looks as if it had been dropped intact from the moon: a landscape of mountainous sands, dry washes, empty basins—one of the hottest, deadliest wastelands in the civilized world. . . . And this conduit, man's longest, spans it all!

4. THE COLORADO RIVER AQUEDUCT, 1938

ISAAC'S MOTHER'S LIST

"Oh, I know these. One must be the Brooklyn Bridge. I practically grew up on that thing! The Eiffel Tower has to be on there. Probably the Sears Tower, too. The Washington Monument. Niagara Falls. What about the Pentagon? And the Hoover Dam, of course."

Flying over the city, below the left wing of the plane, you will see Chicago's Southwest Works, one of the largest and most advanced sewage treatment facilities in the world. It is a veritable modern city, as spanking-looking as if sealed in a fresh-washed bottle, and as motionless and silent as a hospital at night.
5. THE CHICAGO SEWAGE DISPOSAL SYSTEM, 1939

GUY-IN-A-BAR'S LIST
1. A rapid development in our fine and visual arts
2. With all of our technological advancements, a continued sadness among the people
3. Our ignorance of environmental problems
4. Magic
5. The Internet
6. Alaska
7. Hoover Dam

A certain stopper was the fact that the Coulee could only rise to 550 feet. At that height it backed up the Columbia River into a 150-mile-long lake. Any higher and it would have flooded Canada.
6. THE GRAND COULEE DAM, 1941

JOE MILLER'S LIST

"Yeah, this is a message for John D'Agata. I have that information you requested. This is the 1999 list of Modern Wonders of the World:

one is The Golden Gate Bridge;
two, The World Trade Center;
three, The U.S. Interstate Highway System;
four, The Kennedy Space Center;
five, The Panama Canal;
six, The Trans-Alaskan Pipeline;
and seven is Hoover Dam."

It lofts up with the majesty of Beauty itself, and you marvel at what man-
ner of men could have conceived the possibility of building such a wonder.
7. THE HOOVER DAM, 1935 (FROM *AMERICA THE BEAUTIFUL: AN*
INTRODUCTION TO OUR SEVEN WONDERS)

6

Perhaps the Book of Genesis is the first and most famous list of wonders. Today, however, such rosters of remarkable things are common in America.

Whenever I visit a city for the first time, I always notice the gold stars on storefronts—"Voted Best Barbershop," ". . . Mexican Food," ". . . Auto Repair." My brother, who prides himself on his ability to spot "quality trends," as he calls them, has sworn for years by *Boston Magazine*'s annual "Best Of" issue.

He says that living by the list is like living in a perfect world. And the list has grown so comprehensive each year that, these days, my brother seldom has to live without perfection. He has found, for example, a "professional scalper" with the best last-minute Bruins ticket deals, a launderer known for having the best-pressed cuffs, and a sportsman's lodge with the best range for skeet shooting—a sport my brother has taken up simply out of awe of it being listed.

Another purveyor of perfection has gone so far as to publish a book-length list, entitled *The Best of Everything*, which includes the Best Sexy Animal (the female giraffe), the Best Labor-Saving Device (the guillotine), the Best Vending Machine (a mashed-potato dispenser in Nottingham, England), and the Best Souvenir (a shrunken head from Quito, Ecuador).

Not to be outdone, proponents of the worst things in the world have published *The Worst of Everything*. On this list can be found the Worst Nobel Peace Prize Recipient (Henry Kissinger), the Worst Item Ever Auctioned (Napoleon's dried penis), the Worst Poem Ever Written ("The Child" by Friedreich Hebbel), and the Worst Celebrity Endorsement for a Car (Hitler, for the Volkswagen Bug: "This streamlined four-seater is a mechanical marvel. It can be bought on an installment plan for six Reichsmarks a week—including insurance!")

Now Isaac's mother leans over our seats and shows us both another brochure.

"Just think how happy they all must have been," she says, unfolding an artist's rendition of the future across our laps. "I sure wish I lived back then. You know?"

1939. Queens, New York.

She, Isaac, and I have just paid our fifty cents, and before us—miles wide—are promenades, sculptures, buildings, and glittery things, all laid out in perfect grids. "So bright and lovely," she says, "it makes me want to close my eyes." Even the people around us shine, sweaty inside their wool suits and skirts. There are thousands of them, Isaac decides—just like the people who walk around Epcot.

"You know," he says. "The kind who you can't really tell are real or not."

We buy frankfurters, a guidebook, little silver spoons at every exhibition. We are here because—even as far west as Nevada, even as far into the future as 1999—we have heard that this is the greatest fair ever orchestrated on earth.

We start with Isaac's mom's list: the Gardens on Parade, the Town of Tomorrow, the House of Jewels, the Plaza of Light, Democracity.

Then we visit Isaac's list: the Futurama, the Academy of Sports, the Court of Power, the Lagoon of Nations, the Dome of the Heinz Corp.

And by the time we visit my list we have stumbled smack into the middle of the fair, inches from its epicenter, squinting back up at those dazzling fair trademarks known in our guidebook as *Trylon* and *Perisphere*. The obelisk and the globe stand like silence behind the roaring and spurting of ten giant fountains.

The two of them are like fountains behind the silence of our gaze.

One of them is stretched so high it scrapes the color from the sky. The other is arched playfully on its own curved back.

The obelisk, we read, is 610 feet tall ("That's 50 feet taller than the Washington Monument!" our guidebook claims). The sphere is 180 feet in diameter ("The largest globe in the state of New York!").

Both objects are words that never before existed. And despite all the euphoria surrounding them in '39, all the family photos posed in front of them, the silverware and shaving kits and Bissell Carpet Sweepers that bore their images, *Trylon* and *Perisphere* never made it into our lexicon.

At the foot of them, I can't see why.

One is like a list, the other is like a wonder. But I don't say this aloud.

"An arrow and a bull's-eye!" one of us blurts out. And so they are. Perfectly.

Or one is like an ancient scroll unrolled; the other is an orb of indecipherable glyphs. One is how we describe a fantasy; the other is what we've secretly dreamt.

Shoulder to shoulder, we three look them up, then down. Our mouths hang wide—with *awe*—filled with them.

I remember the first list of wonders that I ever knew. One year, an old man on our street told my mother that he had once been a college professor, a master of Latin and Greek. Within days I was studying classics with him. I had just turned eight.

My tutor, Mr. Newcomb, lived along among statuary and plaster casts of temple friezes. Tapestries padded his walls. I met with him each day in the barest room of his house: a desk, two chairs, a lamp, a rug, and seven hanging woodcuts of the seven ancient wonders.

Some days, instead of reading, Mr. Newcomb beguiled me with trivia about the hanging wonders on his walls. And some days, strewn over the years, he divulged their secrets. Why, for instance, the curse of the Pyramids in fact is real; where, in Turkey, the Colossus' body parts are actually hidden; what, according to Vatican documents, which Mr. Newcomb alone had read in Rome, Napoleon "felt" as he pissed on the charred remains of Diana's great temple.

Later, Mr. Newcomb's woodcuts of the seven ancient wonders became mine once he had died. At that point, however, I had only managed to grasp the first conjugation in Latin, so for years after, until I could return to Latin in school, the ancient wonders lived beside me in a parallel present tense.

I have them still. They hang around—dark, worn—reminding me of the last wonderful secret my tutor left: that he had never studied Latin, never read the classics. That he had never traveled to Rome, nor much farther beyond our town.

He had never actually liked school.

Yet what he had was curiosity. Crustiness. An air of scholastic formality. He had a dustiness that was reliable. A home adorned tastefully, lessons always prepared for me, cookies, milk, stories that kept me rapt. He had a knack, which was his lure, for both the mundane and fantastic.

The black-breasted roadrunner, my favorite bird, is that black-breasted roadrunner there.

The bird hurries past our bus, darting up the mountain pass as we slowly descend its peak. I am awakened by our driver's voice and my ears popping as we slide into the valley. Everyone else, everyone except for Isaac and the one-way man, is asleep. They chat across the center aisle.

"I'm gonna live there," says the one-way man, when Isaac asks what he'll do when we arrive at the dam.

"You can live there?" Isaac asks.

"Well, I'm gonna," says the man.

Isaac's mom, I know, would want me to intervene here, tell Isaac the man's just joking with him. Tell Isaac the one-way man is crazy.

But when Isaac starts talking about his computer game, and the one-way man explains how the concave wall of the Hoover Dam would be awesome for skateboarding, it is they who stop, mutually—nowhere conclusive and without any care.

They sit back in their seats, stare forward awhile, and fall asleep.

7

continents, days per week, Deadly Sins, Epochs of Man according to Shakespeare, hills of Rome, liberal arts, perfect shapes, planets in the Ptolemaic system, Pleiades in Greek myth, Sacraments, seas, Sleepers of Ephesus, wives of Bluebeard, wonders of Yemen, Years War

PAUL DI FILIPPO

One Night in Television City

⌒⌒⌒

I'M FRICTIONLESS, MOLARS, SO DON'T POINT those flashlights at
me. I ain't going nowhere, you can see that clear as hubble. Just like
superwire, I got no resistance, so why doncha all just gimme some slack?

What'd you say, molar? Your lifter's got a noisy fan—it's interfering with
your signal. How'd I get up here? That's an easy one. I just climbed. But I got
a better one for you.

Now that I ain't no Dudley Dendrite anymore, how the fuck am I gonna
get down?

JUST A FEW SHORT HOURS ago it was six o'clock on a Saturday night
like any other, and I was sitting in a metamilk bar called the Slak Shak, feel-
ing sorry for myself for a number of good and sufficient reasons. I was down
so low there wasn't an angstrom's worth of difference between me and a
microbe. You see, I had no sleeve, I had no set, I had no eft. Chances were I
wasn't gonna get any of 'em anytime soon, either. The prospect was enough
to make me wanna float away on whatever latest toxic corewipe the Shak
was offering.

I asked the table for the barlist. It was all the usual bugjuice and horse-
sweat, except for a new item called Needlestrength-Nine. I ordered a dose,
and it came in a cup of cold frothy milk sprinkled with cinnamon. I downed
it all in two gulps, the whole nasty mess of transporter proteins and neu-
rotropins, a stew of long-chain molecules that were some konky biobrujo's
idea of blister-packed heaven.

All it did was make me feel like I had a cavity behind my eyes filled with shuttle-fuel. My personal sitspecs still looked as lousy as a rat's shaved ass.

That's the trouble with the tropes and strobers you can buy in the metamilk bars: they're all kid's stuff, G-rated holobytes. If you want a real slick kick, some black meds, then you got to belong to a set, preferably one with a smash watson boasting a clean labkit. A Fermenta, or Wellcome, or Cetus rig, say. Even an Ortho'll do.

But as I said, I had no set, nor any prospect of being invited into one. Not that I'd leap at an invite to just any old one, you latch. Some of the sets were too toxic for me.

So there I sat with a skull full of liquid oxygen, feeling just like the Challenger before liftoff, more bummed than before I had zero-balanced my eft on the useless drink. I was licking the cinnamon off the rim of the glass when who should slope in but my one buddy, Casio.

Casio was a little younger 'n me, about fifteen. He was skinny and white and had more acne than a worker in a dioxin factory. He coulda had skin as clear as anyone else's, but he was always forgetting to use his epicream. He wore a few strands of grafted fiberoptics in his brown hair, an imipolex vest that bubbled constantly like some kinda slime mold, a pair of parchment pants, and a dozen jelly-bracelets on his left forearm.

"Hey, Dez," said Casio, rapping knuckles with me, "how's it climbing?"

Casio didn't have no set neither, but it didn't seem to bother him like it bothered me. He was always up, always smiling and happy. Maybe it had to do with his music, which was his whole life. It seemed to give him something he could always fall back on. I had never seen him really down. Sometimes it made me wanna choke the shit outta him.

"Not so good, molar. Life looks emptier'n the belly of a Taiwanese baby with the z-virus craps."

Casio pulled up a seat. "Ain't things working out with Chuckie?"

I groaned. Why I had ever fantasized aloud to Casio about Chuckie and me, I couldn't now say. I musta really been in microgravity that day. "Just forget about Charlotte and me, will you do me that large fave? There's nothing between us, nothing, you latch?"

Casio looked puzzled. "Nothing? Whadda ya mean? The way you talked, I thought she was your best sleeve."

"No, you got it all wrong, molar, we was both wasted, remember? . . ."

Casio's vest extruded a long wavy stalk that bulged into a ball at its tip before being resorbed. "Gee, Dez, I wish I had known all this before. I been talking you two up as a hot item all around TeeVeeCee."

My heart swelled up big as the bicep on a metasteroid freak and whooshed up into my throat. "No, molar, say it ain't so. . . ."

"Gee, Dez, I'm sorry. . . ."

I was in deep gurry now all right. I could see it clear as M31 in the hubblescope. Fish entrails up to the nose.

Chuckie was Turbo's sleeve. Turbo was headman of the Body Artists. The Body Artists were the prime set in Television City. I was as the dirt between their perpetually bare toes.

I pushed back my seat. The Slak Shak was too hot now. Everybody knew I floated there.

"Casio, I feel like a walk. Wanna come?"

"Yeah, sure."

T Street—the big north-south boulevard wide as old Park Ave that was Television City's main crawl (it ran from Fifty-ninth all the way to Seventy-second—was packed with citizens and greenies, morphs and gullas, all looking for the heart of Saturday night, just like the old song by that growly chigger has it. The sparkle and glitter was all turned up to eleven, but TeeVeeCee looked kinda old to me that night, underneath its amber-red-green-blue neo-neon maquillage. The whole minicity on the banks of the Hudson was thirty years old now, after all, and though that was nothing compared to the rest of Nuevo York, it was starting to get on. I tried to imagine being nearly twice as old as I was now and figured I'd be kinda creaky myself by then.

All the scrawls laid down by the sets on any and every blank surface didn't help the city's looks any either. Fast as the cleanup crews sprayed the paint-eating bugs on the graffiti, the sets nozzled more. These were just a few that Casio and I passed:

PUT A CRICK IN YOUR DICK.
STROBE YOUR LOBES.
BOOT IT OR SHOOT IT.
HOLLOW? SWALLOW. FOLLOW.
SIN, ASP! SAID THE SYNAPSE.
MATCH IT, BATCH IT, LATCH IT.
BEAT THE BARRIER!
SNAP THE GAP!
AXE YOUR AXONS.
KEEP YOUR RECEPTORS FILLED.

"Where we going, Dez?" asked Casio, snapping off one of his jelly-bracelets for me to munch on.

"Oh, noplace special," I said around a mouthful of sweat-metabolizing symbiote that tasted like strawberries. "We'll just wander around a bit and see what we can see."

All the time I was wondering if I even dared to go home to my scat, if I'd find Turbo and his set waiting there for me, with a word or two to say about me talking so big about his sleeve.

Well, we soon came upon a guy with his car pulled over to the curb with the hood up. He was poking at the ceramic fuel-cell with a screwdriver, like he hoped to fix it that way.

"That's a hundred-thirty-two horsepower Malaysian model, ain't it?" asked Casio.

"Yeah," the guy said morosely.

"I heard they're all worth bugshit."

The guy got mad then and started waving the screwdriver at us. "Get the hell out of here, you nosey punks!"

Casio slid a gold jelly-bracelet off his arm, tossed it at the guy, and said, "Run!"

We ran.

Around a corner, we stopped, panting.

"What was it?" I said.

"Nothing too nasty. Just rotten eggs and superstik."

We fell down laughing.

When we were walking again, we tried following a couple of gullas. We could tell by their government-issue suits that they were fresh out of one of the floating midocean relocation camps, and we were hoping to diddle them for some eft. But they talked so funny that we didn't even know how to scam them.

"We go jeepney now up favela way?"

"No, mon, first me wan' some ramen."

"How fix?"

"We loop."

"And be zeks? Don' vex me, dumgulla. You talkin' like a manga now, mon."

After that we tailed a fattie for a while. We couldn't make up our minds if it was a male or female or what. It was dressed in enough billowing silk to outfit a parachute club and walked with an asexual waddle. It went into the fancy helmsley at Sixty-fifth, to meet its client no doubt.

"I hate those fatties," said Casio. "Why would anyone want to weigh more than what's healthy, if they don't have to?"

"Why would anyone keep his stupid zits if he didn't have to?"

Casio looked hurt. "That's different, Dez. You know I just forget my cream. It's not like I wanna."

I felt bad for hurtin' Casio then. Here he was, my only proxy, keeping me company while I tried to straighten out in my head how I was gonna get trump with Turbo and his set, and I had to go and insult him.

I put an arm around his shoulders. "Sorry, molar. Listen, just wipe it like I never said it, and let's have us a good time. You got any eft?"

"A little . . ."

"Well, let's spend it! The fluid eft gathers no taxes, *es verdad?* Should we hit Club GaAs?"

Casio brightened. "Yeah! The Nerveless are playing tonight. Maybe Ginko'll let me sit in."

"Sounds trump. Let's go."

Overhead the wetworkers—both private and government dirty-harrys—cruised by on their lifters, the jetfans blowing hot on our necks, even from their high altitude. Standing in the center of their flying cages, gloved mitts gripping their joysticks, with their owleyes on, they roved TeeVeeCee, alert for signs of rumble, bumble, or stumble, whereupon they would swoop down and chill the heat with tingly shockers or even flashlights, should the sitspecs dictate.

Club GaAs occupied a fraction of the million square feet of empty building that had once housed one of the old television networks that had given TeeVeeCee its name. Ever since the free networks had been absorbed into the metamedium, the building had gone begging for tenants. Technically speaking, it was still tenantless, since Club GaAs was squatting there illegally.

At the door we paid the cover to a surly anabolic hulkster and went inside.

Club GaAs had imipolex walls that writhed just like Casio's vest, dancing in random biomorphic ripples and tendrils. On the stage the Nerveless were just setting up, it being still early, only around eight. I had only met Ginko once, but I recognized him from his green skin and leafy hair. Casio went onstage to talk to him, and I sat down at a table near one wall and ordered a cheer-beer.

Casio rejoined me. "Ginko says I can handle the megabops."

The cheer-beer had me relaxing so I had almost forgotten my problems. "That's trump, proxy. Listen, have a cheer-beer—it's your eft."

Casio sat and we talked a while about the good old days, when we were still kids in high school, taking our daily rations of mnemotropins like good little drudges.

"You remember at graduation, when somebody spiked the refreshments with funky-monkey?"

"Yeah. I never seen so many adults acting like apes before or since. Miz Spencer up on the girders—!"

"Boy, we were so young then."

"I was even younger than you, Dez. I was eleven and you were already twelve, remember?"

"Yeah, but them days are wiped now, Casio. We're adults ourselves now, with big adult probs." All my troubles flooded back to me like ocean waves on the Big-One-revised California shoreline as I said this konky bit of wisdom.

Casio was sympathetic. I could fax that much, but he didn't have the answers to my probs any more than I did. So he just stood and said, "Well, Dez, I got to go play now." He took a few steps away from the table and then was snapped back to his seat like he had a rubber band strung to his ass.

"Hold on a millie," I said. "The wall has fused with your vest." I took out my little utility flashlight and lasered the wall pseudopod that had mated with Casio's clothing.

"Thanks, proxy," he said, and then was off.

I sat there nursing the dregs of my cheer-beer while the Nerveless tuned up. When the rickracks were spinning fast and the megabops were humming and everyone had their percussion suits on, they jumped into an original comp, "Efferent Ellie."

Forty-five minutes later, after two more cheer-beers thoughtfully provided by the management to the grateful friend of the band, I was really on the downlink with Casio and the Nerveless. I felt their music surging through me like some sonic trope. Tapping my foot, wangle-dangling my head like some myelin-stripped spaz, I was so totally downloading that I didn't even see Turbo and his set slope on into Club GaAs and surround me.

When the current song ended and I looked up, there they all were: Turbo and his main sleeve, Chuckie, who had her arm around his waist; Jeeter, Hake, Pablo, Mona, Val, Ziggy, Pepper, Gates, Zane, and a bunch of others I didn't know.

"Hah-hah-hah-how's it climbing, molars?" I said.

They were all as quiet and stone-faced as the holo of a cheap Turing Level One AI with its mimesis-circuits out of whack. As for me, I could do nothing but stare.

The Body Artists were all naked save for spandex thongs, he's and she's alike, the better to insure proper extero- and interoceptor input. Their skins were maculated with a blotchy tan giraffe pattern. The definition of every muscle on their trim bods was like *Gray's Anatomy* come to life.

Now, to me, there were no two ways about it: the Body Artists were simply the most trump set in TeeVeeCee. The swiftest, nastiest, downloadingest pack of lobe-strobers ever to walk a wire or scale a pole. Who else were you gonna compare 'em to? The Vectors? A bunch of wussies dreaming their days away in mathspace. (I didn't buy their propaganda about being able to disappear along the fourth dimension either.) The Hardz 'n' Wetz? Nothing but crazy meatgrinders, the negative image of their rivals, the Eunuchs. The Less Than Zeroes? I don't call pissing your pants satori, like they do. The Thumbsuckers? Who wants to be a baby forever? The Boardmen? I can't see cutting yourself up and headbanging just to prove you feel no pain. The Annies? A horde of walking skeletons. The Naked Apes? After seeing our whole faculty under the influence of funky-monkey that day, I had never latched onto that trip. The Young Jungs? Who wants to spend his whole life diving into the racemind?

No, the only ones who might just give the Body Artists a run for their eft were the Adonises or the Sapphos, but they had some obvious kinks that blocked my receptors.

So you'll understand how I could feel—even as the center of their threatening stares—a kind of thrill at being in the presence of the assembled Body Artists. If only they had come to ask me to join them, instead of, as was so apparent, being here with the clear intention of wanting to cut my nuts off—

The Nerveless started another song. Casio was too busy to see what was happening with me. Not that he coulda done much anyhow. Turbo sat liquidly down across from me, pulling Chuckie down onto his lap.

"So, Dez," he said, cool as superwire, "I hear you are Chuckie's secret mojoman now."

"No, no way, Turbo, the parity bits got switched on that message all right. There ain't no truth to it, no sir, no way."

"Oh, I see, molar," said Turbo, deliberately twisting things around tighter'n a double-helix. "My sleeve Chuckie ain't trump enough for a molar who's as needlestrength as you."

I raised my eyes and caught Chuckie sizing me up with high indifference. Her looks made me feel like I was trying to swallow an avocado pit.

Charlotte Thach was a supertrump Cambodian-Hawaiian chica whose folks had emigrated to TeeVeeCee when the Japs kicked everyone outta the ex-state in the process of forming the Asian-Pacific Economic Cooperative. Her eyes were green as diskdrive lights, her sweet little tits had nipples the color of strong tea.

After she was done sizing me up, she held out one beautiful hand as if to admire her nails or something. Then, without moving a single muscle that I could see, she audibly popped each joint in her fingers in sequence. I could hear it clear above the music.

I gulped down that slimy pit and spoke. "No, Turbo, she's trump enough for anyone."

Turbo leaned closer across Chuckie. "Ah, but that's the prob, molar. Chuckie don't do it with just anyone. In fact, none of the Artists do. Why, if you were to try to ride her, she'd likely snap your cock off. Body to Body only, you latch?"

"Yeah, sure, I latch."

Turbo straightened up. "Now, the question is, what we gonna do with someone whose head got so big he thought he could tell everyone he was bumpin' pubes with a Body Artist?"

"No disinfo, Turbo, I didn't mean nothin' by it."

"Shut up, I got to think."

While he was thinking, Turbo made all the muscles in his torso move around like snakes under his skin.

After letting me sweat toxins for a while, Turbo said, "I suppose it would satisfy the set's honor if we were to bring you up to the top of the George Washington Bridge and toss you off—"

"Oh, holy radwaste, Turbo, my molar, my proxy, I really don't think that's necessary—"

Turbo held up his hand. "But the ecoharrys might arrest us for dumping shit in the river!"

All the Body Artists had a good laugh at that. I tried to join in, but all that came out was a sound like "ekk-ekk-ekk."

"On the other hand," said Turbo, rotating his upraised hand and forearm around a full two-seventy degrees, "if you were to become a Body Artist, then we could let it be known that you were under consideration all along, even when you were making your konky boasts."

"Oh, Turbo, yeah, yeah, you don't know how much—"

Turbo shot to his feet then, launching Chuckie into a series of spontaneous cartwheels all the way across the club.

"Jeeter, Hake! You're in charge of escorting the pledge. Everyone! Back to nets!"

We blew out of Club GaAs like atmosphere out of a split-open o'neill. My head was spinning like a Polish space station. I was running with the Body Artists! It was something I could hardly believe. Even though I had no hint of where they were taking me; even though they might be setting me up for something that would wipe me out flatter than my eft-balance—I felt totally frictionless. The whole city looked like a place out of a fantasy or stiffener holo to me, Middle Earth or *Debbie Does Mars*. The air was cool as an AI's paraneurons on my bare arms.

We headed west, toward the riverside park. After a while I started to lag behind the rest. Without a word, Jeeter and Hake picked me up under my arms and continued running with me.

We entered among the trees and continued down empty paths, under dirty sodium lights. I could smell the Hudson off to my right. A dirty-harry buzzed by overhead but didn't stop to bother us.

Under a busted light we halted in darkness. Nobody was breathing heavy but me, and I had been carried the last half mile. Hake and Jeeter placed me down on my own feet.

Someone bent down and tugged open a metal hatch with a snapped hasp set into the walk. The Body Artists descended one by one. Nervous as a kid taking his first trope, I went down too, sandwiched between Hake and Jeeter.

Television City occupied a hundred acres of land which had originally sloped down to the Hudson. The eastern half of TeeVeeCee was built on solid ground; the western half stood on a huge platform elevated above the Conrail maglev trains.

Fifteen rungs down, I was staring up at the underside of TeeVeeCee by the light of a few caged safety bulbs, a rusty constellation of rivets in a flaky steel sky.

The ladder terminated at an I beam wide as my palm. I stepped gingerly off, but still held on to the ladder. I looked down.

A hundred feet below, a lit-up train shot silently by at a hundred-and-eighty mph.

I started back up the ladder.

"Where to, molar?" asked Hake above me.

"Uh, straight ahead, I guess."

I stepped back onto the girder, took two wobbly Thumbsucker steps, then carefully lowered myself until I could wrap my arms and legs around the beam.

Hake and Jeeter unpeeled me. Since they had to go single file, they trotted along carrying me like a trussed pig. I kept my eyes closed and prayed.

I felt them stop. Then they were swinging me like a sack. At the extreme of one swing, they let me go.

Hurtling through the musty air, I wondered how long it would take me to hit the ground or a passing train and what it would feel like. I wouldn'ta minded so much being a Boardman just then.

It was only a few feet to the net. When I hit, it shot me up a bit. I oscillated a few times until my recoil was absorbed. Only then did I open my eyes.

The Body Artists were standing or lounging around on the woven mesh of graphite cables with perfect balance. Turbo had this radwaste-eating grin on his handsome face.

"Welcome to the nets, Mister Pledge. You didn't do so bad. I seen molars who fainted and fell off the ladder when they first come out below. Maybe you'll make it through tonight after all. C'mon now, follow us."

The Body Artists set off along the nets. Somehow they managed to coordinate and compensate for all the dozens of different impulses traveling along the mesh so that they knew just how to step and not lose their balance. They rode the wavefronts of each other's motions like some kinda aerial surfers.

Me? I managed to crawl along, mostly on all fours.

We reached a platform scabbed onto one of the immense pillars that upheld the city. There the Body Artists had their lab, for batching their black meds.

I hadn't known that Ziggy was the Artists' watson. But once I saw him moving among the chromo-cookers and amino-linkers like a fish in soup, if you know what I mean, it was clear as hubble that he was the biobrujo responsible for stoking the Artists' neural fires.

While Ziggy worked I had to watch Turbo and Chuckie making out. I knew they were doing it just to blow grit through my scramjets, so I tried not to let it bother me. Even when Chuckie— Well, never mind exactly what she did, except to say I never realized it was humanly possible to get into that position.

Ziggy finally came over with a cup full of uncut bugjuice.

"Latch onto this, my molar," he said with crickly craftsmanly pride, "and you'll know a little more about what it means to call yourself a B-Artist."

I knew I didn't want to taste the undiluted juice, so I chugged it as fast as I could. Even the aftertaste nearly made me retch.

Half an hour later, I could feel the change.

I stood up and walked out onto the net. Turbo and the others started yanking it up and down.

I didn't lose my balance. Even when I went to one foot. Then I did a handstand.

"Okay, molar," said Turbo sarcastically, "don't think you're so trump. All we gave you is heightened 'ception, extero, intero, and proprio. Plus a little myofibril booster and something to damp your fatigue poisons. And it's all as temporary as a whore's kisses. So, let's get down to it."

Turbo set off back along the nets, and I followed.

"No one else?" I asked.

"No, Dez, just us two good proxies."

We retraced our way to the surface. Walking along the I beam under my own power, I felt like king of the world.

Once again we raced through the streets of Television City. This time I easily kept pace with Turbo. But maybe, I thought, he was letting me, trying to lull me into a false sense of security. I made up my mind to go a little slower in all this—if I could.

At last we stood at the southern border of T-City. Before us reared the tallest building in all of old Nuevo York, what used to be old man Trump's very HQ, before he was elected president and got sliced and diced like he did. One hundred and fifty stories worth of glass and ferrocrete, full of set-backs, crenellations, and ledges.

"Now we're going for a little climb," Turbo said.

"You got to be yanking my rods, molar. It's too smooth."

"Nope, it's not. That's the good thing about these old postmodern build-ings. They got the flash and filigree that make for decent handholds."

Then he shimmied up a drainpipe that led to the second floor faster than I could follow.

But follow I did, my molars, believe me. I kicked off my shoes and zipped right after him. No disinfo, I was scared, but I was also mad and ecstatic and floating in my own microgravity.

The first fifty stories were frictionless. I kept up with Turbo, matching him hold for hold. When he smiled, I even smiled back.

Little did I know that he was teasing me.

A third of the way up we stopped to rest on a wide ledge. I didn't look down, since I knew that even with my new perfect balance the sight of where I was would be sure to put grit in my jets.

We peered in through the lighted window behind us and saw a cleaning robot busy vacuuming the rugs. We banged on the glass, but couldn't get it to notice us. Then we started up again.

At the halfway mark Turbo started showing off. While I was slowing down, he seemed to have more energy than ever. In the time I took to ascend one story, he squirreled all around me, making faces, and busting my chops.

"You're gonna fall now, Dez. I got you up here right where I want you. You ain't never gonna get to lay a finger on Chuckie, you latch? When you hit, there ain't gonna be anything left of you bigger'n a molecule."

And suchlike. I succeeded in ignoring it until he said, "Gee, that Ziggy's getting kinda forgetful lately. Ain't been taking his mnemos. I wonder if he remembered to make sure your dose had the right duration? Be a shame if you maxxed out right now."

"You wouldn't do that—" I said and instinctively looked over my shoulder to confront Turbo.

He was beneath me, hanging by his toes from a ledge, head directed at the ground.

I saw the ground.

Television City was all spread out, looking like a one-to-one-hundred-scale model in some holo studio somewhere.

I froze. I heard one of my fingernails crack right in half.

"Whatsamatter, Dez? You lost it yet, or what?"

It was the konky tone of Turbo's voice that unfroze me. I wasn't gonna fall and hear his toxic laugh all the long stories down.

"Race you the rest of the way," I said.

He changed a little then. "No need, proxy, just take it one hold at a time."

So I did.

For seventy-five more stories.

The top of the building boasted a spire surrounded on four sides by a lit-tle railed-off platform whose total area was 'bout as big as a bathroom carpet.

I climbed unsteadily over the railing and sat down, dangling my legs over the side. I could already feel the changes inside me, so I wasn't surprised when Turbo said, "It's worn off for real now, Dez. I wouldn't try going down the way we came up, if I was you. Anyway, the harrys should be here soon. The stretch for something like this is only a year with good behavior. Look us up when you get out."

Then he went down, headfirst, waggling his butt at me.

So, like I asked you before.

Now that I ain't no Dudley Dendrite anymore, how the fuck am I gonna get down?

CONTRIBUTORS

Kim Addonizio is the author of several books including *Tell Me*, which was a finalist for the National Book Award in poetry, *The Philosopher's Club*, *Jimmy & Rita*, and a short story collection titled *In the Box Called Pleasure*. She is also coeditor of *Dorothy Parker's Elbow: Tattoos on Writers, Writers on Tattoos*.

Tony Ardizzone is the author of six books of fiction, most recently the novel *In the Garden of Papa Santuzzu*, and the collection *Taking It Home: Stories from the Neighborhood*.

Ken Auletta has written the "Annals of Communications" column for *The New Yorker* since 1992. He is the author of eight books, including *Three Blind Mice: How the TV Networks Lost Their Way*; *Greed and Glory on Wall Street: The Fall of the House of Lehman*; and *World War 3.0: Microsoft and Its Enemies*. He has also been a staff writer for the *Village Voice*, the *New York Daily News*, and the *New York Post*.

J. T. Barbarese's books of poems are *Under the Blue Moon* and *New Science*, and his poetry and short fiction have been published in the *Atlantic Monthly*, *Boulevard*, and the *North American Review*. His translation of Euripides' *The Children of Heracles* was published by the University of Pennsylvania Press in 1999. He is an assistant professor of writing and English at Rutgers University's Camden, New Jersey, campus.

American Book Award winner Helen Barolini has published widely, including fiction (*Umbertina*, *More Italian Hours and Other Stories*) and nonfiction (*Chiaroscuro: Essays of Identity*), and has edited *Dream Book: An Anthology of Writings by Italian-American Women*.

Mary Caponegro was born in Brooklyn of Calabrian and other Italian stock. She is the author of several story collections, including *The Star Café*, *The Complexi-*

ties of Intimacy, and *Five Doubts,* and is a professor of writing and literature at Bard College.

Mary Cappello is a professor of English at the University of Rhode Island and the author of *Night Bloom,* a memoir, and *My Commie Sweetheart: Scenes from a Queer Friendship.* She has taught on a Fulbright at the Gorky Literary Institute in Moscow and is working with Italian photographer Paola Ferrario on "Pane Amaro/Bitter Bread: The Struggle of New Immigrants to Italy." Her grandparents emigrated from the towns of Teano, Campobasso, and Belmonte Mezzagno (Sicily).

Philip Caputo was born in Chicago in 1941 and served in the U.S. Marine Corps in Vietnam. He became a reporter and foreign correspondent for the *Chicago Tribune,* sharing in a Pulitzer Prize for investigative reporting in 1973 and winning an Overseas Press Award. In addition to *A Rumor of War,* he has written three other works of nonfiction, five novels, and one collection of novellas, and is at work on a novel set in Africa. His ancestors come from Calabria, in southern Italy. He has two sons and lives with his wife in Connecticut.

John Ciardi (1916–1986) published twenty books of poetry, much of which can be found in *The Collected Poems of John Ciardi* (edited by Edward M. Cifelli and published by University of Arkansas Press in 1997). He also wrote many books of children's verse, criticism, word history and essays, including the influential textbook *How Does a Poem Mean?* (1959). His translation of Dante is still considered by many to be the best in American verse. Ciardi also had a TV program, *Accent,* on CBS in the early 1960s, and a regular spot titled "A Word in Your Ear" that ran for nine years on National Public Radio.

Rita Ciresi is the author of five works of fiction: *Mother Rocket, Blue Italian, Pink Slip, Sometimes I Dream in Italian,* and her newest novel, *Remind Me Again Why I Married You.*

Gregory Corso (1930–2001) was born in Greenwich Village, served a prison sentence at age sixteen on a robbery charge, and was a major figure among the Beat writers. He published many books of verse, most notably *The Happy Birthday of Death, Gasoline & the Vestal Lady on Brattle,* and *Mind Field.*

John D'Agata is the author of *Halls of Fame* and editor of a forthcoming anthology, *The Next American Essay.* His family comes from the southeast curve of Sicily and then from various Italian-American ghettos. He lives on a beach in New Hampshire.

Michael DeCapite was born in Cleveland in 1962. His published work includes a novel, *Through the Windshield* (Sparkle Street Books, 1998), and *Sitting Pretty* (Cuz Editions, 1999).

Raymond DeCapite was born in Cleveland in 1924. His published novels are *The Coming of Fabrizze, A Lost King, Pat the Lion on the Head, Go Very Highly Trippingly To and Fro,* and *The Stretch Run.* His plays, including *Sparky and Company, Things Left Standing,* and *Zinfandel,* have been produced in New York,

Cleveland, and elsewhere. His people come from the Abruzzi and Basilicata regions of Italy.

Don De Grazia is a professor of creative writing at Columbia College Chicago and the author of the novel *American Skin*. He also edits *F Magazine*, a journal of new fiction. He was born in Chicago to a family that originates in Basilicata and Sicily.

Don DeLillo was born and raised in New York City. He has written twelve novels and two stage plays and has won many honors in this country and abroad, including the National Book Award, the PEN/Faulkner Award for Fiction, and the Jerusalem Prize. His most recent books include *The Body Artist*, *Underworld*, and *Mao II*.

Poet and fiction writer Rachel Guido DeVries's most recent book of verse is *Gambler's Daughter* (Guernica Editions). She is also the author of *How to Sing to a Dago* (poems, Guernica Editions), and *Tender Warriors*, a novel (Firebrand). Her family is of Sicilian and Calabrian ancestry. She grew up in Paterson, New Jersey, and teaches creative writing in the Humanistic Studies Center of Syracuse University.

Pietro DiDonato (1911–92) wrote the classic work of Italian-American fiction, the 1939 novel *Christ in Concrete*, which was a best-seller. (In 1949, Edward Dmytryk directed a film version of the book titled *Give Us This Day*.) A second novel, *This Woman*, was published in 1958, followed by *Three Circles of Light*, a sequel to *Christ*. He also wrote two biographies, *Immigrant Saint: The Life of Mother Cabrini* and *The Penitent*, about the man who murdered Maria Goretti. He spent his life working as a contractor and journalist and just before his death completed a still unpublished novel, *The American Gospels*.

Paul Di Filippo is a native of Rhode Island. He has published many works of science fiction and fantasy, among them *The Steampunk Trilogy*, *Ribofunk*, *Fractal Paisleys* (which was nominated for the World Fantasy Award, Best Collection), *Joe's Liver*, and *Lost Pages*, winner of a Citation for Excellence from the Philip K. Dick Award.

W. S. Di Piero has published numerous volumes of poetry, criticism, and translation. His most recent book of poems is *Skirts and Slacks*. He works as an art journalist and teaches at Stanford University. He grew up in South Philadelphia and lives in San Francisco.

Beverly Donofrio was born in 1950 in Wallingford, Connecticut, into a family that originates in the Caserta region of Italy and in Rome. Her memoir, *Riding in Cars with Boys*, was made into a movie starring Drew Barrymore.

John Fante (1909–1983) was born in Denver but was best known as a writer in and about Los Angeles. He published many short stories, novels, and screenplays; among those still in print are *Wait Until Spring, Bandini*; *Ask the Dust*; *The Wine of Youth* (stories, including a previous collection titled *Dago Red*); *Full of Life*; *The Brotherhood of the Grape*; and *West of Rome*, all of which are published by Black Sparrow Press. His work is also found in *The John Fante Reader*, edited by Stephen Cooper.

Luigi Funaro is a poet and postal worker living in Atlantic City. His ancestors are from the provinces of Chieti and Teramo in Abruzzo and from Palermo in Sicily.

Fred Gardaphe directs the Italian/American Studies Program at the State University of New York at Stony Brook. Born in the Little Italy of Melrose Park, Illinois, he is the author of *Italian Signs, American Streets: The Evolution of Italian American Narrative*; *Dagoes Read: Tradition and the Italian/American Writer*; *Moustache Pete is Dead!: Italian/American Oral Tradition Preserved in Print*; and *Leaving Little Italy: Essays in Italian American Culture*.

Anthony Giardina is the author of three novels, including *Recent History*, a story collection titled *The Country of Marriage*, and a number of plays, including *Black Forest*, which have been widely produced in this country.

Dana Gioia was born in Los Angeles in 1950. He received an M.B.A. at Stanford, eventually becoming a vice president of General Foods, then left business to write full-time. His third collection of poems, *Interrogations at Noon*, was the recipient of the American Book Award from the Before Columbus Foundation. He wrote *Can Poetry Matter?: Essays on Poetry and American Culture* and an opera libretto, *Nosferatu*, which was published in 2001. He lives in Sonoma County, California, with his wife and two sons.

John Giorno was born in New York City in 1936. His father's family came to this country from Aliano, Basilicata, and his mother's from Genoa. He is an innovator of "Performance Poetry," founder of Giorno Poetry Systems (which produces the work of many poets on video and CDs), and inventor of Dial-a-Poem. His many published books include *You Got to Burn to Shine*, *Cancer in My Left Ball*, and the forthcoming *Great Demon Kings & Jane Bowles' Pussy*.

Victoria Gotti has published the novels *Superstar*, *The Senator's Daughter*, and *I'll Be Watching You*. She is a columnist for the *New York Post*.

Barbara Grizzuti Harrison (1934–2002) is the author of *Visions of Glory: A History and a Memory of Jehovah's Witnesses*, as well as a memoir (*An Accidental Autobiography*), a travel book (*Italian Days*), a novel (*Foreign Bodies*), and journalism on a variety of subjects. She grew up in Brooklyn.

Josephine Gattuso Hendin is the author of *The Right Thing to Do*, a novel, and is the Tiro a Segno Professor of Italian-American Studies at New York University.

Evan Hunter is the author of *The Blackboard Jungle* and many other best-selling novels, as well as the screenplay for the Alfred Hitchcock film *The Birds*.

A pitcher with the Milwaukee Braves organization for three seasons, Pat Jordan is the author of two memoirs, *A False Spring* and *A Nice Tuesday*, along with several novels, including his newest, *a.k.a Sheila Doyle*. He lives in Florida.

Maria Laurino is the author of *Were You Always an Italian?: Ancestors and Other Icons of Italian America* and is at work on a book about feminism. She is a third-generation Italian American whose ancestors come from the towns of Conza della Compania and Picerno.

Frank Lentricchia is the author of *The Edge of Night*, a memoir, as well as the novels *Johnny Critelli and the Knifeman*, *The Music of the Inferno*, and *Lucchesi and the Whale*. He is the Katherine Everett Gilbert Professor of Literature and Theater Studies at Duke University. Among his books of literary theory and criticism are *The Gaiety of Language: An Essay on the Radical Poetics of W. B. Yeats and Wallace Stevens*; *Robert Frost: Modern Poetics and the Landscapes of Self*; *After the New Criticism*; *Ariel and the Police*; *Introducing Don DeLillo*; *Close Reading: The Reader*; and *Modernist Lyric in the Culture of Capital*.

Lisa Lenzo grew up in Detroit and now lives near Saugatuck, Michigan. Her father's parents were from Spinozzola, near Naples, and Naso, in Sicily. Her first published collection of stories, *Within the Lighted City*, won the 1997 John Simmons Short Fiction Award.

Dan Leone was born in Ohio and now lives in California. He is the author of *The Meaning of Lunch*, a collection of short stories, and *Eat This, San Francisco*, a collection of humorous restaurant writings. He has a weekly food column in the *San Francisco Bay Guardian*.

Ralph Lombreglia is the author of two short story collections, *Men Under Water* and *Make Me Work* and has contributed fiction to *The New Yorker*, the *Atlantic Monthly*, and the *Paris Review*. He is at work on a novel, for which he received a Guggenheim Fellowship and a Whiting Writer's Award. His ancestors on his father's side are from Foggia, in southern Italy.

Mike Lupica writes about sports for the *New York Daily News*. His work has also appeared in *Sports Illustrated*, *Esquire*, and other magazines and newspapers. He has written many books, among them *Wild Pitch*; *Full Court Press*; and *Summer of '98: When Homers Flew, Records Fell and Baseball Reclaimed America*, and he wrote *Reggie: An Autobiography* (with Reggie Jackson). He lives in Connecticut with his wife and their three sons.

Ed McBain is best known for the series of police novels set in the fictional 87th Precinct, among them *Cop Hater*, *Kiss*, and *Lullaby*.

Theresa Maggio, granddaughter of Sicilian immigrants, was born in Carlstadt, New Jersey, and now lives in Vermont. Her books include *Mattanza: Love and Death in the Sea of Sicily* and *The Stone Boudoir: Travels Through the Hidden Villages of Sicily*.

Jerre Mangione (1909–98) is best remembered for his first novel, *Mount Allegro*, a fictionalized account of life in the Sicilian ghetto in Rochester, New York, where he grew up. He wrote ten more books after that, including a history of the Federal Writers' Project and, with Ben Morreale, *La Storia: Five Centuries of the Italian American Experience*, published in 1992.

Michael Martone was born and grew up in Fort Wayne, Indiana, to a family that hails from Naples. His most recent books are *The Blue Guide to Indiana* and

The Flatness and Other Landscapes, which won the AWP Award for Nonfiction. He lives in Tuscaloosa, Alabama, with his wife and their two sons.

Cris Mazza, whose ancestors come from outside Naples, was born in Southern California and now lives near Chicago. She is a professor of creative writing at the University of Illinois and has published nine books of fiction, among them *Dog People, How to Leave a Country,* and *Your Name Here.*

Robert A. Orsi is the Warren Professor of American Religious History at Harvard University. He is the author of *The Madonna of 115th Street: Faith and Community in Italian Harlem* and *Thank You, Saint Jude: Women's Devotion to the Patron Saint of Hopeless Causes,* and editor of *Gods of the City: Religion and the American Urban Landscape.* A native New Yorker, his father is from Lucca, in Italy, and his mother from the Lower East Side of Manhattan.

Camille Paglia is University Professor and Professor of Humanities and Media studies at the University of the Arts in Philadelphia. She is the author of four books, including *Sexual Personae: Art and Decadence from Nefertiti to Emily Dickinson* and a study of Alfred Hitchcock's *The Birds* for the British Film Institute. Her mother and maternal grandparents were born in Ceccano in Lazio, south of Rome, and her paternal grandparents were born in the area of Benevento and Avellino, near Naples.

George Panetta (1910–71) was a successful advertising executive (for Young & Rubicam), novelist (*We Ride a White Donkey, Viva Madison Avenue!*), playwright (his *Comic Strip* won the Obie Award for best off-Broadway comedy, 1957–58 season), and children's book author (*Jimmy Potts Gets a Haircut*).

Jay Parini, the grandson of immigrants from Rome and Viserla, was born and raised in northeastern Pennsylvania and has taught at Middlebury College for more than twenty years. He has published many books of poetry (including *Anthracite Country, Town Life, House of Days*), fiction (*The Patch Boys, The Apprentice Lover*), biography (*John Steinbeck, Robert Frost*), and criticism. He lives in Vermont with his wife and three sons.

Michael Paterniti is a writer at large for *GQ* and author of the nonfiction book *Driving Mr. Albert: A Trip Across America with Einstein's Brain.* He lives in Portland, Maine, with his wife and son. His paternal grandfather was born in Tortorici, Sicily.

Lucia Perillo has published three books of poetry, the most recent being *The Oldest Map with the Name America.* Her work has appeared in many magazines, including *The New Yorker* and the *Atlantic Monthly*, and has been reprinted in the Pushcart and Best American Poetry anthologies. In 2000 she received a MacArthur Foundation fellowship for her writing. She lives in Olympia, Washington.

Tom Perrotta has published four books of fiction, including *Election, Joe College,* and *Bad Haircut* and *Other Stories of the Seventies.* He grew up in New Jersey and lives in Massachusetts.

Nicholas Pileggi is a journalist and screenwriter who wrote the books *Wiseguy: Life in a Mafia Family* (and, with Martin Scorsese, wrote *GoodFellas,* the screenplay based on it) and *Casino: Love and Honor in Las Vegas* (and wrote the script based on that, for a Martin Scorsese film).

Most famous for *The Godfather* (the novel as well as the screenplays, for which he received two Oscars), Mario Puzo (1920–1999) also wrote *The Dark Arena, The Fortunate Pilgrim, Fools Die, The Sicilian,* and other novels and book-length works of nonfiction.

Ray Romano is a comedian, the star of the TV show *Everybody Loves Raymond,* and author of *Everything and a Kite.*

Richard Russo has written many novels, among them *Empire Falls,* which won the Pulitzer Prize for fiction in 2002. He is also the author of *Mohawk, Nobody's Fool,* and *Straight Man.* He lives in coastal Maine with his wife and two daughters.

Felix Stefanile was born in New York City, the first-generation son of Italian immigrants. He and his wife, Selma, were civil servants in the 1950s when they founded Sparrow Press. Stefanile taught at Purdue University until he retired in 1987. He is the author of eleven books of verse (three of them translations of Italian poets) and has won numerous prizes, including awards from the NEA and the *Virginia Quarterly Review.*

Gay Talese, one of the prime innovators of literary journalism in America, is the author of many best-selling nonfiction books, among them *Unto the Sons, Thy Neighbor's Wife, Honor Thy Father,* and *The Kingdom and the Power.*

Raised in Brooklyn, of half-Sicilian, half-Calabrian ancestry, Marianna De Marco Torgovnick teaches literature at Duke University. Among her books is *Gone Primitive: Savage Intellects, Modern Lives and Primitive Passions.*

Nick Tosches was born in Newark and raised by wolves from Casalvecchio di Puglia. His prose and poetry have been published widely and are represented by *The Nick Tosches Reader,* a collection selected from thirty years' work. He is the author of the novels *Cut Numbers* and *Trinities,* as well as several books of nonfiction, among them *Hellfire,* a biography of Jerry Lee Lewis. His newest novel, *In the Hand of Dante,* is published by Little, Brown.

Joseph Tusiani has published many books of poetry, including *Rind and All* and *Gente Mia and Other Poems,* as well as four volumes of verse written in Latin. He has translated into English *The Complete Poems of Michelangelo,* Tasso's *Jerusalem Delivered* and *Creation of the World* and Dante's lyric poems, among other works. He is a Distinguished Service Professor, retired from City University of New York in 1983. His most recent book is *Dante's Divine Comedy: As Told for Young People.*

Anthony Valerio's books include *The Mediterranean Runs Through Brooklyn, Valentino and the Great Italians,* and *Lefty and the Button Men.* His most recent book is *Anita Garibaldi: A Biography.*

Steven Varni was born and raised in Modesto, California, and now lives in New York City. He is the author of *The Inland Sea* and of a forthcoming novel. He is of Genovese and Sicilian descent.

The haiku of Nicholas A. Virgilio (1928–89), of Camden, New Jersey, can be found in *Selected Poems* (Burnt Moss Press) as well as in *The Haiku Anthology*, by Cor van den Heuvel (W. W. Norton and Company) and other collections. He was a cofounder of the Walt Whitman Cultural Arts Center.

Robert Viscusi is a poet, essayist, and novelist. His work includes the novel *Astoria*, which won an American Book Award in 1996. He is executive officer of the Wolfe Institute for the Humanities at Brooklyn College and president of the Italian American Writers Association.

ACKNOWLEDGMENTS

First things first: My beautiful wife Lisa Mansourian (she's half Armenian and half Napolitana—the good half) and our kids, Lucia and Willie, are the main reason I do anything, especially of a vocational nature (though they would inspire me even if I didn't need the dough). Whatever I don't owe to them I owe to my father and mother, Willie and Sylvia, who—even from quite some distance away—have guided me through this and everything else I do right.

The superb Richard Pine, of Arthur Pine Associates, turned the notion of this book into a reality, merely by fixing a price tag to it and then convincing some publishing company to pay. Without that creative act, this collection would not exist.

Of course, the editor who bit is named Mauro DiPreta, so it's entirely possible that he had some nonmercenary reason for getting involved. Therefore, he is to be doubly commended as a good man who put his money—okay, Rupert Murdoch's money—where his mouth is. I hope it works out. If you won't buy multiple copies of this book for the sake of my two kids, do it for the sake of Mauro's four.

I owe the biggest debt of gratitude to every single writer in this book, of course, for without them it wouldn't be much of a collection. All greeted news of this project with enthusiasm and support and assistance, and I feel nothing less than affection for each and every one. In particular, three aristocrats of contemporary American literature—Don DeLillo, Gay Talese, and Nick Tosches—extended themselves above and beyond the call of whatever duty might be said to exist. Thanks, fellas.

Thanks also to Jay Parini for his extreme generosity.

Certain individuals and organizations have been very helpful in practical ways but also by allowing me and other people to engage in the unruly conversation that is ethnic identity in America today. Among them: Dominic Candeloro and Ben Lawton of the American Italian Historical Association; Ken Ciongoli and Elissa Ruffino of the National Italian-American Foundation; Dona DeSanctis of the Order Sons of Italy in America; Robert Viscusi of the Italian American Writers Association; James Periconi of Round Hill Books, specializing in Italian-Americana; Fred Gardaphe of various crucial postings, among them director of the Italian/American Studies Program at the State University of New York at Stony Brook; Joseph Sciorra (from whom I stole the doowop joke in the intro) and Joseph V. Scelsa of the John D. Calandra Italian-American Institute, of Queens College of the City University of New York; Antonio D'Alfonso of Guernica Editions; and Carol Bonomo Albright and John Paul Russo of *Italian Americana.*

Also, for advice, suggestions, and other goodnesses bestowed upon me, thanks to Jimmy Breslin, Judith Hirsch, Terry Bisson, Alix M. Freedman, Edward Cifelli (my Ciardi consultant), Stephen Cooper (my Fante consultant), Edvige Giunta, Cor van den Heuvel, Claudia DiRomualdo, Lori Andiman, Deborah Foley, Elizabeth Beier, Ron and Eileen Javers, Lois Wallace, Will Blythe, Maria Pia and Michael Gramaglia, Joelle Yudin, Robert Atwan and DeeDee DeBartlo.

On a philosophical plane, I owe John Aiello, whose thinking in matters of culture and ethnicity has long provided direction for my own, and author-scholars Richard Gambino and Richard D. Alba, both of whom contributed a great deal to what I (and everyone else) understands about the power of culture and ethnicity.

Other anthologies I consulted, all of which are recommended to the serious student:

The Dream Book: An Anthology of Writings by Italian-American Women, edited by Helen Barolini (Syracuse University Press).

From the Margin: Writings in Italian Americana, edited by Anthony Julian Tamburri, Paolo A. Giordano, and Fred L. Gardaphe (Purdue University Press).

Beyond the Godfather: Italian American Writers on the Real Italian American Experience, edited by A. Kenneth Ciongoli and Jay Parini (University Press of New England).

Other books that are required reading, I think, for anyone who wishes to understand:

The Italian-American Novel: A Document of the Interaction of Two Cultures, edited by Rose Basile Green (Associated Universities Press).

Bibliography of the Italian American Book, by Fred Gardaphe and James J. Periconi (The Italian American Writers Association and Shea and Haarmann Publishing Company).

Blood of My Blood, by Richard Gambino (Guernica Editions).

La Storia: Five Centuries of the Italian-American Experience, by Jerre Mangione and Ben Morreale (HarperPerennial).

Italian Americans: Into the Twilight of Ethnicity, by Richard D. Alba (Prentice-Hall).

Wop! A Documentary History of Anti-Italian Discrimination, by Salvatore J. LaGumina (Guernica Editions).

At my day job, thanks to Jann Wenner and Bob Love of *Rolling Stone*, who kindly failed to point out my occasional inattentiveness (not to mention all those missing office supplies) as I prepared this ball-buster.

I want to acknowledge the inspiration of my friends and relatives in Comune di Nereto, Provincia di Teramo, Regione Abruzzo, Italia, especially Lucio Addarii.

Finally, I want to say hello to my grandparents Luigi and Lena (née Peca) Tonelli and Pasquale and Carmella "Millie" (née Sinatra) Funaro, whom I hope to join someday (not soon) at their country commune in Yeadon, Pennsylvania. Hello also to my blood as it exists in other bodies—my sisters Lois and Cindy, their husbands Bill and Robert, Bobby, Laura and Allison, Aunt Jo, Aunt Marie, Aunt Rose and Uncle Dom and Aunt Marie Ucciferri, and all my cousins—and to my mother-in-law Angelina Mansourian (née Marsala), Mary D'Anella, Michael Mercanti, Madelaina, Isabella, Michael Vincent, and Mariangela and Dennis Caporiccio.

Hello to the boys from Fifteenth and Moore.

PERMISSIONS